DEC 3 0 2015

THE VERDICT

THE VERDICT

NICK STONE

PEGASUS CRIME

NEW YORK LONDON

THE VERDICT

Pegasus Crime is an Imprint of
Pegasus Books LLC
80 Broad Street, 5th Floor
New York, NY 10004

American copyright © 2015 by Nick Stone

First Pegasus Books hardcover edition December 2015

ISBN: 978-1-60598-923-5

10 9 8 7 6 5 4 3 2 1

Printed in the United States of America
Distributed by W. W. Norton & Company, Inc.

For:
Hyacinth, Dwayne & Aimée,
Janice Brown, Colin Bromfield,
and Nadine Radford, QC

If there were no bad people, there would be no good lawyers.

Charles Dickens, *The Old Curiosity Shop*

I was angry with my friend:
I told my wrath, my wrath did end.
I was angry with my foe:
I told it not, my wrath did grow.

William Blake, 'A Poison Tree'

Prologue

March 16th, 2011

A few hours before his life went straight to hell, Vernon James was thinking about his father. It wasn't something he did very often any more, once or twice a year at the most, and that solely out of a grudging sense of obligation. Neither love nor affection came into it.

Tonight, however, he was making an exception. He was in a bind, the tightest of the tight. He was about to give a speech to a roomful of terminal white liberals who hated his guts, and the one he'd written was all wrong. It was a self-congratulatory list of personal accomplishments, completely devoid of heart, soul and everything in-between. It would confirm their worst suspicions about him. It would bomb and he'd get slaughtered.

The previous week Vernon had been named Ethical Person of the Year by the Hoffmann Trust, a liberal umbrella organisation comprising an international collective of campaigners and pressure groups covering everything from the environment to human rights. He was being recognised for his work in Trinidad, the no-go ghettos he'd helped transform into viable, thriving neighbourhoods, as well as the healthcare and education schemes he'd set up for his employees and their families – schemes he'd initially subsidised out of his own pocket. He'd become a hero of sorts to his workers, while to the British media, he was the new-fangled posterboy for 'Compassionate Capitalism'.

Yet his appointment had been hugely controversial, and reactions to it swift and furious. The award had never gone to a businessman before, let alone a *financier*. Two of the judges had resigned loudly and very publicly. Vernon had beaten out far more suitable people, they argued – an Iranian prisoner of conscience, an anti-government Russian journalist, a woman from Bradford who'd been disfigured with battery acid for campaigning against honour killing. Some had boycotted the ceremony, but the majority had vowed to attend to let Vernon know what they thought of him to his face. And to cap it all the press had decided to cover the event. Despite centuries of consistent progress and civilisation, people still hadn't lost their appetite for a good public hanging.

3

Things had moved so fast he hadn't had time to change what he'd written. And now it was as good as too late. It was zero-sum time and the hour was almost at hand. He had two choices – bail or improvise; flee or fight.

And this was where his father came into it. Vernon decided to go off-script and blindside this well-heeled, braying mob with an exclusive. He was famously – no, *notoriously* – secretive. In the rare interviews he'd given, he offered up little in the way of personal or autobiographical details. Not once had he talked about his family. Journalists and would-be biographers knew better than to probe into his past. He'd ruined three careers and brought down one publishing house with libel suits. The upside had been that he kept his past buried. Yet the downside, as he'd recently discovered, was that people found it easy to loathe him because they knew next to nothing about him. They took the scrappy personal sketch he'd allowed into the public domain – that he was a Cambridge-educated, former banker of early 1990s vintage, who'd established a hugely successful hedge fund, which had made him one of the richest people in the country – and filled in the blanks with their own skewed projections; an association game that saw him the centre of a montage of left-wing hate figures – Thatcher, Reagan, Murdoch, Bush the Second, Dick Cheney et al. He was a multi-millionaire banker, therefore *Conservative*, therefore *Evil*.

He was going to try and prove them wrong.

Showtime imminent.

He checked himself in the bathroom mirror one last time. He spritzed his breath with freshener to kill the vodka fumes. He was OK. He'd only had a couple. He felt good, confident.

There was a knock on the door.

It was a maid. Short and slim, Eurasian features. Not bad-looking, but not his type.

'Turndown service, sir?'

What was that accent? American via somewhere Baltic? He couldn't tell.

'No thanks,' he said.

'Have a good evening, sir.'

He reached into his pocket and peeled a tenner off his clip and gave it to her. She beamed. She'd done nothing to deserve it, but he was now officially in nice-guy mode.

The ceremony was being held in the main banqueting room of the Blenheim-Strand, the hippest hotel in London, thanks to film-star patronage and drooling write-ups. Vernon had booked himself into Suite 18, on the twelfth floor, the main selling point of which was a panoramic view of the South Bank and the city beyond. Not that he'd had the time or space to take it in, let alone appreciate it. He'd been too busy staring defeat in the face and trying not to blink.

He took to the stage to a meagre drizzle of applause, more desultory pats of the palms than fully formed claps. There were some two hundred people in the room, but it sounded like no more than a dozen, with slightly under half bothering to acknowledge him.

Vernon set the prize – a large capital 'E' in solid blue-tinted glass, with his name engraved on the brass plinth – to one side of the microphone lectern. He looked out over the space in front of him, the battlefield, already crackling with opening salvos in the form of inchoate grumbles. He could clearly make out the first couple of rows and the faces around the tables. Beyond that were shadows and silhouettes. A few camera flashes went off.

He cleared his throat and started to speak. He wasn't using notes or an autocue. He'd memorised the whole thing.

'They say awards never go to the right people. And for once they have a point. I don't deserve this.'

He was expecting a reaction of some kind, angry accord at the very least. But no one said a thing. It was so quiet he heard the microphone hum.

He was glad he'd had those few drinks before. Two double vodkas in his room upstairs after he'd run through his speech for the final time, a couple more discreet ones during dinner. While it didn't make him bolder or lighten the immensity of the task before him, it had blunted his fear and loosened him up a little.

He began by complimenting and commiserating with the runners-up. He commended their individual achievements. He'd researched them all thoroughly.

He told the audience things about his co-nominees only a genuine admirer could have known. He got a quick shower of applause from the edges of the room, but it was swallowed up by the cavernous quiet.

Vernon appeared nervous and spoke haltingly at first. This was, of course, deliberate, all part of the plan. As was the voice he was using – what he sometimes referred to as his 'rags to riches brogue'.

It was a Caribbean-tinged variant of the Estuary accent he'd deliberately shed on his eighteenth birthday but wasn't above revisiting whenever the occasion called for it. Tonight the same accent was serving to remind the audience that he wasn't just a racial minority, but of working-class stock too – two kinds of the very person they loved to defend and celebrate more than their own.

It wasn't the only adjustment he'd made. Although a tall, handsome man gifted with that mixture of magnetism and charisma commonly referred to as 'presence', he knew how to turn it off and play humble.

He'd spent the first third of his career having to impress people in one way or another to get what he wanted. Now that he'd long surpassed those initial goals, he had to make a different kind of impression – to appear to be living down his success. That was, after all, the British way. Fake modesty, faker self-deprecation.

He moved on to talk about his work in the West Indies. In-between describing his semi-philanthropic endeavours he took sharp, distancing swipes at sweatshop culture, the evil of child labour, and the corporate exploitation of the Third World. That was delivered with a sudden burst of passion that took the room aback, and made him sound sincere.

It earned him an enthusiastic round of applause. At least half the audience was on its feet. There were even a couple of '*Bravos!*' thrown in. He paused an instant and took stock. He was still far from winning over the crowd, but their antagonism was on hold. Their preconceptions were crumbling. They were there for the taking.

Now for the critical moment . . .

The mother . . .

No.

The *father*lode.

He was about to resume when he sensed he was being stared at.

Yes, sure, *everyone* was looking at him, and a couple of TV cameras were trained on him too, but this was a very *specific* kind of stare. A stare that was calling out to him, clamouring for his attention; a stare that wanted to be met.

He cleared his throat and took a sip of water, using the pause to glance, quickly, to his right, into the pull of the stare.

And that was when he first clapped eyes on his fate; his absolute undoing:

Six feet of long tall blonde in a tight, figure-hugging, bottle-green dress.

He had a clear view of her. Her and her ample cleavage, her dark circumflex eyebrows, high cheekbones and smiling mouth. To say that she stood out in that drab crowd in their limp suits and interchangeable black dresses was an understatement. She was a phosphorescent rainbow in a monochrome desert.

She was sitting at the very front, her chair positioned close to the stage. Chin cupped in her hand, she gazed up at him intently, her hazel eyes finding his. Her dress was split at the side, exposing her leg from ankle to lower thigh. There was a tattoo on her ankle. He searched her hand for a wedding ring, and then remembered his own, glinting in the spotlight.

The sight of her emboldened him. And the booze gave him another boost.

'I said earlier that I've always believed in people. Well, I learned that from my father, Rodney James,' he said, launching the pivotal part of his speech.

He recounted how his father had come to England from Trinidad in the early 1960s. He described the terraced house he'd grown up in in Stevenage; the four of them – his parents, his older sister Gwen and him – sharing two rooms in the basement. Although Rodney had felt unwanted in this new country, he'd absolutely refused to be beaten. He'd worked two jobs: a window cleaner by day and a hospital porter by night. Vernon said that when he was ten, he made three decisions about his future – the first, that he'd work as hard as his father did; the second, that if he ever reached a position of authority over people, he'd make sure no one he employed would ever live as his family did then. People deserved dignity above all else.

That won him a huge round of applause – which sounded unanimous, and thoroughly surprised him. He briefly lost his train of thought.

So he thanked the audience with bashful humility. And then he told them the third vow he made back then – never to eat tinned pilchards in tomato sauce again. His family, he explained, were so poor it was all they had to live on.

That brought the house down. People laughed. People clapped. People whooped! People table-thumped. No one was against him any more. The tide had well and truly turned.

He stole a quick glance at The Blonde. She was still there, looking at him in wonder, hands clasped together. Their eyes connected. Her lips were moving. She was mouthing something to him. But he couldn't linger long enough to make out what it was. Empowered by his success, the mounting blaze in his groin and with the vodka greasing his wheels, he carried on with his speech.

Fifteen years after he first arrived in England, Rodney James opened his own business – a newsagent's directly opposite the railway station. As it was the only one in the immediate area, it did great business. The family were able to move out of the basement, and, for a while, life was good.

Of course, Vernon said, his voice (deliberately) cracking, like all good

7

things, it wasn't to last. Isn't happiness, after all, but a short stopover on a long sad road?

In May 1989, as Rodney was closing the shop for the night, he was robbed and stabbed. He bled to death right there on the floor of a place that had been his pride and joy, his greatest achievement and a testament to his hard work and determination to overcome all obstacles.

Vernon concluded by saying that he thought of his father every day, and that everything he did and had done and would continue to do was always in his memory – the most ethical person he had ever known.

He ended with a simple 'Thank you'.

The room erupted in applause and cheers. The lights went up. The room rose to its feet in ovation. He saw a few tears being wiped off cheeks.

He stepped back from the microphone and savoured the applause, nodding to the crowd, left, centre and right. The Blonde was on her feet too, clapping, beaming, her breasts bouncing under her dress. Their eyes met again.

'I love you,' she mouthed.

People came towards the stage, hands extended. He shook them all, soaking up their compliments, thanking them with humble bows and scrapes.

Yet as the applause rang in his ears, he remembered how things had *really* been when he was growing up. He wasn't sure if his father turned into a monster after he came to England, or if he had always been that way. It didn't matter now. Rodney James had served his purpose. The story Vernon had just told was a big lie strained from the smallest truth, but it was a hell of a tale and that was all that mattered.

He waved to his cheering audience, picked up his award and started leaving the stage. He was happy and his heart was pumping. A celebration was in order.

And he desperately wanted to fuck The Blonde.

But when he turned to look for her, she was gone. The chair she'd sat in empty.

Afterwards everyone went to the hotel nightclub. A DJ with red, white and blue dreadlocks played an array of roots reggae, 1970s funk and rap from an amped-up laptop.

The club was called the Casbah. It had a sunken dancefloor, which glowed overlapping shades of turquoise and gold, and a two-tiered seating area, with tables on one level and booths on the next.

A cheer went up when Vernon walked in. People clustered around him like village idiots to a maypole. They complimented him on his speech. They gushed about how *wonderful*!! he was and how *wonderful*!! the work he was doing was, and they *insisted* they'd always liked and admired him. The backstabbers turned backslappers. He stayed in character, from the false modesty to the faked accent; slicker than grease on ice. He thanked them with his best sincere smile and firmest handshake.

He worked the room. He mingled. He smalltalked. He chatted. He laughed at bad jokes. Strangers offered to buy him drinks, even though they were all free. People wanted to snap photos with him on their mobiles. He complied. Women swooned. Two lost the power of speech. One kissed him on the cheek. He signed a napkin and a couple of menus. An Asian man wanted to know his secret. 'Hard work and aspirin,' he answered and moved on. A pissed sixtysomething northerner asked him if he was a 'tin bath kid'. Earnest types wanted to know his opinions on global warming, the Middle East, the British government, the decline of American power, and whether Ireland and Iceland were safe to invest in again. He gave left-leaning answers to everything. They nodded in agreement like beatified bobblehead dolls.

He didn't mind any of it, the flesh-pressing, the smarming, the insincerity. It was all post-purchase aftercare to him; the promised phone call at the end of a one night stand. This bunch of sorry do-gooders had made him very happy for reasons they'd never know.

Now . . .

Where was The Blonde?

He walked the length and breadth of the club, but he didn't see her.

The guests got drunk enough to take to the dancefloor, as reggae gave way to disco. People danced, some effortlessly, others like they were standing in drying cement.

Vernon retraced his steps, encountering more handshakes and platitudes and flattery. Fistbumps, handpumps, three high-fives and a load of thumb-ups.

No sign of *her*.

The DJ played The Clash, The Jam, The Specials, The Housemartins. The women fled to the edges of the floor and watched middle-aged men pogo wildly for a few seconds, reliving their youth, only to stop, panting and sweating, and looking all embarrassed as time caught up with them and abruptly yanked their chains.

Vernon slipped outside and looked up and down the corridor. Smooth grey carpet and portholes for windows; central London at night, like being in the middle of a gigantic box of jewels.

He took the lift down to the lobby. She was well and truly gone. What a shame, he thought. But he didn't dwell on the disappointment. God had invented escort services for moments like these.

He went back to the party. He decided to give it another hour, then split and order himself up a Nordic cheerleader type. He'd ask her to come in a tight green dress.

Waiters and waitresses were roaming the tiers, taking drinks orders. Vernon ordered a double vodka and went up to one of the booths where some of the judges and Trust board members were sitting. More compliments, more handshakes. A couple of the judges who'd voted against him apologised for misjudging him. He accepted and said he regretted all the controversy. Someone said it had been great publicity and winked.

His drink came. He sipped it and scanned the floor, one more time, just in case.

The music got louder. Tunes everyone knew. A group of men and women had linked arms and were dancing in a circle, singing aloud, high-kicking, butting other revellers out of the way.

No one could hear anyone talk.

Vernon had an ideal opportunity to slip away.

And that was when he saw *her* again.

A flash of blonde on green.

She was standing all the way across the club, near the exit, her back to him.

Vernon excused himself. No one heard him.

He edged around the floor, which was overflowing with people. A woman was being helped over to the booths, hopping, her foot bleeding. Someone called out his name and he turned and smiled and waved without seeing them. He crunched over broken glass or ice cubes and squished olives and lemon slices.

The Blonde was talking on a mobile.

Vernon reached her and stood behind her for a second, waiting for the right moment. He was drunker than he realised. Vodka was the only alcohol he ever touched, because he knew how to pace it and control its effects. He'd had eight – or was it nine? – drinks over a four-hour period and plenty of water in-between. The most he would have usually felt was tipsy. Now his balance was off, his mouth dry and his head caught in a slow clockwise spin.

He tapped her on the shoulder.

She turned around, her phone still to her ear.

'Oh ...' was all Vernon could say when he saw her face.

The dress was ... kind of the same colour, but ... her hair and ... her height and her shape should have given it away.

It wasn't *The* Blonde. Just *a* blonde – a foot shorter, dumpier and only a long-term boyfriend or devoted husband's idea of beautiful.

10

How the hell could he have made such a huge mistake?

'*Yeah . . .?*' She looked at him quizzically.

'I'm sorry. I thought you were someone else,' he said.

'Well I'm not, am I?' she snapped and turned around and resumed her conversation.

Just then a conga line of men burst into the club, singing 'Agadoo'. They crashed into the woman as they hurtled towards the dancefloor. She lost her balance and fell headfirst into Vernon, smacking him hard in the chest. He rocked back on his heels and grasped out for support. His fingers caught her hair and he pulled her down, yelping, on top of him.

They landed on the floor as one, Vernon taking the brunt of the fall and their combined weight on his upper back and shoulderblades. He cried out as pain shot up his neck. They both tried to get up at the same time. In their confusion and momentary panic they struggled against each other, the woman poking his eye, sticking another finger up his nostril and then scratching her nails down his cheek as she attempted to get upright. She'd just about made it, but she couldn't raise her head all the way up because some of her hair was snagged up around one of Vernon's cufflinks. He tried to disentangle her, but she lost all patience and yanked her head away with another yelp.

Vernon was all apologies and concern, even though his shoulders were killing him and the pain had now spread to his jaw.

'Where's my phone?' she yelled at him.

Vernon shrugged and then winced as the bruised muscles flared up.

Then he saw that a strap of the woman's dress had busted and her left breast was slowly spilling out as the fabric fell away.

At first she didn't notice what had happened. She was shouting at him about her phone over the music. But he'd lost all audio. He was looking down at that voluminous left breast of hers.

She followed his stare.

Her mouth formed a perfect capital 'O'.

Then it collapsed into an angry rictus.

'You big *twat!*' she screamed and scampered out of the club in a hunchbacked half-crouch, clutching the front of her dress and trying to contain her modesty.

Vernon looked around to see who was watching. Just about everyone. Most were laughing at him or with him or both.

He switched back to crowd-pleaser mode. He smiled, laughed along, shook his head and held his hands up. It was a perfect moment to leave. He turned, and, as he did, he trod on something.

It was a mobile phone. He guessed it was the woman's.

11

The front was completely smashed.

He picked it up and slipped it in his pocket. He'd hand it in to reception tomorrow.

He left the club and headed down the corridor, grateful to be getting away from there.

He wouldn't need the escort service after all, just bed. He'd been so preoccupied with his speech, he hadn't even had time to look at the suite's bedroom. That was something to look forward to. He was exhausted. The state he was in was more down to the day he'd had than the vodka; it was the tiredness after the adrenalin, the comedown after the triumph, his real self taking over from the forged one.

He headed for the lift.

A group of people came gambolling towards him, drunk, bouncing off the walls, laughing. They stopped him to ask for directions to the club. As he was pointing to it, out of the corner of his eye, Vernon saw a flash of green on blonde go past them, heading away, in the opposite direction.

He remembered the phone in his pocket. He left the group and hurried after her.

'Excuse me?' he called out.

The woman stopped and turned.

And he stopped too.

No ...

No.

Surely not.

It couldn't be ...

But it *was*

Her.

The Blonde.

'Oh hello,' she said, looking him up and down. 'What happened to you?'

'The party's getting a bit wild,' he said.

'And you're *leaving*?' she laughed.

'There's wild I like, and wild I don't,' he said. 'How come you weren't there?'

'I was just going,' she said. She had a French accent – noticeable, but not overpowering.

'You're heading the wrong way,' he said, hiking his thumb over his shoulder.

'Am I?' she smiled.

The bar on the eleventh floor was as good as deserted, with only the bartender wiping down the counter.

12

She took a seat at a corner table by a window, while Vernon got the drinks – a white wine for her and a glass of water for him. He asked the barman to 'make it look like vodka'.

Vernon let The Blonde take the lead with the talking. She'd already introduced herself as Fabia and said she worked in PR. Now she told him she was originally from Switzerland. She'd been living in England for the last five years. She'd married a Kiwi but they'd split up a year ago. She flashed the wedding ring she'd moved to her right hand.

She'd as good as told him she was available.

His move.

Vernon's marriage was essentially solid. Although he and his wife spent a lot of time apart, when they were together they got on fine and the sex was good.

But there wasn't enough of it for him. Nor was it the kind he'd come to like more and more these days. The special kind. For that he went elsewhere.

He rarely picked women up, unless they were a sure thing. He wasn't interested in the chase – too much time and effort to spend on an indeterminate outcome. And he wasn't looking for a mistress or a bit on the side.

So he mostly used prostitutes. High-class ones – expensive, discreet and *always* blonde. It was a simple arrangement: he got what he wanted, paid for it and went home.

Fabia was very different from the kind of women he usually encountered socially. Sure they flirted with him, but never overtly. There was always a buffer, a deniability. Fabia didn't have that. She was direct to the point of bluntness. She wanted the same thing he did. It was there in her eyes when he'd first spotted her, and it was there in the way she was looking at him now.

Vernon told Fabia he and his wife had an open marriage.

'Why wasn't she here tonight?'

'She's in America,' he said.

'What about your entourage?' she asked. 'Bodyguards, assistants?'

'I came alone.'

'That's brave.'

'It's called vodka.'

She laughed. They both sipped their drinks and then gazed out of the window. It was the same view Vernon had from his suite, only slightly lower: the South Bank between the Millennium and Waterloo Bridges, the vista lit up like a giant pinball machine with the cover torn off. Everything washed and burnished and blessed in bluey neon.

'Nice watch . . .' she said, nodding to his wrist.

13

'It was my dad's,' he said.

His father's Datejust Rolex, the only valuable he'd brought over from Trinidad. It had originally been given to his grandfather when he'd retired as manager of the London Bank in 1952. He'd passed it on to Rodney. Rodney used to wear it once a year, on his birthday. They'd found it after he died, in a shoebox at the back of the closet when they were clearing out his clothes. Vernon had suggested selling it, but his mother refused, saying she wanted him to have it, so he could pass it on to his son one day. '*What if I have girls?*' he'd asked. And he had. Three of them.

He'd worn the watch for the first time ever tonight to remind himself to stay on message, to think warmly of the man he'd hated. It was a good prompt. Heavy, like a shackle, the metal cold on his wrist.

'May I?'

'Sure.'

Vernon slipped it off and handed it to her. The watch didn't look flash, the way modern Rolexes did. The lustre had long gone out of the yellow and silver jubilee bracelet, and the glass was scratched.

She took it and felt its heft in her palm. Then she inspected it carefully and he could tell she knew what she was doing.

'This is an antique?' she said.

'Yes. Do you know about watches?'

'My father's a watchsmith,' she said, as she put the Rolex on her wrist and admired it. The strap was too big and the watch slid halfway down her forearm.

'You look like a rapper,' he laughed.

'Birthday or Christmas?'

The tips of their fingers bumped across the table. She took his hand and looked at him. The hold became a light grip as she leaned her face towards his. He felt her warm breath on his chin. She leaned forward a little more, her lips slightly parted, her eyes half-closed.

Vernon pulled back and broke away, looking around quickly to see if anyone else was there. But they were still alone, apart from the barman, who was turned away from them, stacking glasses on a shelf.

'I thought you had an open marriage,' she said.

'The door's always on the latch.'

'Are you staying here? In the hotel?'

'Yes.'

'Well, I guess this is the moment you invite me up to your room to see the view.'

When the lift doors opened, Vernon did the gentlemanly thing and stepped aside to let her pass. He would have done it anyway, because he knew his good manners and how they spoke volumes to the aware, but he also used the opportunity to check her out again and take her in.

Her dress exposed much of her back, all the way down to the absolute lowest limit of her spine, stopping tantalisingly close to the bold convex swell of her buttocks. He let his eyes slide down the groove of her vertebral column and linger on the fine pale down matting her tawny skin. She was perfect.

In the suite, they stood by the floor-to-ceiling window, taking in the view.

'Is this how you see the world?' she asked.

'What do you mean?'

'From up on high, like a god? Everyone small and insignificant and crushable?'

'Just tonight,' he said. It was raining outside, and the glass was speckled and running.

He took her hand gently and turned her towards him. Then he pulled her a little closer. He started kissing her. There was an initial resistance on her part. Her mouth was set and unyielding, her arms down by her sides. He stopped and asked if she was OK.

Instead of answering, she grabbed his head and brought her mouth to his. They tongue-torqued. She nibbled his bottom lip.

Then she bit it.

He stepped back with a gasp and touched his mouth for blood. She apologised with a giggle, said it was over-enthusiasm. And maybe the wine too. He said OK and excused himself.

He went into the hallway bathroom. She'd drawn blood from his lip, but it didn't make much difference to his overall appearance because he looked a mess. He was dishevelled, his face was scratched, his shirt pocket was torn and hanging loose, and the left sleeve of his jacket was wet and filthy with booze and dancefloor dirt.

He splashed cold water on his face, which chased some of the mist out of his head.

When he came out he found her standing by the couch and coffee table in the middle of the room, adjusting her dress about her hips.

'I'm sorry,' she said.

'Make it up to me,' he said.

He took her face in his hands and kissed her. Again he met hard, closed lips. What was the matter with her? This was starting to irritate him. If she was teasing him, he was way too tired and booze-jaded. If she was trying to provoke him, it was working.

He started to say something when Fabia came at him again. She nibbled at his neck and put her tongue in his ear. Then she pushed his jacket off and undid his belt, then his trousers. She licked her fingers and slipped them through the fly of his boxers and freed his hardening prick. He groaned, loving how she was taking the initiative, her aggression.

She stopped abruptly and took a few steps back.

'What's wrong now?' he asked, with a frustrated sigh.

She looked him up and down and smiled – a strange, dislocated grimace, her lips twisted into a sneering parody of happiness. He noticed she was trembling.

'Are you OK?'

She glanced towards the door, then back at him.

'I thought I could do this,' she said, under her breath.

'What?'

'I can't do this,' she said, louder, taking another step away.

His irritation ran to anger.

'What's going on? Is this some kind of game?'

'I'm sorry.' She backed off, holding up her hands, palms out. 'I shouldn't have come here.'

'Why *did* you, then?' he snarled.

She wasn't moving. She certainly wasn't leaving. She was standing there, almost naked in that ultra-tight dress, the material moulding her concave stomach so perfectly he could see the diamond hollow of her navel and the impression of the ring it was pierced with. And her breasts were bulging and subsiding with every deep anxious breath she was taking.

And she wasn't moving.

She wasn't . . .

        going

            . . . *anywhere.*

Which meant:

She *wanted* him . . .

Like this . . .

NOW.

He went for her.

She recoiled and fell back on to the drinks cabinet, sending all the immaculately stacked glassware on top – crystal tumblers, wine glasses, champagne flutes and decanters – crashing to the floor.

She got herself upright, gripping the edge of the cabinet for support.

Vernon came at her again, but his undone trousers had slipped down past his knees and puddled around his ankles, stopping him in his stride. And his dick was poking out through his boxers like the gnomon of a sundial.

As he went to pull up his trousers, Fabia kicked him hard in the stomach. He caught the full wallop of the blow, compacted into the tip of her pointed shoe, right in the solar plexus. He cried out. Vodka and bile shot up to his gullet. He sank to his knees, gagging and gasping.

He tried to get up, but the pain was too much, and he was too pissed, the alcohol all over him like a lead net.

He sat down, briefly, trying to breathe through a tightening chest, the room tilting this way and that.

He tried to get up. He couldn't.

He couldn't even sit any more.

He *had* to lie down.

. . .

just

. . .

HAD to.

And he did, gently lowering himself on his side to alleviate the churning pain in his stomach.

Then he rolled on his back.

Fabia hadn't moved. She was glowering down at him, breathing through her mouth. Her eyes were wild.

He was completely at her mercy.

'Please . . .' he whispered.

She snorted. Her eyes searched the room, quickly. She stared hard at the spume of broken glass on the floor, sifted through it with her foot.

Then she turned to the cabinet. She pushed her fingers through the gap between the wall and its edge and started pulling at it.

It was on wheels, but it was a big heavy thing, hard to shift.

She put her back into it. She grunted and cursed as she pushed and shoved the cabinet across the carpet. The contents rolled and bumped and bashed around inside with every violent twist and lurch. Bottles broke and liquid leaked through the gaps, running trickles at first, and then a steady babble of mixed booze. The stench of alcohol filled the room.

Vernon knew what she was going to do and he tried to move, but he couldn't. The pain was so intense it had virtually paralysed him. He could barely feel his legs, let alone get them to move. And he felt pissed too – really really unbelievably pissed. More pissed than he'd ever been. He wanted to pass out. He wanted to be sick. But he fought it – fought it – fought it.

Finally, Fabia had manoeuvred the bar in range.

She stepped behind it and pushed it towards Vernon with her foot.

The cabinet toppled forward, and the minibar fridge inside slid down

17

with a deep glissando. It smacked into the double doors and threw them open. Then the fridge's doors were flung open and its contents vomited out in a bright wet splash of booze, soft drink and shattered glass, drenching Vernon from the waist down.

But neither fridge nor cabinet fell over. They were stopped at a forward tilt, their full collapse arrested by the parted doors, wedged open on the carpet, and the flex and plug, which hadn't popped out of the socket.

Fabia looked around confused.

Not what she'd expected to happen either.

Then she saw the flex and swore in French at the top of her voice. '*Putain de merde!*'

Vernon lay there, fearing what she'd do next as he gripped at the carpet and tried to drag himself away, knowing it was futile.

Fabia stepped over the flex and glanced back down at him. He could tell she still really wanted to hurt him, but she was exhausted and out of breath.

She looked him up and down, sneering at his shrivelled-up dick, at his very vulnerability.

Then she flounced out of the room, cursing the whole way to the door.

Vernon lay on the floor a while. There was broken glass everywhere. His award was smashed in two. The upturned drinks cabinet was sitting in a pungent lake of blended booze.

He eventually managed to get up.

He was dizzy and unbelievably tired, his internal systems crashing all over. He looked towards the bedroom, but knew he wouldn't make it that far.

He stared at the wall in front of him, which the cabinet had covered.

He thought of the bill he'd get. Thousands and thousands.

He thought of phoning for help . . . security . . . a doctor . . .

But he couldn't even see a phone.

And then he noticed something lying there, on the floor, right under the fridge's taut electrical flex. Something black and small and soft. For an instant he thought it was a mouse, but this thing was the wrong colour, and shape, and it wasn't moving, and . . . the hotel was too new and expensive and . . .

He picked it up.

It was a tiny black thong, with a bright pink bow in the front, a rhombus-shaped hole in the back, and a snap button on the waistband, which was undone.

He slumped down on the couch and held it up. He closed the waist-band and twirled it around his finger.

He guessed it was Fabia's. He'd seen her smoothing her dress down about the hips; maybe she'd slipped off her underwear when he was in the bathroom.

He thought about her and all her potential, and what they would have been doing about now if things hadn't turned out so badly.

Then – unbelievably, to him – he was hard again.

What was that thing she'd done to him?

That thing he'd liked so much?

Oh yeah ...

He licked his fingers and closed his eyes and saw her ...

He jerked off and came quickly in the thong.

When he'd finished, he tossed it at the wastepaper basket.

Bull's-eye.

He chuckled.

Crazy bitch, he thought. At least he'd got *something* out of her.

Then he stretched out on the couch, closed his eyes and fell asleep.

And that is *exactly* how he told me it happened.

PART ONE

Hating Someone's Guts

1

When the news broke that Vernon James had been arrested for murder, I had mixed feelings. Even though we'd once been best friends, I hoped he'd be found guilty and go to jail for life.

But that wasn't the cause of conflict.

Let me explain.

I was working late as usual when the call came.

'Terry? *Terry?*' It was Janet Randall, my boss and partner of the legal firm I was employed by, Kopf-Randall-Purdom. KRP, for short.

I knew Janet was in one of her last-minute/need-it-yesterday/the-end-is-nigh panics, because I could hear her smoking on the other end of the line, taking a deep drag, holding it in. Which meant this was a *serious* panic. She'd quit five or six years ago, but she was one of those ex-smokers who always reached for cigarettes in times of stress. They made her, if anything, even more agitated.

'What's up?'

'Thank God!' she said. I'd taken my time answering the phone, hoping it'd stop ringing so I could finish what I was doing and go home. 'Ahmad Sihl just called me.'

'Who?' I asked, fighting back a yawn.

'Only one of *the* top five corporate lawyers in the country. In fact, make that top *three*.'

'Probably why I haven't heard of him,' I quipped.

There was a double-edged joke in the office about corporate lawyers not being 'real' lawyers because they only saw what a courtroom looked like on TV dramas. And KRP didn't just handle criminal law. The firm also had corporate, tax and marital divisions. Those were the biggest and most lucrative sections of the business, the money-spitting hubs, and boy did they like reminding 'the criminals' – as they called us – who we owed our livelihoods to.

The name Ahmad Sihl did ring a bell, but I couldn't quite place it. I was tired and thinking of home; my wife and two kids, my dinner, the kids' homework.

'He represents Vernon James,' Janet said.

That name I knew, and knew well.

But, initially, I thought I'd misheard.

'Who?'

'Who? *Who?* Are you an owl? *Vernon James.*'

I swallowed. Something in me went cold. My hand tightened to a fist around the phone.

And my legs turned to jelly.

'Hello ... Are you there?'

'Yeah,' I said, trying to stop the tremor from getting at my throat. 'Go on.'

'Do you know who Vernon James is?'

'Sure.' And I reeled off his CV: founder and owner of VJ Capital Management, a hugely successful hedge fund. The *Sunday Times* Rich List estimated his fortune at £145 million. Age: thirty-eight. Homes in New York, Paris, London and Grantchester, a village outside Cambridge. Married, three daughters ...

'I stand corrected! How come you know so much about him?'

'I read the business pages,' I replied, hurriedly. 'What about him?'

'He's been arrested for murder.'

'*Murder? Who? When?*' I couldn't contain my – well, *excitement*; because that's what it was. It went through me in a warm intoxicating surge. I got light-headed, dizzy. I was standing and had to sit down.

Then I realised something was off.

'What's this got to do with us?' I asked.

'Just about *everything*,' Janet said. 'Vernon doesn't have a criminal lawyer. Ahmad's asked *me* to represent him.'

'Oh ...' was all I could say to that. The ground had just given way under my feet, and I was fast-treading thin air.

'Terry, do you know how big this is going to be?' Janet said, puffing away. I could almost see her smiling through the smoke. 'We are talking *the* biggest trial in the country. This is *exactly* what we need. You know how I've been trying to get Sid Kopf to expand our division? This is *just* the kind of case I can use.'

'Sure ...' I said. But I was only half-listening.

'You know what this means for *you*?' Janet said.

Of course I knew. The Call and Response Rule, aka: the Ownership Rule. *It called, you answered, it's yours.*

Although the call had come through to my colleague, Bella, who sat opposite me, I'd picked up the phone, therefore I was working the case.

'Yeah ...?'

'What's the matter?' Janet asked.

'What do you mean?'

'This is the biggest break you'll ever get, Terry. Or do you want to stay a clerk all your life?'

24

'Long day,' I said.

'Better get used to it,' she said. 'You know if this goes well, it could mean you get the nod for the degree?'

And the hits just kept on coming ...

Every two years KRP rewarded its best clerk with a fully funded law degree. No one from the criminal division had ever won it. Our branch was too small, our cases too trifling, too under the radar. The degree invariably went to someone from corporate or tax. The prize was due to be given out this year. Sid Kopf, our CEO, had hinted that he was looking to break with tradition. Now everyone had perked up and started plotting, especially Bella, who'd already been trying to do me over from my first day on the job, three months ago. My catching the most high-profile case our division had ever had was going to mean outright war between us.

'I need you to do something for me right now,' Janet said. 'I have to go and see Vernon at Charing Cross nick in the next hour. I don't have my pen with me. I left it in my office.'

She always used the same fountain pen when she was working a case. She thought it brought her luck. She told me where to find it and asked me to bring it round to her house.

I said sure and hung up.

Then I sat on the floor and put my head in my hands.

Vernon James – arrested for murder.

Of all the payback scenarios I'd conjured up in my head, I'd never once imagined it would be in a judicial setting – and least of all, with me *defending* him.

2

Never bring a bad day home. That was what my wife and I had promised each other after the kids were born. They were entitled to their childhood.

My way of sticking to the tacit pact with my family was to put a buffer between my crises and our front door. I did that by taking long walks whenever I caught a bad situation. We lived five miles from the office, south of the river in Latchmere. The walks would loosen me up a little and give me clarity, even shift my perspective on things.

Unfortunately, I couldn't walk that evening, because I had to bring Janet her talismanic pen. So I took the train. To cap it all, today was St Patrick's Day, which meant exactly this: happy hour every hour till last orders, Guinness and Jameson half price, plenty of shamrocks on display and those stupid oversized bright-green top hats everywhere. Small crowds were spilling out of Victoria Station's four pubs, getting trolleyed before the stumble off home.

St Patrick's Day always makes me think of my parents. They're Irish. Dad's from Cork, mum's a Dubliner. They're both drinkers too, Dad especially. That's where I got it from, my old problem.

I was last to get on the train. The carriage was crammed, every seat taken, people standing in the aisles, holding on to the luggage rack, more commuters stuffed in the doorway, scowls abounding, condensation turning to rivulets on the windows.

As I stood in the cramped compartment, I clearly remembered the day I first saw Vernon James.

October 1978, a midweek afternoon. Me and my brothers were playing football in Wexford Grove in Stevenage, where I grew up. A cab stopped a few feet away from us. Vernon and his sister Gwen got out with their mother. The three of them stood on the pavement, shivering. It was cold and windy, and there were drops of rain in the air. Vernon's teeth were chattering. His dad was arguing with the driver. Vernon spotted us all looking at them. He scrutinised us, one by one. We were staring at him because we weren't used to seeing too many black people – and certainly not in our neighbourhood. Then he singled me out, the smallest, the one most like him, and he smiled and waved. Not at all shy, already confident. I didn't do anything. I just carried on staring. Then he helped his parents carry a suitcase that was almost as big as him into the basement flat two doors down from our house.

The last time I saw him was also in Stevenage, on the High Street in September 1993. That was a year and a bit after we'd fallen out. I had a lot of unanswered questions about all that, like why, and was he sure I'd done what he'd accused me of.

I'd literally turned the corner and bumped into him. We were both surprised, both immediately uncomfortable. I told him we needed to talk and he said yeah sure. So we arranged to meet in the King's Arms the next day. That had been our hangout as teenagers, because it was the only pub in town where the owner didn't care too much about serving underage drinkers, as long as they didn't look it. Vernon and I were already tall enough at fifteen to pass for legal.

He didn't show. I don't know if he deliberately stood me up, or if he was just too scared to confront me. Whatever the reason, I never saw him again.

I took Janet's pen out of my bag. A brushed stainless-steel Parker, shaped a little like a cigar tube. Her initials were engraved on the side in scrolled capitals. 'J.H.H.' She'd been using it since her O levels, for every exam and every test, literal and metaphorical. We all had our baubles, our lucky heather, to ward off the fear of failure. Mine were the shamrock cufflinks my kids had bought me for my birthday a couple of years ago. I always wore them when I thought something bad was going to happen. I didn't have them on tonight.

The train came to the first stop. People got out and the congestion eased.

I opened up the *Evening Standard* I'd picked up at the station. An unidentified Premier League footballer had been arrested for a 'savage attack' on a nightclub bouncer. I flicked through the pages. Riots in Athens, the looming Royal Wedding, the Chicago River dyed green. And then, squashed in the corner of Page Seven, a small heading:

'Body Found at Luxury Hotel'.

The report was short and scant. Maids had found a body in a room at the Blenheim-Strand, and police were currently questioning a man in connection with their enquiries. No mention of Vernon.

His name would be all over the papers tomorrow. The press had their contacts inside every major hotel in London. If that didn't produce results, they had plenty of loose-lipped, underpaid coppers on speed dial.

Of course it was a shock to me. But wasn't it always a shock to anyone who found out a close friend or good neighbour or amiable work colleague was really a serial killer or rapist or some other kind of monster? All we know of other people is what we see reflected of ourselves. Beyond that they're strangers.

When I'd known Vernon, I'd never seen him lose his temper. He'd never been violent, never thrown a punch or a kick. He never even raised his voice. His anger was glacial and controlled, all contemptuous stares and loaded silences. Sure, people changed, but not *that* much.

Yet what did I know? I hadn't seen or spoken to him in almost twenty years.

Pressure was starting to build up behind my eyes, the thoughts swarming too thickly to isolate and break down. There was Vernon and our history. There was me defending him. There was the looming office battle with Bella. And, on top of that, the case itself. Four separate serrating headaches, one head.

I got off at Clapham Junction station and headed for Janet's house, via St John's Road. It looked like every other main street in London. A McDonald's and a Starbucks, then several mobile phone shops, two supermarkets, a bank and an electronics store – all links in those long predictable chains that dragged the guts and soul out of every British town and city.

I passed several pubs, all busy. I walked faster. Pubs reminded me of hell.

Janet lived on Briar Close, off Northcote Road. It was a different kind of environment there, almost genteel, thanks to gentrification and the money that follows it. She was waiting outside her house with her motorbike driver. That was how she got around London, to and from meetings, on the back of a Suzuki GSX-R600. KRP had a firm of riders on call, mostly for deliveries and collections, but Janet used them as a chauffeur service.

'Here you go,' I said, handing her the pen.

'You didn't touch it, did you?' she said as she put the pencase in her rucksack. She had her raincoat on and flat shoes.

'How do you think I got it here?' I joked.

She chuckled as she put her helmet on. She was a good foot shorter than me, with medium-length brown hair and sharp pale-blue eyes. She was older than I was by a decade and change.

'Any more info on the case?' I asked as the rider kick-started the bike and she clambered aboard.

'The victim's a woman,' she said. 'A blonde.'

3

The place I called home was half an hour's walk and a whole different world away from Janet's house.

We lived in a three-bedroom flat in a place called the Garstang Estate, near Battersea High Street – the 'we' being yours truly, my wife Karen, and our two children, Ray and Amy, who were then eight and five respectively.

The estate was a human battery farm – a regimented sprawl of identical brick blocks the colour of toxic factory clouds and bad-tempered skies, consisting of sixty-two apartments and maisonettes, spread over five storeys with communal walkways. Laundry flapped from every other balcony like the sails of a wrecked galleon; satellite dishes clustered at the corners of the walls in an upward creep, reminiscent of an advance of mutant toadstools; and, in the car parks between blocks, a quartet of CCTV cameras were perched atop twenty-foot-high metal shafts, as ineffective against urban evils as church gargoyles.

Dozens of different nationalities lived here, side by side; a regular melting pot, the metropolis in microcosm. There were few friendships

28

on the estate, mainly acquaintanceships. Everyone coexisted peacefully enough, as long as they managed to avoid each other, which most did or very quickly learned to do.

I hung up my coat and went to the living room. The light and telly were on, but there was no sound. Karen had paused whatever programme she was watching because Amy had fallen asleep in her arms. She'd taken the opportunity to snatch a few moments' rest, but conked out herself.

I gazed over them, lying there together on the couch. Karen had her arms around our daughter, who was snuggled up to her, face buried in her mother's armpit, just like she used to when she was a baby. I wanted to kiss them both, but I didn't want to wake them and spoil the perfect image before me. Instead I committed the sight to memory, every nuance – the way their bodies lay, facing each other on their sides, almost, but not quite touching; how they'd both folded their legs up, as if in mid-jump; Amy grasping the sleeve of Karen's T-shirt tight in her little fist.

I tiptoed past them to the kids' bedroom and rapped on the door with my fingertips.

'Come in,' a young voice beckoned imperiously.

My son was sitting in the upper tier of the bunk bed reading *The 39 Clues*.

'Good evening, Ray,' I said.

'Hi Dad.' He smiled and put down his book.

Ray was actually my adopted son. He was mixed race, the product of an on-off relationship Karen had had with a black Brazilian. He'd split for good shortly after he found out Karen was pregnant.

I owed my family and the life I now had to Ray.

I met him first, before Karen, one bright Sunday afternoon at a fête on Clapham Common in 2004. I was working as a part-time 'children's entertainer' then, the Blue Clown – blue of costume, wig and mouth. I wasn't a big draw. My audience averaged one or two kids plus their parents an hour. They'd gawp for five minutes and leave without laughing. Then Ray waddled up to me, on his own, barely two feet tall, all frowns and curiosity. I did my routine for him, which involved walking into a nearby lamp-post and falling over. Ray was as unimpressed as everyone else. Except he stayed put, determined to be entertained. So I repeated the routine with variations, bumping my foot against the post, hitting it with my head, and even twirling around it, but to no avail. I couldn't get a rise out of him. Finally, I resorted to the only other trick I knew, the thing I did at children's parties – animal sounds. He didn't respond to my horse or donkey, my miaowing made him cover his ears and my barking made him cry. But when I did my seal noises – *Ar-Ar-Ar-Arrrrr-Ar-Ar-Ar* – I hit paydirt. Ray's face lit up and he laughed and clapped his hands ... for all of a minute, before his frown returned.

Then Karen appeared. Frantic and tearful, she had a steward and a cop at her side. It turned out Ray had been missing for an hour. He'd wandered off while Karen was buying him a balloon.

I didn't talk to Karen then. She grabbed Ray in her arms and carried him away, sobbing with relief.

That should have been the end of it, but, later the following week, I was working my other job, stacking shelves in Asda, when I spotted Ray sitting in a half-full shopping trolley. Karen was nearby, choosing fruit. Ray stared at me hard, and I swore he recognised me.

It was one of those moments where your life turns on a decision. In my case it was whether or not to make a crappy seal noise. So I did and Ray started laughing and clapping.

I introduced myself to Karen. 'I didn't recognise you with your clothes on,' she said.

And that was pretty much how it started.

'What did you do today?' I asked him.

'I got 85 per cent in maths.'

'That's great,' I said. Maths had never been my strong suit.

'It's very good, but not great,' he corrected me, after a moment. 'Great is 90 per cent or more. Do you know maths is the only subject you can score 100 per cent in?'

Typical, I thought. Not even nine and he was a glass half-empty guy. He was a bright spark, much cleverer than I'd been at his age. He was a quick study and a voracious reader, one of those natural intellectuals who find out everything there is to know about something that interests him.

I looked at my watch. It was almost 9 p.m.

'Can I tell you something?'

'If you want,' he said.

'You won't understand this now, but in time you may,' I said, looking at him. 'Always finish what you start. OK? Every beginning deserves an end. There's nothing worse than unfinished business.'

Ray wasn't one of those kids who simply nodded along to everything you said to make you happy and go away. He liked to think things through. And he was thinking now, furrowing his brow as he tried to make sense of what I'd said. When he couldn't, his brow relaxed.

'I know you're not talking about my dinner,' he said, eventually.

I laughed and tousled his hair – or tried to, because it barely yielded to my fingers.

'Your bedtime's looming. You cleaned your newtons?'

'Newtons' was Manchester slang for teeth. That came from Karen, a proud Mancunian. She kept talking about moving back 'home' at some unspecified point in the future, but every time we went there to visit her parents and she found that another part of the city had changed or disappeared altogether, she started missing London.

Ray shook his head.

'Off you go, then,' I said.

I sat down on Amy's bunk. I was exhausted but knew I wouldn't sleep tonight. Too many thoughts leapfrogging around in my brain. And I didn't have the first clue how I'd face tomorrow, let alone get through it. I needed a plan.

Ray had left his laptop open on his desk and forgotten to turn it off, as he often did. I checked what he'd been looking at. Karen and I made a point of doing that at least twice a week, just to be on the safe side. We were discreet about it.

Tonight he'd browsed Wikipedia and two history websites for a homework assignment.

I turned off the computer.

Moments later Ray came back, followed by Karen carrying Amy.

We tucked them in and kissed them goodnight. Then we went to the living room, where I kissed Karen and gave her a hug, as I always did at the end of the day, when we were alone.

We sat down on the couch. Karen looked ready for bed.

'Your dinner's in the micro,' she yawned. She was wearing a faded New Order *Technique* T-shirt two sizes too big for her.

'Not hungry,' I said. 'I need to talk to you about something.'

She sat up, looked at me a little closer, read trouble the way only she could. A little of the sleepiness left her face.

'Shall I make us some tea, then?' she asked. By tea, Karen meant one of five herbal varieties. They were all supposed to do wonders for you, but I never touched any of them. When they tasted of anything, they tasted horrible.

'Coffee for me. *Not* decaff. And *definitely* not instant either. Real coffee.'

For the first time in God knows how long – what I really wanted – no, *craved* – was a drink. A tall cold Guinness Export: 8 per cent alcohol, a kick in every sip. That's how I'd always started my benders. Five of those, then the spirits . . .

I choked the urge.

'That kind of talk, is it?' she said.

''Fraid so, yeah.'

31

4

There's no such thing as a wholly truthful person. Everyone lies. That's a given. Liars come in two forms – fibbers and omitters; storytellers and editors. I'm the latter, 'economical with the truth', as they say – a rationer of facts. Too much truth can be complicated.

So while Karen was making the drinks, I sat at the living-room table trying to work out how to proceed – what to tell her, what not to tell her; how far to go, and where to stop.

I'd been here before, literally, at this table, in this position. When we'd started getting serious – as in meeting each other's families and talking about cohabiting – I made an executive decision about what to tell Karen about my past. As a single mother raising a young child she deserved to know what she and Ray were getting into. And I didn't want her finding out about me from other people.

That was when we had the first of our coffee talks. Long, serious and all through the night.

I'd told her about my lost years – aka 'The Dark Ages', as we'd come to refer to that period. I'd been open with her – more so than with anyone – but only to a certain extent.

Which meant I hadn't told her about Vernon James and what he did to me. There wasn't any point. But just because he didn't exist in our life, it didn't mean my hatred for him had diminished. If anything it had intensified, because I'd nurtured it in secret. I'd never talked about him to anyone. I didn't like it, not one bit. I wanted to be rid of it, but in the right way. With him paying for every wrong thing he'd done to me.

Karen came in with the coffee and tea and sat down. I looked at her for a moment, mousy blonde hair, eyes the colour of faded jeans, and thin lips she'd finally learned not to try and hide under over-applied lipstick.

'So what happened?' she asked.

I told her about Janet's phone call; the new client – wealthy, high profile and a murder suspect.

Her eyes lit up.

'She called *you* ...?'

'She actually called Adolf, but there was no one around so I answered.'

'Adolf' was our name for Bella – full name: Arabella Hogan. Same initials as Der Führer. Bella hated me, and the feeling was mutual.

'That's great, though, Terry!' Karen said. The way she pronounced my name sounded like 'terror' – *Terruh*. 'That could set you up. The promotion, the degree ... We might finally be able to get out of here!'

'Yeah. That's what Janet said. In so many words.'

On average it took a clerk with a law degree about two years to become a paralegal, as long as they didn't mind taking an industrial dose of shit. An unqualified clerk like me, however, rarely got a look-in – unless a law firm sponsored their degree. Few firms did, but KRP was one of them.

'Hold up,' Karen said. 'You haven't even told me this fella's name yet – the murderer.'

'*Alleged* murderer. Innocent until proven and all that,' I reminded her.

'Sorry, Your Honour.'

'That's American. Here it's "My Lord".'

'Whatever. What's his name?'

I took a deep breath.

'Vernon James,' I mumbled, looking down at the coffee I hadn't touched, meeting my eyes in the cup.

'Sounds like a hairdresser,' she said.

'Have you heard of him?' I asked.

'No. Should I?'

I could've left it there, carried on pretending I didn't know him. But I was in deep trouble. And Karen was great in a crisis. Never lost her cool. Plus she was a company accountant, as good at solving puzzles as creating them.

'There's a problem with me and the case. A big problem,' I said and looked at her. A long, lingering look. This was the moment right before our old life disappeared. Going . . .

Going . . .

Gone.

'I knew Vernon. A long time back. We were friends.'

'In Stevenage was this?'

'Yeah.'

'How come you never mentioned him before?'

'I haven't seen him in eighteen years. Half my life ago. That's as good as never seeing someone again. '

'Yeah, but if I'd known someone who'd become rich and successful . . .'

'Things didn't end well between us. In fact, they ended about as badly as they possibly could.'

'What happened?'

'He fucked my life up.'

'How?'

Then Karen started working something out. She and Ray both frowned their brows into the same walnut furrows when they were thinking hard.

33

I let her do the basic arithmetic.

2011 AD minus 18 years, equals 1993 AD.

'This have something to do with the Dark Ages?' she asked.

'Just about everything.'

Karen pondered in silence.

The Serbian couple downstairs were rowing. Or at least they might have been. It was hard to tell. When they'd first moved in a year ago, all they seemed to do was argue, shouting at the top of their voices, sounding hysterical. We'd gone down to complain – and to make sure the woman wasn't getting battered. Turned out they weren't arguing at all. They were on the phone to their respective families back home. The lines were so bad they had to shout.

Karen clicked into gear.

'Let's isolate the problem, shall we?'

'There's more than just the one problem,' I said, taking a sip of coffee. 'As you know, I've lied on my CV. That's a sackable offence anywhere, but in a legal firm it's castratable. It's all right to represent liars and lie on their behalf, but you can't be one yourself. You've got to draw the line somewhere. As far as KRP are concerned I left school after my A levels. I haven't mentioned my year at Cambridge, the law degree I never finished. I was at Cambridge with Vernon. All he has to do is tell Janet and that's me out on my ear.'

'Why don't you say you can't take the case for personal reasons?' Karen said.

'I could do that. But then I'll have to explain why. And Cambridge'll come up one way or another, whether I tell Janet or he does. And if she hears it from him it'll be even worse: "Yeah, I knew Terry Flynt. He got kicked out of Cambridge for theft."'

'*Theft?*' Karen started and almost stood up.

I hadn't meant to say it the way I did, abruptly like that. I'd intended to build up to it slowly. But it came out anyway.

Karen looked at me like I'd turned into a complete stranger.

'I thought you told me you got kicked out of Cambridge for failing your exams.'

'*And* that,' I said.

She sat back and glared at me. Her eyes had lost their clarity, gone a milky turquoise. If this was a police interrogation, I'd be screwed about now, caught out contradicting my statement; fair copped, guv.

I couldn't hold her stare, so I looked away at the digital photo frame on the mantelpiece. There were pictures of the four of us over the years, going back to when we'd first met, our wedding, me in my clown suit on Ray's third birthday, Ray holding baby Amy, the four of us at Ray's prize-giving. It felt like I was watching the best part of my life flashing by.

'Why don't you start again, from the *very* beginning?' Karen said.

5

'I called him VJ. We were at the same school. He was the only black kid in class.

'We didn't become friends immediately. Though we lived on the same road, the only time I saw him outside school was every other Saturday morning. Him and his sister Gwen would help their mum do the shopping. They didn't have a trolley, so they used this rusted old pram that didn't have a canopy. It was a strange sight, them pushing that thing down the road. The wheels squeaked something terrible. You'd hear them coming a mile off.'

I smiled at the memory.

'The other thing I remember about VJ was that on Mondays he always reeked of bleach. He only had two white shirts for school. His mum'd boil them on the weekends.

'I remember the exact day we became friends. It was in March 1980. It was right after The Jam had gone straight to number one with "Going Underground". This was a big deal in my household. My brothers were massive fans. Paul Weller was their icon, their working-class hero. They cheered when they heard. It was like *they'd* gone to number one.

'Anyway I was on my way home when I saw this group of older kids surrounding him. They were pushing him, hitting him. They'd dumped his books on the floor, ripped pages out.

'I told them to stop. They didn't. There was this skip nearby. It was full of old bricks. So I grabbed one and threw it at the tallest kid. Caught him right on the temple. Then I threw another. Hit a kid smack in the face. Busted his nose, I think. They all ran off. I helped VJ pick his stuff up and walked him home.

'Me and VJ walked to school together every day after that. We got to know each other. He was a total laugh. A really funny guy. Ultra-sharp. King of the one-liners.

'As you know, my family isn't academically inclined. There were no books in our house at all. No one read unless they had to. Not even a paper. I was expected to leave school at sixteen and go into the job market. I was dreading that.

'The options were limited in Stevenage. But, thanks to being around

VJ, I started taking my school work seriously. I saw it as a way out of a pre-planned life, that slo-mo trot to the knacker's yard.

'It was cramped where we both lived, so me and him used to do our homework in the local library. Studying became fun. We pushed each other.

'For the first time, I started doing well in tests and exams. I suddenly had drive and focus. Where I'd been middling before, now I was coming second in the year. VJ was always top, of course. But there wasn't much between us, grades-wise. I got twelve O levels, three A levels. Straight As. And we both got into Cambridge. We were the first people from our school to do that.

'I owe it all to VJ. If he hadn't come into my life, I don't know what would've happened. And I mean that. No matter how bad things turned out later, I'd never take that away from him. And I never will. I hope our kids find a friend like that, I really do.'

I paused there. I couldn't quite believe what I'd just said, the warmth of my tone, the stir of conciliatory feelings.

'Now, VJ's home life was horrible. They lived in two rooms in a basement. His dad – Rodney – was a nasty, *nasty* man. Six foot tall, bald and skinny. Looked like this dark praying mantis. He was bitter as hell, almost permanently angry and hateful with it. You'd be talking to him and suddenly he'd just grow quiet. And he'd get this look in his eye. You'd swear you'd said or done something wrong, but it wasn't that at all. It wasn't you. It was all his rage boiling up.

'Rodney had come over to England from Trinidad. He'd been a "somebody" there – a bank manager in Spanish Town, the capital. When he came here, the only work he could get was manual – or "*de menial*" as he called it.

'He took his frustrations out on his family. VJ, most of all. Not physically, but mentally. Rodney was always putting him down. In public too. Nothing VJ ever did was good enough. Nothing. He just kept on trying to crush him.

'I once asked VJ why his dad treated him so badly. And do you know what he said? "It's 'cause he knows that, one day soon, I'll do something he can't – and that's leave and *never* come back."'

'How old was he then?'

'Twelve or thirteen. Rodney was never going to get in VJ's way, because VJ was one of those people who always knew what he wanted,' I said.

'I think there's three kinds of people in the world. Those that know what they want from the start, and they get it. Then there's those that don't know what they want, but find out later and settle down. And then there's the ones who never know what they want, and they never get anywhere. Life's lost causes, the born losers. They drift and then they die.'

'Which are you?' she asked.

'I've been the second and the third, but never the first. That was VJ,' I said, fiddling with my cup handle.

'In the early 1980s Rodney bought an old betting place opposite Stevenage train station. He reopened it as a cornershop. We used to work there, me and VJ, on weekends. It was one of the busiest shops in town. It was open seven days a week, six in the morning to ten at night. You knew if you ran out of essentials, you could always go to Rodney's. Rodney as good as lived behind the counter. Never took a day off. Except Christmas – and that's only because he couldn't get a licence to open up.

'Every month or so we'd go to France. Calais. We'd load up on cheap fags and drink. This was long before the EU regulations, so prices were low. We'd fill the van up and take the ferry back. Rodney'd sell the fags and booze in the shop cheaper than anywhere else in town. Made a fortune.

'The family moved out of our road and into a semi-detached house in Stevenage Old Town. The posh part. But me and VJ still did our walk to school. I'd stop by the shop to pick him up, because he worked there with his dad in the mornings,' I said.

'Then, in 1989 Rodney was murdered. The police found him in the shop's backroom. He'd been stabbed. Twenty-two times.'

Karen's mouth dropped and her eyes widened.

'*Christ.*'

'The cops reckoned it happened just before Rodney was closing up. He was always on his own then.'

'Did they catch anyone?'

'No. There was no CCTV in the shop. No witnesses.'

'Was anything stolen?'

'Yeah. The safe and till were empty. And a load of fags and booze too.'

'How did Vernon react?'

'He was shocked, obviously, at first. But there were no tears. And I hate to say this, but afterwards he – well, he blossomed. Physically it was like he grew a whole foot taller. He became a lot more confident, socially.

'We never talked much about the murder. He did once say it was a shame his last memory of his dad was a bad one. The morning of the murder they'd had an argument in the shop, right in front of me and all the customers. Rodney wanted VJ to leave school and work in the shop

37

full time. VJ had his heart set on going to Cambridge. Rodney said – or shouted, more like – "*You'll go to university over my dead body.*" And VJ said, "*Hurry up and drop dead, then.*"'

'Famous last words,' Karen said.

'That's one way of putting it,' I said.

Now, we'd arrived at the crossroads moment of our Big Talk.

On my way back from Janet's house I'd decided how much I could afford to tell Karen about my past – how much *more*, that is. My Dark Ages were about to become darker still.

Karen had an expressive face, as good as transparent when it came to telegraphing thoughts and emotions. It made the day-to-day easy in our marriage, as I could foresee potential arguments and conflicts and head them off in time.

Looking at her across the table, I watched the doubts and questions convening quickly behind her brow.

Here it came . . .

the obvious question:

'Did he . . .' she started, and then paused for the right words. Not that there was a delicate way of asking what she wanted to know.

'I mean . . . Do you think he could've . . .'

'Killed his dad?' I prompted. VJ had done me wrong in two big ways. I was about to reveal the first, but not the second. *That* wasn't relevant. Not to Karen, not to the family, and not to the matter at hand. I was keeping *that* out of it.

'Yeah.'

'I honestly don't know. At the time – when it all happened, when we were still friends – I was *sure* he hadn't done it. I was *convinced* he was innocent. Just *knew* it. That's why we gave him the alibi.'

'*The* . . .? You *what*?'

'We gave him an alibi. Said he was with us that night.'

'Whoa! Rewind, Terry. *Alibi?* . . . Your *family*? . . . You're losing me.'

I leaned in, lowering my voice so the kids wouldn't hear.

'His mum and sister were out of town. Up in Birmingham visiting relatives. VJ was home alone that night. He told me he'd been studying.'

'But he had no one to back him up?'

'That's right,' I said. 'Stevenage was a rough old place back then, but murders were pretty rare. Rodney's killing was big news. All anyone could talk about. The police were under a lot of pressure to catch someone.

'The lead detective was a bloke called Quinlan. I forget his first name. He interviewed VJ for two hours. VJ came round mine straight afterwards. He was in a real state. Totally shook up.

'He told us he'd lied to Quinlan. Said he'd been with me that night, in my house. He said he didn't have any choice, that Quinlan had talked to him like he knew he'd done it.'

'And how did you react?'

'VJ was my best friend. My only thought was to help him in any way I could,' I said. 'Luckily for him, Quinlan didn't get round to me for a couple of days. It gave us time to get the story absolutely straight. Yes, VJ was round mine that night, like he said. We did homework and ate dinner with my family.'

'How was your family involved?'

'Almost everyone was in the house when VJ came over after his interview. My mum knew the kind of trouble he was in, what it could mean for him. Arrest, remand, a trial. Even if he was found innocent, it would ruin his life. So she worked out what we'd all say. Her, me, my brothers.'

'What about your dad?'

'He was down the pub that night.'

'So you lied to the police?' Karen said.

'It's called "perverting the course of justice" – but yeah, I lied. We all did. For him.'

Karen was speechless. And then horror crept into her expression. I headed it off.

'Look, I was fifteen, Karen. I didn't know any better,' I said. 'And we all loved VJ. We're not the kind of people who throw their friends over.

'Besides, it was unthinkable that he could have done it. He wasn't violent. He never got into fights at school at all. On top of that, Quinlan didn't have any evidence. The police searched VJ's house and found nothing. No weapon, no traces of blood, none of the stolen goods. Nothing.'

Karen stayed in stunned mode. This was bigger than just me. This was her in-laws too, Ray and Amy's grandparents.

'Was that the end of it?' she asked, after a while.

'Oh no,' I said. 'Quinlan knew something was off.

'He didn't lean on my mum, or my brothers. He leaned on me. Went over and over my story. Kept on telling me he didn't believe me, that I was protecting a murderer, that I wasn't going to help my friend in the long run, that me and my family would go to prison too. But I stuck to my story.

'VJ got it much worse. Quinlan made his life hell. He'd be waiting outside school when we got out, or when we were going in. Staring at VJ. A couple of times he came in to school and pulled VJ out of class for questioning.

'We all used to think that was it, that VJ was going to get charged.

Which was exactly what Quinlan wanted to happen. Start the old rumour mill going. Didn't take much in Stevenage. Everyone thought VJ had done it.'

'Could Quinlan do that to him – legally?'

'This was still the Gene Hunt era of policing, so yeah, he could. And he did – until our headmaster intervened,' I said. 'He said Quinlan was only harassing VJ because he was black, and he got a London lawyer involved. The lawyer complained to Quinlan's bosses. A week later Quinlan got taken off the case. I heard he got disciplined for mishandling the investigation.'

'And the police never caught anyone, did they?'

'No.'

Karen took her cup in her hands and half-raised it off the table, before putting it down.

'What happened next?' she said.

'In 1991 we both went to Cambridge University. Same college. Sidney Sussex. I was doing law, VJ economics.

'It was a whole other world. Full of bright, posh, rich, beautiful people.

'I felt totally out of place there. The first term I was miserable, wondered what I'd got into, couldn't wait to go home. VJ loved it, though. It was the first giant step to where he wanted to be.

'At the beginning we saw a lot of each other. But we were doing different subjects and had different timetables. We also had different kinds of friends. That's when I really started drinking – a lot. And doing a few drugs too. I started having a great time, but I lost focus. I forgot why I was at Cambridge. I was an unremarkable student, neither good nor bad, just doing enough to get by. A coaster in a racer's world.

'VJ fell in with this guy called Anil Iqbal, who was in his final year. Flash, rich. He had invites to all the best parties, and these really stunning girlfriends. Blondes. Always blondes.

'He mentored VJ. He played the stockmarkets, recommended VJ go to work for an investment bank, because, after Thatcher's Big Bang, the City was wide open and there were fortunes to be made if you were hungry, lucky and shrewd enough.

'I didn't get on with Anil. Putting it mildly. He was an arrogant prick. That arrogance of people who've never known a hard day in their lives. Never had to go out to work. Never had to worry about money. They just look down on everyone. He was like that. VJ was fascinated by him. I could tell he wanted – not to *be* Anil, but to have what he had.'

'Sounds like you were drifting apart,' Karen said.

'Yeah, we were, I suppose,' I said.

She stared at me intently for a moment, her face stitched with worry; maybe trying to see how bad my next revelation would be. What was worse than covering up for a potential murderer?

'In the summer term – the final term of the year – we both had exams,' I said. 'The night before my first exam, I was in my room when this note got pushed under the door. It was from VJ. He said his diary had gone missing from his room and could I give it back immediately.'

'His *diary*?' Karen frowned.

'Yeah. Not a diary in the sense of an appointment book, but like a journal, a record of daily happenings.'

'Like *Adrian Mole*?' she asked.

'That's right,' I said. 'It was news to me. I'd never seen it. I never even knew he kept one. And here he was accusing me of stealing it. I thought it was a sick joke.'

'What did you do?'

'Well, I had the exam the next morning. Someone stronger would've put the note aside, dealt with it later. Not me. The note upset me. And I wanted to get to the bottom of it. I actually thought Anil might've been behind it,' I said.

'I went to VJ's room. He wasn't there. Someone told me he was in Magdalene College bar. So off I went. It was a ten-minute walk away. And sure enough, there he was – him, Anil and a whole bunch of girls. I went up to him and said, "What's all this about?" VJ looked at me with the deadest, coldest eyes and said, "You took my diary. I know you've got it." I asked him what proof he had. And his very words were – and I'll never forget this – "*I can't think of anyone else who'd take it.*"'

'He said *that*? To *you*?'

I nodded.

Karen rubbed her forehead and stared down at the table for a while.

'*Did* you steal his diary?'

'Of course I didn't!' I shouted, slamming my fist down on the table. She jumped. 'How can you even ask me that?'

'I had to, Terry. I'm sorry,' she said, softly. 'It's just . . . It just sounds so . . . *weird*, that's all. Him accusing you like that, out of the blue.'

'I didn't even know the diary existed. And I'm not a thief.'

'But why did he accuse *you*? After everything you did for him? How could he?'

'I don't know. I *still* don't know.'

'He had *no* proof?'

'None.'

'I don't get it, Terry. I mean what could've caused him to . . .? Had he seen you steal anything in the past?'

41

'Karen, I thought I just—'

'OK, OK,' she backed off, palms up and out.

I was glaring at her now. She was asking the same questions I'd asked myself over and over. Why?

'What happened next?'

'I told him it was bullshit, that I'd never do something like that. But I was confused, tripping over my words, angry, shouting my head off. Anil, meanwhile, sat there, smirking. Which pissed me off even more. And all those girls with them were giggling. As for VJ – I might as well have been talking to a brick wall. He just kept on looking at me, like he was *sure* it was me, like he was *convinced*.

'Then I got chucked out of the college. I headed back to Sidney. On the way, I passed a group of local lads. Not students. Blokes out on the piss. The pubs had shut and they were getting kebabs. One of them said something to me. I mouthed off back. Next thing I know, I'm on the ground, getting the shit kicked out of me. I got kicked in the head a couple of times. I was knocked out. When I came to, these cops were standing over me.'

And this was where Karen had come in, seven years ago, when I'd told her the first draft of my past.

This was how and when and where the Dark Ages had started: that night in Cambridge, appropriately enough with me lying unconscious on the pavement. That's what the shrink told me at the Lister Hospital. Wires had come loose in the beating, he'd said. He saw a lot of cases like mine, personality disorders caused by head traumas. It was fairly common. And treatable too. Lithium ... those pretty pale-pink pills ...

'They took me to A&E. I got checked for concussion, given pain-killers. By then it was five or six in the morning. A couple of hours later, looking like the Elephant Man, I sat my exam. It was a disaster, of course. The other papers were disasters too. I failed the lot.

'I was called before the review board. Usually when you fail they'll let you carry on and finish your course, but you get a degree without Honours. No letters after your name. They call it a Special.

'Only that didn't happen with me. And they knew about VJ's diary.

'The board told me I should've brought the matter to the college, that my failure to do so showed I had no respect for authority or rules of any kind. Therefore I had no business doing law. So I was sent down.'

'"Sent down"?'

'Cambridge parlance for "expelled".'

'God ... So if it wasn't for the diary ...?'

'I probably wouldn't have got kicked out. But that's all speculation now.'

She rubbed her eyes and sighed. Then she took my hands.

'Why didn't you tell me *any* of this before, Terry?'

'I was long over it when I met you. You and Ray were the present and future. That was the past. VJ didn't matter. After I met you, my life started making sense. It had purpose. Tomorrow was worth looking forward to,' I said.

She stared at me a long moment, looking right into my eyes, probing for deeper secrets. But she saw nothing beyond what I'd told her. I was still the same person she'd met. I hadn't changed, even if my past had – somewhat.

I was relieved.

'What happened when you went back to Stevenage?'

'I didn't tell anyone I'd got kicked out. I couldn't face telling my parents. They were so proud of me, especially Mum. I stayed in my room most of that summer. Then, one day, Mum asked me when I was going to get my things together to go back to college. It was September. I'd barely noticed the time fly. That's when I told her. And Dad.'

'How'd they take it?'

'Mum was livid. She wanted to go round to VJ's house and confront him. Dad . . .? Dad didn't give a shit. He told me they had vacancies on the building site.

'After that things went blurry. I worked in Stevenage. All sorts of stuff. Mostly manual. That thing I'd tried to escape – the pre-planned life? It got me. But I didn't care. I was drinking. Drinking every day. Drinking as soon as the pubs opened, drinking till they closed. I drank so much I couldn't tell the difference between falling asleep and passing out. Then, about a year later, I ran into VJ in the High Street, by accident.'

'What happened?'

'He was pleasant enough, I suppose. But distanced too, like he was talking to a casual acquaintance he hadn't seen in a long while. I said we needed to talk. He agreed to meet me the next day. He never showed. I waited and waited. He never came.'

I left out the next part. How I'd gone round his house that night. Pissed and pissed off. Spoiling for a fight. I'd rung the bell so hard it jammed. Then I started kicking the door. His mum had leaned out of the window and threatened to call the cops. "Call 'em then, you fuckin' black bitch!" And she had. And two coppers came and put me in a car and took me down the station, booked me as drunk and disorderly and stuck me in a cell to sleep it off. The next morning I was given a caution and a cup of tea and sent home.

'That was the last time you saw him?'

'Yeah.'

'So what are you going to do now?' she asked.

'It's a damned-if-I-do, damned-if-I-don't situation. If I tell Janet what I've told you, I'm out on my ear. If I say nothing and go into this with my fingers crossed, VJ will be well within his rights to refuse to work with me because of what happened between us.'

She thought about it a moment, but not for long.

'You're not the judge and jury. You're not a barrister or a lawyer. You just take notes. That *is* your job, right?' she said.

'In a nutshell, yeah.'

'So you can't affect the case or the outcome of the trial. Your role in it's minor. You're unimportant. Vernon'll know that. Secondly, you don't know what happened with his diary. Maybe he found it, or maybe he found out who really took it and was too ashamed to tell you, especially after it got you kicked out of Cambridge. Third, whatever happened between the two of you was over twenty years ago—'

'Nineteen,' I reminded her.

'Whatever. You were as good as kids then. People move on. You have. He has,' she said. 'Plus he'll have more pressing things on his mind. Like the fact he's been arrested for murder ... *Again.*'

'He was never arrested the first time.'

'No,' she said. 'But you can't cheat karma, can you?'

Which was a way of looking at it, I suppose, if you believed that you paid in kind for wrongs you did to others. But if that was the case, that would've meant VJ *had* killed his dad.

'So your advice is: say nothing and hope for the best?'

'What else can you do, Terry? What's the worst that can happen, eh? You lose your job. No big deal. You'll find another.'

'There's a recession on,' I reminded her.

'Recessions only affect people who are picky about what they do,' she said. 'That doesn't apply to you.'

And right on cue, one of life's little ironies happened. A picture of me in my blue clown suit fizzled up in the digital frame. It was the last time I'd worn it, complete with facepaint and big smiling sausage red lips and that blue wig that stained my neck whenever I sweated.

'When are you likely to see him?'

'Maybe as early as tomorrow,' I said.

'The sooner the better. You'll know where you stand.'

'Why is it I feel like I'm still paying for something I didn't do?' I asked her. She had no answer to that.

6

After Karen had gone to bed, I went to the spare room.

Everything we no longer had use for but couldn't face throwing away ended up here, packed, sealed and stacked in cardboard boxes. Clothes, kids' toys, books, videos, unused wedding presents. For the last two years we'd promised to clear the place out, strip the peeling wallpaper, replace the threadbare carpet tiles, but we never did. We simply made another promise and kept on adding to the clutter. It was too convenient the way it was.

Especially for me.

This was where I came to be alone and think; my retreat. Here with all the rejected stuff of our lives.

I kept my big black and brass trunk in the corner, by the door. I'd used it to move my stuff from Stevenage and London. It had belonged to my dad, who'd brought it over on the boat from Ireland to Liverpool a million years ago. He hadn't asked for it back.

I pulled the trunk across the door and opened the padlock with the key I kept Blu-tacked to the back.

There wasn't much in there. My clown clobber, wrapped in clear drycleaner plastic, was the first thing anyone would see. Then, tucked upright, against the side, my framed Sidney Sussex matriculation photo from 1991. I hadn't seen it in ten years. I'd wrapped it in parcel paper, put it in a big jiffy bag and superglued the flap shut.

And in a corner, almost invisible, shrinkwrapped in dull black plastic, was a metal container about the size and shape of a bigger than average shoebox. The box was locked and I'd long thrown away the key. Which had been a pointless thing to do, because I didn't need to see the contents ever again. I'd memorised them years ago, every word, every comma and full stop, every date.

As with everything else in the room, it was waiting to be dumped.

Karen didn't know about the box or the picture.

Just like she didn't know I crept in here when she slept.

Just like she hadn't known about VJ.

And just like she didn't know the rest of the story, the other part . . .

The coda.

Talking about him tonight, about the diary and the beating and getting kicked out of Cambridge, should've brought me some kind of relief, a little clarity. But it hadn't. I felt no differently now than I had yesterday.

I hated VJ.

I'd hated him almost all my adult life.

I wished him ill. I wished to see him destroyed the way he'd destroyed me.

Yeah, I know . . .

Be careful what you wish for, in case you get it.

Well, I was getting '*it*' all right.

By fate or coincidence or plain dumb luck, I'd have a front-row seat to VJ's demise. Justice was being served up by way of the law.

Even if I lost my job at the end of it, it would be worth it; if only to see the look on his face when he recognised me, walking back into his life at the moment he was at his most frightened and vulnerable – and most in need of a friend. He'd know then he was paying for far more than the crime he was accused of. He'd know that what had gone around – a long time ago – had come around.

Karen was right. She'd said it best.

You can't cheat karma.

Can you?

7

The next morning I headed back to the office. Everyone on the train platform at Clapham Junction looked miserable, like they were contemplating jumping on the rails. It was the life of work, and it got to us all. Five days a week, you get out of bed before you want to, go to a place you don't want to be, do things you'd rather not do, and publicly tolerate a small group of people you'd rather not know.

I checked the digital board. The train was delayed. The platform was windblown, wet and dark, with little to no shelter from the elements. The clocks would be going forward soon, but you couldn't guess it would be brighter later. Up ahead, along the rails, I could see part of central London, still lit up as if it were the middle of the night.

I picked up my copy of *Metro*. The arrest had made the front page. 'West End Hotel Murder'.

The report was more detailed. It named VJ as the suspect in custody, and said that the body had been found in a £2000-a-night suite in the Blenheim-Strand, where he'd been staying. The writer couldn't resist mentioning that VJ had been named Ethical Person of the Year just twelve hours before his arrest.

At Victoria I bought all the papers. There was something about VJ in every one. Third, fourth pages. Prominent pieces all. The broadsheets carried a slight variation of the same photograph of him after the award ceremony, posing with his trophy, flashing his broadest smile. 'Murder Horror in Posh Hotel' ran one headline, 'Millionaire in Sleaze Death Arrest' ran another. VJ's trial had as good as started.

I walked out of the station and headed up Buckingham Palace Road. It was close to 8 a.m. and the street was clogged with crawling traffic on both sides. The sun was up, but the light was weak, as if the sky were a dirty window the rays were struggling to penetrate.

I passed the art deco coach station and turned down Elizabeth Street. A short stretch of the road was geared towards one-stop itinerants, the new arrivals and departees coming on and off the coaches. Newsagents, a short row of greasy back-to-back chicken and burger places, souvenir shops selling nothing but Prince William and Kate Middleton memorabilia, and cafés with smokers sat shivering outside.

Two minutes later the whole neighbourhood jumped up three social classes, and you could almost hear the disposable millions fluttering in the wind. I was in Belgravia, one of the wealthiest areas not just in London or Britain, but the world. All grand terraces and great squares of white stucco Georgian houses, fringed with stark black railings gleaming like patent leather. There was a sense of timelessness here, where nothing had lost one iota of its original shade or class or desirability, and the smooth broad streets looked clean enough to eat off.

I crossed to Belgrave Square, home to numerous embassies, each identified by their respective flags flapping from poles outside the buildings they occupied.

At the next square, I turned right and headed for KRP.

Kopf-Randall-Purdom was one of the top private law firms in Britain. They were big, as in highly successful. And they were big, as in they outright owned numbers 15–20 of Cubitt Square. That's a whole block of six-storey nineteenth-century terraced houses; or, roughly £200 million-worth of real estate.

There were fourteen of us in the criminal division – two solicitors, in-house barristers and paralegals, three clerks and PAs, a graduate trainee and a receptionist. We were always busy, keeping the high-value clients' no-good spoilt offspring out of jail – and the headlines – mostly for drug, drink and traffic-related offences. No one we represented had ever been to prison. They got fines, community service, stints in rehab, suspended sentences, but no jail and next to no publicity.

I punched in the access code and the door clicked open.

The first thing newcomers always commented on was the quiet that greeted them when they stepped into the building. Concentrated and intense, it was the silence of a place where secrets come to live for ever.

I stopped, as I always did, to look at the sole ornament filling up the wall of the waiting area. Printed on canvas and hung like a prized painting was a black-and-white photograph of a furniture shop on a street corner. It was a mid-period Victorian structure with steepled slate roofs, whitewashed upper floors and bay windows, propped up by a modern extension that served as a showroom.

The picture had baffled me at first, because it didn't belong here. It was a portrait of drab everyday Britishness, affordable fittings to go in affordable houses in an affordable area, where crime was high and expectations low. Then I'd noticed similar, smaller photographs – black and white, mounted on white card and framed in plain glass – hanging in every room I went to. Our office had a picture of an East End bath house, Janet's a traditional barber's, while a shot of an old bingo hall graced the kitchen.

It turned out Sid Kopf had taken them. The picture in reception had won an award. Kopf was an amateur photographer, and a passionate one. He was always entering competitions and submitting his work to newspapers and magazines. His speciality was local London landmarks, those quirky buildings and businesses that had survived almost unchanged for decades, even centuries, and yet remained invisible to all but those in the know.

I carried on to the clerks' office.

Adolf was already there, at her desk, eyes to her screen, furiously typing away. I supposed she was either sending personal emails or updating her Facebook page, because she didn't type with the same breakneck abandon when she was doing her job.

She didn't look at me when I came in, just scowled grimly, as she always did whenever I was in her orbit.

She was slightly over five feet tall, brown-haired and a borderline beauty. I might have fancied her, if I didn't know her better – or, in fact, knew her at all.

'Morning, Bella,' I said.

No reply. No surprise.

When it came to letting someone know she despised their very existence, Adolf was without parallel. She wasn't merely good, or even simply brilliant at it. With her it came naturally, as if her sole purpose in life were to project hate – of me in particular. At least that's what it felt like, five days a week.

Her weapons of choice were silence and an armoury of black looks she used with such precision it would have been impressive if I hadn't

48

been the target. Her centrepiece was an unblinking glower that got glassier the longer it lasted, as if the intensity of her loathing was making her eyes water. Which was a shame because her eyes were far and away her most attractive feature, the blue of tourist brochure oceans.

There were four of us in the office, along with a junior clerk called Iain, and Michaela, the graduate gopher. Adolf and I sat facing each other, cordoned off from the others by a grey soundscreen.

I turned on my computer and listened to it powering up.

'Sid Kopf wants to see you,' Adolf said without looking at me.

'Bit early for wind-ups, isn't it?' I said.

Kopf only ever summoned clerks to his office when he was firing them.

Adolf carried on typing a moment longer, without comment. Then she turned to look directly at me for the first time.

'I don't wind up people I like,' she said. There was the usual mix of contempt and a dash of poison in the stare she gave me.

I still didn't know if she was being serious. Then my phone rang.

'Is that Terry?'

I recognised the woman's voice – nasal, blue-blooded posh; every 't' crossed with silver, every 'i' dotted with a pearl. It was Sid Kopf's PA. Edwina.

'Yes?' I said.

'Come upstairs.'

No *'please'*. This was an order.

My balls dropped. Had they found out about me?

'Sure,' I said.

She hung up with a crunch.

Adolf smiled at her screen. Her typing accelerated.

8

I saw Janet first when I walked in, sitting opposite Kopf's desk. She glanced briefly my way, then looked down at the yellow legal pad resting on her lap.

Kopf was something of a myth in the company – part legend, part bogeyman. We'd catch fleeting glimpses of him once in a while, always out of the corner of our eyes, going upstairs to his third-floor office, or walking out with a client. Very occasionally we'd hear his voice from the landing, but our experience of him was limited to second- and third-hand tales. He'd stopped practising law twenty years ago to concentrate on running the firm, but in his time he'd been one of the best corporate

49

lawyers in the country, a fearsome and utterly ruthless litigator when he'd needed to be. They used to call him 'the Blond Assassin'.

Kopf pointed me to a free chair facing his desk, and appraised me as I made my way into his office. I knew what he was seeing: the off-the-peg plain navy-blue suit – jacket and trousers bought separately – my cheap blue shirt and non-clashing tie, the polished but worn black Dr. Martens shoes.

I sat down. I was too close to his desk, and far too close to him for my comfort. Janet was out of my line of sight. It was as if she'd already distanced herself from me.

Sid Kopf was a tall man, about my height. He was eighty-two, but could have passed for twenty years younger. He was big on exercise. Only last year he'd done the London Marathon. And he'd run the New York version the year before that. He'd finished both in slightly under four hours. He cycled to the office on good days. He still had most of his hair, which was so white it appeared to hover slightly above him, glowing like a molten halo. His skin was lined and craggy, but still firm. I wondered if he hadn't had work done, but he didn't seem the type to get hung up on personal vanity.

I'd come with a pen and pad, more as props to steady my hands than in expectation that this meeting was anything but a dismissal. I wondered if I'd get any severance. I hoped so. I was a week away from getting paid for the month.

Kopf picked up a document from his desk and flicked through it. Three pages, stapled. My CV.

'How long have you been with us?' he asked.

This already sounded bad.

'Going on four months,' I said. My mouth was dry and my palms damp. I'd gone from mid-level panic to high alert in the space of a minute. Just get it over and done with, I thought. I was already envisaging going to temping agencies this afternoon.

'Hasn't even finished his probation,' he said to Janet.

I'd have to be working here another two months before the firm decided whether they wanted to keep me on or not.

He tossed my CV back on his desk with a scowl.

'Do you come from money?' he asked me.

'What?'

'Are your parents rich?'

I was confused. What did my parents have to do with this?

'No. Why?'

'What do they do?' he asked.

'Sorry?'

'What do your parents do for a living?'

'They're retired,' I said.

He looked at me like I was stupid.

'What *did* they do?'

I didn't like this. I didn't like his questions. I didn't like his sneering tone. And I really didn't like him.

'You're not allowed to ask me that,' I said, straightening up in the chair.

That gave him pause for a millisecond.

'I just did,' he said.

'I'm not obliged to answer,' I retorted.

'Only in an interview situation. Which this isn't. If it were you'd have lost me at "Hello".'

So, I was definitely getting fired. OK, fuck him, I thought. Go down swinging.

'What's the point to your question?'

A hint of a smile flashed across his face.

'Your CV belongs to someone else. Some brat with wealthy parents. A pampered slummer who doesn't understand the concept of working for a living. But who it *doesn't* belong to is you,' he said.

So they'd found out about Cambridge. I braced myself for the chop.

'You're a comprehensive kid. You overachieved at school. Straights As in everything. Then, instead of going to university, which would have been the natural thing to do – and the right one – you went to work. And you've been polishing the bottom rung of the career ladder ever since. Now you're here. That's worrying.'

Kopf had one of those polite accents redolent of money and good breeding, of country retreats and Mediterranean villas.

'Why?' I asked.

'We don't carry people here.'

'I don't think I'm being carried,' I said. 'I made the wrong decision when I was young, that's all. I couldn't see the point of more studying. I wanted to work. What did I know?'

He stared at me without blinking. He had small blue eyes, framed by white lashes, which made his stare even colder. I held his gaze.

'My dad was a welder,' he said, breaking the glaredown. 'I used to pick metal splinters out of his palms every evening when he got home. I had to use a hot needle to get under his skin. He was a good man, but I looked at him and his sore bleeding hands and decided I wasn't going to be him. That's what being born poor's about. Not becoming your parents. How old are you?'

What was he playing at? A little humiliation before he kicked me out? Why not just get straight to it? What did he have to prove?

'It's in my CV,' I said.

He glanced at Janet. Something passed between them. He nodded slightly to her. Had she told him to wrap this up now?

'Thirty-eight,' he said. 'Same age as our newest client, Vernon James.'

'Give or take a few months,' I said. I could hear my heart pounding away.

'And look where he is today?' Kopf went on. 'Millionaire, top of his tree, a few spare homes—'

'And presently in police custody on suspicion of murder,' I interrupted. 'I'd say he'd happily trade places with me right now if he could.'

Sid Kopf smiled. His teeth were the same shade as his hair. A bright cosmetic white that looked ridiculous against his furrowed skin. He sat back a little and studied me, a distinct gleam in his eye.

I felt sweat beading on my back.

'This is already a media-intensive case. It'll probably become a media-intensive trial. Do you know what that entails?'

'I have an idea,' I said.

'Let's say you have *no* idea,' Kopf retorted, leaning forward. 'You haven't handled a media-magnet before. They're a nightmare. There you are, trying to do the best for your client, and all the while you've got to keep the tabloid hacks just about on side so they don't write the kind of prejudicial stories that'll turn a jury. You've got to manage information, give them morsels, a taste but no swallowing. It's a fine balancing act. Bella Hogan has worked media cases, twice before. And both times she's come through with flying colours.'

'Are you saying you'd like me to step aside?' I said.

'That's *exactly* what I'm saying.'

I couldn't quite believe it. I almost smiled. I felt like punching the air and kissing the old man's feet. Relief broke out in me. So I wouldn't get to see VJ burn after all, but at least I'd have my job. I couldn't wait to ring Karen. She'd laugh her head off at the irony, that I'd been unwittingly saved by my office nemesis.

But, of course, here and now, I had to feign disappointment. Play at muted outrage, restrained hurt. Accepting his decision with a mere shrug and rollover would look like I was giving in too easily, lacked the ambition and fibre to stay in the job, wasn't fit to be any kind of lawyer. I tightened my lips and jaw, to make believe I was propping up a drooping mouth – the old 'stiff upper lip' routine that never went out of style.

'What about the ownership rule?' I said.

'I've made exceptions before.'

'OK ...' I shrugged.

'"*OK*"?' he snorted. 'Is that it? I've just suggested I might kick you off the biggest trial in the country, and that's the best you can come up with?'

'What else can I say?' I said. 'Your company, your rules. You don't want me on this, fine. That's your prerogative.'

Kopf looked to Janet again. I didn't know if she was smiling or frowning.

'This isn't a reflection on you or your abilities, Terry. Janet tells me you're good. I'd like to believe it, because she wouldn't have hired you if you weren't,' he said. 'But you're a wild card. And we don't deal those in a case like this. We use what we know. The right barristers, the right solicitor and the right clerk. You've had no experience in this kind of trial.'

'I understand,' I said.

'*But* ...' He raised his hand to silence me. 'Janet insists you're up to the job. So I want you to tell me – are you?'

'Sorry?'

'Why shouldn't I give this to Bella?'

'I can't answer that. I've never worked with her,' I said. That was the wrong thing to say. I should have turned into her cheerleader – extolled her track record, bigged up her experience at the expense of mine, persuaded him to reassign me. But I couldn't bring myself to help out the office viper. She'd bite me anyway.

'You work alongside her, don't you?'

'No. I sit opposite her. That's the extent of our professional involvement,' I said.

Kopf smiled again – archly this time, telling me he knew damn well I couldn't stand her. I think he liked my honesty. And, unfortunately, I also think he was starting to like me.

'Do you want in?'

'Of course,' I said, immediately – even though my head was screaming

NOOOOOOOOOOO!

He looked at Janet again, then back at me.

'Good,' he said. 'Then welcome aboard.'

Eh?

He reached out his hand. Somewhere through my confused daze, I saw myself shaking it and heard myself thanking him for the opportunity he'd just given me. Meanwhile my heart sank all the way to my guts, and every happy relieved feeling I'd had followed it down.

What had just happened? I thought I was off the hook. Now I was back on it. Kopf had been messing with me, seeing what I was made of, if I could take the heat. Had he even intended giving the job to Adolf?

Here's the joke of it:

If it had been anyone other than VJ, I'd have probably failed his test there and then, fallen at the first hurdle, jumped at the first bark. I'd have fought my corner, of course, but I wouldn't have projected the indifferent cool that had obviously won Kopf over. He'd have seen right through me; seen that I wanted the job because I wanted the degree, because I didn't want to come to work in a cobbled-together suit I'd put on in a council estate I couldn't wait to leave.

'Interesting cufflinks,' he said, still holding my hand.

'My children gave them to me,' I said. My talisman hadn't worked. I was in deep shit.

'I thought so,' he smiled, releasing my hand.

As he leaned away from me and back in his chair, I noticed that the wall behind him was covered with about a dozen of his black-and-white photographs. They were different from the others around the office. Each one had been taken at sunset, so all the buildings were almost completely reduced to solid silhouettes. The most striking of the photographs was in the middle. It was of a sunburst over a warehouse. A clear ray of daylight had broken through a hole in an overcast sky and lit up the corners of the building brightly and clearly, while the rest remained in darkness. He was obviously proud of the picture, because it was twice as big as the others and formed the centrepiece of the exhibition.

'Let's roundtable when we get back,' Janet said to Kopf, and stood up. 'Terry, get your things.'

'Where are we going?'

'Charing Cross nick. To meet our new client.'

'Didn't you see him yesterday?' I asked.

'No. They kept me waiting for three hours and then told me there were no free rooms. So let's go.'

9

We took the Tube. It hadn't yet gone nine and there were still plenty of people making their way to work, so it was standing room only.

Janet was in her beige mac and dark trouser suit combo, hair tied back and zero jewellery. She never wore her wedding ring when meeting clients, either because she wanted to keep her professional and private lives separate, or she didn't want her clients knowing too much about her.

I thought about VJ. In the next hour, I'd be walking into a police interrogation room and coming face to face with him again.

How long would it take him to recognise me?

It wouldn't be instant, but it'd be quick. I hadn't changed all that much physically – a little thicker here and thinner there. That was it. So I gave it all of ten minutes max before he spoke my name and pushed a wrecking ball into my livelihood.

Then what?

Could I still come through this with my job intact?

OK, yes, so I'd lied on my CV. But didn't we all, one way or another? Janet and Kopf might even see the irony of my predicament: a lot of people would've killed to have Cambridge on their CVs – even if it was just a year – whereas I'd kept it off. Yet, as I'd told Karen, personal credibility was all in the legal profession. Get caught in one lie, and no one ever believes you again.

My job wasn't supposed to have lasted this long anyway. I'd gone in as a temp at the start of November, to fill in for my predecessor who'd been fired. I was meant to be there a fortnight while they recruited a full-time replacement.

'You handled yourself well with Sid,' Janet said. 'Most people crumble.'

'He wasn't that bad,' I shrugged.

The train stopped at Westminster and the carriage emptied by half.

'Can I tell you something in confidence?' Janet asked.

'Of course,' I said. She gave me a harder look. 'Cross my heart and all that. Who am I going to tell?'

'Sid never wanted to employ you,' she said. 'He thought you were too old.'

'Why did he, then?'

'Because I insisted. I thought you were ideal. Still do,' she said.

Oh. Shit . . .

When VJ exposed me as an (almost) well-educated liar and suspected thief, Janet would look bad. I didn't want that. She was a pretty good boss. Tough, prone to snappiness at times of stress, but basically fair and actually quite fun when she wasn't being biked from crisis to crisis. Her position in the company was rock solid, and she wouldn't lose her job over me, but it would look like she was a bad judge of character – which, myself excluded, she wasn't.

'So you twisted his arm?' I said.

'As much as anyone can twist Sid's arm, yeah.'

'Why? Clerks are ten a penny.'

'You're a natural, Terry. And I don't see many of those in this line of work, believe me. It's just graduates with their senses of entitlement and five-year plans. Keen little drones who know exactly where they'll be in 2016. Who needs that?'

'Was that you once?' I asked.

'Probably. I really can't remember,' she laughed.

'Would you encourage your kids to go into law?'

'It's a noble profession.'

'Spoken like a true lawyer,' I smiled. 'As in: you didn't answer my question, you deflected it.'

'Would you steer *your* kids towards law?'

'More deflections.' I laughed. 'I wouldn't steer my kids anywhere they didn't want to go.' And I absolutely meant it. I wasn't going to push them into fulfilling my failed ambitions.

'You know Sid's thinking about expanding our division?' she said, lowering her voice and looking around. 'Next year we'll be taking on heavier work. Which means we'll be recruiting a few more people, and quite possibly promoting some too.'

She looked at me pointedly when she said that.

'What about Bella? She's been here a lot longer.'

'I'm glad *you* picked up the phone yesterday,' she said. 'I think you'll make a hell of a lawyer.'

'That's very flattering,' I said. 'But I'm still on probation.'

'You're *exactly* what we need in KRP.'

This should have made me feel good, but it made me feel even worse. I *had* to tell her about VJ. Put a stop to this before she lost face in front of both him and Sid Kopf.

I opened my mouth to say 'Look, there's something you should know before . . .'

But the words hadn't finished forming in my head when the train stopped at Embankment and the doors opened. Janet picked up her briefcase and quickly stepped out. I followed her. We were going to change here and grab the Northern Line one stop to Charing Cross. I still had time.

But Janet headed for the exit instead.

'What are we doing?'

'I need to make a couple of calls and have a smoke.'

Which meant I wouldn't have a chance to talk to her after all. 'A call' for her meant at least three; and, as we walked into the police station, she'd be getting her gameface on, which meant psyching herself up to meet both her client and the people who had him in custody. When she

56

did that she shut out all external distractions and went into a trance. I could tell her the worst things about myself and she wouldn't even hear.

10

If you have to get arrested, you could do far worse than be taken to Charing Cross. London nicks really don't get much grander. To the blissfully unaware it's a five-floor cream Georgian building, triangular in shape, stuck on its own island between William IV and Agar Streets. Formerly a hospital, its current identity and purpose are only hinted at by the quaint blue lamps on the street corners, the small blue bulletin board displaying crime awareness and missing persons posters, the irregular sighting of police vans entering or leaving the premises through separate gateways, and the building's name, spelled out in stark but small black metal lettering over the columned entrance. The entrance itself is tucked away on the kind of sidestreet people either find themselves on by accident, or dash down blindly as a shortcut to the train station.

We walked up the stairs and went inside to the reception area. To the left, in a corner, and out of immediate sight, was a solid plate of bullet-proof glass, behind which stood two middle-aged women in pale blue blouses. In the background was a big open-plan office, not dissimilar to any other white-collar hothouse, except for the marked lack of energy or urgency. If you were on the right side of them, police stations were always a bit like this – unremarkable, messy and quotidian; people hunched over desks, tapping away at computers, answering phones, half-expecting something big to happen, quietly hoping it wouldn't.

Janet produced the ID card she'd been issued last night, which had her client's name and the case number written on it. The receptionist tapped away at the computer and brought up the details. I then had to identify myself with my driving licence so I could be logged into the system.

We were told to wait, that it would be a while before someone came to fetch us. They had to bring the client up from the subterranean cells to an interview room, provided one was free. Charing Cross had the busiest custody suite in London, handling not just its own intake, but the over-spill from smaller local nicks, as well as the most high-profile suspects.

We sat on a leather banquette, the only furniture there. It was opposite a black lift, without external buttons.

I felt a bead of sweat dribble down my cheek.

'Are you OK?' Janet asked, noticing.

'Too many layers,' I said, wiping my face with my hand, only to feel

57

more sweat build up around my temples. We'd stepped in from the cold to comparative warmth. I had on a T-shirt underneath my suit and shirt. But I wasn't at all hot. It was nerves.

My heart rate was jacked. The whole way up from Embankment I'd been desperately thinking of ways to get out of this, drawing blank after blank, getting more and more panicked.

I watched Janet read through her notes, close to a dozen pages filled with blue semi-legible cursive handwriting. She was jotting things down in a separate notebook as she read through her pad.

Half an hour later, the lift doors opened and a youngish officer in white shirtsleeves stepped out.

'James?' he called out.

We stood and went to the lift.

'He's in 29,' he said and pressed a button for the third floor.

We rode up in silence. I heard my heart thudding in my chest.

The lift stopped and we got out.

The officer led the way down a corridor. To the right were interview rooms, to the left windows with a view of St Martin's Lane, the Duke of York Theatre and, opposite, the revolving globe atop the London Coliseum's spire, and the roof of the Chandos pub. I saw a small group of tourists pointing their cameras up at it, no doubt marvelling at the mechanical man manoeuvring the barrel of beer on the upper window, looking like he was going to push it into the street below.

Some of the interview rooms were open. A detective was going through his notes in one, two were talking in another. The rooms were different. Some were spartan, white walls, with just a table, three chairs and CCTV. Others were set up to resemble living rooms, with a comfortable couch facing two easy chairs, a carpet and drawn curtains to give the illusion of a window. I guessed VJ would get the first option.

I tried to steel myself as I counted down the numbers to the rooms, but they were random, non-sequential, which may or may not have been deliberate. Room 33 followed Room 15. Then it was Room 7. I kept expecting to arrive at 29 any moment, but we continued walking.

The officer greeted passing colleagues with a nod or a hello. Everyone so far was younger than me. That was a sign you were getting old, when the cops looked fresh out of school and barely acquainted with a razor.

Suddenly we were outside Room 29.

The officer swiped his keycard along a pad next to the door and the lock clacked open. He went in first, holding the door for us.

It was a plain interview room, a white-walls-and-striplight set-up. The next thing I saw was the bright-red panic button on the wall, sprouting out of the brick like a painted toadstool.

And then I saw him. VJ. Not fully, just a glimpse. Sat at the table with his fingers interlaced, dressed in a blue paper boilersuit.

'Who are you?'

A woman was blocking the doorway. She was talking to me.

'I'm ... I'm ...'

The woman advanced, forcing me to step back.

'He's the clerk,' Janet said behind her.

'Solicitor only in here, sorry,' she said, holding up a palm at me.

The woman had short grey hair and a thin, tired face, which contrasted with her broad frame and stout build. I'd seen her before, but I couldn't place her. I guessed she was a detective.

The young officer who'd led us up came out and took me to a waiting room at the end of a corridor.

When he left I let out all the breath in my body, one long, lower-reg whistle of escaping pressure.

In the waiting room, I took off my coat and jacket. My shirt was soaked through.

I sat there a while, without a single thought forming. I got up and had several glasses of water from the cooler. I read and reread the posters and notices on the wall. I checked my phone messages, but had none.

Nicks still freaked me out a little. It couldn't be helped. I've been arrested four times, all in Stevenage. One you already know about, after I'd last seen VJ. The next was a few months later. No charge, just a night in the cells. I'd been out drinking with my brothers, Aidan and Patrick. I don't know how we got separated, but we did and I found myself alone in the street, too pissed to walk home. So I went to the shopping centre and bedded down in a doorway under the arcade. A cop woke me up with his bootcap and took me to the nick, bent on charging me with vagrancy and disturbing the peace. The desk sergeant knew my parents and waived the charge. But I was shoved in a cell just the same. The next morning I got driven home. Dad thought it was funny, said he used to do the same thing in Cork.

The next time he wasn't so amused. I got done for shoplifting. I got tanked up one afternoon and found myself in Sainsbury's, going aisle to aisle, piling up a trolley past the brim. Then I wheeled it straight out of the shop. I made it about halfway down the road before store detectives caught up with me. I was taken back to the shop. Mum was working there then as a cashier, but she was on her break. The staff all recognised me. The cops were called and I got carted off. I got a caution and a ten-year ban from the shop. Mum was humiliated. That was in the summer of 1994.

No one had worked out or understood then that things were seriously

59

wrong with me. The beating I'd taken in Cambridge had caught up with me. Everyone thought it was the drink. I didn't think anything. Most of the time I wasn't even conscious of what I was doing.

A year later I got sectioned. I'd found out that VJ and his family had moved again, to Ashwell, a village outside Stevenage. I got wankered on Guinness Export and Jameson doubles and went out to confront him. On foot. In the middle of the night. The cops found me the next morning, sitting in a field miles away, talking to a scarecrow. We'd swapped clothes. Sort of. I had the hat on and nothing else.

It was then that the collective penny dropped, and I got carted off to the Lister Hospital. The local nuthouse. Bed, meds and four months of therapy:

Tell me about your mother. Let's start with the good things ...

Over the next hour, the waiting room got busier. Solicitors came and went. They talked on their phones. They talked to plainclothes cops. They talked to each other.

And then Franco Carnavale came in. He was one of the CPS's main prosecuting barristers. I'd seen him on the news. He always got the media-friendly trials. He looked better on TV than he did in the flesh – a shortarse in his late forties with thick light-brown hair and a chunky gold watch.

Then the woman from the interrogation room came in. She and Carnavale chatted in whispers and mumbles for a while, before she handed him a thick manila file.

I kept my head down and pretended to be busy studying notes in my legal pad, even though the pages were blank.

'It's all here,' she said.

'Thanks, Carol. Do the away side have this?'

'Minus a few players,' she said.

Carnavale chuckled. He leafed through the file. His pinkie ring and watch kept catching the light and flashing in my eye.

Carol ...?

Carol Reid – DCI Reid, the Met's rising star. A few years back she'd caught the serial rapist they called the 'Polish Pimpernel'. The media loved her. Karen liked her too, reminded her of a TV cop, she'd said.

DCI Reid sensed me staring and looked my way. She recognised me and frowned. Then she whispered into Carnavale's ear and they both left the room.

An hour later Janet came in. She had a file in her hand, the same colour as the one Carnavale had been given, but about half as full.

She was glaring at me, hard. I'd seen her angry before, but never like this.

'What's wrong?' I asked.

Had VJ told her already?

'Everything,' she said.

11

'This case is a loser, Sid,' Janet said.

'Do tell.'

We were sitting in the boardroom on the second floor, the three of us around the conference table, a thick circular slab of varnished mahogany set on a pedestal sculpted into an eagle's claw.

'Where to begin . . . exactly?' Janet said. She was knackered, her face pinched and pale, a vein ticking away at her temple. I could hear the Canning Town roots in her voice, the ones a private education and university had almost completely patioed over, bar the odd recalcitrant weed, which a few drinks or a bad mood pushed up.

She opened the manila folder and separated the contents into three short stacks, which she placed before her – crime-scene photos, witness statements, interview transcripts. Then she flipped through her two pads, backwards and forwards between pages, pausing here and there to quick-scan and cross-reference her notes.

I let my eyes drift around the room. Vast, high-ceilinged and white-washed, with all the warmth and personality of an empty fridge. Apart from the silent clock on one wall, the only thing that broke up the uniform blankness was another of Kopf's black-and-white photographs, hanging above the fireplace – a pie and mash shop, its eponymous menu advertised as stained glass illustrations in its front windows.

Finally Janet was ready.

'The case against Vernon James goes like this,' she began. 'At 6.27 a.m. yesterday morning, he checked out of Suite 18 at the Blenheim-Strand. The receptionist noticed cuts on his hands and scratches on his face. She asked if he was OK. He said he was fine, signed his bill, left and caught a cab to his offices in Canary Wharf.

'At 8.03, two maids went up to clean the suite. Now, it's a big place. Separate lounge and bedroom, two bathrooms, one en suite. The maids entered together and the first thing they noticed was that the lounge had been trashed. Broken glass everywhere, upturned furniture.

'One of them went to check the bedroom. That's when and where she found the victim. White, female, blonde, late twenties to early thirties. The victim was on the bed, face up, naked. Her clothes were on the floor. A green dress, shoes. No underwear. Her name is Evelyn Bates. She—'

'Who again?' Kopf asked.

'Evelyn Bates.'

Kopf frowned and then scribbled in his pad.

'Any other details?' he asked.

'Such as?'

'Appearance?'

'Five five to five seven in height. Chubby-looking.'

'Was she a guest at the Ethical Person awards?'

'No. She was at a hen party.'

Kopf frowned even harder.

'Why are you asking?'

'To get a mental picture,' he said, scribbling some more, still frowning. 'Carry on.'

'The maids alerted hotel security, who called the police. Two officers arrived at the scene at 8.39 a.m. Medics followed a few minutes later. They confirmed the victim was dead. Apparent cause: strangulation, possibly manual. There was noticeable bruising around her neck.'

'What was the time of death?' Kopf asked.

'Preliminary estimate is under eight hours from the time the body was found. The autopsy's being conducted later today, so we'll know more.'

'All right.'

'At around 9.20, police units were dispatched to Vernon James's home and business addresses. DCI Carol Reid and DS Mark Fordham found him at his office.

'Reid states that Vernon's first words to her were: "If it's about the damage, I can explain." She let him talk. He told her he'd invited some people up to his suite after the ceremony. Things got out of hand. The room got trashed. He said he was very sorry, and that he'd pay for any damages.

'Reid then asked him about the dead woman in the bedroom. He said, "I don't know what you're talking about."'

'That wasn't under caution?' Kopf asked.

'No. But it's his word against theirs,' she said. 'At 10.30 he was arrested and taken to Charing Cross nick. He was interviewed under caution two hours later. There he changed his story completely. He said he'd lied about having people up in his room, because he didn't want his wife finding out he'd been with another woman.

'He then proceeded to tell DCI Reid the same story he told me, give or take. He went up to his suite with a woman called Fabia, who he described as white, blonde, around six feet tall, late twenties to early thirties. She spoke with a French accent and told him she was Swiss. And she was wearing a green dress.'

'Like the victim?'

'Like the victim,' Janet said. 'Vernon says Fabia attacked him in the suite and ran off. Shortly afterwards he passed out on the couch in the lounge. He woke up at around 6 a.m. – still on the couch – packed his overnight bag and checked out. He didn't know anything about a dead woman in the bedroom. In fact, he says he never even set foot in the bedroom.

'When Reid showed him a photograph of the victim and asked if she was the woman he was with, he replied, "I'm not sure."'

Kopf shook his head. 'Tell me he didn't say that.'

'It's in the transcript,' Janet said, tapping one of the stacks of paper in front of her. 'Therefore on record, therefore admissible in court.'

'Doesn't he know what "no comment" means?'

'He does now,' she said. 'The first interview was terminated at 1.18 p.m. Vernon was then photographed, had his samples taken – hair, blood, mouth-swab, etc. His clothes were also taken away. Then he got his phone call.

'He called Ahmad Sihl, his business lawyer. Ahmad turned up at 3.30 p.m. He saw Vernon at 4.15. He advised him to say nothing and told him he was going to get him a criminal lawyer. Which is where we came in.'

VJ was no stranger to police interrogations. I was sure he'd remembered Quinlan's grillings. I wondered if he wasn't thinking about those now. Maybe he was even thinking of me. Little did he know . . . for now.

'The police already have enough to charge him with, but they won't until the autopsy report confirms cause of death,' Janet continued.

'Now, we haven't had anything like full disclosure from the CPS yet, but their case so far is pretty damn solid. They already have statements from four eyewitnesses who saw Vernon with a woman who matched the description of the victim – blonde, youngish, green dress. And all four ID'd Evelyn Bates from the photo they were shown.

'Of the witnesses: three were waiting staff in the hotel nightclub where Vernon went after the award ceremony. Two saw him and the victim dancing together. The third says she saw them rolling about on the floor.

'"Rolling about on the floor"?'

'The club got pretty rowdy, apparently,' Janet said. 'The most damning statement so far is from a barman in the Circle, a few floors up from the nightclub. He says he served Vernon and a blonde in a green dress shortly before midnight. They sat in a corner, had a drink, talked, "looked intimate" – his words – and then left together, approximately half an hour later. Again, he positively photo-ID'd the victim as the woman.'

'What did the client have to say to that?' Kopf asked.

'He's sticking to his story. Except for one detail. He had another look at the victim's photo, and now insists she *wasn't* the woman he went to his room with. He says Evelyn Bates looked nothing like this "Fabia".

'But he admits to meeting the victim in the nightclub, by accident. He was looking for Fabia and mistook the victim for her, because they were both wearing green dresses. While they were talking they both got knocked over. She tore her dress and left the club. He then—'

Kopf held up his hand.

'OK. Enough,' he said. 'His story's a mess. Obviously made up on the hoof.'

'My thoughts exactly,' Janet said.

'Did you tell him?'

'I told him how it'll look to a jury. And I outlined the police's case.'

'Did you suggest a plea?'

'Of course. I told him if he pleads guilty now, we could negotiate in his favour.'

'And?'

'He refused. He insists he's innocent. He says he never brought Evelyn Bates up to his room. He clearly remembers lying down on the couch, and waking up there at daybreak,' she said.

'When do you think they'll charge him?'

'The autopsy's due soon. They could have him in front of a magistrate first thing Monday.'

'Any chance he'll change his mind?'

'Not at the moment,' Janet said.

There wasn't even the suggestion of a *presumption* of innocence here. We were a defence team in name only. I might as well have been working for the prosecution. But I held my tongue.

'So we're potentially in trial mode. We need to—' Kopf said, but was interrupted by a knock on the door.

His PA looked in.

'Mr Kopf, I'm sorry to interrupt but Scott Nagle's on the phone. Shall I put it through to here?'

'No. I'll take it in my office,' Kopf said. He looked from Janet to me. 'Let's have a short break.'

After he'd left, I turned to Janet.

'Who's Scott Nagle?' I asked.

'There are people who make you jump, and people who make you ask, "How high?" *before* you jump,' Janet said. 'Nagle is the firm's biggest client. And we're all his pole-vaulters.'

64

'What does he do?' I asked.

'What hasn't he done?' she smiled.

'I mean for a living.'

'None of our clients do anything for a living, Terry. They're way past that. They all have what Americans call "Fuck-Off Money".'

And she went back to her three stacks. I wanted to see the crime-scene photos, but I didn't want to ask right now. Too crude, too voyeuristic for a future lawyer. I needed to concern myself with higher things, like police reports and witness statements – except Janet was working through those.

I pondered VJ's story. Kopf was right. It was bullshit, the kind of desperate lie you conjure up in a cornered panic. It was almost infantile too, a variation of the "twin brother defence" . . . *It wasn't me who broke the window, Miss, it was my identical twin.* I'd found out how useless that lie was when I was five.

Yet something didn't feel right.

If VJ had stabbed Evelyn Bates, I wouldn't have had a problem believing in his guilt – because there could have been a precedent. But strangulation? I remembered those delicate quasi-feminine hands of his; long and narrow, all bone and vein, with thin, tentacular fingers. Everyone had always commented on them, how his hands didn't correspond to his body.

And there was another thing too:

I'd never known him to be violent or even aggressive towards women – not at school, not at university. He'd been close to Gwen and his mother. What the hell had gone wrong with him?

Kopf returned fifteen minutes later, his face like thunder.

'Right then, where were we?'

'Trial mode,' Janet said.

'We really want to avoid a trial, if possible. The CPS will want to avoid one too.'

He caught the baffled look on my face.

'Trials cost the state money, Terry. So the state does its best to avoid them where possible. If Vernon James couldn't afford us and had himself a taxpayer defence lawyer, that lawyer would be doing his utmost to get him to plead guilty. Not for his client's sake, but his own. The state likes a lawyer who keeps costs down. You'll find that they're the ones who tend to get the most work.'

Now I was shocked.

'Welcome to the legal system.' He winked and smiled.

'How do I sell it to him?' Janet asked.

'How old are his kids?'

Seven, five and three, I thought. Family planning at its finest. Equal gaps between each daughter.

'Preschool and primary school age,' Janet said.

'Did the victim have any other injuries – cuts, bruises, broken bones?'

'We haven't had the coroner's report yet, but the preliminary reports didn't mention anything.'

'Assuming that remains the same, we could feasibly go for an involuntary manslaughter plea. Say it was a sex game gone tragically wrong. Happens all the time. People get carried away. The client could even have blacked out. If we're lucky there'll be drink and maybe drugs in his system too.

'So that's a ten-year sentence – maximum. A plea – now – would reduce that to eight, maybe seven. He'll do half that, most of it in a low-security prison. Out in three years. His kids will still be young enough to forget later, he'll have his money minus our fee, and maybe his business too.'

What about his marriage? I thought. Would he still have that?

'He's adamant he's innocent, Sid.'

'It's early days,' Kopf said. 'And we haven't had all the evidence yet.'

'I still think we should be in trial mode,' Janet said.

'Who's the prosecutor on this?'

'Franco Carnavale.'

'Figures,' Kopf muttered. 'High-profile case. *Ergo* cameras. Do you know what Franco's first ex-wife told me? In the five years they were married, he spent at least one of them in the bathroom. Apparently that's why they broke up.'

Janet cleared her throat impatiently.

'Barristers? Are we staying in-house?' she asked.

'With Franco on board, this is going to be a street fight. Our people aren't built for that,' Kopf said.

'So who do we get?'

'Styles make fights. We need his opposite.'

They brainstormed. Names got batted around. All male.

The more they talked and the more people they rejected, I found myself thinking like the jury. What would I be seeing? Two blokes in wigs and gowns getting into a pissing contest. So I spoke up.

'I think the lead barrister should be a woman.'

Janet and Kopf both looked at me like they'd forgotten I was in the room.

'Why?' Kopf asked.

'A woman defending a man accused of killing another woman will make the jury think twice about his guilt,' I said. 'I also think our barrister should be older than our client – and definitely older than the victim. Maybe old enough to have a daughter the victim's age. That'll cloud the jury's mind even more.'

'Good thinking, Terry,' Kopf smiled. 'Who's out there?'

'There's Nadine Radford,' Janet said.

'Oustanding, but currently tied up on two trials, with a third starting before Christmas,' Kopf said.

'Sonia Lawrence?'

'Very good, but a full calendar this year.'

'Janice Brown?'

'She hates me.'

'Lynne Brown?'

'She hates me too. They're sisters. And she doesn't believe in private law firms.'

'Prabjit Khan?'

'Her life's a circus.' Kopf shook his head and winced. 'A *barrister* on a reality TV show, for God's sake.'

'It was a *gameshow*, Sid,' Janet said.

'Same damn difference. Idiots making bigger idiots of themselves.'

They fell silent as they racked their brains. I looked down at the table. There were patterns in the wood, Munch-like faces staring up at me through hollow eyes.

'How about Christine Devereaux?' Kopf suddenly suggested.

'I thought she'd retired?' Janet said.

'She stepped down due to illness. She's since reconsidered and is back at work.'

'But she's still ill?'

'Christine is one of the best barristers ever to step inside a courtroom. She's ideal for this. An absolute fighter. Lethal in cross-examination, and her summaries are grand opera.'

'Sid, she's *dying*.'

'Aren't we all, Janet?' he said.

'No, Sid.'

'What's wrong with her?' I asked.

'What's it matter?' Janet said.

'If she's back at work, she must be functioning. Besides, that can only play to our advantage,' I said.

'We're not using her. Now, who—'

'*How* can that benefit us, Terry?' Kopf interrupted.

'Ailing barrister gets off her sickbed to fight for justice,' I said.

'Are you being *serious*?' Janet asked me, angrily.

I was about to apologise and withdraw, when Kopf spoke up.

'Terry's got a point,' he said.

'Are *you* being serious?'

'I may sometimes laugh at the law, Janet, but I *never* joke about it,' Kopf said. 'Yes, Christine's ill. And obviously so. But think about it. You'll have Carnavale doing his usual routine – flashy, sharp, all withering one-liners and knock-out putdowns. Then you get Christine. Every time she gets to her feet to defend our client, the jury will see and hear the effort she's making, just to even be there. And it'll be almost too painful to watch, but all their attention will be focused on the grand old dame who's using her last thousand breaths to defend our client. And that's before she even speaks. And when she does, she'll wipe the floor with Franco. She'll be flashier, sharper, a lot more withering. And the jury'll love it. And they'll love her. And – who knows? – they might even acquit our client out of sympathy.'

It sounded callous, even cruel. But when the last meal was gone and the cavalry wasn't coming because all the horses had been eaten, people turned to cannibalism.

'You really *do* want her on this, don't you?' Janet said.

'If it goes to trial, then yes, I do,' Kopf said.

After another rummage through her notebooks, Janet reluctantly nodded her assent.

'OK. I'll call her. What about a junior?' Janet asked.

'In-house for that. We just need a backstopper. Liam Redpath springs to mind. He finished up something last Thursday.'

'Don't you want another woman?' Janet asked sarcastically, giving me a cutting look.

Now I wish I'd stayed out of this. Janet was my boss.

'That'll look too deliberate,' Kopf said. 'Juries are often dumb, but never stupid.'

'Liam's a safe pair of hands,' Janet said. 'But no more than that. What if Christine falls ill? He hasn't got the experience to fill her shoes.'

'Then we'll have another trial. Start again.'

Liam Redpath wouldn't have been my first choice either. I'd been in a couple of meetings with him. He was a born yes-man, a middle manager on the make, someone whose entire career seemed to consist of standing with his wet finger in the air, judging which direction the wind was blowing and going with the flow.

'Next. Investigators?' Janet said. 'Terry, any suggestions?'

No, she wasn't being sarcastic now.

Some of the bigger private law firms had their in-house investigators, their PIs, their muck-rakers. KRP didn't. It kept them at arm's length. Payroll snoops were convenient but also potential PR disasters waiting to happen. Investigators work in a grey area, where legality and illegality get blurred and often entwined for the sake of expedience. It was condoned as long as none of it came to light.

One of my first jobs had been to hire an investigator to look into the boyfriend of a client's daughter.

'I've worked with Colin Bromfield twice,' I said. 'Very good, very discreet. He'd be my first choice. If he's booked up, there's Stan Dommett, then Mike Egan. Not much between them in terms of quality.'

'Call Bromfield,' Janet said.

'No, don't,' Kopf said.

Janet sighed loudly.

'You know the problem with today's investigators?' Kopf continued. 'Like most of the under-forties in this country, they don't get out enough. They do everything by computer. And they're too literal. You tell them what you want and that's all you're going to get. They'll overlook all extras, no matter how important. Why? Because you didn't ask. You have to do their thinking for them.'

He looked at Janet. 'You're not going to like this one bit, but I want the old-school touch on this ...'

Her face dropped.

'Sid, *no* ...'

'I want to roll the dice.'

'Tell me you're not thinking of—'

'Yes. I am.'

'Not Andy ... *Swayne*?' Janet as good as shouted.

I'd never met him, but Andy Swayne was a byword for fuck-up in the company.

'Sid, you *fired* him,' Janet said, once she'd calmed herself down.

Kopf nodded and shrugged.

'He's a fucking *alcoholic*.'

'A *recovering* alcoholic,' Kopf reminded her.

'Crawling between wagons,' Janet said.

'Mr Kopf ...' I said. 'This case is far too delicate, and too high-profile to take a chance on someone like him.'

'Andy Swayne was – even on a bad day – head and shoulders above any of these ex-military, disgruntled coppers, chronic voyeur types who do a correspondence course in surveillance and pass themselves off as investigators these days,' Kopf said. 'You said your people are very good, Terry? Well, Andy was *brilliant*. He saved our hide more than once.'

Kopf looked at Janet when he said that.

'Past tense,' I said.

'Sorry?'

'You said he *was* brilliant. That's not good enough for this,' I said. 'I haven't read the files, but from what Janet's been saying they could convict our client right now on what they've got so far. If there's any chance we have of proving his innocence, we need solid people on this. Besides, I thought I was your only wild card.'

'Andy isn't a wild card,' Kopf said. 'He's a straight arrow who flew into a hurricane. I've heard he's back to his best now.'

'Did *he* tell you that?' Janet asked.

'Trust me on this. This trial – should it happen – is going to generate a lot of publicity. We need someone who won't be fazed by that. Someone who won't blink in the glare,' he said.

'Have you forgotten that burglary?' she said.

'No, of course not,' Kopf said, keeping his absolute cool. 'I haven't forgotten *anything* about Andy.'

I didn't want to get in the middle of them. There was ancient history I didn't know about, nor really want to know.

They stared at each other, Janet glowering, Kopf calm and steely, yet faintly amused too. I could sense the telepathy, Janet cursing Kopf, Kopf taking the barrage, but standing his ground and enjoying himself.

After a moment, Janet broke the stare-off with another long loud sigh and nodded, but with great effort, like her neck was in plaster. Kopf turned to me.

'Terry, you'll be managing him.'

'Sure,' I said.

'Some dream team we've got here, Sid. A dying barrister and an alkie investigator,' Janet said. 'I really hope this *doesn't* go to trial.'

'They're brilliant, that's their problem,' Kopf said. 'Brilliant people tend to pay a steep price. Andy drank because of the things he saw and did. Christine was too busy turning around impossible cases to take care of her health. Sometimes I think it's better to be merely good at what you do, instead of brilliant. Mediocrity always outlasts genius.'

'Speak for yourself,' Janet said.

'I just did,' Kopf smiled. He had the best smile money could buy.

Janet shook her head. She was pissed off. I couldn't understand the dynamic here. It was her case and she was senior partner, head of the criminal division, yet she was letting Kopf pick the key players. And not only was he not a practising lawyer any more, he'd never been a criminal one.

'You said it yourself, Janet, this one's a loser. And it is. One way or another Vernon James is going to prison. But we're still going to defend him. And I believe these are the best people to do it. You know why? Talent aside, they're both hungry. Andy wants to redeem himself

70

and, as this'll probably be Christine's last trial, she's going to make it count.'

Janet stared at him for a long moment. I could see her trying to think of a way round it, and for a moment I thought she'd found it. But then the tension left her face and she conceded with a blink of the eyes.

'Let's move on,' she said.

For the next hour we discussed other experts we'd use in rebuttal. I had a shortlist of contacts to call when we were done. We tried to anticipate as much as we could, but we were stabbing in the dark. VJ had yet to be charged and we didn't know what other evidence the prosecution would come up with.

I got so involved in what I was doing, that for a sweet moment, I forgot it was VJ we were defending, and I forgot all about the deep water I was in.

12

After the meeting I went back to my office to start making calls. It was a full house. Everyone was in: Iain, Michaela and, of course, Adolf.

They'd been talking about me an instant before, as they often did when they thought I wasn't around. I heard my name followed by laughter as I came down the stairs. When I walked through the door all conversation died instantly. Michaela's stunned embarrassment made her grin wilt into a crinkled oval, Iain looked down at once, and Adolf went into multitask mode, picking up the phone with one hand, tapping at her keyboard with the other, while simultaneously avoiding my gaze and pulling her best pissed-off pout.

My situation wasn't anything new. Nor was it exclusive to my profession. You'll find someone like me in every office in every country everywhere in the world: the one no one likes.

It was entirely Adolf's doing. She was a dab hand at backstabbing in numbers. She'd turned the office against me, and they were too scared for their jobs – and of her – to resist.

In some ways, I didn't blame her. From the outside looking in, I even empathised. Adolf had worked her way up from office assistant to senior clerk. She was good at her job, and, by rights, should have been in pole position for promotion. Instead I'd been dropped right in front of her like a boulder in a thin gorge. I was an obstacle she had to either blast through or bypass.

It hadn't always been bad between us. We got on fine in my first week, when I was temping. She didn't think I'd be there long, so she went out of her way to be helpful, showing me the office systems and giving me tips about note-taking in court. But when Janet offered me the job on the Friday and we'd all gone out for a welcome-to-the-company drink, her attitude shifted from hospitable to hostile, and my new colleagues got in line.

Adolf now knew I'd caught the Big Case. It was up on the office white-board. The clerks' names were grouped in seniority, and then arranged alphabetically, with our respective cases written up alongside them. Red for new, green for ongoing. I was top of the board, over Adolf. The salt had been rubbed in and it was burning like hell. She'd also got a brand-new case, by the looks of things. Someone called Regan – but that wasn't going to make any difference. I'd bagged the Big One, which meant I was an even greater threat to her career ambitions now than ever. In other words: we were at war.

I turned on my computer. As it powered up and the hard drive started humming and whirring, my stomach threw in a little accompaniment of its own: deep growls followed by high-pitched mewlings. Adolf looked at me in disgust.

'Afternoon, Bella,' I nodded and smiled. That was the way I handled her, with passive-aggression, wind-ups and a unique ingredient of my very own. Confronting her or trying to sort out our differences amicably would have been a complete waste of time. The only thing that would make her happy was if I resigned, got fired, or – preferably – was hit by a bus.

'Where've you been?' she asked, tapping away, looking at her screen.

'Client visit,' I said, even though it was actually none of her business.

I could tell she wanted to know more about VJ but was too proud to ask. She had a fascination with the rich. Always buying *Hello!* magazine, *Harpers & Queen*, *The Lady* and *Tatler* to see how the other half lived, those ennobled debutants with their triple-barrelled names and in-bred connections to the Royal Family. I once overheard her tearfully telling Michaela how she and her fiancé had been invited to a rich friend's wedding, and she'd got so depressed at the ostentation she burst out crying, realising that they'd never ever be as rich as that.

'Who's your client?' I asked.

'Pepe Regan,' she said.

'Who's he?'

'The Chelsea player.'

'Pass,' I said. I didn't follow any sport – especially not football. 'What's he done?'

'He's *alleged* to have assaulted a bouncer.'

I'd read about that in yesterday's *Standard*. Regan hadn't just beaten up said bouncer, he'd pissed on him afterwards too. That was this year. Last year he'd shagged his best mate's wife, got her pregnant and was now denying the kid was his. The year before that he'd wrapped £350,000's worth of Porsche around a lamp-post outside a school. The same month he'd also been charged with racially abusing the goalkeeper of an opposing team. He'd called him a 'snowflake bitch'. He'd been acquitted when his defence team had successfully argued that the comment had been directed at the cold weather not the keeper: '*It's* a snowflake, bitch.' Then, as now, he was represented by KRP.

Adolf's phone rang.

'Hi babe!' she beamed.

'Babe' was Adolf's fiancé, Kev Dorset. Kev had recently landed his dream job, as a reporter for the *Daily Chronicle*. Except he was in a precarious position, because they'd started him as they did all their new reporters, on a twenty-four-hour contract. If he didn't come up with the goods, he was out on his ear without ceremony. He called Adolf every day at roughly the same time to tell her he hadn't got the chop. She'd congratulate him and tell him how good he was. If I hadn't known her better, I would have found her loyalty and devotion quite touching.

They made a very odd couple, Kev and Adolf. Kev was six foot five, Adolf almost one and a half feet shorter in heels, a midget manqué in flats.

I went to the kitchen to get my sandwich.

I brought the Tupperware container back to my desk and took out my sandwich. It was a wholemeal bap with a tinned tuna, pesto, lemon juice and caper mix. It was layered between lettuce, cucumber, onions, tomato and spinach. I watched Adolf's eyes widen as she said sweet nothingkins to the poor bastard who'd agreed to marry her next year.

I took my first bite, savouring the clash of pesto and capers, and brought up the contacts database on my monitor. I tapped in Andy Swayne's name.

Adolf finished her call and I sensed her looking in my direction.

I dialled Swayne's number. The phone started ringing.

Adolf came over to my desk, picked up the other half of my sandwich and took a big bite, eyeballing me as she chewed, daring me to say something, knowing full well I wouldn't. Then she turned and looked over at the juniors' section, standing on tiptoe and holding up my half-bap, her trophy. She was showing it to Iain, her main ally.

'This is *so* nice. *Much* better than yesterday's,' she said, without looking at me.

This had been going on since the start of my second week at the company, when Adolf helped herself to half a sandwich I'd left on my desk when typing up my trial notes. I reached for it and it was gone. I looked around, on the floor, under my desk, and then I saw Adolf in her chair, looking at me defiantly, munching.

I'd immediately clocked what she was up to, trying to provoke a confrontation, luring me into her comfort zone. So I didn't say anything. I simply closed the empty container and went back to work.

The next day, she did it again. I'd left the half-sandwich in exactly the same place. This time she didn't wait until my back was turned. She got out of her chair, came over, took it and bit into it.

It was a crude and very blatant power play. By taking half of what was mine, she was asserting her authority, showing me who was boss. It was also a test to see how I'd react, whether I was aggressive or passive, a fighter or a flea.

Now she thought she had my number. When we'd last had anything close to a civil conversation, she told me she had a degree in psychology from some flyblown university I'd never heard of. In other words, she was a failed shrink.

What Adolf didn't know, and hadn't actually considered – today, or any day since she'd officially declared hostilities open by eating my sandwich – was that I'd spat in the tuna mix. In fact, the only time in the last two and a half months Adolf hadn't ingested my flob was the first time she'd helped herself to my food. I had thought of spiking one half of the sandwich with a volcanic dose of Scotch Bonnet pepper, elephant laxative or worse, and be done with her once and for all, but why ruin a perfectly good sandwich? So this was better. My secret, my laugh on her.

Swayne's phone rang into double figures before he answered.

'Swayne.'

'Hello, my name's Terry Flynt,' I said. 'I'm a—' I saw Adolf looking at me, listening as she chewed, pretending to work. 'I'm a clerk at KRP.'

'April Fool's two weeks away. Christmas was last year. And I no longer count my birthdays,' was the response. His voice was deep and croaky.

I thought he was pissed. Then I realised he was kidding.

'This isn't a joke,' I said.

'Flynt, did you say your name was?'

'Yes.'

'You must be new.'

'I started a few months ago. Why?'

'Herr Kopf dispensed of my services last century.'

'He's reconsidered,' I said.

'Well, he's either desperate – which I doubt – or he's got a very tricky trial coming up,' he laughed. I wondered how far he and Kopf went back.

'Can we meet up to talk the case over?'

'You can give me the details right now, if you want.'

'Our client's going to be charged with murder.'

'You mean Vernon James?' Swayne asked.

'As you know, we never reveal a client's name until the investigator has signed our confidentiality agreement.' I smiled. 'Are you free on Monday?'

Swayne laughed and the laugh provoked a cough which ended in a retch and spit. I glanced over at Adolf. She'd finished her tuna, pesto and flob special.

'Yes,' I said. 'Where do you want to meet?'

'The Cedars of Lebanon café on Edgware Road,' he said. 'Say, two o'clock?'

'See you then,' I said.

13

Back home.

After everyone was sound asleep, I crept into the spare room.

I sat on the trunk and read the newspapers I'd bought this morning.

The broadsheet pieces read like obituaries, the first fistfuls of dirt landing on his reputation. VJ's arrest was being presented as a definitive full stop to a life already behind him. Guilt is always assumed by the media, hoped for, pushed. It makes a good story, a perfect narrative; the rise and fall, who goes up must come down – or be brought down. Success can only defy the laws of gravity so long.

I should at least have been satisfied with what was happening to him. But I wasn't. No matter the evidence, I didn't believe he'd killed on purpose. It had been an accident. Surely.

Then again . . .

This was the same person who'd accused me of stealing his diary, out of the blue. Like that. No proof. No motive. No basis in past behaviour. His word against mine. His absolute certainty of my guilt over my claims of innocence.

I can't think of anyone else who'd take it.

Where had that come from? Totally out of character, totally unexpected, yet said with utter conviction. Maybe the diary had been the start of something going bad in him, just as it had been for me – but for different reasons.

Was that really it? Or was he always on this path?

Rodney's murder . . .

Maybe Quinlan had been right, maybe VJ *had* killed him.

As I put the scrapbook away, my fingers brushed against the jiffy bag that held the matriculation photo. Suddenly I had the urge to look at it again, a need riding the back of a powerful impulse.

I took out the envelope and ran my fingernail along the edge of the seal. It was loose, but not quite open. The glue had dried and came away in flakes on my fingers. Still, there was no way I could get at the contents without ripping up the packaging.

I hadn't seen the photo in a long time, more than a decade. Couldn't face it. Too many bad associations, triggers and tripwires.

But I couldn't do much about my memory of it. Four rows of fresh-faced undergraduates and postgraduates, assembled on tiered benches and chairs in Sidney Sussex courtyard. Everyone in gowns, some in first or second formal suits; most smiling. I was in the bottom right of the first row. VJ was next to me, smiling, confident, chin up. My eyes were closed. I'd blinked at the very moment the shutter clicked. I was smiling, though. Happily, sincerely.

Mum said I look pissed in the picture, but I wasn't. I was happy because something had happened right before the photo was taken. As we were taking our places . . .

My mobile was ringing outside the door, loud enough to wake everyone up. It was in my coat, hanging in the hallway. I could tell from the designated ringtone – the theme from *Tales of the Unexpected* – it was Janet.

'Hello?'

'They've charged him with murder,' Janet said, quelling a yawn. She'd gone back to Charing Cross after our meeting with Kopf. It was almost midnight now.

'What about the manslaughter plea?'

'No go. He insists he's innocent,' she said. 'Not that it would've made any difference anyway. The police have got a very strong case for murder, Terry. There've been new developments.'

'Like what?'

'More witnesses have come forward. A waiter called Rudy Saks says he took a bottle of champagne up to the suite after midnight. He saw Evelyn Bates in the room with Vernon.'

That sounded like an open and shut case to me.

'And he's still saying he didn't do it?' I asked.

'I'm beginning to wish I hadn't taken this sodding thing.'

'We haven't even started working on it yet,' I said.

'Come on ...' she said.

'Which magistrates' is he going to?'

'Westminster,' she said. 'Meet me there on Monday at 8 a.m.'

We said our goodbyes and I ended the call.

On Monday VJ would have his first moment in court, where he'd state his name and officially enter his plea to the charges.

And on Monday I'd surely come face to face with him.

14

70 Horseferry Road, the building that used to house Westminster Magistrates' Court, was dreary going-on drab. Skirted by a broad pavement and nudged a little further back from the road than its neighbours, it was half a dozen floors of functional redbrick rectangle with no discernible entrance and small, dark, dirty windows too high up to see through. Only the large royal crest moulded into the front wall hinted at the building's higher purpose; but the design was buried under so many layers of white paint it had as good as disappeared, suggesting that the pale wall was either all that remained of a grander structure that had once stood in its place, or that the building itself had been started from loftier blueprints, only to be downgraded a quarter of the way in, to the car park manqué it was now.

Yet Westminster Magistrates' was – arguably – the most famous court of its kind in the land. Its eight courtrooms played host to virtually every high-profile, media-intensive case spat the way of the judicial system, from ruptured terrorist cells to transgressing celebrities of every alphabetical grade.

Janet and I sat together in the waiting area on the third floor, killing time until our case was called. We were due in Court 2 and we were running late. This was the nature of the game, a big part of the process – the hanging around, waiting for things you had no control or influence over to happen, to take their course.

The hallway was a cheerless, striplit, utilitarian stretch of dull black marble floor and mint-green perforated metal benches set out like rolls of particularly obnoxious carpet.

Today the press were out in force, all here for VJ. TV, papers, radio, internet, sitting around and waiting, like us.

Lawyers milled about, making phone calls, conferring with colleagues, cops and court staff; or else they chatted to witnesses or to the family and friends of defendants. All conversations were whispered or muttered. No voices were raised. Like church without God or religion.

Meanwhile VJ was sat downstairs, in one of the basement cells. He hadn't seen daylight or felt the sun on his face or breathed fresh air in at least forty-eight hours. He'd simply exchanged one subterranean hole for another. I knew what was going through his mind. Same as everyone else in his position – fear, disbelief, incomprehension.

I kept myself busy reading the copy of the disclosure file Janet had handed me when we'd met outside the courtroom earlier this morning. This was a big deal. Clerks didn't usually get to see any of it, unless absolutely necessary, to clarify a point or crosscheck a reference. I'd been fully integrated into the case at ground level.

The file was slender. Five witness statements, police interview notes, an autopsy report and photographs.

I started with the photographs. Not the victim's, but VJ's. Police mugshots, his face against a plain pale-yellow background, bathed in harsh light. His expression was neutral to downcast, his eyes both wired and dazed. It was the face I remembered; that of the friend I'd grown up with. Seeing it set off a mix of conflicting emotions, a warmth of recognition coupled with an immediate, corrective anger. I wanted to help him, but mostly hang him.

His lower lip was split in the middle and swollen, as if he'd been punched. Scratchmarks on his cheek were visible in the front-view photo, and clearer still on the profile shot. In the next image they had enlarged the injuries: a trio of abrasions that started as deep gouges on his upper cheekbone and ran down, thinning and breaking into dotted lines before stopping just above his lower jaw.

Next were front, side and back photographs of his upper body. He had a large dark bruise on his belly, consistent with a punch or a hard blow from a blunt object. There were pinprick wounds and small gashes on his back and shoulders. His left palm and fingers had small nicks and cuts on them, some fine and straight, others curved and deep. If I didn't know differently, I would have said he'd been the victim of a low-key assault or in a semi-serious car crash.

Then I turned to the crime-scene photos.

The hotel suite's lounge area. The minibar – the biggest I'd ever seen – in the centre of the photograph, leaked contents soaked into the carpet, blossoming up and out and across like a dark mushroom cloud. The bar was suspended, half off the ground, in mid-tilt, held in place by its flex, plug and socket. Its double doors were flung open, and its contents were piled up in front of it, smashed. There was a lot more broken glass on the floor – including VJ's Ethical Person of the Year award, broken in half, the capital 'E' on its side and inverted, so it looked like an 'F' with a fang-shaped stem. White on black numbered plastic evidence markers had been placed everywhere.

I looked for a list corresponding to the markers, but I didn't find one in the file. Typical brinkmanship. Although it wasn't allowed, it was common practice for the police and prosecution to withhold key evidence from the defence until very close to the trial start date, so the defence would have very little time to prepare a rebuttal.

There were no photographs of the bedroom, only one of the victim.

She stared through the picture with open eyes, which were as good as painted on. Their whites bore the tell-tale signs of the manner of her murder – petechial haemorrhages, small red spots where the capillaries had burst as the asphyxiated blood stagnated in her facial area because it couldn't flow back to her heart. There was no hint of pain in her expression, even though she must have been in agony as his hands closed around her neck, and she'd realised she was about to die. Her face had the waxen quality of corpses in the first eight to twelve hours of death, and with the curly blonde hair framing her face, she looked like a plump doll – albeit a doll with lipstick smeared past her parted lips and dark marks across her cheeks, where the mascara had run with the last tears she'd cried.

On the back was her name, written in blue biro.

Evelyn Bates.

I turned to the autopsy report. It confirmed that she'd died by strangulation, and that the killer used his hands, because the sides and back of her neck, as well as her throat, bore 'finger-shaped' bruises. And her killer had been strong, because there were petechiae in her mouth too.

I went back to the photograph of VJ's torso. The autopsy report listed Evelyn's weight at 152 pounds, and her height as five foot four. VJ was six foot two and weighed 187 pounds.

We'd been typical front-desk swots at school, strong of mind, puny in body. We'd been useless at sports. We'd played football twice a week with our class in a local playing field, where we'd be put in goal or defence because of our size. So we'd spent the next hour or so shivering and talking. VJ had since made up for his lack of athleticism. He looked after himself. His body was lean and muscular. He'd become strong enough to kill Evelyn.

I closed the file and looked up and saw Franco Carnavale. He was sat opposite us, staring at Janet, his small, clear blue eyes the colour of ice cubes floating in a chilly swimming pool. I don't know how long he'd been there. He wore a low-watt smile dipped end to end in smugness. He had a surprisingly youthful face for a man close to fifty, his skin scored with only the lightest of lines. He looked like he'd never been in a fight and whatever dangers he'd faced, he'd evaded or bullshat his way out of.

Then I noticed a flashing in the corner of my left eye. I turned slightly and saw that it was the light catching Carnavale's pinkie ring. He was tapping his little finger on the empty seat next to him – except the seat wasn't quite empty. He'd put a file there – a manila file, just like the one I had in my hands. Except his was twice as thick as mine.

I knew why he was smirking. He had a big head start on us. He knew things about the case we didn't. The police had handed him everything they had so far. He'd shared as little of it as possible with us – just the stuff he intended to base his argument on today. He was under no obligation to do any more than that, and he wouldn't. That's the way things are. The trials may be fair, but the system isn't. It's geared towards putting people away. Better to be a prosecutor than a defender.

Moments later we were called in to Court 2.

Magistrates' Court means different things to different people. To the defendant – the accused – it's the opening salvo, the formal declaration of hostilities by the justice system, the taste of what's to come, the beginning of the end.

To us, the lawyers, it's the starting pistol that launches the sack race to trial. We get the date and venue of the main event, and then we're off, slowly, awkwardly, hands and legs bound by the thing we simultaneously step upon yet faithfully uphold – the law.

And to the rest – the press and, by extension, the general public – it's a little bit of theatre, a curtain-raiser for the main event. The accused is seen for the first time in the flesh, and confronted with his crimes. The justice system squares up to him.

The legal term for what was about to happen is a Plea and Directions Hearing. The defendant pleads guilty or not guilty to the charges the police have brought against them, and the magistrate directs his or her fate, immediate and future. They fix the day the trial will begin and either free the defendant on bail or remand them to prison until then.

What the public don't know is that practically everything's been agreed beforehand. We already knew how VJ was going to plead, and it was a given he wouldn't get bail because of the charge, and because he was a flight risk. As for the trial date, the first thing Janet had told me this morning was that it would be July 4th. Carnavale was free then, and so was Court 1 at the Old Bailey, the grandest legal stage in the country.

The only unknown to us going into court was the prison VJ would be remanded to. That was down to wherever there was space, and was within reasonable commuting distance for the legal team. It wouldn't be an open prison, but a high-security one. The central London prisons were all full to overflowing, so I guessed VJ would end up in Belmarsh, on the outskirts. Not that it would really matter much to him where he was sent, initially. Prison would scare the living shit out of him.

We took our places in court.

Janet and Carnavale sat at the front table, facing the three magistrates, who were behind a long desk on a raised podium, with a big royal crest as a backdrop. A ruddy-faced, bespectacled man sat in the middle, flanked by two women also wearing glasses. He was the senior magistrate, the one who'd be officiating. A tier below them, in profile, sat the court clerk, a slight woman with a pointed nose, dressed in a white blouse.

I was behind Janet, next to the CPS clerk.

And directly behind me was the dock VJ would soon be standing in; a box of thick blond wood and bulletproof glass, louvred at the front so the defendant could speak and be passed papers if necessary.

Next to that was the public gallery, another wood and glass box, the same as the dock, only half the height and twice as deep, with two tiers of folding seats and speakers indented into the graffiti-marked wood. It was full today, mostly with members of the press, freelance writers who were already prepping their true crime books on VJ, and members of the public – the one-off visitors who were there out of chance and curiosity, for something to do and talk about over dinner.

We waited. DCI Reid came in, bowed to the magistrates and handed Carnavale a few stapled sheets of paper. Janet read through her notes.

It was quiet, except for the shuffling of papers; a very British kind of silence, the silence of people looking at their feet, of the air going out of conversations. Everybody avoided making eye contact with people they didn't know, and everybody tried to look like they were busy doing something other than waiting for VJ to come into the dock.

Carnavale being here was highly unusual. The CPS usually sent a solicitor not a barrister to Plea and Directions Hearings, but the press were out in force, so they'd rolled out their big gun early. Or maybe Carnavale and his titanic ego had had a meeting and decided he should do this part himself.

The magistrates whispered among themselves. The press mumbled into each other's ears. I tried to stay calm. I'd positioned myself in such a way that all VJ would see of me was the back of my head. I wasn't going to look at him, or let him see me. The time wasn't right for that.

My heart was thumping. I had a knot in my stomach, a dry mouth, and pressure at the nape of my neck.

Then I heard him coming. When their case was called, defendants were marched up several flights of stairs from their cells to the dock. They were cuffed, hand and foot, the chains long enough to allow them to walk, but not run. The court's walls absorbed the high notes the metal made on the concrete, so the sound that echoed up the hollow stairwell and cut into the officious silence was the heavy swoosh of ankle chains, like a pile of heavy coins being scooped up into a sack.

The door of the dock was unlocked. I heard the press behind me shift in their seats, as they no doubt craned forward to get their first glimpse of the accused. Then I heard the chains clinking as they dragged across the dock.

He was here. Just a few feet behind me. My pulse started racing. I tried breathing through my nose, but my nostrils were constricted to points. I lowered my head and looked down at the blank page of my pad. I uncapped my pen. My fingers slipped on sweat.

The court clerk looked over at the dock.

'Please state your name, address and date of birth,' she said.

'Vernon James,' the voice came behind me. 'Clemons Mews, Cheyne Walk, London. June 18th, 1973.'

From his voice alone, I wouldn't have known him. He didn't sound remotely like the person I remembered. Not even a trace of his old Stevenage Estuary accent.

'You have been charged with the murder of Evelyn Bates on or around the night of March the 16th, 2011. How do you plead?'

'Not . . . guilty,' he said. Pausing between words, for emphasis.

Carnavale stood up to outline the charges for the magistrates, and for the record.

'The defendant has been charged with the murder of Evelyn Bates on the night of March 16th, 2011.

'The facts are these. Evelyn's body was found in the bedroom of Suite 18, in the Blenheim-Strand hotel. The defendant was a guest at the hotel, staying in the same suite. The autopsy report confirms that Evelyn was strangled. No object of death has been recovered from the scene – no noose, no cord, or anything of the kind. Circular bruise patterns around her neck indicate that her murderer used his bare hands to asphyxiate her.'

Carnavale went on to outline the prosecution's case. The lie VJ had told DCI Reid about having a wild party in his suite, how he didn't initially deny that Evelyn was the woman he'd been with, the fact that he'd fled the scene. Next, he detailed the witness statements – six in all now.

82

Every one of them had seen Evelyn with the defendant, and every one of them had identified her from the post-mortem photograph they were shown.

Hearing it all again, in court, from another party, in a stranger's voice, made the case seem utterly indefensible. I didn't have a clue how we were going to play this. And we hadn't even had the science yet – toxicology, DNA, hair and fibre, fingerprints.

When he'd finished, Carnavale sat down. He'd been very good, I had to give him that. He had no one to impress here, but he'd impressed me.

The magistrates conferred. Their mouths moved, but they made no sound. Janet flipped through her notebook. I kept my head in the same position, completely turned away from the dock. My upper back was starting to ache from the strain of maintaining the same posture.

The senior magistrate cleared his throat.

'The trial date is set for July 4th, at the Old Bailey,' he said. 'Because of the seriousness of the charge, and taking into account the fact that the defendant poses a significant flight risk, I'm going to remand him in custody at Belmarsh until the start of his trial.'

Belmarsh. Inmates past and present referred to it as 'Hellmarsh'.

I heard the door of the dock being opened and VJ walking out to a heavy jingle of chains. I was sorely tempted to turn around then, but I stayed put. A drop of sweat ran down the middle of my forehead and fell on my pad with a solid *tak*. I looked at it soaking into the paper, spreading out. I worried that the notes I'd taken would be ruined, unreadable, but then I realised that the page I was staring at was blank. I'd been so busy listening and worrying and hiding that I hadn't written a damn thing.

'The court will rise,' the magistrate said, standing up, indicating that the proceedings were over.

I hadn't heard the door close, although I knew VJ had left the dock, otherwise the magistrate wouldn't have called time.

I turned around slowly. The dock was empty, but I could hear the chains following him down the stairs as he was led back to a cell to get ready to be transferred to the next.

15

I stood on the pavement opposite the court and watched as they drove him away to prison in a white van with blacked-out portholes; one of those long cattle trucks that housed half a dozen prisoners in separate boxes little bigger than gym lockers.

There was a small crowd of photographers by the back exit. The van slowed and then stopped to wait for a break in the traffic that had clogged up the road. TV reporters were already filming their two-minute accounts of the proceedings that would get played on repeat on the news channels later in the day. They'd describe what VJ had worn, what he'd said and whether he'd been bailed or remanded, and then they'd cut to the scene I was watching now.

The photographers rushed the van. They did the window bob and weave, pushing and shoving and jostling each other to get their camera lenses right up against each black pane. Today they had it really easy. The van wasn't going anywhere because of the traffic blockade. Plenty to go around.

The TV news crews just kept on filming the van as it pulled on to the road and rolled away.

16

I took the Tube from Westminster to Bond Street, and walked down Oxford Street to Marble Arch.

While we'd been in court the day had steadily brightened up, and a preview of summer hit me like a sharp slap. Sharp light, blue sky, warmth. All in one. I stood on the pavement for a moment blinking, disorientated, feeling like time had jumped forward a few months.

The small parks by the arch were full of office workers enjoying the last dozen minutes of their lunch breaks. Shirts undone, sleeves rolled up, shoes off, bovine smiles.

I crossed over on to Edgware Road and headed to meet Andy Swayne.

He'd told me he'd be in a Lebanese place called the Cedars, but almost every restaurant and café down Edgware Road was Lebanese. No surprise. Lebanese refugees had settled in the area in the mid to late 1970s, when they'd fled their country's bloody and ruinous civil war.

The first third of the road was all scaffolding and shop signs with Arab subtitles. The newsagents sold nothing but Arab dailies displayed in racks; there were Arab food stores, banks, book and record shops, and a video rental place that had more VHS tapes than DVDs. It was like the internet had never happened. And it was all the better for it. There was a low-key vibrancy here, a sense of community, of a home away from home.

No sign of a place called the Cedars of Lebanon. I cursed myself for not thinking to look it up before I'd gone to court. Cursed myself even more for not asking Swayne if he had a mobile.

After the Connaught Street junction, the Middle Eastern influence petered out and Edgware Road became a concrete funnel of inter-changeable household names, with pubs, betting shops and fast food places wedged in-between.

And it was somewhere here that I passed the Cedars of Lebanon. It was next to a tired and empty-looking newsagent's displaying dusty fruit and wilted flowers outside. I might have missed it altogether, if it hadn't been for the Lebanese flag painted in the middle of the window.

Swayne was already there, a tall, thin man in a light-blue shirt, maroon tie and steel-rimmed glasses, sat deep in a far corner, back to the wall. He was the only customer in the café. We made eye contact and he gave me a slight nod.

The place was sombre and poky, a dead-ending corridor that had been reclaimed, roofed over and reinvented. It reeked like a mound of ripe dishcloths. I couldn't imagine anyone coming here more than once unless they owned it or had a fetish for one-star eateries.

To the right of the door was a counter, pastries arranged on trays, no more than four or five on each. They looked pale and dry, except for a couple of baklavas that were as good as drowned in congealed brown syrup. A tubby man with glasses and thick stubble stood behind the counter, following me in with a wary look, his mouth caught between a smile and a scowl.

I introduced myself to Swayne and held out my hand.

'You're a bit old to be a clerk at KRP, aren't you?' he said, looking me up and down.

I'd heard far worse alternatives to 'Hello', but I hadn't expected hostility from him. I kept my surprise in check, pulled out a stool and sat down.

Swayne was in his seventies and looked it. His short grey hair was thinning all over and the scalp below was spattered with liver spots. He had a vulpine face with a skin tone that ranged from cloudy red to semi-translucent, like raw meat wrapped in greaseproof paper.

Even if I hadn't been told, I'd have known he was an alcoholic. Like the drunks they start out as, alcoholics come in two varieties – sweet or sour. Swayne was meanness personified. He had the look of someone who wakes up every morning and realises that that's the best he's going to feel all day, and decides to hate his every conscious minute in return.

'What do you want?' he asked.

'Sorry?'

'To drink.'

'I'm fine for now,' I said.

'Suit yourself.'

He crossed his arms and sat back. I noticed he was wearing a brand-new shirt that he hadn't bothered to iron. It had those just-out-of-the-packet vertical and horizontal creases across the chest and arms.

'How long have you been at KRP?' he asked. His voice was slightly raspy, like he was recovering from a cold. And I heard the remnants of a Geordie accent in his pronunciation.

'Four months.'

'How are you finding it?'

'OK,' I said.

He sniggered. Or at least I thought he did. His shoulders spasmed, and he smiled and creased his face into a thousand furrows, yet the sound he made was more like a wet sneeze that had got stuck between his palate and nose and was fighting to get out.

'What's so funny?'

'That wasn't a laugh,' he said.

I was getting annoyed. He was the drowning man you risk your life saving, only for him to cuss you out for messing up his suicide bid. If it had been up to me I'd have told him to sod off, but it wasn't and I couldn't.

'Now, this case we talked about yesterday . . . This is what we have so far,' I said, pulling out a copy of the disclosure file.

He took what I handed him and quickly flicked past each page with barely a glance. Then he screwed the lot up in his fist, scrunching and compacting the paper until it all disappeared under his fingers. He kneaded and squeezed it tight, his forearm shaking with the effort, before opening his hand out and letting the tight paper ball he'd made of the legal documents roll off his palm and on to the table.

For a blank moment all I could do was watch the ball expand and loosen, popping and crackling as it did, like a huge piece of popcorn.

Then I looked up at him. His face was the same, still channelling vinegar and bile and God knows how many million grudges and resentments.

I was almost grateful for his behaviour. Now I had all the excuse I needed not to use him. As I unravelled and then flattened the paper, I was already thinking of which investigator I'd put on the case.

I slipped the pages back in my bag.

'Thanks for your time,' I said.

I stood up and started for the door.

'You might want to take this with you, boy wonder,' he said behind me.

I heard something heavy thud on the table. I turned around. A thick A4 manila file was lying there.

86

I knew what it was, but he told me anyway.

'That's what *they* have so far. The CPS disclosure file for Case No. 3375908. Everything to date on *L'Affaire James*.'

'How d'you get it?'

'The investigators you usually use can't and won't go to the places I can. That's why Sid sprung me from the gulag,' he said.

Right up until then, I'd thought I had some leeway as to whether or not I worked with Swayne. That was how Kopf had sold it to me – or, rather, to Janet. But that wasn't the case at all. I was stuck with this odious twat whether I liked it or not.

I went back to the table and opened the file. It was divided into two parts – what the CPS had already given us, and everything they hadn't. Our material took up under a quarter of the file. The rest comprised a lot more – crime-scene photographs, additional witness statements, complete transcripts of each of VJ's police interviews, and an inventory of materials taken from the crime scene that ran to ten pages.

'I can't take this,' I said.

'Why?'

'It's illegal.'

'There's nothing there you won't be getting all or part of eventually. Think of it as a head start. A levelling of the field.'

'It's stolen property,' I said.

'It was a gift,' he said. 'I asked and I received.'

'It's *still* stolen property.'

He sighed. 'You obviously don't know your place in the scheme of things, so let me enlighten you. I fetch, you carry. You're just a gopher here – at best,' Swayne said. 'If you've got ethical issues about any of this, you're in the wrong profession. And *definitely* with the wrong firm.'

I understood straight away. Janet and Kopf knew Swayne would give me the file, but they couldn't legally know I had it, or that I'd even seen it. I couldn't take the file back to the office. I was going to have to keep it at home, where I'd study it, comparing what the prosecution had given us against what they hadn't. I'd feed the information back to Janet unofficially – and not in writing. We'd then be able to work out what their case was going to be; who they were going to call as witnesses, what evidence they were going to present, what the narrative would be. This was gold dust. It was also a major violation of ethics, the kind of thing that could get a lawyer disbarred.

I took the file and put it in my bag.

He held out his hand.

'I'm Andy Swayne.'

'Terry Flynt.' We shook. Swayne's grip was strong, his skin tough. He may have been an alcoholic, but there was an implacable hardness to him, a cold core no amount of self-medication could warm, let alone melt.

'You'll need a bigger bag, because there'll be more where that came from,' he said.

'Is that how you operate?' I asked.

'It's one of the things I do,' he answered.

A proactive investigator, I thought. That was a first.

'What's the worst thing you've heard about me?' he asked.

'That you used to be the best at what you did,' I said. I could've mentioned the burglary Janet had brought up in the meeting, but I really didn't want to know.

'Why's that so bad?'

'Nothing worse than living in your own shadow,' I said.

He considered that a moment. Then seemed to file it away.

'What do you know about the James case?' I asked him.

'Only what I've seen on TV.'

'You haven't read the file?'

'No.'

'Why not?'

'I'm a snoop, not a lawyer. And, besides, I really don't give a fuck.'

In that respect he was no different from any other investigator, just more upfront about it. The best investigators are the ones who remain aloof from what doesn't concern them; they locate the pixel but ignore the picture.

'Do you work with Bella Hogan?' he asked.

'We share an office,' I said.

Swayne read between the lines and smirked.

'I guess her time is almost at hand.'

'What do you mean?' I asked.

'The degree, the promotion.'

'I don't know anything about that,' I said.

Swayne grinned and I saw the uneven grey stumps he had for teeth.

'You mean Janet hasn't given you that little talk of hers? About how you're her favourite, the best clerk in the company – words to that effect?'

I didn't say anything, but I felt myself blush and he had his answer.

'I worked for KRP for close to thirty years, on and off. They always pull the same crap on people they're going to get rid of,' he said.

I went cold inside. 'What are you talking about?'

'I don't know why they do it,' Swayne continued.

'What *are* you talking about?' I said.

88

'Did Janet drop a big hint about promoting you after this trial?'

Again, I said nothing.

'Won't happen,' he said, looking at me.

'Why not?'

'Look at yourself. You're too old to be a lawyer – especially one of theirs. By the time you start practising you'll be what – early forties? Your peer group'll be fifteen years younger. Their bosses will be your age. You'll be a lightweight who looks like a heavyweight. Who wants that?'

'Are you saying I'm going to get *fired*?'

'Yup.'

'When?'

'When this trial's over. Probably after sentencing,' he said.

'*Sentencing?* The trial hasn't even started,' I said.

'Please! There's only one possible verdict here. It's open and shut. And, anyway, what can you do about it? You're a *clerk*, for fuck's sake. Which barrister are they using?'

'Christine Devereaux.'

Swayne laughed out loud this time, but it was hollow and joyless, an echo of a laugh coming from a deep dark place.

'They're sparing no expense to lose this one, are they? You think I'm over the hill? She's all the way at the bottom. They gave you a loser, Terry, because they want to lose you.'

But they *hadn't* given it to me. Janet had called Adolf's desk, long after Adolf had gone home.

Or was that simply how I was seeing things? I thought back to that day. Adolf had left work early to go to the dentist. Janet had been in the office then, so she'd known Adolf was out. And I'd stayed late, as was my habit. Therefore Janet *knew* I was going to pick up the phone when she called.

But if that was true, and they were planning to fire me, why had Kopf tried to get me off the case? Or had he been bluffing?

I didn't trust Swayne. And I didn't want to believe him. Yet, for all I knew, he could have been telling the truth. He had an axe to grind after all.

'I just thought they were interested in promoting the best person for the job,' I said.

'Oh they are. But that's not you.'

'How do you know?'

'I know Bella. She's their kind of person. Hungry, ambitious, no feelings,' he said. 'If I'd handed her that file just now, she'd have taken it with both hands and no questions – and definitely no complaints.'

89

I said nothing.

Why had he told me what he had? It didn't have anything to do with me or my welfare, that was for sure. But there was an element of self-projection to it. He was bitter at Kopf and the company for firing him, and was letting me know the kind of people I was working for. Maybe they'd fooled him like they'd fooled me, hinted at his indispensability one day and kicked him out the next. I was now curious as to what had happened, but I didn't want to ask him yet.

The man who'd been behind the counter walked over to our table. He smiled at us and said something in Arabic. I was about to tell him I didn't understand, but Swayne replied – in Arabic. This led to a short conversation between the two of them, the patter quickfire and guttural. For the second time in the twenty minutes I'd known him, Swayne had surprised me – only this time it was pleasant, or as pleasant as things could be around someone with the personality of an irate viper caged in barbed wire.

The man went away a few moments later.

Swayne saw my curious look.

'Cities are like the devil,' he said. 'They speak in many tongues. It's always good to know a few of them.'

Then we heard someone pissing in the toilet, behind the wall Swayne was propped up against.

'Have you been to the crime scene?' Swayne asked.

'The hotel?'

'The room itself. Suite 18.'

'Of course not. It's restricted.'

'Only if you don't belong there,' Swayne said.

'Breaking and entering's a crime,' I said.

'Who said anything about breaking and entering?'

'You're just going to walk in?'

'Uh-huh.'

'That's impersonating a police officer, which is a crime.'

'Only if you identify yourself as such,' Swayne said. 'If somebody mistakes you for one that's their bad judgement. What have you got to lose? And don't say your job, 'cause that's already gone.'

If he hadn't told me about Adolf and KRP's machinations, I'd have refused on the spot. But I was falling through layers of self-belief. And part of me was curious as hell to see where VJ had killed Evelyn Bates, where it had all gone down.

'It's another thing I do. Another of my bespoke services. View the scene while it's still live. Take my own pictures. You'd be surprised what coppers miss. Or choose not to see.'

90

'When are you thinking of going?'

'Now,' he said.

'How are you going to get in?'

'That's the easy part,' Swayne smiled. He picked up a medium-sized black rucksack from the floor. 'You already look like a cop. You carry yourself like one – that certain whiff of moral rectitude, that walk like you were born with a stick up your arse. It's as right as your suit. Cheap, but well looked after. A cop's suit. Only your shoes need shining.'

'I cleaned them this morning,' I said.

'Cops' shoes are always spotless. They gleam. Like mirrors. So they can admire themselves from on high,' Swayne said. 'There's a shiner down the road. Shall we?'

17

I slipped the plastic covers over my gleaming DMs and wondered why the hell I'd bothered getting them polished. The covers were the disposable kind – white and opaque, with elasticated openings – and they went all the way up to my ankles.

Swayne snapped on his latex gloves and handed me a pair. He noticed me frowning at my feet.

'You build a character from the ground up, don't you know?' he whispered. 'Fundamental rules of acting.'

We were on the twelfth-floor corridor of the Blenheim-Strand, close to Suite 18. The door had been wedged open a crack, but I couldn't hear any sound coming from the inside.

We'd had no trouble getting in. The suite was located in the part of the hotel known as the Chimney – the sixteen-storey tinted glass tower that rose out of the middle of the building and housed all the upmarket rooms, starting with the superior, then deluxe, before moving on up to the suite variants and the penthouse.

The last two were served by an exclusive lift that could only be accessed by a guest's keycard. We'd got around that problem by taking the fire escape. I'd expected to find police at the doors to the twelfth floor, but their only presence was a nominal strip of blue-and-white barrier tape stuck across the entrance.

'Nervous?' Swayne whispered.

Nervous? No. I was terrified.

Here I was, about to break the law. Why and what for? I was just a clerk, a nobody with a notebook. But Swayne had goaded me into it – and it hadn't occurred to me to say no. Adolf would've come here without hesitation. No way was I going to wimp out where she hadn't feared to tread.

Yet that wasn't quite the only reason. I was curious too. I wanted to see where the crime had happened; gain some kind of perspective on what VJ had done.

'No,' I said, glancing at the door. 'You?'

Swayne grinned and it was a perturbing sight, a leer so wide the ends of his mouth almost touched the far corners of his eyes. And there was a cruelty to his mirth, as if he'd just watched someone he hated go down in flames on a freezing cold day and was warming his hands on the pyre.

He was a totally different entity now. Something had fully awoken in him. He'd shrugged off his defeatism and lethargy, and whatever powers he needed to do his job had come off the sidelines and manifested themselves. Only his unpleasantness remained, but I suppose he needed that to do the things he did.

We were about to go in. Swayne checked his camera. I looked up and then down the long curving corridor. There was no one coming.

'Follow my lead,' Swayne said, handing me his rucksack. 'And walk with purpose.'

We'd barely got inside when we were ambushed by a very familiar smell. We had the same reaction. We froze. For a few seconds our senses kicked our brains into freefall. We forgot where we were, who we were meant to be, and what we were supposed to be doing.

Stale booze in a closed, warm space. Sticky-sweet, rancid, pungent, welcoming. The smell of pubs. The smell of drinking. The smell of trouble.

We should have been ready for it. If Swayne had read the file, he would have known about the overturned minibar in the middle of the room, and the minor lake its smashed contents had made on the carpet. As for me, I'd forgotten all about it – one of those important minor details that slipped between bigger ones.

The stink took me back to my old Stevenage haunt, the Griffin. As a kid I'd walked past it at lunchtime and seen the hardened drinkers sitting inside, alone, pints on the tables, cigarettes on the go. That had been me a few years later. The midday boozer. Four drinks in and I'd feel better. Five to seven and I'd feel good. Then the demons would come-a-knocking and I'd let them all in.

Swayne was in that zone too. Only it was hitting him harder, I could tell. I'd just had a drink *problem* – as in a problem with it; as in I couldn't drink too much otherwise I went crazy and blacked out. Swayne had had it worse. He was an alcoholic. A dependant. He was an addict. He couldn't function without the stuff. And he'd only recently gone on the wagon. Learned to live again. So this was a serious test for him.

I saw him standing there confused for an instant, almost dizzy, trying to pick the past from the present.

But his pride must have slapped him out of his stupor, because he shook it off fast.

He took a short breath through his mouth, and then nodded in the direction of the living room.

We carried on in.

It was a shockingly big space, the size of my entire flat and the one next door combined, maybe even bigger still – and that was without the bedroom, which was at the opposite end.

Two thousand *a night* – and this wasn't even the biggest suite.

Acres of thick khaki-toned carpet, towering, natural stone walls, and a vast ceiling garnished with a crystal chandelier, looming brilliantly over the centre of the room. And then there was the view from the floor-to-ceiling window, which added another dimension to the immensity of the suite, making it seem more expansive, almost limitless: south London between the Blackfriars and Hungerford Bridges; mile after mile after mile of charred blacks and seared browns and sooty greys, ending in the green fields and hills of Surrey, just about visible on the horizon.

I looked away and back to the room. After the busy, crowded city view, the interior seemed empty.

What furniture there was, was arranged in three individual groupings with plenty of empty space in-between. The only thing on the left side of the room, facing the window, was a long and wide cream leather couch, no doubt meant for contemplating the vista. At the far end of the room, to the right, was a desk the size of a grand piano, equipped with an orthopaedic chair, footrest and green banker's lamp.

The crime scene was in the middle of the room.

We headed towards it.

I heard sound – a light scraping. Or was it a rustling? Or a bit of both?

And then, in the lounge area, I saw ...

People.

Cops!

Three forensics officers in white boiler suits were working around the coffee table and couch. They were on their knees, their backs to us.

They hadn't seen us.

I stopped.

They weren't supposed to be here.

We weren't supposed to be here.

93

Why the hell hadn't Swayne thought of this?

Why hadn't *I* thought of this?

It wasn't too late. They hadn't noticed us. We could slip out.

I started turning, but Swayne grabbed my arm. He shook his head. I rolled my eyes and nodded at the scene in the middle of the room – the *live crime scene* we were trespassing on.

He shook his head again and pointed forward.

We weren't backing out. We were going in.

He hadn't let go of my arm, and his grip was tight and stronger than his puny, booze-corroded frame implied.

'I lead, you follow,' he whispered.

We moved into the room, heading left, towards the window.

I kept my eyes on the cops. In their all-in-one white coveralls, with their hoods up over their hair and their attention focused on minutiae, they were hermetically sealed off from the outside. One was sweeping small quantities of broken glass into a white dustpan, sifting through it, and dumping it into one of two plastic containers, marked 'A' and 'B'. Another was shining a small torch into the gaps between the couch cushions, and scraping it with a glass wand. The last was dusting the side of the upturned minibar for fingerprints.

The minibar was the scene's centrepiece, almost another body. Practically the size of a horizontal family freezer, and originally concealed in a faux mahogany cupboard, it was no longer suspended in mid-topple. Now it was safely upright, on its base. But the double doors had been left open and the contents were piled in pieces on the carpet. The leakage had spread out in a broad, rusty-brown circle, almost the same shade as week-old blood.

Number markings had been placed around the area, but these were different from the ones in the photographs I'd seen – black on yellow as opposed to black on white.

This was another sweep. They were either looking for something else – something they'd missed – or gathering corroborative evidence, backing up theories.

A thick aura of desperation hovered about the scene. It would have taken considerable strength to tip over the minibar, but if a person was being attacked and fighting for their life, adrenalin kicked in and sometimes made up for physical shortcomings. VJ had said Fabia had used the fridge as a weapon. It didn't seem that way from here. The skewed angle of the bar suggested the fridge had been used defensively, possibly as a shield to block an assailant's advance.

The rest of the area was oddly tidy. The long L-shaped couch was perfectly aligned. The coffee table and its lavish display of now arid lilies and orchids were intact. Also on the table was an unopened bottle of champagne, still in its bucket, and two glasses.

The damage wasn't in fact as extensive as the pictures had suggested. The vastness of the space made it seem even smaller, confined, close to trivial.

We'd given the forensics trio a wide berth, staying close to the window as we edged our way towards the bedroom. I had the manila file in my hand, stuffed with some of the scene photographs and the manifest of logged evidence.

I stayed close to Swayne, behind him, as he'd instructed. He had his camera out, and was taking pictures as fast as he could, barely pausing to look at the screen. All the while we were edging towards the bedroom.

As we got within reach of the steps, I noticed that a wide area of the carpet had been cordoned off with police tape, marking a rough triangle. There were three markers on the ground, one placed near a large stain. And, circumscribing the stain, and the areas above and below it, was an outline – a bright-red chalk outline, in the shape of a body.

Someone coughed behind us.

I turned round and found myself looking at one of the forensics officers, who was staring right back at me. He had round rimless glasses and a snubby nose. His mouth was open, in surprise. He straightened up a little, his eyes narrowing and brow contorting.

I'd managed to keep to the calm side of nervous up until now. Swayne's confidence, his sureness, had bolstered my own.

But now it hit me.

Panic . . . fear.

Panic . . .

Fear.

Fuck.

We looked at each other across the room, the real deal and the impostor. I froze up.

Swayne stepped on my toes with his heel. *Keep it together.*

'Anything new?' Swayne asked the man, in an officious, impatient tone that bordered on the snappy, and had just the right amount of volume to carry across the room. The other forensics people stopped what they were doing and looked our way. They all had the same look. Trying to place us, work out how senior we were.

I didn't move.

'Uh . . . yes,' the man said to Swayne, nervously, wilting before perceived authority. 'Found some . . . um . . . hair on the side of the couch.'

'How much longer are you going to be?' Swayne asked.

'Few hours yet. We'll be done tonight.'

'As you were,' Swayne said.

'Yes, sir,' the man said and went back to work. The others followed suit.

We headed for the bedroom. Swayne in the lead. I could see him grinning that big ugly beam of his.

Swayne pushed the door shut behind us, leaving it open a crack.

'That was close,' I whispered.

'No, it *wasn't*,' he snorted. He took out his camera and started snapping away.

If the suite had consisted of the bedroom alone, it still would have been the biggest hotel room I'd ever set foot in. Evelyn Bates had been murdered in the lap of luxury.

The bed where her body had been found dominated the room; two king-sizers rolled into one, its heavy wooden frame bolstered by an arching padded headboard, which was a radiant white, like a movie screen showing a close-up of a blank piece of paper. Forensics had removed all the sheets and pillowcases, exposing the dense slab of memory foam that was the mattress.

In keeping with the lounge's theme, the rest of the furniture was elegant but kept to a minimum, boosting the sense of space instead of filling it. The bed was flanked by glass-topped cabinets, which had a phone, lamp and alarm clock on each. A flatscreen TV faced the bed, its borders painted the same grey-stone tones as the walls, which made the screen appear indented. To the left was a dressing table and chair.

Swayne opened up the walk-in closet. There was a wall safe at the very back, the door open. He photographed it once.

Then we went into the en suite bathroom, which was gleaming and echoey. The glasses were still sealed in plastic, the towels folded and plumped up, and none of the complimentary toiletries had been used.

'Didn't even wash his hands afterwards,' Swayne said.

I went back into the bedroom and took out the crime-scene pictures. They were numbered and arranged in the order they'd been taken.

I glanced from the photographs to the mattress, mentally juxtaposing the printed images on to the reality before me.

The first few showed Evelyn Bates as the hotel maid had found her – face up on a huge bed, naked, one arm drooped over the mattress, the other flung across the middle of the bed, palm out. Her head was partly propped up on the edge of the pillows.

There was something deeply sad about the way she'd been laid out here; whole, yet broken, like a shopfront mannequin no one had any use for. She was on the left side of the bed, nearest the door. She would have been the first thing everyone saw when they walked in. If she'd been alive, she'd have scrambled to cover up her nakedness before a stranger. She couldn't now. But she'd been accorded a minor dignity in the way her mussed-up hair fell over much of her face, making enough of a mystery of her features.

Next were photographs of her dress, a crumpled pile of shiny green fabric on the floor by the bed, directly below her hand. Both her shoes were at the foot of the bed, green patent leather stilettos. One was upright, the other on its side, its heel snapped off at the stem.

Next were close-ups of her face, with and without the hair veiling her features; zoom-ins on her blood-speckled eyes, the cloudy bruising to her neck and throat, the lipstick smeared like the shaft of a tick across her left cheek, her torn earlobe and the hooped earring on the mattress.

And then I saw something that completely threw me, that didn't make sense.

A picture that didn't belong there.

I checked the log sticker on the back, and cross-referenced it with the evidence manifest. Case number, scene letter, picture number and a brief description of the object in the photograph.

3375908/A/34 – Chocolate.

A diamond-shaped chocolate piece wrapped in a royal-blue wrapper with 'Marquis' printed across it in gold cursive script.

I went back to the very first photograph. I looked at the sandbag arrangement of pillows behind Evelyn's body. They were easy to ignore, given the context, but there was a piece of Marquis chocolate on the middle and last stack of pillows, placed right in the centre.

Room service had turned the bed down while VJ had been out.

But then I noticed something else.

The pillows hadn't been moved at all. And the sheets under and around Evelyn were barely disturbed.

I went to the last photograph. It was the bed after the body had been moved. The space had been outlined in bright-red chalk.

Which meant . . .

Jesus.

'Ready?' Swayne said as he came out of the bathroom.

I beckoned him over and pointed to the pillows in the photo.

'She wasn't killed here,' I said. 'She was killed next door. He carried her in here afterwards, stripped her and laid her down on the mattress. And he did it very gently. He didn't drop her or dump her. See the chocolates on here? They were on the bed before she was murdered. He was careful.'

'So?'

'It was like she was posed, or put here deliberately.'

In other words: this wasn't manslaughter or even a run-of-the-mill murder. There was something twisted about it. Fetishistic, ritualistic ...

'You know what differentiates successful people from failures?' Swayne asked. 'Successful people mind their own business. Failures mind everyone's business *but* their own. I fetch, you carry – remember?'

I opened my mouth to ask him if he thought he defined success, but we heard voices coming from the lounge.

I went over to the door and looked through the gap.

Fuck.

DCI Reid and Franco Carnavale had walked into the suite. They too were wearing latex gloves and overshoes.

And they were heading straight for the bedroom.

The forensics team had stopped what they were doing. One of them spoke to DCI Reid. I couldn't hear what they were saying.

Carnavale turned towards the window and didn't move for a moment. That view had him hooked. He started walking towards it, almost involuntarily, as if he were being reeled in.

'Gimme the file – bag – phone,' Swayne said behind me.

I handed him everything.

He started leafing through the file, as he walked towards the bathroom.

Reid finished chatting to forensics and called to Carnavale. He came away from the window, reluctantly.

I turned and looked at Swayne. He was standing by the bathroom door with the phone to his ear.

The pair were making a beeline for the bedroom, crossing the lounge, their eyes fixed on the gap I was observing them from.

Then I heard a ringtone. A pounding funky piano riff, all lower keys. I recognised the theme from *Police Woman,* a forgettable American TV series from the 1970s. I would have laughed if I hadn't been so damn scared. Reid and Carnavale were but fifteen feet from the door.

Reid stopped, swore under her breath and took out her phone. She glanced at the screen and answered.

I heard Swayne mumbling behind me.

'DCI Reid?'

'Yes?' she said outside.

'This is the Deputy Commissioner's office,' Swayne said. 'He'd like a word. Are you alone?'

'Um ... no. Give me a moment,' she said, looking around her, first at Carnavale, then behind her at the forensics team. She held up an index finger to Carnavale, mouthed something to him, and then turned and started walking away. She passed the forensics team and then left the suite.

I heard her voice on my phone.

'Can you hold?' Swayne said. 'He'll be on the line shortly.'

Swayne came quickly back to the door.

Carnavale had sauntered off back to the window.

Swayne handed me a small white plastic bundle.

'Put it on,' he said. It was a forensics coverall.

I was going to question the wisdom of what we were doing, but Swayne was already pulling his suit on over his legs.

I dragged the coverall on, pulling the hood over my head.

Swayne dropped the file in his rucksack and gave me my muted phone.

'Keep it on,' he said. 'Let's go.'

He opened the door and we stepped out of the bedroom.

Carnavale was by the window, admiring the view, his gloved hands folded behind his back. He didn't turn round as we passed him.

I kept my head down as we walked. The forensics team were engrossed in their individual tasks.

We reached the front door. Swayne opened it, looked left and then right.

He slipped out into the corridor. I followed.

DCI Reid was standing to the right of the door, facing the window with the phone to her ear. She glanced briefly at our white forms, but made no eye contact. I kept my mobile hidden loosely in my hand.

We walked as normally as possible. I wanted to speed up, but didn't. I stayed in step with Swayne, who was almost sauntering.

We reached the fire escape.

Swayne opened the door.

A uniformed cop was sitting on the stairs opposite us.

'What are you doing here?' he asked me.

Again I completely froze up and lost the power of speech.

'Have you got a key for the lift?' Swayne asked quickly, his tone more subservient than before. 'We've only got the one for the whole team.'

The cop sighed and tutted, but he got up and led us back out into the corridor.

We walked down a short stretch until we came to the lift. He took the card out of his breast pocket and swiped the side of a keypad.

Swayne thanked him. The cop went away without a word.

We waited for the lift to come. I looked at the phone. DCI Reid was still connected.

'I blocked your number,' Swayne said.

The lift pinged and the doors opened. We headed down without saying a word, keeping our heads lowered because of the CCTV camera in the corner of the lift. Swayne hummed the theme from *Police Woman* under his breath, then he did his wet laugh.

We changed in the toilets and Swayne stuffed everything back in his rucksack.

Five minutes later we were back outside, walking away from the hotel.

'Now *that* was close.' Swayne grinned his crooked railtrack smile.

I didn't say anything. I speeded up to a near jog, needing to get as far away from the hotel as possible, half-expecting to hear a police siren coming our way.

Swayne was keeping up. He was revelling in the buzz, energised.

'Exhilarating.'

No, it *wasn't*. We'd almost got caught.

But I didn't regret going:

What I'd seen hadn't proved guilt, yet it had certainly cleared away some of my doubts.

I didn't say anything to Swayne. He didn't care, so it would have been a waste of breath.

We were on the Embankment now, walking up towards Waterloo Bridge. It was after four. Traffic was getting heavier.

'Turned you on, didn't it?' Swayne almost shouted.

'No,' I said. Then I thought of Adolf doing this. 'I bet that never happened with Bella.'

'Why would it?'

'You told me you took her to crime scenes.'

'I never said *that*.' Swayne smiled.

'But ...'

I thought back to what he'd *actually* said in the café. And, of course, he'd said no such thing. He hadn't even suggested it. He hadn't even said he'd *worked* with Adolf.

Swayne looked at me, smirking, eyes twinkling. He'd read my thoughts as clearly as if they were ticker-taping across my forehead. I wanted to punch him.

Then I remembered my phone. I hadn't ended the call. It was in my pocket, on mute. I took it out. DCI Reid was still holding.

I put her out of her misery and turned it off.

When I looked up Swayne had vanished.

18

'Daddy, you're on TV!' Amy said, almost jumping up from her seat.

We'd finished dinner and were watching the news, all of us bunched together on the sofa.

There was a short report on VJ's appearance at Westminster Magistrates'. It showed his arrival – in the prison van, the crowd of photographers jostling each other, camera flashes bouncing off the glass – and then cut away to a young male reporter, standing outside the court building, describing the little that had happened inside. The last details were spoken off-camera, his voice overlaid on a shot of the van driving off down Horseferry Road.

Ray rewound to the moment where the van started moving away down the road. The camera pulled back and he paused the TV, right at my split-second cameo.

I was standing on the pavement with three other people I'd never noticed, a gawker among gawkers. Except I was looking straight at the camera and through the screen, probably watching the photographers rushing to get a shot of the real vehicle that was ferrying VJ to Belmarsh.

Amy clapped and Ray smiled.

'Who was in the truck, Daddy?' Amy asked.

Ray answered before I could.

'Vernon James,' he said.

I was shocked to hear him say that name. Any parent would have been proud that their child was so attentive and focused. But not me, not about this. A chill went down my neck and back. It was, for a horrible moment, as if all the hatred I'd nurtured and stoked over the years had somehow jumped from me to my son, like a terrible virus.

After we'd put the kids to bed, we did the dishes. Karen washed and I dried and stacked.

I asked her about her day, but she knew from the way I was 'hmming' and 'yeahing' along to her rundown that I was only being polite and waiting to talk about mine, so she cut to the chase and popped the question.

'How'd it go?'

I told her everything in order – the court, Swayne, the CPS file I'd brought home, how I'd be getting fired after the trial and breaking into the crime scene . . .

'What were you thinking, Terry – doing that?' she said, after I'd finished telling her about our two close shaves.

'I wasn't thinking at all.'

'Why d'you do it?'

I wasn't going to tell her the truth.

'I wanted to be sure,' I said.

'Of what?'

'His guilt.'

'You're supposed to be the defence.'

'It was a stupid thing to do,' I said.

'You can say that again.'

She scrubbed away at a pot.

'Do you believe him, that man, that investigator? That you're going to get fired after this?' she asked.

'What he said makes sense. He couldn't have known what Janet told me – about getting promoted and all that.'

She carried on scrubbing. I saw her reflection in the glass, her downcast stare and knitted brow. It meant she was thinking things through.

'It doesn't seem like the kind of thing Janet'd do,' she said, after a moment.

'Exactly what I thought,' I sighed. 'But I've only known her four months. I knew VJ most of my life and look what happened there.'

Karen stopped what she was doing and turned to look at me.

'You know what you should do? When the verdict comes in, you should quit,' she said.

'Quit?'

'Resign. Hand your notice in. Don't give them basstids the satisfaction of firing you, all right? Take their sting away. Play it for references – and salvage a little dignity in the process.'

She was right. Jumping before I was pushed was my only option, leaving on my terms instead of theirs. But I was going to be out of the best opportunity I'd had to make a better life for my family, to get us out of this place.

'Then what?' I asked.

'Then you get another job,' she said, rinsing suds off a plate and handing it to me.

'Doing what? I can't go back to hustling for pennies when I was earning pounds.'

'You'll find something.'

'I can always dust off the clown suit.'

'Best job you ever had, that was,' she said. 'It's how you met us.'

Typical Karen. She wouldn't blink or bow before a crisis. She'd weather storms that would uproot and break others. To her every problem came bundled with a solution, and every setback was a chance to find another way up. And she always had an unerring faith in things working out, even if they took time to get there.

We finished the dishes and Karen put her arms around my shoulders. Dishwater dribbled down my nape, but I didn't mind. I drew her close and we embraced and kissed.

These days we didn't have sex as often as we used to. Spontaneity was a thing of the past. We either didn't have the time, or when we did, we didn't have the energy. And on the occasions we had a little of both to spare, something else got in the way – usually the kids.

I pulled away from her a little so I could look at her face and lose myself in her big brown eyes. I stroked her cheek with the backs of my fingers, feeling the smoothness of her skin, its warmth.

'I know what you want,' she smiled.

I moved in to kiss her again, but there was a knock at our front door.

I groaned. She frowned. I wasn't going to answer it. She was thinking about it.

'God or gas, I bet,' I mumbled. The only people who came to our door at night were either Jehovah's Witnesses or energy supply salesmen.

There was another knock.

Karen went to the door. I followed.

She looked through the spyhole. Stood back. Looked again. And then she clamped her hand over her mouth and started laughing.

'What is it?' I asked.

'Take a gander.'

I did. And I almost laughed too.

It was Arun, our next-door neighbour. Twenty-something going on fifty-something; more plonk in his bloodstream than plasma. He was standing at the threshold, shivering. Holding a quilt around his waist. It was all he had on.

He knocked on the door again with his free hand.

He knew we were in, so he wasn't going to go away until we answered.

I dropped the chain and opened up.

'Yeah,' I said quietly, but aggressively.

'I'm sorry if this is … random,' he began. 'I've … I got a … an appointment tomorrow with me probation officer and I ain't got no clothes. I 'ad an argument with me missus a few hours ago. I went ta bed, right, an' when I woke up she'd gone and took all me cloves.'

I wanted to slam the door in his face. But I couldn't be that heartless.

'Just a sec,' I said.

Karen had cleaned out our wardrobe and bagged up some old clothes we were going to take to the charity shop. The bag was by the door, waiting to go. I found some old jeans, a denim shirt and several stray socks.

I handed the clothes to Arun.

'Cheers, mate,' he said. 'You's a good geezer.'

'No, I'm not,' I said and closed the door.

Karen looked at me and smiled.

'Where were we?' she said.

We started kissing again, right there in the doorway, up against the wall. I slipped my hands under her sweatshirt. She giggled and caught my arms by the wrists and brought them down.

Then she led me towards the bedroom. We got inside and started undressing. She'd got my shirt off and I was fumbling with her bra hooks when there was another knock at the door. Louder, heavier than before. I thought of the kids waking up.

I stomped back to the door, pissed off, ready to give Arun an earful. But when I opened it, there was no one there. I looked left and right down the corridor. It was empty.

I was about to close the door when I saw something lying at my feet. A stiff-backed envelope, too big for the letterbox. It had my name on it, in large black felt-tipped capitals.

I took the envelope into the kitchen and opened it up.

It was from Andy Swayne. And it wasn't good.

He'd left me a small sheaf of colour photographs, taken in the lounge of Suite 18. But they weren't of the crime scene. They were of me *at* the crime scene.

In other words: he was letting me know he had me by the balls.

The two-faced, double-dealing wanker.

'What you got there?' Karen asked from the doorway.

I told her.

'The sooner you leave that place the better. It's nowt but trouble.'

19

'Just so you know, I'm dying. But not today,' Christine Devereaux said.

She was joking, but only just. She was falling apart at every nail, and it was a terrible thing to see. Life was deserting her.

She'd been waiting for us in a chair in the middle of her office. She used a thick walking stick to stand up to greet us – and to help her sit back down. She was the colour of milk in moonlight. Pale, faintly blue, and with a lot of darkness about her. I wasn't sure she'd be able to get through our meeting, let alone make it through the trial.

We pulled up chairs around her in a semicircle, Janet, me and Liam Redpath – the designated junior barrister, the second in command.

She started by giving us a rundown of her ailments. She'd been battling lupus for the last four years. It had been misdiagnosed twice. The doctors had told her it was fatigue, then the flu. They didn't call the illness 'the great imitator' for nothing.

There was no cure for it. Now it was attacking her from every front. She was on a cocktail of painkillers, heart medication and immunosuppressants. She tired easily, found it difficult to concentrate for long periods of time and was becoming forgetful.

'The other symptom is that I can't be exposed to sunlight for too long,' she said. 'So that's ruled out my tour of the ten places to see before you die.'

Her words made a vacuum in the office. That tense silence where someone's said something uncomfortable and no one knows how to respond, where to look, what to think. And no one wants to be the first to break the silence lest they make things worse. The indefinite pregnant pause.

We all heard life carrying on through the door and walls. Phones ringing, conversations along the corridor, the whirr of the computer fan coming from her desk, the broken drone of traffic several floors below on Fleet Street. Any quieter and we could have heard the hairs on our collective heads growing. Two barristers and a solicitor, professional mouthpieces with years of billable hours between them, and not one of them could think of the right words.

So I blundered right in.

'Not to be insensitive or anything, but ...'

'Will I croak before or during the trial?'

It wasn't what I was going to ask, but that didn't matter. The tension had left the room.

'Highly unlikely.' Christine smiled at me. 'The doctor's given me six months of mobility. He's reliable. He told three of my friends when they'd die and he's been right so far.'

She said the latter with a glint in her eye. Typical British humour: the bleaker the situation, the better the quips.

'Have you had a chance to read the files I sent you?' Janet asked her.

'Yes,' she said.

'And?'

'Horseshit,' Christine said.

'Which part?'

'Our side. Our story.' The fact that she was referring to the case in the possessive meant she was already immersed in it, taking ownership. VJ was now part of her, part of us. He was already our client, but his trial was *our* trial.

'That's a bit . . . negative.' Redpath leaned in, frowning.

'He's been charged with *murder*,' she said, lancing him with a look.

Liam Redpath was mousy-haired and mousy-eyed, of medium height and narrow build. We were the same age, but his face was as fresh and uncreased as newly spun cotton, as if he'd never known a moment of hardship or anguish.

Christine handed out a two-page timeline of VJ's story, and gave us a minute or two to study it before she started.

'As we're already familiar with what he's claiming, let's concentrate on the problem areas – of which there are many,' she said. 'James checked into the Blenheim-Strand at 5.30 p.m. His PA booked the room, Suite 18 on the twelfth floor.

'He worked on his speech in the lounge between 5.40 p.m. and 7.30 p.m. He says he never set foot in the bedroom at all. He claims he didn't even know what it looked like until he saw the crime-scene photographs. And that's the first problem. Where did he change his clothes? He doesn't say anything about that here.'

Janet and I made notes. Redpath looked around the office and lightly drummed his fingers on his pinstriped trousers.

'Next point, his drinking. Not one witness has described him as drunk or even tipsy. But according to his statement he had six vodkas. Neat. Doubles. Two in the suite. Two more at the awards dinner, before he made his speech. He was discreet about those. He tipped the waiter who was serving his table £50 to have the drinks waiting for him at the bar. He downed them on his way to the lavatory. Then he had two more at the Casbah club, before he ran into Evelyn Bates. He switched to water at the Circle bar on the eleventh floor, where he was with the woman he says he went up to his room with – the *other* blonde in the green dress. "Fabia." Six big drinks. That's about half a bottle, depending on the measure. That would have affected his powers of observation and recall.'

Christine looked at us one by one to make sure we were in agreement. Then she continued.

'Now, this . . . "Fabia". He claims he first saw her while he was making his speech. She was sat very close to the stage, directly in front of him. What are the two immediate problems with that?'

She was looking at me.

'The dinner was invite only. There's no Fabia listed on the hotel's table plan,' I said. The police had been quick to check out VJ's story. A guest list from the Ethical Person's award ceremony was included in the initial disclosure file Janet had been handed at Charing Cross nick.

'Where are we with CCTV?'

'Still waiting on that,' I said.

106

'Channel 4 filmed the speech. Contact them to get footage. With any luck Fabia will be on the tape. If we find her and she backs up his story, the prosecution's case will be much harder to prove.

'Terry, you're to look for her – or at least for concrete evidence that she was there with him. Who's your investigator?'

'Andy Swayne,' I said.

Christine winced and looked at Janet in surprise. Janet shrugged, as if to say it was out of her hands.

'What if she's a figment of our client's imagination?' Redpath asked.

'Our job is to believe him,' Christine said, shooting him a cutting look. 'We have to know, one way or another, if she – or someone matching her description – was at the dinner. If it turns out she wasn't, and she doesn't show up on CCTV or on any other recording, then we'll have to tell our client to stop wasting our time and tell us the truth.'

Fair enough, I thought.

I knew where to start – at my desk, with a few phone calls.

'Now to the difficult part – the initial statements Vernon made to the police,' Christine said.

She quickly summed up the contradictions and outright lies VJ had told DCI Reid.

'Any suggestions as to how we explain away what's tantamount to a confession? Liam?'

'It's a tough one,' Redpath said.

'Illuminating,' she sighed.

'How about putting it down to duress?' I said. 'When the police came to see him, he was tired, hungover, confused and in shock too, because he'd been assaulted. They tell him a woman was found dead in his hotel room and arrest him for murder. He doesn't have a clue what's happening. It could happen to anyone in those circumstances.'

It was my turn to get one of Christine's howitzer looks.

'Have you met Vernon James?' she asked me.

My stomach tightened. I didn't know how to answer.

'Not yet,' Janet interjected.

'When you do, you'll realise that he's not just "anyone", Terry. He's a multimillionaire. He runs a hedge fund that manages £6.8 billion's worth of investments. The jury won't accept that he's like them – that he's "anyone". They won't believe someone that rich gets confused, frightened, that he even knows the meaning of duress,' Christine said. 'The prosecution will make hay with the social disparity angle. It'll be his word against DCI Reid's. His Oxbridge vowels against her Essex ones. The elite versus the masses. She'll say he lied to her, which he did. And no one will believe a thing he says after that. Even if it's true.'

The three of us said nothing.

'What else is wrong with his story?' Christine asked.

Janet studied her notes. I looked at mine. Redpath glanced through a witness statement. The CPS had sent us more disclosure this morning: crime-scene photos, including the actual murder scene, on the lounge floor, an evidence manifest, and more witness statements. It still didn't come close to matching what Swayne had given me.

Christine held up a photo of the victim on the bed.

'Anyone notice anything *really* obvious?'

Silence. Everyone craned forward.

Blanks all round.

'The bed's barely ruffled,' she said. 'The prosecution will say he killed her next door, carried her into the room and *posed* her, in that way. In other words, they'll put a pathological slant to this, and any hope we have of a manslaughter defence is gone.'

More silence in the office. More sounds of phones ringing and conversations coming through the walls. I heard car horns and conversations on Fleet Street.

'Our options here are limited,' Christine said. 'Best-case scenario – Terry or the police find Fabia. If she confirms our client's story, there might not even be a trial. Worst-case scenario is we go to court.

'Now, we can mount one of two kinds of defence. Stupid or Ugly. If we go Stupid, we take on the prosecution's case witness by witness, expert by expert. We rebut their testimony with ours. The drawbacks to that are major, not least that we bore the jury.

'Alternatively, we go Ugly. We attack the victim. Dig up whatever dirt we can find, expose it, expose her. Tarnish credibility, destroy reputations. We do the same with the witnesses, the people who gathered the evidence, the arresting officers. It's very risky. If we're too brutal, we alienate the jury.'

Again, more paralysed silence.

'When are we getting DNA?' Janet asked me.

'Monday week. Maybe sooner,' I said. Swayne would get the report before we did.

'Then I say Stupid,' Janet said.

'I don't think we've got much choice,' Redpath said.

Christine nodded. They'd agreed.

'Could you all stop writing now please,' she said.

We did as asked.

'What I'm going to say is off the record and doesn't leave this room. We'll speak about this today, and then never again. Agreed?'

We nodded in unison.

'Liam – do you think our client is innocent or guilty?'

'Guilty.'

'Why?'

'The evidence against him is overwhelming.'

'Janet?' Christine asked.

'Have you ever defended anyone innocent?'

Christine laughed.

'What about you, Terry? What do you think?'

'I think he's innocent – till proven guilty,' I said.

'But do you think he did it?'

Yes, I think he could have done it, Christine. But I'm not sure if it's because I want it to be so. Or because I know he may have killed before. Or because I genuinely feel he did it. I'm almost convinced he killed Evelyn Bates. But I still have a doubt. In him, and in myself.

'We haven't had all the evidence yet,' I said. 'So I'm keeping an open mind – for now.'

'Lawyers don't sit on fences,' she said.

'I'm not a lawyer.'

'. . . yet,' she smiled, and then turned to the others. 'I'm going to be frank. The chances of us getting a not guilty verdict are slim to non-existent. And if forensics puts our hands around her throat, slim leaves town. But don't worry. I've been here before – defending a certified loser, and I've won most of them. Unfortunately, this time out, things are different. The prosecutor is Franco Carnavale – not only one of the best barristers in the country, but *the* best prosecutor in the land. I should know. I taught him.'

Was *that* why Kopf had insisted on her – because she had the inside track?

'Franco started his career here, in these chambers. I mentored him. The first thing I taught him was always to think like the opposition. He knows how I fight. And he knows me,' she said. And then she moved herself round so she was facing me. 'When you're faced with insurmountable odds, there are three things you can do: Fight, fold or cheat. Fighting losing battles isn't my style. Folding isn't my style either. And I *definitely* don't cheat. At least, not knowingly.'

She wasn't only looking straight at me, but straight into me.

'This is where you come in, Terry,' she said. 'We're going to need some silver bullets here, something that kills or at least fatally weakens the prosecution's case. And you're going to have to find them.'

'How?' I asked.

'You're to interview all the police witnesses, especially the barman

109

who says he served Vernon and Evelyn Bates before midnight, and the waiter who delivered the champagne to the room.'

'How's that going to help?' Janet asked.

'The police showed the witnesses this picture.' Christine held up a post-mortem photograph of the victim, cropped to show just her head. 'It's prejudicial. They need to see another picture of Evelyn Bates, alive and preferably smiling. Show that around and ask again.'

'OK,' I said.

'When you interview the witnesses, look for weaknesses – contradictions in their statements, anything I can use against them on the stand. If they're vague on details, plant doubts in their minds. For example, if they say they're not sure if the dress was green or blue, make them believe it could have been blue. Check things like their eyesight, alcohol and drug history. Research them. Know them. Get their medical and bank records if necessary. Identify the nervous types too, the ones who are likely to crack under pressure. And I want to know everything about the victim too. Get me dirt.

'One thing to bear in mind is that the witnesses are under no legal obligation to talk to you – especially if you identify yourself as a member of the defence team. Andy Swayne knows his way around that particular loophole. Work with him.'

So she was indirectly asking me to impersonate a cop – or at least a member of the CPS – to get her evidence.

I couldn't believe it.

I glanced at Janet and Redpath. No reaction. This was standard business for them.

'Are you up for it?' she asked me.

'Sure,' I said.

What else could I say? No point in protesting the ethics of what she was suggesting I did, because she'd suggested no such thing. I was assuming she had. Just like I'd assumed Swayne and Adolf had infiltrated live crime scenes. I had a lot to learn.

How many other KRP clerks had done this? And was it just restricted to my firm, or were they all at it? Is this how you got on in the law? Is this what Janet and Christine had done when they started out? I could almost see it. But *Redpath* . . . in his nice bespoke suit with the white silk hanky in the pocket?

'I'm sure I don't need to point out we never had this conversation,' she said.

In other words: I was on my own. If I got caught, the 'I was only following orders' defence wouldn't stand, because they'd deny everything and claim I'd acted off my own bat. Their word against mine.

I thought of quitting there and then.

But I couldn't. I had responsibilities, mouths to feed, lives to protect and nurture.

'What conversation?' I said.

'Excellent!' Christine beamed. 'I'll book a prison visit to see our client. Terry, you'll be coming with us to that.'

'Fine,' I nodded.

Shit, I thought.

The meeting broke up soon after. Christine stayed seated and we all shook her hand and then headed for the door.

Once we got outside, I turned my phone back on to call Swayne.

'Keep tomorrow free,' Janet said to me.

'Why?'

'We're seeing Vernon.'

My stomach knotted up. 'When was that arranged?' It usually took between a week to ten days to set up the first prison visit.

'There was a free slot,' Janet said.

Which meant strings had been pulled, markers called in.

'Oh ...'

'Is there a problem?' she asked me, searching my face.

'Not at all,' I said.

20

When you're strapped to the railway tracks with no means of escape and nothing left but the certainty that the end is near, what might your thoughts be?

Tomorrow I was coming face to face with VJ, the in-bound train.

And my fledgling legal career would be over.

Face it. It was always going to happen. Our meeting had been an inevitability from the moment I'd picked up Adolf's phone. Yet I hadn't expected it to come so quickly, so unexpectedly. I'd thought I'd have advance notice and a little time to plan for it, to prepare.

'Are you OK, Terry?'

That was Adolf, looking at me all concerned from across her desk.

'Yeah. Why?' I said.

'You look like you're having a bad time.'

'I'm all right.'

'No, you're *not*,' she sneered and grinned.

Someone behind her laughed.

I didn't react.

There were a few hours left on the clock, and fretting about tomorrow wasn't going to do me any good, so I carried on with my work.

I called Channel 4 about footage of VJ's Ethical Person award speech. I was put through to a woman in their legal department.

'We've already given the tapes to the police,' she said.

'You must have copies, though?'

'We do, but it's up to the CPS now,' she said. 'If they want to put the footage into evidence and use it in their case, they'll provide you with a copy. If they don't, there's no need for you to have the tapes because they won't be relevant.'

I'd gone to the wrong department. They were by the book and no exceptions. I should have asked the camera crew.

I moved on to the Hoffmann Trust, to get hold of contact details of the award dinner guests.

I hit a wall there too. They didn't give out members' addresses, the snotty receptionist told me, mentioning the Data Protection Act before hanging up.

Two minutes later I rang back and asked to speak to her boss. She took that personally and said she wasn't going to put me through because her boss was very busy and would tell me the same thing anyway. She was about to hang up again when I dropped VJ's name.

Silence.

Then she put me on hold. I got a helping of music.

Another woman's voice came on the line, posh and imperious, like God might address a microbe.

'Pamola Hoffmann. How can I help you?'

Founder, owner and CEO of the eponymous Trust. VJ had sat right next to her at the ceremony.

I told her what I was after. She gave me the Data Protection runaround. But I could tell from her tone there was more to it than that.

I needed her on side. Without her cooperation Operation Find Fabia would be a tough slog.

'Can I ask you a couple of questions about that night?' I said.

'I'm very busy,' she said.

'Won't take long. Did you happen to see a blonde or fair-haired woman sitting close to the stage when Vernon was giving his speech? She was wearing a green dress.'

Pause.

Then:

'No.'

'You didn't see anyone fitting that description?'

'Mr ... *Flynt*, is it?'

'Yes.'

'I appreciate you're just doing your job, and that you're not responsible for who your firm represents. And I also have an absolute respect for and belief in an individual's right to a fair trial, but Vernon James is someone I dearly wish I'd never met.'

'Why's that?'

'He's made an absolute mockery of our award, and he's dragged the Trust's reputation into the mire. The press have had an absolute field day with this. Their sniggers will follow us around for years.'

One of the first jobs I'd had when I first moved to London was telesales. Cold-calling. I'd been pretty good at it. The trick was to keep the potential customer – aka 'the mark' – on the phone.

There was a moment in every cold call when you had to show your hand, ask for what you wanted, go for the close. Except, before you got there you had to hook the mark, build rapport and get them interested. I was in a precarious spot here. I'd only succeeded in holding her attention, and that was waning fast.

'I'm sorry to hear that,' I said. 'I know you do a lot of good around the world, and it's very unfair about the media, but there are aspects of this case that haven't been made public. It's not as cut and dried as it appears. And—'

'Are you saying he's innocent?'

'I can't really talk about it, I'm afraid. But I know you support political prisoners. People who've been unfairly locked up.'

That was a wild guess. I knew nothing about the Hoffmann Trust's work.

Pause. Then it stretched to silence again. A longer one. I braced myself for a hang-up, or another dose of music.

But she didn't put me on hold. She didn't do anything.

I strained to hear through the silence.

Nothing. Not even background noise.

Then she sighed. A slow, pained whoosh; the sound of surrender. I'd got to her. I'd closed. Her fear of appearing a hypocrite outweighed her feelings towards VJ and what he'd done. And she didn't know which way the trial would go. She wouldn't want to risk being on the wrong side of the verdict; turning her back on VJ only for him to be acquitted. Think of all that glorious good publicity if they stood by their man – their *Ethical* Man.

'Look, Mr ... It's Terry, isn't it?'

'Yes.'

'Terry, I really can't give out our members' contact details. But ... I can ask them to get in touch with you, if they want,' she said.

'That'd be a great help,' I said. 'Thanks.'

21

If you're not a criminal, getting into Belmarsh Prison takes time and perseverance.

The cab dropped us off outside the visitors' centre, a separate building in the jail's grounds. The authorities had done their best to make it comfortable and hospitable, even disarming, but it was what it was – the gateway to the end of the line.

We queued to get in. Lawyers and cons' families and friends, some thirty or forty of us. It was slow-moving, just two people checking paperwork and IDs, and doing the biometrics – fingerprint scans and photographs that were entered into the database.

Once we'd been processed, we went to the waiting area. A shuttle bus would be coming to take us all to the prison. Bags and phones were put into lockers, and then everyone went to sit among their own kind, voluntarily separating into two distinct groups either side of the room.

Lawyers read through files or chatted to colleagues. Kids stared across at them, curiously. Babies wailed. Mothers, wives and girlfriends looked weary, put-upon and baleful.

Janet made smalltalk about her forthcoming holiday. I heard her and nodded along, but I wasn't listening to a thing she said.

I'd had a sleepless night, working myself up so much about the meeting I'd now attained an almost zen-like state of neurosis.

Karen had told me to call in sick. I'd nixed that. Too cowardly, too temporary. I wanted this over and done with. And, above all, I wanted to see him – here, in prison – and to read the look on his face when it all sank in, when he realised that what had gone around had come around. No one cheats karma.

After that, I was happy to walk away from it all. I'd follow the trial on TV and the internet.

The bus arrived and we all got on.

The drive was short. Smatterings of conversation died out as soon as the first of the prison wings loomed up in the windscreen. Low-lying, with thick brown walls and deep-sunken windows of impregnable glass, it resembled the hand of some monstrous mechanical grabber at rest. Even the babies stopped their mewling.

Moments later, the bus pulled up outside B Wing and we filed out and made for the entrance.

Another stuttering queue and more ID checks. On we went through layer after layer of security.

First, the metal detector. Coats, jackets and absolutely everything metallic – including any loose change in wallets – went into plastic trays that were sent dribbling up a conveyor belt through a scanner.

One by one we walked through the electronic gantry. One by one we were patted and wanded down by a man or woman in latex gloves. They were all smiles and courtesy and in absolutely no hurry to get to the next person.

A pair of sniffer dogs sampled our feet and legs, each one getting their turn. They were sweet-looking brown-and-white spaniels with floppy ears, wet noses and keen, darting eyes. Their handlers probably gave them a treat for every catch.

We picked up our belongings and moved on, chaperoned by two wardens. A heavy metal door rolled back into the wall. We heard it shut behind us with a big, dull, definitive boom after we'd walked through; our first taste of confinement. Now we couldn't get out until we were let out.

Next came the orifice scan. We each sat on a grey plastic chair for two minutes and got our cavities X-rayed. You felt nothing, just heard the hum of mechanised software searching for secreted drugs and mobiles.

After we'd left the room we were led deeper inside the prison.

The further we walked, the more the place lost its personable edge and bared its teeth. The floors went from carpet squares to hard light-brown lino, and the walls lost their matt grey tones for a glossy putrid pale yellow. It got hotter and smellier, disinfectant barely masking the stench of stale sweat and rotting vegetables. And then there was the noise.

The prison was loud. We'd heard a faint banging as soon as we walked into the foyer, as if construction work was going on somewhere deep within the building. The volume increased incrementally the closer we got to the cellblock. Now it was almost at its peak. A metallic cacophony of gates opening and closing, of feet hitting metal, pounding up and down stairs, pounding on floors. Then the voices, hundreds of them – shouting, screaming, hollering from all directions; every single one trying to make itself heard above the others.

Two more retractable gates later and we were in the visiting area. Again we separated into our different groups, this time deliberately. The civilians stayed downstairs, the legals went up to the next floor.

We were assigned a plain room with a bolted-down metal table and grimy yellow walls, dotted with no smoking signs and printed reminders not to pass anything to inmates.

I sat down next to Janet.

It was 2.10 p.m. Visiting hours started in five minutes.

The door was open, so I could see the cons walking past us to their lawyer meetings.

Then he came in.

Vernon James.

VJ.

You can brace yourself for impact all you want, imagine what the collision will be like, how far you'll get thrown and how much of you will be left after you land. But when it actually happens, it's like you never saw it coming.

My body went into lockdown, seized up and stopped its every function.

I'd told myself not to look him in the eye, but I did.

We locked for an instant.

And my throat dropped into my stomach.

His expression didn't change. Not a flicker or a frown of surprise. No reaction at all. Just a blank, as if he'd never known me.

Then he looked away, scanning the room, seemingly lost.

'Vernon.' Janet waved him over.

He approached, a semi-smile on his face. He was wearing green tracksuit bottoms, a white T-shirt and mismatched trainers.

I don't think I breathed.

'Hi.' He greeted Janet with a handshake. He didn't look at me.

She beckoned him to be seated.

He sat opposite her.

My heart was now pounding so hard it was making my whole body reverberate.

'This is Terry,' Janet said. 'He'll be liaising between me, the barristers and you.'

VJ turned to look at me.

'Hi.' He nodded.

'Hi,' I said back. Or at least I think I did. I'm not sure my voice made it out of my tight chest.

No recognition from him whatsoever.

None.

What . . . so . . . *EVER.*

He turned to Janet.

'What's going on with my bail?' he asked.

'We're appealing the decision and putting in another application next week, but I wouldn't get your hopes up. We're going to offer sureties. You'll have to pay maybe half a million, a million. Can you do that?'

'Of course,' he said, like someone had asked him if he could get his hands on a tenner.

'I'll warn you now, I can't promise anything.'

'Which means it's unlikely.'

116

'Which means we'll try,' she said, slowly and firmly.

He tutted and sighed and sat back, crossing his arms.

'I could surrender my passport, wear a tag,' he offered.

'You still have the resources to go to any non-extraditable country you want,' she said. So far she'd handled him the way she handled all her clients. No deference whatsoever. The firm hand, letting him know who was in charge.

He pursed his lips.

'I know it's hard for you.'

'Hard?' He snort-laughed.

Then he flicked me a glance, a flash of a stare. Still zero recall. But more than that – I didn't count here. To him, I was the help. A person of no interest, sway, or importance.

I was deeply confused. In all the years I'd imagined coming face to face with him again, I'd never expected him not to recognise me, not to know me.

He was a little more grizzled than in his pictures – there was frost in his stubble and glints of silver in his coal-black hair – but it was definitely him, my old friend, my ex-friend.

'How are you doing?' Janet asked him.

'I'm in prison, awaiting trial for something I didn't do,' VJ said, with a hint of sarcasm.

She didn't acknowledge it. 'I talked to Nikki, your PA. We're sorting out your clothes and money. How's your cell?'

'It's shared accommodation,' he said. 'Compact but *bijou*.'

'How many people are you in with?'

'Three. I don't know what they're in for. Haven't asked. I can't sleep with one eye open.'

'They treating you OK?'

'They're well informed. They know who I am, why I'm here.'

'But they're not threatening you or . . .'

'Not yet,' he said.

'Let me know if anything happens,' Janet said. 'If it's any consolation, you'll find that having money – being rich – will make your life easier in here than most.'

He nodded. He understood.

He was cornered and stressed and tired. But he wasn't scared. I could see he was holding it together. It wasn't a front. He'd already got the measure of the place, worked out how to survive. That was rare, especially for someone like him, softened to warmed-over butter by his prior lifestyle.

'What about my family?' he asked.

117

'Your daughters are fine. They haven't been told yet. I spoke to your wife. She's in America. She's back next week.'

'How much does she know?' he asked.

'Almost as much as I do,' Janet said.

'Does your firm handle divorces too?'

Janet ignored his attempted joke and pushed a copy of the CPS file over to him. 'Your barrister, Christine Devereaux, will be visiting you next week to start preparing for your trial. You have to read the file. It's the prosecution's case. Some of it. There'll be more to come.'

He opened the file and started leafing through it. I'd put it together for him this morning.

'Is she any good?' he asked.

'For this kind of trial, she's the best. She fights dirty before she fights clean. But so does Franco Carnavale, the prosecutor. You'll have to be absolutely primed for this,' Janet said.

He nodded.

'There are gaps in your story we'll need to plug,' she said.

'Gaps?'

'Things that need explaining.'

'Like what?'

'You brought a change of clothes with you to the hotel?'

'Sure, to wear to the event.'

'You say you never went into the bedroom. Where did you hang the clothes?'

'In the bathroom,' he said.

Janet frowned. 'Why didn't you use a closet?'

'The bathroom was closer,' he said. 'I had a lot on my mind. My speech wasn't right and I only had a couple of hours to fix it. When I got to the suite, I set up in the lounge and went straight to work.'

'Did you shower before you went down?'

'Of course.'

'Did you move your clothes?'

'From the bathroom? Sure, I must have. I can't remember doing it.'

'Where did you change?'

'In the living room.'

Janet frowned again. 'Why not the bedroom?'

'I probably put my clothes in the living room.'

She shook her head. 'Not "probably", not "maybe". You *left* your clothes there. That's what you have to say.'

'Will they ask me about that?'

'Your defence hinges on the fact that you say you can't remember anything between 1 a.m. and 6 a.m.'

'I was passed out on the couch.'

'Exactly,' she said. 'You were *unconscious* when the victim was murdered. But you have to *appear* to be able to recall and account for everything you did up to and including that moment.'

'To make my unconsciousness more credible?' he asked.

'That's right,' she said. 'The jury know you're going to say you didn't do it. But it's *how* you say it. The impression you make. They have to be able to follow your story. No gaps, no contradictions. Everything has to make sense.'

All the while I'd been keeping my head down – almost literally. I was bent over my notebook, my head turned away from him, writing down what he said; as well as trying to trace the person across the table back to the one I'd last seen on Stevenage High Street, the person I'd grown up with. I couldn't find him. He was long gone.

He may have looked just about the same, but that was it. He was a different person now. Cold, distant, haughty, assured. If anything, he was the same dead-eyed stranger who accused me of stealing his diary.

Again I considered what he was accused of, and wondered if he'd really killed Evelyn. It no longer seemed impossible. My doubt was shrinking.

I checked on the body language. He was talking and moving his hands backwards and forwards slightly, as if describing the shape of small waves. Janet was craning forward, getting in his face. That was what she called her 'silent partner' posture, something she'd picked up in police interrogation rooms. Two cops would sit in front of a suspect, one would ask questions, the other would say nothing, just lean forward slightly and observe.

It meant that she wasn't buying what he was saying.

VJ really had no idea how bad this was for him. His lawyer didn't believe him, his barrister didn't think she'd win the trial, and I wanted to see him suffer. He was the only person who thought he was getting out of this.

For the remaining half-hour they talked about the awards dinner, and how many drinks he'd actually had. He'd said two, but he thought it might have been more.

So Janet made him start again, from when he'd had his first drink. She took notes. I took notes. Very little progress was made.

Then a guard called time on the meeting. Janet told VJ Christine Devereaux would be in touch, and to contact her or me if he needed anything.

He had to wait for us to leave first.

He stood up when we did. He shook Janet's hand and looked at me very briefly, and still blindly. He gave me a curt nod and sat back down.

Then we left the room.

I let out a deep breath. I was suddenly knackered.

'What do you think?' Janet asked, as we headed down the corridor.

'I don't know,' I said, but not in answer to her question.

How was it that VJ hadn't remembered me, when I'd never forgotten him?

22

The next morning, I was about to add the finishing touch to my sandwiches when my mobile rang. *Tales of the Unexpected.*

'Hello, Janet.'

'Did I wake you?'

It was 6.15. I'd gone to bed early and slept better than I had all week.

'No,' I said. 'What's up?'

'Vernon's PA left me a message last night. She can't face the idea of going to the prison. So you're going to have to drop off his clothes.'

'Sure.' It only meant going to the visitors' centre. I wouldn't have to see him.

'It has to be now-ish.'

'What's the address again?'

'Clemons House . . . no Clemons *Mews*, Cheyne Walk.'

'*Cheyne Walk?*' I repeated.

It shouldn't have come as a surprise. He'd given his address out in court, and it was in the file, yet I'd totally missed it. He lived a mere fifteen minutes' walk from my flat, right over Battersea Bridge.

All this time we'd been as good as neighbours.

Again.

23

Cheyne Walk is a genteel exclusion zone, a gated community in all but name, where the British establishment live cheek by jowl. You can't simply buy a house there and move in. Your money has to be old, your pockets deep, and/or you have to know the right people.

The road is quiet and sombre, sheltered by trees and bushes on the right, which mute the view of Chelsea Embankment and the river beyond. The houses are mainly eighteenth- and nineteenth-century Georgian, set back from the road and enclosed by black wrought iron railings, many of them wreathed in ivy. Almost all are listed, and several have blue plaques honouring their most famous inhabitants.

VJ's home was about halfway down. A detached redbrick townhouse, four floors high, with bay windows and a converted attic space. The front garden was pale pebbles and controlled explosions of red barberry bush, crossed by a granite flagstone path to the front door.

I buzzed the intercom in the gatepost.

'Yes?' a woman's voice crackled through the speaker almost immediately.

'I'm from Kopf-Randall-Purdom,' I said.

'Come in.'

The gate unlocked with a click that sounded like a sharp '*Tut!*' and I followed the path to the door, which started opening moments before I reached it. A woman with short red hair, a blue skirt suit and white blouse stood there to greet me.

She extended her hand as soon as I was within range.

'Nikki Frater, Vernon's PA,' she said.

'Hello,' I said, shaking her hand. I didn't give my name.

She ushered me into the hallway, which was tiled in brown and white mosaic and ended at a broad staircase, midway into the house. I smelled fresh coffee and the rich warm tones of mahogany.

'This way, please,' she said before I could take in any more.

We went to a reception room on the right. It was high-ceilinged, cream-walled, varnished wooden floors decorated with a pair of red Kashan rugs. There was a bronze statue of Shiva on the marble mantelpiece, but no other decorations save a large gilt-framed antique mirror. The decor was tasteful, but thoroughly impersonal. There were no self-celebratory awards, mounted magazine covers, or personal portraits. That wasn't VJ's style at all. He'd never been flash.

'It's there,' she said, pointing to a black bin liner by the fireplace. Suitcases weren't accepted in prison.

Nikki Frater hadn't quite met my eyes. She had the same air of defensive embarrassment you see on well-to-do parents accompanying their law-breaking kids to court.

I picked up the bag and followed her back out of the room. I now had to get to Belmarsh in the rush hour, which was going to be grim.

'Terry?'

The voice had come from the stairs, behind me.

I knew who it was.

She wasn't supposed to be here. She was supposed to be in America.

I stopped. I didn't want to turn round. I wanted to keep on walking, out of the door, out of here, and well away.

But, of course, I couldn't. For all kinds of reasons. Professional ... and personal.

So turn round, I did.

And there she was, coming tentatively down the steps.

Mrs James. Mrs *Melissa* James – née Sylford.

'My God, it *is* you,' she said. 'I saw you from the window, but I ... I wasn't sure. I ... I ... What are you doing here?'

'I work for your husband's solicitor,' I said.

'Hello Melissa' would've been the thing to say, but that moment had passed.

I was calm. The shock of seeing her again hadn't hit home yet.

She was dressed down – albeit very expensively – in a black pullover, skinny blue jeans and leather trainers. Her once long black hair now stopped above her shoulders, in a swaying bob. She still had her high cheekbones.

'This *is* a surprise,' she said, drawing up to me.

'I thought you were out of the country,' I said.

'I got back this morning. The children ...'

She wasn't wearing any make-up, and was even more beautiful than I remembered. Flawless caramel skin, *those* hazel eyes, *that* broad, bee-stung mouth. Yet there was now a remoteness to her, something not just unattainable, but utterly out of reach, like a photograph of a long dead model or film star. The Melissa I'd known and fallen in love with at Cambridge, the one who drank Newkie Browns, smoked roll-ups and swore in a broad Leeds accent was long gone. She'd become a Society lady.

'It's been *such* a while,' she said, crossing her arms.

'Hmmm.' Almost two decades was more than 'a while'. I wondered if she'd counted the years as I had. Of course she hadn't. Better things to do. Like marry my nemesis and have his kids.

'How are you?' she asked.

'OK.' I shrugged, tightening my grip on the bag, which made a dry munching sound in my fist.

'You're looking so ... *well.*'

Was she as nervous and thrown as I was? If so, she was doing as good a job at hiding it as I hoped I was.

I'd last seen Melissa on August 16th, 1992. I remembered the date because they were playing Elvis songs all over Stevenage that day in honour of the fifteenth anniversary of the King's death. I'd barely been out of my bedroom in close to two months when she'd come round, unexpectedly.

She broke up with me that October, by letter:

Dear John ... well, Dear Terry. She was splitting up with me because she couldn't have a one-way relationship. She hoped I got better. She hoped I got myself together and sorted myself out. There was so much about me that was great and lovable, and I had so much to give and so much to live for. She'd miss me and she hoped that in time we could be friends. Love Mel.

I later locked the letter away in an old metal box my dad had used to keep the household tools in. The letter rested at the bottom, pressed down by all the other letters and postcards and notes and cards she'd given me, or sent me, or slipped in my pockets or under my door. Every single one of them, from the very first scribble, thanking me for the three espressos I'd bought her at Don Pasquale's café on Cambridge Market Square, right after we'd had our matriculation photo taken. I still had the letters. Locked up in the box, and hidden in my trunk. I'd thrown the key in the Thames so I couldn't read them like I used to. And I'd had the box shrinkwrapped in black plastic.

Melissa Sylford – now James – was my first love.

And yes – and no – I'd never got over her.

I took the break-up badly. I went out and got seriously tossered. I picked three different fights with three different groups of people and they all united and chased me down the road. I got away by climbing up a tree and staying there. The idiots wound up beating each other up instead.

I'd cut ties with everyone I knew at Cambridge after I got kicked out, so I didn't know Melissa had got together with VJ until I read they were married.

That was in *Business Age* magazine in 1999. They'd done a big feature in the colour supplement on potential movers and shakers of the twenty-first century. 'Faces of the New Millennium.' VJ was there under 'Finance'.

James is married to television producer Melissa Sylford. The two met when they were students at Cambridge University.

That had ruined the rest of my year, and some of the next.

I was shocked. Devastated, if you will. And hurt. And pissed off like you wouldn't believe.

'We're old friends,' Melissa said, past my shoulder, to Nikki, with a hint of reproach.

'Oh,' the PA said. She quietly slipped by us and went back into the reception room.

Now it was just us. I desperately wanted to get out of here, out of this. Out of her presence. Nineteen years later and it was all still so damn raw.

I looked at my watch.

123

'I really have to get going,' I said.

'Let me walk you out.'

I wanted to say no, it's OK, please don't. But we were five steps from the door, so what difference did it make?

Except she walked me to the gate.

'How've things been for you, Terry?'

'What do you mean?' It was a strange question. She hadn't even asked about her husband.

'Since we last saw each other?'

'Your path's too short,' I said.

She let out a one-note chuckle.

'So you're a lawyer now?'

'Not quite. Paralegal,' I lied. 'Halfway there.'

Would the truth have mattered?

We were now at the gate. She looked through the bars, across the road, at the bushes, as if trying to see the river through the gaps in the leaves.

'Do you live locally?'

'Not around here,' I said.

It was a weak attempt at a bitter joke – or a bitter attempt at a weak joke. Either way it missed its mark.

'Do you have a family?'

'Yeah. Two kids. A boy and a girl,' I said.

'We should get together when this is all sorted out.'

Get together, I thought. Why and what for? What could you *possibly* want with me? And what the hell did I have to say to you? You, who'd made a life with the man who'd ruined mine. How *could* you?

But I couldn't even bring myself to say something noncommittal. I just looked at the gate, willing it to open.

'Will Vern get bail?' she asked.

Vern . . .? She used to call him *BJ*. She never liked him when we were together. And the feeling was mutual. Or so it seemed then.

'You don't get bail on a murder charge,' I said.

'So he has to stay in prison?'

'Yeah,' I said, and looked at my watch again.

She pushed a red button in the wall and the gate clicked open.

'I'm glad it's you,' she said.

'*What?*'

That came out too sharply, too aggressively.

'I'm glad you're involved,' she said.

'Why?'

'You were good friends.'

124

Once, I felt like adding and emphasising. But, naturally, I said nothing.

I pulled the gate open and stepped out to the street and started walking. I didn't look back, but I could feel her watching me as I hurried away. Or I thought I could. Or maybe I wished it.

24

I handed the bag in at Belmarsh visitors' centre.

The receptionist tapped away at a keyboard and printed off a label, which she stuck to the side. The bag would be taken over to the inmate's wing, where its contents would be emptied, searched, scanned and dog-sniffed before being passed on to their intended recipient.

'Can you take a seat, please?' the receptionist said.

'Why?'

She nodded at her computer screen. 'There's a note on the system, says you have to wait.'

'What for?'

'Take a seat and you'll find out.'

I sat among the lawyers and listened to courtroom gossip and mumbled smalltalk about holidays.

A prison guard walked in, went to the receptionist's desk and was pointed in my direction. Short, stocky and strictly no neck.

'You James's brief?' he asked.

'I work for the firm representing him, yeah.'

'He wants to see you.'

'Me?'

'Yeah.'

'Me *specifically?*'

'You *are* his brief, right?'

'I don't have a visitor's order.'

He leaned in closer and lowered his voice. 'Don't worry 'bout that.'

VJ had already started spreading his money around.

Same room as yesterday.

I wasn't remotely nervous, or even apprehensive. It was just me and him now. Nothing to hide and no one to hide it from. Besides, seeing Melissa again had wrung me dry. I'd thought I was long over her. But I wasn't. Not even close. On the way here, she was all I thought about.

She was the reason I could neither look at the college photo – nor throw it away. She was on the row behind us, exactly – and appropriately –

between VJ and me, smiling demurely. Of all the new faces that morning, she'd stood out the most, in her leather jacket, jeans and monkey boots. Her Ramones look. Everyone else had come in their finest formal clothes. When she got up on the tier behind me, she put her hand on my shoulder briefly, for balance. That was how we first got talking. And that was why I was smiling in the photo.

VJ arrived, still dressed in green and white. But he'd shaved and looked rested. He had his file with him, tucked under his arm, ready to work.

'Hi,' he said as he sat down. Again, not a hint of recognition in his face. I guessed he hadn't spoken to his wife yet.

'Thanks for bringing my things.'

'No problem,' I said.

He opened his file, turned over a few pages until he came to what he wanted – the list of crime-scene evidence.

'I've remembered something about that night, something I didn't mention in any of my interviews,' he said.

I opened my notebook. 'Go on.'

'The watch I wore at the event. A Rolex. I've been through the evidence log twice. And it's not there. It's not listed.'

'Why didn't you mention it before?'

'I didn't remember until this morning,' he said.

'Were you wearing it when you left the hotel the next morning?'

'No.'

'Are you sure?'

'Positive.'

'When did you last have it?'

'You know the woman I met – Fabia?'

'Uh-huh.'

'I think she took it. In fact, I'm sure she did,' he said. 'When we were having that drink at the Circle bar, she noticed the watch and asked if she could see it. She told me her father was a watchsmith. So I gave it to her – *handed* it to her, I mean.'

'Why?' I asked.

'Why not? A beautiful woman asks to try on your watch, you wouldn't turn her down, would you?' he said, smiling.

'If it was a Rolex, I would,' I said. 'Which hand did she put it on?'

'Sorry?'

'Which hand did she put the watch on?'

He squinted, frowned, racked his brains.

'Left, I think.'

Whenever clients add to their statements, they're usually lying.

They've had their first taste of prison and started panicking. I'd just used a classic interrogation tactic on VJ, something I'd seen in every suspect interview video, something Quinlan had used on me – and him too.

They'd let a suspect talk for a while, get into a comfortable flow, and then they'd interrupt him, make him go back over seemingly trivial points – colour of shoes, what the weather was like that day, what was on TV. Then they'd let him carry on with his story, find his rhythm again, and then they'd ask him the same questions they'd asked before, only in a different order. If the suspect gave different answers, they had him.

'Carry on,' I said.

'The watch didn't fit her. It slid up and down her forearm. I joked about it. I told her she looked like a rapper. And that's the last time I remember seeing the watch.'

'So you're saying she kept it on the whole time you were with her?'

'I suppose so. She must have. I don't remember seeing it again.'

'Did she have a handbag with her?'

'Yes.'

'So you gave someone – a stranger – a piece of your property, and you forgot all about it?'

'Yes. My mind was on other things.'

'Like what?'

'Getting laid,' he said.

I thought of Melissa. How long had he been cheating on her? This didn't sound like it was the first time. Did she know?

And how *could* he?

'Consider the circumstances,' he said. 'I was going up to my room with this *really* hot chick. The last thing on my mind was what she had *on* – if you get my drift.'

'So you're basically saying that this woman – Fabia – had your watch on when she was in the room with you? Which means she would have had it on when she attacked you?'

'That figures, yeah.'

'And when she left the room she was still wearing it, or had slipped it in her bag?'

'Yeah,' he said. 'The only other explanation I have is that the maids or the police stole it.'

'Unlikely on both counts,' I said. 'The maids walked in on a trashed room and a dead body. The only thing they'd be thinking of was raising the alarm. As for the police, we're not talking loose cash or something that could be easily missed. Tell me about the watch itself.'

He cleared his throat.

'It's a 1951 Datejust Rolex. One of the earliest models in that range. Stainless steel, with a gold rim around the glass. Ivory face, jubilee bracelet. Serial number is 7353.'

I froze a second and stopped writing.

I knew the one he meant.

It was his dad's Rolex.

I carried on writing fast. If I stopped, my hand might start shaking. And I thought of what I'd say to him next, about how I'd look for it. I'd handle the official channels – the jewellers', watch shops, eBay – and get Swayne to ask around the fences.

'The watch was my grandad's, originally. He passed it on to my dad,' VJ said. 'You remember my dad, don't you ... *Terry*?'

Now I stopped writing. My head had been bowed over my notebook, as I was scribbling down the details.

I blinked a couple of times. Dry swallowed.

I finished what I was writing, put my pen down and looked up at him.

He was sitting back, arms crossed, wearing a sardonic smile – and black-framed specs.

That's why he hadn't recognised me yesterday.

'I didn't know you wore glasses,' I said.

'It's been contacts for the last twelve years,' he said. 'They won't let me have them in here. I only got these last night.'

'I see,' I said, close to a whisper.

He chuckled at my unintentional pun. Or maybe it was the shock on my face that amused him. Or maybe how my hand was trembling.

I suddenly couldn't think any more. My head was blank. I didn't know what to say, what to ask him, where to begin, where to go. I was lost and intimidated. It might as well have been me in his shoes, him in mine.

'I thought I recognised you yesterday, but I wasn't sure,' he said.

'Is that why you got me here?'

No reply. Instead he looked me over, inspected me, his eyes dashing back and forth over my face like a pair of fat wet flies. I couldn't tell what he was thinking, but I knew he was seeing my frozen panic.

'They don't know about you, do they – your firm?' he said.

'No.'

'I didn't think so.'

What did that mean? Was that a threat or an observation, or a bit of both? Then the guard who'd walked me in opened the door.

'Sorry, gents,' he said to VJ. 'Time's up.'

No.

We needed more time. *I* needed more time.

VJ closed his file and stuck out his hand.

'It's good to see you again,' he said.

I stood up like some summoned zombie and remotely shook his hand.

The guard cleared his throat.

'Best move it along now,' he said.

VJ leaned in closer.

'I didn't do this, Terry. I know what it looks like, but I didn't do it. You *know* I didn't do it.'

25

On the Tube, rattling and clunking back into town . . .

. . . thinking:

What was *that* about?

Not what I'd expected.

Not what I'd expected *at all*.

It's good to see you again.

He'd been . . . friendly. Not suspicious, not hostile, not even questioning.

Friendly.

As in: we were long-lost mates.

As in: he acted like he didn't know I hated him.

As in: all the stuff that had happened between us was trivial, a mere 'tiff', just water under a bridge – the diary, getting me kicked out of Cambridge, marrying my ex-girlfriend.

Maybe he saw things Karen's way. He thought I'd moved on with my life, as he had with his. Maybe he even thought I'd *forgiven* him.

He'd have to be naive and stupid to believe that.

Or . . .

They don't know about you, do they – your firm?

If VJ was really innocent, surely he wouldn't have wanted me on his defence team. How could he? I could jeopardise things. If not actively, then passively – by doing something close to nothing, the absolute bare minimum.

My best guess was that he *was* guilty, he'd done it – he'd killed Evelyn Bates – but he was going to use me to try and wriggle his way out of it. He was going to make me do things – unethical things, illegal things – to get him off the hook. Just like I'd done before.

If I refused, he'd tell Janet about my past.

He had me . . .

Or so he thought.

But he didn't know I was going to get fired anyway; that I had nothing to lose.

So, really, I had him, right where I wanted him.

At my mercy.

What was I going to do?

I didn't know. I didn't have to make a decision right now, but the options were clear. I could quite easily screw him over. Do unto him as he'd done unto me. What if I found that piece of evidence that could exonerate him ... and I lost it. Or what if I found Fabia ... but never found her.

But could I live with myself, if I did that?

Irrespective, today I'd learned my first real lesson in how to be a defence lawyer:

You don't have to believe in your client's innocence. You only have to *make believe* you do.

26

Back at my desk, I'd taken out my sandwiches and turned on the computer when Janet walked in, with Sid Kopf right behind her. Time busted a spring and everything stopped dead. Everyone looked up and gawped. Kopf had never graced us with his presence.

'Where've you been?' Janet asked me. 'I've been trying to reach you.'

'My phone was off, sorry,' I said.

Adolf was typing, pretending to mind her own business, but I could see her smirking away. Kopf stepped out from behind Janet.

'Where were you?' he asked.

'Client visit,' I said.

'You didn't have a VO.'

'Didn't need one.'

'Eh?'

'Our client's bought himself a friend,' I said.

'Why didn't you call in?'

'No time.'

He glowered at me.

Adolf kept typing.

'What did he want?'

I told him about the watch. I tried to include Janet in my explanation, but she was hanging back, behind her boss.

Kopf shook his blanched mane and let out a theatrical sigh.

'So, he gives a valuable family heirloom to some woman he's just picked up?'

'That's what he said.'

'Do you really believe someone that clever would do something that stupid?'

'Everyone can be stupid sometimes,' I said. 'He was drunk and horny.'

'I'm not the jury. And if I was, I still wouldn't believe it. The watch probably doesn't even exist.'

'It does exist,' I said.

'How do you know?'

'I've seen it.'

Then I realised what I'd just said.

'What I mean is . . . I've seen . . . I know the one he means. He was very specific.'

Adolf stifled a laugh.

Kopf looked at me like I was talking crap. Which, of course, I was.

'Terry,' he said, putting both his palms flat on my desk and leaning in, pivoting his weight. 'The only thing that interests us here is *proof*. All right? Maybe you can *prove* this watch exists, but can you *prove* he actually wore it that night?'

The office had fallen silent. Everyone was listening to me getting a dressing down from the Big Boss Man. Even the phones had stopped ringing. I could imagine Iain and Michaela exchanging gleeful grins across their desks, suppressing sniggers. Much like Adolf was. She'd gone red with the effort. She couldn't even pretend to type now. She didn't want to miss a beat of this. They probably thought I was about to get fired.

'Good point,' I said.

And someone laughed in the far corner.

'But here's the thing,' I continued. 'I may work for you, but *we* work for our *client*. And *our* client met me today and gave me instructions. And those instructions concerned finding his missing watch. If I find the watch and it leads to Fabia, that won't just help our defence, it'll *make* it.

'Ultimately, it's your call. If you don't want me to look for it, say the word. But then that same burden of proof falls back on us. If I can't *prove* that I made a serious enough attempt to find the watch, our client will be well within his rights to use the incompetence of his defence team as grounds for an appeal.

'If it comes down to that, and his appeal is upheld, we'll get investigated. I'll be legally compelled to say I didn't look for the watch because you told me not to. And I'll have four witnesses to back me up, because everyone here's heard what you've just said. That will look like you instructed me to ignore our client's instructions. And that could have serious consequences for both you and this firm.'

It's amazing just how big your balls grow when you've got nothing to lose.

Kopf pushed himself away from the desk and straightened up. He eyeballed me like he wanted to kill me *at least*. Then he quickly glanced around the office, and back at Janet, before returning to me – cold, furious, but cornered.

And then he left, quickly. Janet followed him out, eyes straight.

A long minute later we heard his office door slam three floors up.

'Bet you wished you hadn't picked up my phone,' Adolf said, smiling.

PART TWO

Can't Cheat Karma

27

On March 31st, exactly two weeks after VJ's arrest, we got the police lab report. A dozen pages of DNA and toxicology analysis, plus a one-page summary in bullet points.

It was devastating. All the prosecution would have to do to get a conviction was stand up and read the report out to the jury. From now on in, any defence we mounted would be irrelevant, strictly for show, an exercise in legal box-ticking at best. Nothing we could say or do would make any difference. The outcome was as good as preordained, the verdict beyond doubt.

VJ was officially fucked.

'Slim's left town. Sends his regards.'

That was Janet, breaking the uncomfortable silence that had settled in Christine's office as soon as we'd taken our now usual places around her.

Christine retorted with the thinnest of smiles and a grudging nod.

Touché.

She was leaning on her walking stick, hands folded over the top, pressing down on it hard like she wanted to gouge a hole in the carpet. There was a distant look in her eyes, and her face was a study in dourness.

Janet couldn't hide her dejection either. She'd known the case was a loser going in, but now it had turned into something far worse – an *absolute* loser.

'Let's assess the damage, shall we?' Christine said finally, resting her stick against the chair and opening the case file.

The report had come in first thing this morning. Swayne had called me at 5 a.m. to tell me he'd scored a copy, but there was no point in my getting a preview, because it was already on its way to us.

I knew that meant it could only be bad. The prosecution only show and tell early when they have a solid piece of evidence, something incontestable. It's gamesmanship disguised as cooperation; helping us prepare our defence while letting us know we've as good as lost anyway.

I'd read the report in Janet's office. At first I thought there'd been a major mix-up at the lab, that someone else's results had been swapped around or misallocated.

Then I read it again. And again. Confusion ceded to disbelief, and then to disgust.

Who *exactly* were we defending?

'The prosecution contends that Vernon strangled Evelyn Bates in the lounge. He then moved her body to the bedroom, where it was found,' Christine said.

She looked at the three of us individually, left to right, her eyes pausing a moment to take our measure, before moving on.

Then she came back to Janet. They stared at each other. And I picked up a little of what was going on. These two seasoned pros, for whom setbacks and defeats were par for the course and nothing to get worked up about, had never been blindsided quite like this. They weren't just in uncharted waters. The boat was leaking, the sharks were circling and neither of them had the slightest clue what to do.

'Now, the report . . .' Christine said.

We all looked at our stapled, photocopied pages.

'The first item is a black iPhone. It was in the pocket of the jacket Vernon wore that night. It belonged to the victim. The glass is smashed, but the phone still works.

'Vernon says Evelyn dropped the phone in the Casbah when she fell into him. He found the phone on the floor and put it in his pocket, intending to hand it in at reception. He failed to do that when he checked out. In fact, he forgot all about the phone.

'The prosecution will say Vernon took the phone off Evelyn in the suite and smashed it. Maybe she was going to call for help. They found fragments of glass from the phone in his jacket.'

She turned a page.

'The phone was found when the police searched Vernon's offices in Canary Wharf. It was in a bin liner containing the clothes he'd worn the night before – a blue two-piece suit and a white shirt. The trousers were alcohol-stained. The jacket was missing buttons and the shirt pocket was torn. There were also small bloody holes in the back of the shirt – probably from when he fell on the broken glass in the lounge. He'd stuck a Post-it note on the bag. "Nikki, please dispose". "Nikki" is his PA, Nikki Frater.'

'So, they'll say he was planning to destroy evidence?' Janet said.

'Of course. And they'll call Ms Frater as a witness. She's proved to be *most* cooperative with the police's inquiries so far. It was her who gave them the bag.'

'Come again?' Janet said.

'They missed it when they searched his offices. She'd already put it in with the general trash. She went and got it for them. And she also told them where Vernon kept his personal laptop – not just the one in his office, which they'd taken away.'

'What laptop? And how do you know this?' Janet asked.

'Didn't you get Franco's fax?'

She handed Janet a single sheet of paper.

'It's an addendum to the report,' she explained to me. 'It says that computer forensics are going through Vernon's laptop, as well as looking at the mobile phone and three SIM cards they found with it.'

No one said anything, but we were all thinking along the same lines. Why did he have a separate laptop, phone and SIM cards? Because he wanted to keep something separate from his professional life. And why did he keep them out of sight? Because whatever they were for was private, therefore secret.

What could it be?

Women, I guessed.

I remembered Nikki Frater from the time I'd gone to VJ's house. She hadn't been able to look me in the eye. Never a good sign. Maybe she knew what her boss was really like, thought what had happened to him was inevitable.

Christine returned to the report.

'Next. Fibre analysis. Evelyn Bates was wearing a dark-green, silk-look dress from H&M. Part of the 2010 Lanvin range. The dress was found on the floor at the side of the bed. It was torn in two places – the left strap, and the side split had been ripped upwards. The material is 85 per cent polyester, 15 per cent elastane.

'Forensics found matching fibres in three main areas of the suite, identified as A, B and C:

'A is the area nearest the steps leading up to the bedroom, where they believe Evelyn was murdered. That had the highest concentration of the victim's fibre, hair, tissue, bodily fluids – predominantly urine – and some faecal matter.'

'*Faecal matter?*' Redpath interrupted.

'Don't you know what happens to the body during strangulation, Liam? Everything goes. Would you like me to elaborate?' Christine asked.

He blushed. 'No, it's all right. Sorry.'

'Fibres were also found in Area B – the bedroom – and Area C – the couch,' Christine continued. 'Matching fibres were retrieved from Vernon's jacket and trousers. Hair from the victim's head was also found on Vernon's suit, as well as in the aforementioned areas of the lounge.'

She paused there, closed her eyes and pinched the bridge of her nose. She'd done that when we met VJ in Belmarsh earlier in the week. She said the medication she was on made her dizzy sometimes, especially when she was concentrating. Clamping her nose and holding her breath for ten seconds stopped the spin cycle. I found myself counting with her.

'Sorry,' she said, and found her place on the list. 'The shirt had red lipstick and a trace of petroleum jelly on the rim on the collar. Both came from Evelyn.'

'Petroleum jelly?' Redpath asked.

'Makes thin lips look plumper,' Christine said. 'You should try it. Though not when we're in court.'

I almost laughed. And when I saw Redpath self-consciously touch his mouth, I almost laughed again. He was the butt of Christine's barbs, whether he'd done or said anything to deserve them or not. I felt a little sorry for him, and threw in a twinge of empathy, because he was getting a variant of the Adolf treatment. Christine obviously didn't want him as a junior. I couldn't tell if it was political or personal, or if she simply thought he wasn't up to it. So far, I'd failed to see why Kopf had picked him. He hadn't made a single useful contribution in any of our case meetings.

'The victim's hands and feet were bagged by forensics ninety minutes after the discovery of the body,' Christine said. 'During autopsy, the fingernails were scraped, and the hands and feet swabbed. A trace of Vernon's saliva was found on Evelyn's right middle finger. The scrapings from three fingers of her left hand contained skin tissue and blood matching his DNA profile and blood group.'

Christine cleared her throat and turned another page.

'Toxicology. Blood tests show that the victim had an alcohol content of 0.11 per cent. That would have made her noticeably "merry". The test also revealed the presence of flunitrazepam. Anyone know what that's commonly known as?'

I did.

I'd been prescribed it during my first few days at the Lister, when I was going through alcohol withdrawal.

Medically: a sedative and muscle relaxant.

Criminally: mixed with alcohol it can cause incapacitation, blackouts and amnesia. Its effects last up to twelve hours, depending on the dose.

'Rohypnol,' Janet said.

Aka the date-rape drug.

Like I said, VJ was fucked.

But there was a little more to come, the finishing touch, the *coup de grâce*.

We'd almost reached the end of the report. Christine glowered at the pages in her hands, her fingers tensing and then trembling. She looked up again, briefly, at Janet. More telepathy. More lost in the wilderness without a compass looks. Then she continued.

'The contents of the wastepaper basket in the lounge were removed and analysed. There were several torn-up drafts of the speech Vernon gave at the award ceremony. And, on top of those, was a black thong. The thong had a substantial quantity of semen on it. Tests show the semen is Vernon's.'

Redpath shifted in his chair. Janet didn't move. Christine pinched her nose and held her breath. Ten, nine, eight . . .

She continued:

'The prosecution will contend that he drugged Evelyn with Rohypnol. He took her up to his suite. For some reason the drug didn't kick in as quickly as he'd expected. He tried it on with her, but she resisted. They fought. The room got smashed up. He overpowered her on the floor and strangled her. He then carried her to the bedroom, undressed her, and arranged or posed the body in a tableau. Once he had her looking the way he liked, he masturbated into her underwear. He then left the room and dumped the thong in the bin.'

She rested the report on her lap. Silence filled the room like air to a vacuum; the silence of not knowing what to say next, of words evaporating before they're half-formed.

'Our client has lied to us,' Christine said. 'When I met him this week, I asked him if there was anything else he'd remembered from that night. He said no.'

Redpath and I had been at the meeting in Belmarsh. We'd gone through VJ's statement with him. He'd been absolutely consistent in the answers he gave Christine – and convincing with it. He made me doubt his guilt a little more, and I thought he might have won Christine over too. But after he'd gone back to his cell, she told me she wasn't sure if he was telling the truth, or a brilliant salesman.

Christine caught my eye and smiled like she'd just read my mind.

'Janet, if you'll indulge me, I'm going to break things down in layman's speak, for Terry's benefit. He needs to be able to follow the process.'

Janet nodded her consent.

'In any trial, there are two separate juries. The twelve members of the public, and then the judge. The prosecution has to satisfy both to get a verdict. The jury has to be convinced by the evidence, and the judge has to be sure that the crime is being prosecuted according to the rule of law.

'Let's focus on the judge. What is a crime, in legal terms? It's a compound of two separate elements, like a chemical compound.

'The elements of a crime are called *mens rea* and *actus reus*. Latin for "guilty mind" and "guilty act". Thought and deed. It's not a crime to have a guilty mind alone. You can't be prosecuted for *thinking* you want to kill someone. And a guilty act can't exist without a guilty mind behind it.

'For example. A man is on trial for killing his cheating wife. The prosecution will say that he intended to kill her because of her infidelity. That's *mens rea*. The guilty thought. Then he acted on those thoughts and killed her. *Actus reus*. Thought plus deed equals crime. OK?'

I nodded. I remembered studying this at Cambridge.

'Had this lab report been limited to hair and fibre, and the tissue under the nails, the prosecution would have had a big problem proving *mens rea* – that Vernon *intended* to kill Evelyn when he invited her up to his room. As far as we know, he'd never met her before that night. She wasn't even a guest at the event he was attending. Why would he kill someone he didn't know? No motive. No premeditation. His intentions towards her were sexual, not murderous. If his mind was guilty, how was it so?

'Yet he's being tried for murder, not manslaughter. The prosecution are saying he *intended* to kill her when he invited her up to his room. Now, any judge would know that the legal case is weak for murder, but strong for manslaughter.

'My original intention – before the report came in – was to tailor my defence, not at the jury, but at the judge. In other words, use legal argument and play the trial for a reduced sentence. If found guilty, our client would get a life tariff, sure, but with a ten-year maximum. In other words, he would be found guilty of murder, but serve time for manslaughter. Unfortunately, that's no longer possible.'

Christine sighed and shook her head. Then she addressed all of us.

'Who jerks off over dead bodies?' she asked.

'A seriously sick bastard,' I said.

'Exactly. A seriously sick bastard. Someone who gets sexual gratification out of killing another person. Famous examples: John Wayne Gacy, Jeffrey Dahmer, Dennis Nilsen, the Son of Sam – all notorious serial killers.

'Vernon James isn't a serial killer – that we know of – but he's like them. Depraved, twisted. A "seriously sick bastard". He killed Evelyn for kicks, to get a hard-on. And that's all the motive and intention the prosecution need. That's their guilty mind. It doesn't have to make any sense, legal or otherwise, *because it doesn't make sense*. He's a sick bastard. That explains everything – without explaining anything. Why did Dennis Nilsen kill and dismember fifteen men? Because he was a seriously sick bastard. Case closed.'

'So what's the damage?' Janet asked.

'It'll be argued that Vernon James poses a risk to both women and society as a whole. A crime of this nature, with the drug and fetish element – the posed body, the post-mortem masturbation – suggests an escalating pattern. If he isn't locked up for a long time, he'll do it again. And again. So he's looking at twenty-five to thirty years minimum.'

'Is there any way around this?' Janet asked.

'He can spare himself a trial and plead, but he won't get a reduced sentence.'

'What about claiming diminished responsibility?' Redpath asked.

'That won't hold,' Christine said. 'The mad-not-bad angle only works if the accused is deemed mentally incapable of understanding court proceedings. Nilsen tried it, and failed. Ian Huntley tried it, and failed. They're both in prison, not an asylum. A few hours before he killed Evelyn, Vernon was up on a podium delivering a clear, articulate, well-constructed speech.'

'When are you seeing him next?' Janet asked.

'Monday morning.'

'I'd like to be there.'

'I've already booked us all in,' Christine said.

Twenty-five to thirty years. VJ would be in his sixties when he got out. And prison added an extra decade to a body. He'd be a very *very* old man. The life he'd known and worked for and built would be long gone. His kids would be adults, Melissa would've divorced him and his business would have been taken over. Even if he deserved it, it was a horrible fate.

'Where are we on the research?' Christine asked me.

I filled her in. So far so slow and getting nowhere fast. Swayne and I had managed to interview three of the thirteen witnesses the police had so far. All of them had confirmed their original statements and hadn't stumbled. Two were at the hen party with Evelyn, and had told us she'd been drinking, but not excessively. The other person we'd spoken to had been in the Casbah nightclub. He said he'd been pissed that night, but he clearly remembered seeing VJ and Evelyn talking together. We were still working on setting up meetings with the rest of the witnesses.

We'd also made no headway finding the watch.

'What about CCTV?' Christine asked.

'Still waiting on that,' I said.

'Footage from the speech?'

'Channel 4 turned their tapes over to the police.'

'The CPS will only share those with us if they intend to use them at trial. Which I can't see them needing to, given what they already have,' she said.

141

'Fabia could be on that tape,' I said.

'You mean that woman you haven't been able to find any trace of in the last fortnight?'

Yes, the same. I'd drawn a complete blank there so far. Swayne had spoken to some of the waiters who served at the awards dinner. None remembered seeing someone matching her description. And none of the Hoffmann Trust guests had called me.

'Do you want me to carry on looking for her?'

'Are you also a brain surgeon, Terry?' Janet asked.

'No.'

'That's a pity – because the only place you'll find Fabia is in our client's head.'

28

The next day I went on the witness interview round with Andy Swayne.

It was my third time passing myself off as a cop, and I wasn't happy about it – not one bit. It didn't make any kind of sense, risking every-thing for someone who didn't deserve it, who was going down anyway.

So why was I doing it?

Simple. I couldn't afford not to. I was pretty sure what Swayne would tell Janet if I refused to go the distance to get information. And I still wanted a career in the law. Christine was relying on me to bring her 'silver bullets'. If I did this job well and helped her build an impressive enough defence case, I could come out of it looking good enough to a prospective employer.

Besides, I was starting to get the hang of the fakery.

Compared to your average conman, we had it easy. We weren't there for money, only information; so lying, not stealing. We'd already got the hard part out of the way – gaining trust and access – because our marks hadn't just invited us in, they'd picked the time and place. Sometimes they even made coffee. And there was no doubt in their minds we were the real deal, as we had copies of their sworn and signed statements. All we had to do was turn up, look the part – weary of face and suit (not a stretch for either of us), cantankerous, but holding it in – and talk like satnavs reading out an Ikea assembly manual, and that was that. Job done. So far, no one had asked us for ID or even to repeat our names. They were too distressed and overwhelmed by what had happened – and so very keen to help us any way they could.

*

I'd arranged to meet Swayne at a Caffè Nero on Regent Street at nine on the dot. I got there early, but he'd beaten me to it. He was sitting at the back, chatting up one of the baristas – in fluent Portuguese.

As I got my double espresso, she was heading back to the sinks with a tray full of dirty cups and a smile on her face. He was following her with a melancholic look. I guessed he hadn't pulled.

'*Garota de Ipanema*,' he said, as I sat down.

'Hello,' I replied.

'Brazilian,' he said, still watching her. 'They look their best when they're walking away.'

'Let's go through what we're doing today,' I said, putting the interview file on the table.

I was strictly business with Swayne, all about doing the job and getting out of his orbit as fast as possible. I didn't try to hide it either. No point. I hadn't mentioned the pictures he'd taken of me in Suite 18, because I knew he'd done it for insurance; as something to have over the firm. I almost didn't blame him, because I guessed Kopf had burned him in the past, but I also wondered if he hadn't deserved it, wittingly or unwittingly, because of his drink problem, and his way of doing things.

'So this isn't goodbye?' he said.

He knew about the lab report.

'I'd have done that by phone,' I said. 'It's business as usual.'

'Lawyers are born optimists.'

We went over today's witness list. We were meeting more of Evelyn Bates' friends, among them the woman whose hen party she'd attended.

It wasn't just about cross-checking information and identifying potential blindspots and contradictions in their statements. We were also looking at the people themselves, how they answered, how they came across, how well they handled pressure. The more presentable and empathetic the witness, the more likely they are to sway or even swing a knife-edge verdict.

And, of course, we were also digging for dirt on Evelyn. Anything that might have made her complicit in her own demise. Promiscuity, childhood traumas, substance abuse, drink issues, choking fetishes or related fantasies.

But so far we'd found exactly nothing.

Evelyn Bates had been well liked by her friends. They all said the same things about her. 'Nice', 'bubbly', 'a right laugh', and 'a good listener'.

Yet something struck me as odd. No one we'd talked to seemed to have known Evelyn very well, or got close enough to her to get past a good first impression. This could mean she'd been an open book, a what-you-see-is-what-you-get type. Or it was all a front, and she'd been hiding something.

I was leaning towards the latter.

If Evelyn had been a listener, and a 'good' one, it meant she didn't talk much. Which in turn meant she'd given nothing away, that she liked to get to know people before committing to them.

I knew this for a fact, because I'd never been the same after VJ's treacheries. I'd gone from open to closed, accepting to suspicious, outward to inward. And do you know what people said about me?

They said I was a good listener.

29

We took the train to Waterloo, then the Tube to Piccadilly, where we got off and walked to our first meeting.

It was warm and sunny; too bright and too hot for this time of year, which meant summer had come prematurely and the real one was going to be a washout. Just like last year. And the year before.

Regent Street had been done up for the Royal Wedding. Big vertical Union Jacks, five in a row, twelve feet apart, were suspended over the traffic and pavement bustle; hovering straight and still, in staggered tiers, their colours sharp and vibrant against the tawny Georgian buildings and clear blue sky. Tomorrow it would be a postcard, but today the scene was almost magical; as if the flags had come off every pole and awning in the city and gathered here, in orderly formation, waiting for the Oxford Circus lights to change so they could progress towards Portland Place.

Our first interview was with Clare Oxborrow at her workplace on Beak Street. She'd given the most detailed of all the hen party statements. No surprise there: she was an analyst for a management consultancy, which meant she made a living out of specifics.

She met us in the company boardroom. Tallish in flat leather pumps, with medium-length dark blonde hair and a clear complexion suggesting regular exercise, a healthy diet and zero vices, she was a steel blade sheathed in a designer suit. Everything about her seemed figured out in advance, geared towards making the right impression for the moment at hand. She was happy to help, but on a clock.

We refused her offer of coffee or water and got to work.

I may have been running the investigation, but it was The Andy

144

Swayne Show. He was both frontman and conductor, carrying the burden of our deception on his thin shoulders and setting the pace and tone of each interview. And he was loving every minute of it. For today's turn he'd opted for the kind of no-budget dark-blue suit you'd bury an unloved relative in, a mauve-and-black tie woven from the finest polyester and, to cap his throwback cop shtick, a 1970s vintage Timex watch he'd got off eBay. He'd also tailored his voice to match. Compassionate, with enough restrained gruffness about it to let witnesses know he was on a leash, playing nice and polite strictly for their benefit.

I was his opposite – the strait-laced, by the book, younger cop who'd been through PC camp and sensitivity training. We hadn't agreed on these roles beforehand, merely improvised off each other until we'd found our respective places. Not that they were too far removed from reality. Swayne dug for dirt, while I sat on the sidelines, making notes and avoiding eye contact.

I'm not sure anyone actually noticed these details. In fact, I think the whole act was more for Swayne's benefit than the outside world's. He'd been a broken man long before I met him, his confidence buried so deep within him it'd fossilised. Dressing up as someone else allowed him to escape himself. For a few moments he got to be a person who hadn't completely messed up their life – even if it was only a moderately successful public servant. And for that same short space of time, I actually admired him. He may have been a fraud, but he was a sincere one, fooling himself as much as he did others.

Swayne walked Clare through her statement.

There'd been fifteen of them at the hen party. They'd all rendezvoused in the hotel lobby and had a cocktail before they went to their rooms on the fourth floor. Everyone doubled up except for Hazel, the bride to be. She had her own room, paid for by the others.

They went to the spa at around 4.30 p.m. Sauna first, then a swim in the heated indoor pool. Two hours later they went out to the Paramount in Centre Point for dinner. The Paramount was a private members' club on the thirty-first floor, where the food competed with a God's-eye view of the West End.

Swayne stopped her there.

'Who was a member of the club?'

'Penny,' she said. 'Penny Halliwell.'

She was next on our list.

'Did you talk to Evelyn much?' Swayne asked.

'Not really. I think she mentioned she was auditioning for a reality TV show.'

She said the last contemptuously, and then blushed when she noticed

145

Swayne had caught her tone. She knew it betrayed her attitude to Evelyn, that she'd thought her shallow and frivolous. To her credit she didn't try to backtrack and undo the damage. She stayed silent, standing by what she'd said, no matter how it made her look.

Carnavale wouldn't want her on the stand – a career woman with an empathy bypass. That's all the jury would see. I put a cross by her name and wrote 'Cold, going on freezing.' So far I'd crossed everybody off. 'Forgetful.' 'Vague.' 'Unreliable – too pissed on the night.'

Swayne continued with her account.

Dinner had lasted two hours. Then they'd gone to Heaven, the famous gay club under Charing Cross arches. Penny had wangled them a table in the VIP area. They drank champagne, and then switched to their favourite tipples. Clare had taken it easy, because she had to be at the office the next day.

She remembered Evelyn leaving them at around 10.30 p.m. Couldn't fail to notice her, because she was the only one at the party in a green dress.

No one in the group noticed or commented on Evelyn's absence until around 2 a.m., when they were all debating whether to carry on drinking somewhere else, or go back to the hotel. They noticed she hadn't touched her drink. It was still on the table – a shot of tequila, complete with salt and lemon. They wondered if she hadn't met a man and slipped away. Not that they paid her much mind beyond that. They were drunk, happy, sentimental and distracted. The club was dark, the music loud, and the bride to be was the centre of attention. This was Hazel's time, not Evelyn's.

Swayne pushed Vernon James's mugshot across the table to her.

'Did you see or meet this man at any time that night?'

'No,' Clare said.

'You're sure of that?'

'Positive. I would've remembered.'

He asked her for her personal observations about Evelyn.

'I'd say she was probably a nice person.'

Jesus, I thought. Not another one. Luckily Swayne had had enough too.

'You implied she was stupid earlier,' he said.

'The two aren't mutually exclusive,' she said.

I wanted to laugh there – in complete agreement.

'We didn't have a lot in common,' she added. 'Maybe if . . .'

Then, all of a sudden, out of nowhere, a tear ran down Clare's face and the rest of whatever she was going to say was curtailed into a stifled sob. It seemed to take her by surprise, as much as it did us. She looked

146

from Swayne to me and back to Swayne, blinking and confused, like she'd woken up from a deep sleep to bright lights and strange faces.

She patted herself for a tissue, but didn't have one. Swayne took out a packet he carried around with him for moments like these – of which there'd been a couple. She took one and wiped her eyes and blew her nose.

'I'm sorry,' she said. 'I barely got to know her ...'

'It's OK,' Swayne said.

I changed my cross to an emphatic tick. If she cried when – or if – Carnavale decided to use her, he'd have his first star witness. She looked good in tears.

'I thought about Evelyn afterwards, thought about her a lot,' Clare said. 'And, this'll sound strange, but I realised I'd never met her before that night. I thought I had. Somewhere. But I hadn't. The only thing I really know about her is that Vernon James murdered her. How sad is that?'

Penny Halliwell had organised the hen party and shared a hotel room with Evelyn. She'd also been the first person to be notified about the murder.

We'd arranged to meet in the restaurant of the Architectural Association on Bedford Square, off Tottenham Court Road. She worked for a music publisher on the same block.

Even if the place hadn't been almost empty, recognition would've been instant. The detective who'd interviewed her had written 'Myra Hindley' in brackets next to her name in the notes accompanying her statement. One look at her and I understood what he meant.

It was probably the hair that did it. A peroxided bouffant, complete with a batwing fringe which exposed the middle of her forehead and covered her temples. Or maybe her interrogator had been struck by her passing resemblance to the infamous Hindley mugshot – that dead-eyed, faintly pouty expression where the Moors Murderess looked like she was about to blow her photographer a kiss before telling him where she'd buried his kids. Either way, I got it. She was definitely not Carnavale material.

We sat at a small corner table meant for two. Penny was tell-tale nervous. Darting eyes, involuntary blinking, hands fidgeting from her empty teacup to imaginary lint on her black jacket. Swayne did his best to put her at ease, layering on the avuncular charm; nothing-to-worry-'bout-luv, just a few questions and we'll be on our way; you're not under arrest. She responded to the last with a thin laugh that was meant to be ingratiating, but was too short and shrill to mask her stress.

We got started.

After they'd come out of the hotel spa, they went to their respective rooms.

Evelyn and Penny had changed for dinner. Then Evelyn had gone to the bar for a couple of 'liveners' – shots of silver tequila. She'd said she was a bit nervous about the evening ahead and how it would go, because she didn't know anyone that well.

Penny barely noticed Evelyn after they got to the restaurant. She was too busy making sure everything ran smoothly and on time; and then catering to Hazel's every need. Hazel was her best and closest friend. They went back fifteen years. Like me they were satellite town refugees, Norwich being their dark star.

They'd stayed in Heaven until closing time, at around 3 a.m. Some of the party had left for their hotel beds. She, Hazel and a couple of others had gone off to a private drinking den on Dean Street. They'd stayed out until just before five. Then they'd gone back to Hazel's room, where Penny had fallen asleep.

Penny checked out at 11.40 that morning. Before she left, she noticed Evelyn's things were still in the room, and she found a note on her bedside table:

@ Private party @ Suite 18. Evey x

That's when she realised Evelyn hadn't been back. But she was too hungover and knackered to think about more than getting home and going back to bed. She left the note where she'd found it.

All pretty much what she'd told the police, when they'd come round her flat later that day.

Swayne looked back over her statement. Or pretended to. He was just buying time, letting her stew a little. Penny rubbed her fingernails. They were painted black.

'What drugs did you do that night?'

The question might as well have been a slap for what it did to her. She sat up, eyes wide, mouth agape. Her hand started trembling.

To be honest, it threw me too. I was glad Penny was too shaken up to notice the shock on my face.

'You're not under oath,' Swayne said. 'And this is all off the record. But I do need to know.'

'I . . . I . . . did some coke.'

'What about Evelyn?'

'No,' Penny said.

'None at all?'

'No,' she said.

'Who else did coke?'

148

'I . . . I . . . I'd rather not say.'

'I don't need names,' Swayne said. 'A ratio or percentage'll do.'

'Why d'you need to know?'

'A member of your party disappeared right under your noses – forgive the pun. No one seems to have noticed. Or cared one way or another,' Swayne said. 'We've established that Evelyn left Heaven at around 10.30 p.m. The place closed at 3 a.m. She was gone over four hours. I just need to work out why and how that could happen. Now I have. Coke makes you feel like you're the centre of the universe, top of the world. Of course you wouldn't have noticed.'

Silence.

Swayne had his answer. Most of them had done coke.

He let her dangle for a while, while he went back to her statement. She was blinking like crazy now.

'Why did Evelyn leave the club?' he asked.

'I don't know.'

'Did someone say something to upset her?'

'No.'

'Are you sure?'

'Yeah. I would've heard about that.'

She glanced at me, quickly, then looked away. I knew she was holding something back. A fellow omitter. Takes one to know one, and all that.

Swayne opened his file now and turned over some stapled documents.

'What else can you tell us about Evelyn?' I asked her.

Out of the corner of my eye I saw Swayne stop what he was doing.

'What do you mean?'

'You shared a room with her for a bit. What did you talk about?'

'Hazel, the wedding . . .' And then she smiled, and I saw that some of her red lipstick had come off on the tip of her canine. 'When I say "the wedding", I mean *the* Wedding. As in the *Royal* Wedding. Kate 'n' Will's.'

And she pulled a dismissive, conspiratorial face, as if she were sure I found the subject matter crass too.

Then something clicked.

I remembered my first week at Cambridge; the daily get-to-know-you parties, trying to make conversation with the cooler than thou types. The universal icebreaker was, 'What did you do in your year off?' And you were meant to listen while the stranger you were hoping to find common ground with told you about their gap year, and then you told them all about yours. Except I hadn't had a gap year. I went straight from school. So I'd tried another tack. Music. But grunge was the big hip new thing

149

then, and I knew close to nothing about it. What I'd heard sounded like bad heavy metal – the only heavy metal there is. I said I was into Paul Weller. They looked at me like I'd just beamed in from Planet Sad.

And suddenly I felt for Evelyn. The deepest empathy. She'd spent the last few hours of her life with a bunch of people who didn't give a toss about her.

'None of you liked her much, did you?' I said.

I heard Swayne catch his breath.

Penny opened her mouth in surprise. That red-tipped canine again.

'It wasn't like that,' she said, hurriedly. 'I can't say I liked her. No. I mean ... OK. This ... this'll sound horrible but I ... I thought she might've been a bit of a slapper.'

'Why?' I asked.

'It's just an opinion I had.'

'*Why?*'

'Something she wrote on her Facebook page that day – "No VPL tonight".'

'What's VPL?' Swayne asked.

'Visible panty line,' she said.

'Oh,' he said, frowning.

I'd seen Evelyn's Facebook page. She'd posted two pictures of herself in her green dress – from the front, and from the back – both taken in the mirror with her iPhone. Under the backshot, she'd written 'No V-P-L 2nite!'

So she'd worn a thong instead, I thought. Big deal.

'You thought she was crude and crass, didn't you?' I said. 'Unsophisticated, non-too-bright Evey, with her cheap green dress. Right slapper, eh? With her reality TV ambitions. Maybe the kind of girl you might've been if you hadn't moved to London. Is that it, Penny?'

She was tearful.

I'd got her absolutely right.

But I'd messed up in the process. And badly.

Before we started the interviews, Swayne told me we weren't to draw attention to ourselves. We didn't want to be remembered. Carnavale was bound to call some of the people we were talking to as trial witnesses. They'd probably recognise me in court, but they wouldn't necessarily be able to place me if I kept a low profile now – not in the heat of the moment, being cross-examined in a murder trial. I'd just gone and guaranteed that Penny Halliwell wouldn't forget me in a hurry. And that could cause big problems further down the line.

'Look, can we please forget what I said?' she croaked. 'I was out of line. I'm sorry. I didn't know her well enough either way. I'd only met her once or twice before that night.'

'Once or twice?' Swayne jumped in, before I could say anything.

'Yeah,' she said, almost relieved to be talking to him again. 'I can't exactly remember. Hazel introduced us, I think.'

'She was Hazel's friend?'

'Yes.'

'Right.'

We were seeing Hazel Ellis later.

Penny looked around the room again, quickly, then down at the table. Swayne closed the file. We were done here.

'I'm really sorry about what happened,' she said, eyes going from me to Swayne. 'I feel bad about it. Really bad. We all do.'

'It's not your fault,' Swayne said, reaching into his pocket for the tissues.

'I can't help but feel . . . responsible. In some way.'

'Don't,' Swayne said. 'Evelyn died because she was killed by a sick and twisted man. No other reason. It's not fate, God, or karma. And it's certainly not you or anything you did, or could've done differently. It's just what it is, and what it's always been. Bad people doing bad things. That's it. That's all.'

Fifteen minutes later Swayne and I were on Tottenham Court Road, heading for the Tube.

Swayne was furious.

'What was that about?'

'She was holding out on us.'

'Bollocks! That was personal with you.'

'It got results.'

'It got us *nothing*, Terry!' he snapped and abruptly stopped walking. We were almost at the Tube entrance. 'If you think you can do this better than me, be my guest.'

I looked at him like he was bluffing.

'You bet your life,' he said.

'I'm sorry,' I said.

'You know what makes a good lawyer? Solicitor, barrister – whatever? They never get personally involved. And they fake every emotion. So whatever crap you've had in your past, deal with it in your own time.'

I could have pointed out that he'd told me I was getting fired at the end of the trial anyway, so his advice was just hot air. But I didn't want to push him so he walked out on the case when we still had interviews to do. For now, I needed him more than he needed me. Who else was I going to find to get me to the places he had?

We took the Central Line to Shepherd's Bush. It was packed with a lunchtime crowd, all sweaty and uncomfortable.

'Tell me you don't feel just a *little* bit sorry for Evelyn,' I said.

'Welcome to London, Terry. No one gives a shit about anyone here. It's eat or be eaten. I heard this story once. A man got on the Circle Line to go to work one morning. Had a heart attack and died in his seat. He slumped against a window, eyes closed. His body went round and round all day until the Tube shut at midnight. Nobody noticed until the cleaner came in at end of play.'

I'd heard that story once too. Tom Cruise told it in *Collateral*. Except that was in LA. And it probably hadn't happened there any more than it had here.

Hazel Ellis lived in Croydon.

Poor her.

I'd lived there too, when I first moved to London; a ground-floor bedsit on Montague Terrace. One light socket, no heating, an ingrained smell of burned fish, and a brown stain on the ceiling. It was all I could afford. It was either that or go back to Stevenage. So I stuck it out and saved up for somewhere better. I worked two jobs – catalogue telesales by day, door-to-door gas company sales by night. Within nine months I'd done a midnight flit to Battersea. I still owed my old landlord £375.

The first thing we saw when we got out of the train station were ugly towers of 1960s vintage. The buildings sapped the edge out of the sunlight and left the low-lying area around it in semi-dusk, as if a designated raincloud were hovering over it, waiting for God to look away long enough for it to unload and wash it off the map.

The Ellises lived in a semi-terraced house off Reeves Corner. The street was quiet enough, but the retractable metal gates on all the windows said this was burglary central.

Swayne rang the intercom and announced us.

As we waited I checked out the surroundings. There was a shop on the other side of the road called the House of Reeves. I recognised the mostly white-painted Victorian building almost immediately. It was in the blown-up picture on the wall of our reception, the photograph Sid Kopf had won his award for. Superimposing memory on actuality, I realised Kopf must have been standing almost where we were now when he'd taken it.

The door opened behind us.

'Hazel Ellis?' Swayne asked.

Hazel Ellis – née Jensen – nodded. Short, skinny and with too much naturally frizzy blonde hair for her small head, she greeted us in a dark-grey sweatshirt and jeans.

She led us up a flight of stairs to her apartment, and showed us into the lounge.

Swayne and I sat on the couch, while she pulled up a dining-table chair and positioned herself so she was facing me.

Swayne did his introductory preamble.

'Is it OK if Richard sits in?' Hazel interrupted him as he was telling her none of this was on the record, more of a dotting and crossing exercise. Richard was her husband of two weeks.

It was against protocol. The police always interviewed adult witnesses alone.

'Sure,' Swayne said, before I could say no.

'*Rich!*' she called out. She had a chirpy, bird-like voice, but when raised it was a glass-shatterer. She'd be impossible to beat in a row.

The door opened and Richard Ellis walked in. Tall and broad, with glossy black hair that stopped a couple of inches off his shoulders, he had the kind of classic dark and handsome looks you see in American soaps and aftershave posters. He shook our hands and went and sat next to Hazel.

'Why are you investigating us?' Hazel asked, looking directly at me. She had the same informed wariness about her as a particularly perceptive cat. Penny had obviously told her I was the bad cop here.

'We're not,' Swayne said. 'We're just tightening up our case.'

'It's pretty solid already, though, yeah?' Richard said. Deep voice. Region-free accent. Apart from the *yeah*. That was street, but an affectation, a hint of prole he might have picked up from living in places like this and needing to blend in. Minor public school, I reckoned.

'We can't discuss that, I'm afraid. It's still an open investigation,' Swayne said.

'But you caught the guy?'

'Innocent until proven guilty in a court of law,' Swayne said. 'Let's crack on, shall we?'

Hazel told us she'd talked to Evelyn when they had drinks at the start. Inconsequential smalltalk, mostly; couldn't remember their final exchange at all. She didn't speak to her at dinner, nor at the club. Too wrapped up in being the centre of attention and having fun.

'So you didn't notice she'd gone missing after 10.30?' Swayne asked her.

'Personally, no,' Hazel said.

Richard was looking at us – studying us, more like. Taking in details, crunching and computing them. Whenever his eyes stayed on me too long I'd look up from my notes and catch his gaze ducking out.

'How well did you know her?' Swayne asked.

'Not that well. She was Penny's friend, I think.'

'Penny's?'

Swayne and I exchanged a look.

'Penny Halliwell,' Hazel prompted.

'We've talked to her,' I said.

Hazel gave me a slight smile. *I know.*

I noticed Richard fiddling with his wedding ring, twisting it back and forth on his finger. I'd done that too, the first month of marriage. My ring was a little too wide for my finger and used to itch. I never bothered getting it fixed.

So what was this all about? Evelyn had been invited to a hen party for someone she barely knew, by someone she barely knew. And no one could remember originally meeting her. She was like the gatecrasher you don't want to throw out at a party in case they've come with someone you might know and offend.

'Who organised the party?' I asked.

'Penny.'

'How? Invite? Phone? Email?'

'Facebook. That's how we all keep in touch.'

That explained it.

Evelyn was a Facebook 'friend' to Penny and Hazel. I wondered if they'd ever really met. What were the chances? What if Penny had put a message up about Hazel's hen party and Evelyn had simply invited herself?

Suddenly, the intro to 'Step On' by The Happy Mondays started playing. Just the keyboards, on a loop.

It was Richard's phone, ringing in his pocket.

'Sorry,' he said, pulling it out, glancing briefly at the screen and killing the call.

He shifted in his chair, repositioned himself slightly, leaned forward.

'It's OK,' I said. I warmed to him a bit. I'd loved The Mondays. Karen and I had bonded over them.

Swayne carried on asking questions. I was beat. Really wanted to get out of here and get home. We weren't going to get any dirt on Evelyn. The whole day had been a near waste of time. Then again, I could have said that about our entire investigation.

As they talked, I glanced through the file. Swayne had handed me a new bit of disclosure this morning – a list of calls Evelyn had made and received from her mobile. I hadn't had a chance to look at it. I did now.

The last call had been incoming. At 11.07 p.m. The network was Vodafone, but the caller was unidentified because it was a pay as you go number. She'd made two calls to the same number before that, neither lasting longer than a minute. The person hadn't picked up and she'd left a message.

But it wasn't the only time she'd called the number. The list was three pages long and the ingoing and outgoing calls were all listed in a single column, going back two weeks. Most of the calls were to the same Vodafone number.

Facebook.

If Evelyn had been a Facebook friend of Penny and Hazel's, as opposed to a real one, it meant they'd all had someone in common.

But it wasn't anyone at the hen party. It was someone connected to it.

So I played a hunch.

I discreetly slipped out my phone and tapped in the number on the list.

The sound was off, and I'd blocked my number.

I stared at the screen.

And 'Step On' started playing again.

'*Richard!*' snapped Hazel.

Again he took out the phone and looked at it to see who was calling.

I killed the call.

The song died in his hand.

'Who was it?' Hazel asked.

'Dunno,' he said. 'Number withheld.'

30

'When did you guess he was doing her?' Swayne asked me.

'Not a guess,' I said. And I broke it down for him, my rationale. The Facebook theory.

As he listened, the two stretched worms he had for lips scrunched up into a condescending half-pout which stayed in place until I'd finished. He was telling me he not only knew a whole bunch of things I didn't, but another whole bunch of things besides that too.

We were still in lovely Croydon. Some dump called the Laughing Camel, round the back of the Whitgift shopping centre.

His choice of venue surprised me. A pub, of all places. And not any old pub either, like a chain one, with its two-for-one vodka pitcher offers and pre-set menus of everything with chips. This was a professional drinker's pub.

It was full and getting fuller, the clientele almost exclusively middle-aged to old men. They were sitting or standing solo or in pairs, nursing shots and chasers.

Swayne was drinking ginger ale and eating Big D peanuts.

'Not bad, but slow,' he said. 'I knew for sure as soon as I saw Hazel. She's just an upgrade on Evelyn Bates. Look.'

He opened his file and passed me a photograph. Colour, glossy A4 photo paper.

Evelyn, alive.

I wouldn't have recognised her. Not because she looked all that different in life than she did in the police photographs or the ones in her green dress, but because I was used to seeing and imagining her another way – not as a person, but as a victim. VJ's victim.

Yet here she was smiling – smiling like she was enjoying herself, caught in the middle of a happy moment.

It was a holiday snap. Clear blue sky and a blurred palm tree in the background. She was wearing a plain white T-shirt, which offset the pinkish glow to her face, and her wavy blonde hair. She was looking straight into the camera, cupping her chin in the ball of her palm, eyes full of tenderness. A lover's gaze.

Swayne was right. She did take a little after Hazel, or vice versa. The fundamentals were similar. Hair, eyes, not unattractive, but no head-turner either.

'Find any pictures of her and Richard?'

'No,' he said. 'But he was one of her 217 Facebook friends. He calls himself "Poolboy". And yes, all the hen party crowd were her "friends" too.'

'You could've said something sooner,' I said.

'Why spoil the fun?'

'Fun?'

'Watching you blunder on to the truth,' he said. And he smirked. *Wanker.*

'Remember you told me I should know my place?' I said. 'Well, that cuts both ways. You work for us. Which means you work for *me*. So don't waste my time again, all right?'

He didn't reply. The smirk thinned to crooked threads.

'Anything else you've discovered?' I asked.

'Not yet.'

I didn't believe him, but I wasn't going to push it again. The day was over. I had a free-ish weekend to look forward to. And he'd had his warning.

He chomped more nuts and washed them down with ginger ale. I hadn't touched my water. The glass had come clouded with finger-prints.

'What are you doing in a pub anyway?' I said.

'What do you mean?'

'Aren't you ex-alkies supposed to avoid them?'

'Pubs were never the problem,' Swayne said.

Yeah, right, I thought.

'Why d'you reckon the police haven't interviewed Richard? He was the last person to talk to her,' I asked.

'Why bother? He didn't have anything to do with it. They've got the killer, they've got eyewitnesses, and most of all they've got DNA. Do you know what DNA stands for, in legal terms? Do Not Argue. Case closed.'

He finished his Big Ds and screwed up the pack.

'Tomorrow I'll set up meetings with Evelyn's proper friends and her family. They'll know about Richard. How long it'd been going on. Then Christine'll make him part of her case. Put him on the stand.'

I thought about the implications. This was going to cause a lot of unnecessary damage.

Swayne seemed to read my mind.

'Fetch and carry, Terry,' he said.

'But these are people's lives here. Innocent people. We'll be ruining a marriage and Evelyn's reputation.'

'So what? That marriage is doomed anyway and what good's your reputation when you're dead?'

'How did you get this way?' I said.

Suddenly loud music started playing in the pub. A chug-a-gug-a-lugga guitar riff.

Then the first and only woman I'd seen in the pub brushed past us and got up on a nearby table. Long russet-brown hair, tight white blouse, half undone over her cleavage, spray-on black bellbottoms, killer heels.

She went into the bog-standard stripper routine – air humping, arse shaking, tit grabbing, tongue lolling, crotch caressing.

I looked at Swayne. He was gawping, all beige vulpine grin and twinkling eyes.

I'd never been to a strip club before, let alone seen a live stripper. Not my thing. Couldn't see the point.

She tore off her blouse and I heard the rip of Velcro fasteners splitting apart. Shouts and growls and a catcall or two came from the crowd.

She had a tattoo on her left shoulder blade. We were close enough to read it. Five letters of the lowercase Greek alphabet in a single blue line across the upper blade.

She headbanged to the beat, then tossed her hair back and slid her fingers slowly down her abdomen, flat and ribbed from crunches. Her nails disappeared under the waistband of her bellbottoms. She turned, gyrating and grinding her hips, then bucked like she was riding a … yeah, a camel.

VELCRO!

Off came the trousers and away to the left they flew. Punters grabbed and flailed after them, reminding me of refugees and shipwrecked evacuees reaching for manna or a helicopter rope. But they were caught by a black bouncer type, who was also holding her blouse.

Swayne was gone, eyes on stalks, brain set to dumb by the stripper, now in her bra and thong. I wouldn't be getting anything more out of him.

I was well out of sorts, embarrassed going on uneasy at being here with these sad, horny, but above all lonely, old blokes. And Swayne, close to drooling all over his cheap disguise.

VELCRO!

The stripper lobbed her bra over her shoulder and there was something like a scrum to get it. Bouncer beat them to it. A voice shouted, 'You promised!' over the music. The stripper blew a kiss its way and jiggled her breasts and winked and jiggled her breasts some more.

Swayne leaned forward. I swore I heard him panting. I hoped to hell he wasn't wanking under the table. I pulled my chair away from him.

The song cross-faded into another number.

Then something hit me smack in the face. I jolted back. What was it? I searched the table, around me, didn't see anything. The stripper was on her table, stark naked but for her heels and tattoo, still doing her thing. Except she was also looking our way, a big smile under cold eyes.

I knew what had just happened.

She'd thrown her thong at me.

I felt myself blush.

Then I looked at Swayne.

He was watching the stripper, now pirouetting deftly on one foot and stretching her leg out and up in the air. The crowd were in ecstasy, whooping, shouting, groaning, corrr-yeahhhhing.

The song ended and the stripper slipped off the table and sashayed off. The bouncer chaperoned her through her audience, slapping or glaring away potential gropers and graspers.

Time to go.

'I'll call you Monday,' I said, gathering my things.

'Better places to be?'

'Yeah. Home.'

'You *sure?*'

I didn't like the way he said it, like he wouldn't swap lives with me if I paid him.

'Don't you want this?' He held up the stripper's thong, waving it back and forth like a pendulum.

'Call it a bonus,' I said.

31

Sunday afternoon and I was sat at the bedroom computer, staring at the screen, trying to make a decision between the lesser of two evils.

I'd written two versions of the investigation report. One was the truth, the other my take on it. Or Evelyn with and without the dirt. I liked the truth better, from a professional point of view – it was solid work; an investigation that had yielded a definite result, the kind of thing that made me look good. But the abridged version was the one I could live with.

If I went with the truth, Swayne and I would have to confirm the affair with Richard Ellis by interviewing some of her family, conning our way into their lives, walking in on all that grief and pain and torment, pretending to be people who cared, who wanted to make things right and fair and just. We'd weasel out Evelyn's secrets and intimacies, and then turn them on her – and her loved ones – in court. I wanted no part of that.

It would have been different if I thought VJ was innocent, or that we had even a halfway chance of getting an acquittal. But I didn't. Yes, he was entitled to a fair defence. But this was neither a defence, nor was it fair. It was pointless, gratuitous damage.

At that moment, Karen came in the room. She had my chiming phone in her hand.

Tales of the Unexpected.

'How are your inquiries going?' Janet asked.

Never mind the formalities, the pleasant smalltalk, the apologies for today being Sunday . . .

I gave her the summary, but stuck strictly to the facts.

'We had some new disclosure on Friday afternoon,' she said, when I was done. 'Evelyn's phone records. Have you got a copy?'

'No,' I lied. Again, the CPS had released the information fast.

'Makes for interesting reading,' she said. 'The list goes on for half a dozen pages, but says the same thing over and over.'

'What?'

'That she spent the last two weeks of her life calling and texting the same number. She made more than eighty calls to it, none longer than a minute. Which means she left messages, or kept getting voicemail and hanging up. And she was calling at unsociable hours too. Early morning was her favourite time – 3, 4 a.m.'

Janet let that hang, inviting me to offer an opinion. Even if my thoughts hadn't been scrambling every which way and my mouth wasn't as dry as salt on a hotplate, I wouldn't have said anything for fear of giving myself away.

'Evelyn Bates was a stalker. A restraining order just waiting to happen,' she said. 'It wasn't all one way. The person she was harassing did call her back. Once. At 11.08 p.m., on the night she died. They were the last person she ever spoke to on her phone. The police didn't look into it, because they've got their man. But I have looked into it.'

She paused there. I heard a conversation in the background.

'What've you found out?' I asked.

No answer. A tap was running. I heard her filling a receptacle, maybe a kettle.

'Sorry about that,' she said. 'The number she was calling was pay as you go. Vodafone. Next to impossible to trace if they're one-off or casual users, because they rarely register on the website. But they tend to if they're regular customers. So I gave it to Dean.'

'Dean?'

'Our computer guy. He has this system that matches mobile numbers to handsets. Took him under an hour to find the person in question.'

'Oh . . .' I said.

'The handset belongs to Richard Ellis,' she said.

I played the ignorant-savant card.

'Hazel Ellis's husband?'

'Yes.'

'We met him on Friday. He sat in on the interview.'

'I bet he did,' she chuckled. 'He's a worried man.'

So was I. I was just glad we weren't having this conversation face to face, because Janet would've picked up on my edginess.

'I'm guessing what happened is, he had a thing with Evelyn and broke it off as the wedding got closer. Evelyn didn't accept it and went berserk,' she continued.

'That figures,' I said. I realised I was coming across as clueless: I'd sat right there in front of the victim's lover, and Janet would think I hadn't picked up on anything. I had to salvage a little dignity here.

'Have you seen her Facebook page?' I asked.

'No,' she said.

'I was going to put this in the report – strictly as a supposition. No one we interviewed from the hen party knew Evelyn very well. They all thought she was someone else's friend,' I said. Then I told her how she'd used Facebook to invite herself to the hen party.

'Do you think she was going to tell the bride to be all about her husband to be?' Janet asked.

'Possibly. But she didn't do that. She walked out of the party at around 10.30.'

'Either lost her nerve or came to her senses.'

'Could be. Not sure we'll ever know.'

A longer silence at the other end of the phone.

'So what do you want me to do now?' I asked.

More silence. Then the rustle of paper. I'd never been inside her house, but I imagined she had her own office there, away from the road, overlooking the back garden, few distractions.

'Forget Evelyn,' she said.

'But—'

'I know Christine loves to bring this kind of thing into the defence, but Evelyn's behaviour is irrelevant. It doesn't prove our client didn't kill her. It's not even enough to raise a reasonable doubt,' she said. 'But I can still put what we've got in the bank, as potential leverage with Carnavale.'

'How so?'

'You know what a filibuster is?'

'Yeah. Talking until the clock runs out.'

'Right,' she said. 'We employ similar tactics in court. When you want to make a jury forget some damning testimony, you introduce a semi-relevant piece of evidence to cushion the impact. You spend a day or two on it, bring in your experts. Bore the jury to sleep.

'In this particular case, we could wheel on a rent-a-shrink to explain that Evelyn displayed obsessive behaviour – stalking an ex-lover – which means she was suffering from some kind of dissociative mental disorder. And, at a push, we can say she was possibly suicidal.'

'Asking for it, in other words?'

'To coin a phrase.'

Normally I would've been appalled, but at that moment I was relieved to be off the hook. My conscience was turning into a delayed luxury.

'You ready for tomorrow?' she asked.

The lot of us were seeing VJ in the morning. He didn't know about the forensics report yet. I wondered what the hell he was going to say, confronted with the evidence. Was he going to confess and change his plea?

'Yeah,' I said.

'Good. Send me and Christine your report,' Janet said. 'Add in a theory by way of a conclusion. Reference Evelyn's SIM card information, and say it all suggests she'd had an affair with Richard Ellis. Say you noticed the number – obviously – and called it up. In fact, do exactly that for the record. Speak to him, get him to confirm his name. That way we'll have this ready to submit, if necessary.'

I wanted to laugh at the irony. I really did.

'How's Andy Swayne working out?' she asked.

'Fine.'

'He's not drinking?'

'Not that I know.'

'Has he talked to you at all?'

'About . . .?'

'Himself. His past.'

'No. It's strictly professional between us,' I said. 'Why, what's his story?'

'Alcohol, a divorce, more alcohol, a daughter who doesn't talk to him, even more alcohol, prison . . .' she said.

'*Prison?*'

I knew she hadn't meant to say that. It had just slipped out. I remembered her mentioning a burglary in the meeting we'd had with Kopf, when we were choosing the defence team.

'Never mind,' she said. 'Enjoy the rest of your weekend.'

After I'd emailed the report I went to the lounge. Ray was out with his friend Billy, but Amy and Karen were in there, on opposite ends of the couch, reading.

I stood and watched them. My wife and our daughter held their heads over their books exactly the same way, leaning into them like they were listening to whispers, their eyes following the lines back and forth down the page with the same transfixed gaze.

My phone rang again and broke the spell. Karen and Amy looked up at me, accusingly, ordering me out of their zone.

'Hello.'

'Terry? It's Mel.'

I looked at Karen a moment, her finger saving her place in the book, her expression impatient to borderline irate.

I stepped out into the corridor.

'Melissa?' I asked, lowering my voice.

'You used to call me Mel, remember? Sorry, is this a bad time?'

'What can I do for you?'

'I'm in the neighbourhood. I was wondering if you were free to meet up.'

162

'Now?'

'I'm in a French place on Battersea High Street.'

There was only one. Chez Manny's, practically over the road.

'Yeah,' I said. 'I can be there.'

I stuck my head into the lounge.

'I've got to pop out for a second,' I said to Karen. 'Work thing. Won't be long.'

'Who's Melissa?' Amy asked.

I left before I lied.

It could have been the bright light, but Melissa was already starting to take on the appearance of a con's wife. Tired and harassed, shadows under her eyes and that frayed restlessness where too little sleep meets too many worries.

She was dressed, possibly deliberately, definitely appropriately, in black – jeans, polo shirt, shoes. She was sitting close to the back, a cup of coffee and her phone on the table.

'Does this count as work?' she asked.

'Depends what you want to talk about,' I said. I'd ordered a single espresso. I didn't intend to stay long.

'I saw Vern yesterday,' she said.

'How is he?'

'He thinks this'll all be sorted soon.'

Still in denial. Or still holding out hope. Or both.

'Have you talked to Janet?' I asked.

'Did that yesterday too,' she said. 'She doesn't share his optimism.'

Lawyers are like doctors. You get the bad news as soon as the results are in. And then they tell you how long you'll get.

'Do you think he did it?' she asked me.

'My job is to believe he didn't,' I said.

'You used to be so direct, Terry. Always spoke your mind.'

'Not a good quality in an aspiring lawyer,' I said.

'Tell me,' she said. 'Please.'

'Why?'

'We should be honest with each other.'

I knew what she was after now, why she'd called. She wanted a friend. She had plenty of those, sure, but none who bridged the gap between her life and her husband's present situation; someone to explain things, someone who cared.

There was a lot I could've said to that, aired some archived resentment and recrimination. But this wasn't the time or place. For all intents and purposes, I was on duty.

163

'It's above my paygrade,' I said. 'You should ask Janet.'

'Please. As a . . . a friend.'

Whose friend, I felt like asking. The question rolled to the tip of my tongue, poised for launch.

But no . . .

'I can't. I'm sorry.'

I could've told her about the lab report, but that would've been unethical, because we hadn't discussed it with VJ yet. I could've told her about the personal laptop and the separate phone and three SIM cards.

But no. I couldn't go there either.

She'd soon find out. Like tomorrow.

I could have told her it wasn't looking good.

But she knew that.

She looked at her cup of coffee. The sugar and little biscuit were still in the saucer, both wrapped. She was beautiful, even at this, her lowest ebb. I wished I wasn't thinking like this. She was vulnerable.

The café was lively with laughter. Early evening drinkers, all of them well-heeled but catalogue-styled. That was the thing that hurt most about London; everyone around you seemed to have a better life than yours, and by extension a better time.

'I knew he cheated on me,' she said, looking up. I noticed how long her lashes were. I don't think I had when we were together. Too busy being swept away to remark the small things.

'I never asked him, and we never talked about it. But I knew,' she said.

No surprise, obviously. Just bewilderment.

'How . . .' I started, then clammed up because I couldn't finish. I'd meant to ask, 'How could he cheat on *you*?'

'Female intuition,' she said, saving me from a potentially awkward moment. 'It wasn't anyone steady, like a mistress or something. That's not his style. He said he never understood the point of mistresses. Why swap one wife for another?'

I smiled, but I didn't find it funny or clever. He'd married my first love, and then gone and cheated on her . . . over and over. How much more could I hate him?

'And you were all right with it?'

'Realistic, not all right. He was away a lot. Always abroad. He likes women. And they like him.'

There was bitterness in her resignation. Why had she accepted it? Out of love, for the sake of the kids, because she was too used to the lifestyle? I wanted to know more, much more.

But no . . . that was yet another place I couldn't go.

I had to keep a professional distance, stay uninvolved.

Act.

Fake it.

'Vern used to say that everyone wants a piece of you when you're successful, and no one wants any of you when you fail.'

'Have people started staying away?'

'Some. Torrents always start as trickles.'

'Well, at least, when it's over, you'll know who your real friends are. And there's an upside too.'

'What?

'Fewer Christmas cards to write.'

She laughed. Our eyes met again, properly. Then she scanned my face, as if she were trying to read me, figure me out; or maybe compare her memories to the present, as I was doing.

'Do they know . . . at work?'

'Know what?'

'About you and me, you and Vern . . .'

'No,' I said. 'And I'd like to keep it that way.'

'We will,' she said.

We will . . . They'd talked about me yesterday. That was obvious. She was here to sound me out.

'How's your mum doing?' she asked.

'Fine. Why?'

'Just asking. I liked her.'

And she liked you, I thought. She liked you a *lot*. Said we made a lovely couple. Even saw us having a few cute kids. Mum was a lousy soothsayer.

'How's Stevenage?'

'Still there,' I said.

I hadn't been back in twelve years, but I wasn't going to tell her that. Because if I did, I'd have to explain why. Which would mean talking about the past. And I knew I'd get angry and spoil what we were having here.

So it was time to go. I made a show of looking at my watch. I hadn't touched my espresso any more than she had her coffee.

We walked out together. Her car was parked on the road. A four-door Merc, so clean its tyres looked like all they'd ever rolled on was spotless shag carpet.

'Thank you.'

'What for?'

'I wasn't in the neighbourhood.'

'I guessed that,' I said.

'I really wanted to see you,' she said.

165

'Why?'

'I've been thinking about you, Terry.'

Likewise, I thought. I hadn't stopped thinking about her from the moment I'd met her.

'Call me, if you need anything.'

Now why did I have to go and say *that*?

Because I *wanted* her to. That's why.

We stood there in the road, very close. She was swaying ever so slightly, her eyes locked on mine. And then it just happened. We walked into each other, both of us taking the first step. She slipped her arms around me and held me like she used to when we slowdanced around in her college room. I held her too, trying to keep it casual and platonic, but I couldn't help myself and pulled her in closer. It felt good, and unbelievably wrong in a million and one ways. I smelled her perfume and felt the valley of her spine. Yeah, you could say, I was just holding a friend, offering comfort. But it wasn't just that, was it? Melissa rested her head on my chest. I wondered if she had her eyes closed like she used to when she'd held me. That was exactly how it had started between us, in October 1991, on Garret Hostel Bridge in Cambridge. With a hug. Like this.

She kissed me on the cheek and got in her car. A few moments later she'd pulled out and driven away with a wave.

I stood there the whole time, exactly where I'd held her. I couldn't move.

32

At Belmarsh, Christine and Redpath sat in front of me at the bolted-down table, going through their notes, unfazed by the racket going on beyond the interview room. I couldn't take my eyes off the panic button on the wall behind them. It appeared to have been well used. I wondered what the response time was, the distance between alarm and salvation.

Redpath had laid out his yellow pad and poncey Montblanc pen. Two hundred quid's worth of sodding biro. Was it a gift or had he bought it to round off his spiv look? And what was he thinking, coming on a prison visit in a navy-blue pinstripe suit, dressed up in bars? Was he trying to send VJ some kind of subliminal message? Hard to tell, because the only time we ever spoke was when he remembered to say hello or goodbye.

Each time I saw her, Christine seemed to be inching a little closer to death. Today her skin had the hue of day-old boiled eggs, and her breathing was slow and arhythmic, with long pauses between the in and out, as if she were having to prompt herself every time.

I didn't know how she was still doing this, let alone managing to function the way she was. And why was she spending her precious time defending someone she knew to be guilty? Did she believe in the law that much, or merely love what she did more than whatever life she had left?

Janet hadn't made it. Only room for three here. I was her eyes and ears.

VJ came in and greeted us with a smile and a handshake. He was wearing the clothes I'd brought him – an unbranded blue sweatshirt and tracksuit bottoms, white Asics trainers with the laces removed, and his glasses.

He and Christine made smalltalk for a minute or two. How was he? Fine, keeping his head down, minding his own business, working on his case. How were things, generally? OK, again. Not that bad, once you got used to it. He'd had himself moved to a single cell recently, because prison rules stated that a non-smoker could not be made to share a cell with a smoker, as all his initial cohabitants had been. So now he was in comparative luxury. God bless the EU and the Court of Human Rights.

I could tell prison was getting to him, though. He'd lost weight, his haircut was growing out, and the lower half of his face was coated in a few days' grey-white stubble. He was letting himself go. First sign of depression, that, when you start neglecting your personal appearance. I'd been there, knew exactly what he was going through.

And all the while, the evidence against him just kept piling up. It was a lot like being slowly buried alive; accusation after accusation dumped on you, until that's all you can see, all that's around you. I'd been *there* too. Knew *exactly* what he was going through. It was how I'd felt when he accused me of stealing his diary.

'The glasses are a good look. They soften your face,' Christine said to him. 'Wear them in court.'

'Those kind of things work?'

'Juries aren't sophisticated, Vernon. They're blunt instruments,' she said. 'Glasses, on the right kind of face, project intelligence and physical weakness. You have the right kind of face.'

'Thanks,' he smiled. 'What about the wrong face?'

'That says you're a nonce.'

'Right.'

She opened her file and he opened his.

'We've had some new disclosure. But, prior to discussing that, I need

167

to ask you something I should've asked sooner,' she said. 'Do you have any enemies?'

'Enemies?'

'Business rivals, competitors, colleagues. People with something to gain with you being out of the way. Or maybe people you've crossed or upset in the past – ex-friends?'

It was a routine question, but it still made my heart skip a beat.

'Not that I know of,' he said. 'All my business deals have been legal, above the board. I've never cut corners. And I've always made a point of giving back – to charities and stuff. But I'm sure plenty of people hate me anyway.'

'Why?'

'People hate success. Especially in this country. Way it goes,' he shrugged. 'Which reminds me ...'

He sifted through his file, pulled out a couple of sheets of paper.

'Ahmad Sihl, my business lawyer, has put together a list of all the ongoing deals I had before my arrest. They were at various stages, some close to conclusion, others in mid-air,' he said, passing her the pages. 'He's got a team of investigators looking into my competition.'

'Are you saying you were *set up*?' Redpath asked, with a hint of amusement.

'There's no other explanation for all this. Don't tell me it never occurred to you?'

Redpath didn't answer. Of course it hadn't occurred to him. Or to me. Or to Janet, for that matter. It was one of the first questions she would've asked him. Yet no one had raised the subject, let alone considered it. Why? Because there was no conspiracy here, no frame, no set-up. He'd killed Evelyn Bates.

As for Christine, I don't think she believed it either. Otherwise, she would've been kicking up a stink right now, about another lawyer getting involved in her case, potentially undermining the defence she was putting together. But she hadn't reacted.

And what about Ahmad Sihl? What was he doing? Squeezing one huge paycheque out of his client while he still could? Being a friend – a *real* friend – and therefore in denial? Or did he believe VJ was innocent?

Redpath passed me VJ's pages and I caught his eye, saw the sardonic gleam in them.

I looked through the list. Over a dozen deals in date order, their status and rival bidders by company or organisation. Most had individual names alongside them. No one I'd heard of. Many were foreign. A couple of deals had been crossed out and marked 'Non-Applicable' – Stratford Quakers and the Chelmsford Co-Op.

'Has Ahmad come up with anything yet?' Christine asked.

'No,' VJ said. 'He has your contact details, though. He'll be in touch.'

Christine handed him a copy of the lab report.

I watched him read it. He scanned it fast, too fast, I thought. Either he'd learned to speed-read in the last twenty years, or he already knew the contents.

When he'd finished, she talked him through it.

She kept her tone neutral, and her eyes fixed on him, as she linked each piece of evidence to the prosecution's case. He listened to her, hands flat on the table, occasionally nodding, sometimes taking notes. Hair, fibre, tissue, blood, saliva, sperm.

'That's the Crown's case against you. So far,' she concluded.

'You mean there's more?'

'You tell me.'

'There's an innocent explanation for all of this.'

'Innocent?' Christine said. '*All* of it?'

'Yes,' he smiled.

'Even the Rohypnol?'

He lost the smile. Fast.

'*What?*' he said.

'You know what that is?'

'Of course I do.'

'It was present in Evelyn Bates's body. It's there in the autopsy. It was found in her blood, which means she ingested it mere hours before her death. The effects of Rohypnol last between eight and twelve hours, depending on the dose and the individual's metabolism. It's at its most potent early on. It starts wearing off as the body eliminates it, which it does fairly quickly. All trace of the drug disappears from the bloodstream within twenty-four hours, and the rest is eliminated through sweat and urine over the next one or two days.

'Looking at Evelyn's toxicity report, the Rohypnol-to-blood ratio is very high. This is in part because she was dead when the sample was taken. Blood coagulates post-mortem and becomes concentrated, as do the various elements and toxins within it – including any drugs. Irrespective of this, the Rohypnol percentage is still high enough to suggest she was very much under the influence of the drug when she was killed. Which means she'd taken or been given the substance between one and two hours before her death.'

'That wasn't me. I barely talked to her ten seconds!'

'You've read Rudy Saks's statement. He's the waiter who—'

'That didn't happen. He never came to the room.'

'Saks said – and I quote – "The woman was sitting up across the

169

couch, with her shoes off. She looked stoned, like she'd smoked a strong joint or something. Her eyes were fluttering and she had this stupid smile on her face."'

'That didn't fucking happen!' VJ snapped.

Christine ignored him and his anger.

'We've had more disclosure relating to Saks's account. The Suite 18 phone log shows you – someone – making a call to room service at 12.43 a.m. on March 17th. It lasted a minute and a half. Your finger-prints were found on the phone. You have to press "3" for room service. Your print was on the button.'

'Of course it was,' he said. 'I ordered a bottle of vodka as soon as I got to the room.'

'At around 5.40 p.m., the previous day?'

'That's right. What I didn't do was order champagne. And I didn't open the door for Rudy Saks – or anyone. And Evelyn Bates was not in my suite. At 12.43 a.m. I was passed out on the couch.'

'So you keep saying. But the evidence says differently.'

'Damn the evidence! I was passed out!'

Christine closed her file.

'What about the thong they found in the bin?' she said.

'*That* I remember.'

Redpath grinned at me. His eyes said, I can't wait to hear *this*.

'I had a wank,' VJ said, matter-of-factly.

Christine looked him right in the eye.

'Why is it we're only talking about this now?'

'What d'you mean?'

'You never said anything about masturbating at the scene.'

VJ glanced at me for an instant, then back to Christine.

'It's not how it looks,' he said.

'And how's that?'

'Like I'm some kind of . . . freak. A . . . a sick fuck.'

'That's *exactly* how it looks, Vernon,' Christine said. 'It looks like you drugged Evelyn Bates, strangled her on the floor, carried her to the bed-room, stripped her naked, posed her and jerked off in her panties.'

VJ held his head in his hands, rubbed his temples, breathed deeply through his nose. It was warm in here, and the air reeked of industrial floor cleaner, heavy on bleach and artificial citrus.

'I didn't mention the thong before, because . . . because . . . Because when you're arrested for *murder*, the last thing you're going to remem-ber is the wank you had the night before.'

'When *did* you remember?'

'I don't know,' he said.

'Before or after you were taken to the station?'

'After, when I was in the police cell.'

'Why didn't you say anything then?'

'I didn't think it was relevant.'

'A thong with your sperm all over it, in the same radius as the body of a naked woman in a room you were staying in, is *very* relevant, don't you think?'

'I was confused, wasn't I?' VJ said, testily. 'All I could think was, What the hell's going on? How hard do I have to pinch myself to wake up?'

I'd been writing everything down. I didn't look up. I didn't want to catch VJ's eye. I didn't want him to see I thought he was talking crap.

'Vernon, this is the *first time* you've said anything about a thong. A *key* piece of evidence. A *damning* piece of evidence. *Why?*'

'I've just told you!'

'You could – and *should* – have told Janet about it, on the four or five times you met her. You could've told Terry. And you could – and *should* – have told me. Instead you wait for us to hear about it from the prosecution. You're doing their job for them.'

'It was ... I don't know ... *embarrassing*. OK? I didn't think it'd ... *Shit!*' He slammed the table and looked away.

'Is there anything else you haven't told us about that night?' she asked him.

'That's everything.'

'You're sure?'

'Yes.'

'So I'm not going to get any more surprises from the CPS – find out things you were too "embarrassed" to tell me?'

'No,' he said, through clenched teeth.

Christine had maintained a steely tranquillity, never once raising her voice, not even when she'd been skewering him. VJ had completely lost his cool. He'd gone from affability to tipping-point anger in a matter of seconds. The man sitting next to me, seething and looking daggers at his barrister, had a short fuse. And he was every ounce and inch capable of violence. I could see it, and so would a jury. All Carnavale would have to do was push him – and not even that hard.

'OK, now tell me what happened with the thong,' Christine said.

'I ... I jerk – *masturbated* into it and threw it in the bin afterwards.'

'We *know* that, Vernon,' Christine said. 'I want to know as to why and when. What possessed you to do something like that?'

'What *possessed* me?' He laughed, mockingly.

Christine glowered at him. He raised his hand in apology.

'Let's start with why,' she said.

171

'As I've said from the start, I didn't take Evelyn Bates up to my room. So the thong's not hers,' he said.

'Whose is it?'

'Fabia's.'

'*Fabia's?*'

'Before she attacked me, I told you she bit my lip?' he said.

Christine nodded. *Go on.*

'She drew blood. I went to the bathroom to clean up. When I came out, I saw her smoothing her dress down like she was straightening it. A little later we fought. She beat me up, knocked me over and tried to push the minibar on me. Then she ran out of the room. A while later, I got up. I saw the thong lying on the floor. I supposed it was Fabia's. I thought she'd taken it off when I was in the bathroom. And so—'

'Where on the floor was the thong?' Christine asked.

'By the wall.'

'Which one?'

'Where the minibar is – was.'

Christine frowned. Then she pulled out the police photographs of the hotel suite, pawed through them until she found the one she wanted. She slid it across to him.

'Show me.'

VJ looked at the photo and pointed.

'You're sure?' she asked.

'Pretty much.'

I tried to see what he was pointing at, but couldn't without craning over.

'You previously stated that Fabia pulled the minibar out?' she said.

'Yeah.'

'Did you see Fabia holding the thong – or see it in her hand at any time?'

'No.'

She took the picture back from him. 'Go on.'

'Well, I . . . I picked it up and . . . you know . . . looked at it, and, um . . . I jerked off. Masturbated.'

Redpath guffawed. VJ shot him an angry look.

I didn't find it funny. I thought it was a really stupid, desperate lie. Just like the conspiracy theory angle he was trying to work.

Christine stayed inscrutable.

'So, you're saying that this woman – Fabia – attacked you. *Assaulted* you, quite seriously. And, instead of calling hotel security, or a doctor, you *masturbated* over her underwear?'

'That's what I did, yeah,' he said.

172

'Why?'

'Why did I jerk off, or why didn't I call security?'

'Both.'

'I jerked off, because I had an erection and nothing better to do with it. I didn't call security because . . . I was embarrassed about getting . . . Call me unreconstructed, or whatever you want, but I was embarrassed about getting beaten up by a woman.'

'What did you do with the thong after you'd finished?'

'Threw it in the bin,' he said, miming an overhand lob.

Christine looked through her notes. Turned the pages of her pad back, read those. Frowned. Turned more pages, loudly. Air-treading tactics, silence to make him feel uncomfortable. It was working. He'd slid to the edge of his seat and was leaning forward, fingers interlaced.

'Vernon, I saw the pictures of your torso. You had heavy bruising on your abdomen, consistent with a big kick or a punch. You must've been in some pain.'

'I was,' he said.

'But you masturbated instead of getting help?'

'What can I say? It was a sexy thong. I imagined Fabia in it. Nature took its course.'

Christine shook her head. 'Fabia? The same woman who beat you up?'

'Yeah.'

'Did you like it? Getting beaten up?'

'What?'

'Is that your thing? You're not a sadist like the prosecution say, but a masochist? You like women kicking the crap out of you?'

'No,' he said. 'Right before Fabia attacked me, we were in the first throes of foreplay. I had a hard-on, as you do. I still had a hard-on when she was attacking me. Not because it turned me on, not because I bloody *wanted* one, but because these things have a will of their own. All head and no brain.'

'And that's your defence, is it?'

'Yes,' he said.

'Franco Carnavale will have a field day with this,' she said. 'Do you know what he's going to do?'

VJ didn't answer.

'He's going to make the jury laugh,' she said.

'So what? It *is* kind of funny. Even I can see that.'

'You don't understand,' she said. 'When a jury laughs *at* you, they no longer take you seriously. And if there's one thing Carnavale knows how to do, it's to make a jury laugh.

173

'He has a particular tone he uses to ridicule someone. A kind of nasal, upper-register sneer. It's so famous in legal circles it has a name. "The Kazoo". As in the plastic wind instrument that sounds like a wasp serenading a dentist's drill. That's how he'll sound when he's cross-examining you. Trust me, it works.'

VJ sighed and slumped back, every spring in his body suddenly lax, as if half the life in him had been sucked out.

He took off his glasses and rubbed his eyes.

'They're going to find me guilty, aren't they?' he mumbled.

Christine looked at him dispassionately.

'We're beyond innocence and guilt now, Vernon.'

He swallowed hard and blinked a few times.

'What are you saying? You think I did it?'

'No. But I don't believe you, Vernon. I don't believe you're telling me the whole truth.'

'I am.'

'The evidence says you're guilty. You don't have an alibi, and you have no witnesses to back you up. The only thing you have in your defence is your word. And that, frankly, counts for nothing at the moment.'

Redpath and I exchanged a look. We were both confused as to what was happening.

I found myself thinking back to Rodney James's murder, and VJ banging on our door after he'd been interviewed, virtually hysterical, fear and panic in his eyes. *They're saying I killed him!* I wondered if the same memory wasn't playing somewhere in his mind now. And if it was, how ironic was he finding the situation – to be accused of another murder, with me, once again, cast as his potential saviour?

Christine leaned forward.

'As of now, I – *we* are going to have to approach your defence from a whole new angle. We're no longer going to say that you didn't do it. That's the wrong way to fight this.'

'Why?' he said.

'Because that's what they're expecting us to do. That's what the prosecution is preparing for.'

'I don't understand,' he said.

I did.

Christine had told us what she was going to do when we'd first met her. She'd just been waiting for the right moment to reveal it to her client – namely when she had a clearer picture of what she was up against.

'Do you know what I mean by "beyond a reasonable doubt"?'

'Yeah, I think so. The jury has to be absolutely convinced of a person's guilt before convicting them.'

'Who has to convince them?'

'The prosecution.'

'And how?'

'With the evidence.'

'Exactly. The evidence,' she said. 'A juror's worst nightmare is getting it wrong – sending an innocent person to prison. I intend to give them those nightmares, those reasonable doubts – every day of the trial. In other words, I'm not going to defend you, I'm going to attack the evidence against you.'

The 'Stupid' defence.

'Franco Carnavale is going to build his case primarily on the evidence he's already given us. He's so sure of it that he hasn't sat on it like they often do. And I can see why. It's a very strong case.

'However, every case is invariably flawed. Think of it as a house of cards. The cards represent all the evidence – witness accounts, police reports, lab reports, physical evidence. One layer supports another. But the whole thing can only stand up as long as a card – a key piece of evidence – isn't removed.

'Better still, if two or more cards go, so does much of the case. You can then take the stand, look Carnavale right in the eye and say with a straight face, "Yes, I masturbated because I had an erection and nothing better to do with it." It'll sound crude and rude, but the jury won't see you as a "sick fuck". Just a drunk, horny bloke who had a wank in the privacy of his hotel room. Do you know why you'll be able to do that?'

'Because the prosecution's case will lack credibility?'

'Exactly.'

Simple but stunning, I thought. Simple in its imagery, stunning and convincing in its delivery.

And then she went on, outlining flaws in the case I hadn't seen or thought of. Hairline fractures that could be worked into gaping holes. Evelyn could have popped Rohypnol voluntarily. It was also used and abused as a party drug, the anti-E, something clubbers took to come down. Yes, yes, he had called room service seven hours before and ordered up a litre of Grey Goose. That easily explained his fingerprints on the phone. Don't worry about that. As for that waiter – we were already looking into his background . . .

Not to worry . . . not to worry . . .

She spoke to him with warmth and sincerity, doing her best to reassure him that he had an absolute warrior at his side, fighting for him all the way. She promised him everything and guaranteed nothing.

It was pure bullshit to me, but it seemed to work on VJ.

When we got up to leave twenty minutes later, VJ rose with us and helped Christine to her feet, tenderly, like a devoted son. Then he hugged her and said, 'Thank you.'

And he shook my hand too, with a double grip, and winked at me with both eyes. That chilled me to the marrow. He'd done exactly the same thing the day he'd found out Quinlan had been taken off the investigation.

He was guilty then. He was guilty now.

I knew it. I didn't doubt it.

He'd killed Rodney. And he'd killed Evelyn Bates.

No way was he getting away with it again.

No way.

You can't cheat karma.

'That was incredible, Christine,' Redpath said, on the Tube back into town. 'You even had me convinced.'

'All part of the service,' she said, bowing her head in acknowledgement. 'But I meant some of it.'

She was sitting between us, leaning on her stick, staring through the window.

'You don't think he's *innocent*, do you?' Redpath asked.

'You know what the biggest problem with this case is, from the prosecution's point of view?' she asked him.

'Where they're going to celebrate after the verdict's in?'

She shook her head.

'Vernon James got a starred first in economics from Cambridge University.'

'So?'

'Getting *in* to Cambridge is hard enough. Coming out of it with the highest mark you can get is next to impossible.'

'So? He's very bright. Big deal. Some sociopaths are.'

'That's just my point. Vernon is a highly intelligent, highly educated man. *So*, Liam, why would he go and kill someone in his hotel suite, and just leave the body on the bed while he merrily went about his day?'

'Are *you* saying he was set up too?'

Christine shifted a little in her seat, so she was looking directly at him. For the first time that day, she smiled.

The train stopped and the doors opened. No one got on or off.

She didn't answer his question. Which meant she either knew some-

176

thing and was keeping it to herself, or she was bluffing us like she'd just bluffed her client and was keeping that to herself too.

33

Back at the office I went on the trail of the missing Rolex, and stayed on it for the rest of the day. It was a numbers game, laborious as hell, working my way through a list of over six hundred jewellers, watchsmiths and pawnbrokers up and down the country.

And I'd made exactly zero progress, just as I'd expected.

Still, though it may have been water-treading work, right now it was useful, because it took my mind off what was going on in the office. Adolf had gone and pulled another of her petty divide and conquer, stick and twist moves.

Today was Michaela's birthday. She'd turned twenty-four. She'd got a card from the department, which everyone had signed – apart from me. The first I heard about it was when Adolf and Iain started singing 'Happy Birthday' shortly after I got back from Belmarsh. Probably planned that way.

Now they were all getting ready to go out together after work, my colleagues and their partners and friends. One big happy gang. Needless to say, I hadn't been invited.

I'm not going to pretend it didn't get to me. Yet I wasn't going to give Adolf the satisfaction of a confrontation. I couldn't afford that. I had to keep my head down and get through this until the verdict was in. I was almost looking forward to unemployment, to never having to put up with this crap again ... Until the next time.

I called up Allen & Sons, a jeweller's on Bond Street.

'Grenville Allen.'

'Good afternoon. My name's Terry Flynt. I work for Kopf-Randall-Purdom, a law firm. We're trying to track down a missing Rolex on behalf of a client, and I'm calling to find out if you might've come across it recently.'

I didn't use the word 'stolen' when talking to dealers, because that would put them on all kinds of defensive and stymie cooperation.

'The watch is a 1951 Oyster Perpetual Datejust. Stainless steel with a gold rim around the glass. Ivory face, steel and gold bracelet,' I said.

'Let me just check our records for you. Please bear with me.'

Adolf was over by Michaela's desk, talking to her in whispers and giggles. She'd done herself up for the night ahead, let her hair down to her shoulders and ditched the usual corporate two-piece and blouse for jeans, heels and a tight black Ed Hardy T-shirt. I hated to admit it, but she looked pretty good.

'I've acquired five Rolexes this past month,' Allen said. 'A Paul Newman Daytona, a Cellini Cestello, a President and two GMT Masters, but no pre-1970 Datejusts.'

'That's OK,' I said. 'If you come across it, can you please give me a call?'

'Of course,' he said.

I gave him my direct line. He read the number back to me. He had an old, well-bred voice that made me think of that bygone generation of Englishmen who stood up when women walked in the room, or tipped their hats when they passed them in the street. He also sounded like he had all the time in the world to talk. Everyone else I'd spoken to so far couldn't get off the phone fast enough when they found out I wasn't calling about business.

'You said it's a 1951 Datejust. Those rarely sell for more than £800 to £900, depending on their condition,' he said.

'It's barely been worn,' I said.

'Do you have the box?'

'Yes.'

'Can you describe it?'

Off I went to the memory bank. I was amazed at how quickly and clearly it all came back. I was fourteen, standing in James Newsagent's with VJ and his dad. Rodney was performing his birthday rite, putting his prize Rolex on; babbling away about the watch's history, interweaving the Swiss company's story with that of his Trinidadian patriarchs. He'd placed the box on the shop counter and very carefully taken the watch out, slipping his index fingers under the bracelet, as if handling a sacrament. Then he'd wriggled it on to his skinny wrist, a touch of luxury in that realm of the humdrum – stacked tabloids, canned food, cigarettes, porn mags and booze.

'The box is black leatherette, with the crown logo stamped in gold on top,' I said. 'The inside's dark-red velvet.'

'Hinged?'

'Yes. The inside lid is printed with the logo and a legend below it: "Accuracy That Is Truly Remarkable",' I said.

'That's a gift box,' Allen said. 'What's the watch's history?'

'It belonged to the client's grandfather, who got it as a retirement present.'

'What did he do, if you don't mind me asking?'

'Managed a bank in Trinidad.'

'Ah,' he said. 'Do you have the serial number to hand?'

'Yes. It's 7353.'

'Seven-three-five-three. That's it?'

'Yes.'

'Are you sure? Not six digits? As in seven-three-five-three-zero-zero?'

'No. Why?'

'Rolex watches manufactured after 1937 have six-digit serial numbers. In 1955, they went to seven digits. This dropped back down to six in the late 1980s, but they were prefixed by a capital letter,' he said. 'I don't wish to be rude, but are you sure your client's watch is authentic?'

'Pretty sure,' I said.

'I'll need to do some research, but four-digit serial numbers for a mass-produced watch are highly unusual.'

'So it could be valuable?' I asked, remembering that Fabia had supposedly told VJ her father was a watchsmith in Switzerland.

'All Rolexes are worth something, Mr Flynt. What they're worth depends on the collector. There are various types of collector, just as there are various makes of Rolex.'

'One for each?'

Allen laughed. 'You could say that. Some collect by make, some by face colour, some by year. And yes, some collect by serial number. Three- and four-digit watches are extremely rare in themselves because they tend to be highly limited runs. Prototypes are even more limited. Sometimes less than five will ever be made. You said the watch was missing? Was it stolen?'

'We're not sure,' I said.

'The serial number – 7353. It sounds familiar. I need to look it up. Are you OK holding again?'

'Sure.'

I checked the office clock. Almost 6 p.m. This would be my last call of the day. Then I'd head off home. On Thursday I'd be back on the interview round with Swayne, talking to the Blenheim-Strand staff who'd given statements.

'*Hi babe!*' Adolf called out, jolting me.

Kev Dorset, her fiancé, had just walked in. It wasn't a smooth entrance. He was so tall and broad he had to stoop and swivel to get in the room.

We'd never been introduced, but he knew who I was. He strode right past me without a word or a look, his big feet cratering the carpet. I could tell he'd come straight from the office. His grey suit was slightly crumpled, his tie undone and he had a leather manbag slung over his shoulder.

'Hiya,' he said, jovially. He had a naturally loud, room-filling voice, and an oafish, yawning way with his delivery, which reminded me of the way the semi-deaf speak.

Adolf hugged him. He had to stoop again, this time all the way down like he was getting fitted with a lei, so she could drape her arms around him and plant a smacker on his pursed lips.

'I got that thing you wanted,' he said, reaching into his bag.

She shushed him angrily, looking my way.

I was turned away from them, still seemingly staring at the bath house picture, but really watching the middle of the room in my peripheral vision, missing nothing.

Kev passed Adolf a large envelope from his bag and looked over his shoulder at me, to see if I'd noticed. He fell for it too.

Adolf took the envelope over to her desk, bent down and put it in the bottom drawer.

Then Grenville Allen came back on the line.

'Mr Flynt. I've checked the serial number you gave me. Seven-three-five-three. Are you *absolutely* sure of this?'

'Yes,' I said.

I heard him breathing hard, panting almost.

'May I ask who your client is?'

'I can't tell you that, I'm afraid.'

'Of course,' he said. 'I'm sorry.'

'It's OK. Just rules.'

'Well, his – or her – or *their* watch . . . It's the holy grail.'

'Come again?'

'There are only two of that particular model in existence. One's in the Rolex corporate museum in Geneva, and the other belongs to your client,' Allen said. 'It's known in collector circles as the "Three E".'

'The Three E – as in the letter "E"?'

'Yes. Rolex pride themselves on perfection. If a batch of watches is in anyway flawed, they'll recall the lot and replace them,' he said. 'Several things are special about your client's watch. First of all, it's a prototype. The Datejust models were still in their infancy in 1951, only five years old. Rolex were still modifying the design, adapting it for modern times.

'The Three E is so nicknamed, because the "e" in the brand name on the face is back to front. As is the "e" in "Datejust". The third reversed "e" is found when you open up the watch, the brand name etched on the inside of the back cap is also flawed.

'Prototypes are never meant to enter public circulation. A few have in the past, either because they've been sent out by mistake, or they've been stolen. Rolex are known to be highly efficient at tracking them down. And they also pay substantial rewards for the ones that are still outstanding.'

'So, if a Rolex collector, or someone familiar with the watches came across the Three E, they'd know what they had?' I asked.

'Without a doubt.'

'How much is it worth?'

'The last flawed Rolex, which had a back-to-front dial, was sold at auction in 1992 for £150,000. It's widely believed the company bought it. They don't like having dodgy products in the public domain. Bad for the image,' he said. 'I'd estimate the Three E to be worth close to double that. Much more with the box and paperwork.'

'Say you were offered this watch, face to face? Do you have a protocol or a procedure?'

'Of course. I'm a Rolex-approved trader,' he said. 'I'd handle it no differently from any Rolex I got offered. First, I make sure it's not fake. That's easily done. All you need to do is take the back off and check the engine. Counterfeiters can replicate a Rolex shell easily enough, but the mechanics take time, talent and money, which will defeat the whole purpose of a forgery. Then I'll call the company to formally authenticate the watch and make sure it hasn't been reported stolen. Almost all Rolexes are registered under their owner's name. This is because of repairs and servicing.'

VJ wouldn't have registered the watch. It would still be under his grandfather's name. Or maybe even the bank that had given it to him.

'What about an unlicensed dealer, or a pawnbroker?' I asked.

'They probably wouldn't buy the Three E, because they'd notice the flaw and think it was a fake,' he said. 'If the watch turns up in sanctioned Rolex trader circles, I'll know about it. We're a village, Mr Flynt. We all know each other's business.'

'Will you please call me if you hear anything?'

'Of course I will,' he said. 'And can you please call me if it turns up. I'd *love* to see it.'

'Yes. Count on it.'

'Good luck in finding it.'

'Thanks for your help,' I said.

I was now alone in the office. Everyone had left.

I sat back, pondered.

Going on VJ's version of events, where Fabia existed and everything had happened the way he said: she'd asked to see his watch, noticed the reversed E in the logo, and either knew what it was or thought it highly unusual, and possibly valuable. She'd kept it. Maybe she'd even beaten him up because of the watch – assaulted and robbed him.

181

It was a good enough theory for Christine to run with. But for it to be viable, we had to prove that Fabia wasn't a figment of VJ's imagination. And, so far, she seemed to be.

Swayne had drawn a complete blank there. And we only had four weeks to find her.

I typed up my notes and emailed a copy to Christine, Janet and Redpath.

It was almost 6.30. I'd be home in time for dinner.

I stood up, stretched, yawned and rolled my neck to get the kinks out.

Then I remembered the envelope Adolf had stashed in her desk.

What didn't she want me to see, or know about?

Not exactly hard to figure out. She was on a high-profile case featuring a newsworthy footballer, and Kev was angling for a permanent contract at the *Daily Chronicle*. I could smell an ethics violation ...

What the hell? She'd have done the same to me.

I went over to her desk.

The brown envelope was the only thing in the bottom drawer. It wasn't sealed. The flap was tucked in.

Inside was a ten-page transcript of a conversation between a mobile and a London number.

No idea what this was about. Tapped phone evidence couldn't be used in court anyway. Adolf knew that. Maybe she was helping Kev out. How? Looking into one of our cases for him, perhaps? Then she'd be violating client-lawyer confidentiality. If it was that, I'd *really* have a lot more over her than just adulterated sandwiches.

I slipped the transcript back in the envelope. It wouldn't go all the way in. Something was blocking it from the bottom. I shook it out.

A thick white business card landed on the desk.

> **NW5**
> *PRIVATE INVESTIGATORS*
> **DAVID STRATTEN**
> **07423 814921**

David Stratten?

That was the same name and number listed as a contact on VJ's list of ongoing business deals – one of the two that had been scrubbed out.

I checked the list again.

Yup.

Stratford Quakers. Contact: David Stratten. 07423 814921.

Was Adolf looking into *my* case?

34

I'd got the key in my front door, when Arun came staggering out of his flat, face bloated and blotchy, moving like a cork trying to stay upright in a whirlpool.

'Awrite, Terry?'

I nodded to him.

Piss off – fast!

He burped loudly, put his fist to his mouth afterwards, giggled at the memory of manners past. I smelled the beers he'd had for breakfast and lunch, the ones he was having for dinner.

'I got sumfin' for you.'

'What?'

'This geezer dropped it off.'

'Where is it?'

'Left it with me, dinn'e?'

'Where *is* it?'

'He gave it me ta safekeep for you.'

'*With YOU? Where* is it?'

He pointed to his flat. I heard his baby crying inside.

'Can I have it, then. Please?'

'Yeah, sure ... 'course. But ... um ... ur ...'

He scratched his thatch of chestnut hair. A scrap of tin foil floated out and rested on his shoulder.

'I was finkin', right. I don't wanna be ... *vague* or nuffink ... but can I get like a ... a reward, please?'

'A *what*?'

'A reward.'

'You want me to *pay* you for holding my mail?'

'Lotta dishonest people around 'ere, you know, Tel? And I coulda nicked it m'self for all you know.'

I took a step towards him.

'Arun. Get me my mail – *now*!'

He burped again.

'Awrite, bruv, awrite.' He backed off towards his door. 'No need to get stressed. Bad for yer elf.'

Swayne answered on the first ring, like he'd been expecting my call.

'What's on this?' I asked, looking at the unmarked DVD he'd dropped off.

'CCTV from the hotel. Footage from the nightclub entrance. Evelyn Bates is on it. So's the Strangler.'

'*One* disc?'

'All they've got for the evening of March 16th. They had some kind of power failure. Took out most of the cameras. There's nothing from the lobby or any of the floors or lifts.'

'How convenient,' I said, suspicions crowding in.

'Shit happens.'

'The day of the murder?'

'Way it goes sometimes. But look on the bright side.'

'What?'

'The CPS haven't got that disc yet.'

'How come?'

'They got given a dodgy DVD. They haven't got round to requesting a replacement,' he said.

No point in asking how he knew that. The information had probably come from the same place he got the disc.

Christine and Janet were going to want to see the footage first thing tomorrow. Which meant I was going to have to view it now, sort the relevant from the useless.

I turned on our PC.

'Have you heard of an investigator called David Stratten?' I asked him.

'Is the Pope a Nazi?'

'Do tell.'

'Dodgy Dave, or Diamond Dave, depending on whether you're snoopee or snooper. He's a techie. Speciality: phone and computer hacking. Also a dab hand at surveillance,' he said. 'Up till a few years ago he worked for the papers, whichever one paid the most. He had a good thing going with the *Daily Chronicle*. He was their go-to poop-scoop.'

'What happened?'

'He reinvented himself as a CSC – a corporate security consultant. Theoretically he sets up internet firewalls and secure phone connections for businesses. In reality he's a spy.'

'Hacking the competition?' I said.

'Whatever they desire. City banks have a lot of CSCs on the payroll. It's the next level up from insider trading.'

So what did Stratten have to do with VJ and the Stratford Quakers? I'd looked them up before I left the office. They were a Quaker group who'd been based in Stratford since Victorian times. They ran a homeless shelter and soup kitchen in the area. It really didn't fit at all.

'Why d'you want to know anyway?' Swayne asked. 'I know you're not replacing me with him.'

'Don't flatter yourself.'

'Sid'd never employ a PI who worked for the press.'

'Why not?'

'They're mercenaries. No discretion, no loyalty. Nature of the sewer they swim in.'

'And you're different?'

'I've never crossed a client. And I've never worked for their competition,' he said. 'I'm going to hazard a guess here. Stratten's name came up in connection with Vernon James.'

'Our client thinks he's the victim of a conspiracy.'

'Course he does,' Swayne said. 'You know Elvis runs al-Qaeda from a chipshop in Bradford, right?'

'So I keep hearing,' I said.

The PC had powered up. I smelled the dinner waiting for me on the table, heard Amy talking next door, and I thought of getting the first of what would be several pots of coffee ready for the all-nighter ahead.

'Have you examined CCTV footage before?' Swayne asked.

'No.'

'It's an art,' he said. 'Never watch it the same way twice.'

'Could you be a little more cryptic?'

'You'll figure it out. You went to Cambridge.'

'What did you just say?'

'You heard.'

And he hung up.

35

'What do you think?' Janet asked.

'We haven't formed a fist yet, but we've certainly got a finger to poke in the prosecution's eye,' Christine said.

The defence team had convened in a windowless office in Christine's chambers and watched the CCTV. Actually, 'watch' doesn't describe what we'd been doing for the past two hours. We'd *scrutinised* the footage, all but put it under a microscope and prodded at it with probes and needles. It had been played half a dozen times, twice at normal speed, then in slow motion, then significant parts had been reviewed frame by frame, not to mention magnified and brightened too.

I hadn't had much sleep. I was running on fumes, will-power and coffee with a Red Bull chaser. I'd been up all night doing the exact same thing we were doing now. Watching footage of Evelyn and VJ in the Casbah nightclub.

'This affects their take on motive,' Christine continued. 'Prior to this video, the prosecution would've had it that Vernon went up to Evelyn *specifically* in the club. As in: he chose her. As in: her murder was premeditated.

'The tale of the tape has it differently. His motive for going up to her was commonplace. Sex. He fancied her – from a distance, with her back turned. But when he saw what she looked like from the front he either changed his mind – or, as he has it, realised he'd made a mistake, and backed off. Quickly.'

We'd seen exactly that. VJ approached Evelyn while she was on the phone, her back to him. He tapped her on the shoulder. She turned round. They appeared to have a brief exchange of words. Then VJ backed off – almost immediately – palms out in apology and the name of peace.

'Beer goggler's remorse,' Redpath chuckled. 'That'll play well with the men in the jury.'

'And lose us the women, Liam,' Janet said, sharply.

But what he'd said made me think of something.

'Liam isn't all that wrong.'

Janet turned her icy blue beams on me.

'Vernon's eyesight's not too good,' I said.

'He's short-sighted. So? He had his contacts in that night,' she said.

'When was his last eye test?'

'What's your point?'

'Assuming he takes the stand, he's going to have to explain how he mistook five-foot-four, plump Evelyn Bates, for a woman he's described as "six foot and slim, but curvy". Their only resemblance is hair and dress colour. He wasn't pissed enough.'

'Good point. Talk to his optometrist. With any luck he was overdue a check-up,' Janet said.

Christine took a sip of her herbal tea and cleared her throat.

'From what we've seen here, Vernon and Evelyn barely spoke, never danced, and definitely did *not* leave together.'

'And he didn't spike her drink with Rohypnol there either,' Redpath added.

I looked at the screen. The image was frozen on the empty entrance, seconds after VJ had walked out at 11.19 p.m. He'd spent slightly over an hour there. Evelyn had left at 11.13. Six minutes apart.

'We have to figure out how Carnavale will spin this,' Christine said. 'His initial theory, that Vernon met Evelyn in the club and developed enough of a rapport with her to invite her for a drink, and then to his room, simply does not hold. So where's he going to go now? Remember,

186

he has to prove murder, not manslaughter. And his narrative has to be consistent.'

She paused. I was getting to know her through her pauses. She'd sometimes use them for dramatic effect – the quiet before she hit you with a motherlode of insight; or, when going over VJ's statements, to communicate very subtly that she thought he was talking crap. And then there was *this* kind of pause, which was really a time-out silence while she ordered her thoughts and chose her words.

'What I'd do in his place is play a variant of the wounded pride angle,' she said. 'Vernon went up to Evelyn and tried to chat her up. She told him where to go. That hurt his pride. Got his blood up. To a Master of the Universe like Vernon that was an insult. He saw Evelyn as a *challenge*. He *had* to have her – out of principle. This then introduces the anger, the *rage* that compelled him to strangle her later.'

'But how did he get her up to his room?' Janet asked. 'He didn't follow her. He left six minutes after she did.'

'She'd ripped her dress. She was exposed, embarrassed,' Christine said. 'Where would she have gone? The club is on the first floor. Her room is on the fourth. She'd have to get a lift up there. And there were plenty of people around. She wouldn't want to be seen going around half naked. Where did she go?'

Christine looked at me to state the obvious.

'The nearest bathroom?'

'Yes. It's on the same floor, between the club and the lifts,' Christine said.

'Vernon says that after he left the club, he walked to the lifts. It's perfectly feasible he met Evelyn as she came out of the bathroom. He apologised to her. He was sincere and charming. They went up to the bar on the eleventh floor.'

'She fixed her dress in *six minutes*?' Janet said.

'More like four, or even five.'

'Impossible,' Janet said.

'Not to a red-blooded man like Franco. To him all she had to do is tie a knot and walk out. Nothing about adjusting the dress, making it look presentable,' Christine said. 'And, of course, she would've done her make-up too – all of which I'll be sure to highlight for the *women* in the jury.'

She addressed the last to Redpath, who winced on cue.

'What about her phone?' Christine asked.

'She lost it when she got knocked over by that conga line,' I said.

Now that bit of video had made everyone laugh when they first saw it. Evelyn, seconds after she'd talked to VJ, getting crashed into by someone in the conga line that had burst through the door almost at the same time. She went flying face forward off the screen.

'He said he picked it up and put it in his pocket. He said he was going to hand it in,' I said.

Christine coughed and cleared her throat.

'This video isn't a silver bullet, but it's definitely a silver dart,' she said. 'We can discount some of the prosecution witness statements – the waiters in the bar, who saw them "dancing" and "frolicking around" together. It's obvious from the tape they were doing no such thing. She fell over, or was pushed. And she landed on him and they both went down.

'Vernon says her hair got tangled up in his clothes and she scratched his face while trying to stand up. That explains the hair on his person, and on the couch. It also explains the lipstick on his collar, his skin under her nails, and his saliva on her fingers.

'And it's also obvious, from the way she's moving when she leaves the club, that her dress is torn and she's holding it in place. She hurries out, hunched over, holding her modesty by the straps. So, from that we can assume the dress was ripped during the melee with Vernon. That accounts for the matching green fibres the police found on his suit and in his *suite*. In other words, we've just moved a chunk of the forensic evidence out of the suite and into the club – well away from the crime scene.'

It was a great argument. And I could see a jury wavering, hesitating, *doubting*. I wondered what Carnavale's comeback could be.

'That's good,' Janet said. 'But we still need to account for one thing – one key piece of evidence against us.'

'What?' Christine asked.

'The body in the bed.'

36

The next morning I decided to visit David Stratten.

I wanted to know what Adolf was up to. She hadn't wanted me to see what Kev was giving her. That quick, sneaky look my way, that sharp '*Shush!*'. She was either looking into VJ's case, or she was violating ethics while working on hers.

This was about her getting the paralegal job. I may have been getting fired, and the promotion and the degree were as good as hers, but I wasn't just going to roll over and accept my fate. She didn't deserve that easy a ride.

I called Janet, put my thumb up my left nostril and told her I was ill. I assured her I'd be in later.

She said I sounded terrible and wished me a speedy recovery.

Stratten's offices were in a three-storey semi-detached in Tufnell Park. Thick, shiny ivy covered the lower walls, but advanced no further than the window. The tendrils had been pruned back to preserve the effect and the house itself.

I rang the bell.

The short squat man who answered had a worried look on his face he was trying to cover with a smile. He'd missed shaving for a day or two, and didn't appear to have slept in as long either. His skin had the yellowy texture of fresh dough, and his small, bloodshot eyes were suspended in shadows. I couldn't tell what colour they were.

'I'm looking for David Stratten?' I said.

'That's me, yeah. Come in.' He stepped aside and beckoned me in.

Not what I was expecting. I didn't move.

'David Stratten, the investigator?'

'Yes, the same,' he said, impatiently. 'Come in, come in.'

The foyer made me think of how an upscale brothel might've looked in the swinging sixties. Oak beams on the floor, garish turquoise and black tiles on the walls, and a gilt-framed theatre mirror complete with bulbs.

I smelled coffee and burned toast in the air.

Stratten led me into the front room, which was his office. There were filing cabinets, wall-to-wall shelves stacked with ring binders, and an expensive-looking orthopaedic executive chair.

He was dressed like he was running late for a business meeting. He had on plain dark-blue suit trousers and a blue-and-white gingham shirt with silver cufflinks.

'That's all the receipts and invoices,' he said, pointing to three cardboard boxes on a desk, stuffed to subsidence with paper. 'Over there's the bank statements, credit card statements and whatnot.'

Those were in a trio of splitting orange recycling bags.

'Um . . .'

'Sorry, they're in a mess and out of sequence,' he said sheepishly. The ingratiating smile grew. 'I had a couple of mishaps when I was pulling it all together. It was a bit short notice.'

'Who do you think I am?' I asked.

'Inland Revenue, right?'

'The taxman?'

'Aren't you?'

189

'No,' I said.

'Oh ...' The smile disappeared and his round cheeks deflated like a stabbed soufflé. 'Who are you, then?'

'My name's Terry Flynt. I'm from Kopf-Randall-Purdom, the solicitors.'

'*Solicitors?* I didn't call you.'

'It's about some work you did for a client of ours. You looked into the Stratford Quakers?'

Stratten thought, head back, hands in pockets. His eyes traced an arc across the ceiling before they came back to me.

'This isn't a good time,' he said, gesturing to the boxes. 'I'm busy.'

'Tax inspection?'

'Yeah. Due any minute. Fuckin' nightmare.'

He moved towards the doorway and beckoned me to follow him out.

The situation was slipping from my hands. I racked my brains to remember what they'd taught us back when I was door-to-door selling in Croydon. *Always assume the close.* Act like you've already got what you want. And, most of all ...

Stay put.

'It's just a couple of questions, really, then I'll be on my way. Won't take long,' I said.

He looked down the corridor at his front door, and then at his watch. He wasn't wearing one.

'All right then. If it's quick.'

His hands went back in his pockets. His hair was several shades of brown at the top and greyish-white at the temples.

'The work you did on the Quakers. What did it entail?'

'What's this in relation to?'

'We're defending Vernon James. And we're looking into all his business deals. It's just routine. Your name was on a list of contacts.'

'Right,' he said, nodding. 'I wasn't investigating *them*. And, for the record, I didn't know I was working for your guy. Not officially.'

'I don't follow.'

'His lawyer hired me. Not Vernon James himself. Never met the fella. That's the way things usually work in our trade. A second- or third-party approach.'

'A middleman?'

'Yeah.'

'So dirty hands stay clean?'

That got him smiling again. No obsequiousness now, but a sly, knowing grin that put small, deep dark rhomboid dimples in either cheek. Diamond Dave.

190

'What did he want with the Quakers?'

'Not that I asked, 'cause I never go into ulterior motive, but he was looking at bidding on some of their land. The Quakers were being coy about who his competition was.'

'And he was using you to find that out?'

'Yup.'

Then he laughed and shook his head.

'It was one of the hardest cases I've ever worked.'

I frowned.

'The Quakers didn't do business over the phone or by computer. Everything was face to face. I'm into techy stuff. Hacking, basically. So I was like Spider Man in the desert here. I had to do it old school – go in and bug their HQ. Hadn't done that in years.'

'Where's the HQ?'

'Stratford. Your bloke was after the land.'

'Did you find out who the competition was?'

'Yeah.'

'And . . .'

'Client confidentiality, mate. Ahmad Sihl knows, obviously.' Stratten winked. Dodgy Dave.

I still hadn't got to first base with him. I couldn't just bring up the *Daily Chronicle*, even if time was short and getting shorter.

The sales manual oracle needed consulting again:

When you sense a close coming over the hill, get closer – be a friend, work the empathy angle.

'What's this about a tax inspection?' I asked.

He blew out his smile in a long woe-is-me sigh.

''Bout a month ago I was due to meet some clients. I had a set of meetings scheduled. Including Ahmad, funnily enough, to talk about the Quakers.

'Eight-thirty in the morning, the bell rings. I go to the door. A man and a woman are standing there. Smart – suits, coats. But officious too. I thought they were cops, right? Except they've got this big bald bugger behind them. Bouncer type, you know?

'The woman shows me ID and a warrant. Inland Revenue. HMRC. Says I've got undeclared earnings going back three years, and asks – no, *demands* – to come in and inspect my business premises.

'So I let them in. What choice do I have? Death and taxes, right? Always get you. They start removing everything – computers, hard drives, flashdrives, paperwork, you name it. I complain. I say, "This is interfering with my business. You can't do this." And the woman says, "Yes we can, 'cause it's been authorised by a magistrate.

191

Read the warrant." So I check it again. There's an official stamp on it.

'They took *everything*. All my gear. The muscle loaded it up in a van outside. They were dead polite, the lot of 'em. *Thanks for your cooperation*, and all that. The woman gave me a card and told me to call the next day, to find out what the next stage'd be.'

Stratten rubbed his face and made his bristly chin crackle.

'That fucked me up, let me tell you. Not only was I facing God knows what they were going to throw at me, but they'd just cost me about two hundred grand's worth of business. One of the computers they took had all my active jobs on it,' he said.

'When did this happen?' I asked.

'St Paddy's Day . . . um . . .'

'March 17th?'

'Yeah, that's it. Anyway, I called the number on the card the next day,' he said and smiled again. Shook his head. He'd gone a little red.

'And . . .'

'Have you ever called the tax office?'

'No.'

'Consider yourself lucky. I got put on hold for about forty minutes, waiting for an answer. All the while this pre-recorded message is telling me to go on the website! *Sorry, I can't do that. You took my fuckin' computers!*

'Then someone *finally* came on and told me an adviser would be with me shortly. "Shortly" took for ever. At this point I'd been on the phone something like two hours.

'When the adviser came on, I tell 'em why I'm calling. They didn't say anything. They just transferred me to another department. Didn't know what it was called.

'No holding this time. Phone's answered immediately. I give this woman on the other end my name, NI number and the case reference number from the warrant. "How can I help you?" she says.

'I asked to speak to Heather Gifford. That was the name on the inspector's card. "Sorry, no one here by the name."

'I told her why I was calling, what had happened. She told me it wasn't them. First of all, they would've written to me before coming round. And they wouldn't have taken my stuff.'

'So you got robbed?' I said.

'Yeah,' he said. 'I mean this lot were good. They didn't even have to give me a fake phone number, 'cause they knew most people lose the will to live trying to get through to the right tax department on the phone.'

He chuckled.

'They got everything on every case I've worked on in the last five years. And I didn't suspect a sodding thing. Everything about them looked legit. Right down to that warrant.'

'Weren't you due to meet Ahmad Sihl on March 17th?' I asked.

'Yeah. But he wasn't the only client I had meetings with that day. The others were *much* bigger fish with a lot more to lose, if you know what I mean.'

Now my head was churning.

'Who do you think's behind this?'

'Got a list of suspects as long as my dick,' he said.

'You said earlier that Ahmad knows who the competition was? He got that from you?'

'Course. I remembered the names. I had a lot more information that I'd recorded, but the fuckers got all of that.'

I still wanted to know about the *Daily Chronicle*, but now it wasn't such a priority. The Quakers' land deal was. It was too much of a coincidence that Stratten had been robbed the day VJ had been arrested.

'So you've got an *actual* tax inspection now?'

Dodgy Dave smiled and shook his head again.

'Here's the kicker. The minute you ring up the tax office – for anything – you're on their radar. And I *definitely* raised a flag, ringing up about a raid,' he said. 'A couple of weeks ago I got a letter from an inspector saying they were coming round to look at my books.'

God had a twisted sense of humour, I thought. But He was funny with it too. God *had* to be Irish.

'I'll tell you something for nothing, though, 'bout your bloke,' he said.

'What?'

'He's guilty.'

'Why do you say that?'

The bell rang.

'That'll be the *real* taxman,' Stratten said.

'Tell me. Please.'

'Ask Sihl. You're both on the same side, right?'

37

Now I remembered.

Stratford was where VJ had planted the cornerstone of his property empire and raised the flag on his illustrious career.

I'd read about it in *Business Age* in 1999.

VJ had made the cover – standing on a stretch of bare ground, loose bricks and tufts of wild grass about his polished shoes, and the Canary Wharf tower, meagrely lit up in the background. It was still big on space and short on takers then, a white elephant disguised as a robot's darning needle.

Inside was a profile of a dozen of the UK's future captains of industry – whizz-kids judged 'most likely to succeed' in the new millennium. They had one thing in common, apart from being youngish, hungry gogetters. They'd all set up their headquarters in or around Docklands – then still very much a wasteland of rubble and rusty cranes and derricks, after the much-vaunted regeneration programme had stalled when the bottom fell out of the property market in the last recession.

In the article, VJ had talked about his new investments. He'd bought up most of the land he was photographed standing on; an area off Pudding Mill Lane, known as the Kite. So named because that's exactly what it looked like in aerial photos – a quadrilateral divided into four individual plots by two roads.

The remaining segment belonged to the Stratford Society of Friends, a Quaker group that ran a hostel and soup kitchen for the needy in what had once been a warehouse.

The side of the building featured prominently in the photograph of VJ inside the magazine. Its wall was covered in a faded and flaking mural of the Quaker Oats cereal packet logo – the plump, rosy-cheeked face of a middle-aged man in a black hat, with thick white hair covering his ears and a smug smile playing on his lips.

The reason the article came back to me so clearly now was because it was there that I'd found out that VJ and Melissa were married. In his interview, he'd said he was buying the land in Stratford in lieu of setting up a trustfund for his future children – such was his faith in the area's potential.

Boy, had *that* hurt.

I stepped out of Stratford station and walked into one great big busy building site.

The Olympics were coming to town next year and much of it was taking place right here, in the heart of the East End. Construction was in overdrive. The 80,000-seater stadium, 10-million-litre Aquatic Centre, and a 370 ft commemorative steel sculpture that looked like a barbed wire helter-skelter were all going up simultaneously to the left. Further away, to the right, the 2800 apartments comprising the Olympic Village were being built from scratch; while almost on top of the station loomed the soon-to-be-opened Westfield shopping centre – a hybrid of beached cruise liner, car park and aircraft hangar. Even the station itself was being altered and expanded around the commuters, with new extensions, entrances and walkways being bolted on and blasted in.

I headed for the Kite.

The sun was out and a warm breeze was blowing gently through the neighbourhood. It reeked of wet cement and raw metal, and tasted of fine dirt and chemicals.

VJ's property was fenced off with high steel netting, topped with razor wire and plastered with security company placards illustrated with the heads of German shepherds. That hadn't deterred people from using it as a dumping ground for everything they could heave over. The lower part of the fence sagged under the accumulated weight of broken furniture and household appliances, much of it pre-plasma coffin TVs and pre-flatscreen computer monitors not even charity shops wanted.

The Stratford Friends House stood at the far end, a huge square brown-brick building with big windows and outside metal stairs and gangways. It looked deserted going on uninhabitable, the sort of place where you'd expect to find the detritus of a staved-in roof when you opened the door.

A white food van was parked near the front of the building, the side flap open. People were queued up outside, in a short line. All tramps, in heavy overcoats, despite the heat. The main door was open, and they were taking whatever was being doled out at the van and walking into the building by way of a concrete ramp.

The Friends House was in far worse shape, the closer I got. The walls were fissured and most of the windows boarded up.

I queued at the van. A couple of the tramps turned to look at me weirdly. I didn't blame them. I was the outsider here, in my suit and tie.

A stout middle-aged woman with sweat running down her brow was serving. I smelled curry coming from the big steel pot on the stove.

'Bread?' she asked, pushing a polystyrene cup my way. Thick bright yellow soup with something paler floating in the middle, that was either a piece of boiled potato or a clump of rice.

'No thanks,' I said. 'Is the manager around?'

'Go inside and ask for Fiona.'

Despite being a wide-open space with a high ceiling, the warehouse smelled close and musty, and much of it was steeped in semi-darkness. The front and back doors were open, as were most of the windows, but the light only came through in solid concentrated slants and didn't dissipate.

The warehouse was empty, save three long dinner tables set up in the middle, slabs of wood balanced on packing crates, and the benches flanking them were variations of the same. A few tramps were sitting and eating, miles apart from one another.

They were outnumbered by men and women of various ages – the Quakers, I assumed – most in jeans and T-shirts, some in shorts. They were eating and talking quietly among themselves. A few heads turned as I passed and all nodded or smiled at me.

I asked one of them for Fiona. He pointed to the back of the hall, where someone was sitting alone.

When I reached her, I saw she was working through a stack of paper, tapping away on a calculator and jotting numbers down on a pad.

I introduced myself and said I wanted to talk about Vernon James.

She asked me to take a seat, she'd be with me in a moment.

I watched her work, head down.

She was a small woman with a pair of large square specs whose frames reminded me of old portable TVs. Her hair was straight and black and tied up in a bun. She was wearing a man's shirt with a frayed button-down collar, open over a plain white T-shirt. Her fingers were rough and calloused and her hands were veiny.

Beyond the door the artillery of construction work was drowning out the sound of passing trains.

After a few minutes, Fiona stopped what she was doing.

'You're defending him, you say?'

'I'm part of the team, yeah.'

She appraised me, quickly. Clothes, bearing, demeanour. She had my position in the pecking order all figured out by the time her eyes found mine again.

'How is he?'

'It's not easy for him,' I said.

'I can only imagine,' she said. Her voice was quiet and calm. 'We were all very surprised when we heard the news. Shocked, really.'

'You know Vernon?'

'We've met a few times over the years. He's been a good friend to us, to our community.'

I noticed the grey glinting in her hair, the lines around her mouth, the paleness of her skin, her general thinness.

'How so?'

'Support, donations, advice. He always had time for us.'

'So, not just at Christmas, then?' I quipped.

'Quakers don't celebrate Christmas, Terry,' she smiled. 'Every day's special to us.'

'Sorry,' I said, feeling a blush shooting up my neck.

'It's OK. The only thing people seem to know about us these days is oats.'

I laughed and she joined in.

'Vernon wasn't – *isn't* – your typical businessman, only interested in his profits,' she continued. 'When he bought the land around here, he came to see us before he called in the diggers, to let us know what was happening. That was required, but he did something else too. He rented a space for us, not too far from here, so we could carry on our work. Not many people would have done that, let alone taken us into consideration. He truly valued – *values* – what we do here.'

Not as much as he values your land, I thought.

VJ had seen these people for what they were – decent, selfless sorts – and played them accordingly; seduced them with kindness and charity, softened them up. Mr 'Compassionate Capitalism'? *My arse.*

'That was good of him,' I said.

'Yes it was,' she said. 'How can I help you exactly?'

'We're looking into Vernon's affairs, before his arrest. Ongoing deals he had. That sort of thing. Just routine, really. Checking things off.'

'OK?' She frowned.

'I understand he was in the middle of negotiations with you, to buy this place?'

'No, he wasn't.'

'I thought he was.'

'He did discuss it with us, once, last year, when we told him we were thinking of selling up. But it never went beyond that.'

'So he never made an offer?'

'No,' she said.

'Ah ...'

Had Dodgy Dave bullshitted me?

'We were surprised he didn't bid,' she said. 'He owns the rest of this land. And he would've been our ideal buyer.'

Now it was my turn to frown.

'The sale wasn't just about money,' she said. 'We needed to find the right person. We've had a presence in Stratford for over two centuries. We didn't want someone just coming in and building luxury flats here. We wanted someone who'd give something back to the community. Continue – if not our actual work – then something of our tradition. Even if it was just affordable housing.'

'I understand,' I said. 'Have you found this person?'

'Yes, I think we have.'

'Who?'

197

'The deal hasn't been finalised yet, so I can't go into that. Sorry,' she said, politely but firmly.

It didn't matter anyway, because I'd come here for nothing.

I thanked her for her time and picked up my bag, mulling whether to go back home or to the office. Neither appealed. The flat would be empty and the alternative was Adolf and mundane phoning around.

Suddenly I thought of Melissa, of calling her, seeing her again, just dropping by. I crushed it quick.

Fiona walked me out, talking as she did about how full the Friends House used to be, the beds they'd once had for runaway kids and women who'd fled abusive relationships. Stratford had changed a few years ago, gone more upwardly mobile as Docklands had sprouted into the high-rise global financial centre it was now, and its workforce had bought up the area. New money had washed away the old casualties, further out towards the Essex borders. She sounded almost rueful as she spoke, seeming to miss the old days, but then she perked up as she told me they'd be relocating to Walthamstow once the deal was done.

I wished her luck. I meant it. I liked what she did here. Genuinely good people were hard to come by anywhere, but in twenty-first-century London, they were an endangered species.

'Can you please pass on a message to Vernon from . . . us?' she said, as we reached the door.

'Of course.'

'Please tell him he's in our prayers.'

No, I wasn't going to tell him that, because he didn't deserve her, these people or their prayers.

'I'll do that,' I said. 'I'm sure it'll mean a lot to him.'

Heading back to Stratford station, I turned my phone back on.

Moments later it started ringing, the tone playing the theme from the *X-Files*.

That meant number withheld/unknown caller.

'Hello?'

'Is that Terry?'

'Yes?'

'This is Ahmad Sihl. Are you free to meet up?'

38

The person Janet had dubbed '*the* top corporate lawyer in the country' wasn't much to look at. But then very few people's professional reputations complement their physical appearance. Same goes with mass murderers. You go in expecting gods or monsters, and you come face to face with the likes of Ahmad Sihl.

He *was* sort of god-like in looks, I suppose. Think a Buddha in a pin-stripe suit and you'll pretty much get the idea. His body was piled up, puffed out and compressed together, compensating in girth what it lacked in height and stature.

He thanked me for coming at short notice, asked if I wanted anything to drink, praised the glorious day, and then motioned me to sit in the chair opposite him.

There were no hide-bound legal megatomes in Sihl's seat of power. In fact there were no books here at all – legal or otherwise. His office was a trading-room on the upper floors of the NatWest Tower, in the heart of the City. The plasma TVs on each available wall were set to Bloomberg, CNN and BBC 24 News, the volume muted. On his desk a four-panel computer screen showed technical analysis graphics and share prices. He was either monitoring his investments or projecting an image, telling his clients he was exactly like them.

He switched to smalltalk, all of it about me. How long had I been at KRP? What had I done before? I stuck to my most recent CV for answers.

That pretty much ended the prelims. All the while I'd sensed he was coming in low and easy, feinting while he checked me out. His eyes were the tell. Nothing soft and flabby about those. They were a brown so dark I couldn't differentiate iris from pupil, and they didn't look at you, so much as hover, moving in dips and zigzags, searching for somewhere to settle.

'What did you want with Dave Stratten?' He had a Scottish accent, shorn of its thickness and much of its burr, yet still berthed in the Glens.

'Didn't he tell you?'

'He said you asked about the Quaker building.'

'That wasn't what I was seeing him about,' I said.

He waited for me to continue, but I didn't know how to proceed. I'd answered without thinking. I should've lied.

If I told him the truth, it would look beyond bad. Here I was, wasting critical time playing petty office politics, while his good friend and top client was in prison. No way.

'This a bit embarrassing . . .' I began.

Now his eyes stopped moving and fixed on mine. I was staring into twin sinkholes to oblivion. The rest of him was utterly still too, not a twitch.

'I was helping out a colleague,' I said. 'We're a pretty solid team, the clerks. We always look out for one another. If someone's overworked or on a tight deadline, we pitch in. A colleague of mine is working on a case, and David Stratten's name cropped up. She needed to know more about him. I was curious myself, and I offered to check him out for her.'

I'd left myself open to questions, but I was on fairly safe ground. It was the truth, give or take quite a bit.

Sihl glanced over at the grey phone on his desk. He reached for it, then hesitated and withdrew his hand.

'Do you know what KRP stands for?' he asked.

'Kopf-Randall-Purdom?'

He shook his head.

'Kill-Rape-Plunder. As in: Kill your parents-Rape your friends-Plunder their pockets. That's your firm in a nutshell. That's its ethos,' he said. 'So you *weren't* "helping out a colleague", Terry. That's bullshit. Because, if it even *occurred* to you to help out a colleague at KRP, you wouldn't be working there. You'd be somewhere else entirely. The Samaritans, Amnesty International, Save the fucking Whale and Bring Back the Honey Bees while you're at it. That kind of place.

'So, let me ask again: what did you want with David Stratten?'

It was too late to come clean, and anyway, I'd look pathetic doing it.

'A colleague is working on a case indirectly related to something Stratten did for the *Daily Chronicle*.'

'This to do with Pepe Regan, the footballer?'

'That's right.'

'So?'

'We're in the process of putting together Vernon's defence,' I said. 'If things go our way in court, this trial could come down to brass tacks. Vernon's character will come into play. The prosecutor has a reputation for curveballing. He'll look at everything and everyone from Vernon's past – especially dodgy associates with any connection to sex and sleaze. Stratten was a tabloid investigator.'

I paused to check how I was doing. I hadn't lost him so far. Even though I was winging it, making it up as I went along. Even my vocabulary. *Curveballing?*

'In order to avoid surprises, I decided to check Stratten out, to assess his character. You have to anticipate everything, no matter how small,' I said.

Sihl rolled his chair back a little, folded his hands on his stomach.

'There's nothing linking him to Vernon,' he said. 'I employed Dave. And it's all legit.'

'I didn't know that until this morning,' I said.

He considered that a second.

'Either way it's beyond irrelevant. Christine Devereaux would squash that one dead.'

Sihl rolled himself towards the desk.

'Stratten could've been the loose end that tripped us up. He turned out not to be, but better safe than sorry, right?' I said.

That worked. Back he rolled again.

'What did you make of Dave?'

'Tosser,' I said.

Sihl laughed. 'That he is.'

I waited for the jolly cloud to pass. I glanced past him and took a hit of the view. It was a lovely afternoon outside. Blue skies, bright sun. This was my favourite time of all in London, not too hot, but far from cold, the sun out and people comparatively pleasant and laid-back.

'Why did you bullshit me, Terry?'

Now I could tell the truth.

'I was afraid this would look trivial to you – a waste of precious time, and our client's money.'

'It is,' he said.

'No, it wasn't.'

I needed to salvage a little of my reputation. I couldn't leave him thinking I was the weak link in the defence team, the inexperienced clerk who'd spent three billable hours on a wild goose chase for next to no reason.

'Didn't you find it odd that Stratten got robbed the day he was coming to see you?' I asked.

'That didn't even surprise me,' he said. 'Dave's burned more bridges than he's crossed. He's got so many enemies they've probably got a union. He's lucky it was just his equipment they took this time.'

'*This* time?'

'He's been beaten up, had guns pulled on him, axes aimed at his head. He's been hit by cars, even hung off a bridge. I'm sure he deserved all of it. Like you said, he's a tosser.'

'Why d'you employ him?'

'He gets the job done. And he's loyal to a fault – as long as you're paying.'

I thought of Swayne for a moment. I was seeing him tomorrow. Hotel staff interviews.

'Stratten had information for you, about the Quaker deal,' I said.

'That's right. But that was also the first thing Vernon crossed off the likely suspects list.'

'Why?'

'It wasn't a high-value deal,' he said.

'It's right next to the Olympic Village.'

'And Vernon owns all the surrounding land,' Sihl smiled. 'That doesn't mean he wasn't interested in buying the Quaker plot. Of course he was. Always has been. He's spent the last couple of years getting close and cosy with the Quakers. He's been very generous to the hostel they run there.'

'Buttering them up?' I suggested.

'Of course. Why else?' Sihl said. 'He knew that sooner or later they'd have to sell up. The building's close to being condemned. Unfortunately, the Quakers aren't just about money. They wanted the buyer to honour their legacy in the area, in some way.'

'Someone of proven ethical character?' I suggested.

Sihl grinned. 'You're a sharp one, Terry.'

What had I just said to deserve that?

I let him think I was as perceptive as he thought I was.

'Vernon should've been a shoe-in for the Friends House,' Sihl said. 'Except they had an offer on the table from a man called Hal Peterson. A Canadian property developer. He's what's called a "flipper". He'll buy up a property, improve it in some way, and then sell it on for a profit.'

'Exactly the kind of buyer the Quakers don't want,' I said.

'Technically, yes. Except Dave found out that Peterson is a Quaker. He went to a Quaker school here in England. He was classmates with one of the board. His offer was £3.5 million, and he guaranteed he'd build a dozen affordable homes. If you ask me, the offer was way too high.'

'What was Vernon going to offer?'

'He wasn't going to pay above 1.75. But he *was* going to meet the board in person and guarantee to build a new Friends House. Much smaller than the existing one, but they were going to have it completely free, right down to the bills.'

'Very generous of him,' I said.

'Very smart too,' Sihl said. 'The Quakers aren't naive. They know they're dealing with sharks. But the hostel'd work out cheaper than a bunch of affordable homes.'

'In other words, there's more likelihood of it actually being built.'

'Exactly ... Well, *assuming* it was ever going to be built ...'

'Vernon was really going to sell the land on?'

'Of course,' Sihl said. 'His share of the Kite is currently worth twenty times what he paid for it.'

'He was going to sit on it until the price was right?'

'Yes.'

I wondered what Fiona Grant would think if she could hear this.

Bastards together, I thought. VJ the manipulator, Sihl the facilitator. What a pair. They truly deserved each other.

I kept my thoughts from showing, and just smiled and nodded.

I thought back to what Stratten had said to me before I'd left his house – that VJ was guilty, and Sihl knew it. I could've raised that now, but it wouldn't have been the right thing to do. It would have prompted Sihl to ask if I agreed. He'd have been watching my every facial twitch for a tell as I answered – and he'd have read my mind; he'd have known.

Sihl looked at his watch.

'I've got a meeting now. But thanks again for coming in.'

'Pleasure,' I said.

Well, the view had been.

He stood up to signal we were through. He walked me to the office door, making more smalltalk as we went. Where did I live? Did I go for river walks along Battersea Embankment? He had when he'd lived there, many years ago.

Then, as I was about to step out he clapped a fleshy hand on my shoulder.

'One more thing . . .'

I turned round.

'What was Vernon like, back then?'

'When?'

'In Stevenage.'

I'd been expecting a variation of this from the moment I walked into his office. I knew VJ had told him about me. Sihl hadn't called me here because of Stratten. He wanted to check me out, to see if I wasn't a serious liability.

'He was my best friend,' I replied.

39

Home, well in time for dinner.

I should've been happy, here with my family, but I was too knackered to appreciate it. The traipsing around had worn me out, and all I had to show for my efforts were more unanswered questions, a fresh barrel of doubts, and a blockbuster headache.

The kids were doing all the talking. Usually Karen and I took it in turns to referee the conversation, keep the volume down and the babble manageable and civil, but today they had free rein. They were going to be on their Easter holidays next week and they were excited.

Karen was as tired as I was. She'd had a hard day, getting the company accounts together for the annual tax audit. After the run-up to Christmas, it was her most frantic, stressful time at work, because books had to be balanced and bank accounts reconciled. I thought of Stratten being ripped off by those phoney tax inspectors and nearly told her about it – the ingenuousness of it – but I didn't want to cut into what she was saying.

Dinner was one of the microwavable ready meals we kept handy in the freezer for when neither of us were up to cooking. This evening's pre-cooked delight was shepherd's pie with mixed veg, and a sachet of thaw-'n' pour gravy.

Amy was holding court at table. She was at that stage in life when everything she said was a question. She wanted to know why things were the way they were in the world; how they worked, why we needed them, how we lived before they existed.

Our answers always had to be on point. She wouldn't accept fob-offs or shortcuts, and woe betide you if your reply was patronising. I suspected she'd be a lawyer one day, or failing that a cop.

'Daddy? *Daaad?*'

Amy was talking to me.

What had I just missed? I looked at Karen, who was looking at me. Amy had obviously asked her for something and Karen had deflected the request to me, as she always did when she didn't want to be the one saying no.

'Can I have an iPhone?' Amy asked.

'What d'you want one of those for?'

'To talk to my friends.'

'Don't you talk to them at school?'

'I'm not in school *now*.'

'We've got a phone here. Call them after dinner,' I said.

'How can I do that when I don't have their numbers?'

'Don't you have them written down?'

'No.'

'Why not?'

'Because I've got nowhere to keep them. If I had an iPhone, I'd have somewhere to keep them.'

Karen and I exchanged a grin at our daughter's logic.

'Why does it have to be an iPhone?' Karen asked.

'Sophie's got one.'

That figured. Sophie Colvin was Amy's best friend. Her parents spoiled her rotten.

'We'll get you a phone, Amy,' I said. 'But not now. You don't need one.'

'Yes, I do,' she said.

'No, you don't. And you *definitely* don't need an iPhone,' I said. 'I don't have an iPhone, and neither does your mum.'

'But you're not on Facebook, are you?' she said.

'*Facebook?* What's that got to do with an iPhone?'

'If I had an iPhone, I could be on Facebook.'

'You can't be on Facebook until you're thirteen.'

'Yes, I can.'

'How?'

'I can pretend.'

Karen suppressed a giggle. I didn't find it funny.

'Now, Amy, you mustn't lie. You know that. It's bad.'

'But *Ray's* on Facebook!'

Karen and I looked at Ray. He was the perfect picture of red-handed surprise.

'Is that *true?*' Karen asked him.

He couldn't look at her or me. He lowered his head and scrunched up his brow, thinking.

'How long have you been on Facebook?' I asked him.

Ray stared at his plate and said nothing.

'Answer your dad, Ray,' Karen said.

'About a year,' he said, sheepishly.

In other words, for about the same time he'd had his computer.

When had he started becoming sneaky? And why hadn't he asked us if he could go on Facebook?

I was angry at him, but not as much as I was surprised and hurt. I thought we were liberal, tolerant parents – the kind he could come to, talk to, be honest with.

'All my Facebook friends are real. From school,' Ray said. 'I know all about the danger of paedophiles pretending to be teenagers, if that's what you're worried about.'

There goes our every notion of protective parenting, I thought.

Karen was dumbstruck.

Thankfully that part of the conversation was lost on Amy. Not that she wasn't listening and trying to understand.

'We'll talk about this later, Ray,' I said. 'Finish your dinner and go to your room.'

Ray gave Amy an angry look and went back to his shepherd's pie.

We ate on in silence for a moment.

'So can I have an iPhone?' Amy said.

Karen let out a short laugh.

'The only reason you want one is because Sophie's got one, right?' I said.

She nodded.

'Well, that's the *worst* reason to want something, Amy – because someone else has got it,' I said. 'Besides, Sophie's not going to be your friend for ever. In fact, the friends you have now you won't have in a couple of years. None of them. You know why? Because friendships never last. OK?'

Amy didn't answer. She stared at me across the table, looked into me without blinking.

Her eyes slowly silvered and her face reddened from the cheeks out. Then her face crumpled and creased and she closed her eyes and let out a long, braying sob. Moments later she was bawling loudly and uncontrollably.

Karen got up and led her out of the room, turning back to glower at me as she left.

Ray quickly finished his dinner and went to his room without a word.

I sat at the table with the dirty plates. Amy was still crying.

I hadn't meant to hurt her. I felt terrible.

But I'd meant every word of it, just the same.

40

The next morning I met Andy Swayne in the lobby of the Blenheim-Strand. He was sitting at a table close to the reception desk, halfway through a family-sized coffee pot.

Though we were here officially and legally this time, he hadn't got the memo. He was dressed in yet another of his off-the-peg combos – three different shades of man-made blue, his tie a striped medley of the same.

He flashed a supercilious grin when he saw me.

First things first.

'So you know about Cambridge?' I said.

'And a very good morning to you too,' he said.

I'd considered avoiding the subject altogether, but I knew Swayne had an agenda and I wanted to know what it was.

'Are you going to make this a problem?' I asked him.

'No more than you already have.'

'Meaning?'

'Give someone your National Insurance number, you hand them your life on a plate.'

'So they know at KRP?'

'You think a company like that doesn't do background checks?' he said. 'Usually happens between first and second interview.'

I'd never had a second interview, let alone a *first* – at least not a formal one. I'd come in as a temp. I'd met Janet, talked over the basics of the job and that was it. No tough questions. A handshake and I was straight in, started the same morning.

Swayne had been fishing. No more than that.

'Did Sid Kopf get you to investigate me?' I asked him.

'No. But be sure he has.'

'Why am I still here, then?'

'Must be your charming personality,' Swayne said and flashed me a punch-magnet of a smirk.

We were here to interview staff who'd given witness statements, and to tour all the places VJ had been, starting with Suite 18 and finishing at the Circle bar on the eleventh floor. This was standard practice for defence and prosecution, getting a feel for the crime scene, visualising their respective cases.

Our guide would be the hotel's head of security. He'd been the third person to see the body, after the maids. And he'd called the police.

He arrived on time, greeting Swayne first.

'*Hola, Andy. ¿Cómo estás?*'

'*Muy bien, Albert,*' Swayne smiled, standing up to shake his hand.

Swayne then introduced us. His name was Albert Torena.

'Thank you very much for your help, Mr Torena,' I said, shaking his hand. 'I know you're very busy, so we'll try and get this done as quickly as possible.'

'No problem. Call me Albert. Please,' Torena said. He was a trim, swarthy man with a shaved head, rimless glasses and a goatee so immaculate and dark it looked photoshopped. His accent was Spanish shade.

'I didn't know you and Andy knew each other,' I said.

'We go back a few years,' he said, smiling at Swayne. 'Shall we make a start?'

He led us through the split-level lobby, walking slightly ahead, with his chest out, his chin up and his feet splayed, like a particularly self-satisfied duck. He nodded to every staff member he spotted – cleaners, waiters and waitresses, bellboys and receptionists. They all responded in kind.

The lobby was a spacious sweep of gleaming cream and red-veined marble, whose centrepiece was a huge chandelier suspended over a sunken floor like a stalactite of tiered glass and trapped light. One of the walls consisted entirely of a water feature, a slab of rough granite washed over by a stream that fed into an aquarium filled with koi carp. Another was a solid plasma screen showing Sky News.

We reached a vast carpeted atrium, eight floors high. It was practically the same layout as the cruise ship Karen and I had taken our honey-moon on, with wraparound interior balconies, and three giant silos for lifts.

Torena motioned us to the VIP lift, on the right. It was matt black and there were no call buttons, just a card slot. He proudly explained how the system worked, showing us the two different keycards issued to guests – black for rich, white for everyone else. His was blue.

It occurred to me that if Swayne was so tight with Torena, why had we bothered to break in? Surely he could have asked him to let us into the suite after forensics had left.

Except he'd already been testing me then, seeing what I was made of, how far I'd go. And how gullible I was.

It made perfect sense.

The lift came and we got in.

Suite 18 still reeked like a bar-room brawl, but the smell didn't smart as much. Its sting was broken, its pungency dissipated.

The only police presence today were the poles and blue-and-white tape sectioning off part of the lounge and the area near the stairs where Evelyn had met her end. The minibar had been left in place, its doors open, the scene's skewed nucleus. Much of the broken glass was still on the carpet. The coffee table was missing its flowers and champagne; the couch had had rectangular patches of leather cut out of its seat and arm-rest, exposing the white padding.

We moved to the bedroom. It was unchanged from our last visit, except for greyish dust that had settled on all the surfaces in a dirty frost.

Torena explained where the body had been lying on the bed, and talked me through what had happened when the police and medics turned up. I half-listened and took a few notes.

'I don't know what it is about this place. It always attracts trouble,' Torena said, when we left the bedroom.

'Like what?'

'Oh, you know – parties that get out of hand. Musicians and bankers and footballers stay here a lot. The bankers are the worst, when it comes to bad behaviour. They're like spoilt brats on steroids,' he said.

'How long have you worked here?'

'Since the place opened. Three years.'

'Any deaths in your time?' I asked.

'A couple of near misses. Death hit the post.' He smiled at his wit. 'This whole suite is going to have to be remodelled,' he said. 'We've been getting a few enquiries from people wanting to stay here. Sick, no?'

*

In the lift back down I noticed the round security camera in the ceiling.

'What about those problems with your CCTV the night of the murder?' I asked.

'The fuses tripped out and killed the cameras around 7 p.m. Our maintenance guys said it was a power surge.'

That used to happen in our flat whenever Karen dried her hair. She'd plug the dryer into a multi-socket extension and the power would automatically cut out in the living room.

'Couldn't you have flipped the circuit breakers back on?' I said. That's what we always did.

Torena chuckled. 'You didn't hear this from me, OK?'

'Fine.'

'The power in all the cameras went – except for the ones in the Casbah club and the casino. Those still worked. The surveillance guys, watching the screens upstairs, called maintenance – the contractors who installed the CCTV. They said, "We'll come out and fix the problem, but we'll have to charge you extra because this isn't covered in the contract." To save money, hotel management didn't take out a twenty-four-hour repair contract, only one for office hours.

'Surveillance called the hotel manager. When he heard the casino cameras were still working, he said to wait until the next day. He only really cares about the casino. That's where the hotel makes most of its money. The maintenance contract has been upgraded now, of course.'

'What was the problem with the cameras?'

'Just what you said. Circuit breakers. All they did was flip them back on and everything was back to normal. Nothing we couldn't have done ourselves.'

'Why didn't you?'

'Rules. We're not allowed to handle the fuseboxes. That's why we pay electricians.'

'Can I see these fuseboxes?'

They were in a room in the basement. Plain grey door, keypad entry. His fingers punched in the code:

1-2-3-4.

Inside, more grey – walls, floor, ceiling. The fuseboxes were in mounted metal cabinets, all stencilled with alpha-numeric codes and also keypad-locked. A very faint drone emitted from them, making me think of beehives at the height of summer.

1-2-3-4.

He opened one of the cabinets and showed me two rows of circuit breakers fitted with dark-blue plastic levers. The general power switch was at the end.

'So, the casino and nightclub cameras were working, but all the others went down?' I asked.

'That's right.'

'Odd,' I said. 'The cameras run off the same circuit. Surely they should have all gone out?'

Torena shrugged.

'What did the maintenance people say happened?' I asked.

'System overload.'

'That's it?'

'Yeah.'

'What about the police? What did they say?'

'They talked to maintenance, were told the same thing, I guess.'

'So they just accepted that almost all the CCTV was down the night someone got murdered?'

Another shrug.

'Who knows the entry codes?'

'Security and the management.'

'That's it?'

'Yes.'

'Have the codes been changed recently?'

'No.'

I typed the code into the keypad on the cabinet door. It clicked open. Torena looked at me with surprise and suspicion.

'1-2-3-4 is a common factory preset,' I said. 'Anyone could come in here and switch off the power.'

The ballroom was being prepped for a gala dinner of some kind. A cleaner was going over the tiles near the entrance with a floor polisher, while waiters and waitresses were dressing the round tables in brilliant white cloths.

On the stage at the end, technicians were wiring microphones to a lectern and fitting filters to the spotlights.

All these goings-on were being supervised by a slim brunette in a dark-blue suit, standing in the middle of the room, a clipboard in hand, reading glasses perched on the end of her nose.

Torena introduced her as the banqueting manager.

We shook hands and exchanged pleased-to-meet-yous. Then, without prompting, she ran through her job description. She was in charge of running the hotel's corporate events from planning through to execution.

'Did you work on the Ethical Person of the Year awards?' I asked her.

210

'Yes. I put that one together.'

'Were you at the event?'

'Yes.'

'Do you remember seeing a woman in a green dress that night?'

'No.'

'About my height, blonde – long hair?'

'There were a lot of people there, but I don't remember anyone in green.'

'What about Vernon James? You know who I mean?'

'Of course.'

'Do you remember seeing him?'

'Yes. He gave the speech.'

I looked at the seating plan for the Ethical Person award dinner. Twenty-one tables, the highest numbers at the back, the lowest at the front; eight to ten guests on each.

'Mind if I check something from the stage?' I asked.

'Go ahead,' she said.

I stood at the lectern, and looked out across the ballroom. As to be expected, it was impressive, even in the bare broad daylight. The ceiling was finished in black satin and supported half a dozen boat-shaped chandeliers.

In his statements to Janet and Christine, VJ had described first seeing Fabia to his right, out of the corner of his eye. I tried focusing my gaze ahead of me, while scanning my peripheral vision.

I couldn't see the tables to my right very clearly. They were set too far back from the stage, a good three metres away at least.

It would have been much darker when VJ was stood here, and the stage lights would have been in his eyes – eyes that were already impaired, whose short-sightedness he corrected with contacts.

How could he have seen Fabia?

He couldn't, unless she'd been directly in his line of sight – so sitting or standing *between* the tables and the stage.

Nightclubs and daylight don't mix. The Casbah was no exception to the rule. It may have scored five stars out of five in all the London hotspot listings, but here and now it was dismal going on depressing; like an out of season summer resort in the middle of a cold snap.

Swayne and I sat in the same VIP booth VJ had. Down on the dancefloor, a young woman was on her knees, chipping and prising away gobs of pancaked chewing gum with the blunt edge of a knife.

I looked out the window, at Sea Containers House and the Oxo Tower across the river. And then I came back here and noted the chips

211

and nicks on the table, the grime on the red velvet ropes around the booths, the stains on all the seats; and how the place couldn't shift the rank, bittersweet whiff of booze, stale perfume and staler sweat.

Swayne was handling the interviews, which were almost entirely pointless, because the CCTV footage had rubbished all but one of them. Yet we still had to go through the motions, so there was no comeback from VJ – and, I suppose, to add to his bill.

The only person we really wanted to talk to was the final name on the list – Rudy Saks, the waiter who'd delivered the champagne to Suite 18 at 1 a.m.; the last person to see Evelyn alive.

The witnesses came in individually and in order, and went through their statements.

Four waitresses. Swedish, Czech, Polish and Turkish.

We got the story in random fragments, according to the teller.

The Czech saw VJ and Evelyn talking together when she passed them on her way to drop off empties at the bar. She didn't hear what they said, simply noticed the tall black man talking to the blonde. She said they didn't get a lot of black people at the club, or the hotel. She looked embarrassed when she said that.

Swayne told her not to worry. He showed her the pictures. VJ's mugshot first, then two of Evelyn – the post-mortem headshot, and the self-taken picture of her in the green dress she'd posted on Facebook.

The waitress positively ID'd them as the couple she'd seen.

We thanked her for her time.

The next two witnesses assumed more than they'd actually seen, but we didn't let on.

The Turkish waitress had narrowly missed tripping over Evelyn and VJ on the floor. She thought they were both pissed and rolling around on the ground like they were 'lovers in a field', she said.

She thought they were both gross, but 'typical English'.

That made Swayne and me laugh because she was right, despite being wrong.

After she left, I put a star next to her name. She'd be worth putting on the stand to back up our explanation as to how VJ had got so much of Evelyn's DNA on him, and vice versa. Just what Christine wanted – prosecution evidence she could turn and use in the defence.

Next up was Rudy Saks. I reread his statement. It was detailed and precise, and absolutely damning.

Torena came into the club.

'Sorry, guys,' he said. 'Just heard Rudy phoned in sick this morning. He won't be coming in today.'

*

Our last stop was the Circle bar.

It was a mock country pub with a mock Tudor interior, uneven white plaster walls and black timbering. It had a fake fireplace, plump leather armchairs with footstools, a small library and an upright piano. Pewter tankards hung above the bar, and the drinks menu was chalked on a board – real ales, wines and spirits.

The barman looked the part too. Gary Murphy, his name. Pinkish, plump and bald, with the sort of open, welcoming features you rarely saw anywhere in London.

'Please talk us through what happened that night,' Swayne asked him once we'd got the formalities out of the way and sat down.

'The two of them came in before midnight,' he said, in an Australian accent.

'This man?' Swayne showed him VJ's mugshot.

'Yup, that was 'im. He was with a bird. She went and sat right over there, in the corner by the window,' he said, pointing to a two-seater table across the room to the right. 'I remember his order, 'cause it was odd. He asked for a white wine for the lady, and a water for himself. 'Cept he got me to make the water look like a large vodka, said he'd pay for it like it was vodka. And he did – even left a tip.'

'How was he? Drunk, sober?'

'A bit pissed. Unsteady. Trying to hold it together. His clothes were a mess, though. The jacket was wet and a bit dirty, like he'd fallen over.'

I looked down his statement. It was short, barely two pages.

'That's not what you told the police,' I said.

'They didn't ask.'

I made a note.

'Carry on,' Swayne prompted him.

'He had ... er ... cuts on his face. Scratches on his cheek. Quite deep. They'd drawn blood.'

This wasn't in his statement either. This was *good* for us and bad for the prosecution. It backed up VJ's story that Evelyn had scratched him when they'd fallen over in the club.

DS Fordham had taken both the barman's statement and Rudy Saks's. He hadn't asked either about VJ's appearance. Why?

'Did you ask the man what had happened?' Swayne said.

'No. You gotta be discreet here. I just served him his drinks.'

'How were they together, him and the woman?'

Murphy frowned and his shiny forehead folded downwards from the temples and pouched up along his brow.

'Were they arguing, or friendly?' Swayne asked.

'I didn't look at them all that much 'cause I was startin' to pack away.

But whenever I did look over they seemed close – intimate. Low voices, leaning over the table, looking into each other's eyes – if you know what I mean.'

Swayne pushed the picture of Evelyn in her green dress across to him. 'Was this her?'

Murphy looked at the picture.

'Nah.'

'No?'

'Wasn't 'er, mate.'

Up until that moment, I'd believed Swayne when he said he didn't care about the case. He'd cruised through the entire process with rock-solid indifference, only breaking a sweat when he was winding me up.

But what he'd just heard made him start, the same as me.

'Are you sure? Look at it again,' Swayne said.

'That was *not* 'er.'

'You identified her from this photo.' Swayne held up the post-mortem headshot.

'No, I didn't. What I told the copper was it *might've* been her. Check my statement. It's right there. I reread every word before I signed it.'

I looked over his statement.

That was *exactly* what he'd said, when DS Fordham had shown him the crime-scene picture of Evelyn.

That could've *been her, yes.*

Fordham hadn't asked him to confirm or elaborate. He'd missed it. And so had we. I guessed the prosecution had too.

'What did the woman who came in here *actually* look like?' I asked him.

'I didn't see 'er face too well, but she was blonde – long straight blonde hair. And she had this *dress* on. *That* I remember. I can as good as see it now.' He smiled. 'It was dark green, split down the thigh and open at the back. And tight too. Trouble. Showed off her curves. Not like that sheila you showed me *at all*.'

Murphy was practically drooling at the memory.

None of that was in his statement either – only:

The woman was blonde and had a green dress on.

Nothing else.

'How tall was she in relation to Vernon James?' I asked.

'Who?'

'The man. How tall was the blonde next to him?'

'Same height. A real Amazon type.'

VJ was six foot two. She would've been wearing heels, so take off a couple of inches. That meant she would've been around six foot.

214

Evelyn Bates was five foot four. Definitely not an 'Amazon type'.
This was a breakthrough.
This was Christine's silver bullet.

'Haven't you had enough excitement for one day?' Swayne asked through a yawn, as we rattled along on the Tube going west, to Acton.
'You can get off at the next stop if you want,' I said.
He kissed his teeth.
We were on our way to see Rudy Saks.
Rereading his statement after interviewing Murphy, I could now see at least two tell-tale gaps in it:
No references to VJ's physical appearance. He'd have had scratches on his cheek at 1 a.m.
Vague description of Evelyn Bates again – *Blonde, twenties, green dress.* Nothing about her height, body shape, hairstyle. Nothing about the style of the dress. And like the rest of the witnesses, he'd identified her from a post-mortem photo.
What if it wasn't Evelyn Bates he'd seen in the room, but Fabia?
I won't pretend I wasn't excited.
Of course, I was. This was a *rush.*
I wasn't thinking of VJ here. I wasn't thinking of getting him off the hook, or even considering the slim possibility that he might not have done it, that he really could have been set up.
No, I wasn't thinking along those lines *at all.*
I was thinking about myself, and how good I'd look if I pulled this off – if I, through my efforts and intuition, gave Christine enough to torpedo the case.
Christ – they might even keep me on at KRP. I could get that promotion . . .
Imagine that.
'I want you to look into DS Fordham's background,' I said to Swayne.
'What are you after?'
'Procedural irregularities. Any cases that got thrown out of court, convictions that got quashed on his watch. Falsified statements, complaints against him. In fact, get me his life. Everything and anything you can find.'
'Yes, Mr Kopf.'
I ignored that. I was on too fast a roll.

Rudy Saks lived down Berrymead Avenue, a sloping road of terraced houses with steepled slate roofs, short wrought gates, regular speed bumps and neighbourhood watch signs.

215

We weren't supposed to be here, let alone even have Saks's home address. It was in the CPS case file Swayne had given me the day we'd met, on a recruitment company form the hotel had in their personnel files. I recognised the company's name: the Silver Service Agency. I'd almost gone to see them about work when I moved to London.

A muscular man in a plain blue T-shirt and baseball cap opened the door just as I was about to ring the bell. He was on his way out, sports bag in hand. He froze in mid-motion when he saw us.

'Rudy Saks?' I asked.

'Me? No. Rudy moved out yesterday,' the man said, in a foreign accent with an American twang. He looked Scandinavian, although he wasn't tall enough.

'Where did he go?'

'He— Who are you, man?'

He looked me up and down, small brown eyes gauging me. His jugular vein jutted thickly out of his neck.

I was stuck for an answer. I didn't want to say we were cops. He wouldn't believe me. His eyes were too shrewd.

'We're private investigators,' Swayne said over my shoulder.

'For real?' he said, surprised and a little bit impressed. 'Is Rudy in trouble?'

That question was aimed at me.

'No,' I said. 'We were hoping he'd be able to help us with something. Is he still in London?'

The man put his bag down and leaned against the doorway, using his elbow to keep the door ajar. His inner forearm was tattooed with a black lion's head inside a Star of David, encircled in a green laurel leaf. There was some kind of writing underneath.

'Yeah. He's moved in with his girlfriend.'

'Do you have an address or a number?'

The man looked from me to Swayne, and then back to me.

'Why don't you give me your details, and I'll leave Rudy a message?' he said.

'Are you likely to see him soon?'

Again the man looked me over.

'He's coming back sometime tomorrow to get the rest of his stuff.'

I took out a blank KRP business card and wrote my name and mobile on the back of it.

The man took the card. 'In case he asks, what is this about?'

No point in lying.

'It's to do with something that happened where he works,' I said.

'You mean the murder?' he asked.

216

'You know about it?'

'It's all we talked about for a week, man. I'll make sure he gets the message.'

'Thanks. What's your name, by the way?'

'Jonas.'

'Thanks, Jonas.'

He was about to go back inside when Swayne said something to him in a language that sounded Arabic.

Jonas looked taken aback.

'You know *Hebrew*?' he asked Swayne.

'The writing on your arm – *Lo tishkach* – it means "Never forget", doesn't it?' Swayne said and smiled.

'That's right. How do you know?'

'I've seen the design before. A long time ago.'

'What was the tattoo?' I asked Swayne as we walked back to the Tube station. That he knew Hebrew didn't quite surprise me. In the short while I'd known him, I'd heard him speak Arabic, Portuguese, Spanish and English.

'Postcard from the past,' he said.

'Care to elaborate?'

'No.'

41

I came home to an empty flat.

Karen had taken the kids to Manchester for the weekend. It was her dad's birthday. A few weeks ago, she'd asked me if I was coming. I'd begged off, claiming I'd probably be busy with the case. This was half-true. I liked my in-laws a lot, but their birthday parties were always an excuse for a piss-up – therefore slow-motion torture for me.

I slumped down on the couch and closed my eyes.

The Serbs downstairs were shouting down the phone to their relatives back home. Arun was having an argument with someone next door – at least I assumed there was someone there. You never knew with him.

Tonight the loudest sounds were coming from outside. One big draw-back to living here was that when the weather was good all the school-age kids would come and hang out right under our window. The plonker who'd designed the estate had thought it a great idea to stick concrete benches on the edge of the back passageway linking the houses. For some reason I'd never been able to work out, the kids and their

217

friends favoured our bench over the five others. It was their hang-out and meeting spot, their youth centre and clubhouse. They'd come and they wouldn't go. And their numbers would swell. Twenty or more barely broken voices would babble loud and fast and all at once, projecting that inner city melting pot argot through the double-glazing, under our skins and into our heads.

There were maybe a dozen of them on the bench now, blowing my attempt at chilling out and unwinding.

I did what Karen always did. I turned on the TV and jacked up the volume.

Peace of sorts.

The local news was on. Royal Wedding preparations followed by football match previews.

I channel surfed.

Nothing hooked me.

I turned on the digital recorder and remote-clicked through the list of programmes Karen had taped and stored on the hard drive. She had a thing about recording whole series and watching them after they'd finished, an episode a day.

She also had a thing for Billy Wilder films. There'd been a complete season of them on the BBC last summer, and I knew she'd recorded some of those. I liked a few of them, *The Apartment* and *Sunset Boulevard* in particular – and the one about alcoholism, of course, *The Lost Weekend*.

I moved the blue highlight bar down the contents page, passing titles and recording dates.

What did *that* just say?

I went back.

The Hoffmann Trust's Ethical Person of the Year Award. Channel 4. March 16th, 2011.

I gawped at the screen for a long moment.

Then I remembered.

I'd read about VJ winning the award in the papers in January, and found out the ceremony was being shown live on Channel 4 for the second year running. I'd set the machine to record it a few days before the broadcast.

But I'd forgotten all about it after VJ's arrest, and my subsequent involvement in the case.

I pressed play.

The Blenheim-Strand ballroom again, looking suitably glitzy. A still-famous, once-funny comedian was on stage, warming up the well-heeled crowd with fastball cracks at the current government, and softball digs at a few of the showbiz guests in the room – actors and musicians – who laughed on cue when the camera picked them out.

He was followed by three short videos highlighting the Trust's work around the world.

And then it was time for the presentation and VJ's speech.

I'd read the transcript a few times over, so I knew that practically everything he told his audience was a lie with a few truths slipped in the pockets.

Yet I wasn't ready for the *way* he said it. I don't know if it was something he'd been taught, or something he'd picked up and made his own, but he exuded the type of sincerity they give out Oscars for. It was in his occasionally tearing eyes, and his voice, which constantly threatened to be engulfed by the emotions he was trying to control when talking about his 'beloved' dad. He made most of the crowd laugh, and a good few of them cry.

Boy, was that bastard good.

So good I had to pause and rewind to make sure he wasn't allowing himself just the one sly smirk somewhere, that he didn't have his fingers crossed the few occasions the camera left his face and concentrated on those long and slender hands of his, weaving small concentric circles in the air.

And then it dawned on me:

If Christine put him on the stand, and he played the jury like he was playing this crowd – this initially hostile, sceptical crowd – he could very well get off. He'd do what he was doing here, but far better. He'd make them believe he was innocent, that he was *incapable* of murder. Factor in the weakening prosecution case, and things were looking pretty damn promising for him.

I thought back to the Stratford Quakers. I saw him sitting where I had, sweet-talking and soft-pedalling them over to his side.

And I thought of Melissa, and imagined him doing exactly the same thing to her; making her fall in love with him. What line of crap had he fed her? And how had she been so duped? Melissa who'd been so smart, so sharp, so worldly beyond her years. Melissa who knew what he'd done to me, what he was capable of.

And all the elation I felt about today's little win crumpled into a tight, hard ball and rolled away.

This was who I was defending – *what* I was defending. Not just a consummate liar, but a shameless, calculating one too. He was pimping out the father he'd hated – and maybe killed – recasting him as some kind of martyr, for no reason I could think of, except to make this audience like him.

Then the camera that was on him did something strange. Instead of focusing on VJ, it zoomed in on the lectern in front of him and held the shot. The lectern was empty. He wasn't using notes. Camera-to-viewer subtext: this speech is coming straight from his heart to them, to us – to me.

He was near the end. I noticed how his gaze had been roaming as he spoke, in a slow left to right pan, so he included every section of the room.

He was talking about the lessons his totally fictitious dad had taught him and how he – a daddy himself – was passing those on to his children.

The camera cut away to the audience for a few seconds, as it had been doing throughout the speech.

And if I'd blinked, I would have missed it.

But my eyes were wide open.

And I saw:

Green.

A hint of green, to the right of him.

I hit pause and rewind. I went back too far.

I got off the couch and squatted in front of the TV.

I played it back in ultra-slow motion, frame by frame.

As I'd suspected, standing on the same stage this morning, he couldn't have seen the audience clearly from where he was. They would have been a constellation of dark-orange blobs, all individual features blurred by distance and dim light.

I paused the video.

There she was. Exactly where he said he'd seen her.

A woman was sitting between the middle and last table on the right. She was a couple of feet in front of both, so that while they were misted in darkness, she was clearly visible – unmissable, in fact.

I couldn't make out her face, because it was out of focus. But the rest of her was clear enough – the shoulder-length fair hair, and the dress. It was long, emerald green and split down the thigh.

'Hello, Fabia,' I said. 'Where the hell are you?'

42

'We can't use this.' Christine paused the DVD I'd made of the awards ceremony.

'Why not?' I asked.

'It merely confirms what Vernon told us in his statement, that he saw a blonde in a green dress from the stage. But that's *all* it does. It's no gamechanger. No silver bullet. Sorry.'

Janet looked pissed off, Redpath tutted, and my high spirits took a dive. It was a very sunny and very warm early Sunday afternoon, the kind of day that almost never falls on a weekend in England. Yet we were all spending it here in Christine's house in Richmond, on a hastily arranged meeting that now needn't have happened.

'What about Gary Murphy's statement?' I asked, pointing at the screen. 'Look at the dress. It's the one he described.'

'That's a rubber not a silver bullet. It'll only bruise the prosecution's case – if that,' Christine said. 'They'll say the barman never saw Vernon and Fabia together *after* they left the bar. He doesn't know what they did or where they went. There's only an *assumption* that they went up to Suite 18 together. Maybe they did, maybe they didn't. But that doesn't change the fact that Evelyn Bates was not only found dead in the suite, she was seen there a few hours later by Rudy Saks.'

Christine was the colour of grout, and her clothes – a loose plain-black kaftan and open-toed leather sandals – gave her the air of a ghostly mother superior without the wimple.

Janet cut in.

'Finding Fabia is now your priority, Terry,' she said. 'You've proved she exists, and that our client at least talked to her. How are you going to find her?'

I'd been thinking about that since Thursday.

'Fabia's obviously a pseudonym,' I said. 'There's no record of anyone by that name at the dinner, let alone the hotel. The dinner was invite-only. There was security at the door. She couldn't have snuck in.'

'Right . . .'

'Someone at the dinner knows her, knows who she is and where she is,' I said. 'None of the guests have got back to me yet. So I'm going to go to them. Andy Swayne can get us the contact details. In-between I'll talk to the TV camera crew, and anyone who worked front of stage that night – waiters, light people and so forth.'

'Good,' Janet said, and then she looked at the others. 'Who thinks our client's still guilty?'

Redpath held up his hand. 'The evidence is still against us, namely the body in the bed and Rudy Saks's statement.'

'Christine?'

'Vernon may well have met and talked to Fabia, but until we know otherwise, I don't think she went up to the suite,' she said.

'Why not?'

'A complete absence of proof. Besides, I don't trust Vernon at all. He's already withheld information from us,' she said.

'Terry?'

'What if he was really set up?' I asked out loud the question I'd been asking myself.

'Why d'you think that?'

'Look at the way Fabia's sitting, and where.' I rewound the DVD and froze it on the shot of the crowd, with her at the forefront. I knew the timings off by heart. 'She's pulled her chair out, away from the rest of the tables, so she's in the light, where he can't miss her. She doesn't want to see better, she wants to be seen. Vernon said she was mouthing sweet nothings at him all through his speech.

'He'd been named Ethical Person of the Year. What an embarrassment it would be – to him, and the Hoffmann Trust – to get caught *in flagrante* with a woman who wasn't his wife.'

'Apart from a blurred image of a woman showing a lot of leg, where's your proof?' Christine asked.

'It's just a theory.'

'A *conspiracy* theory at that. Judges hate them, juries laugh at them. As for motive – exposing Vernon James as an *adulterer*. Come on. Who cares if he cheats on his wife in this day and age?'

She does, I thought.

'What do you think, Janet?' Christine said.

'I don't know,' she said. 'Something seems to be off about all this. But I don't trust Vernon either – even when he's telling the truth.'

Given her previous stance, her certainty of his guilt, this was progress, I supposed.

I glanced around the room. It had taken a lifetime to get this way. The furniture was antique, lots of dark polished wood with shiny brass or copper fixtures. There were rugs on the floor and landscape paintings in baroque frames. Family photographs were displayed on shelves and massed on a mantelpiece, including one of Christine, her husband, their four grown-up children and their grandchildren. Yet for all its cosiness and warmth, the fresh flowers by the window, the evergreen plants in every corner, the place smelled of slow death and medication; the metallic whiff of whatever painkiller cocktails and get-me-to-tomorrow pills and potions Christine was living on.

'As we're here, we might as well talk about the PCMH on the 26th,' Janet said.

PCMH stood for Plea and Case Management Hearing. On the surface this was a bit of costumed bureaucracy. The defendant would be brought to criminal court, and face the judge who'd try him. The

222

prosecution would submit all or most of the evidence and witnesses they intended to present in the case, as well as what was referred to as 'unused material' – evidence they'd discarded, witnesses they'd discounted. The judge would then give the defence fourteen days to present their statement – their case. The judge would also set a date when the trial would start. This would either be the date originally determined by the magistrate, or, if the prosecution needed more time to get its case together, a new date.

PCMH was just over two weeks away.

'Our only play, at this stage, is to accept the prosecution's evidence and build a defence from there,' Christine said. 'They have all the aces. The body in the room, no signs of forced entry, the eyewitnesses, the DNA evidence, and the incriminating statements. Oh, and that thong too.'

'What about the hotel CCTV?' I asked.

'We're not meant to have that yet,' Christine said. 'And we don't technically know if they're even going to submit it. I expect they will.'

'How does that help their case?' I asked. 'Doesn't it disprove the club staff's statements?'

'No. The footage only shows the victim and the accused having contact, but only for a few seconds. We see Evelyn falling over, but we don't see her falling *on* Vernon. Neither do we see them wrestling around on the floor, or her scratching him. All of that happens off screen.'

Christine's trial strategy was becoming clear to me. She didn't have one, because we didn't have much of a case. She was relying on me to bring her stuff she could use, because she couldn't find it herself. Why? Because it wasn't there. The case was still a lock for the prosecution and we were shut out.

So, on the surface, nothing much had changed: VJ was still in deep shit and there was nothing we could do about it.

But I'd changed. A little. I didn't think he was innocent, but I wasn't so sure he was guilty. I was having my first reasonable doubt.

Why?

Because everything he'd told us so far had been true.

43

Monday morning, I got to the office early and went straight to work.

I plugged a pair of headphones into my computer, fed it the DVD and watched the award ceremony again. As it played, I jotted down a list of all the people who could have come into contact with Fabia:

31 guests
7 waiters and waitresses
2 camera crew
2 stagehands

Total: 42 potential witnesses. And that was just for starters. There were bound to be others, once memories were jogged.

Next, I reread all of VJ's statements and highlighted everything he'd said about Fabia. I now had a pretty vivid picture of her.

She had a 'medium-sized' tattoo above her inner right ankle, either a rose or a snake, or a combination of both. Hazel eyes, dark eyebrows.

In his words:

'Beautiful, severe features.'

'Nordic-Latina.'

'Fire trapped in ice.'

'Pneumatic.'

'Coke-bottle figure.'

'Big breasts – implants?'

'Hard body.'

'Legs for days.'

'Pierced belly button.'

And then, of course, there was the dress. *That* dress. VJ had spent so many billable minutes talking about it, it was as if the dress had worn her and not the other way round. Emerald green, plunging at the front, split up the side, open at the back, *so tight you could count her pores.*

The few audience shots in the video showed a conservatively dressed, older set. The men were in black tie and lounge suits, the women in ballgowns or standard dark dresses. Fabia would have stood out a mile.

No way had she been missed.

Before I knew it, it was 9 a.m.

The office was full, but not for long. Iain was going to be spending his first week in court, clerking for one of the barristers. He'd got his hair cut and bought what looked like a new suit for the occasion.

Adolf was off to court too. Southwark, near London Bridge. It was her thug footballer's PCMH.

She'd donned her dark-blue business garb, pinned her hair up and back, and laid off the aren't-my-eyes-beautiful make-up. She was camera-ready professional, right down to the trolley case she'd be carrying the files in.

A couple of weeks ago, I'd overheard her giving Iain grooming tips for court attendance. Press and TV cameras were always rolling, so you had to look your best, but never flash, she'd advised him. Always reflect the profession and the gravity of your responsibilities. Dress in boring tones; dark shades of every colour, as long as they're blue, grey or black. Good advice I'd memorised for future reference.

I waited until they'd left before picking up the phone and starting my calls.

Rudy Saks first.

I called the Blenheim-Strand. They told me he was still off sick. Did I want to leave him a message?

No, but . . .

I asked for the names and contact details of all the waiters and waitresses who'd served at the awards dinner.

Sorry, they didn't have that information because they were all temps. Why didn't I try the Silver Service Agency, who'd sent them? They'd also originally sent them Saks.

I called the agency.

The number was engaged.

I moved on to Channel 4. I'd got the names of the camera crew off the credits at the end of the video.

I was put through to the personnel department and rattled off my spiel. Strictly no bullshit, totally above the board. Who I was and why I was calling – give or take. I didn't mention VJ by name.

They said the camera crew were freelancers. They couldn't give out their contact details because of the Data Protection Act, but they were happy to take a message.

I made instant coffee and threw cold water on my face.

I tried Silver Service again. Still engaged.

Swayne called me. Yesterday I'd given him the names of all the award dinner guests and asked him to get me their numbers and addresses.

He'd already come up with twenty-five. I was impressed.

I got calling. I was rebuffed by twenty-five smooth-voiced, female gatekeepers.

Who was I? What did I want? No, they couldn't put me through because their bosses were all busy/in meetings/not available. Could I please give them my number? Of course. Thanks. Bye.

It was lunchtime now.

I'd got nowhere.

I phoned Silver Service again. Another engaged tone. I checked their address: 75 Gloucester Road. That was fifteen minutes away, via the District Line. I decided to go over there.

I called Swayne again. I needed back-up.

*

It took a couple of walk-bys to locate the entrance to the agency – a grimy white door slipped between a pizzeria and a patisserie which advertised 'traditional fish and chips' in several languages after English. Easy to miss, especially as we were looking for something a tad more obvious – like a sign.

I rang the intercom. A sing-song voice announced the name of the company and buzzed us in without asking who I was.

We went up a narrow flight of thinly carpeted stairs. Then another. The agency was on the top floor, but before we reached it I understood why their phone had been perpetually busy.

A queue of people was lined up on the staircase all the way down to the lower landing; youngish men and women, most carrying small bags of one description or another, some still wearing that stunned, unfocused look of fresh-off-the-bus newcomers.

'Aren't we in a recession?' I mumbled.

'Tables don't lay themselves,' Swayne quipped.

We squeezed up past the line, earning hostile glares and a few protests. I suppose they were wondering what we were doing here, or if we hadn't come to steal their jobs.

At the top of the stairs was a varnished brown door bearing the company's name, printed in black on white paper and taped to the door. No expense spared there, then.

A man in a denim jacket came out and inched past us.

A red-haired woman poked her head around the door and beckoned me in.

We stepped into a surprisingly bright space that made me blink.

'One at a time, please, gents,' she said, in a South African accent.

She sat at a desk to our left.

'We're not here for work,' I said. 'Are you the manager?'

'No, that'd be Bev.' She pointed across the room to the window, where a much older blonde woman in a white rollerneck was on the phone. 'Who are you?'

'Investigators,' Swayne said. 'We're trying to track down some of your employees.'

'Oh . . .' she said, looking worried.

The older woman eyed us and continued her conversation as we came over. Small, thin features set in tanned, lined skin. When she smiled, as she frequently did during her call, I thought of worn leather.

There were four of them in the room, all women, all on the phone except the redhead, who'd already summoned the next person in. Their workspace was no-frills functional. Desks, computers, phones. The floor was spotless grey linoleum and the only thing hanging on the walls was a whiteboard with a long list of hotels and restaurants in black and, next to them, numbers in red. That was it. No plants, photos or any other kind of personal knick-knacks around at all. They came, they worked, they buggered off home. Repeat five times over.

The manager finished her call.

'How can I help?' she asked, looking from me to Swayne, and flashing a professional smile. Her face was late fifties, her hands added a decade.

And she was also South African.

I introduced myself and asked for the names or numbers of the temp waiting staff she'd sent to the Blenheim-Strand on March 16th.

I gave her the list of names. She studied it carefully.

'I don't know how much I'll be able to help you here, Terry,' she said.

'Data Protection, right?'

'Not just that,' she smiled. 'We've got a very high turnover of people here, as I'm sure you've seen. Most of them are only on our books a month or two. More than half work for us just the once.'

No surprise there. They were a *temp* agency.

'Don't you have regulars?' I asked.

'Oh sure. For more specialised work, like chefs and stuff. But they're not on here,' she said, tapping the list. 'Waiters and bartenders are ten a dozen.'

'Right.'

'Tell you what. Why don't you let us contact these people for you – the ones we can get hold of. We'll give them your name and number. How's that sound?'

Like a professional brush-off.

'This is pretty urgent,' I said.

'Do you have a card?' she asked.

I took one out of my wallet and scribbled my mobile number on the back. She put it on her desk and then opened a drawer and handed me her business card.

Beverley Wingrove, Managing Director.

'That's my direct line on there. Call me Wednesday and I'll let you know the state of play,' she said.

'Great. Thanks for your help,' I said.

So I'd got her wrong.

Good.

'That reminds me,' I said. 'We've been trying to get hold of someone called Rudy Saks.'

'I know Rudy,' she said.

'Do you have a number for him?'

227

She turned to her computer and rattled her fingers across the keyboard.

'The only number I've got for him is a mobile,' she said and read it out to me.

I took it down and read it back.

Then I was about to bid her goodbye and wish her a pleasant day, when Swayne said something to her in a language I took to be Afrikaans.

Beverley Wingrove frowned at him.

'I don't understand,' she said.

'You're not South African?' he said.

She shook her head.

'Rhodesian,' she corrected him.

That threw me.

'Don't you mean Zimbabwean?' Swayne asked.

'No,' she frowned. 'I really don't.'

'Fairly common attitude among certain ex-pat Rhodies,' Swayne said, taking hold of his coffee cup by its two ear-shaped handles.

He'd insisted on finding a Costa to talk in, because it was the only chain where a large coffee meant supersize. It came in a deep bowl with a dainty double handle. Swayne ordered it black and dumped in half a dozen sugars. I stuck to a single espresso.

'There was mass emigration when Mugabe took over in 1980,' he went on. 'Over a third of the quarter million white population split. Some came here, some went to Australia and America. Most crossed the border to South Africa. I'm pretty sure Beverley Wingrove was one of them. I'm guessing she only moved to London after Mandela got in.'

'She didn't understand Afrikaans,' I said.

'Tough language to master,' he said. 'Unless she was pretending.'

'What did you say to her?'

'"*Ons sal lewe, ons sal sterwe.*" It's from the old South African national anthem, the apartheid-era one. It means "We shall live, we shall die."'

'You were testing to see if she was a racist?'

'No,' Swayne said. 'That's the only Afrikaans I know.'

I laughed.

Customers were scattered about the café. There was a big group of young mothers by the window. They'd pushed four medium-sized tables together and set up a kind of encampment: them, their babies and their space-buggy-looking prams parked in a cordon around their space. The infants were all bawling their little lungs out. I thought of Amy and two years of nappy changes, colic and teething.

'We need to refocus our investigation,' I said.

228

'On the Green Goddess?'

'Yeah.'

'Thought so.'

I laid out my honeytrap theory. It didn't stack up to much more than a regurgitation of the relevant parts of Vernon's statement, with weak circumstantial evidence holding it together by a thread. Swayne listened attentively, neither touching his coffee, nor letting his gaze wander. This was a first. No snide gleam in his washed-out eyes, no condescending smirk. Was he hungover?

'It's plausible, even possible,' he said. 'But if it is what you think it is, you're not going to find the honey.'

'Why not?'

'She's long gone. Either out of the country, or – given what happened to Evelyn Bates – dead,' he said. 'This would've been a professional job, exactly like a hit. It would've been subcontracted by someone via a middle man. No direct ties. The people who did it would've been a three-, four-, maybe five-man team – including the Green Goddess. She was the bait. They reeled in the catch. Then they were in the wind.'

'So what are you saying – there's no point looking?'

'You're a clerk, remember – fetch and carry? Leave it to the cops.'

'They're not interested. They think he's guilty – *remember*?' I said. 'If you don't want to do this, I'll find somebody else.'

'Oh, I want to do it all right, Boy Wonder,' he said. 'It's money for nothing, as far as I'm concerned. 'Cause that's what you're going to find. Nothing.'

'Enjoy your coffee, Andy. Pleasure as always,' I said and stood up.

'Sit down, Terry. We need to talk.'

'We just did.'

'Sit down. Please.'

I didn't move.

'Why are you doing this?' he asked.

'What?'

'Defending that dick?'

'It's my job,' I said.

'You stopped doing that the minute you walked into Suite 18 with me. That wasn't doing your job. That was something else entirely. That was about you and him.'

He wasn't fishing now. He was telling me he had the goods on me. Everything. All of it.

I sat down.

He slurped some more coffee. When he took the cup away his lips were framed in a wet brown Cupid's bow.

'I couldn't figure you out at first,' he said. 'If you really were a late starter like you claimed, you wouldn't want to blow that second chance at a new career by breaking the law before you'd even sat your first exam. Come to think of it, most first-timers wouldn't do that either. There had to be something else about you. It took me all of three phone calls to get your sorry little life. I've had harder times ordering pizza.'

I kept my cool, even though I was already on the boil.

'Boy, did you ever miss the boat, Terry Flynt,' he said. 'You peaked at eighteen.'

'Fuck you. At least I didn't go to prison.'

Swayne moved his bowl aside and craned across the table at me, blowing coffee breath in my face.

'There are all kinds of prisons, Terry. They let me out of mine. You're still in one.'

'What do you mean?'

'You and Vernon were tight friends. Until you stole off him.'

Here it comes, I thought.

I sat back.

Let's have it, then.

'Sorry, I mean *allegedly* stole off him. I know you didn't do it,' he said.

'Slay me with your acumen,' I said.

'If you had it in you to fuck over your best friend, you wouldn't be a clerk at KRP. You'd be senior partner.'

Wow, thanks, dickhead, I thought.

He pulled his coffee bowl back by the handle.

'And then, of course, there's Melissa . . .'

'And that was a long time ago.'

'Not long enough,' he said.

'For what?'

'For you to get over her.'

I was stumped there.

Swayne snort-laughed again, then shook his head. 'For the first time in my long and undistinguished career, I know everything about a person, but I *still* don't understand.'

'What?' I asked.

'Why you're going the extra mile for someone who fucked up your life,' he said. 'Even if you prove this theory of yours, and he gets acquitted as a direct consequence of your work, there's no glory at the end of it for you. There's nothing at all. You're still getting fired. And for what? For *him*?'

'What would you do then, in my place?'

'Something close to nothing. As little as I could get away with. And

230

if I did find that one piece of exculpatory evidence, I'd bury it. I'd bury it deep and then I'd pour the concrete.'

I looked from my espresso cup to his bowl, half-empty and cooling by the second.

'Have you ever hated someone?' I asked him. 'I don't mean disliked or not liked, I mean *hated*. As in wished them ill. As in hoped to see them on their knees begging forgiveness for the things they'd done to you. Have you ever felt like that about somebody?'

He shook his head.

'I have. And I do. I hate Vernon James,' I said. 'I've hated him longer than I ever liked him. I've hated him longer than my kids have been alive, longer than I've known my wife. It's the only constant, consistent thing I've ever done. I can't let go. I want to, but I can't.

'It's like having a terminal illness that refuses to kill you. It gets into everything you do. It gets in front of you. It walks behind you, and either side of you. It stops you moving on. It's what you do *best*. It's *all* you do, and all you *can* do. Because it defines you.

'What hurt most about what Vernon did wasn't that he fucked me over, that he dragged my name through the mud. It wasn't even *quite* that he took up with my ex. It was that he got away with it. That he wasn't punished in kind. That nothing happened to him. Every time I'd open the paper, there he'd be, doing a lot better for himself than the last time. Doing as well as I was doing badly. He'd cheated karma.

'But, you know what? I want this to stop. I really do. I want to feel nothing for him. I want to let go. I want to be able to say it's all water under the bridge – and *mean* it.'

Swayne surprised me with his lack of reaction. He stared mostly into his cup, as if trying to read the future in the stains. Was I making him feel awkward, embarrassed? It seemed that way.

And what was I doing telling him all this? He was the wrong confessor. He wasn't on my side. But I really didn't care. He started this. He triggered it, set me off with his questions, and his taunts. It was too late to stop. And I wasn't finished.

'I don't want my kids to turn out like me,' I continued. 'I'm going to prepare them for life's disappointments – the biggest of which always involve other people. So I'm going to tell them about all this one day. About the best friend who turned into my worst enemy.

'But I hope to tell them how I had a chance to take my revenge, to get even. But I didn't take it. On the contrary, I did everything I could to help him. Because I wasn't going to do to him what he'd done to me. Because that was wrong. I'll tell them never to hate a person, no matter what they've done. No matter how downright evil they are. I'll tell them

231

it all passes, in time, even the worst things. But only if they let it. Because to hate is to hold on, never to move on. And if you don't move on, you stay put. And if you stay put, you sink and rot.

'So if the verdict comes back "guilty", I'll honestly be able to say – to myself, but mostly to them – that Vernon James was punished for the things he did, but not for the things I didn't do. Do you understand?'

Swayne nodded, and sighed, quietly.

Then he finished his coffee in two gulps and wiped his mouth with the back of his hand again.

'So you want closure?' he said.

'Something like that,' I said. 'This ends when the verdict comes. Whichever way it goes.'

'Closure's a myth invented by Americans,' Swayne said. 'Even if he gets found guilty and put away for twenty years, you'll still hate him, you know that? Sure, it'll get turned down a few notches, but it won't go away. Ever.'

'I can live with that,' I said.

'Can you?'

44

Back at the office: no calls.

I called Rudy Saks. It went to voicemail. I left a message, said it was very important.

Then . . .

Nothing.

I figured that was all I was going to get by asking politely, following correct procedure. At this stage we couldn't compel anyone to give evidence or make statements on VJ's behalf. We'd have to wait until we got to court. And then we'd need good grounds, not hunches and theories. What else could I do now but write up a (non) progress report, make five copies, file one and cross my fingers.

I called VJ's optometrist. VJ had been issued with a new prescription for contact lenses six months ago. His vision was fine the night of the murder. Bang went our explanation for how he'd mistaken Evelyn for Fabia.

I spent the rest of the afternoon closing out the Rolex dealer list. Sorry, no watch of that sort had turned up. Was I sure about the serial number? Yes, of course they'd let me know if they came across it. Thank you. You're welcome.

At around six Adolf and Iain came trotting back from court together.

Adolf had had herself a good little day, judging from her chirpy tone and how she accidentally smiled at me a few seconds before she realised what she was doing. Iain was all buzzed about being inside a courtroom for the first time. To commemorate the grand occasion he'd bought a documents trolley – a four-wheeler with a telescopic handle, exactly like Adolf's. I was sure she'd helped him pick it out. She was making him in her image.

Jesus.

Time to go.

I started packing up, putting papers back into my case file.

The phone rang.

'Hello, is that Terry Flynt?'

'Speaking.'

'This is Rudy Saks. I got your message.'

I reached out to grab a pen and sent my case file flying off the desk. It spilled crime-scene pictures as it crash-landed on the carpet, not too far from Adolf's zone.

I left it.

'Thanks for getting back to me, Rudy.'

'No problem. What can I do for you?'

He sounded like he had a cold; otherwise, he spoke with the same Americanised foreign accent as Jonas, his housemate.

'I work for the law firm that represents the man accused of murdering Evelyn Bates at the Blenheim-Strand.'

'You're defending him?'

'That's right.'

Silence

. . .

'Are you recording this?' he asked.

Tread carefully.

'No, I'm not.'

Silence

. . .

'Am I allowed to talk to you?'

He's clued up. Play it straight.

'It's perfectly legal – as long as it's voluntary,' I said. 'If you don't want to speak to me, you can hang up. I'd rather you didn't, but that's your right.'

Silence

. . .

I heard my heart thudding, the scratching in my throat as I tried to swallow, the tremor in my breath.

'OK. Let's see how things go,' he said.

'Thank you, Rudy. By the way, I really appreciate you calling,' I said, remembering a key tenet from my telesales training: *Empower the listener – make the mark feel like they're in control.*

'I wanted to ask you a couple of questions about the statement you gave to the police. There's a few things we're not quite clear about.'

'OK.'

'First question. How come you went to the suite?'

That was a Swayne tactic. Softballs to start – obvious answers, get the guard down.

'I was working the night shift for room service. There were three of us on duty. We took it in turns to answer the calls.'

'Were you busy that night?'

'No. We don't get a lot of business weekdays. Maybe one or two calls an hour, mostly for drink.'

'So you answered the phone call from Suite 18?'

'Yes.'

'How did you know who the caller was?'

'We have caller-ID. The rooms are displayed by number, the suites by numbers prefixed with "S" – for "Suite", of course. S18 came up.'

His English was very good. I wasn't going to risk alienating him with a compliment he might deem patronising.

'What did he order?'

'A bottle of Cristal champagne, on ice. Two glasses,' he said.

'Is that a popular choice?'

'Yes and no. Footballers always order Cristal. All the rappers sing about it.'

I laughed.

He did too.

We had rapport.

'What time was this?'

'A quarter to one, in the morning.'

'How did you know that?'

'I entered the order on the computer, so it would get billed to the room. The time was on the computer.'

'Then what happened?'

'I took the bottle and two glasses up. I used the VIP elevator.'

'Did you see anyone in the corridor?' I asked.

'No.'

'Was anyone else in the lift with you?'

'No.'

'What happened after you knocked on the door?'

234

'He – the guest – opened it.'

'How do you know it was him?'

'Who else would it be?' he said.

'What were your initial impressions of him?'

'What do you mean?'

'What did he look like? How did he appear?'

'Tall black guy. Thirtysomething. Seemed fine. Normal.'

'How was he dressed?'

'White shirt, dark-blue trousers.'

'Was he drunk?'

'He didn't look drunk.'

'Please carry on,' I said.

He'd said nothing about the scratches on VJ's face. Maybe he hadn't noticed.

'I carried the tray into the room and that's when I saw the woman – the one who . . . who died.'

'Where was she?'

'On the couch in the middle of the room. She was sitting up, with her legs stretched out. She wasn't wearing any shoes.'

'Can you describe her for me?'

'Yeah. A young blonde, in her twenties. She was wearing a green dress.'

Now my heart started pumping.

Please tell me it was Fabia.

Please tell me it was Fabia.

'What she was like physically – height, weight, that kind of thing?'

'Urm . . . short. I'm around five ten. She was shorter. Five four, five five . . .'

Oh no.

'. . . She was – not fat – not fat at all. But not really in shape, if you know what I'm saying?'

'Plump, then?' I said.

'That's the word. "Plump",' he said.

Evelyn Bates.

'Can you describe the dress a little more for me?'

'Yeah, it was kind of a bright green, like fake grass. It stopped above her knees.'

'What else did you notice about it? Was is long-sleeved or short-sleeved?'

'Long sleeves. And it had straps on the shoulder.'

Definitely Evelyn Bates.

I wanted to hang up now.

'You said she was blonde,' I continued. 'What was her hairstyle like?'

'Her hair was curly, wavy. Medium length.'

'How did she appear to you? Was she happy, sad, scared?'

'She wasn't scared. Not at all. She was definitely drunk – maybe stoned, I don't know. But she was happy drunk, if you know what I mean? Like she was having a good time. She was giggling.

'The guest told me to put the champagne down on the big table near the couch. As I was doing that the woman said hello to me. I said hello back. She asked me what my name was. I told her. Then I asked the guest if he wanted me to open the bottle, and he said leave it. And then the woman said, "You can open *my* bottle any time!" And she started laughing again. The guest thanked me and gave me a tip. Forty pounds. I wished them goodnight and I left. Took the lift back downstairs.'

'What time was this?'

'I don't know. A little after 1 a.m. Say, ten past. No later.'

Saks was a perfect witness. He hadn't just stuck to his statement, but he'd added minor details to it as well, which reinforced what he'd told the police.

'Thanks for your call, Rudy,' I said.

'Is that it?'

'Yes.'

'Thank you, then ... Oh, there is one other thing I remember – about Mr James. You asked me about his appearance, when he opened the door?'

'Yes?'

'He had scratches on his cheek.'

'Thanks, Rudy.'

Thanks for sinking us.

I sent Janet, Christine and Redpath an email about the call.

So what had happened between VJ leaving the club and turning up at the Circle bar with Fabia? And what had happened after they'd left? There was at least an hour unaccounted for, between them leaving the bar and VJ ringing room service for champagne. Had he tried to get Fabia up to his room, but she'd turned him down, and then he'd gone back downstairs and run into Evelyn again?

One thing I'd forgotten to ask Saks was whether VJ had been angry or annoyed at Evelyn Bates for flirting with him. I felt like calling him back, but what difference would it make?

When he'd interviewed me about Rodney James's murder, Detective Quinlan had laid out pictures of the body on the table in front of me. They were taken in the morgue. Twenty-two stab wounds. Half of them had been to his face. The killer had stabbed him in the eyes and mouth –

especially the mouth. Rodney was missing most of his lips, and seemed to be grinning at me in a way I'd never seen him do. Quinlan said the facial wounds had either happened post-mortem, or very near mortem, because Rodney was already on the floor. He reckoned the killer had hacked at the mouth because it was likely Rodney had abused him or her verbally, and they were focusing on the part of him they hated the most. Rodney had never hit VJ. But he'd constantly put him down.

'I've seen this kind of death before,' Quinlan had said. 'It's what people who bottle things up do to people who pop their corks. A moment of madness after a lifetime of self-control. Your friend Vernon's started young. If this isn't dealt with, he'll do it again. Do you want that on your conscience?'

Is that what had happened with Evelyn? She'd pissed VJ off, because she was drunk and giggly; because the Rohypnol he'd slipped her hadn't taken effect fast enough; because she hadn't wanted to screw him?

So he'd strangled her. And . . .

Was Evelyn's death my fault, for lying for VJ?

No.

Don't go there.

That was enough for one day.

I turned off my computer and picked up the case file and crime-scene photos from the carpet.

I packed everything into my bag and headed for the door.

'Terry,' Adolf called behind me.

I turned round.

'Don't forget your knickers.'

'Eh?'

She frisbeed something at me. A photo. It fluttered and flapped and turned crudely a short distance before landing at my feet, face-up.

Evelyn Bates's black thong, photographed against a plain white background.

As I bent down to pick it up I started blushing.

And then I flashed back to that Croydon pub, and the stripper's thong hitting me in the face.

VELCRO!

This was the same kind of thong.

45

The next morning, as I was brushing my teeth, my mobile started playing the theme from *Tales of the Unexpected.*

'Got your email about Rudy Saks,' Janet said. 'Good work.'

'Thanks. Shame about the result.'

'What did you expect?' she asked. Like me she was still at home. 'I never expected us to win this trial. That's not the reason I took this case.'

'Why, then?'

'Sometimes you don't pick a case, it picks you. I had to prove to Sid that we can handle the big numbers.'

'Because you're looking to expand the division? And this is a test. If you pass, Sid gives you the go-ahead,' I said, remembering what she'd told me that day on the Tube.

'That's right,' she said. 'Remember Scott Nagle?'

'Your biggest client.'

'*Our* biggest client,' she corrected me. 'Fifteen years ago – before I started – he got himself into some serious trouble – or rather, got himself into serious trouble *again.*

'One of his properties – a townhouse on Rittenberg Grove – got occupied by squatters. Thanks to our crap tenancy laws, it can take years to get rid of squatters. And even when you do, they've done so much damage to your property its value's dropped through the floor.

'Scott Nagle allegedly took matters into his own hands. All fifteen of the squatters were sent bullets with their names engraved on them. Then two disappeared one day, never to be seen or heard from again. Police arrested Nagle when they matched fingerprints on the bullets to one of his employees. The man claimed Nagle had paid him and another employee to kidnap the squatters and drop them off in the New Forest. He was offered a reduced sentence in exchange for testifying against his boss.

'At the time, KRP – or Kopf-Purdom as we were then – didn't have a criminal division. Sid said there was no money in criminal law, so what was the point? He outsourced the case to my old firm.'

'And you defended Nagle?'

'With Christine Devereaux as the lead barrister,' she said. 'She destroyed the witness on the stand. And she systematically destroyed the case against Nagle, exposing a web of police corruption in the process. Nagle was acquitted.'

'And Sid offered you a job?'

'More than that,' she said. 'He offered me automatic senior partner and my own division within the firm.'

Your own division after a fashion, I thought. Sid's still calling the shots.

'Fast forward to 2006,' she continued. 'Remember the two squatters who disappeared? Their bodies were discovered buried in the New

Forest. They'd been shot in the head, execution-style. The Rittenberg Grove case was reopened and Scott Nagle was charged with conspiracy to commit murder.

'We didn't defend him that time either. I had to outsource the case to another firm. You know why? We simply weren't big enough to handle our biggest client. Which is a shame, because the case against him was so flimsy it never even went to court. The charges were dropped because of insufficient evidence.

'The trouble is, that wasn't the first or last time I've had to turn down major cases because we didn't have the time or resources. I got sick and tired of seeing serious business go across the road to our competition, because for Sid it's all about profit and loss. So last year I gave Sid an ultimatum gift-wrapped as a proposal – expand our division, so we can not only provide our clients with a vertically integrated firm along American lines, but we can also do non-client work – practise *real* criminal law. Or else I'd quit.'

'Were you serious?' I asked.

'Yes. Sid had turned me down twice before, but this time he gave me the go-ahead – on one condition. We had to prove we could take on and deal with a non-client "marquee case".'

Enter Vernon James.

'Ahmad Sihl and I go way back. We were law students together. When Vernon was arrested he called me up for a lawyer recommendation, not representation. I persuaded him to give me the case.'

'I see,' I said. 'So if we win, you expand—'

'This case isn't about winning and losing, Terry. It never was,' she said. 'It was a loser from the off. But in the best possible kind of way for us – it's a *high-profile* loser. It's publicity. It's our name in the papers and on TV and on the internet every day of the trial. It's our showcase, our launch, our coming out as a major player.'

Jesus.

She didn't give a shit about VJ.

She never had.

'Yet, here's the thing,' she continued. 'Though we know it's a loser, we have to look like winners. We have to put up a hell of a fight in court. This can't be a walkover for the prosecution. We go down swinging and look good doing it. That'll put us on the map.'

While VJ gets a life sentence for murder . . .

Twenty-five years *minimum* before he got out.

He may have been guilty, but this all seemed so wrong.

'Unfortunately, as things stand, we don't have much to fight back with. Christine, Liam and I have gone over all the statements and the evidence, and none of us know how to attack this thing. All we've got is the barman, but his testimony is as good as irrelevant because of Rudy Saks. The club CCTV? So what. There's plenty of evidence on the suite's carpet, not to mention the body in the bed.'

'What do you want from me, Janet?' I said.

She missed the spiky weariness in my tone.

'The same as Christine, only different. Forget silver bullets. We need roadblocks and roadbumps, diversions, smokescreens, black ice. Anything and everything to throw Carnavale off course. As long as it doesn't come back on the firm, I don't care how you get it, or what you do.'

I couldn't help myself, I had to say it.

'Without breaking the law, of course?'

She didn't reply. I heard traffic in the background and then the sound of a motorbike getting louder. She was now outside her house waiting on the company courier to take her to the office. I hadn't even got dressed yet.

'Do you know why I became a lawyer, Terry?'

'No.'

'I grew up in Canning Town. It was very poor, very rough and crime was a way of life. My mum and dad ran the local bakery. All my friends were the sons and daughters of career criminals. Every other week one of their dads or brothers or uncles was getting arrested. Most of the time they were guilty, but sometimes they weren't. Yet it was always the same story. Their lawyers were rubbish. Their lawyers failed them. Their lawyers were corrupt. I thought this was outrageous, and I swore when I grew up, I'd do something about it. I'd help them. *My people.* I'd keep them out of prison. I'd fight for their rights. Do you know the closest I get to Canning Town these days? It's whizzing through it on the Tube, going to and from Belmarsh. The first thing to go in this profession are your principles.'

But I didn't have any principles to lose, not really, not the way she meant. The only thing I held sacred was my family. And I'd never sacrifice them for anything – or anyone.

She'd got me all the way wrong.

I didn't want to be a lawyer when I came to KRP. I was a *temp*:

... just 'whizzing through', filling in, a £10 an hour transient worker ...

And when Janet had offered me the job, I hadn't thought of it as a stepping stone, or a way back into the future I'd missed out on nineteen years ago. No, I'd just thought of it as a bit more money and a little more security.

Look at me now:

Janet had just expanded my responsibilities far beyond the case. She'd tasked me with furthering her career, building her empire.

'What if I can't come up with anything else? What if I don't find Fabia?' I asked. 'What if there's nothing I can do?'

'Then I hope your CV's up to date.'

46

VELCRO!

What was that Torena had said when we were up in Suite 18?

I don't know what it is about this place. It always attracts trouble.

I rang him and asked him to send me a list of people who'd stayed at Suite 18 from January through to the day before VJ had become its last guest to date.

Thirteen people had stayed in the suite.

Over half were private individuals, like VJ. The rest were corporate.

At the office I picked up the phone to make my first call. The question I was going to pop was intrusive, indelicate and embarrassing. If I phrased it wrong, people would hang up on me in a reflex.

I ran through my spiel a couple of times, once in my head, once *sotto voce.*

I checked around the office. Adolf was in work mode – both hands at her keyboard, her shoulder cradling the phone. If I kept my voice down, they wouldn't hear.

I called the first number on the list.

It was answered immediately.

A nice, airy, posh woman's voice announced the company name and asked if she could help me.

'I hope so. Can I speak to Joe Finder, please? . . . It's David Stratten. *Detective Inspector* David Stratten, from the Metropolitan Police.'

'Were there strippers in the room?'

That was the question. I asked it twelve times. Got ten 'No's, one 'No way!' and an imperious '*Certainly* not'.

But it wasn't quite a dead end. I went back to the first person I'd called – Joe Finder, a junior analyst at a merchant bank. I hadn't got to speak to him because he was no longer with the company.

He hadn't left, they specified. He'd been fired.

It took a couple of bounced-around internal calls and some polite insistence on my part to track him down.

I got Finder out of bed and talking like he had back to back hang-overs. When he heard I was a cop he sharpened up and started pleading his case before I could get a word in edgeways. He'd used his former company's Amex card to throw a retirement party for a cleaner who'd been with them thirty years. He didn't think his company had been generous enough to their longest-standing employee, so he took matters into his own hands.

He'd booked Suite 18 at the Blenheim-Strand, got the hotel to lay on food and drink for thirty people, as well as paying for the guest of honour to stay on at the hotel an extra night, all expenses paid, no expense spared.

'Were there strippers in the room?' I asked him.

'Yeah. One.'

Her stagename was Breeze.

I called her agency. I dropped the cop act. I said I was interested in booking her for an appearance, but I'd need to meet her first, talk a few things through.

Breeze rang my work number and picked the time and place for our meet 'n' greet.

The Violet Room was a bar modelled on a stripclub – or at least my idea of one.

The decor was deep purple on pitch black, with dashes of bright yellow. There was a shiny brass pole in each of the four corners, heavy velvet drapes covering the walls, and strategically hung and angled mirrors that made the room look wider and deeper. A few touches undid the mannered sleaze, like the bar with its underlit display of spirits bottles, stacked in eight columns, reminiscent of a grand church organ. And the tables, all set with small purple tea candles, floating in bowls sprinkled with violet petals. Ideal for marriage proposals and the infidelities that followed.

The stripclub theme extended to the prices, except here the rip-off was by the glass, not the bottle. The 'Historical Cocktail' range started at £120 for a daiquiri made with pre-Castro vintage Cuban Bacardi; £280 would get you a manhattan prepared from pre-Prohibition bourbon; a White Russian concocted out of Tsarist vodka cost £370. I ordered the cheapest thing on the menu. A Coke at £10.50.

The bar was completely empty.

'Are you Terry?'

Right on time. Six-thirty, on the dot.

242

'I'm Breeze,' she said, holding out her hand.

She'd come straight from work. Her other job, that is – the one she wrote on her mortgage application form. The dark-grey trouser suit she was wearing was pure high street bank or building society, or maybe a department store: smart, but characterless and unshowy, designed to blend in with an overall aesthetic, to reduce a person to a specific function.

With less bright lipstick, she'd present well to the jury. She didn't come over like a stripper. She was normal, ordinary. The men wouldn't be turned on, the women wouldn't get turned off. They'd see someone doing an extra job on the side; someone almost like them.

Good start.

A waiter came over.

She ordered a glass of house champagne.

Sixty-five pounds.

I'd let the silence drag a little too long while I was trying to think of a casual kick-off topic. So I said the first thing that sprang to mind.

'Do you come here often?'

Had I just asked her that?

Yup – a *pick-up* line. And the naffest of the naff.

She smiled.

'Never been here before, actually,' she answered in an accent that was pure Essex outback. 'You?'

'First time too,' I said.

Her eyes moved over me, in stop-start blinks. She was totting me up. My watch, which looked cheaper than it was. My shirt and tie, as cheap as they looked. Suit, ditto.

The waiter came back with her champagne.

She sipped it and savoured it a moment.

'That nice?' I asked. I didn't know good champagne from bad – or champagne from sparkling wine for that matter.

'Why don't you tell me about this booking,' she said.

So much for the prelims. Straight down to business. I was ready for that.

'Before we go into that, can you tell me about your act?'

'My "act"?'

'Your routine. Do you have a set one . . . A speciality?'

She grimaced. 'Like what, ping-pong balls?'

'Pardon?'

She looked at me like I was stupid.

Then the penny dropped. She did *that*?

'Never mind,' she said. 'Probably wrong for your crowd. You're lawyers, right?'

243

'Yeah. They're a bit conservative,' I said. 'Not that they think they are, but—'

She interrupted me.

'Uniforms. I do uniforms.'

She was as good as wearing one now, I thought.

'Maid, policewoman, nun, nurse, traffic warden, teacher, schoolgirl . . .'

Schoolgirl? Did she have kids?

I took out my notebook and turned to a blank page.

'What are you doing?' she asked.

'It's so I don't forget. There are other people involved in the planning. We're going to have to work out roughly when to, erm . . . insert you.'

'*Insert* me?' She giggled.

I blushed, which made her giggle harder.

But she was looking at me suspiciously. I was now sure she worked in a bank. I could picture her refusing loans, repossessing houses, closing down small businesses.

'You were recommended by an acquaintance of mine, who booked you for the Blenheim-Strand,' I said.

'Where that fella killed that girl?'

Did anyone *not* know about VJ?

'Yes . . . Can you talk me through the routine you did that night?'

'Didn't your mate – sorry, "acquaintance", tell you?'

'He was a bit vague,' I said. 'But, you obviously made quite an impression.'

She smiled coyly. Her eyes were cold.

'That night was a bit different,' she said. 'I usually use my own clothes, my costumes. But the fella who was organising it got me to dress up in the hotel uniform. I was a waitress. I went up there with a trolley and a bottle of bubbly. The party was for this old geezer.

'When I got to the suite, it was chaos. They'd moved the furniture around. And there was this chest of drawers or big cabinet in the middle of the room. I got on top of it, blew a whistle – which is what I do to get everybody's attention – and then I did my thing. Do you want me to tell you 'bout that?'

'Do you take off all your clothes?'

'I'm a stripper, ain't I?'

'I meant *all* of them?'

'The full monty, you mean? Yeah I do that. I throw my bra and thong out to the chaps. Souvenirs.'

This was the wrong moment to do this, but there wasn't going to be a right one.

I took out the picture of Evelyn Bates's thong and held it up to her. 'Is this yours?' I asked.

'What's this about?'

'Please look at the picture then I'll tell you,' I said, more firmly.

She took the picture, studied it, frowning.

'It's definitely the make I use,' she said. 'HKs. Hot Kittys. But I don't know if it's mine.'

Now she was plain hostile. Her voice was snappy.

I took the picture back.

'This ain't about a booking at all, is it? Are you even a lawyer?'

'I never said I was. I'm a clerk at the firm. And I *do* have a booking for you. Not in a hotel, though.'

'Where is it?'

'Court. We'd like you to appear as a defence witness.'

Although she knew I'd completely wasted her time and that she wouldn't be getting any more out of me other than that glass of champagne, it hadn't quite sunk in.

'Why didn't you say so before, then?'

'I didn't think you'd come,' I said.

'You're right about that.'

'You could be really important to us. You might be able to help keep an innocent man out of prison. He—'

I didn't get any further. She tossed what was left of her champagne at my face. I'm not sure if she'd meant to get it in my mouth, but that's where most of it went.

It was a hell of a way to fall off the wagon.

'Fuckin' timewaster!' she shouted.

I gagged and spat the booze out. It landed on my shirt and tie and trousers.

She flounced out of the bar, stomping across the floor, flinging open the door.

Well, I'd blown that.

Big time.

No witness. My word against hers. Why hadn't I thought to record the conversation?

I looked at the glass. A single drop of champagne was making its way slowly to the bottom.

Then I had an idea.

47

Tuesday, April 26th
Plea and Case Management Hearing

The Central Criminal Court – better known as the Old Bailey, after the street on which it stands – is the most famous court in the world.

It's housed in a pair of crudely conjoined buildings; a domed neo-baroque structure originally opened in 1907, and its modern extension, an armoured barn built of stone slabs and bulletproof glass called the South Block.

Yet, despite the building taking up half the road it's on, a novice could easily walk past it and be none the wiser. It's almost self-effacing, barely noticeable in the long shadow of St Paul's Cathedral, half a mile away, and partly swallowed in the quiet grey tones of its surroundings.

What fixes the Old Bailey in the memory, what makes it instantly recognisable, even to someone who's never been there, is the statue that stands on top of its cupola. Twelve foot tall, twenty-five tons in weight, and painted gold, the statue of Lady Justice, brandishing a broadsword in her right hand and a pair of scales in the other, dominates the building, reducing it to a functional, if anonymous, plinth.

There are three ways into the court, depending on what you do and what you've done.

The legals, police, witnesses and bailed defendants go through the main entrance on the South Block.

The spectators – the general public, including families and friends of the defendants and victims – are admitted to the viewing galleries via a separate entrance, a few yards away. It's strictly first come first served; the higher-profile the trial, the longer the queue.

The third entryway is for the defendants on remand. The prison vans bring them in through a secure gateway off a side road, and then on to the holding cells, located below ground, where they'll be kept until they're called to go before the judge.

It was there that we met VJ.

He was shown into the meeting room by a squat and scowling female warden.

He had his file with him, and was dressed in a no-brand dark-blue suit and cheap tie. His face was gaunt and his eyes were bloodshot and puffy.

The room was the size of a large cupboard and smelled of stale cigarettes and nervous sweat. Dust pocketed densely in the corners and the white walls were cracked and chipped, but graffiti-free. Christine and Redpath sat opposite, on bolted chairs, at a bolted table with a bolted ashtray in the middle.

'How are you?' Christine asked him.

'I feel like I'm going to meet my maker,' he said.

'It won't be that bad today.'

'Great,' he muttered.

She ignored his sarcasm. 'You don't have to impress anyone. There'll be no jury here. They don't get sworn in until the trial starts. The PCMH is really an admin meeting in fancy dress,' she said.

She and Redpath were in their court clothes, a uniform unchanged since the eighteenth century – long black robes with billowing sleeves, wing collars and bands, and white horsehair wigs. They weren't allowed to wear the wigs outside court, so they'd put them on the table like cowboys resting their stetsons on the bar of a rotgut saloon.

'What'll happen today is this: the charges will be read out and you'll be asked to enter your plea. As it's "not guilty", the prosecution will outline their case and present all the material they intend to use – the witnesses they'll call, as well as the physical and documentary evidence.'

'Right,' he said.

'Once that's out of the way, the judge will ask the prosecution to estimate how long the trial will last. I'm thinking two weeks. It really shouldn't take any longer than that. The judge then sets the trial date, and that's it.'

VJ nodded grimly.

'Do you have any questions?'

He shook his head. He was scared. I'd only ever seen him like this once before, when he'd come round our house after Quinlan had first interviewed him. Now, he was in an alien environment he couldn't control, and facing an outcome he couldn't predict or influence. Above all, he was having to trust and rely on people who were virtually strangers. Including me.

For an instant I remembered my old friend again, everything that had been good about him. I wanted to say something reassuring to that person, let him know I'd be there for him. But I couldn't, in every sense.

'The judge is Adam Blumenfeld,' she said. 'The phrase "tough but fair" could've been coined for him. He runs a tight ship. He doesn't put up with any nonsense. The media like him because he hands out the stiffest possible sentences. And he's never been successfully appealed against.'

'Wish I'd stayed in bed,' VJ quipped.

247

No one laughed or cracked a smile. He might as well have said he wished he hadn't killed Evelyn.

We were in Court 1, where all the high-profile murder cases are tried.

Situated in the baroque building, the courtroom is among the oldest in the Bailey, and far and away its most notorious. Many a criminal career has ended there. The Yorkshire Ripper, Dennis Nilsen, Ian Huntley, the Kray Twins, Ruth Ellis, Lord Haw-Haw, Dr Crippen all got their comeuppance in its dock, as have hundreds more. Acquittals are rare, life sentences common.

In keeping with its legend and reputation, the courtroom radiates an arcane malevolence. Its bright whitewashed walls and thick dark oak panelling and furniture have all the austerity of postwar classrooms ruled by cane-wielding teachers, or fundamentalist chapels presided over by demented preachers.

The legals sit at long tables in the middle of the court, facing the jury bench, which will remain empty until the trial kicks off. To the left is the dock, raised several feet above the floor and shielded by a high wall of bulletproof glass. The judge's podium is directly opposite, and elevated to the same level, so that judge and defendant are eye to eye. The podium is lined with high panelling and dominated by a sculpture of a portico. Suspended from a bracket in the middle of the portico is a long sword in a gold-and-black scabbard, its tip touching the royal crest embedded at the heart of the sculpture. The sword, identical in shape and length to the one brandished by Lady Justice, is reminiscent of a church crucifix, albeit inverted. Some might say this is deliberate, because all evil is summoned here.

The public gallery, which overlooked and slightly overhung the well of the court, was predictably packed. But there was no sign of Melissa. I was glad about that.

The prosecution team sat at the table in front of us. Carnavale, his junior barrister – a thirtysomething woman with short straight blonde hair – and their clerk, a young man in a pinstriped suit.

Although she was using a thick cane to get around, as well as sit and stand, Christine was in the best shape I'd seen her yet. It was her first time in court in over a year, and being here had given her a boost. She was alert and comparatively robust, her illness sidelined.

Carnavale handed us each two lists of evidence – the one he intended to present to the judge and use in the trial, and the other consisting of material he'd discarded.

He talked to Christine. All dulcet tones and purring concern. He was *so* delighted to see her again, he said, and commented on how well she looked, before asking after her husband and family.

The prosecutor was groomed like a lawn. Even his wig looked good and absolutely right on him, as if he'd been born to wear it.

We were about to start. The court clerk – a tall black woman with a bygone curly-perm – was on the phone, managing to talk without making a single sound, as if miming.

Carnavale went back to his seat.

'All rise,' the court clerk said.

We stood as Judge Blumenfeld entered from the side of the podium. Draped in silk violet robes and a black sash, he was a lanky, gangling man with swarthy skin and medium-length grey sideburns that stole out from under his wig.

He reached his chair in four strides and took his place. He appraised us all with a fast sweep of the eyes over his lowered glasses. His face was stern, but not unpleasant; a tyrant with a line in good jokes.

Carnavale stood over a small lectern at his table, and did the preliminaries for the record.

'My name is Franco Carnavale, and I am appearing in this matter on behalf of the Crown,' he said to the judge. 'Also appearing on behalf of the Crown is Lisa Perez, acting as junior counsel. Appearing on behalf of the defence are my learned friends Christine Devereaux and Liam Redpath.'

It was tradition to refer to a fellow barrister as 'my learned friend'. Like the uniform, this was another custom from a bygone age, when the legal profession had been a small club where everyone knew each other.

'Are you ready to proceed, Mr Carnavale?' the judge asked, in a mellifluous voice that carried a hint of thunder about it.

'I am, My Lord.'

'Please bring in the defendant.'

Carnavale sat down. The court clerk got on the phone.

Moments later the door at the end of the dock opened, to a rattle of keys on a heavy ring. We all turned to watch VJ being brought in-between two barrel-shaped security guards. I heard the spectators in the gallery, the wood creaking under the shift of bodies as they leaned in and turned and half-rose to get a view. I glanced up at them.

And I saw her.

Melissa.

She was sitting right at the front, in the near right-hand corner, ideally positioned to see her husband entering and leaving the dock. Her expression was pure deadpan, but her eyes never left him.

The three of us hadn't been in the same room together in twenty

249

years. In our first term we'd all gone out for pizza and then to the Arts Cinema to catch a late show. The film? *Presumed Innocent.*

VJ stood in the dock and faced the judge.

The court clerk read out the charges and asked him to state his plea.

'Not guilty,' he said.

'Please be seated.'

Carnavale went back to the lectern.

'My Lord, it is the Crown's case that the defendant, Vernon James, murdered the victim, Evelyn Bates, between the hours of midnight and two o'clock on the morning of March 17th. The evidence we wish to submit in support of this charge is as follows . . .'

He went through the witnesses he intended to call, giving their names and occupations, and briefly explaining their relevance. Nightclub staff, Gary Murphy, Rudy Saks, the hotel receptionist, DCI Reid, DS Fordham, and a forensics expert. The judge followed the list with his pen, as did Christine and Redpath.

There were two surprises – none of the hen party attendees had been called, but Nikki Frater, VJ's PA, was listed. She'd given the prosecution a statement about disposing of VJ's clothes. Nothing incriminating, but borderline ambiguous.

'Next, the physical evidence.'

Carnavale read out the items – the note Evelyn had left Penny Halliwell saying she was at a private party in Suite 18; her green dress, thong, mobile phone; VJ's trousers, jacket and shirt. Each was prefixed by 'Exhibit' and assigned a consecutive number.

He concluded by submitting DVDs of VJ's police interviews, and the nightclub CCTV. Then he sat down, indicating he'd finished.

'Mrs Devereaux?' the judge said.

Christine stood up slowly, using her cane handle for support.

'You can sit, if you prefer, Mrs Devereaux?'

'Thank you, My Lord, but I'd rather be on my feet.'

'As you wish,' he said.

'My Lord, we accept all of the Crown's submissions, bar one item in the physical evidence. We request that Exhibit 3 be removed.'

The judge and Carnavale both consulted their lists. Carnavale turned to Christine, puzzled and amused.

'Exhibit 3 is an item of clothing belonging to the victim. Namely her underwear,' the judge said.

'Yes it is, My Lord.'

'And you'd like it . . . *removed?*'

'From the *list*, My Lord.'

The judge smiled. 'On what grounds, Mrs Devereaux?'

'We do not accept that Exhibit 3 belonged to the victim. And we believe it to be irrelevant to the case, and therefore inadmissible as evidence against the defendant.'

Carnavale looked at her like she'd gone mad.

Christine cleared her throat and shifted a little at the lectern.

'The item in question – a thong with a detachable Velcro clasp on its waistband – is one commonly worn by strippers. It's designed to be removed in haste. Whipped off, if you will, My Lord – thus.' She illustrated what she meant by pinching at the air near her waist and flinging her arm out. She accompanied the motion with a sideways bump of her hip, which made the judge grin, and earned her a ripple of laughter from the public and press.

'Fascinating,' the judge said, still smiling. 'What proof do you have, Mrs Devereaux?'

'The defendant told us he first saw the garment in the living room of the hotel suite. It was on the floor, close to a skirting board. As you will be aware, a large item of furniture – a minibar – had been displaced. Its usual position was between a sideboard and a chest of drawers. The minibar had previously covered this space up.'

'And that's where he says he first saw the ... Exhibit?' the judge asked.

'Yes, My Lord,' she said.

The judge made notes. Christine continued.

'We have spoken to a previous guest at the same suite. His name is Joe Finder. He used the room on March 11th of this year for the purposes of a private party, which at least twenty people attended – including a stripper, whom he hired. The stripper danced on the same minibar. Mr Finder said that he and two of his guests had moved it out to the middle of the room to serve as a stage. The stripper removed all of her clothes, including her thong, which she threw into the crowd. Mr Finder has given us a sworn statement to that effect, which I would like to share with both you and my learned friend.'

Christine handed Carnavale and the judge's clerk copies of the statement Finder had given to Janet the previous morning. Carnavale took it and read it, his face slowly reddening.

Christine let the judge finish with the statement before resuming.

'We have spoken to the stripper. She recognised Exhibit 3 from a police photograph. She stated that it was the same make as the thongs she habitually uses in her routine.'

Christine stopped there, turned to me and nodded. That was the signal.

I handed her what she asked for.

'My Lord, we have here a DNA sample, which we believe will match that found on Exhibit 3.'

She held up a sealed evidence bag containing the champagne glass I'd swiped from the Violet Room, after my encounter with Breeze. As she'd stormed out before I could get round to asking her to give us a statement, I'd grabbed at the only straw going.

Christine was on very thin ice here. You needed legal consent to take a person's DNA. Breeze hadn't given it to me. Christine was gambling that the judge wouldn't ask as to the legality of the sample, as long as she didn't request the glass to be entered into evidence. This was really about calling Carnavale's bluff and planting a warning flag in the judge's mind.

So far it seemed to be working. Carnavale was glowering at his junior barrister and especially at his clerk. They obviously hadn't thought to check Suite 18's previous guests.

'I would like to ask if my learned friend can confirm that Exhibit 3 was tested for the victim's DNA as well as the defendant's. And, if this was done, was the victim's DNA found on the exhibit?' Christine said and sat down.

'Mr Carnavale?'

'The Crown was not informed of this development until now, My Lord.'

'What "development"?' the judge asked.

'We were unaware that the defence had approached previous guests at the hotel suite, My Lord.'

'You mean you were unaware that the defence had done its job?' the judge said.

Redpath smiled. So did I. Christine was po-faced.

Carnavale blinked. He had no comeback.

'Mr Carnavale, can you confirm to me that Exhibit 3 was tested for the victim's DNA?'

'One moment, please, My Lord.'

Carnavale asked his junior for a file, which he looked through as they conferred in sharp whispers. I couldn't make out what they were saying but I thought of two snakes spitting venom at each other over a hotplate.

'My Lord, that doesn't appear to be the case.'

'You mean to say that you wanted to enter into evidence an item of clothing you weren't actually certain belonged to the victim?'

'No, My Lord, that was not my intention. That would imply I was seeking to deceive the court, which I would never do.'

'I should sincerely hope not, Mr Carnavale,' the judge said. 'Yet in your submissions here, you clearly state Exhibit 3 as belonging to the victim. Can you explain to me why DNA testing on this item was selective?'

'I have no explanation for that, My Lord. I'd have to ask the lab. I personally submitted the Exhibit in good faith, assuming DNA testing had been carried out with the same thoroughness it was on the other items presented into evidence.'

'You assumed wrong, Mr Carnavale,' the judge said. 'How long will it take to get the exhibit retested?'

'At a guess, between six to eight weeks, My Lord.'

Judge Blumenfeld scribbled a few notes.

'Are you otherwise ready to go to trial?'

'Yes, My Lord.'

He made more notes.

'On what grounds did you include Exhibit 3 into evidence?'

'The item was found in the wastepaper basket of Suite 18. There was a quantity of semen on the item, which DNA tests showed was the defendant's. It is the Crown's contention that the defendant masturbated into the victim's underwear either prior to or after murdering her.'

There was silence in the courtroom. I thought of Melissa, who was possibly hearing about this for the first time.

'Where was the wastepaper basket located?'

'In the living room.'

'And the body was found in the bedroom?'

'Yes, My Lord. But the victim was murdered in the living room.'

'And where were the victim's other clothes?'

'In the bedroom.'

'But not her underwear?'

'No, My Lord.'

'In other words, Exhibit 3 was found in a separate part of the suite?'

'Yes.'

'Were there traces of semen on any of the victim's other clothes?'

'No, My Lord.'

'Why did you assume Exhibit 3 belonged to the victim?'

Carnavale hesitated, looked down at the file on his lectern.

'It was the only item of female underwear found at the scene. That's Presumption of Fact, My Lord. Archbold 10.1.'

He was referring to the lawyer's bible – *Archbold: Criminal Pleading, Evidence and Practice* – an elephantine tome covering every aspect of criminal law and the cases that shaped it.

'Did the police, to your knowledge, investigate or speak to previous guests at Suite 18?'

'No, My Lord.'

'Please sit down.'

The judge made a few more notes.

'I will have to rule on this,' he said. 'Let's have a twenty-minute break. Could you please return at 11.45?'

He stood up.

'All rise!'

We got up and watched him leave.

VJ was led away from the dock.

Carnavale walked out of court, thumbs under the collar of his gown, followed by his team.

'How do you think it'll go?' Redpath asked Christine.

'Hard to say. The judge won't want to delay the trial by two months, that's for sure,' she said.

Carnavale returned fifteen minutes later with Lisa Perez in tow. He didn't look at us, just went straight back to his seat. His clerk wasn't there. Probably been fired.

I sneaked a look up at the gallery. Melissa wasn't there.

'All rise!'

Judge Blumenfeld took his seat. VJ was led back into the dock.

'In the matter of allowing Exhibit 3 into evidence,' the judge began, looking briefly at Carnavale and then at Christine, before pushing up his glasses and reading out his ruling.

'It is the prosecution's duty to prove its case beyond reasonable doubt. This extends to all evidence submitted in support of that case. That evidence must always be credible. And in a case such as this, where serious charges have been brought, there can be no margin of error.

'The Crown has submitted into evidence an undergarment believed to have been worn by the victim at the time of her murder. This was recovered from a wastepaper basket in the living room of Suite 18 of the Blenheim-Strand hotel, and marked "Exhibit 3". The Crown confirmed that the item was tested only for DNA of the defendant, not that of the victim.

'The defence contends that Exhibit 3 does not in fact belong to the victim, but to another party, who was a guest in the same room on the weekend prior to the events of March 17th, 2011. To support its argument, the defence has provided a sworn statement from the guest – named Joe Finder – who rented the room.

'Mr Finder confirmed that the room was used to host a party, and that he hired a stripper as part of the evening's entertainment. As part of her routine the stripper threw her underwear – a detachable thong, similar to Exhibit 3 – at her audience.

'The defence asserts that the owner of Exhibit 3 is not the victim, but likely to be the stripper. The defence contends that Exhibit 3 was found by the accused on or around the early morning of March 17th after the hotel minibar had been moved from its normal place. The defence contends that Exhibit 3 is likely to have been behind or under the minibar before the accused first entered the suite.

'Having read Mr Finder's statement and taken into account the prosecution's confirmation that Exhibit 3 was not tested for the victim's DNA, I am inclined to conclude that there is a higher probability that the item marked *Exhibit 3" did not belong to the victim.

'On this occasion, the prosecution has not been able to provide any proof, nor a satisfactory argument that the item was ever worn by the victim. I therefore rule Exhibit 3 inadmissible as evidence in this trial.'

He banged his gavel.

Redpath clenched his fist in triumph. Christine gave me a respectful nod.

Carnavale took the blow with his eyes wide open.

The courtroom was otherwise silent. A little piece of the earth had shattered and no one else had heard it.

'That's what's known as a "technicality",' Christine said to VJ, back in the meeting room. 'It was a significant bit of evidence against you. Now it's gone.'

VJ was a little perkier than he'd been earlier, but he was still going back to prison. This triumph had been ours alone.

'We got lucky today,' Christine continued. 'Franco was complacent, thought he had it in the bag. That won't happen with him again, trust me. He's at his worst after a setback.'

VJ didn't know the part I'd played. I'd asked Christine to keep that quiet, saying it was best if he saw us as a team instead of individual components. He'd feel more secure that way. But, really, I didn't want him thinking I was anything more than a powerless underling. That way, if something went wrong, he wouldn't be able to blame me and our past history.

'Where does this leave us?' VJ asked.

'In a better place than we were a couple of hours ago. The judge ruled the evidence inadmissible. This means it can't be brought up in trial. The jury will never know that you masturbated into the thong. And that's a big deal, because if they *had* heard about it, they wouldn't have forgotten it. That would have set them against you.'

'Can the prosecution bring it up at all?'

'He may try, but I'll object, and the judge will support me,' she said. 'Remember, the order of things. The police brought the charges, and the

255

prosecutor is trying you based on their evidence. You didn't say anything about masturbating in your statements to the police, so he can't ask you about something you never said. Secondly, the judge has ruled Exhibit 3 inadmissible. Which means that legally, it didn't happen.'

'Can't the prosecutor ask me what I did after I got beaten up in the suite?'

'Yes, he can. And I will object to the question. The judge will know what Franco's doing and warn him off. If he persists, he'll be held in contempt.'

'So I don't have to answer?'

'No,' she said. 'The judge may ask you to answer according to what you told the police. In which case you say you lay down and passed out.'

'Isn't that perjury?'

'No. It's the law. The judge has set the boundaries and you'll be sticking to them.'

VJ nodded.

The judge had set the trial date for Monday, July 25th. We had three months.

'What about Nikki Frater, the PA?' Christine asked. 'Is she going to cause us any problems?'

'No. She's a rock. She's been with me from the start. She followed me over from my last job.'

'Probably Franco playing mindgames with us, then.'

We fell quiet for a moment. Outside, in the corridor, we heard the shuffle of feet and the voices of barristers and their clients, the locking and unlocking of cell doors. Just another prison.

'The Royal Wedding's on Friday,' VJ said. 'You know they're giving us an extra hour in bed and a choc ice, as a special treat? I can't believe I'm saying this, but I'm actually looking forward to it.'

'I remember when Prince William's parents got married,' Redpath said.

'Me too,' VJ said, and he glanced at me for a split second.

We'd spent that day together, my family and his – apart from Rodney – round my house, watching the telly. The Jameses didn't have one.

July 29th, 1981. Charles and Di.

That was the day I had my first ever drink. Yes, my parents had been giving me a nip of what they were having every now and then, but I had my first full, proper glass then. Me and VJ helped ourselves to a can of my dad's Guinness. VJ hated it on first sip and didn't want any more. I thought it was pretty good, like sweet black coffee. I polished it off. We were eight years old.

48

I'd barely had time to sit down at my desk when the phone rang. It was Edwina, summoning me upstairs.

Sid Kopf was putting something back in his filing cabinet when I walked in. On the wall directly above him, the muted flatscreen TV was showing what the Bank Holiday weather had in store for London. Cloudy, with a chance of sun.

I hadn't quite noticed how big Kopf's office was. It seemed to stretch the length of the building, as if three rooms had been knocked into one. At the far end, I spied a running machine.

'Take a seat,' Kopf said without looking at me.

I went to the same chair I'd sat in before, opposite his desk. For a moment I had my back to him.

I knew he was observing me. I could feel it. I'd developed a sense for being watched when I was at the Lister. The wardens used to monitor us surreptitiously, from a distance, looking out for signs of regression. Their eyes were like tiny, fleet-legged insects, scarpering across my skin before I could catch them. That's what I felt now. Except this was a bigger insect, and it didn't need to run.

I gazed at the black-and-white pictures on the wall, noticing how they'd all been taken in the late afternoon, as the sun was starting to set and the shadows were longer and thicker, obscuring at the least a third of every image in darkness. Did he just like the look, or was there some symbolic intent here?

Kopf came and sat down behind his desk. He was in shirtsleeves and a waistcoat.

'Nicely done today,' he said.

'Thanks, but it was all Christine. I just—'

He cut me off with a wave of the palm.

'Spare me the shopfront modesty. Good days are rare in this racket – and you always pay for them in kind. A day in the sun, a month in the rain. It all evens out.'

He sat back and stared at me for a few seconds. The whites of his eyes matched his hair. Through the door I heard Edwina's phone ring twice before she answered it.

'The reason I wanted to see you is that I have some concerns about your methods.'

'My "methods"?'

'There's a fine line between ambition and recklessness, and you've got both feet planted on it. Only luck has stopped you going over so far,' he said. 'In the few weeks you've been on this case, you've obtained a DNA sample illegally, trespassed on an active crime scene, and impersonated a police officer – "Detective David Stratten".'

The shock on my face made him smile.

Fucking Adolf!

She'd grassed me up.

And so had Andy Swayne.

I don't know which I was least surprised and more pissed off about.

'I set the bar very high here for a reason,' Kopf said. 'It's the only way I know how to get the best out of people. Pressure. Some you squeeze, they fold. Others flourish. The law's a tough game. Not everyone's invited, and not anyone can play.'

Was I getting *fired*?

He leaned forward and crossed his forearms on the desk.

'Janet was right to hire you. She said you were a natural, and you are. You're bright, sharp, tenacious, persistent, analytical, inquisitive, argumentative – when you need to be. Core qualities in a lawyer.'

His tone was pleasant and conversational, no clouds on the horizon. He could have been asking what my bank holiday plans were, if we were going to watch the Wedding at home or on the street.

'*But* – and consider this a *very* friendly warning, but a warning nonetheless – a lawyer who breaks the law is no longer a lawyer, Terry. He's a fraud. An impostor. And an idiot. In short, he's not the kind of person I want here. Lawyers never get their hands dirty. That's why we have investigators. Do you understand?'

Still no harshness to his tone.

'Yes.'

He studied me for a moment, made sure I wasn't just telling him what he wanted to hear.

'I understand,' I said.

I did.

And I didn't.

I was confused all over the place.

Andy Swayne had not only conned me into going into Suite 18, then told Kopf all about it, but he'd also tried to keep me in line, tell me my place. *Fetch and carry* ... Don't get above your station.

Then both Janet *and* Christine had implied that I was to get them results by any means necessary.

And now Kopf was calling me out on my methods.

Who was the true master here?

'In the meantime' – Kopf opened a drawer and took out a white envelope, which he pushed across the desk at me – 'that's for you.'

From the heft and outline of the contents against my fingers, I knew it was cash – a wad of twenties. It must have been a grand, at least.

'Enjoy your day in the sun, Terry. You've earned it.'

49

I fell asleep during the Royal Wedding, missed the whole show. After breakfast we'd all sat down together to watch it. Aerial views of Westminster Abbey and the masses of people carpeting the pavements all the way up to Buckingham Palace filled the screen. I closed my eyes and promptly conked out.

I couldn't help it. The week had caught up with me. I'd finally come down from the high of the court triumph and crashed.

I opened my eyes a few hours later, just in time to see Prince William driving his new bride out of the gates of Buckingham Palace in an open-top Aston Martin and speeding up the Mall. That was the coolest thing the Royal Family had done since they got rid of Oliver Cromwell.

The kids laughed at me, still dazed, yawning and rubbing my eyes, my hair all porcupined. They said I snored so loudly through the vows, they had to turn the volume up.

We went to the public street party in Battersea High Street. It was Karen's idea. She wanted to give the kids a memory to go by, and spend a little time together as a family.

Half of Battersea had thought the same way. The street was full to capacity. Long tables and benches had been laid out in the middle of the road, and every seat taken. People were doubling up, sitting on each other. The pavements were overspilling with human traffic, proceeding slowly in either direction.

There was music in the air. A red double decker bus was parked at the top of the road and Capital Radio was broadcasting live from inside. On a big stage down the opposite end of the road, an eight-piece Cuban band was playing wild salsa. Cooked food was on sale at stalls – Jamaican, Thai, Chinese and Indian. And in-between the tables were tents hosting samba and rumba classes.

Ray and I got ourselves some rice and peas and curry goat from the Jamaican stall and ate as we watched Karen and Amy getting samba lessons. Amy was taking to the dance well, finding her steps and rhythm. She was graceful and briefly no longer a child. Like me, Karen wasn't one of life's natural dancers, and quietly gave up to watch our daughter from a corner.

A woman in a Union Jack T-shirt and leggings stepped into the tent. She had a riot of brown and blonde-tinged curls. She knew all the moves and was showing the others how it was done. One of the instructors stepped up behind her and they started dancing together, moving their hips in time, the man looking over his shoulder at his colleague and winking.

And just like that, I started thinking about Fabia.

If only we could find her – *I* could find her. Someone other than VJ *had* to have seen her at the dinner. But no one had come forward, no one had called me back – not the Hoffmann Trustees, not even the Silver Service temps. I was going to have to step up my game.

Ray nudged me in the ribs.

I snapped out of it. I'd been gawping at the woman in the tent, without seeing her, chasing my thoughts.

'It's not what you think, son,' I said.

Ray frowned and made that cauliflower pattern with his brow.

'What do I think?'

'That I fancy her or something,' I said, nodding at the woman, who was now sandwiched between two instructors and dancing with her hands in the air.

Ray looked at her and then back at me, quizzical and confused.

'Wasn't what I was thinking,' he said. 'I've been talking to you for the last five minutes.'

'Oh . . .' I said. I hadn't heard him. 'What did you say?'

'Doesn't matter,' he said, sadly.

There was a large manila envelope waiting for me on the doormat, when we got back. Another Swayne delivery. He obviously hadn't taken the day off.

It was a single sheet of paper with a black-and-white photograph run off on a printer whose ink was starting to run low. It showed a young woman in semi-profile, from the torso up, dressed in a beret and a white T-shirt, holding an automatic pistol in a double-handed grip.

I phoned Swayne.

'What's this?' I asked.

'A recruitment poster for the Rhodesian police.'

'So?'

'That's Beverley Wingrove.'

'Is it?'

I looked again. The woman's face hadn't come out particularly well because of the poor resolution and poorer print quality. It could've been anyone. So I had to take his word for it.

'The very same,' he said. 'I've dug up some interesting stuff on her.'
'Like what?'
'Not on the phone,' he said.
'Are you being bugged?' I asked, sarcastically.
'My battery's running low,' he said.
'Where are you now?'
'Looking at Michael Caine Towers.'

Swayne meant the Belvedere tower in Chelsea Harbour. A high-rise block with a brass-coloured roof shaped like a witch's hat. Michael Caine was said to live – or have lived – in the penthouse, hence its nickname. It was the centrepiece of an upscale apartment complex, with appended marina, where all manner of flashy boats were docked. A whole other world.

Swayne should have been waiting for me on the opposite side of the river, on Battersea Embankment, but he wasn't. As I approached, I saw him standing outside a nearby block of flats called Archer House. He was talking to a black woman. She was about his age, with short grey hair, round glasses and a pair of long white earrings.

They were standing too close together to be strangers. I stopped to observe them. Swayne was smiling, laughing. And when he wasn't, he was looking at the woman affectionately – and she at him. He was a completely different man, one briefly freed from the weight of all the bitterness and poison he carried on his back like a life-support system.

A moment later he left the woman, kissing her on the cheek, before he crossed the road and made for the embankment. She watched him go and then turned and walked through the gate into the building.

I gave it two minutes before I went to meet him.

He'd found himself a bench, taken off his jacket and undone two buttons on his shirt. He was gazing across the river at the Belvedere. On the grass verge behind him, a family of five was having a picnic.

'I remember when that didn't exist,' Swayne said, pointing to the tower. I was now used to the absence of any kind of greeting – formal or familiar – from him when we met. 'It used to be nothing but rubble, weeds, squatters and scummy water.'

'You lived around here?'

'Just across the road.' He hitched his thumb over his shoulder. 'We used to come here all the time.'

'"We" . . .?'

'My wife and daughter. Well . . . my *ex*-wife and daughter.'

I hadn't picked him as the sentimental sort. Too disappointed in humanity. Yet here he was, literally back on memory lane.

'My wife is from Zimbabwe,' he said.

'Not Rhodesia?'

'Definitely not. She's black.'

So, that's who the woman was. I was surprised at how affectionate they still were towards each other. I wouldn't have thought Swayne the type to have amicable break-ups – quite the opposite.

It also explained his interest in Beverley Wingrove.

'What about your daughter?' I asked.

'We don't talk,' he said. 'Kids grow up, that's the trouble. They start out looking up to you, then they look through you, then they look down on you.'

'When was the last time you saw her?'

'Ten, twelve years ago. Can't quite remember. Bright girl. Pretty too, full of life. Nothing like me. Thank God.'

I thought of Ray and how I'd upset him. And I remembered making Amy cry at the dinner table. All because my head was elsewhere, on the case, on VJ – on things that would soon pass. The idea of losing them, of someday telling a near-stranger a story similar to Swayne's, made me shudder.

'I'm sorry to hear that,' I said.

'But you're not surprised?'

'That you were an arsehole? No.'

Swayne laughed.

There was a smell of seawater in the air. The tide was low. The river had retreated over the bank, exposing drying green-brown sludge and dumped bricks and masonry, plus acres of rubbish, much of it bottles and cans.

'Tell me about Beverley Wingrove.'

'I recognised her name from years back,' he said. 'She wasn't in the Rhodesian police, just modelled for the propaganda. But her husband – Oliver – was in the force. He was a captain in PATU – the Police Anti-Terrorist Unit.

'In Rhodesia, as in South Africa, a "terrorist" was anyone black who'd taken up arms against the regime. PATU basically hunted them down and killed them where they found them. No mercy,' he said.

He looked off into the distance, his expression grim.

'I take it you were out there?' I said.

'I was, yeah,' he said. 'Forget what you think you know about Rhodesia, what liberal-peddled lies you've swallowed as truth. There was no right and wrong in that conflict, no good guys and bad guys. They were both right, and every bit as bad as each other. Just look at what's happened there since. Who's worse? Mugabe or Ian Smith?'

'What were you doing?'

'I've led what boring people call an "interesting and colourful life",' he said.

I knew he wasn't going to cough up any more details.

'And what's this got to do with Vernon James?'

'When Rhodesia turned into Zimbabwe, the Wingroves moved to South Africa, and then they came here in 1984. Oliver got a job at the South African Embassy. Security. His wife went into catering. When apartheid ended and Mandela was elected, there was a change of staff at the Embassy. The Wingroves stayed in London,' he said. 'Now, do you know what I mean by the Truth and Reconciliation Commission?'

'Yes. It was a public inquest into the apartheid regime, that happened during Mandela's presidency.'

'It wasn't all public. Some hearings were done in secret. The sensitive stuff. Don't forget that South Africa was a front in the Cold War. The CIA were out there. So were MI5, Mossad, you name it. Then there were the Commies on the other side. Russians and Cubans.

'A few of the former South African secret police bigwigs agreed to testify in exchange for immunity. They had a hell of a story to tell.

'One of them turned over these classified lists and files to the Commission. Dossiers on the old regime's opponents. All anti-apartheid activists. Nothing out of the ordinary there. All governments keep files on people they don't like. But these weren't South African activists. They were Europeans and Americans. And they were all dead.

'Someone high up in the old regime had authorised a death squad to take out their opposition abroad. Not the high-profile set, the public faces, the celebrity mouthpieces, but the people behind them. The wealthy backers, the accountants, the lawyers, the journalists. The death squad was called *Die Blanke Spoke* – 'The White Ghosts'.

'The Ghosts had a simple mandate. Search and destroy. But it could never look like murder. Too obvious.

'The Commission's supergrass spilled the names of the White Ghosts. One of them was Oliver Wingrove.'

'Did he get extradited?'

'No. Our government said there wasn't enough proof.'

There was a row of houseboats in front of us, all beached now that the tide had gone out. On one, the bow had been transformed into a mini-garden, complete with a bench.

'What's this got to do with Vernon James?' I repeated.

'Fuck all, probably,' he said. 'Oliver Wingrove died of cancer in 2001.'

'So why d'you bring me out here?'

'It's a theory you could use.'

'A *theory*?' I said, tetchily. 'As in: Vernon James was set up by a bunch of – what? – *apartheid-era assassins*, who may or may not have even existed. And they used the Silver Service Agency as a front to infiltrate the hotel? Is that what you're saying?'

He didn't reply, or look at me.

'You're *billing* me for this bollocks, aren't you?'

'Something isn't right about Silver Service.'

'Really? You know I checked them out, right?' I said. 'They're totally legit. They're a limited listed company. They've being going sixteen years. They supply practically every four- and five-star hotel in London with staff. They've got a solid reputation. Just because the owner said something to you that provoked a guilt trip about your fucked-up marriage doesn't mean she was involved in this. And these White Ghosts of yours? They'd be in their fifties and sixties now. A bunch of middle-aged men getting old.'

'It was just a theory, Terry,' Swayne said, wearily.

'You got me out here on a *bank holiday* to tell me *that*. Were you bored?'

'Were you?' he asked.

'I'm not paying for this crap, all right? It's probably not even Beverley Wingrove in the poster.'

He didn't reply. The light was starting to fade and the sky was taking on the hue of raging flames. People were coming back from the street party, swaying and singing, some still wearing masks.

I got up to go, angry as hell.

'Shame about David Stratten, eh?' Swayne said.

'What about him?'

'Didn't you hear?'

'No?'

'He's dead.'

'When?'

'Couple of days ago. It was in the *Standard*.'

That stunned me. I suddenly saw him again. Dodgy Dave who'd been ripped off by dodgier people impersonating tax officers.

'What happened?' I asked.

'They're not sure if it was suicide or an accident. He was pissed as a fart and jumped or fell in front of a Tube train in Tufnell Park in the afternoon.'

'Poor sod,' I said. I sort of meant it. What a horrible way to go.

'There is one small problem,' Swayne said.

'What?'

'Dave didn't drink.'

*

264

I got home four hours later. It was dark. The kids were up, watching TV with Karen. I popped my head around the door and said hello, sheepishly. Ray looked at the floor, Amy smiled and Karen stared right at the screen, furious. They were watching the news, replaying the crowd cheering outside Buckingham Palace. I guess that was when William had kissed Kate.

I knew there'd be hell to pay for shooting off the way I had this afternoon.

I went to the bedroom to get changed. Karen came in moments later.

She always tried her best to give me the silent treatment, but she could never stay quiet long enough to pull it off. She wasn't a natural hoarder of hurts. She liked to clear the air immediately, settle things and move on. The complete opposite of me, in other words.

'Where've you been?' she asked.

'Work,' I said.

'You're on *holiday*, Terry.'

'Something came up.'

I'd left Swayne and wandered over Battersea Bridge.

Cheyne Walk was close by. I'd gone down to VJ and Melissa's house. I stood outside the gate and thought about ringing the bell. If she answered I would say I was in the neighbourhood and thought I'd drop by and see how she was doing. Or something like that. My index finger hovered over the buzzer, trembling. It felt like the first step to adultery. Then a car pulled up at the house next door, and two little blond boys bounced out. I remembered it was the school holidays and realised Melissa's kids might be home. It would be awkward, meeting those little VJ-ettes. I'd start imagining how our kids might have looked, the ones Melissa and I might have had if . . .

So I'd moved on, headed into Chelsea, drifted aimlessly; up King's Road to Sloane Square, back down King's Road to the redbrick high-rise estate called World's End, where Joe Strummer had written *London Calling* while looking down at the river he lived by.

I'd thought about what Swayne had told me. Although it seemed like complete rubbish at the time, he was utterly serious about it. No snideness in his tone, no smirk. He could have been putting me on, but I didn't think so.

And, of course, I thought about David Stratten too. Was his death a murder, like Swayne seemed to have implied? He'd been robbed the day he was going to give Ahmad Sihl information for VJ. Some people would call that a coincidence. Others would call it a conspiracy.

I'd found an internet café and looked up Oliver Wingrove. There were only a few scraps of information about him, which I printed off and brought back.

265

But first there was Karen to get past.

'I don't know what's going on with you, Terry, but I don't like it,' she was saying. 'Ever since you started working on this case, I've been seeing this whole side of you I never knew existed. If you'd shown it sooner, I'd have run a mile.'

This was unexpected.

'What are you talking about?'

'You're turning into a stranger, you know that? You're shutting me out, shutting *us* out. You don't tell me anything. You barely talk as it is. You come home and say three words if you say that much. Ray says you don't even come in and see him any more after work.'

I hadn't realised. Yeah, I'd been coming home late. The kids would be getting ready for bed or already fast asleep. And when I got home in time for dinner, my head was on the case. It was always on the case.

But what was I supposed to do? Share all that stuff with them at the dinner table? About how I was helping a man who may or may not have murdered a young woman? Or explain what my job actually consisted of? The hours of phone calls, the interviews where I'd impersonated a cop, the day I'd spent finding out about Evelyn Bates's sad life? Besides, it was illegal to discuss a case with an outside party. Not that that ever stopped anyone.

Karen was spoiling for a fight I wanted to avoid.

'This'll be over soon,' I said. 'When the verdict's in, I'm still quitting. That hasn't changed.'

'I don't believe you,' she said.

'What do you mean?'

'You're not acting like someone who's quitting.'

'How am I acting?'

'Have you been looking for another job?'

'No.'

'Have you updated your CV?'

'No.'

'Course you haven't,' she said. ''Cause you're not coming to the end of anything. You're in the middle, you're in *deep* – and you *like* it. You're like a pig in shit.'

OK. She had me. *Like* was the wrong word. But I *was* enjoying the job – and I'd *loved* it on Tuesday, playing a big part in that court win. It was the first time in a good long while I'd taken pride in something I'd done. Not since school, in fact.

I hadn't told her about the bonus Kopf gave me. I hadn't even told her what happened in court. It would've confirmed what she suspected – that I really *didn't* want to leave. And I didn't. I was getting a taste for the law, getting to like it. I could even see myself doing it for a living.

Kopf had sent out ambiguous signals yesterday. Why give someone a '*very* friendly warning' – and a bonus – if you're planning to fire them? All he had to do was keep quiet and then use my infringements to justify getting rid of me.

What if they intended to offer me the paralegal's job and the degree – except I resigned before they got round to it?

'Have you got anything to *say*, Terry?' Karen said.

Here was the thing. Although I was genuinely sorry I'd been neglecting them all, I couldn't just come out and say so yet. Karen and I didn't argue all that often, once or twice a year, if that. Yet when we fought, there were rules of engagement. Ours were simple. Karen had to have her say, make and score her points, and then leave the room with a dramatic slam of the door. That was the way things worked. That was our balance.

So I couldn't apologise before she'd done that because, to her, it wouldn't be sincere. She'd think I was trying to avoid a tongue-lashing, duck a conflict altogether or – worst of all – stop her from saying what she had to say.

She'd said she was feeling shut out, so I had to let her in a little way.

'This case *is* getting to me, you're right. I can't help it. Given the circumstances. It's brought things back, dredged up things I never thought I'd have to face.'

'Like what?'

'It's made me see things in a different light. A *harsher* light.'

'What things?'

'Myself, mostly,' I said. 'I had opportunities once, and I never took them, never made the most of what was right in front of me, on a plate. It's like I took a wrong turn a long time ago, and just kept going.'

'*A wrong turn?*' She frowned. 'Does that "wrong turn" include us? The family you made along the way – the daughter you brought into this world, the son who loves you? Does that include *me*?'

Talk about putting your big fat foot in it.

'No ... of course not, Karen. I ... I didn't mean that.'

She took a couple of steps back, her face furious and pained, her eyes shining with tears.

'Everyone means what they say, Terry. They just don't mean to be understood so *fucking clearly*!'

'I'm sorry, Karen, I—'

She left, slamming the door.

*

267

In the spare room, I looked over the stuff I'd got on Oliver Wingrove.

There were several short reports on the failed attempt to extradite him from Britain in 1997. No reasons were given for the extradition. Wingrove's lawyer had issued a statement saying his client had been a South African Embassy employee in London from the mid-1980s, and denied any wrongdoing.

The other pieces dated back to the early 1960s. Wingrove had been in the Rhodesian police when the country was still under British rule. He'd been in charge of an investigation into the suspected kidnapping of a farmer called Michael Zengeni.

Zengeni was a British citizen. In November 1961, he'd been due to visit his family in Britain, but disappeared on his way to the airport.

A month later his body was found in the back of his Land Rover. He'd been shot. The remains were too badly decomposed for identification, but Zengeni's passport and plane ticket were found at the scene.

In 1962, Wingrove appeared at an inquest into the kidnapping in London. The very short article had the only photograph I'd found of Wingrove – a big, dark-haired man with a full beard. He was shown arriving at the inquest with his wife, Beverley. She was wearing a raincoat, headscarf and wraparound sunglasses. She'd been very attractive then, like a young Britt Ekland.

I compared that photograph with the one Swayne had put through my door. Despite its poor quality, I could see the woman holding the gun was definitely *not* Beverley Wingrove.

What was Swayne playing at?

50

Tuesday morning. The holiday was over. Back to work.

I was relieved. Things had been tense in the house all weekend. Karen sparing with her conversation, the kids surly – especially Ray. I'd stayed away from the case, and done my best not to think about it; put the family first. I took the kids out to Battersea Park on Sunday, and then for pizza. Karen didn't come, told me she had work to do. Yeah, *right*.

I went to the kitchen, put a pot of coffee on and started making my sandwiches.

I was buttering a roll when the phone went. Not my mobile, the landline.

I dashed out and grabbed it.

Janet.

'We're in serious trouble,' she said.

'Why, what's happened?'

'I'll tell you on the way to Belmarsh.'

VJ knew something was wrong as soon as he saw us. Janet and Redpath were there with me, but I was the only one looking at him. Janet had her head down over the stack of papers she'd brought with her, and Redpath, who was facing me, didn't turn round.

'We've had new disclosure from the prosecution,' Janet said.

'I thought we'd passed the cut-off date,' VJ said, frowning.

'Technically, yes. Practically, there's no such thing,' she said. She slid across a couple of sheets of paper. 'First, your toxicology report.'

She let him read it.

He took off his glasses and brought the paper up close to his face.

'Flunitrazepam . . .' he muttered. 'That's—'

'Yes, Rohypnol,' Janet said.

He put the paper down, smiling.

'What did I tell you? I was set up. I was drugged. This helps the case, surely?'

'It might have done.'

'What do you mean? Evelyn Bates had Rohypnol in her body. If I'd really killed her, I wouldn't have taken the same stuff I'd used on her, right?'

'That's one way of looking at it,' Janet said.

He stared at her, then at me, then Redpath; his smile fading as he passed from each of us.

'What's going on?' he asked.

She pushed more papers his way.

I watched him, watched his expression change as he read, his eyes tracking back and forth along the lines. Confusion, trepidation, consternation and, finally, fear. His eyes widened. He started blinking and breathing deeply through his nose, making a sound like dry leaves being stuffed into a plastic bag. That was a variation of how I'd reacted, reading the very same thing on the train. Except I'd also been disgusted. Sickened.

'Well?' she asked, when he'd finished.

'What is this?'

'You tell me.'

He went back through the pages. He separated the colour photographs that came clipped to every other page and set them out in a row before him.

'There are no names here,' he said. 'Witness A, Witness B, Witness C, Witness D . . . Who are they?'

'That's called Special Measures. Witnesses are granted anonymity in certain circumstances, sexual offence cases being one of them,' she said.

Now he was confused again – or acting that way. Still studying the pages, looking at the photos, shaking his head, frowning.

'When did you get this?' he asked.

'Carnavale biked it over to me yesterday afternoon. You know what this means in terms of the trial?'

'No,' he said.

What was he doing? Had he turned stupid in here, or was he too shocked to tee up another few lies?

Janet laid it out for him:

What it meant was this – the prosecution had its motive back; all the motive it needed, and then some.

Welcome back to square one.

Of the three laptops the police had taken from VJ's office, two had been for work, the other for play – if you can call what he did for kicks 'play'.

'Do you know the surest and safest way to delete something on a computer?' Janet said. 'You smash it up, take out the hard drive and throw it in the river. What you don't do is press "Delete" and "Empty trash". That just takes something away and buries it – in your machine.'

'The police found the pictures?' he said, quietly, almost whispering.

'And the emails,' Janet said and sighed. 'Why didn't you tell us you'd been blackmailed?'

'I . . . I didn't think it . . . I didn't think they'd find out.'

'Well, they have,' she said.

VJ had used his personal laptop and the mobile phone they'd found with it to set up meetings with escorts. He contacted them via email. He kept their names, contact details and photographs in a database on the laptop.

The women were all the same type – tall, blonde, athletic, well proportioned. High-class hookers, working out of expensive rented flats in expensive parts of town. Yet they weren't the standard courtesan types. They were into S&M.

The police had tracked down and interviewed eight of the eleven women he'd been with. All told a similar story. VJ's thing was 'rough sex', specifically slapping and choking. Fine, but not the way he did it, they said. He'd always start gently, testing the boundaries the first few times, then he'd go further and further – and then *way* too far. He liked using his belt to choke them.

Four of the witnesses had agreed to testify in court, on condition of anonymity. They'd been codenamed Witness A, B, C and D.

VJ had been rougher with them than with the others, and they'd decided to do something about it. They'd each originally threatened to go to the police and report him for assault. They'd emailed him pictures of their swollen faces and bruised necks. He'd offered to pay them off. They'd made a deal.

Witness A had received £20,000 for her silence.

Witness B, £15,000.

Witness C, £30,000.

Witness D, £100,000 – in three instalments.

All the women said the money was delivered by an intermediary – a man they met somewhere public. Witness D had a friend photograph her meeting, 'just in case'.

The man was David Stratten.

To make the point absolutely clear, Carnavale had reincluded the autopsy photos of Evelyn Bates, along with the ones of the battered women they'd dredged up from VJ's laptop. All the women had bruising around their necks.

VJ put the statements down.

'It's not what it looks like,' he said.

Janet pulled an expression of mock-surprise. Or maybe it was genuine surprise with an overtone of mockery.

'This was about sex not violence. It was consensual. They knew the risks. That's what I paid them for.'

When she didn't reply, when the harsh stare she was giving him started to burn, he looked at me. I glared at him. I was thinking about Melissa. She was all I'd been thinking about since the second I started reading the witness statements. Had he done these things to her too – slapped her, choked her, battered her? He clocked the disgust on my face and turned his head away quickly.

'I never meant to hurt them – beyond what we'd agreed,' he said. 'I might have got a little carried away on occasion. I may have squeezed a little too hard, once or twice. I could have slapped them a bit harder than they . . . than we'd agreed. But it wasn't deliberate. It was *never* deliberate. It was an accident. Heat of the moment. We were having sex – intense sex – and I . . . maybe I didn't hear the safety word.'

'Because your belt was around their throats?' Janet said, calmly and quietly, but her tone was pure ice, sharp at both ends, frozen in-between.

He didn't answer.

'Who arranged the pay-offs? You?' Janet asked.

'Ahmad Sihl, through a private investigator.'

'David Stratten?'

VJ nodded.

'So Ahmad knew?'

He nodded.

Janet scribbled something. Why hadn't Sihl told her?

'Did you kill Evelyn Bates?' she asked him.

'No,' he said.

'The jury's going to see this.'

'I know,' he said, slowly.

'Do you want to change your plea?'

'To what? "Guilty"? I'm not. I didn't kill her. I'm innocent,' he said, but without any kind of force or energy, or much in the way of emotion, a non-believer reciting a creed from memory.

What had happened to him? When had he started doing these things to women? And why? Did it have something to do with his childhood, something he'd seen or gone through and never told me about? Had Rodney abused him? I was repelled, sure, but I really wanted to know how he'd got so twisted.

'Do you only go with prostitutes?'

'No.'

'So you've slapped and choked non-professionals too?' she said, her voice all serrated edges.

She'd never told me, never given it away, but she'd never liked him.

Now she flat-out hated him – hated him for what he was, and what he liked doing to women. And she hated him because she had to represent him. We weren't just going to lose this trial, we were going to lose it *big*. We were going to have to defend the indefensible, and look stupid doing it. This would get KRP noticed for all the wrong reasons.

'Not the way you mean it,' he said.

'How do I mean it?'

'Like it's an act of violence.'

'I do retort,' she said, sarcastically. 'Let me rephrase that: did you ever *lovingly* slap and choke women you didn't pay for the privilege of doing so?'

'Not unless they were into it. If it's not consensual, it's assault and battery. And that's not me,' he said, through clenched teeth. And without a *hint* of irony.

She could have had fun with that one, but at that moment the guard outside banged on the door. We had five minutes left.

'Where does this leave us?' he asked.

'About a hundred miles up shit creek,' she said. 'Not only does the prosecution now have all the motive it needs, but we've also lost any possibility of impartiality from the judge. He must feel like a bit of a tit right now. He made the wrong decision in excluding the thong from evidence.

He'll make us pay for that in court. And when it comes to his summary, at the end of the trial, just before he sends the jury away, he'll direct them to find you guilty.'

'Can he do that?'

'In so many words, yes. He can't tell them what to do, but he can drop big hints as to what he thinks. The smarter juror will know he has the evidence in front of him – used and unused, admissible and inadmissible, and that he's made his mind up.'

VJ looked at the wall next to him, then the ceiling.

'What are my options?' he asked.

'Much narrower than they were at the start,' she said. 'You can go to trial and say you're not guilty, or you can change your plea and take your chances. The sentence will now be the same either way. With this new evidence, you're looking at a minimum of twenty-five years.'

For a split second I swore I saw his soul leave his body; and he became an upright, unkempt shell in a baggy white T-shirt, waiting for his brain to switch off the rest of him.

'The defence is client-led. We can only be as good as you make us,' Janet said. 'If you withhold vital information from us – as you've done twice now – we're going to get blindsided by the prosecution. So I'm going to ask you again, for the last time, is there anything else we need to know?'

'That's it,' VJ said.

'Are you sure?'

'Yes.'

'What about his dad's murder?'

That was Redpath, talking to Janet like VJ wasn't in the room.

My mouth went dry. And my heart stopped and my blood froze in my veins.

'He was questioned but neither arrested nor charged,' Janet said. 'It's completely irrelevant. It won't come up.'

I let out the breath I'd caught and held.

'What do you think, Terry?'

That was VJ, looking right at me with a blank expression.

Both Janet and Redpath turned to me, puzzled and questioning.

'About ...?' I managed.

'The case,' he said. 'How does it look to you? What do you think?'

Here's what I *really* think:

I wanted you to be guilty, not so you could be punished for killing Evelyn, but so we could be even. That was hatred corrupting my judgement.

Yet, I wasn't sure you actually were.

I had a reasonable doubt.

273

It shrank, then it grew again. Then it shrank back.

But now, with all this evidence . . .

I think you're guilty. I think you're fucking *guilty.*

I think you took Evelyn Bates up to that suite of yours, with its two huge rooms and its devil's-eye-view of London. You spiked her drink with Rohypnol, and then you strangled her.

And here's what else I think.

You're a sick depraved twisted fuck who deserves to go away for life meaning life.

But, do you know what else I think?

You killed your dad too.

We lied for you.

We kept you free . . . so you could kill again.

So you could kill Evelyn Bates.

I wish I'd listened to Quinlan.

He said you'd do it again.

And he was right.

You did.

That's what I *think.*

'I think I'm going to need all the information you can remember about Witnesses A to D,' I said. 'Names, descriptions, where you met, how you met, any phone numbers and email addresses that come to mind. Everything.'

'Why?'

'Because I'm going to put our investigator on this. Christine's going to cross-examine those witnesses on the stand. She's going to need to know everything about them.'

Janet looked at me, surprised but a little impressed.

To her, to VJ, to the outside, it looked like I was keeping my cool in the face of mounting pressure.

'You didn't answer my question,' VJ said.

'It doesn't look good,' I said. 'But when did it ever?'

51

One glance at me and Adolf knew my case had gone to bits. Defeat was on my face, in my body language, pinned to my sleeve. She didn't hide her glee. She cracked a big grin that mixed spite and cruelty with pure joy in one ultra-brite explosion of small, imperfect teeth.

To think, another lifetime ago – a parallel one where everything had worked out – I'd actually been looking forward to coming into the office today, all flushed with success and propelled by that pat on the back from Sid Kopf. I was going to go one better than last Tuesday, work on getting us another big win. For a brief instant it had seemed that this was going to stop being about VJ, and start being about me – doing a good job and getting that promotion.

Oh, well . . .

I sat down. My mind was blank. I didn't know what to do or where to go from here. Did I stick to being a note-taker and bag carrier to Belmarsh? Strictly fetch 'n' carry, while I got my CV together and started planning for life after KRP? Or did I work on somehow turning this nosedive around? The other question was – did I want to help out a double murderer?

On the way back Janet had talked about getting in an expert witness to testify that S&M practitioners rarely became killers, that it was all a bit of harmless fun, adult play-acting. It wouldn't sway the jury at all. Never did. They always saw through mercenary mouthpieces. But the case was now purely about maintaining appearances; so we had to be seen to be mounting a defence, doing everything possible. She'd put me in charge of finding and recruiting a courtroom psychologist, someone who sounded good and didn't cost the earth.

I dug out the witness directory from my bottom drawer, thumbed through it until I found the relevant section and started marking up potential names.

As I reached for the phone to make the first call, it rang right under my fingers.

'Is that Mr Flynt?'

'Speaking?'

'This is Grenville Allen of Allen & Sons. We spoke about a Rolex a few weeks ago. The Three E?'

'Yes, I remember. How are you?'

'I have some very good news,' he said. 'The watch has turned up. A colleague of mine phoned this morning, to say someone brought it into his shop.'

I sat up.

'Are you sure?'

'It matches the watch you described in every way.'

'What's your colleague's name and number?'

He told me. It wasn't a London number.

'Where's he based exactly?'

52

Southend. Forty-five miles outside London, right on the coast. Sand, sea and sun, British style – so, grim beaches, freezing iron-coloured water and zero sun.

It was here that Cecil Norcross lived and worked. He owned a pawn shop, specialising in cheap and shiny bling, which was why he hadn't shown up on my radar. But he also doubled up as a private Rolex collector. To those in the know, he was the go-to man for the rarest models – the one-offs, the recalls, the limited editions, which he'd either flip to collectors, or sell back to the company in Geneva, if it was on their wanted list.

When I'd spoken to him on the phone he'd told me this:

A French-sounding woman had brought the watch to his shop yesterday afternoon. He'd asked to see ID, as he always did with strangers. She'd shown him a passport and driving licence. He described her as tall, youngish, with short and spiky black hair. She'd left the watch with him overnight for authentication. She knew the drill. She also knew about the company reward.

Her name was Fabia Masson. And she was due back this afternoon at around 4 p.m. to hear his offer.

'Mr Flynt?' Norcross said when I walked in at 4.15, dishevelled, soaked and dripping on his parquet floor. It had been spitting rain when I was on the train, and the skies had opened up as soon as I came out of the station.

Norcross was a skeletal man in browline specs, a silk cravat and a double-breasted grey pinstriped suit. He was on his own. The shop was a glorified cupboard, most of the space taken up by an L-shaped glass counter with silver and gold chains, bracelets and rings displayed on upright red felt stands. There couldn't have been room for more than two customers at a time.

'Have I missed her?' I asked.

'Sort of, I'm afraid,' he said, frowning. 'Look, I'm sorry you've come all this way, but . . . I did try and tell you when we spoke.'

'Tell me what?'

'That I was going to call the police. I run a respectable business, and I have a reputation to maintain.'

He wasn't the same jolly jovial old chap he'd been on the phone. The accent and manners were all there, but I saw the wheeler-dealer behind the façade, the type who drove a very hard bargain and prided himself on squeezing everyone down to the last penny.

'Where is she now?' I asked.

'The police station, I suppose. They took her away about fifteen minutes ago.'

'Where is the station?'

'Victoria Avenue,' he said, and gave me directions.

'And the watch?' I asked him.

'The police took it,' he said. 'You know it's worthless, don't you?'

'What d'you mean?'

'I also tried to tell you that on the phone. It's a fake.'

'That's impossible,' I said. 'I've seen the case, the paperwork . . . That watch is older than I am.'

'Maybe it is. But that only makes it an old fake,' he said. 'It's an occupational hazard, in this circle of ours. For every rare and sought-after item, there are always twenty counterfeits. The Three E is no exception. Your client's is one of the best I've ever seen, admittedly, but a fake's a fake. The more serious counterfeiters will go to some length to pass their goods off as genuine. It's easy to get real cases and easier to falsify paperwork.'

Had Rodney James known his Rolex was fake?

As I ran out of the shop, I allowed myself a smile. I wondered if VJ would see the funny side too.

53

The custody suite was in an annexe around the side of the main building, across a parking lot scattered with police vehicles.

I rang the intercom. It was answered as soon as I took my finger off the button. I asked if they still had Fabia Masson in custody.

I was buzzed in.

The only people at reception were police, working behind the big desk at the back, tapping at computers. No surprise to find it so quiet. It was early in the week, still daytime and pissing down with rain.

'You got here quick,' the desk sergeant said. He was a big bloke with all his white hair. Boxer's nose, faded forearm tattoos, still in good shape, but only five years from his pension and war stories.

As I reached the desk, the penny suddenly dropped. He thought I was a duty solicitor, the state-paid lawyer.

My gut told me to walk away.

My balls told me to stay.

My brain abstained.

'What are the charges again?' I asked.

277

'Trying to sell counterfeit goods, possession of a fake driver's licence and possession of stolen credit cards,' he said. 'Sign in and come through.'

The interview room was warm and poky and smelled of burned plastic and spilled coffee. There were no windows or any kind of ventilation, just the white walls, bolted-down furniture and strip lighting.

As I'd rushed over from London, I'd brought no pen and paper, or a tape recorder with me. And I'd had to leave my phone with keys at reception.

A young officer poked his head round the door.

'Mason?' he asked.

I nodded.

She came in. The door was shut behind her. We were alone.

Dressed in black jeans and a V-neck jumper over a white T-shirt, she could have passed for a catwalk model in her downtime. Her hair was a mess – too short for her long face, and dyed too dark for her complexion – but that didn't make much difference. She was stunning. I knew exactly what VJ had seen in her.

She sat opposite me.

Up close, she was even more beautiful. High cheeks, bright hazel eyes, long lashes, naturally pouting lips.

Right then, looking at her, my brain froze. I lost the power of thought and speech. She saw it too. Smiled, very slightly.

Reset. Focus. Concentrate.

'What's your name?' I asked.

'Fabia Masson. Not *Mason*. Or Massoon,' she replied.

'That's not your real name, though, is it?'

She shrugged.

'French?'

'Swiss,' she said.

'Now I want you to listen to me very carefully. We don't have a lot of time. My name's Terry Flynt. I'm not your lawyer. But I am here to help you,' I said.

No reaction.

'I work for the law firm that's defending Vernon James.'

That got her attention. First surprise, then anxiety. Her eyes darted left and right, past my shoulder, where the panic button was, then over to the door.

'How did you find me?'

'The watch,' I said.

'It is a fucking fake. I thought I was going to sell it and get out of here.'

'On a fake passport too?'

'What do you want, *Monsieur* Flynt?'

Her aggression was masking fear.

'I want to know exactly what happened between you and Vernon James in the Blenheim-Strand that night. Everything. All of it.'

'I'm not talking to you.'

'Why not?'

'I just want to get out of here. Forget everything that happened.'

She spoke perfect, precise English, her voice on the deep side.

'Vernon James is in prison,' I said.

'I know,' she said. 'So?'

She'd been following the case.

'Who are you running from?' I asked.

'Who said I was running?'

'You've changed your hair.'

'Women do it all the time. Men too.'

'It doesn't suit you,' I said. 'You did it in a hurry.'

'Are you a hairdresser too?'

If we'd been together in a pub or a café, I would have laughed.

'I know you're in trouble,' I said. 'You came here to sell the watch and catch a plane to Europe.' Southend had a small airport, with regular flights to Holland, Spain and Ireland.

She looked at her nails.

'Who are you running from?'

Still no answer.

'I'll tell you what'll happen if I leave here right now,' I said. 'You'll be charged with trying to sell counterfeit goods, possession of fake ID and stolen credit cards. That's two years in prison,' I said, bluffing it.

That got her attention again.

'What are you offering?' she asked.

'A way out,' I said. 'But I need to know what happened with Vernon James first.'

'How do I know you're telling the truth?'

'You don't. You're just going to have to trust me.'

She laughed.

'I trust no one.'

'Me neither. That's why I work in law not hairdressing.'

Another laugh.

She weighed me up. Same socio-economic biopsy as Breeze, the stripper. She focused on my wedding ring, then my eyes, then my mouth. She was too scared to trust me. Luckily for me, she hadn't worked out that I wasn't supposed to be here; that I'd blagged my way in.

'Who are you running from?' I asked again.

Outside I heard people coming down the corridor. They stopped right by the door, talking. The words were muffled. Then they moved on.

'If I tell you everything, will you get me out of here?'

'Absolutely,' I said.

She scanned my face up and down, looking for lies and agendas. I passed.

'I was paid to seduce Vernon James in the hotel, the Blenheim-Strand,' she said.

Time stopped and my brain froze.

I told myself to keep calm, get the story, get it now, get it fast.

'Who by?'

'I don't know. I never met anyone in person. It was just a voice on the phone. Always the same man. English.'

'Did he give a name?'

'Yes. Bill.'

'What do you do for a living?'

'Can't you guess?'

'Tell me anyway,' I said.

'I'm an escort.'

'How long have you been doing that?'

'What is this, career guidance?'

'Background,' I said.

'Four years, in London. I work through an agency for new clients. But I also have regulars I deal with directly. Some recommend me to their friends also. I have a separate phone for them. On March 1st I got a call from Bill. He said he wanted to book me on March 16th. He needed a date for a black-tie event at the Blenheim-Strand.'

'He called you directly?'

'Yes. On my private clients line.'

'Did he say who'd recommended you?'

'No.'

'Didn't you get suspicious?'

'I always get suspicious. But not anyone has that number, and I've been recommended in the past. I assumed he was a high roller, big bucks.'

'Go on.'

'I asked to be paid in cash, as usual. My outcall rate is £4000 for an evening. I always ask for half upfront, the rest when I meet the client.

'He asked where I wanted the money delivered. I said a café in Knightsbridge. I thought he would come in person, but a courier delivered it in an envelope. I signed for it. It was my full fee, not half. I thought he'd made a mistake, or misunderstood me.

'Two days before we were due to meet, Bill called again. He told me to wear a dress that would "stand out".'

I nodded.

'I had just the thing, but it was emerald green. I asked him if that was OK. He said he wanted me to make an impression. I thought, Typical older rich man – wearing women like a wristwatch. Showing off.

'On March 16th, I went to the hotel. We had arranged to meet at the cocktail bar in the lobby at eight o'clock. I ordered a drink. A waiter came over to me and handed me something – lipstick, it looked like. He said, "This is for you," and went away before I had a chance to say anything.

'Then my telephone rang. It was Bill. He told me he was watching me and I had to do exactly as he said. Open the lipstick. I did. Instead of lipstick, there was a small glass ampoule inside, about the size of my little finger. It was filled with clear liquid.

'Then he told me what I *really* had to do: go to the ballroom and pick up Vernon James. Then I had to get him alone, go up to his room with him, and put the liquid in his drink. The man said the liquid would knock him out. Once he was unconscious, I had to call room service and order champagne.'

'Champagne?' I asked.

'Yes,' she said. 'After I made the call, I was to wait in the room until someone came. They would take pictures of Vernon James and me in "compromising positions". Then I'd be paid again. My full fee *again*.'

'So they wanted you to pose for blackmail pictures?'

She nodded.

'I told the man no. I wouldn't do it.'

She took a deep breath, looked off to the side.

'And?' I prompted.

'He said, "You will do as you're told. You try and walk out of here, you'll never walk again. You try and warn Vernon James or anyone, you'll be sorry." I got scared. Then he called me by my real name. Not Fabia – my *real* name. He also told me other things too – very personal things, private matters. He made me understand that . . .'

She closed her eyes. Two tears ran down her face.

'They'd looked into you?' I said.

She nodded.

And I got the chills.

'They knew everything. I knew I'd been *picked* for this. I had to do it. I had no choice.'

'So you went to the ballroom?'

'Yes. The event had started. I just walked in. There was one security guy at the door, but he didn't stop me.

'Vernon James made his speech. I sat in the light, directly in front of him. He noticed me as soon as he started talking. He couldn't stop looking at me. I tried to meet him after he had finished, but there were too many people around. One of the men on the table near where I'd been sitting asked if I was going to the afterparty. I asked him where it was, and he told me. So I decided that was where I'd approach Vernon James.

'I didn't go there immediately. I was very nervous. I was shaking inside. I had a drink in one of the bars. I stopped in the bathroom to freshen up and get myself together.

'While I was there, another woman came in. She was wearing a green dress too – bright green, like leaves. One of the straps was torn, she was holding the dress up, crying. She kept trying to tie it together, but she could not. There was an attendant in the toilet. She said she could fix the dress for her.'

'You saw Evelyn Bates?'

'Who?'

'That was the woman they found in Vernon's suite.'

She looked confused.

'What time did you see her?'

'I don't know exactly. But that was not the only time I saw her,' she said. 'When I came out of the bathroom, I went to find the club, but I went the wrong way. I turned round and retraced my steps. That's when I saw him, Vernon James.

'He was coming down the corridor. His suit was dirty. He seemed drunk. We talked a little. As we were talking, the girl – Evelyn – passed me. She was going in the direction of the club. I saw her talking to a man.'

'What did he look like?'

'I think he was hotel security. He was a bodybuilder type in a black suit with a name-badge, a shaved head, and a plastic earpiece.'

'Did you hear what she was saying?'

'No. Too far away. There were other people in the corridor.'

'What about you and Vernon James?' I asked.

'We went to a bar on the eleventh floor. He bought drinks. He had vodka straight. I noticed his watch. The Rolex. I asked to see it, so I could distract him. He had problems taking it off. That was when I put the liquid in his glass. He drank it all. Didn't notice. A little later we went upstairs.

'We got inside his room. We talked for a bit. Then he started kissing

282

me. I went along with it, but I was confused. He was supposed to pass out. But he wasn't showing any signs of being more than just drunk. In the back of my mind I was really scared. Paranoid. I didn't know what was going on. Was I being set up instead of him? Was this a cop sting? Or one of my ex-clients playing a trick, I didn't know.

'He started getting rough. He pinched my nipple, twisted it hard. I bit his lip. He was bleeding. That's when he went crazy. He touched his mouth, saw the blood and smiled at me. Not a nice smile. This cruel smile. Then like *that* he slapped my face. *BAFF!* I screamed. He hit me again. And then he jumped on me.

'I lost my balance and fell on the drinks counter. I knocked all these glasses over. Everything was smashed, there was broken glass everywhere. He tried to pull me on to the couch. I held on to this piece of furniture. I thought it was fixed to the wall, but it moved. It was on wheels.

'He flipped me around and pinned me down with his body so I couldn't move. He put his belt around my neck, like a noose, and started pulling it tight. It was hard to breathe. He pushed my dress up over my arse. He forced my legs apart. I thought he was going to rape and kill me.

'I was trying to fight, trying to breathe. But I couldn't. I was trapped by his body. My head was getting light. I was seeing stars.

'And then, suddenly it just stopped. He backed off. I turned round and I saw him standing there, with his trousers down around his ankles and his erection in his hand, but he was dizzy, stumbling. He looked like he didn't know where he was, what was happening.

'I got the belt off my neck. And then I just freaked. I wanted to kill him. I kicked him in the stomach. He fell over on his back, straight on to the glass. I tried to push the big minibar on him. It went halfway over and everything fell out, all over him. Everything in there was broken. All the bottles. Then I ran out of the room.'

'So you never made the call – for champagne?'

'Of course not. I didn't even think of that.'

'Then what happened?'

'I left the hotel. I was scared. I did not go home,' she said.

'Wait,' I said. 'When you ran out of the room, did you take the lift down?'

'No. It needed a special card. I used the stairs.'

'What time was this, do you know?'

'It was around 12.20 a.m.'

'That specific?'

'Yes,' she said. 'I was still wearing his fucking fake watch.'

Rudy Saks had told the police – and me – that he'd found the suite undamaged when he'd been up there at 1 a.m. – to deliver champagne.

Rudy Saks had lied.

This changed absolutely *everything*.

'Did anyone see you leave the hotel?'

'I don't know.'

'What did you do after you left?' I asked.

'I went home. Changed my clothes, packed a bag. Then I left town,' she said. 'Southend is a good place to lie low. I knew I could get a passport made here, and sell the watch too.'

'And you were going to leave the country?'

She nodded.

It was time to bring Janet in.

'Don't say anything about this to anyone. If the police interview you again, say no comment,' I said. 'You'll go back to your cell. I'll get you a lawyer. She's coming from London, so it'll take a couple of hours. Please sit tight, OK?'

I got my stuff back at reception and signed out. The sergeant nodded to me as I left.

Once outside I called Janet.

'Terry, where the hell are you?' she asked.

'Southend nick,' I said. 'I've found Fabia. You've got to get over here – *now*.'

I went down the road, looking for a café. Nothing doing. It had gone six, so they were all shut. I found a pub instead. Not ideal, but the rain was coming down harder, and I needed somewhere to sit and think for a while.

I ordered coffee and went to a corner table.

I eyed the beers. Then the bottles of spirits all lined up at the back, inverted, ready to pour. Spotted the Jameson . . .

Just *one* . . .?

And a Guinness.

No!

I was shaking – not for want of booze, fighting all that temptation – but because of what Fabia had told me, what it meant.

VJ was innocent.

He *had* been set up.

He *hadn't* killed Evelyn Bates.

So who had?

My theory: the people who'd hired Fabia had intended to murder her in the room, while VJ was passed out. They'd known about his sexual

284

proclivities, and the type of women he went for. And they'd set him up for the fall.

Things had gone wrong: the Rohypnol hadn't kicked in fast enough. Then Fabia had fled and messed up their plans, so they'd grabbed Evelyn instead.

How *that* had happened, I didn't know.

But she'd been drugged, taken up to Suite 18 and murdered.

Fabia had last seen her talking to someone from hotel security:

A bodybuilder type with a shaved head.

David Stratten had mentioned 'a big bald bugger'.

So, where to now?

The trial would definitely still go ahead. But with Fabia as our main defence witness, it would be very difficult for Carnavale to prove his case beyond a reasonable doubt. Pretty much impossible.

VJ would either be acquitted, or the trial discontinued.

And it would all be because of what I'd done today.

My work. My win.

Me.

I'd handed Christine her silver bullet and the gun to fire it with.

Hell, I'd handed her the silver bombshell . . .

My chest swelled and I grinned, and I really wanted to punch the air.

But not quite . . .

Look at who this was all for, who I was defending.

VJ may have been innocent of murder and the victim of a frame-up, but he'd as good as attempted to rape Fabia, and he got his kicks hurting women. The thought of setting him free, putting him back in circulation, made me suddenly very uneasy. This may have been the law, but it wasn't *any* kind of justice.

Was he ever going to pay for *anything*?

Janet pulled up outside Southend nick on the back of a dispatch rider's motorbike at 7.45 p.m. The rain was bucketing down.

She'd come in her raincoat with waterproofs underneath. She handed the rider her helmet and we headed inside.

As we crossed the parking lot, a squad car pulled up and two uniformed cops got out in a hurry. They keyed open the door. We followed them in, quickly.

An alarm was sounding. A long loud pulsing drone, with a couple of seconds' silence in-between. The counter was unmanned. There was no one around at all.

Janet and I looked at each other.

What was going on?

Phones were ringing. All of them at once, it seemed.

We stepped up to the desk and waited.

The sergeant who'd signed me in came through the door leading to the cells and interview rooms.

He looked at us, at me specifically.

'That's him, that's the fucker, right there,' he shouted, pointing at me.

Next thing I knew, my arms were grabbed from behind and I was pushed face down on the desk.

'What's this? What's going on?' I yelled.

The sergeant was now back behind the desk, looking down at me.

'You're under arrest for the murder of Fabia Masson.'

PART THREE

The Verdict

54

They put me in an interrogation room and left me alone to stew for a couple of hours.

It was a narrow space of perforated walls and thin grey carpet, much of it filled by a big metal desk, shaped like a sawed-off grand piano, with only a cramped sluice to manoeuvre in. I sat with my back to the wall, flanking what I guessed was a two-way mirror. The chair was too small, the room too hot and too bright, but there was exactly nothing I could do about it. The basics were now officially out of reach, beyond my control. This was the sharp end of the law. Next stop: prison.

I was in a daze. I knew it wasn't a nightmare, but reality had slipped its moorings all the same. I didn't have a clue what was going on, except that I'd been arrested for Fabia Masson's murder.

When had she died? What had happened?

No one had told me anything, except that I'd killed her.

It didn't make sense.

I started rationalising. This was all a high-stakes misunderstanding. They'd figure that out soon enough and let me go. It was just a matter of time. All I had to do was be patient.

Outside, through the door, there was plenty of activity. Feet popping back and forth along the floor, multiple voices rising and then fading, the world going by fast. In here time stood still.

Then it hit me: VJ would have felt exactly the same way when he was arrested. The bewilderment, the confusion, the sensation that you've crashed through the looking glass into some other world where everything is upside down and coming at you fast, from every angle.

I wondered where Janet was. Had she been arrested too?

And then it was back to Fabia. Had she *really* been murdered?

I couldn't believe it. We'd just talked. I could still hear her voice, her French accent and perfect diction.

And I couldn't believe I was here.

As more time passed and no one came, I started suspecting things weren't going to turn out in my favour. And that's when I started getting scared. Scared I'd been fitted up like VJ, scared of being locked up for something I didn't do, scared of not seeing my family, watching my kids grow up . . .

A pair of detectives came in. Shopworn middle-aged blokes with pouchy eyes, damp hair and sparkling black leather shoes that made me think of Swayne. They introduced themselves, but I didn't catch their names. One was in a grey suit, the other in blue.

Grey Suit sat opposite me, Blue Suit took the desk.

'You're in a lot of trouble, Terry,' Grey Suit began, his soft voice belying his appearance of a jowly panther at rest.

'Where's Janet Randall?' I asked.

'Who?'

'The woman I was with when you arrested me?'

'You mean your accomplice?' Blue Suit said. He was louder and snarlier; theatrically or personally the nastier of the two.

'She's my boss,' I said.

'She put you up to this?' Blue Suit asked.

'Put me up to what?'

'Murder.'

'She didn't put me up to anything,' I said. 'She's a solicitor, and I'm her clerk.'

Blue Suit laughed and winked at his colleague.

'We got a smart one 'ere, eh, Phil. Phoney lawyer who stays in character. Method actin', I believe they call it,' he said, then turned to me. 'You can drop the act now, son. Show's over.'

'I don't understand what's going on,' I said to Grey Suit.

'You impersonated a lawyer to gain access to the victim, Fabia Masson. Is that right?' Grey Suit asked.

Was that true?

Think. Fast.

'You haven't charged me with anything.'

'*Yet*,' Blue Suit said.

'I've not been advised of my rights.'

Blue Suit ground his teeth and glared at me. Then he shot Grey Suit a quizzical look.

'I apologise for that oversight,' Grey Suit said. 'You don't have to say anything. It may harm your defence if you do not mention in evidence something which you later rely on in court. Anything you do say may be given in evidence against you. Do you understand?'

'Yes. Thank you, Detective,' I said. 'When I get the phone call I'm entitled to after this interview's over, I'd like to speak to DCI Carol Reid of the Metropolitan Police.'

Two hours they kept me in there, asking variations of the same thing. Once or twice I was close to answering when I remembered the golden

290

rule a lawyer always drums into a client. When interviewed alone by the police, say nothing. The generic term for this is 'No Comment'.

So:

Had I killed Fabia Masson?

'No Comment.'

Had I poisoned her?

'*Poisoned . . .?* No Comment.'

Had I injected her with poison?

'Eh . . .? No Comment.'

Had she ripped me off? Was that why I killed her?

'No Comment.'

Was I a hitman?

'*WHAT?* No Comment.'

When they were done, Grey Suit told me they'd pick this up later.

'I'd like to call DCI Reid now,' I said.

And I did – after they'd fingerprinted and photographed me, taken DNA samples, and made me change out of my clothes and into a white paper suit.

Then they took me to the cells.

The next morning they brought me back to the interrogation room.

DCI Reid was sitting at the desk, Blue Suit opposite me.

I was almost pleased to see her.

'Sit down, Terry,' she said, without looking at me. She was leafing through a file on the table, steel-rimmed glasses perched midway down her nose.

Blue Suit took the chair opposite mine.

'This isn't the first time you've called me, is it,' she said.

It was a statement, not a question. I didn't know what she was on about.

'Nor is it the first time you've trespassed on a police location.'

She turned over a couple of pages in the file. She still wasn't looking at me.

'And neither is it the first time you've impersonated someone.'

Ah . . .

Oh . . .

Fuck.

She knew I'd been in Suite 18, when she'd come in with Carnavale; knew the call had come from my phone. Easy enough for the police to trace a withheld number.

'So that's one count of impersonating a police officer, to go with one of impersonating a solicitor. The penalty for each is at least a year in prison – and you'll never work in the law again, obviously.'

291

I suppose now was the time to offer an apology, only I knew she wouldn't have been interested.

She took off her glasses and looked at me.

'Why am I here?' she asked me.

'I wanted you to hear what I found out from Fabia Masson before she died.'

'She didn't "die", Terry, she was murdered. Big difference,' she said, levelling an icy gaze at me.

'I didn't kill her,' I said.

She didn't so much as blink.

I tried to swallow but my mouth was dry. The reflux felt like a hand at my throat. I thought of my kids again, Karen.

She tapped the file.

'Do you know what this is?'

I shook my head.

'You. Your record, from the Hertfordshire police,' she said. 'Makes for interesting reading.'

'It was a bad time,' I mumbled.

'I'd say. So you know Vernon James?'

'*Knew* him. A long time ago ...'

No reaction. I glanced at Blue Suit. He was making notes in his pad.

If I didn't keep my wits about me, this situation had the potential to get way worse.

'There's no friendship between us, DCI Reid. Hasn't been for years.'

She closed her file.

'Then why are you here?'

'I was following a lead,' I said. 'I've been trying to track down Fabia Masson from the moment we got this case. She is – *was* – a key witness for us. And – for the record – I had no intention of going into the interview room or passing myself off as a solicitor. That happened by accident.'

'Come again?' she said.

'The desk sergeant buzzed me in. He didn't ask for ID, but I showed him my business card anyway. It doesn't say I'm a lawyer. It doesn't even have my name on it.'

'You mean this?' she said, and held up one of the KRP cards I carried around in my wallet.

'Yeah.'

'Why the interest in Fabia Masson?'

'Vernon James claims it was her he took up to his hotel suite that night, not Evelyn Bates. I wanted to verify that that was so.'

'Did you?'

292

'Yes.'

'What was her story?'

I told Reid almost everything Fabia had said. I began with VJ's watch and my search for it and ended back here, in the other interview room. The only thing I left out was the part about VJ assaulting Fabia.

'And that's what you wanted me to hear?' she asked, when I'd finished. She'd listened without interrupting me, showing absolutely no reaction.

'That's right.'

'Why?'

'It proves Vernon James is innocent,' I said.

'It proves nothing of the sort,' she said. 'Maybe she really told you these things, and maybe they're even true, but she's dead and you have no record whatsoever of the conversation. All we've got to go on is your word. And you're biased. You work for the firm representing the accused, and you two were childhood friends. See what I mean?'

Yes, I did. All too clearly.

I'd done this for nothing.

Fabia was dead.

And I'd messed up. *Massively.*

'You are going to look into what she told me, aren't you? You're not going to push this under the carpet, are you?' I said.

'Her murder will be thoroughly investigated,' she said.

Official speak for: *That's all I'm going to tell you for now.*

We sat in silence. Both detectives looked through their paperwork. I glanced at the mirror.

'How was Fabia killed?' I asked.

'After you left the station, the desk sergeant went on his break. A woman came in and said she was Fabia's solicitor. She showed the officer at reception her ID and was directed to the same interview room as you. Fabia was brought back in from the cells.'

'Wait a minute. You said *a woman* came in. I thought I was the main suspect.'

'Detectives reviewed the CCTV from the custody suite reception last night and they've eliminated you as a suspect.'

'Why didn't anyone tell me?'

'You wanted to see me,' she said. 'We thought it best to hold you until I got here.'

Blue Suit choked a guffaw.

'To continue,' she said. 'As you know, lawyer-client conversations are confidential. The meetings aren't taped or filmed by us, and there's never an officer present. There should, however, always be an officer

293

standing outside, but for reasons that aren't quite clear at the moment, there wasn't one. I'm guessing they're short-staffed here.

'At some point Fabia was injected with a fatal dose of poison. Her killer pricked her at the side of her neck. We don't know what it was yet. But it was fast-acting. When they found her, she was face down on the table like she was asleep. Didn't look like she had time to put up much of a fight. Job done, the killer left. She even signed out.'

'*Christ*,' I said, shuddering at the coldness of it.

It was a hit.

An assassination.

And a *daring* one at that.

Someone had wanted Fabia dead so badly they were prepared to take the greatest risks, go to any length to do it – even if it meant walking into a police station and killing her.

I thought of Swayne and what he'd told me . . . the White Ghosts, the Wingroves, Silver Service. I'd dismissed it at the time. Did he *know* what was going on?

'You said you had CCTV of the killer? Can I see it?'

'Not at the moment.'

'What did the killer look like at least? You said it was a woman, I might've seen her.'

DCI Reid nodded to Blue Suit, who read from his notepad.

'Caucasian with Oriental features. Five foot six or seven. Medium-length dark hair. Late twenties, early thirties. She was wearing a beige mac and carrying a briefcase.'

'Did you see anyone fitting that description?' she asked.

'No,' I said.

'Right then. You'll give Detective Rose here a statement about your interview with Fabia. Then you're free to go,' she said. 'As to how you got in here . . . Let's just say we'll overlook that in exchange for your full cooperation with our investigation.'

I was let out three hours later. Janet was pacing in the lobby. She had a face like thunder, with a hurricane following right behind. I knew she couldn't wait to bite my head off.

55

'What is it we do here, Terry?' Sid Kopf asked, a few long beats of silence after I'd finished talking to him about Fabia. It was the fifth time I'd gone over what happened.

294

'Pardon?' I asked.

'What is our business? Our trade? How do we make money?'

Outside it was raining. A steady, unending soak of slanted wetness that pinged off the lattice window and metal balcony, and filled the office with a light background noise akin to a distant stampede.

'We're a law firm,' I said.

'What does that mean?'

'Where's this going?' I asked.

'Humour me, please.'

'We provide a full range of legal services to our clients.

'*Legal* services. As opposed to *il-legal* ones, yes?'

'Yes.'

'What you did was *il*-legal. Are you aware of that?'

'Yes.'

'But you knew before you did it, didn't you?'

'Yes, but—'

'You did it all the same? We talked about this last week, remember – your "methods"?'

No comeback to that, and he wasn't expecting one. Point made, he leaned in and parked his elbows on his desk.

'Why didn't you wait for Janet instead of going in?' he asked.

She was sat to my left. Neither of us had taken our wet coats off. We'd come straight up here from the train station. I'd stood outside while Janet briefed him with the door closed. Fifteen minutes. Then I finally heard her voice, irate and snappy. I thought of my parents and how they'd always had their domestics where they thought we couldn't hear them. When a room wasn't free, they'd stand out in the street and bollock each other.

Janet hadn't bitten my head off as I'd expected, not when I recounted Fabia's story. It stunned her. She went pale, looked frightened. Then she took out a digital recorder and got me to repeat what I'd said. I tried to apologise for the trouble I'd caused, but she wafted that away like it was of no consequence.

'I wasn't sure Fabia was the right person,' I said. 'I didn't want Janet to come all the way out to Southend for nothing.'

'In other words, you did this to cover your back and save face?'

'I suppose so, yeah, but—'

'You thought it best to put the firm's reputation on the line instead of your own,' he said. 'Do you know the kind of trouble you almost landed us in?'

'I'm sorry about that, I truly am,' I said.

'A firm's reputation is everything in this business. A firm cannot be

295

seen to violate the very thing it represents. It's unethical. And this is one of the few sectors where ethics count as much as winning and losing trials. Did any of that even occur to you?'

'I decided . . .'

'Wrong. You had *no* decisions to make. You know why? You don't make decisions. You're not *qualified* to make decisions. Solicitors and barristers make decisions. Not clerks. You just write them down, type them up and file them away. You follow orders. And, most of all, you know your place.'

Not even a week ago this same man had slipped me a cash bonus.

'I thought you encouraged initiative,' I said.

'What you did was not initiative. It was good old-fashioned stupidity. And that I *don't* encourage.'

We stared each other down. After what I'd been through last night and this morning, not to mention the eight hours I'd spent in a cell in-between, this old man with his motionless white hair wasn't even close to intimidating me.

'With all due respect, Mr Kopf, I think you're missing the point,' I said.

'*Really?*'

'Have you taken into account *anything* I've just told you?' I said. 'Fabia Masson – a witness who could well have put a stop to this trial – was murdered in custody. I think it's fair to assume she was killed to stop her becoming that witness. *Our* witness. Just like I think it's an equally fair assumption that she was murdered by the same people who killed Evelyn Bates and framed Vernon James. And you're sitting there, waffling on at me about ethics I violated, while a person I talked to yesterday in connection with this case is lying dead on a slab – and while *our* client is in prison for something he didn't do.'

Kopf didn't so much as flinch.

'You're the one that's missing the point, Terry. Innocence is nothing without *proof* of innocence,' he said.

'I *know* that,' I said. 'But this case is now about more than a man killing a woman in his hotel room.'

'Not to us. We're lawyers, remember, not the police.'

'What would you have done in my position, then?'

'I wouldn't even have *been* in your position.'

'You haven't got where you are without taking risks.'

Kopf looked at Janet in disbelief. She found her wet shoes more interesting.

'You want to talk about risk, do you?' Kopf said. 'Stephen Purdom and I started this firm in 1962. We had all of one client then. A man like us, just starting out.

'That was the biggest risk I've ever taken. And we're still here, forty-nine years later. You know why? Some of it was down to luck, some of it down to hard work, but most of it was simple maths.

'The risk I took then was calculated. I worked out the pros and cons in advance. I weighed up how much I could afford to lose by how much there was to gain. When gain outweighs loss by a significant amount, take the risk. But never be blinded by the gain. Always remember what you have to lose. You were blinded by the gain, weren't you?'

'I didn't think about it that way,' I said. 'It was about doing the best for our client.'

'Rubbish!' Kopf thundered. 'This was about getting ahead here – and don't pretend otherwise.'

'Yes, *that* too,' I said. 'But I'm more interested in winning this trial.'

'Why?'

'Because Vernon James did *not* kill Evelyn Bates. And you can go on about the law all you bloody well want, but our client is *innocent*. And Janet knows it. Don't you?'

I looked to her for support. But her shoes still had her hypnotised. What the hell was wrong with her?

Kopf sighed.

'In a way, I should thank you for your candour. It's quite obvious to me you don't care about yourself any more than you do this firm. You haven't even tried to pretend otherwise,' he said. 'Ambition is all very well and it's nourished and cherished here, but it has its limits. What you did was reckless, foolhardy and completely wrong. A lawyer must be cold, rational and detached. They must also look before they leap. You're obviously completely wrong for this firm, but also, I think, for this profession. So I want you to get your things and leave. If you're not out in five minutes, I'll call security.'

Now I couldn't meet his eye. I'd been expecting this from Janet when I was released from Southend nick. But then, on the train back, seeing her reaction to what I told her, I thought I'd be OK, that we'd be devoting our energies to proving Fabia's story. Funny how it was turning out here. When I expected to be fired, I wasn't. When I didn't . . .

I looked over the photographs on the wall behind him, hanging off the wood panelling like flaking monochromatic scales, all except for the larger one in the middle; the centrepiece, that big sunstruck building with the black Morris Minor parked close by.

Then I walked out.

I only had three personal effects in the office: a birthday card Amy had painted me, and an essay Ray had written for school a couple of years ago. It was called 'My Hero: My Dad'. I kept them there as a kind of talisman, something to look at and remind myself why I was putting up with all the crap Adolf threw my way. The last was my lunchbox in the fridge, and the sandwiches and apple I'd brought to work yesterday.

As I sat at the desk, with my wet coat still on, I almost laughed. My lunchbox was empty. Adolf hadn't just eaten the sandwiches, but the apple too, which was a first. All she'd left me was a crumpled, lipstick-stained napkin and a few crumbs.

I put everything in my bag.

'Bella?'

Adolf stopped typing and glowered at me, irritated.

'This is goodbye,' I said.

Surprise.

'But, before I go, there's something I've wanted to tell you for the longest time.'

The others had heard. Keyboards stopped chattering. Iain peered over his cubicle.

'You're a sad, pathetic, mean-spirited little squirt. If you put half as much effort into your work as you do into protecting the trivial pisspot Reich you run here, you'd probably do quite well for yourself. But you don't, so you won't. This is the best it'll ever get for you. Enjoy.'

She was incredulous, open-mouthed, crimson.

I slung my bag strap over my shoulder and stood up.

'Oh, and by the way – you know that sandwich you helped yourself to? I spat in it when I made it yesterday morning. Just like I have in every one of the sandwiches you've helped yourself to. *Bon appetit* and fuck you very much.'

And, head held uncommonly high, I walked out of the office.

I didn't get far.

'Terry!'

It was Edwina, hailing me from the stairs.

'Can you come up, please?'

They had to give me my P45.

I followed her upstairs.

Kopf's door was open. Janet was still sitting there, but no longer watching her feet. It was Kopf's turn to ignore me. He was leaning back in his chair, arms folded, staring off into space.

'Close the door,' Janet said.

I did as asked and took a couple of steps in, staying out of their immediate radius.

'I *personally* think you did the right thing yesterday. You just went

298

about it the wrong way,' she said. 'The truth of the matter is, I wouldn't have come to Southend based on your hunch. You had no way of being sure it was Fabia. And there's no way you could have verified her identity without talking to her. Firing you, in that respect, is *completely* unfair. Besides, if things hadn't gone so wrong, you would've been a hero.'

I didn't look at Kopf.

'We're also far too close to the trial to lose you, frankly. We're a good team. Christine likes you. And Vernon will want to have familiar faces around him. It'll be bad for his morale if a key member disappears. So Sid and I have talked this over, and he's prepared to withdraw your dismissal – on one condition.'

I glanced at him. The old bastard was inscrutable.

'You can only leave the office during working hours accompanied by me, Liam or Christine. No more unsupervised field trips. That includes doing the rounds with Andy Swayne. And strictly *no* investigating Fabia's murder. That's the police's job. Ours is to prepare for trial.'

Grounded, like a disobedient kid.

'Are you prepared to accept those conditions?'

So 'safe' for three more months. Time to get my CV together and start looking for another job.

'Yes, I am,' I said.

'All right then. Go back to work.'

It's one thing to despise people you have to work with every day, and quite another to tell them. They should never know.

When I walked back to the office, freshly reinstated, the three of them all stared at me in silence and with predictable surprise. Yet there was also something else in their looks – wariness. The last time I'd provoked that particular collective reaction was in Stevenage, back in the Dark Ages, when I used to walk into pubs, binge-primed.

I took off my coat and jacket and rolled up my sleeves.

It was going to be a long few months.

56

As a rule, I don't cry. It's in my genes. I come from undemonstrative stock. The Flynts are born pessimists and stoic with it. We were weaned on spilled milk. But when I walked into the living room that night and saw my family sitting around the dinner table, the tear dam almost ruptured. Knowing I'd come so close to losing them, to never seeing them like this, doing something as simple as eating together, almost overwhelmed me.

'Where've you been, Dad?' Ray asked, stern-faced.

'Occasionally, in this job, you have to work overnight,' I said, helping myself to dinner. Karen had made spaghetti Bolognese.

'Mum was worried,' he said, reproachfully. In his dark eyes, I saw the adult he was becoming; the stern parent too.

I looked at Karen. I'd phoned her an hour ago. I hadn't told her much, except that I was coming home and would explain everything. She'd sounded equal parts relieved and pissed off.

'I know. I'm sorry. I really am,' I said.

I took Karen's hand and squeezed it, gently. Amy beamed at us. All was right in her world. Her dad was home. Her family was together. And she was eating her favourite dish. It didn't get any better than that for her.

'It's all right,' Ray shrugged. 'Just this once.'

Amy laughed.

And I did too.

Then Karen, and, lastly, Ray.

Thank God I was home.

Later, Karen made coffee and we sat alone at the table. I hadn't slept in over thirty-six hours. I was drained. But we had to talk.

So, for the sixth and final time that day I reeled out what had happened at Southend nick. Except now I was barely conscious of what I was saying. I felt my mouth moving and heard sounds coming out, and saw it all apparently making perfect sense to my wife, but I might as well have been talking in my sleep.

'*Un-believable . . .*' she said at the end.

'Yeah . . . I know I—'

'You used the one and only phone call you had to call that copper.'

'What was I supposed to do?'

'You could've called me,' she said. 'You *should've* called me.'

'I had *one* phone call,' I said.

'I was worried out of my mind when you didn't come home last night. And then, this morning, when I got up and you weren't there . . . I was *scared*, Terry. I didn't know what had happened to you!'

'Look, I know, I—'

'Why didn't you call me?'

'I—'

'You didn't even call me from Southend when you were waiting for Janet,' she said, getting angrier and redder, and fighting to keep her voice down so the kids wouldn't wake up.

'I called you as soon as I could, but—'

'You should've called me *from the fuckin' station!*'

'What could you've done?'

'I could've got you a lawyer and called DCI Reid. That's what I could've *done*, Terry.'

'Yeah, but . . .'

'Did you even *think* about us? Your family? Your kids asking where you were? You didn't, did you?'

'Of course I did, Karen.'

'Bollocks.'

She was cutting me off at every corner. We both knew she was right. Despite my tiredness I was sticking to the rules of domestic combat.

'You care more about this bloody case, don't you?' she said, bitterly, tearing up.

'No. That's not it.'

'One phone call you get. *One!* And you don't even call me.'

What could I say to that?

I hadn't. Janet had been locked up, and I wanted DCI Reid to hear Fabia's confession.

'You don't understand, Karen. This was . . . This wasn't . . . Look, I didn't want to involve you, all right?'

She gawped at me, stalk-eyed with amazement.

'But I *am* involved, you daft twat! We all are. *All* of us here. We're your *family* for Chrissakes! You got locked up on a *murder* charge! What if you were still locked up?'

I was too knackered to think.

I looked at the digital photoframe on the mantelpiece. Our marriage seemed to be flashing before my eyes in slow motion. Us on our wedding day at Wandsworth Registry Office, Ray in-between; us on our honeymoon, Ray wearing my sunglasses; us with Amy in hospital, Ray cradling her with a proud smile on his face; Amy's christening at St Mary's Church on Battersea Embankment; the four of us celebrating our first Christmas in Manchester.

Then I yawned. I couldn't help it. The reflex kicked in before I had time to catch it.

'You know what, Terry? I'd call you selfish, but selfish people only put themselves first. You don't even do *that* much. You put that bloody case before *everything*.'

I could barely form coherent thoughts, let alone muster up the words to answer.

'What are you going to do when this is all over, eh? Have you thought that far? When they kick you out of that firm? When there's no more trial and no more Vernon James? What are you going to do then?' she asked.

'What do you mean?' I said.

'I've never seen you so motivated in your life. I've never seen you chase anything with this kind of ... *passion* before. Not even me. This case is the first thing I've ever seen you *really* care about. It's all that matters to you. All you think about. And it's scary. And *you're* scary. 'Cause you can't see what it's doing to you, to us.'

'And what would that be?'

'I rest my case,' she said. 'You can sleep on the fuckin' couch.'

57

May

Back at the office the next day, my colleagues arrived together, which they'd never done before. Adolf and The Other Two. All smiles and jokes, extra-friendly with each other. They didn't look at me. Not so much as a glance in my general direction.

Michaela announced a tea-making rota. They picked their slots. She wrote it down and it went up on the corkboard. I wasn't asked.

The message was simple: I no longer existed.

Nothing I could do about it, but ignore it by staying busy.

I called Swayne. I wanted to talk to him about the Wingroves and the White Ghosts. He'd brought them up for a specific reason. He knew more than he was letting on – a lot more.

He didn't answer. I left a message.

Then Janet emailed and asked me to write a full report about Fabia and run off four copies. We had a client meeting at Belmarsh to go to.

'Well, at least it proves my defence, doesn't it?' VJ said.

I'd been spared regurgitating the Southend nick debacle. Janet played narrator this time. Because she told it chronologically, VJ's face went through a time-lapsed sequence of hopes raised and dashed expressions – exhilaration to disappointment to sick, quaking shock at the conclusion.

It took him a few moments to regain his composure. He got up and paced and took deep breaths. He'd lost so much weight, his clothes were barely staying on him; his sweatshirt slipped and slid towards his shoulders, his tracksuit billowed about his legs like oversized sails.

'To us, yes,' Christine said.

'Can't you put Terry on the stand?' VJ asked.

Christine shook her head.

'That's a minefield. Legally, Terry is a "Bad Character" – a witness who committed an offence in obtaining evidence. Franco Carnavale would destroy him.'

It was a good call on her part. Besides the pitfalls she'd mentioned, I would have to admit my past relationship with VJ, and that would make what I'd done look even worse than just some overeager underling getting in over his head. None of the defence team – nor anyone at KRP – knew about us. *If the truth came out reputations would take a hit.*

'What about the police? They know the truth.'

'They know what Terry said, but there's no one to back it up.'

'How's their investigation going? Are they close to catching someone?'

'We don't know. They're under no legal obligation to tell us, unless it directly affects you and the trial. For now, to them, it's a separate matter,' Christine said. 'And I wouldn't get your hopes up that they'll catch Fabia's killer. It was a professional hit. Professionals don't get caught.'

VJ groaned and rubbed his temples. I saw new greys there.

'But you *will* bring Fabia's murder up in court, right?'

Christine and Janet exchanged a look that told me they'd already discussed this and agreed what they were going to tell him in advance. Janet gave her a nod.

'We can't so much as *hint* at it,' Christine said.

'*Why?*'

'Without a signed statement from Fabia it's inadmissible. Hearsay.'

'Doesn't the prosecution know what happened?'

'Probably. But that's not the point, because, legally – so far – it doesn't affect the case. As I said, we cannot enter Fabia's conversation with Terry into evidence. Therefore it's not part of our defence, and not part of the trial,' Christine explained.

'The bottom line is that unless the police catch Fabia's killer and get a confession out of her, the fundamentals are unchanged. Evelyn Bates was murdered in your room. Even if Fabia was still alive and talking to us, it wouldn't prove you didn't kill Evelyn. You'd still have a case to answer. The trial would still go ahead.'

The following morning, Redpath came down to the office with his and Janet's Belmarsh notes and asked me to type them up, run off three copies, email another to Christine, and put the spare in filing.

No problem there, exactly, but him and Janet both had PAs for that, and I wasn't a trained typist. I was a one-finger seek and peck keyboardist. But all I said was:

'Sure.'

'Looks like you're coming full circle,' Redpath said as he left.

And that pretty much set the pace for the rest of the month.

Overnight, my job became simple and undemanding. Basic clerical work – typing and filing.

I'd arrive in the mornings to find a small heap of badly scrawled notes and dog-eared legal pads in my in-tray. By late afternoon I'd have turned them all into typescripts. They also got me covering for the receptionist when she took her lunchbreak.

Demotion did have its upsides. The pressure was suddenly off. I didn't have to come up with anything that might turn the trial around.

I stopped spitting in my sandwiches.

I started taking all my lunchbreaks. And I also got to leave the office dead on six, so I saw much more of my family. I was home well in time for dinner every night and my weekends were free again. I made up for the last few weeks, by helping the kids with their homework and hanging on their every word. I read to them at night.

I mended things with Karen in a big way. One Friday we got a babysitter and had our first date in God knows how long. We went to dinner on Battersea Embankment and spent most of the night holding hands across the table and looking into each other's eyes, me apologising for ever putting the case before them, vowing it wouldn't happen again.

Unfortunately, I didn't mean it.

Really, I was bored stiff. The prospect of going to work and knowing exactly what I was going to be doing from day to day began to gnaw at me after the second week.

I tried to look on the bright side. I hadn't been fired. I'd been given a three-month grace period to get my act together and have a job to go to when this one ended. And I was luckier still. It could have been even worse. I could have gone to prison. Yet that's the thing about luck: you never know you've had it till it's run out.

But mostly, I couldn't stop thinking about the case.

I didn't have a clue what was happening because I was shut out. Janet and Redpath weren't keeping me in the loop at all – and I knew better than to ask them.

I kept trying to reach Swayne. The first two weeks, straight to voicemail. Then, on the third week, an automated voice told me I couldn't leave a message because his inbox was full. By the end of the month his number was no longer in service.

I called DCI Reid to find out how the investigation was going. Her response was predictable: 'I can't discuss ongoing police affairs. If anything relevant to you or your client comes up, we'll be in touch.'

There'd been nothing on the news about Fabia's murder. Nothing at all. Even on the internet. Like it had never happened. Maybe it was too embarrassing, or maybe there was something else afoot, something bigger than a dead prostitute.

And as for what I now thought about VJ:

Well . . .

I won't lie.

I wished he was guilty. That had been easier to accept, and easier still to believe.

I was disappointed he was innocent. The tag didn't suit him. Good people were 'innocent'. Not him. He wasn't 'good'. He wasn't even blameless in the fate that had befallen him. If anything, he deserved it. Actions have consequences. *You can't cheat karma*, and all that.

But, now, above all, what I really wanted to know was who was behind it. And – especially – why? What had VJ done to them?

58

June

Another month of pure drudgery. I didn't leave the office at all.

It was sunny, then it rained, then it was sunny again.

I got my CV together and sent it out to law firms and recruitment agencies. I had no response from the former, and a few introductory meetings with the latter. Those all ended the same way – nothing for someone with my skillsets at the moment, but they'd call me back if they had anything.

So – when the verdict was rendered, irrespective of how it went, my law career was looking over.

What was I going to do?

Karen suggested I retrain, pick a trade specialising in something people would always need, that I didn't need to be young to do, or lie my way into; something it wasn't too late to start.

Like what?

'Plumbing,' she said. 'There'll always be a future in shit.'

59

Friday, July 8th, 2011

With the trial starting in just over two weeks, I was finally let out of the office to do some real work. Christine and Redpath were prepping VJ for the witness stand. They needed me to sit in as a notetaker and soundboard.

VJ had aged another half-decade since I'd seen him last. His face was seemingly held together by wrinkles and an untamed black-and-white beard covering his neck and creeping up his cheeks in a patchy spread.

'You look tired,' Christine said, diplomatically.

Not that she could talk. Her eyes were pink-rimmed and glassy. She'd dozed off on the train over and filled the carriage with phlegmy and hissy breathing, occasionally punctuated by a heavy cough that exploded midway in her chest.

'Haven't been sleeping much,' VJ said. 'I keep having these dreams. Nightmares, really.'

'You need to focus,' she said, gently.

'I know.'

He ground his teeth and rubbed his chin. I noticed he'd chewed his nails to the quick.

'You're going to have to give evidence. The jury will want to hear you say you didn't kill Evelyn Bates. We're going to make you convincing. You need to work on everything, from what you say to how you say it. Voice, attitude, posture, eye contact.'

'Will that make any difference?' he asked.

'The British jury system is inherently flawed. It's based on the assumption that an ordinary member of the public is intelligent enough to follow hours of complex legal argument delivered by men and women in powdered wigs, spouting a version of English last spoken in 1811. The assumption's wrong. Nine out of twelve jurors don't understand what's going on. So they look at things they can understand. Simple things. Do they like the accused? Does he look guilty? Does he sound guilty? Could the victim be their daughter? At the end of the day, a trial is nothing more than a high stakes reality show, a popularity contest where your fate gets voted on by idiots.

'You're going to have to be ready for Franco Carnavale in a way you've never been ready for anything and anyone in your life. He not only possesses a fine legal mind, but he has that special thing too – he has a performer's sense of audience. He knows how to work a jury, how to get them on side. But if you get through one of our sessions, you'll make it through ten of his.'

VJ looked around the room, at those now very familiar four pale-yellow walls, pausing at the panic button.

'OK,' he said. 'Let's have it.'

'Carnavale's going to wind you up,' she said. 'He'll come at you from all angles. He'll do everything to unsettle you. His objective will be to make you angry, to provoke you into losing your cool. Fall for that and the jury will see a man who lacks self-control, a man who could kill in anger. So, the first rule is to stay absolutely calm. Don't ever raise your voice.'

'OK.'

'Next, when answering questions, always remember the word "squid".'

'Pardon?'

'S.Q.U.I.D. Squid,' she said. 'Keep your answers:

Simple – Answer yes and no at all times. If you have to say more, use as few words as possible.

Quick – Don't hesitate. If you do, it means you're thinking. And if you're thinking, it means you're inventing.

Unambiguous – Stick to your version at all times. Don't go off statement.

Informative – Answer the question asked. Tell him exactly what he wants to know.

Decisive – Be firm when answering. Remember you're telling the truth.

'*SQUID*. Got it?'

'Got it,' VJ said.

Christine leaned in.

'Now we can begin. Terry, ask the first question, please.'

I hadn't been briefed on any of this, but I knew what she wanted. Something that would put him on edge and get a rise out of him. I had quite a few of those – not all of them relevant. Like 'Who really stole your diary?' and

'When did you first cheat on your wife?'

VJ tensed up immediately.

'*What?*'

Christine jumped in.

'Never answer a question with a question, Vernon. It looks like you're playing for time. And watch your tone. Keep it flat. Emotionless. Ask him the question again, Terry.'

I did.

'We weren't even married the first time,' he said, scowling at me.

'So why get married at all?'

'It was her idea,' he said. 'We both wanted children, a family. I thought she'd make a good mother.'

'But not a good enough wife?'

'Melissa's a perfect wife,' he said.

'But you're an imperfect husband?'

'Yes,' he said.

'Excellent!' Christine said. 'Remember that, Vernon. You're an "imperfect husband".'

'I will,' he said, giving me a cutting look.

'Good. Let's carry on.'

Monday, July 11th, 2011

I got into the office early, buzzing from Friday. I was renewed, determined, primed. I really wanted to be a lawyer. I was going to *fight* for it.

And then, the instant I saw my desk, I deflated faster than a balloon colliding with a hedgehog. There was the now habitual pile of to-be-typeds teetering in my in-tray, but two box files had been left on my chair, with a Post-it note from Janet on top: 'For archiving.'

'Archiving' was a fancy euphemism for one of my other tasks – filing.

Both boxes related to VJ's case. I went through them, sorting bills, invoices, copies of Janet's correspondence and unused CPS material. There was plenty of the latter – evidence Carnavale had discarded.

I went through it, just in case. Plenty of crime-scene and post-mortem photographs, statements from witnesses who wouldn't be called or used, lab reports about carpet fibres.

And then ...

This:

VJ's bill from the Blenheim-Strand.

There were only two things listed. The cost of the room – £2011 – and a bottle of Grey Goose vodka for which he'd paid £275. That was about ten times what it cost in a supermarket.

But where was the champagne he'd supposedly ordered?

I opened my case file and found the list of evidence the police had taken from the suite.

1 bottle Cristal champagne 75cl (unopened) in a bucket, two glasses.

Rudy Saks told me he'd entered the order into the office computer as soon as he'd taken it, 'so it would be billed to the room'.

In his statement to the police, Saks hadn't mentioned doing that. His witness account focused on delivering the champagne to the room before 1 a.m., and seeing Evelyn Bates on the couch.

From Fabia's account, I knew that Saks was in on the set-up.

How to prove it?

First up, if VJ really ordered the champagne, how come it hadn't appeared on his bill?

The CPS had entered the phone log from Suite 18 into evidence, showing that a call was made to room service at 12.47 a.m.

Second, there were no signs of forced entry. The CPS had included a print-out of the log from the suite's keycard lock.

The log was a simple table:

S18 – Door Lock

Day	Time
16.3.11:	17.38pm (gk040973)
16.3.11:	20.52pm (pk15t)
16.3.11:	23.57pm (gk040973)
17.3.11:	08.03am (pk15t)

gk – Guest Key
pk – Passkey

Conundrum:

17.38 p.m. – VJ entered the suite.

23.57 p.m. – VJ entered the suite with Fabia.

The door to Suite 18 was not opened from the outside again until the maids went in at 8.03 a.m. the next day.

So how did Evelyn get in the room?

Theory:

Someone let Evelyn in, someone *already* inside the room.

Not VJ. He was unconscious on the couch.

Then who?

Fabia was supposed to call room service for champagne – that was to let Saks in.

Saks could have killed Fabia alone, but there was always the risk of something going wrong – Fabia fighting back, or getting away, as she had.

So there must have been at least one other person in the room, to make sure everything ran smoothly.

309

When had the second person come in?

The answer was right in front of me.

I took out the crime-scene pictures and went through them until I came to the shots of Evelyn in the bedroom; the close-ups of her head resting on the crisp, unruffled pillows with the Marquis chocolates still on them.

I rang Albert Torena at the hotel.

'What time is the turndown service?' I asked him.

'Between 7 p.m. and 9.30 p.m.'

'What's the process?'

'The topsheet and duvet are turned back and a mint is placed on each pillow.'

'A mint? Not a chocolate?'

'No, the chocolate's for when the guests arrive. A little welcome gift.'

I *knew* it.

The photograph of the bed showed it hadn't been turned down at all.

VJ told us a maid had knocked on his door while he was getting changed for the awards dinner. It was the turndown service, and he'd sent her away. She hadn't come into the room.

Yet someone *had* entered Suite 18 at 20.52 p.m., after VJ had left, using the maid's passkey.

And they hadn't left. They'd stayed there the whole time.

Would this stand up in court?

No. It was pure speculation.

I needed evidence.

And I needed to find out what had happened to Evelyn in the last two hours of her life.

Tuesday, July 12th, 2011

Fabia had met Evelyn Bates once, in the bathroom near the Casbah nightclub. She'd then seen her in the corridor, talking to a man who looked like hotel security.

At some point after that Evelyn had returned to the room she'd shared with Penny Halliwell and left her a note on the side table:

@ Private party @ Suite 18. Evey x

Penny hadn't noticed it until she left the next morning.

Timeframe:

Evelyn left the nightclub at 11.13 p.m.

Went to the bathroom. Seen by Fabia (*circa* 11.15 p.m.).

VJ left the club at 11.19 p.m.

Met Fabia in the corridor (*circa* 11.22 p.m.).

Evelyn talked to hotel security man in the corridor (*circa* 11.22–11.25 p.m.)

VJ and Fabia went upstairs to the Circle bar (*circa* 11.30 p.m.)

Evelyn was murdered between 12 and 3 a.m.

Slightly over an hour and a half for her to:

1) Accept an invitation to Suite 18.
2) Go to her room, leave Penny a note.
3) Get drugged with Rohypnol – which starts to take effect within ten minutes of ingestion.
4) Go to Suite 18.

There were two ways up to Suite 18 – via the fire escape, which was alarmed and would have sounded if the door had been opened; or the VIP lift, which was only operable with the right keycard – either a room key or a staff passkey.

Where to start?

Here:

Talk to the security guy.

Get keycard info for Evelyn's room for March 16th and 17th.

Back to Torena I went.

'Do you have someone working for you who's well built and has a shaved head?' I said, after I'd got him on the phone.

'That's most of them. Even the girls,' he quipped.

'I need a list of all security personnel who worked the night of March 16th. And I'll also need the keycard data for Room 474 on the same date. Can you help with that?'

'Sure. I'll have the information for you in a couple of days. Give me your personal email.'

Back on reception duty.

The Gang of Three went out to lunch in formation, led by Adolf.

Edwina left ten minutes later.

The office was quiet.

At times like these, when I had nothing better to do, I thought about my future. If I wanted to be a lawyer, I'd need a degree. I didn't need KRP for that. There were plenty of courses for mature students. I could apply for a loan. I had a fair chance of getting one too, seeing as I'd once been good enough to get into Cambridge.

I looked up courses on the internet.

311

The phone rang.

'It's Edwina. I think I may've left my mobile upstairs. The trouble is, I don't know where. If I call the number, can you locate it for me? You'll recognise my ringtone. It's "The Dambusters March". I'll hang up and call now.'

I trotted off upstairs.

I didn't hear anything ringing around Edwina's desk. I wasn't even sure I'd recognise the theme from *The Dam Busters*. Hadn't seen it since I was a kid.

I looked on the floor around her desk, tried the drawers. Had she even called the number?

And then I heard a faint sound.

It was coming from Kopf's office.

I put an ear to the door.

A tune was playing. One I recognised all too well, but I remembered it better from an insurance advert. Or was it carpets?

Dam Busters.

Kopf obviously wasn't in, but I knocked anyway.

No reply.

I tried the door. It was unlocked. I pushed it open a crack, enough to see his desk.

I walked in.

The ringtone was coming from deep in the room.

The phone was on top of the filing cabinet.

I picked it up.

I saw Adolf's name on the screen.

'Hello?'

'Took your time,' Edwina said.

'It was in Mr Kopf's office,' I said.

'Oh . . . Can you leave it on my desk?'

'Sure.'

She hung up.

So, she'd gone out to lunch with Adolf and Crew: I'd never stood a chance here.

I should've turned and left then, but my curiosity got the better of me. I was standing in the middle of Sid Kopf's inner sanctum, the brains and soul of the company. What was it that made someone like him tick, exactly? Why was he so interested in photographing crumbling old London buildings – therefore preserving the past; therefore prone to reflection and sentimentality – yet so ruthless in the way he ran his business?

Kopf's personality was all over the room. The furniture was antique

312

and obviously expensive, but as tasteful as it was solid and durable. There were no framed degree certificates here, no photographs of him with any of his famous clients, and no pictures of the family I knew he had from stray office gossip. This was his seat of power. This was where he ruled.

I went and stood behind his desk. I sat down. The backrest of his chair resisted my attempts at getting comfortable, refusing to yield, so I found myself leaning precariously over the desk, on the verge of tipping over.

I pushed one of the levers under the seat. The chair dropped down suddenly with a hydraulic hiss. I tried another and the chair sprang back up and bucked forward, slamming my kneecaps painfully into the desk.

OK. Time to go.

I readjusted the chair to roughly how I'd found it. Then I scanned his desk to make sure I hadn't displaced anything.

All in order.

Except for Edwina's phone. I'd left that on top of the filing cabinet.

As I got up to fetch it, I noticed that the bottom drawer of the cabinet wasn't quite closed.

I opened it.

There were two hanging files, one pretty much stuffed to capacity, the other only partially filled. The files were index tagged 2008–10 and 2011–.

I reached into the latter.

There was a single document. A will, made by Scott Nagle. It was a three-page document. I scanned it quickly. The man was worth multi-millions. He'd left his estate to his three sons, and put ten million in a trust for each of his seven grandchildren. He'd bequeathed money to his PA, his driver, cooks and cleaners. Decent bloke, I thought.

And then something caught my eye.

A name:

Miriam Zengeni.

He'd left her the deeds to a flat in Archer House, Vicarage Crescent, Battersea, and set up a trust in her name.

Archer House?

That was the block of flats near Battersea Embankment where I'd seen Swayne talking to his ex-wife.

Nagle had also left a million pounds to a Bridget Zengeni.

Zengeni . . . ?

Where did I know that name from?

I put the will back.

I opened the top drawer. More hanging files, again indexed by year.

313

The first was for 1962 – the year the firm had started. The other drawers held files all the way to the present, grouped by decade.

I opened the penultimate drawer, randomly reached for the 1992 file, and took out the first document I found.

Scott Nagle Associates had bought a block in Oakley Street, Chelsea. Kopf had overseen the deal.

I looked in the 1999 file, and found a letter from Sid Kopf to Wandsworth Council. He expressed his client's 'profound disappointment' that his bid to redevelop Battersea Power Station had been rejected. His client was Scott Nagle Associates.

I looked in another drawer. Pulled out a file: 1981 – a different property deal. Three houses in Powis Square, Notting Hill. The buyer was Scott Nagle Associates. The law firm: Kopf-Purdom. Before Janet's time.

Then I went to the top drawer and pulled out the very first file: 1962. Scott Nagle Associates had bought a penthouse in Lancaster Gate. Sid Kopf had represented him.

Scott Nagle was Kopf's only client, or so it seemed.

The next document in was another will – or a draft of one. There were annotations in several pages in red. Every corrected line had initials in the margin. 'SK'.

The will was that of Thomas Nagle. He'd divided his estate evenly between his two sons, Scott and Michael. Michael's share of the inheritance was conditional on his changing his family name from his mother's to his father's.

Michael's maternal name was 'Zengeni'.

Michael *Zengeni*.

Now I remembered.

I'd looked up Oliver Wingrove and the White Ghosts on the internet after Swayne told me about them. I'd found all of one thing about Wingrove. He'd appeared at an inquest into the death of Michael Zengeni in Rhodesia.

Michael Zengeni was Scott Nagle's half-brother.

Not for the first time did I ask myself the following questions:

What the hell was Swayne getting at?

And what did this have to do with VJ?

60

Contrary to popular belief, you can't find everything you want on the internet. This especially applied to information on Scott Nagle. He didn't have a website, nor any other official internet presence, and there were no photos of him.

An hour's trawl turned up all of a single paragraph in Wikipedia:

Scott Nagle (born on March 8th, 1932) is a British businessman, financier and real estate tycoon. His father was Thomas Nagle, the British property developer. The Sunday Times has estimated him to be worth £1.2 billion [citation needed]. In 1979 he won undisclosed damages from Private Eye, the satirical and current affairs magazine, over an article suggesting complicity in his first wife's death.

After work I schlepped over to the British Library's newspaper archive in Colindale, north London. I bought a one-day pass, found a place in the reading room and started searching.

Call it fate or coincidence or just the way things happen to shake out, but I'd crossed paths with Scott Nagle long before I started working at KRP.

My bedsit in Montague Terrace, Croydon, was his. Nagle had owned not just that house, but almost *every* house in that miserable street, where the trees were either dead or had been set on fire, and most of the cars were on blocks or not worth nicking.

He was a slumlord.

Evening Standard, March 8th, 1962

Property Developer Laid to Rest

The funeral service of Thomas Nagle, the property tycoon, took place at Brompton Oratory in South Kensington. Nagle, a former Quaker, had converted to Catholicism ten years ago. He is survived by his wife Sybil and his son, Scott.

(There was a picture accompanying the piece. Taken in the street, outside the church, it showed Scott Nagle, in profile. A tall man with

315

dark wavy hair and a thin face, dominated by a long and fleshy nose. His eyes were hidden behind wraparound shades. He had on a black suit and tie, and winkle pickers. Standing next to him were two women in dark coats. The youngest wore her hair in a beehive and stared straight into the camera, all smouldering, pouty model poise. The woman at her side was older and blonde. She'd lifted up her dark glasses to dab at a tear on her cheek. The fourth person in the photo was blonde too. He was partially turned away from the photographer and seemed to be talking to Nagle. It took me a while to recognise this figure in the double-breasted black suit. It was the hair that threw me, a short and stylish pompadour complete with medium-length side-burns. It was Sid Kopf.)

Daily Mail, May 22nd, 1962

Zengeni Inquest Returns Open Verdict

An inquest today on the death of Michael Zengeni, illegitimate son of late property developer Thomas Nagle, recorded a verdict of unlawful killing.

Zengeni, a British citizen living in Rhodesia, was first reported missing in November 1961, when he failed to arrive at Heathrow airport on a flight he had been booked on.

Captain Oliver Wingrove of the British South Africa Police, who headed up the investigation into Zengeni's disappearance in Rhodesia, told the coroner how Zengeni's badly decomposed body was found in the back of his abandoned car, some twenty miles outside Salisbury the following month.

Zengeni's body was identified by Wingrove with the help of dental records from England.

During the course of the inquest it was revealed that Michael was the son of Thomas Nagle and a black South African woman, who Nagle is believed to have met on a business trip to Rhodesia. Michael and his half-brother Scott were born days apart, with

Michael being the eldest. Although Thomas Nagle never publicly recognised Michael as his son, he paid for his education in England.

Miriam Zengeni, Michael's widow and mother to their one-year-old daughter, stated that the family had experienced 'hostility and threats' from both white and black Rhodesians while living on their farm outside the town of Hartley.

Evening Standard, April 11th, 1972

World in Action Injunction Upheld

An injunction taken out by real estate magnate Scott Nagle against Granada Television and the producers of current affairs programme *World in Action* was upheld today in the Royal Courts of Justice.

The programme, *Lucifer's Landlord*, was to have aired last November. Mr Nagle was granted the injunction against the broadcast on the grounds that it was defamatory.

Scott Nagle is believed to own over a thousand rental properties in the country, predominantly in London and the South-East. It has long been rumoured that Nagle has forced owners out of properties he has wished to acquire through various forms of intimidation. These are believed to include installing prostitutes and drug dealers in neighbouring houses, and encouraging West Indian immigrants to use his property as 'sha-beens' – illegal drinking dens – complete with 'sound systems' (playing loud reggae music). There have also been allegations of anonymous threats and violence.

Sid Kopf, Mr Nagle's lawyer, said his client had 'no comment to make at this stage'.

Crucified Man Identified

The body of a man found nailed to the door of a squat in Ladbroke Grove, west London, on Christmas Day has been identified as that of Roland White. White was one of eight people illegally occupying the five-bedroom house.

The property was purchased last year by controversial real estate baron, Scott Nagle. Nagle served the squatters with an eviction notice, which was successfully challenged in court by White, a trainee solicitor.

Police are appealing to witnesses to come forward with information.

Sunday Times, June 24th, 1979

Property Tycoon's Wife Found Dead

Estelle Nagle, wife of controversial property tycoon Scott Nagle, was found dead at her home in Holland Park. The couple, who had separated earlier this year, were said to have started divorce proceedings. A police spokesman declined to comment on the investigation.

Evening Standard, October 30th, 1979

Property Tycoon's Wife's Death Ruled "Accidental"

An inquest into the death of Estelle Nagle, the estranged wife of property mogul, Scott Nagle, has returned a verdict of accidental death caused by electrocution.

Mrs Nagle was found dead in the bathtub of the Holland Park home she had shared with her husband and their two children. A hairdryer was also found in the tub, still connected to a wall socket. It is believed Mrs Nagle may have been drinking at the time. She had started divorce proceedings against her husband.

Sidney Kopf, Mr Nagle's lawyer, said his client had 'no comment to make at this stage'.

Guardian, May 3rd, 1981

Court Reduces *Private Eye* Libel Damages

The £500,000 in libel damages awarded to Scott Nagle against *Private Eye* last December has been reduced to £50,000 on appeal.

Nagle, a property tycoon thought to own more than five thousand homes in England, sued the magazine over a piece in the magazine's Grovel column. Referring to the tycoon as 'Scotty Nailgun', the article suggested that he was complicit in his wife's death.

Estelle Nagle was found dead in her bathtub in 1979 after a hairdryer fell in the water. An inquest ruled her death as accidental.

Evening Standard, September 26th, 1999

Council Rejects Nagle Battersea Power Station Bid

Wandsworth Council has rejected a £300-million bid by property tycoon Scott Nagle to redevelop Battersea Power Station. The Grade II listed building has stood empty for more than two decades, as owners and redevelopers have come and gone.

Wandsworth Council officially stated that the bid was rejected because it included no provision to create affordable housing in the area. A source close to the Council's Planning Approval Committee told the *Standard* that there were also 'gross irregularities' with Nagle's bid.

The tycoon is believed to have bid for the property 'quasi-anonymously', using an offshore company based in the British Virgin Islands and an Egyptian frontman, Waleed Dallal.

Sid Kopf, Mr Nagle's lawyer, said his client had 'no further comment to make at this stage'.

Financial Times, September 7th, 2001

Nagle Quits UK Property Market

Scott Nagle, the controversial and equally reclusive property tycoon, has quit the British property market. Nagle sold the last of his 18,000 UK properties last week.

No official reason has been given for his decision. A spokesperson from Nagle's law firm, Kopf-Randall-Purdom, said their client had 'no further comment to make at this stage'.

It was gone 10 p.m. when I left the library. I went to King's Cross to get the Tube back to Victoria.

I was equal parts relieved and frustrated. I was glad to be done, because I was tired and my eyes were hurting. But I wasn't sure if I'd gone and wasted the last four hours. I'd come here thinking I'd find what Swayne had been getting at, and maybe tie it into VJ's case, but I had nothing whatsoever.

What did Scott Nagle have to do with VJ? Apart from the fact that they shared a law firm, there was no obvious connection. They weren't rivals. VJ ran a hedge fund, and the little real estate he owned here was land. And besides, Nagle had retired.

This much I knew:

There *was* a link between the Silver Service Agency and Evelyn Bates's murder, in the shape of Rudy Saks.

And there was also a link between the Nagle family and the agency, because Oliver Wingrove had investigated Michael Zengeni's disappearance.

But how did the two fit together?

Or did they fit at all?

Swayne was the common bond, the glue. But I couldn't reach him.

At the station, I felt a melancholy pull. I could quite easily have bought a ticket and caught the next train to Stevenage. I'd be there in under an hour, ringing my parents' doorbell fifteen minutes later.

My first couple of years in London, I'd gone back to Stevenage once a month. I loved my parents dearly, but I hated those weekends and couldn't wait to leave. All those bad bad memories from the Dark Ages; every pub I'd got chucked out of or barred from, every shopfront I'd passed out in, and the faces of all the people who'd seen me at my worst, the nudges and whispers to their friends when they saw me, the finger-pointing. So it was best to stay away. Which I'd pretty much ended up doing. I hadn't been 'home' in twelve years.

My phone rang.

Melissa.

'Are you free to talk?' she asked. She sounded pissed.

'What's the matter?'

'I need someone to talk to. Are you at home?' she asked.

Definitely pissed.

'No. Just leaving work,' I said.

'Can you drop by?'

Going to see an ex-girlfriend at night, when she's alone, half-cut and vulnerable, isn't just a bad idea, it's a *really* bad idea. Just say no. Sorry, got to get home. See my wife, see my kids, have dinner, fall asleep ...

'Sure,' I said. 'I'll be there in half an hour.'

61

Melissa wasn't as far gone as she'd sounded, but she was working on it. There was half a bottle's worth of white wine in a large long-stemmed glass in front of her. The rest she'd poured into the glass she'd pushed my way.

We were in her kitchen, sat at the granite-topped island in the middle, surrounded by sleek chrome appliances and white cupboards and shelving. The place was as sterile as an empty operating theatre.

'Be honest with me, Terry. Did he do it? Did he kill that girl?'

'No,' I said.

She cut me off before I could continue.

'Actually, I don't care if he's innocent. Makes no difference to me. I'm divorcing him.'

She sipped her wine. How much had she had already?

'I won't be at the trial,' she said. 'I'm leaving the country on Sunday.'

'Where are you going?'

'America. The girls are all at summer camp. I want to be with them.'

'Have you told him?'

'No.'

More wine went back.

We used to drink together all the time in Cambridge. We drank like couples have coffee or dinner. We'd go to student-free pubs, old men's hangouts that served room-temperature ale and peat whisky you'd still be tasting three days later. Melissa handled her booze a lot better than me. She never got out of control. The only way to tell she was tossered was by the way her Leeds accent got broader and her language filthier. And she asked me to roll her cigarettes for her, because she couldn't quite manage. She always had a tin of Old Holborn tobacco with her. Sober, she could roll them one-handed, which I thought was dead impressive at the time. But then everything about her mesmerised me.

'Why don't you tell me what happened? What set you off?' I said.

'*Set me off?* Like a bomb, you mean?' she sneered.

'It's just a figure of speech. What I mean is, why now? Why are you drinking like this?'

She pushed a lock of hair back from her eyes so she could glower at me unobstructed. She looked a state, possibly wearing the first things she'd grabbed when she got out of bed – grey tracksuit bottoms, a loose black T-shirt and flip-flops. Yet even pissed and pissed off, she was stunning.

'Janet called yesterday. She wanted me to give evidence for Vernon. Say what a great bloke he is and ... I agreed. Then ...' She smiled bitterly and wiped a tear with the back of her hand. '*Then* she told me what's going to come out in court. The whores – the S&M ... all that sordid stuff. She asked me if I knew.'

'Did you?'

'It's more complicated than yes or no.'

'You suspected?'

'I *knew*, Terry. I knew. Not because he told me. I knew what he was into. How he *got off*.' She sniffed. 'But, you know, he's a great father. Really loves those girls. Dotes on them. And we were so happy. That's all I chose to see and believe.'

'If it's any consolation, it shocked me. I don't know where it came from,' I said.

I was on duty here, still working, representing the firm. That's how I'd decided to play it. Professionally, keeping my distance. Although who was I kidding? I'd told Karen I was going to be working late at the office, going through files with Redpath.

'Does it have to come from anywhere?' she said.

'On an academic level, he doesn't fit the profile,' I said. 'Sexual fetishists usually compensate for their public lives by doing the opposite in private.'

'Save me the textbook patter. Vernon's just another cheating husband with twisted fetishes,' she said.

'That wasn't the person I knew, the bloke I grew up with.'

'None of us are.'

'But there's always a hint of the person you'll become, somewhere,' I said.

'Maybe you weren't paying close enough attention.'

'Or maybe he already knew how to hide things from those closest to him,' I retorted.

No comeback from her, except to drink more wine. She'd necked over half the glass now. I couldn't help but notice. That was the ex-drinker in me, one part smug, two parts alarmed.

'You said you knew?'

'We'd always experimented. Almost right from the start, at Cambridge ...'

I didn't want to hear this.

323

'Role play. Handcuffs. Uniforms. Toys. Threesomes ...'

But how could I stop her?

'We had an orgy once – not all they're cracked up to be. Have you ever had one?'

I'd been a virgin when I met her.
She wasn't.

I shook my head.

'Didn't think so,' she said, laughing.

What was that supposed to mean?

'Vernon liked variety, trying new things. It was exciting – *he* was exciting,' she said, smiling coyly.

I wished my hands weren't on the table so I could clench my fists. I tried balling up my feet instead, but it wasn't the same.

Had she fancied VJ when she was with me?

Had he coveted her all along?

I wanted to know all the things I didn't want to know.

Why the hell had I come here? I *knew* it was a mistake.

'What Vernon really liked was rough sex. Spanking, biting, slapping, choking. Pain. Giving, not receiving. I'm not the submissive type. I hated it. I mean I tried ... I went along with it, to please him. I thought it was another phase, something he wanted to try out and would get bored with.

'But it wasn't a phase. And he didn't get bored. He went further, until he was outright hurting me. We'd have rules. Safety words and signals. But he'd ignore them. One night he choked me so hard with his belt I thought he was going to kill me. I told him I'd had enough. That I wasn't into any of it. Never had been. That I hated it. Sorry, am I embarrassing you?'

No, *horrifying me*. I remembered what Fabia had told me.

I shook my head. 'Did he stop?'

'Yeah,' she said. 'But he was distant with me afterwards. Things weren't right. I tried talking to him about it, and he was evasive. We almost broke up.

'Then he went away with Ahmad to New York for a couple of weeks, touting for clients. It was a very successful trip. When he came home, he was back to being himself, back to being the man I loved. We had sex for the first time in ages, and it was totally normal – no hitting, no choking. It was like we'd never been to those other places. And it stayed that way.'

'He never slapped or choked you again?'

'No, all that stopped. He even apologised for what he'd done, said he'd gone too far. And I didn't think any more of it. I got pregnant and our lives changed,' she said. 'We were so happy – *so, so* happy. But now I know why. He was going out for what he couldn't get at home. Just like every other man who uses whores. I don't think we could ever be happy again.'

'I thought you told me you knew.'

'I didn't *know*. I assumed there were others. I never asked him because I didn't want him to lie,' she said.

'I'm sorry,' I said, quietly, reaching across the table to take her hand. She didn't notice.

'Aren't you going to have that?' she asked, pointing at my glass.

'I don't drink,' I said.

'At all?'

'No.'

'Poor you.'

She took my glass.

I was still holding her hand, which hadn't moved.

What was I doing here? I didn't even know her any more. I'd been listening to a stranger who happened to look a lot like someone who broke my heart a long time ago.

Melissa went over to the sink, and turned the taps on full.

'I've got to get going,' I said.

She didn't turn round. I didn't think she'd heard me over the jets of water. This was going to be an easy enough exit.

Then I noticed she was crying.

I couldn't leave her like this. What had she done to me anyway? It was almost twenty years ago. I wasn't going to see her again. Probably.

So I could finally say goodbye, wish her the best. And mean it.

I went over to her and put my hands on her shoulders. She was wearing a man's T-shirt. One of VJ's, I bet. She might be leaving him to his fate, but she still loved the bastard. And she always would, no matter how much she hated him.

The taps were roaring. I could hear her sobs, feel her quaking.

I reached over and closed the taps.

She turned round and gazed up at me. Her eyes were red and wet and puffy, her cheeks were glistening with tear streaks and her nose had started running. And do you know what? Despite every damn thing I've just said, she was the most beautiful woman I'd ever seen – or known.

She put her arms around my waist and pulled me in tight and rested her head on my chest. She wasn't wearing a bra and I felt her breasts pressing against my shirt.

I really couldn't help it. My dick went rock hard.

I hugged her closer and stroked the back of her head. I remembered how she'd liked me doing that.

Then I kissed her forehead.

And our eyes locked. I stroked her face, and she was still holding me tight, tighter, not letting go.

She raised her face slightly and closed her eyes, which was what she'd always done right before we kissed.

I bent my head down and our lips touched. And touched again. And then they met. Her eyes were still closed. Her mouth opened and our tongues met. I tasted wine, and I knew that if this went any further my life was well and truly over. Marriage, family ... I'd be a weekend dad ...

No.

It wasn't worth it.

Nothing was.

I pulled away.

'We shouldn't,' I said.

She looked at me, blinking, confused, like she wasn't sure what had just happened.

'I'm going to go,' I said, moving towards the door.

She nodded, but not at me, more to herself.

I walked out and went down the corridor. She followed me.

I opened the front door. The wind was up outside, rustling through the leaves, carrying with it the smell of the sea.

She was right behind me.

'You know what the difference between you and him is?' she said.

I didn't answer. There was a bite to her voice.

'Same as it always was, Terry. He always knew what he wanted and he always had the balls to take it.'

And look where it got him, I thought.

'Goodbye, Melissa.'

I crossed over Albert Bridge, walking fast; relieved and saddened – but mostly relieved.

The bridge was a beautiful thing to behold, all lit up like a fairground attraction; four thousand bulbs making its frame and gently swaying cables twinkle as though they were made of gold.

I took out my phone to turn it back on. I noticed my cuff was undone. One of my lucky green shamrock cufflinks was missing. It had probably fallen out at Melissa's house. *Damn.*

My phone screen blinked on. I had a message.

Meet me top of Wellington Arch. Tomorrow. 6.30 p.m.
Andy Swayne

326

62

He was already there when I arrived, hands in the pockets of his blue raincoat, which he'd buttoned up to the collar, looking up at the huge black brass sculpture that dominated the roof of the arch. The Goddess of Peace descending on a four-horse chariot going full tilt. The horses were frozen in mid-gallop, front hooves raised, heads twisted and turned in different directions, the outer two looking panicked, as if they'd realised they were about to drive the carriage into thin air and certain death.

How many times had I passed this monument sitting in the middle of a busy road outside the walls of Buckingham Palace? I'd lost count. I'd thought nothing of it. Yet until Swayne had arranged to meet on its roof, I'd never known the arch was hollow inside; that it had three floors with a museum and a café, that it was even open to the public.

'Beats your usual choice of venue,' I said, knowing better than to say hello and ask him how he was.

Swayne glanced briefly in my direction then moved over to the parapet, and gazed out across the park towards Hyde Park Tube.

It had been raining all day. Thunderstorms in the morning, heavy showers in the afternoon, and now a light and constant drizzle was falling over the city like wet dust.

'I found Fabia,' I said.

'And she's dead?' Not even a flicker of a reaction.

'How do you know?'

'You wouldn't be talking to me if she wasn't.'

'What's Scott Nagle got to do with Vernon James?' I asked.

'You *have* been busy,' he said, sarcastically.

'Tell me.'

'After Vernon fucked you over, you must've thought of shopping him, telling the cops you'd made up his alibi.'

'Every day,' I said.

'Why didn't you?'

'The police never had enough evidence to charge him. Vernon wouldn't have been prosecuted for his dad's murder. And I would've implicated myself and my family for nothing.'

'Now you know how I feel.'

'Are *you* implicated in this?'

He laughed and shook his head.

'You're closer than you know, but further than you think, Terry. Time is not on your side. If you haven't got the proof to exonerate Vernon by the time the trial starts, they've won.'

'Who's "they"?'

'You know that answer.'

'Scott Nagle?'

'Remember the first time we met, and I asked you who the lead barrister was? What did I say when you told me? What were my exact words?'

'I don't remember. I was too busy trying to figure out how the hell I was going to work with a dickhead like you.'

Swayne stared straight ahead. The monument was surrounded by a small park, with a path threading under the arch. The only person there was a woman in a short black raincoat standing by the Australian War Memorial, reading the names off the curving grey granite. The grass was an unnatural shade of green, the colour of cheap processed peas and pool table baize.

'All right. Let's start with me, then. How did I get this job?' he asked.

'It wasn't through you. And it *definitely* wasn't Janet Randall.'

'Sid Kopf insisted on you.'

'Even though I hadn't been an investigator for twelve years?'

'He said you were the best person for the job – for this kind of case.'

'Was I?'

'I never had any complaints – apart from your obnoxious personality.'

'What was I good at, in particular?' he asked.

'What is this – an appraisal?'

'Indulge me.'

'I liked the way you ran the interviews. That was impressive.'

'That was acting,' he said.

'You got hold of the CPS stuff.'

'That was bribery.'

Enough of this already.

'Listen,' I said. 'I've had a long, boring day. I'm tired and I'm standing out here in the rain, when what I really want to do is go home. So why don't you spare me your famous donkey and carrot act.'

Swayne finally deigned to look at me through his speckled glasses. I was expecting his usual reaction to my annoyances – that punchable half-smirk – but his expression stayed neutral.

'How good an investigator was I *really*, Terry? How effective was I? Did I bring you results? Did I find you Fabia Masson? Did I even do a good job – or any kind of job?'

Rating him on that scale, no he hadn't. None of the breakthroughs in the case had come via him. They'd come from me. But surely that was all down to good luck and diligence on my part?

Swayne moved to the opposite corner, where we could see over the barbed wire-topped wall surrounding Buckingham Palace and the gardens beyond.

'Let's try this again,' he said. 'What do you think of your junior barrister?'

'Liam Redpath? I don't know.'

'You've been working with him for three months and you don't know?'

'I've got nothing to go on. I've never seen him in action, in court.'

'What about meetings – client meetings, case meetings? What's he like in those?'

'He doesn't say much,' I said.

Swayne let out a short snort.

'What do barristers do, Terry?'

'Defend a client.'

'And how do they do that? With their fists? Their wigs?'

'Verbally. They talk.'

'They *talk*. Exactly! All barristers *talk*. They love the sound of their own voices. That's why they're barristers, not solicitors. Yet you've told me Redpath doesn't say much. Don't you think that's a bit of a problem? A mute barrister? What good's he going to be in court?'

I could have argued that Christine and Janet did most of the talking during meetings, but Redpath had never made his presence felt in any of them. He'd said little and contributed less.

Just then I had a sense of foreboding about where this was all going. I was starting to see how the broken pieces Swayne was tossing me might fit together.

Swayne misread my silence as ongoing cluelessness and sighed impatiently.

'How about Christine, then? What's the first thing that comes to mind when you think of her?'

'She's terminally ill,' I said.

'So what's she doing defending a high-profile murder case?'

'She's still good.'

'When she's not on two kinds of morphine-based painkillers that make her nod off in her soup, you mean?'

'She's *still* good.'

'Put your personal feelings aside, Terry, and ask yourself: is that *really* true?'

I thought back to when Janet, Kopf and I had put the defence team together. I'd suggested using a female barrister. Kopf had insisted on Christine over Janet's objections.

It made perfect sense then. The case was a loser. We all thought VJ

329

was guilty. Kopf wanted to bamboozle the jury; smuggle reasonable doubt in the pockets of sympathy. It was a good plan. Janet bought it. As for me, I thought it was cynical genius. I still did.

Yet how good had Christine actually *been*? She'd only got around to asking VJ about his enemies a month into the interviews. She never even *considered* the possibility he could have been set up until I found Fabia. She'd missed things, obvious things. And she was going to trial in under two weeks.

But that wasn't the only thing wrong with the picture that was slowly coalescing in my head. Redpath, as junior barrister, would have to replace Christine if she was too sick to attend – or continue. He couldn't carry this trial. Franco Carnavale would shred him.

'The penny dropping yet, Terry?' Swayne said, and moved off again.

I stayed put, out of his range. I needed space to think.

What kind of defence team were we, exactly? A dying barrister, a crap junior, a washed-up investigator, and me – an inexperienced clerk ... with a grudge against the client.

What kind of defence team were we?

No.

Impossible.

Yet who'd brought us all together?

No.

It *couldn't* be.

It wasn't possible.

It made no sense at all.

Unless ...

I walked over to Swayne.

'Are you saying Sid Kopf *wants* to lose this trial?' I asked.

'It's like I told you the first day we met: "They're sparing no expense to lose this one."'

Now I remembered him saying that. I hadn't picked up on it. How could I? *Why* would I?

I was too stunned to think. My eyes suddenly lost all focus. The view blurred.

'Ultimately, KRP is the house Scott Nagle built,' Swayne said. 'Kopf owes him everything.'

We were looking out over Constitution Hill, and the broad pinkish stretch of road disappearing behind the dense foliage of the flanking trees. Above, on the horizon, was the Big Ben spire and the clockface marking 7.10 p.m. To the left was the London Eye, the spokes and capsules already illuminated.

330

Spotlights came on under the statue. The horses and carriage looked like they'd sprung from the depths of a tarry pit.

'Did you work out how they found Fabia?' he asked me.

'They followed her.'

Swayne shook his head.

'They didn't follow *her*, Terry. They followed *you*.'

'*What?*'

'Like they followed you here,' he said, nodding towards the park. 'See that woman by the memorial?'

I knew exactly who he meant. I'd noticed her when I first arrived. Dark hair, black raincoat, jeans and trainers. She was standing in exactly the same spot now, half-turned to us.

We'd gone around the sculpture three times, stopping at each point of the compass, pausing at the different views. But Swayne had always lingered here, facing Hyde Park Corner Tube. When I thought he was looking out at the dual carriageway that went into Knightsbridge, he was really checking up on her.

'She's waiting for you to leave,' Swayne said.

He saw the alarm in my face.

'You have nothing to worry about for now. They're just keeping tabs on you. They know the police are involved and Nagle won't want anything getting in the way of the trial. They won't make a move unless they have to,' he said.

'Unless they *have* to?'

'Put it this way: if you get killed any time soon, you'll die knowing you were on the right track.'

'Thanks,' I said.

'You're welcome,' he chuckled.

They must have started following me from the moment I went to the Silver Service Agency.

Wait ...

What if this was more of Swayne's bullshit?

Only one way to find out.

'Are they following you too?' I asked.

'I don't interest them.'

'Which way did you come here?'

'Piccadilly.'

The opposite direction to me.

I led him back around the sculpture, so we were out of sight.

'Give me your coat,' I said, unzipping my waterproof.

'Why?'

'I want to see if you're telling the truth.'

331

'This isn't a game, Terry. I'm being very serious.'

'We'll see. *Coat.*'

'This really isn't a good idea – for either of us.'

'Because you're lying?'

'I'm not lying,' he said. 'You don't know—'

'*Coat!*'

Swayne emptied his pockets – phone, wallet, keys, his spectacle case and a pack of tissues – and handed me his raincoat.

'Go back the way you came,' I said, trying to button up his mac. It was tight around my shoulders and wouldn't do up without looking ridiculous.

Swayne started heading for the exit.

'Terry . . .'

'Go back the way you came,' I said. 'I'll be watching.'

He left.

I went back and looked at the woman at the memorial. She hadn't moved.

I started cursing Swayne and his too small raincoat and his bullshit and riddles. He was probably pissing himself laughing now.

A couple walked past the woman.

I turned to Constitution Hill.

I glanced back at the memorial.

The woman was gone.

I searched the park. No sign of her.

Then I spotted her, on the path, right before she disappeared under the arch.

I turned my head. There was Swayne, moving away, his hood up, walking at a steady pace.

The woman reappeared on the other side of the arch, keeping her distance from Swayne, but keeping him in sight.

And that's when I got seriously scared.

And I ran.

63

I jumped on the first bus that came along. I didn't know where it was going, and it didn't matter.

All I could think about was my family.

I took out my phone and called home.

'Karen, it's me.'

'Where've you got to?'

'Please listen very carefully and promise to do exactly as I say. I don't want to discuss it or anything. You just have to do it, OK?'

'What's going on?'

'I'm being followed, possibly by the same people who got Fabia.'

Silence. I hoped she'd heard me. I was speaking as quietly as I could, my hand over my mouth.

'Are you there?'

'Jesus ... *Christ!*' she shouted. 'You're going to the police, right?'

'I will,' I said. 'But first, it's best you all leave town. Don't tell me where you're going. Call me when you get there, OK?'

'But, Terry, I ... I ...'

'Please, Karen. You *have* to do this. It's not safe. Trust me. You know what they can do.'

64

Five hours later I was sitting in my kids' empty bedroom.

I'd talked to Karen. She didn't tell me but I knew she was in Manchester, at her parents' house. I heard them talking in the background. The kids were asleep, she said. They wanted to know when I'd be joining them.

I lay down on Amy's bunk, put my hands under my head and closed my eyes.

My head was churning.

The easiest thing, and the safest thing, was to do nothing. Keep my head down, see out the trial and quit when the verdict was rendered. There was still an outside chance VJ would be acquitted. We could get lucky. I wasn't counting Christine out. I'd seen her in court and, irrespective of how Swayne had it, she was still a force to be reckoned with.

But it felt wrong, sitting by while an innocent man went to prison. It didn't matter that it was VJ. He was innocent. If I wanted to be any kind of lawyer in the future, this was where I had to take a stand. If I didn't, if I took the easiest option and did nothing or looked the other way, I wouldn't be able to face myself, let alone my kids, for the rest of my life.

Yet what could I actually *do* without putting my family in harm's way – not to mention myself?

Nothing.

I couldn't do anything.

I couldn't go to the police, because I had no proof.

I couldn't look for the evidence because I didn't know what to look for. And besides, I was being watched.

But, there had to be *something* I could do.

I closed my eyes and thought about the case.

I went over it again, bit by bit.

Sid Kopf.

What did he want out of this? What was his goal – his *motive*?

I considered the case from his perspective – as the prosecution, *not* the defence.

I saw Evelyn Bates first, strangled to death, left naked on a bed, her cold rigid flesh almost the same colour as the sheets. Most murders are committed by people known to the victim. She hadn't even had that dubious distinction.

Poor, poor Evelyn.

Murdered by a hitman.

Why her?

Fabia had split.

They'd *needed* a victim.

They'd *needed* a body in the bed – anybody would do.

Because they already had everything else in place . . .

The elements of a crime:

Mens rea

Actus reus

And Rudy Saks – the bogus witness.

They'd just needed a dead woman's body.

Anybody.

Any . . . body.

Evelyn's fleeting encounter with VJ?

Evelyn being a blonde in a green dress?

Luck.

The objective of the set-up hadn't only been to frame VJ for murder. He had to be *convicted* of it too. The crime had been *designed* with a trial in mind – the goal a guilty verdict.

Swayne knew. Swayne had known all along.

So why the hell hadn't he told me?

I opened my eyes. Feelings of futility and uselessness turned to rage.

I lashed out, threw a punch up in the air. Except I'd forgotten I was lying on a child's bunkbed. My knuckles smacked into the slats of Ray's berth above. The mattress bounced up and the whole frame shook.

I'd knocked a plank out of joint.

I sat up and pulled it back. And as I did, something small and dark and hard fell and hit me in the face.

A flashdrive with a blob of Blu-tack stuck to it.

What was it doing under Ray's bed?

I turned his laptop on and plugged in the drive.

There was a single folder.

I froze when I saw what it was called.

VJ

It held miscellaneous TV news clips about VJ's case. BBC TV, Channel 4, Sky. His arrest, his appearance at Westminster Magistrates', the PCMH.

Seeing all this here, in my kids' bedroom, gave me the chills; the same as when Ray had said VJ's name when we were watching the TV after he'd appeared at Westminster Magistrates'.

I checked his internet history. Naturally he'd wiped all trace of his searches, but left his school homework enquiries intact.

First his secret Facebook account, now this.

Ray wasn't just sneaky. He was turning into a liar.

Where had that come from?

The blob of Blu-tack on the flashdrive told me everything I needed to know.

He'd learned by example, the way kids learn all things, good and especially bad.

I went to the spare room.

The box of Melissa's letters, and my Cambridge college picture.

The shrinkwrap around the box was intact. But the jiffy bag had been opened. Ray had looked at the photograph. He'd worked the Sellotape off the brown paper wrapping and done his best to fold it back the way it was, but he'd got it wrong. He still had a little more to learn about deceit.

What had I gone and done to my family?

I was shocked but I wasn't angry at Ray. I had no right to be. It was my fault – directly or indirectly. I'd led by example.

I wanted this whole thing to stop now. VJ, the case, the firm, the job. I wanted out.

I was looking at the college photograph, for the first time in sixteen years.

It hadn't changed.

There we were. VJ and me, side by side, still teenagers in our first ever suits and the black gowns we'd rented for the day. On the row behind us, and standing directly between us, was Melissa. All three of us were smiling. VJ was beaming because he was genuinely glad to be there; Melissa, because that was what you were supposed to do in pictures; and me, I was grinning like an idiot because I'd fallen in love with her five minutes before.

And then, suddenly, from nowhere, it came to me.

335

I knew what to do.

There *was* a way out of this. And an easy one.

VJ could *fire* KRP. The trial would be postponed while he got new representation. It wouldn't get him off the hook, but he'd definitely get a fair shake that way. His new team would know about Fabia and use that as a starting point.

As for me – I'd be free and clear, no longer a target because I wouldn't be working on the case any more.

I was seeing VJ next Thursday at Belmarsh. I'd tell him then.

65

'You look bloody awful,' Christine said to me, as she dabbed at the sweat above her lip. Her eyes were fixed and glassy like a teddy bear's, and her perfume was fading into the sour metallic odour it was masking.

It was Thursday morning in Belmarsh and we were waiting on VJ.

I was supposed to tell him to fire us today, but I'd been so busy being paranoid I hadn't worked out how I was going to do it. I didn't have a plan. I hadn't even remembered to make sure I sat next to him. Redpath was where I was meant to be.

So how was I going to broach it? I couldn't just blurt it out. He wouldn't take me seriously. Plus I didn't want to do that to Christine. She deserved better.

I had to find another way. Something discreet.

In walked VJ with his case notes, an air of confident purpose and a new haircut.

Christine waited for him to settle in his chair.

'Today we deal with your police statements,' she said.

'OK,' he said.

'Why did you lie to the detectives who came to your office?'

'I didn't,' he said. 'I thought they were coming about—'

'SQUID rules, Vernon. You *did* lie to the police. You've admitted it. Why?'

'They didn't tell me what it was about. I assumed it had to do with the damage to the room. I didn't want to admit I'd been there with another woman, in case my wife found out,' he said.

'So you made up an elaborate story about throwing an impromptu party in the suite instead?'

'Yes.'

'Hypothetically: let's say the police had *only* come about the damage – what did you hope would happen?'

336

'I'd offer to pay all costs and that would be it,' he said.

'In other words, you'd write a cheque and the problem would go away?'

'Yeah.'

'You do know wrecking a hotel room is a crime, don't you?'

'Of course.'

'Then you've just sunk us.'

'How?'

'No one likes the rich, Vernon. You're the easiest people to hate. Carnavale's going to play on that. He's going to remind the jury they're *not* your peers. He's going to rub it in – the ends they can't make meet, the mortgages they'll never pay off, the things they'll never have. Because once they think that way, they're going to see you as completely different from them; as 'other', as alien. What goes for them, does *not* go for you.

'If you say you *thought* all that was going to happen when the police came to your office was you'd pay for the damages and they'd go away, the prosecution will say you think your wealth puts you above the law. In other words, in your mind, you can trash a hotel room and walk out, certain that you'll buy the problem off. Therefore, by extension you think you can kill someone and walk away, because you believe ordinary rules don't apply to you.'

'That's a ludicrous theory,' he said.

'That's not for you to decide – but it *is* for you to disprove,' she said. 'You have to convince the jury that although you are not like them now, you were once. Remember your award speech? Four to a room in a cold basement in Stevenage? We need *that* Vernon James on the stand.'

VJ caught my eye and smiled. He was remarkably chipper for someone going to trial next week, the odds still stacked against him.

'So, again, why did you lie to the police?' Christine asked him again.

'I was . . . disorientated.'

'And? How did you feel that morning? What had happened to you the night before?'

'I'd been attacked – and drugged.'

'Scratch "drugged". You didn't know that,' she said. 'Remember: stick to your story at all times. Every answer you give must relate back to your story. You were in shock. You'd been brutally attacked by a woman who wasn't Evelyn Bates. You were also still pissed from the night before. You didn't know *what* you were saying. You get it now?'

'Yes.'

'Good,' Christine said. 'So, once again, why did you lie to the police?'

I'd been writing everything down, questions and responses, the strategy. It was good. Christine was sharp and on the ball today. Who

337

wouldn't want her in their corner? Then again, this was only a rehearsal, and it didn't count.

In-between taking notes, I'd written a message on a separate page in my pad.

VERY _VERY_ IMPORTANT!
Please call me this afternoon on 07663 700900.
Terry

I'd pass it to VJ on the way out.

When he called, I'd tell him everything.

I quietly detached the sheet of paper, folded it into a small square and slipped it into my jacket pocket.

Christine asked VJ the same questions a third time. His answers were perfect now.

She started wrapping up the session. She talked about what we'd cover next week. She went through the strategy she'd worked out – getting the prosecution to defend rather than attack; put them on the back foot from the start and keep them there.

She sounded confident, almost excited, like she couldn't wait to get to the courtroom. I felt a pang of guilt at what I was going to do. But I had no choice. I'd made a decision to help VJ as best I could, and I was sticking to it.

A knock on the door interrupted us. Our time was up.

We started packing our things away.

I slipped the note out of my pocket and moved it to the middle of my palm, holding it in place with my thumb. I'd shake VJ's hand on the way out and pass him the paper.

The door opened. The sounds of the prison rushed in – the banging, the yelling, the buzzers.

In walked Sid Kopf.

What was _he_ doing here?

'You made it. Better late than never,' Christine said.

Kopf strode across the room towards VJ, a warm smile on his face.

'Hello, Vernon. My name is Sid Kopf. I'm CEO of Kopf-Randall-Purdom, your solicitors.'

VJ stood and shook his hand.

'I just wanted to meet you in person. You're that rarest of things in this profession – a truly innocent man.'

'Thanks,' VJ said, a little confused, but smiling.

'I also wanted to personally reassure you that the _entire_ firm is fully

338

behind you. We are absolutely committed to you. We will fight for you the whole way. We won't let you down.'

You platinum-coated piece of shit, I thought.

'That's very reassuring. I appreciate it,' VJ said.

He lapped it up. And why not? He didn't know any better. Kopf oozed avuncular warmth and cold-headed authority.

Christine and Redpath had already left.

But not me. I stood there dumbfounded, watching Kopf smooth-talking VJ, promising his 'every possible assistance' and saying that he was at his 'complete disposal'.

I stepped around the table. VJ and Kopf were by the wall.

I got slightly in-between them and held out my hand to VJ, the note secreted under my thumb.

'See you next week,' I mumbled.

VJ gave me an annoyed look, like he was irritated at me for interrupting his pep talk.

He took my hand and gave me a perfunctory shake, barely gripping my hand. The note slipped between our palms and landed on the floor, right at Kopf's feet.

Kopf and VJ both looked down at the square of pale-yellow paper.

I picked it up before either of them had time to say anything and left the room, cursing under my breath.

66

'Thanks for doing that,' Christine said, on the train back to Charing Cross.

'Your suspicions are unfounded,' Kopf said, sitting next to her, their shoulders gently bumping to the train's vibrations. 'He's not going to dump us.'

Eh?

'I needed an outside opinion,' she said.

'That's unlike you,' Kopf smiled, still full-on oleaginous.

'*I'm* unlike me these days, Sid.'

'That's not what I saw at the Bailey.'

'You're very generous,' she said.

'You know me better than *that*, Christine.'

They exchanged a conspiratorial smile.

'I was your idea, wasn't I?' she said.

'My first and *only* idea.'

'Thank you,' she said to him.

'No, Christine. Thank *you*.'

She got tearful.

I couldn't believe it. Yet who was I to deny a dying woman a last few moments of joy – no matter how illusory?

I glanced over at Redpath but he was engrossed in his session notes; an ostrich in a pinstripe suit.

'So . . . Terry. What do you think about our client?' Kopf asked. '*Was* he having second thoughts about retaining us?'

For one deep-fried scary instant I thought my paranoia had taken a flying leap into the paranormal; that Kopf hadn't only worked out that I'd been trying to pass VJ a note, but what its purpose was. As in he'd read my mind.

'He seemed about the same to me,' I said.

'When a person's facing judgement day they like to know who they can count on. Wouldn't you agree?' Kopf said.

He wasn't smiling at me, nor speaking in that impassioned purr he'd used on Christine and VJ. This was Kommandant Kopf addressing his minion – the bastard who sat behind his desk with my bollocks in one hand and my windpipe in the other. And just what was he getting at here? Was he talking about VJ, me – or himself?

'Goes without saying,' I answered through a dry mouth. 'If I was in Vernon's position, I'd be happy to have this team here. Christine, Liam, Janet – and Andy Swayne too. He really couldn't ask for a better . . . set-up.'

Emphasis on *set-up*. But my delivery was deadpan. And I looked Kopf straight in the eye as I spoke, looking for a blink or a flash of realisation, or maybe trying to see into him, to glimpse the dark machinery that had driven him to conjure all this up in the name of his main client. Fat chance of that. Sid Kopf was as cool and opaque as a statue.

'You didn't include yourself,' Kopf said.

'I'm just a clerk.'

'I'd say you're a little more than that.'

What did *that* mean?

The train was over the river now, getting close to the station.

'Which reminds me,' Kopf said. 'I have some bad news. The police called the office today. Your investigator is dead.'

'My inv— you mean Andy Swayne?' I said.

He nodded.

'He's *dead*?'

Another nod.

My legs might've gone if I wasn't sitting down.

First thought: you killed him.

340

Second . . . I'd been trying to call Swayne all week. His phone had been switched off.

'*When?*' I asked.

'Yesterday morning. He was found at home. In bed. Apparently.'

'What happened?'

'They said it was drink-related. He had some kind of seizure.'

'Natural causes, then,' Redpath quipped.

All kinds of things I could've said to that, and a few more I could've done too, but I let it go. I was too shocked. Too panicked.

'He hadn't had a drink in years,' I said.

'That you know of,' Kopf said. 'You know where he lived, don't you?'

'No.'

'Above *a pub* in Croydon. A dump called the Laughing Camel.'

That stripper place.

VELCRO!

'First thing they tell you in rehab and AA is to avoid temptation. Andy rented the flat right above,' Kopf continued.

I thought of David Stratten, a non-drinker who'd jumped in front of a Tube train pissed. Is that what they had planned for me too?

'Andy was a good man,' Kopf said. 'But I always knew it was going to end like this. Some people plan their demise, the way others map out their lives.'

He was staring right at me as he spoke, not even a suggestion of sympathy or sadness about him. I understood what he was telling me. All too well.

The train had stopped.

67

I waited until I got home to crack up.

Swayne had been murdered. No doubt in my mind, whatsoever. I sat in the living room staring into space.

A thunderclap made me jump. Then a flash of sheet lightning brightened the room.

Then it pissed down with rain.

I went and got Swayne's coat and put it over the back of the chair. I turned the chair round and stared at it.

'Who killed you?' I asked.

Yes, I know, crazy thing to do, but what is panic if not a breakdown on fast-forward?

'Well . . .?'

I sat down on the couch.

Had Swayne being wearing my waterproof when he died? Was his death *my* fault? Had Fabia's killers got to him?

Or was it really just the drink?

I was stuck with his cheap raincoat, a size too small.

I didn't want it. I could take it down the charity shop, but that didn't feel right.

No. I was going to give it back to him.

68

Saturday. The regulars got in early at the Laughing Camel. They were on their second or third rounds, well away down the slow slope to oblivion when I walked in. A few glanced expectantly my way, as if they hoped I'd be someone else, most ignored me.

The barman was swaddled in a bright pink-and-green Hawaiian shirt and bopping along to 'Club Tropicana', which was playing at a semi-obtrusive volume.

'What'll it be, mate?'

'I'm here about Andy Swayne,' I said.

'You family or plod?'

'Neither,' I said. 'We worked to—'

'You're Terry, aren't you?'

That was a woman's voice, to my right. Thirties, pale skin and eyes the exact same shade of dark brown as her eyebrows and long straight hair that cascaded over part of her face and fell past her shoulders . She was sat on my side of the bar with a mug in front of her.

'I am, yeah.'

'That's Andy's coat,' she said.

'I'm returning it.'

'No use to him now,' she said.

The barman chortled.

'Did you know him?' I asked.

'Don't you remember me?'

'Sorry?'

'We've met before,' she said.

Had we?

Yes . . . of course we had. Then as now, she'd been the only woman in here.

VELCRO!

'I'm sorry, I didn't . . .'

'Recognise me with my clothes on?'

We both laughed. How many times had she heard that one?

'I'm sorry about Andy,' I said.

'Want to see where he died?'

Swayne had lived in a single room, but it was a bright and spacious studio apartment overlooking a derelict cinema. There was a small kitchen area in one corner and a dining table in the other.

'Your place or his?' I asked.

'He was already here when I met him,' she said. On the way up, she'd introduced herself as Steff.

The furniture was plain but sturdy, obviously bought as a long-term investment. There were a couple of rugs on the dark parquet flooring, and a couch opposite a big silver Sony Trinitron TV. No books or music, no DVDs, no photographs. Nothing on the walls, apart from a corkboard by the window.

'Did he mention me at all?' she asked.

'We didn't talk about personal stuff,' I said. She sucked on her bottom lip, her eyes silvering. Please don't cry on me, I thought. You need a sincerer shoulder. 'How long were you together?'

'A couple of years, if you can call what we were "together".'

'What do you mean?'

'We were lovers who weren't in love. Do you understand?'

Yes, I did. Swayne had been some kind of low-rent sugar daddy. He'd had a little joy in his life after all.

'We met downstairs,' she said.

'When you were st—'

'*Dancing.* I call it dancing,' she said, quickly. She looked a few years older in daylight, closer to her forties than her thirties. 'You get to know your regulars by sight. Andy'd always be there at the same table, always in a suit and tie, always with a ginger ale and a little bag of peanuts. He never missed one of my shows . . . until Wednesday night.'

'Was that when he died?'

'He was well on his way.'

The double bed was unmade, the duvet piled on the floor, the sheet half off the mattress. There were two pillows on the couch, where I guessed she'd been sleeping.

'I found him here when I got back,' she said, pointing to the bed. 'He was passed out. He *stank* of booze. I tried to wake him. I was yelling at him, shaking him, slapping him. I was so angry. I couldn't believe he'd been drinking.

'When he didn't wake up, I had a bad feeling. I felt his face. He was cold and clammy, his breathing was shallow. I called an ambulance. He died in hospital early Thursday morning. Alcohol poisoning.

'The doctor said he was twenty times over the limit. The binge killed him. He hadn't had a drink in God knows how long, and his body couldn't cope. The exact same thing happened to my dad, you know. He was an alcoholic too. He'd have these dry spells, swear he wasn't going to touch another drop for the rest of his life, and just when you thought he might mean it, he'd go on a week-long bender. He died of liver failure.'

She teared up again.

'When did you last see Andy alive – conscious?'

'Wednesday morning. We had breakfast together.'

'What was he like?'

'Fine. Normal. The usual,' she said.

'Did you have any indication he might start drinking again?'

'It doesn't work like that with alcoholics. My dad was exactly the same. You never knew when he'd go off. I don't think he did either. He didn't just wake up one morning and decide to get pissed. It just happened. He said it was a compulsion. A "magnetic pull", he called it. Everything'd be fine and then the next thing you knew he'd be in the pub with nine double brandies in him, or down the park with two carrier bags of lager.'

It was all too familiar, what she was saying. I'd been there, my willpower broken by that powerful undercurrent; every vow broken. Maybe Swayne hadn't been murdered after all. Maybe his death was accidental – or even suicide.

'Did Andy say anything about being followed?' I asked.

'No.' She frowned. 'Who was following him?'

'Did he talk about what we were working on?'

'No. He was enjoying it, though, whatever it was. He said it was going to make things right.'

'What things?'

'He once told me he had one big regret in life, one thing he'd take back and undo in an instant if he could. He refused to say what it was, except that it was something so terrible, it led to every other bad thing that happened to him,' she said.

Had he kept her out of the loop for her sake, or his?

'Did he ever talk much about his past?' she asked.

'Not really,' I said.

'If you find out what that bad thing he did was, please don't ever tell me. I only want to remember him as I knew him.'

344

'Of course.'

In spite of what she'd said, she'd loved him. Even if only a little, but that was enough. Had Swayne loved her back? I hoped he had, but it was hard to imagine someone as hateful and as bitter as him having any room for tenderness in that dried-up cactus he'd had for a heart, but what did I know? I'd thought he lived alone with his ghosts and his demons, a broken old man whose existence was in a holding pattern until the final landing. As it turned out, Andy Swayne had been shacked up with a woman three decades his junior. Some people would say he hadn't done too badly, all things considered.

'I knew he was a bit dodgy. He had that look about him,' she said.

'Did he tell you he'd been to prison?' I asked.

'Yeah. For burglary, right? Do you know the story?'

'No.'

'It's a bit of a funny one. This lawyer he used to work for – Sid – asked him to get some documents from a rival law firm. The job should've been easy for Andy. Breaking and entering, a bit of safe-cracking, then out. Except he was drinking back then.

'He gets into the lawyer's office just fine, but his hands start shaking as he's trying to get the safe open. Can't keep his fingers steady. He finds a bottle of Scotch in a desk drawer and knocks some back.

'He opens the safe, takes the documents and leaves. Two days later he gets arrested. The police have found his fingerprints on the whisky bottle. He hadn't realised it, but he drank most of the bottle. His prints were on file, because he'd had a drink-driving conviction the year before.

'The cops offered him a reduced sentence if he shopped Sid. Andy kept his mouth shut. Got ten years. Served eight. Sid did all right by him, when he got out.'

Hush money. Which was how he'd been able to afford this place – and her.

So why had he turned on Kopf? Was it linked to this 'one big regret' he'd had in his life? And what did that have to do with VJ?

'Did he talk about Sid much – apart from that?'

'No. I knew he was scared of him, though.'

'How?'

'I was here when Sid called him out of the blue, last year.'

Last year?

'Andy was really surprised to hear from him. They hadn't spoken since he came out of prison. The call upset him. Upset him a lot. He was really down. And scared. I'd never seen him like that.'

'What did Sid want?'

'He wanted Andy to investigate someone.'

'Who?'

'You know that bloke who got arrested for killing that girl in the hotel?'

Christ . . .

'When was this, do you remember?' I asked.

'Last Easter or thereabouts.'

'Did he talk about the investigation? Tell you what kind of things he'd found out.'

'No,' she said. 'I only knew the bloke's name because Andy left some stuff lying around, copies of old newspapers he'd marked up. Stuff about him killing his dad.'

So Kopf had got Swayne to do the background work on VJ. He'd used someone he knew he could trust – or, better still, someone he had a hold over.

Kopf had done more than just rig the defence.

'I'd better give you your anorak back,' she said, holding her hands out to take the coat.

I went over to the corkboard. It was slightly askew. Swayne had pinned my mobile and office number up there on a piece of paper, along with two colour postcards and a black-and-white photograph of three people standing with their arms around each other.

The photo was of a black man and woman, with a younger, shorter white man in-between them. They were all laughing, as if sharing a joke with the photographer.

Steff came back with my waterproof.

'Who are these people?' I asked her.

'That's Andy there in the middle . . .'

Really?

I looked again.

I hadn't recognised him at all. He couldn't have been older than mid-twenties there. Short, neat dark hair with a parting and medium-length sideburns. In his open-necked white shirt, and the pen in his breast pocket, he could have passed for a Mormon missionary. But it was the sight of him happy that threw me. This was him before the corrosion had entered his soul.

'That's his mate Michael.'

'Michael . . .? Michael who?'

'Andy only put the board up on Tuesday. He just said the guy's name was Michael.'

The man was a head taller than Swayne, light-skinned and hand-some, with a dignified bearing. I thought of a leaner Muhammad Ali in his prime. They had had the same bright wit about their eyes.

'And the woman is Miriam.'

Miriam? Miriam Zengeni. Had to be. She was marginally taller than Swayne and far darker than Michael, with an almond-shaped face and strong cheekbones. Her rimless pebble specs gave her a serious air.

'Do you know anything else about the picture? When or where it was taken?'

'No.'

'Did he tell you anything about Michael and Miriam?'

She shook her head. 'He didn't talk much about his past. He said he couldn't remember much about it because of all the drinking he did.'

Yeah, right . . . What if he'd drunk to forget?

'Did Andy have any friends at all? Any people he saw regularly, people who dropped by?'

Again she shook her head.

'You didn't find that odd?'

'Not at all,' she said. 'Some people are happy being loners.'

The colour postcards were of Wellington Arch and a train station surrounded by fields.

I took them down. The back of the train station card had the number '7' written on it in blue biro.

Frant Railway Station, Bells Yew Green, East Sussex.

'Ever been to this place?' I showed Steff the postcard.

'No.'

I checked the pockets of the waterproof to make sure there was nothing of his there. I found a packet of tissues in one, and a small, square-handled brass key in the other. The key had a number felt-tipped on the handle: '7'.

I checked the postcards again.

Swayne had put the board up on Tuesday.

He knew he was a marked man. He'd guessed I'd come here, looking for answers.

So he'd left me a message.

We'd met at Wellington Arch.

The set-up was linked to Michael Zengeni. Go see Miriam. I knew where she lived. Archer House, near Battersea Embankment. I'd seen them together. Had that been deliberate on his part?

'When my dad died, my mum said she felt like the lone survivor in a plane crash, stumbling around in a daze all the time, wondering what she was doing here, what life was all about,' Steff said behind me. 'I didn't know what she meant then. I do now.'

I felt sorry for her. And I felt sorrier still that I'd taken Swayne away from her – even if I hadn't meant to. He must have had kindness and decency in him, for her to be missing him like this. Or maybe she was still in shock.

'Do you want a cup of tea or anything?' she asked.

'No thanks,' I said. 'I've got to get going.'

69

Frant station was two hours and two train changes out of London.

First stretch: East Croydon to Tonbridge.

The train was at the platform. I went to the last carriage and got in.

Five people were already there, two men, three women. All middle-aged.

I sat right at the back, so I could see who was getting on.

Pure tactics. I didn't know if I was being followed.

Funny. Even in death, I still didn't trust Swayne. He was the sort whose ghost would lie. He was an alcoholic – therefore an addict. Addicts are chronic liars. And yes, I'm speaking from personal experience.

No one boarded the carriage.

The train idled on the platform.

An announcer apologised for the delay. They were waiting for a driver.

I watched the doors – the entrance, and the inter-carriage one – waiting, hoping, *praying* no one else would get on.

Another announcement: the driver had arrived and we'd be leaving in a few minutes. Once again, apologies for the delay and thanks for our patience.

The train finally left.

And no one had got on after me, or entered the carriage through the connecting door.

I was instantly and overwhelmingly ...

Relieved.

I relaxed. My bunched-up neck and back muscles loosened, my fists unclenched like a pair of unsprung traps, and my nerves stopped nagging my brain.

Now I needed a piss. The toilet was in the middle of the train, down two carriages. Off I went, through connecting doors, past a couple of young families, some pensioners and their grandkids, a few solo travellers with wadded backpacks.

When I was done and going back to my seat the pre-recorded station announcement was saying that Redhill was the next stop.

I pushed open the door to the second from last carriage and started heading down.

And then I saw her.

A young woman with short dark hair, sitting on her own in the middle, looking out of the window.

At least that's what she was doing now.

I'd *sworn* I'd caught her looking my way an instant ago – a quick glance, then back to watching the view rushing by in a blur.

The woman who'd followed Swayne out of Wellington Arch had had short brown hair. And a slight build. And . . .?

So had the woman who'd killed Fabia.

Could it be her?

Wait . . .

What was I thinking?

First up:

I hadn't seen the Wellington Arch woman's face. I was too far away.

Second:

I didn't know what Fabia's killer looked like. Just the description. *Oriental features.* This woman looked Eurasian.

But . . .

If she was following me, surely she'd have sat in the same carriage, not halfway down the next one, with her back to the interconnecting door.

So, I was being . . .

Totally paranoid.

So paranoid I hadn't noticed the train had stopped at Redhill and the doors had opened, and people were getting out, and others were waiting to get in.

As for the woman – she stood up and got off the train.

I was still standing there, in the middle of the carriage.

Paranoid twat.

I went on back to my seat.

The train carried on to:

Nutfield.

Godstone.

A man got on with his daughter. I thought of Amy and taking her and Ray down to Stevenage.

Edenbridge.

Penshurst.

Then I thought of my mum taking me to London and showing me the sights for the first time. The Tower of London, Tower Bridge,

Madame Tussauds, Harrods at night, Westminster Abbey to light a candle even though she never went to church. She'd always made sandwiches and packed a can of Sainsbury's own-label crisps and lemonade for the trips.

Leigh.

High Brooms.

Tonbridge.

Last stop on this part of the ride.

Change for Tunbridge Wells to Hastings, via Frant.

I found the connecting train and got on the last carriage again.

Seven fellow passengers. No one from my carriage came on.

OK. I absolutely, *definitely*, was not being followed.

Thank God.

That was all that mattered.

I enjoyed the view. Fields, lakes, golf courses, woodland. The pre-recorded station announcement reminded all passengers that the train would divide at Tunbridge Wells and those of us wanting to continue on our journey should move to the first four carriages.

I got out of the train and headed up to the other end of the platform.

And then I stopped bang in my tracks.

What was *she* doing here?

Hadn't she got off at Redhill?

Yes, she had.

The dark-haired woman was standing in the middle of the platform, staring straight ahead of her – at a blank wall.

I'd got it right the first time.

She *had* been following me.

Without thinking, I hurried towards the exit.

I navigated my way through the clump of passengers and went up the stairs, moving as fast as I could.

I looked over my shoulder.

She was coming after me, but was also caught up in the crowd, queuing to get up the stairs to the exit.

At the top of the stairs I had a brainwave:

The exit was to my right.

To my left was a covered footbridge leading to the opposite platform.

I ducked down and crouch-ran along the bridge.

I went down a few steps, squatted down.

Then I peeked around the side.

The woman hurried up the stairs and rushed out of the exit.

350

I counted to ten.

Then I crouch-ran back down the bridge.

Took the stairs two at a time, made it on to the original train platform.

The train had been separated in two.

First four carriages.

First one. I tried the door. It wouldn't open.

Next. The same.

The train was on the verge of leaving.

Then I saw the guard leaning out of the front carriage, beckoning to me.

I dashed down the platform and leaped on.

I looked out of the door.

Fuck.

The woman had rumbled me.

She was back in the station, bounding down the stairs.

She reached the platform and jumped into the nearest open carriage.

Except . . .

She'd got on the wrong part of the decoupled train. She was going back to London.

The guard closed the door.

Moments later we left for Frant.

I collapsed in a seat.

Sweaty.

Relieved.

Scared.

Confused.

All I could think about was my family: a future widow and two orphans.

And for what?

For who?

Why?

70

Frant station was a ragstone block structure of tiled steepled roofs, chimney stacks and recessed windows, more nineteenth-century rectory than train stop. I could see why Swayne had picked it: a blink-and-miss place, strictly in the know and right in the middle of nowhere.

I was the only person off the train, and the only person on either

351

platform. There were fields directly in front of me, sheep grazing in one, and acres of swaying wheat in another. The only sound I could pick up was the breeze caressing the trees and the sound of a single car driving up a nearby road.

The stationmaster was sat behind the ticket counter, reading the *Daily Chronicle* with the radio on in the background. He jerked to when I tapped at the partition.

'I've come about this,' I said, holding up the brass key.

He squinted through the glass. 'Locker?'

'Yes.'

'Number?'

'Seven,' I said.

'Name?'

'Swayne.'

He got up and took a file down from a shelf behind him. The radio was saying something about a demonstration in central London.

I looked around the small office: at the season ticket poster; at the leaflet rack stuffed with tourist brochures for Historical Hastings, the Kent coast and, angled in one slot, a stack of postcards identical to the one in Swayne's flat. When had he last been here?

The stationmaster unlocked the door to a room opposite the ticket office and waved me in.

There were a dozen numbered lockers fixed in two rows along the wall, all fitted with different-sized padlocks.

When I opened up locker 7 I found a large manila envelope propped up at the back. Nothing else.

The envelope contained a single sheet of plain paper, folded over several times.

I opened it up on the ground.

It was the size of a large poster.

I was looking at a professional drawing of a floor plan. I noted a reception room, a kitchen, toilets, multiple units – and a handwritten legend in a small box in the right-hand corner.

> Nagle Building
> Construction Drawing
> Ref: E151LW/1960/0507

There was nothing else in the envelope.

*

An hour later I was on the train back to London.

What did I do now?

I was *definitely* being followed.

They had me.

They'd lost me.

They *knew* I was on to them.

Should I go to the police? Call DCI Reid?

What could she do? Put me under police protection? Hardly. Not enough grounds. And zero proof. The best – and the most she'd offer – was to take a statement and file it away for future reference.

In other words, I was out on my own here.

The train started slowing. Next stop: Tunbridge Wells.

As the platform came into view, I tensed up and slid down in my seat and searched the faces of the waiting passengers for the brown-haired woman.

I didn't see her.

Charing Cross was crowded. Nothing unusual about that in itself but there was something wrong with the scene. No one was moving. People in the main concourse were standing around, talking on their phones, talking among themselves, their expressions worried to bemused. Small crowds were spilling back out of both exits, all heads turned to the outside, as if they'd been stalled by heavy rain and were waiting for it to let up. No one looked like they wanted to leave.

As soon as I got on to the Strand I understood why.

There was a big demo happening in Trafalgar Square, but it had started going wrong. Small groups were running up the road, all wearing balaclavas or bandannas, wielding baseball bats and bars. They were stopping just long enough to take swings at shop windows. One group was attacking a McDonald's. Clubs to the window pane, then feet, then their shoulders. A couple of bins were on fire.

No police around at all.

I stood in the street, near the zebra crossing, gaping at what was happening, fascinated and fearful.

There was a silver chopper in the air, hovering low almost directly above me. I looked up and squinted into the bright blue sky. I thought it was the cops. But no, it was Sky News.

And then, suddenly, I was grabbed.

Hands locked around my upper arms, lifted me off my feet and propelled me forward towards the road. A car with tinted windows screeched to a halt in front of me. The back door was flung open.

I turned to my left. A bald man had one arm. To my right was the brown-haired woman who'd been following me. I couldn't believe how strong she was.

They pushed me towards the car.

I tried to get free, writhing and wriggling; but their grips were tighter and faster than tourniquets.

I kicked out. Got a foot to the passenger-door window, another to the rim of the roof and pushed back.

I heard shouting all around me.

'It's the fucking cops!'

'Let 'im go!'

A semicircle of people, all bandannas and baseball bats, had formed around us.

Suddenly the hand on my left arm went.

I fell to the ground, hitting my arse on the kerb. The woman started dragging me towards the car.

The bald man punched one of the bandannas in the face, and circle-kicked another in the jaw. They went down simultaneously. A third swung at him with a bat. Baldie punched him in the throat. His attacker dropped his bat and fell backwards, both hands reaching for his throat, his body convulsing.

Next thing I knew I'd been dragged into the back of the car. Baldie got in next to me. The door slammed.

'Fucking *drive!*' yelled Baldie.

What was that accent? *American?*

I knew him.

I *recognised* him.

It was *Jonas*, the man who opened the door when Swayne and I went to Rudy Saks's house. Swayne spoke to him in Hebrew, translated the writing on the tattoo on his arm.

David Stratten had said the 'tax inspectors' came to his house with a *big bald bugger.*

Fabia had said she'd last seen Evelyn Bates talking to a *bodybuilder-type with a shaved head.*

It was *him*.

Was that Rudy Saks at the wheel?

The car took off fast.

Still I struggled. Or tried to.

The woman took out a syringe and grabbed my forearm. She shot a short jet of clear liquid out of the needle.

Something smashed into the car.

Then . . .

WHUMMP!

Bright white light filled the windscreen.

Then it was covered in flame.

The woman had let go of my arm an instant and covered her eyes.

The car braked.

The tyres screeched.

We all jerked forward.

My head went over the passenger seats, then I was thrown back.

I saw the syringe still in the woman's hand. Our eyes locked for a second, just as they had in the train. The adrenalin kicked in.

The woman went for my arm with the needle, but I was faster.

I grabbed her by the wrist, and slammed her syringe hand down on the driver's seat.

I meant to knock the syringe out of her hand, but instead the needle plunged into the driver's neck.

'*Aaarrggh!*'

He grabbed at the syringe sticking out of him.

Then he slumped hard over the wheel.

The car shot forward.

A bump, a sharp jolt, then we hit something.

The car stopped moving for a couple of seconds. Then it started skidding sharply to the left, the tyres screeching on the road.

The front of the car was still on fire, the window covered in flames, as thick black smoke and petrol fumes poured in through the vents.

Jonas threw a fist at my face. I ducked. The punch slammed into the woman's temple instead. Her head smashed into the window, cracked the glass and left blood. She slumped down.

A mob had surrounded the car. They were kicking and pounding at it with bats.

The windows were going. First the front, bursting in a shower of flame. Then the sides. Then the back.

Suddenly I was grabbed from behind again. A chokehold round my neck.

I was dragged out of the car, fighting for air.

I landed heavily on my shoulders.

Gasped.

Screamed.

Gasped again.

I was surrounded by dozens and dozens of people, all masked. They were battering the car. Eight or nine or more of them had their hands to the sides and were rocking it, trying to turn it over. The tyres on the back wheels had ripped, and the rubber was flapping ragged around the still-spinning, sparking tyres.

355

One of the mob picked me up.

My head was spinning, my vision was going in and out of focus; my chest was burning, my mouth tasted of petrol and plastic.

'Run, bruv! Run! *RUN!*'

I was pushed away with force. I stumbled and fell. Then I picked myself up. Trafalgar Square on one side. Nelson's Column, the lions, the fountain. And people. *People.* A mass of people. Everywhere. Running, shouting, yelling. Someone crashed into my shoulder and span me round.

I heard sirens.

I breathed in, deep. Smoke. Petrol. Rubber.

My head cleared.

And my body got another dose of adrenalin.

And I ran.

I just ran.

And ran.

And ran ...

71

... all the way to the pub.

I didn't even stop to think about it.

I wanted a drink.

Nothing else would steady my shaking hands, and still my quaking legs.

I wanted ...

No.

I *needed* a drink.

The Falcon in Clapham Junction had three kinds of Guinness on tap – standard, Extra Cold and – my all-time/old-time favourite – Export. They were also doing a two for one on Jameson. Pure Irish-combo heaven.

The order popped right out of my mouth without hesitation and right on cue, like a line I'd been rehearsing in the mirror for years.

I took my pint and double J and went and sat at the back of the pub, under a stained glass dome covering a skylight. It was cool and sombre there, dark wooden floors and panelled walls strung with faded satin drapes.

I looked at the drinks on the table. The whisky fumes were sharp and heady, already making my head reel.

Did I *really* want this? To do this, and undo everything else? My family, all those years of abstinence, the life I'd made since leaving the Lister ...

I'd last had a drink in 1994.

That was 6205 days sober. Give or take.

Think of:

The pickled ruins in the Laughing Camel; and the creatures I saw through the window in *this* very place every Saturday morning.

Did I want to end up like *that*?

And wasn't I just doing my would-be killers' job for them?

I still had a choice. It wasn't a done deal yet. I could still get up and leave my transgression unconsummated, just like I had with Melissa ...

Yeah ...

RIGHT.

I'd never ever cheat on my wife, but I'd always be true to my real mistress, the one I'd never got over or got out of my system; the one I'd always missed.

Booze.

Truth was: I hadn't just *liked* drinking ...

I'd fucking *LOVED* it.

The happy buzz the first few glasses gave me? Better than any drug I'd tried. I loved the way the high intensified; how the rush turned to soothing balm. And I loved the way I could forget my woes for a while, the six-to-eight-hour head holidays. I liked pubs. I liked talking to strangers, the pub philosophers and politicians, the barstool footballers and boxers and tennis players, the world-to-righters and the world-done-me-wrongers. No, I hadn't liked the hangovers. I really hated those. And I hated the blackouts too. They scared me. And the morning-after depressions were horrible. All the lies I told – to others, and mostly to myself. All the friends I lost. Every single last one of them. But ... that was a long *long* time ago. I was a different person now. I could handle it.

Besides ...

I'd come *this* close to getting killed today.

THIS close!

Hell ...

I deserved a drink.

I took a pull of Guinness. Just half a mouthful, telling myself that if it tasted disgusting or made me sick I'd stop immediately.

Fat chance.

It tasted good.

Damn good. Like the brandy in my morning coffee used to.

Then I had a nip of whisky.

I closed my eyes and smiled as I slipped away a little inside.

The punters around me were mostly young; social drinkers getting tanked up before hitting the Grand up the road for an all-night rave. Over half were done up in fancy dress; the men out-dafting each other in fluffy yellow bird and black gorilla costumes, the women got up as porno nurses and cheerleaders, hems ultra-short, necklines a-plunging and heels high and spiked. The few old-timers and bar-proppers leer-licked their lips and clucked their dentures. Everyone was happy. Even the staff.

Half an hour later I was on my second round.

A group of blokes came in and took over the tables next to me, pushing them together to make their own little island. They were dressed in a uniform of jeans, plaid shirts and second- or third-attempt beards – ex-students reviving the grunge look, I guessed. They looked appropriately miserable too, sitting around their pints not saying much of anything, as if all their teams had lost and their girlfriends had run off with their best mates, and the only music on their iPods was Pearl Jam.

Round three now. The tremors had stopped and my fear had lost its fangs, but I wasn't even close to getting trolleyed. My head wasn't giving in. I downed my J in one and chased it with a quart of Guinness.

The grunge contingent's ranks were increased by several newcomers. Even surlier than their mates, they slouched in with downturned mouths and a weight of the world dip to their shoulders. They had hand-shaped white placards tucked under their arms, printed with Big!-Bold!-Black!-Imperatives!

HANDS OFF!!!
OUR
PENSIONS!

HANDS OFF!!!
THE
NHS!

HANDS OFF!!!
OUR
EDUCATION!

They'd come from today's demo – the whole lot of them.

And the reason they weren't talking was that their eyes were glued to the TV I'd failed to notice, above the bar.

It was showing the news.

Sky News.

'Could you turn that up a bit, please?' one of them asked the barmaid, who obliged.

On screen: an overhead shot of a car, the front covered in flames. It was reversing away from a masked man dancing jubilantly on a traffic island in the middle of the road.

That was the car I'd been in. I hadn't noticed the colour – dark blue – or the make – a Renault Megane.

The car shot forward at a sharp angle, away from the line of the road. The dancer ran across to the opposite pavement as the Megane headed straight for the traffic island. It bumped over the kerb and ploughed into the lightpost, flattening it in one, before rolling forward a few feet and skidding to the left as its back axle dragged the toppled traffic light with it. The car stopped. Its wheels were still spinning, smoking up on the asphalt, but the car was stuck. And still on fire.

Someone ran across the street and took a flying kick at the passenger window. Then three more people were pounding it with bats and bars. Seconds later a small mob was all over the Megane, rocking it backwards and forwards, oblivious to the flames.

Reporter:
'One man is in critical condition. Another passenger – believed to be a
woman – is also in hospital with burns and head injuries. A third
person is being sought by the police. He is described as being around six
feet tall, white, with dark hair, wearing a blue top and black trousers.'

Shit. That was *me.*

And how I was the *third* person? There'd been *four* of us in the car.

The screen cut to now.

Still an overhead view. The Strand was empty of all traffic, except for stationary police vehicles and ambulances. The Trafalgar Square end had been cordoned off, as had all the side roads from Covent Garden and Charing Cross. There was a horizontal line of forensics officers stretching from pavement to pavement, crouched down in the road, fingertip searching for evidence.

News anchor:
'Do you have any more information on the shooting in Adam Street?'

Reporter:
'It's still unclear as to exactly what happened. Eyewitnesses told us

they heard shots as the car was being attacked. We don't yet know
precisely where the shots came from.'

The screen had cut back to the mob swarming over the Megane.

Reporter:
'An armed man was seen running up the Strand moments after the
car was overturned. Officers from SO19 – the police's armed-
response unit – have confirmed that a man was shot and killed in
Adam Street, a few blocks from here. Witnesses have described him
as white and bald.'

Now the reporter was talking to camera, standing in Trafalgar
Square. Behind him, uniformed police were guarding the perimeter.
The camera was zooming in on the Megane. It was on its roof, in the
middle of the road, lying in a halo of shattered glass, all four doors flung
open, the front blackened.

So . . .

The driver and the woman were in hospital in critical condition.
Jonas had been shot and killed.
And the cops were looking for *me* – the 'third' person in the car.
My hand started shaking again as the fear returned.
My mouth was dry and my guts were churning.
I had to get out of here.
I stepped out into the street. The light pierced my head with white-
hot spears. I turned the corner on to Falcon Road and the start of the
long walk home.
That's when the effects of my first round of drinks in 6205 dry days
hit me, all in one go, like a wrecking ball had skimmed off the tip of a
tsunami and smacked right into me.
My balance went as my centre of gravity turned into a greasy puck
bouncing around an ice rink. I was a passenger in someone else's body.
People veered out of my way. People looked at me strangely. People
looked at me knowing full well.
Déjà vu time: summer in Stevenage, doing the wino shuffle from the
Griffin to the Naseby through the town centre.
I hoped to high heaven I didn't see anyone Karen knew.
I managed to make it to Falcon Road railway bridge, where it was
permanently dark and always cool. That was a relief. I slid along the tiled
walls, deafened and threatened by the roaring traffic, the booze sloshing
around in my stomach.
When I made it out of the bridge the sunlight as good as blinded me.

I closed my eyes. My head whirled like a flicked coin inside a spinning top.

I opened my eyes and puked my guts out in the street.

72

Home to:
Water.
Coffee.
Bed.

Last thoughts before I konked out fully dressed, my shoes still on:

I'm never ever ever drinking again
I'm never ever ever drinking again
I'm never ever ever drinking again
I'm
Never
Ever
E-V-E-R
drinking
again
(*ever*)

The phone woke me up.

I was convinced it was early Sunday morning, 3 a.m. or thereabouts.

It was dark. The car park lights were on in the estate, flooding the room with an orange sodium glow. A party was going on in the opposite block, reggae bass so loud the bedroom window rattled in its frame.

I tried raising my head off the pillow but my skull felt like it was stuffed with loose rocks and balls of razor wire, and held together by crooked rusty screws. Pain alternately thudded and stabbed my brainpan. The only relief I got was putting my head back where I'd found it.

The phone kept on ringing.

Why wasn't the answering machine kicking in?

I pulled the duvet over my face.

No good. The ringing still got through with the music and now the inside of my head felt like it was getting mashed in a blender.

I forced myself out of bed and grabbed the receiver.

'Terry? *Terry?*'

Karen.

It was Karen. And it wasn't Sunday morning, but 10.15, Saturday night.

'Yeah?'

'Where've you been?'

'Out.'

'I've been calling all day. Tried here, tried your mobile. I was worried.'

Wurried.

'I was out,' I said, leaning back against the wall.

'Are you OK?' she said. 'You sound ... You sound ...'

She didn't want to say it. She'd never seen me drink, or drunk. But she knew my history. Knew it was a sensitive area. Knew better than to go there.

'I was asleep,' I said.

'All day?'

'I went out, I told you.'

'Have you seen the news? That shooting in Trafalgar Square?'

'What about it?'

'Amy swears that's you on TV.'

Eh?

'The fella they're looking for,' she said.

'What fella?'

'Haven't you seen the news?'

That's when I properly heard the tone of her voice. Panic, fear, borderline hysteria. I saw the answering machine button was flashing red. I bet she'd filled up the tape with messages – and done the same with my mobile. Where was my mobile anyway?

'They put this picture up on the news, this CCTV image of the bloke they're after. Amy saw it and said, "That's Daddy!"'

I swallowed. Or tried to. My mouth and throat were as dry as burned paper. I could hear my heart beating over the party's bass waves, hitting the exact same deep notes, except my heart was going way faster. It's not that I didn't want to tell her what had happened, but I was in no fit state to explain. And I didn't know what was going on now. I had to get to the TV first.

'It *isn't* you, is it?' she asked.

'I haven't seen the news,' I said.

Wrong answer.

Quick correction:

'I've been here all day.'

Wrong *again*.

'I thought you said you were out!' Karen shouted.

I needed to get off the phone quick.

'I was out ... this morning,' I said, standing up. The room span around me, as if I was mid-ride on a merry-go-round. I sat back down on the bed.

'Look ... I'm not really with it,' I said.

'You can say that again! Why are you slurring?'

Was I?

How long before she popped the magic question? *You haven't been drinking, have you?* I could almost hear it forming in her head, over the line.

'Give me a few minutes,' I said. 'I'll call you back, all right?'

Amy was right.

I'd made every news programme on every channel.

Thankfully, the image wasn't the best. I was caught mid-sprint – legs galloping, arms pumping. Most importantly, my head was tilted down, so much of my face was obscured. Strangers wouldn't recognise me.

But my family had.

I switched channels. They showed more of the picture. I wasn't the only person running. There were two rioters right behind me, faces half covered with bandannas. One was looking over his shoulder, the other straight ahead of him, his eyes bulging in terror.

I hadn't known where I was heading after they pulled me out of the back of the car. I legged it as fast as I could, paying no attention to my surroundings, just wanting to get as far away from my potential kidnappers as possible.

In the picture I was tearing up the Strand. I had no memory of that. None whatsoever.

I sat gawping at myself on the screen, switching channels whenever the report cut from the picture until I saw myself again. It looked slightly different every time. The three of us – me and the rioters – could have been running a race, with me ahead.

Then I noticed the ticker scrolling at the bottom of the screen:

Central London Bloodbath: Second Death.

Sky News again.

The video of the burning car reversing and then darting forward into the traffic light.

The same reporter as before, talking live from his spot on a now dark corner of Trafalgar Square. Spotlights had been erected along the Strand, and the forensics teams were visible in the background, shapes standing in the middle of the street like frozen ectoplasm.

Reporter:
'The gunman came out of the car and ran up the Strand towards Charing Cross. He opened fire. At the time there were anti-capitalist demonstrators vandalising shops along the road. Four were hit. One – believed to be a man in his twenties – was hit in the head and died instantly. A woman was seriously wounded. The survivors have been taken to hospital. Their condition is described as critical.

'I spoke to someone earlier, who was taking part in the union demonstration in Trafalgar Square and saw the Renault Megane being attacked.'

Cut to: the same old car as bonfire-on-wheels footage. Then to the witness – a young man in a zip-up top.

Bystander:
'People were attacking the car. I heard them yelling something about "police brutality". I thought the police had nabbed one of the anti-capitalists. The car was on fire. Then this cheer went up, you know, like a football crowd goes when they get a goal. And then I heard shots. Bang! Bang! Bang! Loud. Everyone started running away. It was mental. And I saw this man, this big bald bloke come out of the car and start running up the Strand. Shooting. I hit the deck. I didn't know what the hell was going on. It was mental. Totally totally mental.'

Cut to: a police press conference. A senior officer in uniform was giving a statement.

Officer:
'We are looking for the man in this photograph. He was seen running up the Strand shortly before the shooting started. He is white, six feet tall, with short dark hair. He was wearing black trousers and a navy-blue top. We are asking him to come forward to help with our inquiries. And we are appealing to anyone who recognises him to contact us immediately.'

Then my picture flashed up on the screen again.
And I understood *exactly* what had happened now.
Jonas had been shooting *at me*. I was in such a dazed panic I didn't even hear the shots.
The normal thing to do – and the right thing to do – would be to go straight to the cops, tell them my side; tell them absolutely everything – proof or no proof.

364

But I didn't want to do that. They'd take me into custody, and I'd be there while they cleared things up. Fabia Masson had been killed in custody. I wouldn't be safe.

I was still alive. The people after me were either dead or had been caught.

I'd take my chances.

73

Sunday:

I went home, back to Stevenage, for the first time in twelve years.

Old Stevenage dates back to medieval times, a quaint little place with period houses, homely shops and a whiff of gentility. Linked to it via metal bridges and underpasses, is the New Town; a cheerless sprawl of small, near-identical houses corralled into estates, purpose-built in the 1950s and 1960s, and added to in the ensuing decades, to accommodate the London population overspill.

My parents still lived in one of these houses, the same two-up two-down in Wexford Grove I'd grown up in.

Mum opened the front door.

I take after her the most. We're both tall, pale-skinned, blue-eyed and have the same dark-russet hair. We're also cursed with expressive faces, the kind that let you know what we're thinking.

A miscellany of emotions washed over Mum's face when she saw me standing there, a bunch of cheap flowers in my hand. Surprise. Confusion. A little consternation, and then, at the end of it, joy.

She smiled, put her arms out and hugged and kissed me.

'Come on in. We're just going to eat.'

There was astonishment all around the dinner table. That and the smell of booze. Dad had been down the Naseby like always on a Sunday. My brothers Aidan and Patrick had joined him. They'd both moved back home, temporarily they'd each said then, two and three years ago respectively.

'Look what the mangy cat dragged in,' Ade said, standing up unsteadily, for a hug.

'Drink, Terry?'

That was Dad, waving a can of Guinness Draught.

'No thanks,' I said.

We shook hands, as we'd always done, even when I was a kid. Dad wasn't big on displays of emotion. But I knew from the twinkle in his eyes that he was glad to see me.

'Still off the sauce, then?' asked Pat.

Sober for sixteen hours, I thought.

'You look good, man.'

'Wish I could say the same for you.'

Pat laughed. He was a state. Two chins, with another on the way; a dome of a belly straining the stripes of his Celtic football shirt.

He'd been the sporty one in the family. He wanted to be a boxer, but he didn't have the right mentality. Too short-tempered. He'd been kicked out of every gym in the county. He took up bodybuilding instead. Then he met an Irish woman called Molly and followed her back to our ancestral homeland. Once there he went the whole hog and became Irish, right down to developing a mannered brogue and a line in blarney to go with his Cork address and Irish passport. Somewhere along the line he decided that he couldn't call himself fully Irish without drinking himself stupid too. He lost his job, then Molly and their daughter, before retreating here. The brogue was long gone now too. But not the drinking.

'Get y'self a plate and a seat,' Mum said. 'I've made stew.'

The living room hadn't changed. The plastic-coated map of Ireland still hanging on a string holder on the wall; and photos of us as kids, then all our kids too – my nephews and nieces. I had six, two of them mixed race like Ray. The only daughter-in-law on the wall was Karen. She was the last one standing.

'What brings ye back, son?' asked Dad.

Impulse. Fear. I hadn't really thought about it. As soon as I woke up this morning, hungover and dry-mouthed, I decided to come here.

'Been a while,' I said.

'Bollocks!' Ade said.

'Guilt more like,' laughed Pat.

Mum didn't say anything.

'How's the family?' asked Dad.

'Good.'

'Karen ain't kicked you out yet, then?' Pat said. He'd never met Karen or the kids, just knew them through photos and family gossip.

'No,' I smiled.

'Give it time,' Ade chimed in.

'You'd know, right?'

This was brotherly banter. We'd always taken the piss out of each other. Although it had been well over a decade since we'd all last sat at this table, eating together, it was like yesterday.

366

OK, some explaining to do.

My family are alcoholics. All of them.

My parents wouldn't label themselves as such. They both started drinking young and never stopped. They're disciplined daily drinkers, with strict limits on what they knock back. Dad's is five pints of Guinness and a whisky to round off. Mum likes her three cans of Mackeson's stout and a couple of brandies in-between. I've never seen either of them drunk, or even tipsy.

That doesn't go for the rest of us. Alcohol has blighted our lives.

Me, you know about.

Ade had been my hero. I'd looked up to him, wanted to be him. He used to be lithe and wired, all style and dash: the Jam fan who dressed like Paul Weller and tooled around town on a Lambretta. He was the only person I've ever known who could pull off the Weller look. Everyone else always got it wrong, Sta Press imitators with crap mullets.

Ade and Pat had been the local hardnuts. Everyone in town was wary of them. They never met a scrap they didn't like. I had an easy time growing up because of them and their rep. That extended to VJ too, once we became friends.

But Ade was fucked now. He couldn't keep his spoon still. His hair was all grey and thinning, and his face looked like a dirty handkerchief after a nosebleed.

He used to run a nightclub in Brighton but it was closed down after a girl took Ecstasy and went into convulsions on the dancefloor. Turned out Ade was getting backhanders from a dealer who sold in the toilets. There was a trial. Ade was acquitted through lack of evidence, but he lost a civil lawsuit brought by the girl's parents. He hit the skids soon after, winding up homeless and sleeping on park benches when his wife kicked him out after one drunken row too many.

That was why I'd stayed away all these years, and why I'd never brought my kids here. I was scared. Alcoholism may not be genetic or hereditary, but it felt that way to me. I didn't want Ray or Amy being exposed to it; and yeah ... I didn't want to be reminded of what I'd escaped.

But you know what?

Sitting here with them, joking and laughing, I wish I'd been stronger than that. I loved my family, each and every one of them, warts and all – especially the warts.

'D'he do it, then?' Pat asked me.

'Eh?'

'VJ. D'he kill that girl? You're his brief, right?'

I hadn't even spoken to my parents since VJ's arrest. How did ...?

'Lorraine told me,' Mum said.

Lorraine was VJ's mother.

'Didn't know you two were talking again,' I said. As far as I knew, Mum hadn't said a word to Lorraine since she'd insisted I'd stolen her son's diary. They'd had a full-on row, right in the middle of the town shopping centre. Ireland vs. Trinidad. Two forces of nature, neither yielding.

'You should come 'ome more often then, shouldn't ya?' Ade said.

'Let's talk in the kitchen,' Mum whispered to me.

'You know he never comes back neither, does Vernon? Hasn't been back since he moved to London. Not once. He supports Lorraine, but never sets foot here. I see Gwen around, though, now and then. She's got a family in Norwich.'

I was helping Mum dry the dishes. The kitchen was new, flagstones instead of lino on the floor, and the appliances all modern, but it still looked and smelled exactly the way I remembered.

'So, *did* he do it?' she asked.

'No,' I said.

'Are you sure?'

'Positive.'

'Funny how things keep coming around, isn't it? Him in big trouble, you still defending him,' Mum said.

There was some truth in that, but it wasn't the *whole* truth.

'Why d'you get us to lie for him?' I asked.

When VJ had come to the house, terrified and tearful, after getting grilled by Detective Quinlan, neither me nor my brothers had known what to do. We'd been watching *Top of the Pops*. We all gawped at him like cows distracted from grazing. It was Mum who took charge. She turned off the telly and got him to repeat what he'd said. Then she told him not to worry, she'd tell the cops he was with us that night. She gave him his alibi, and we backed her up. That's what really happened.

'Rodney used to beat Lorraine all the time.'

'I didn't know that,' I said.

And I hadn't. VJ never told me. Not even a hint.

I didn't see Mrs James all that often when Rodney was alive. I was never invited into their house. She was little more than an outline in the kitchen window, waving us off to school.

'He used to hit her,' she said. 'And Vernon and Gwen used to see him do it. Lorraine told me he tried to strangle her once or twice too – with

368

his belt. We went to the cops about it. Know what they told her? "We don't interfere in domestic matters." So Rodney got what was coming to him. All tyrants fall, one way or another.'

'Did VJ kill him?'

'I don't know about that,' she said. 'But I'll tell you this much. If I had to do it over, I wouldn't change a thing. I've never regretted it. Not even when you and him fell out. Men shouldn't hit women.'

I stayed a few hours more.

The trial was starting tomorrow, and I had to get back to prepare, but I didn't want to go. I kept on putting off leaving by an hour, then another, until the rain that had been falling in London this morning made its way to the house.

We all sat around the living room. The cans came out. They all toasted my health and put the telly on and we sat there watching a film, barely speaking.

Dad and Mum sipped their beers. Ade and Pat seemed to be in competition over who could drink four cans the fastest. They both had jobs to go to tomorrow, but you wouldn't have known it. Ade was working on the railways, Pat on a building site.

Yeah, I felt the urge to join them for a brew or ten. I'd kicked open those gates yesterday and it would take a while to get them closed again.

After nine I knew I had to go. The trains would run less frequently, and then they wouldn't run at all.

I said my goodbyes and see you soons and headed for the door, Mum right behind me.

I stood on the doorstep, looking at the wet road and the rain falling orange against the streetlights.

'I don't think I ever told you this, Mum, but I appreciate what you and Dad did for me back then – when things were really bad,' I said.

Mum looked me over.

'Are you in trouble?' she asked.

'I'm OK,' I said.

She knew I was lying. She always had.

'Come see us when you can, Terry. Bring the family.'

'I'll do that. Soon as this thing's over. Promise.'

'Say hello to Vernon for me. Tell him I'm thinking of him.'

74

Latchmere, London, 1 a.m.

Here's what I now believed:

Sid Kopf had masterminded the whole set-up.

Scott Nagle wanted VJ out of the way for whatever reason, but he couldn't use his old methods, either because suspicion would fall on him, or because VJ was too rich and too high-profile. Some squatter's murder would be quickly forgotten, blamed on drugs or bad luck, but not a financier handling powerful people's money. Nagle needed a whole new approach.

Enter Kopf.

He got Swayne to research VJ. Swayne discovered VJ's penchant for escorts and S&M.

The narrative of the fit-up fell into place. Frame VJ for killing an escort, by strangulation.

Find him his type of woman (Fabia), get her to be noticed with him (the green dress), drug him and go up to his room. Then kill her. He'd wake up and find her dead. He'd get arrested for murder.

The case against him would be textbook.

You've got:

Mens rea – motive/intent. VJ intended to slap and choke Fabia when he took her up to his hotel room. It's what he liked doing. He'd done it before, to others.

And you've got:

Actus reus – death by strangulation.

Hard to argue against a clear behavioural pattern – and the body in the bed.

But that wasn't *quite* enough.

And here's what jarred, what separated this from an ordinary fit-up. Rudy Saks.

He was in on it, part of the team. Assassins don't hang around the scene of the crime. They always disappear.

VJ had been locked up for murder. Mission accomplished, surely? Why give the police a witness statement two days after his arrest?

Because their job wasn't quite finished.

Saks's statement was pivotal to the case against VJ. It was clear proof that he'd been in the room with the victim close to the time of her death. It would ensure a conviction.

So the purpose of the set-up wasn't simply for VJ to get arrested for the murder of a woman, but for him to be *convicted* for it too.

Kopf had designed this as only a lawyer could – with a trial in mind, and a guilty verdict as the objective.

What about Swayne?

Why had he broken rank and started dropping hints – Silver Service, Oliver Wingrove, the White Ghosts?

Why hadn't he simply come clean, and told me what he knew?

Swayne was scared of Kopf. Scared enough to keep his mouth shut and do eight years in jail, when he could have given him up and walked. Maybe he was implicated too, or maybe he'd feared for Steff's life.

Now he was dead. And that was on me.

As was Fabia's death. I led her killers right to her.

Not strictly my fault, I know, but I *was* to blame.

So what were my options?

Go to the police?

With what? Attempted kidnapping? Yes, but I had nothing else to give them except unsubstantiated conspiracy. I'd lost the drawing I found in Swayne's locker when I was grabbed.

Which left Janet.

How much did she know?

She was the senior partner in the firm and had Kopf's ear. But, ultimately, he called the shots.

Ahmad Sihl had contacted her out of the blue, not to represent VJ, but to recommend a lawyer. She'd fought to get the case because it was high profile and would put KRP on the map as a criminal law firm.

She'd been genuinely pissed off about Christine and *especially* Swayne being brought in on the case.

So, that meant she didn't know.

The phone rang and rang. I hoped I wouldn't get the answering machine.

I didn't.

I got a snarling yawn.

'Janet? It's Terry.'

'Terry? It's one o'clock in the fucking morning.'

'We need to talk. Now. In person.'

75

Regina v Vernon James
Case No. T20119709
Court 1, Central Criminal Court
(Old Bailey)

Day 1

We met in Christine's chambers at 7 a.m. sharp.

One glimpse of her and I feared the worst. She looked about as ill as I'd ever seen anyone look: haggard, skin close to translucent, make-up clinging to it like overnight frost on a windscreen. I was positive she was going to tell us she was stepping down and handing over to Redpath ...

But no. The first words out of her mouth were orders:

'We're to meet up here every day at the same time. We'll review the day's order of business, and then get a cab to court. It's imperative we're seen arriving and leaving together – as one, a team, a united front. OK?'

We nodded. I felt like saluting.

'Terry, do you know how to do the court walk?'

'No.'

'The media will be out in force today. TV in particular. They always film the lead barristers going in on the first day. They repeat the same clip on every news item about the trial until it's over. Your entrance must be just right.

'So: walk at a medium pace. Head up, back straight. Do not look at the cameras, and do *not* smile. That's *very* important. We're arguing over a person's future, sometimes the rest of their lives. Wear a serious expression, but not a stern one. Be human, but not humane.

'Normally I walk on the outside for the cameras, but I don't look my best today so I want you to take my place. I'll be next to you. I'll be moving a little slower than usual, playing up my frailty. I'll be holding on to your arm for support. We'll pretend we're deep in discussion. I talk, you listen and nod along. All right?'

'OK,' I said.

Redpath cleared his throat.

'What about me?' he asked.

'You're on trolley duty,' she said. 'Stay three or four steps behind.'

The taxi dropped us off at the corner of Newgate Street. I helped Christine out and we set off down the road, arm in arm to the Old Bailey.

The press were camped on the pavement opposite the South Block entrance, a dense grey clump of photographers and camera crews already training their lenses our way.

It was warm but overcast, the sky a solid grubby white matt rolled over the city, blocking out every hint of blue and the sun beyond it. The faint breeze smelled of brewing rain.

Christine walked ultra-slow but talked non-stop. She explained how she'd written two very different opening statements, dry and dramatic. She'd know which one to use once Carnavale kicked things off. She'd worked out her strategy, she said. *We were going to win.*

Then she was telling me about opening-day nerves, how she still got them after all these years and well over a hundred trials. Good barristers had to be like boxers; scared going in – scared of failure, scared of ridicule, but most of all scared they'd let their client down. If they didn't have that fear, they no longer cared and had no business being here.

Was that really the case? I asked her. Oh yes, she said. All the best silks are nervous wrecks the night before a trial; zombies (insomniacs) or chuckers (pukers). Take Carnavale, for example. The Walking Dead.

I didn't tell her I was nervous too, probably as much as her – if not more.

I kept my head averted as we walked past the press pack. Yesterday, I'd made the front page of every newspaper, fleeing a gunman.

We waited in the Great Hall for the courtroom doors to open.

Carnavale stood across from us with his junior barrister and clerk, the three of them inadvertently lined up in descending height-order, the tops of their heads forming a step arrangement. They were juggling individual phone conversations and going over a document that was passing back and forth between them. The clerk handed to the junior who read and scribbled as she babbled into the phone in her other hand. Then Carnavale got the document, looked it over and made an annotation of his own before passing the paper back to the clerk via the junior. The clerk then read the document down the phone.

There were about a dozen accredited journalists hanging around with their hands in their pockets or thumbing through notebooks. A few came over and said hello to Christine. None of them asked about the trial or VJ, just after her. I sensed the length and depth of the relationships. Christine must have used them as much as they'd used her.

I played tourist and took in my surroundings.

The Great Hall lived up to its name. We were in the very heart of the Old Bailey, under the dome and thus directly below the golden statue of Justice. Every inch was decorated or dramatically illuminated with yellow lighting or opened up into vaulted skylights. The floor and walls were black-and-white marble, the ceiling strung with arches that had friezes on every abutment and moulded stucco squares on their undersides. Half-moon frescos fanned out above the entrances to the courts, depicting the building's four mainstays – God, the Law, the Establishment and London. Court 1's painting showed Justice on the steps of St Paul's Cathedral, with Alfred the Great – the lawmaker king – to her left, and on her right, Moses receiving the Ten Commandments. The subtext was clear: if we don't get you, God will.

'Here he comes,' Christine whispered to me.

Carnavale was heading our way, heels snipping at the floor.

'How are you?' he said to Christine, grinning.

'Well. You?'

'You know . . .' he said with a shrug. 'Are we going to be straight out of the gate?'

'I don't see why not.'

'You're not going to contest anything?'

She shook her head. This was the way things were often done, Christine had explained to me. Deals were struck between defence and prosecution – a kind of bartering where both sides agreed to drop repetitive evidence and inessential witnesses to speed things up. They all had other trials to go on to, other cases to work on. Unlike America, there was also an unspoken agreement not to submit new evidence in the middle of proceedings. It wasn't unusual for opposing barristers to be good friends, so they tended not to burn each other either. And, even if they weren't friends, the law was a small world where favours were accumulated along with grudges. But as this was Christine's last trial, she had no intention of observing niceties.

Carnavale changed the subject. He asked about her family. And then they were off, chatting about kids, grandkids, houses . . .

I tuned out.

We'd come here from the cells downstairs. We'd seen VJ. He was calm, all smiles and quiet confidence, as if he thought this the beginning of the end of his ordeal, that it would be over soon; just one mountainous hurdle to get over and he was home free.

Christine had talked him through what would happen today. Jury selection and opening statements. Setting up the pieces on the board. The fun, she said, would start tomorrow.

Carnavale said his goodbyes to Christine, a quick hello to Redpath and went back to his team.

'That's a worried man,' she said.

'Seems confident enough to me,' I said.

'Barristers are the best fakers. Ergo good actors. Franco's Oscar material.'

'All rise.'

Judge Blumenfeld came in with a swish of his robes and a bounce to his wig.

We sat down after he'd taken his place at the podium. The clerk was the same woman with the same outdated curly-perm.

'Anything before we start?' the judge asked, looking at Carnavale, then Christine.

Both barristers shook their heads.

'Bring in the defendant, please,' he said to his clerk, who picked up a phone and spoke inaudibly for a few seconds.

Our seating arrangements were slightly different from the PCMH. Prosecution and defence barristers habitually sat in the first two rows, with their clerks behind them, but Christine had brought me on to her row and sat me next to her. More pieces being arranged on the chess-board.

A security guard led VJ to the dock. A chorus of murmurs and whispers rose up from the packed public gallery. Christine glanced at him as he reached the bulletproofed dock. We all exchanged nods. He was expressionless.

'Let's proceed with jury selection,' the judge said to the clerk. Another silent phone call.

A few minutes later twenty people entered the courtroom. Mostly mid-twenties to mid-fifties men and women, all carrying a single sheet of paper.

The clerk addressed them.

'The court requires twelve of you to sit as jurors. I will call out the number you've been given. If your number is called please come forward and let me know if you are available for this trial. If you are not available, you will be asked to explain your reasons to the judge, and to provide relevant evidence on your behalf. Do you all understand?'

She scanned their faces.

'I will now call the first number,' she said, running a finger down the list she was holding. 'Fifteen.'

A young Asian woman with shoulder-length hair came forward. The court clerk spoke to her. Then she motioned her to take a seat on the jury bench facing us.

'This is where you start earning your keep,' Christine whispered to me. 'I want you to read the jury.

'First thing to remember is that these people don't want to be here.

They've been ordered to do this. Most will stay resentful for the duration, wishing the whole thing be over. They're the best and worst kind of juror. They barely listen. So when it comes to making a decision they'll side with the majority just to get out of here as fast as possible.'

The clerk read out the next number.

'Seven.'

A squat man in a blue blazer and silver-rimmed specs approached her with the waddling stomp of the seriously overweight. A few murmurs and head bobs later and he'd joined the Asian woman on the bench. He smiled as he sat down. And then he looked up at VJ, looked at him a little too intently for my liking. He didn't like what he saw. If this had been America, Christine could have cross-examined him to root out bias or pre-judgement. Unfortunately in Britain we don't have the luxury of not liking someone's face. Jury selection was random. We were stuck with who we got.

'Juries are dictatorships,' Christine continued. 'The verdict will be decided by three or four people at the most. Those are the ones who'll follow the trial carefully, who'll determine how the other eight vote. You're to be my eyes on this. I want you to identify the main players and observe their reactions. I need to sway at least two.'

'What should I look out for?'

'Note takers, obviously. They're the keenest. Also watch for how they react to me and Franco. If they smile when I speak and scowl when he does, that kind of thing.

'The most important juror of all is the foreman. The other eleven choose him or her as soon as they're sworn in. It's almost invariably a default decision. The person who volunteers for the role gets it. The foreman is the authority figure, the organiser. The weaker jurors always think as the foreman does. So he's worth a couple of extra votes.

'Last thing. Don't let them catch you looking at them – especially when you're helping me up or down. They'll know it's an act then and we'll lose their trust.'

'Did you teach your esteemed pupil this?' I asked.

'Of course,' she smiled. 'What do you think his clerk's doing right now?'

I resisted the temptation to turn round.

The proceedings took all morning. Several of those selected wanted to be excused and had to go before Blumenfeld to plead their cases. The judge made it hard on them from the off, glowering intimidatingly as they stood looking up at him on his podium, and asking them to speak up so the whole court could hear them. I knew what he was doing – making any potential shirkers think twice about trying to wriggle out.

The first person – a redheaded woman in a pinstripe skirt – had a valid excuse. She was getting married next week and everything had already been booked before she got the jury summons. She stammered as she spoke and trembled as she produced the paperwork, which the judge scrutinised like it was incriminating evidence, his expression thunderous. Then, with a smile and in a purring tone, he told her that was fine and she was excused. He wished her well in her marriage.

He wasn't so accommodating to those who followed. There was a writer on a tight deadline. Blumenfeld asked him what he wrote. 'Crime fiction.' The judge's lip curled ultra-sardonically and there was laughter from both press and public. 'Then you should regard this an ideal research opportunity,' he said and sent him to the bench. The writer was furious. We had our first potential problem juror.

By 12.30 p.m. the jury had been sworn in. Ten men, two women. They chose as their foreman the fat man in the blazer. The worst choice.

'We'll break for lunch now,' the judge said. 'Let's reconvene at two for opening statements.'

Janet joined us in the canteen, motorbike helmet in hand, file under her arm.

She didn't so much as glance at me, never mind say hello. She went and sat several tables behind me, where Christine joined her. I couldn't hear what they were saying, but I knew what they were talking about.

Janet and I had talked till sunrise, mostly on her patio, because she'd chain-smoked her way through a whole pack of Silk Cut.

It hadn't started well. My fault. I hadn't prepared, hadn't planned what I was going to say. I spouted my theory about Kopf. She greeted it with predictable disbelief and outrage, but also fury. She shouted, slammed her hand on the kitchen counter, called me everything from stupid to nuts – all in pure, unadulterated Cockney. In-between she spat out chunks of Kopf's career history, to underline his lifelong honesty and integrity. She dismissed everything I said as baseless paranoid delusion without a shred of evidence to back it up. Then she told me to get out – out of her house and out of the firm.

I made it to the door when her husband intervened. The commotion and cigarette smoke had woken him up. He'd come down to see what was going on.

That was when I told Janet how I'd spent my Saturday – minus the drinking.

That got her attention.

She fished her copy of the *Sunday Times* out of the recycling. She recognised me, even though my face was a blur. When she found out

377

that one of Rudy Saks's housemates was the gunman, she told her husband to fetch the whisky.

But that wasn't what swayed her.

What did it was when I came clean about my past – VJ, Stevenage, Rodney, Melissa, Cambridge, the Lister.

'But Sid had you vetted,' she said. 'I read the report. It matched your CV.'

'Who did the vetting?' I asked.

Only one person it could have been:

Andy Swayne.

I'd been part of Kopf's plan too.

Janet drained the whisky I hadn't touched in a single gulp.

Then she asked me to go over my theory again. Out had come her notepad.

'This changes everything,' she said, when I finished.

And that's how we'd left things.

Carnavale stood at his lectern and looked briefly at the judge, and then slowly over the faces of the jury as he began to speak in a precise and even tone, pitching his voice at just the right volume to carry around the court.

'On the morning of Thursday, March 17th this year, the body of a young woman was found in the bedroom of a hotel suite. The woman's name was Evelyn Bates. She was twenty-seven years old. She worked as a receptionist at a hairdresser's. She was loved by her family, to whom she was daughter and granddaughter, sister and aunt. And she is sorely missed by all her friends, who called her "Evey".

'Evelyn was strangled to death. She fought for breath as hard as she fought her killer. But he was much bigger and far stronger. He crushed her windpipe with his bare hands. Her last few moments of life must have been absolutely agonising.'

He paused there. Good beginning, I thought. He'd told the jury that this was about justice for the victim first and foremost. And the victim could be one of their friends, their daughter, their sister. In short, one of them.

He'd also fired the first class warfare salvo, by establishing what she did for a living. And – above all – he'd started with the strongest bit of evidence against VJ: the body in the bed.

'Later the same day, the police arrested and charged the person you see in the dock before you. His name is Vernon James.'

Another pause. All the jurors looked at VJ. Some stared at him, others glanced. I scanned their faces for a reaction. None. Early *early* days.

378

'The reasons he was arrested are straightforward,' Carnavale continued. 'He was the only guest in the room at the time of Evelyn's murder. He was present in the room at the time of her murder. And several eyewitnesses saw him with Evelyn in the hours leading up to her murder.'

Carnavale methodically went through the evidence against VJ, in the order he intended to present it. The autopsy report establishing time of death, forensics, eyewitnesses, the police interviews, the note Evelyn had left for Penny Halliwell. He would be taking the jury through his case chronologically, telling them what he believed happened that night at the Blenheim-Strand. Most took notes, pencils scratching away at pads.

I had to hand it to him. Carnavale knew how to spin a yarn and hold attention. He varied tempo regularly. He focused on a different block of the jury, yet didn't make eye contact with anyone specific. And he completely avoided looking at VJ, or mentioning him by name. He was 'the accused', 'the man in the dock', 'the man the police arrested'.

'Members of the jury, I can imagine what you're thinking, because I thought the very same thing,' he said. 'How is it that someone clever enough to be a multimillionaire before the age of forty could be *stupid* enough to walk away from a hotel room where he'd just murdered someone, without even making an effort to conceal the body? He left Evelyn Bates where he killed her. Naked, on top of the bed. He didn't even cover her with a sheet. No. He simply checked out of the room the next morning and went to his office.

'Yet, over the course of this trial, you will learn enough about the accused's character to understand, if not *why* he did this, then *how* he could do this. You will see that the accused is no ordinary man. He is a self-made millionaire. He can buy practically anything he wants. Maybe even, in his mind, any*one* he wants. He's someone who has created his very own personal exclusion zone. A golden bubble where he believes he's beholden to no one. That he can do what he wants, when he wants, *to whom* he wants. He is no ordinary man, so to him, the rules that bind others – that bind you and me, that bound Evelyn Bates – simply do not apply to him.

'You will also understand his state of mind. You will hear how he's done this sort of thing to women before. How he was violent with them, how he indulged in *extreme* sado-masochistic practices for his own sexual gratification. The consequences may not have been fatal then, but had he been reported to the police, he would have been held to account in a court of law. That he wasn't, is because of one thing and one thing only. His money. He paid off his previous victims. He bought their silence. And he bought the freedom to continue his depraved acts. And, by extension, in his mind, he bought himself the right to kill Evelyn Bates.'

Carnavale sat down.

The court was absolutely silent. Silent like it was empty. Silent like all the air had been sucked out of it. Both female jurors sneaked a look at the dock. This wasn't good.

'Mrs Devereaux. Would you like to proceed now or shall we have a break?' Judge Blumenfeld asked.

Christine put one hand on her stick, and I took her arm and helped her stand. She was slow and let the effort and pain play a little on her face. I took a quick look at the jury. No reaction.

I was hoping we'd have a recess, so we could put some distance between what we'd heard, let people forget a little.

'My Lord, I'd like to proceed. I won't take as long as my learned friend,' Christine said.

She looked at the jury.

'I don't like Vernon James,' she said.

What?

'I don't like him one bit. I don't think he's what you'd call a "nice person", or a "good person". Over the course of this trial, I expect you'll agree. He's been physically abusive to women. He's a sexual sadist, a serial adulterer, a habitual user of prostitutes. He's betrayed and shamed his family. He's also shamed the venerable institution that elected him Ethical Person of the Year the night before he was arrested for murder. In short, Vernon James is an absolute disgrace as a human being. Yet, he is not on trial for any of these failings. And neither is he on trial for being rich. He is on trial for murder. The murder of Evelyn Bates.'

A pause. So far so dreadful.

What the hell was she doing?

'Ladies and gentlemen of the jury, I will ask only one thing of you. Please consider the evidence against Mr James very *very* carefully and ask yourselves if it really adds up, if it *really* proves he killed Evelyn Bates. I do not for a moment believe it does. Thank you.'

'What the *fuck* was that about?' VJ said to Christine when we met him in the cells, half an hour after the judge had dismissed us for the day.

I didn't blame him for being angry. Neither did Redpath. Janet wasn't even there. She'd torn out of the courtroom, her phone already on.

'Did you see the jury's faces?' he asked.

She hadn't, but I had. Universal confusion. As in: w*here's the defence?*

'You didn't even say I didn't do it,' VJ went on.

380

'Because that's what they were expecting me to say,' Christine said, finally.

'No kidding! That's what *I* was expecting you to say!'

Me too.

'Did you follow the prosecution's opening statement?' she asked.

'Yeah ...'

'I wrote two very different openers – "Dry" and "Dramatic",' she said. 'If Carnavale had gone the melodramatic route, acted like every lawyer always does in American films, my response would have been "Dry". I would have laid out the facts of the case bit by bit and explained how I was going to dismantle them. But that was the direction he took.

'Never bore a jury. Always give them something to talk about, something to remember you by. Carnavale took almost an hour to say he thinks you're guilty. I was brief. I gave them drama. And I stole the prosecution's thunder.'

'How?'

'I told the jury the worst thing they'll hear about you – that you're into rough sex with prostitutes. It won't come as a surprise when they hear it. And I've also sided with them, distanced myself from you as a person, but not as a client.'

None of us were buying it. It was a clever enough tactic in theory, but she hadn't pulled it off. The jury didn't get it. They'd heard a defence lawyer say she didn't like her client, that she found him despicable. And they hadn't heard her state his innocence either. They'd heard her say the evidence against him was flawed. In other words, he did it, but the prosecution can't prove it.

'I hope you know what you're doing,' VJ said.

I went down the road to Ludgate Hill to hail us a taxi.

As I was standing there waiting, it started to rain. Not heavily; a few stray droplets peeled off the clouds and fell on the pavement and on my face.

Then Sid Kopf turned the corner. He'd been in court, watching from the public gallery, I guessed. He was with a much younger woman in a dark-grey suit and sunglasses.

I didn't recognise her until they got closer.

Melissa.

She hadn't left the country after all. She was standing by her man.

I ignored them and looked up the road. A cab was coming along. I held out my hand. The taxi stopped in front of me.

'Do you mind if we grab this one?' Kopf said, catching up to me.

'Be my guest,' I said.

He asked the driver to take them to Kensington Roof Gardens and opened the door for Melissa.

'Oh, sorry – have you two met?' he asked me.

I looked at Melissa, saw my double reflection in her opaque glasses, caught there like twin locusts in an oil slick.

'I don't believe we have,' she said, holding out her hand. 'I'm Melissa *James*. Vernon's wife.'

'Terry Flynt,' I said, shaking her hand, which was as cool and smooth as a flat stone in a stream.

'Terry's the clerk,' Kopf said to her.

'Not a paralegal, then?' she said.

Nice . . .

She got in the cab. Kopf followed her in. Then he stopped mid-stoop and looked over his shoulder at me. He shifted his eyes to the taxi and then back to mine. And he winked.

76

'Miriam Zengeni?'

'Yes?' a woman's voice answered the Archer House intercom.

'I'm a friend of Andy Swayne's.'

'Andy? You mean *Andrew*?'

'I'd like to talk to you about him and Michael.'

There was a long pause.

'Number 75, third floor,' she said and buzzed me through the gate.

She brewed up a pot of ginger tea and carried it with cups on a tray into the living room. We both sat either end of a light-brown leather couch.

The conversation started small; about the ruined, rainy summer; then how the building had changed in the last fifty years, going from a state-owned working-class council estate to the private, exclusive gated community it was today. She said the joy had gone out of the area. Poverty had bound people together. Wealth divided them. There'd once been a school just outside the block, which her daughter had gone to. It had been converted into luxury flats too. She missed the sound of children playing.

I took in the room, the grey porcelain praying hands and red rosary beads on the mantelpiece, a variety of snow globes from all over the world, and the photographs – so many photographs.

I noticed, in a frame on the shelf, the same black-and-white photo

Swayne had pinned to his corkboard, but larger and clearer. Miriam was pregnant there and just starting to show.

'I thought Andrew had stopped with the drinking nonsense long ago. Especially after—' She caught herself. 'How well did you know him?'

'Only a few months. He told me about his time in prison, if that's what you mean,' I said.

'He must have trusted you. He didn't make friends easily. If at all.'

She spoke in a surprisingly strong, clear baritone for someone her age. And her accent was pure bygone English, all clipped and proper, what used to be known as BBC English. She'd banished any and every hint of Mother Africa.

'We weren't friends exactly, more work colleagues,' I said.

'*Work?* I thought Andrew was retired.'

'He was helping me with a case.'

'A case? You mean an investigation?'

'Yeah,' I said, sipping the tea. It was sweet and spicy and surprisingly good, considering I wasn't a tea person.

'He didn't tell me anything about that.'

'Did you see him often?'

'I saw a lot of him this year. He'd come by once a week, usually Tuesday or Wednesday. We'd have lunch, sometimes go for walks when the weather was good,' she said, looking out of the window. 'Before that our contact was irregular.'

'When did you last see him?'

'He came twice last week, Monday and Tuesday. He borrowed that photograph you see there,' she said, pointing to the picture of the three of them on the shelf. 'He brought it back on Tuesday.'

The day before he'd died.

She sipped her tea.

'Are you a private detective as well?'

'I'm with a solicitors' firm – Kopf-Randall-Purdom.'

'You work for *Sid Kopf?*'

'Do you know him?'

'Of course. My daughter – Bridget – works for him.'

Now this was awkward.

'Which division?' I asked.

'Commercial. She's a partner there. Done well for herself,' she smiled, proudly.

My turn to stare out the window, at the moored barges bobbing on the rusty grey Thames, then Chelsea Harbour and the brass pagoda-like roof of the Belvedere.

'The reason I came to see you is that Andy – Andrew – died quite suddenly, just as I was getting to know him. I was curious about his past. He talked a bit about you and Michael.'

'What did he say?'

'Him and Michael were good friends.'

She frowned and shook her head. 'They only met twice.'

'Oh . . .' I was a little thrown, but not surprised. Typical Swayne; still messing with me from the grave. 'Did they meet in Zim— in Rhodesia?'

'Yes,' she said. 'What do you know about Michael?'

'He was Thomas Nagle's son.'

'Michael's father brought him over to England when he was four. In South Africa, mixed race children were rejected by both sides of apartheid. So he pulled some strings, got Michael a British passport and sent him to live with a couple who had a young son about his age. Thomas paid for his upkeep and education. Michael went to boarding school.

'Apart from that, his father had no involvement in his life. There was no contact, and he never recognised Michael as his own. He simply wrote cheques. Which, I suppose, is a lot more than most men would do in the circumstances.

'Michael lived in England until he graduated. Then he cut all ties and moved to Rhodesia. He had ambitions. He was interested in farming.'

She fetched a photo album down from a shelf, sat closer to me and opened it on her lap. Michael as a young boy, in shorts, cross-legged in a back garden next to a slightly older white boy. Michael and the boy at the seaside, building a sandcastle together. The pair outside a small terraced house, in cowboy outfits, aiming toy sixshooters at the camera. Michael at a school prize-giving, Michael holding up a silver cup.

'I met Michael when he was out buying feed in the market one day. Not the most romantic of encounters. I was a teacher. We married, moved to a farm. I fell pregnant. And then, one day, Andrew turned up with a letter from Michael's father.'

'Was that the first time you met Andrew?'

She nodded. I glanced up at the picture on the shelf.

'My mother took that with her camera. We'd bought her one for her birthday. She was trying it out.'

Swayne knew I'd come here too. He'd *wanted* me to talk to Miriam.

'What did the letter say?'

'Thomas wrote that he was dying of cancer and wanted to make amends. He wanted to meet Michael in London as soon as possible,' she said. 'Michael didn't want to go. He'd grown up knowing he was illegitimate, that his father was white and rich and British. He had a lot of anger about all that.

'He said his father didn't want to know him all his life, so why should things be any different now? But I insisted he went. He was about to become a father himself, and I thought it was only right he make peace with his own. I've regretted that ever since.'

She wasn't sad when she spoke those words, but I felt sorry for her. She'd unwittingly sent her husband to his death. From the other photos on the walls, I don't think she'd remarried, maybe never even had another significant relationship since. There were no other men in the pictures. Only her, her daughter, and two young, light-skinned girls I took to be grandchildren.

'Michael agreed to fly to London to meet his father,' she said.

'Where was Andrew?'

'He left after he delivered the letter. Went back to England. He telegrammed Michael to say he'd meet him at Heathrow when he got off the plane.'

'So, on November 27th, 1960, Michael left for Salisbury airport in his Land Rover. He never made it. They found his body a month later, hands tied behind his back. He'd been shot. We'll never know what happened. Maybe the whites killed him because they were jealous of how well the farm was doing. Maybe the blacks killed him because he was a traitor. Or maybe it was just a robbery.

'Scott Nagle – Michael's half-brother – came to Rhodesia a week after he disappeared. He got the police to investigate. If he hadn't come, nothing would have happened. The white police weren't interested in blacks going missing. The more the merrier. They found the car two weeks later, with the body in the back. Badly decomposed.

'Michael was identified by the officer in charge of the investigation. Wingrove. He had to use dental records from England.

'Thomas Nagle pushed for an inquest and a full investigation. He was determined to bring his son's killer to justice. But he died and they never caught Michael's killers.

'Scott arranged for me and Bridget to come to London for the inquest. That was forty-nine years ago. We've never left.'

I finished my tea.

'Do you know Scott Nagle well?'

'Bridget's Uncle Scott – of course,' she smiled. 'He's been very good to us. Thomas didn't leave anything for Michael in his will, but Scott took care of us. Always has. We've wanted for nothing.'

Thomas Nagle's will. I'd seen a draft version in Kopf's office. The father had split his estate equally between his sons. Maybe it had never been ratified because Michael failed to show; because he'd been murdered.

'You know, it's strange to hear that Andrew talked about Michael with you. He never did with me. Not until he asked to borrow the picture.'

'What did he say?'

'He said he thought about Michael all the time, that he hadn't stopped thinking about him from the day he died. And if there was one thing he could take back and undo, it would be the letter he brought.'

77

Day 2

The first witness called was the receptionist from the Blenheim-Strand, a fair-haired man in his early twenties.

He told the court how VJ had checked out of the hotel at around 6.30 in the morning. He'd noticed scratches on VJ's cheek and cuts on his hands and lip – 'like he'd been in a fight' – as well as his dishevelled appearance. The receptionist had asked him if he was all right and VJ had replied he was 'fine'. Then he'd signed for his bill and left.

Carnavale thanked him and sat down.

It was a short opener, both curtain-raiser and scene-setter.

Christine stood up with my help.

'Was Mr James drunk that morning?' she asked the receptionist.

'I don't know if I'd call it "drunk". He was a bit unsteady on his feet, his voice was slurry, and he reeked of alcohol,' the receptionist replied.

'Why didn't you say this to Detective Fordham in your statement?'

'He didn't ask me.'

Christine checked the witness statement – or rather pretended to, for the jury's benefit.

'DS Fordham spoke to you on March 21st, four days after the body was found. Correct?'

'Yes.'

'Could it be you'd forgotten that Mr James was drunk?'

'No,' the receptionist said. 'I've got a pretty good memory. The detective didn't ask me if he was drunk.'

'Thank you. No further questions,' Christine said.

Carnavale got up as Christine was still sitting down.

'Are you *sure* the accused was drunk?' he asked.

'Absolutely,' the receptionist said. 'We all know what drunks look like.'

Laughter.

'Why didn't you mention this in your statement?'

'The detective didn't ask me anything about that. I was asked about Mr James's appearance.'

'But you've just told the court he *appeared* to be drunk,' Carnavale said.

'He didn't "appear" to be drunk. He *was* drunk,' the receptionist replied, to more laughter.

Carnavale consulted the receptionist's statement. 'Detective Fordham asked you – and I quote – "Did you notice anything odd or unusual about him?"'

'And I said I'd noticed the injuries on his face and hands.'

'But you didn't find it odd or unusual that a guest was drunk at 6.30 in the morning.'

'No,' the receptionist answered. 'We get a lot of footballers at the hotel.'

More laughter.

Carnavale sat down.

Next up was one of the two maids who'd found Evelyn Bates's body. Spanish, with dyed pink hair that was growing out and a nose ring. She'd since left the hotel for another job.

She described how she and her colleague went to the suite to clean it at 8 a.m., as soon as their shift started. She described the wreckage in the lounge, the displaced minibar, the broken glass, the stench of alcohol. She remembered the bottle of champagne in the bucket on the coffee table, and the two glasses. While her colleague called hotel security as per procedure, she went to check the bedroom.

She initially thought Evelyn was asleep, but then noticed her eyes were open. She knew something was very wrong. She left the bedroom and waited for Albert Torena – the head of security – to arrive.

The court clerk passed a crime-scene photo to the jury foreman. It was Evelyn as the police had first found her – naked on the bed, her head slightly propped up on the pillows.

'Watch the jury,' Christine whispered. 'If anyone looks at Vernon after they've seen the picture, we've lost them.'

'How's that?' I asked.

'They already think he looks the part.'

Not one of them looked at VJ. And only the crime writer lingered over the picture, scribbling furiously. He'd probably realised he could use all of this as future material. He'd also become a key juror.

Christine's cross-examination was brief.

'Did you or your colleague move or touch the body in any way?'

The maid answered empathically. *Definitely* not. They'd been trained to call security immediately in an emergency.

'No further questions. Thank you.'

Albert Torena took the stand. He told the court he'd known Evelyn was dead 'on sight' because he'd been a cop in the *Guardia Civil* in Spain. He'd called the police and also found out the name of the guest staying in the room to 'help them with their enquiries'.

No questions from Christine. Torena looked disappointed when he was told he was done.

After a short recess, we heard from the coroner who'd performed the autopsy. He confirmed that Evelyn Bates had been murdered, the cause of death manual strangulation. He estimated the time of death as between midnight and 3 a.m.

He was precise as he described her crushed windpipe, the burst capillaries in her eyes and her swollen and distended tongue. I suppose dispassion came with the territory. He believed the killer to be right-handed because there was heavier bruising to the right side of the throat than the left. VJ was right-handed. So were most people.

I handed Christine both the autopsy and the forensics reports, which she placed on the lectern before her.

'Was there bruising to the victim's face?' she asked.

'No,' he said.

'So she wasn't slapped or punched prior to being strangled?'

'No,' he said. 'There was no indication of that.'

'What about elsewhere on her body? Were there any injuries – bruises, contusions, wounds?'

'Nothing recent,' he said. 'There was some old scar tissue on her left forearm, which appeared to be from a small cut.'

'Was there any indication that she'd been tied up or handcuffed in any way?'

'No,' he said.

'One further question,' Christine said, running a finger down a page of the autopsy report. 'I noticed you mentioned finding traces of several chemicals around the victim's neck. Polychloroprene, aluminium, carbon and other substances. What are those commonly found in – if you know?'

'This was from the fingerprinting process carried out by the forensics team. It's in the report,' he said.

'Please explain for the benefit of the jury,' she said.

'The polychloroprene is found in glue. Carbon and aluminium are found in fingerprint powder. Forensics would have dusted the body for fingerprints. It's very difficult to get a print off skin – living or dead. In death the body decomposes. The skin loses its elasticity and contracts, which would mean that any fingerprints will be distorted.

'Forensics officers use a process called glue fuming, which involves blowing a mixture of steam and household glue over the area they wish to fingerprint. The heat expands the skin back to its prior state, and the glue seals whatever's on the surface. They give it ten to fifteen seconds to dry and then apply standard print powder.'

'Thank you, doctor,' Christine said. 'No further questions.'

We broke for lunch.

Everyone rubbed shoulders in the Old Bailey canteen – prosecution, defence, witnesses, clerks, solicitors, police, press and the accused who weren't on remand. It wasn't uncommon to find yourself sharing the same air as newsworthy sex offenders, fraudsters or even killers on a break from their trials. This was where the business of justice was conducted. Courtroom opponents broke bread – literally – and discussed possible deals. Cops and barristers gave reporters off the record interviews. Solicitors and freelance clerks touted for work.

Christine, Redpath and I sat at a table by the window, overlooking the main road. It was raining outside, had been since yesterday night.

Christine stuck to bottled water and the contents of a small bright-red pillbox, its quartered tray carrying a different coloured and shaped tablet apiece. I had an apple and black coffee. Redpath was eating a jacket potato, tuna and grated cheese.

'What do you think of the prosecution's tactics, so far?' she asked me.

'Methodical,' I said. 'Carnavale's spoonfeeding the jury. He's walking them through the case step by step: the accused leaves the hotel with facial injuries; a dead body is found in his room; the police are called; time and cause of death are established. It's a straightforward linear narrative from crime scene to courtroom.'

'Is it working?'

'Seems to be,' I said. 'No confused looks or yawning from the jury.'

'Any avid note-takers?'

'Three. The Asian woman and the crime writer are the busiest, then the foreman,' I said. 'They and the only other woman – who was middle-aged and wore thick square glasses – were the jurors who'd stood out so far, who I could even remember.'

'Do I have any fans among them?' she asked.

'Not yet,' I said.

She smiled at me. She appreciated my honesty. 'How many times have you read the witness statements?'

'Three, four times.'

'And you can't see what's coming?'

'No,' I said.

'Stick around. All will be revealed,' she said.

The afternoon session began with DCI Reid taking the oath on the witness stand. Dark-blue two-piece suit, white blouse and black loafers – police uniform colours, I noticed. Subliminal messaging or an institutionalised imagination on wheels?

Carnavale got her to talk briefly about her career – fourteen years on the force, all at the Met. He referred to her by her longform rank the first few times – Detective Chief Inspector. Subtext one: senior officer, lot of experience, top of her game. Subtext two: you can trust her.

He eased her into the cross-examination. What was her role in the investigation? She headed it up. Had she been in charge of similar investigations before? Yes, several – unfortunately. Why 'unfortunately'? Because they were all murders.

Nice touch. A caring copper, a regular bleeding heart.

It worked too: five jurors smiled, including the foreman.

'Can you please tell the court what happened when you first encountered the accused?'

'Myself and Detective Sergeant Mark Fordham went to Vernon James's offices at One Canada Square, Canary Wharf—'

'When you say "offices", you mean the London headquarters of the business owned by the accused?'

'Yes.'

'Which occupies two floors?'

'Yes.'

Point: Vernon James is very rich and *very* successful. His offices are in London's second financial centre.

Jury: no reaction. We already *know* he's rich, thanks.

'When we were shown to Mr James's office, we found him standing in the middle of the room. Straight away I noticed scratches on the right side of his face, and his swollen bottom lip. We identified ourselves as police officers and introduced ourselves by name.

'Mr James said, "I know what this is about. It's about what happened in my hotel room, isn't it? I can explain everything. You really don't need to be here."'

'Those were his exact words?' Carnavale said.

'Yes.'

'You have very good recall.'

'DS Fordham wrote everything down in his notebook,' she said.

'Please continue.'

They'd rehearsed this. There was a lack of spontaneity to their exchanges.

'Mr James went on to say he'd got drunk in the hotel nightclub after the award ceremony and invited a group of people he'd met there up to his room. Things had got out of hand and the room was damaged as a result. He promised he'd pay for everything – and asked us to apologise to the hotel on his behalf.'

There was a stray chuckle from the press area.

'What was his demeanour?'

'Nervous, edgy. He couldn't look us in the eye.'

'Did he appear to be drunk?'

'No.'

'Was he lucid when he was making this unsolicited statement about a party in the room?'

'Yes. Totally. We could follow everything he was saying.'

'Please continue.'

'I informed Mr James that a dead body had been found in his suite, which is why we'd come to see him.'

'And how did he react?'

'He was surprised. His exact words were "What are you talking about – a body? What kind of body?"'

Laughter from the press section. Judge Blumenfeld glowered at them until the laughter stopped. Carnavale waited for silence before asking DCI Reid to resume.

'I then informed him that a body of a woman had been found in the bedroom of his hotel suite. Mr James replied, "I never went in the bedroom. I passed out on the couch."'

'We told Mr James we were arresting him on suspicion of murder and taking him to the station for questioning.'

'And what was his reaction?' Carnavale asked her.

'He said nothing. He sat down on the couch.'

'He said *nothing*? He didn't deny it?'

'No.'

Another pause.

I checked the jury. They were *all* riveted.

I checked Christine. She was listening, casually.

I checked Redpath. He was listening, glumly.

Carnavale continued his cross-examination.

DCI Reid talked the court through VJ's first interview at the police station. That was when he changed his story. There hadn't been a party at all. It was just him and another woman there. He'd tried to seduce her and she'd attacked him 'out of the blue, just like that'. Why had he lied?

Because he didn't want his wife to find out he'd been with another woman – and, more importantly (his words, she stressed), it would be highly embarrassing, given the award he'd just won.

That elicited a gasp and a 'No!' from a juror, and a shake of the head from the foreman.

Carnavale heard it. He cut off his cross-examination and asked for the video of the interview to be played for the jury.

No matter how many times I'd seen the tape, watching it in open court with a jury was like seeing it for the first time. Every inconsistency in VJ's story was exposed and magnified. He looked and sounded guilty. His version of events came over as made up on the spot. DCI Reid would back him into a corner and he'd lie his way into a tighter one. He spoke haltingly, his voice rising and falling in pitch. His hands trembled. The most damning moment came when he was shown the post-mortem photograph of Evelyn Bates and asked if that was the woman he'd been in his room with. He studied it for a long moment – a whole minute – before saying, 'I'm not sure.'

Carnavale paused the tape right there – VJ looking up at DCI Reid, his palms flat on the table, Evelyn Bates's photo between his hands. It was a close-up of her face, dead eyes still open. That was a clever little move: on the screen VJ looked like he'd just strangled her again.

The jury wouldn't miss it.

Carnavale asked DCI Reid about the second interview, three hours later.

That was when VJ had been shown Evelyn's photograph again and had said no, it wasn't her. No way would he have even talked to someone like that, unless she worked for him. Why not, asked DCI Reid. 'Because she's no looker,' he'd said.

Both female jurors frowned at that. Angrily.

VJ went on to describe the woman he'd been with. He gave her name – Fabia – and physical description. What had she been wearing? A green dress and high-heeled shoes.

Carnavale stopped the tape there and turned to DCI Reid.

'We heard the defendant describe the clothes the woman he claims he was with was wearing. "A green dress." Had you or DS Fordham mentioned a green dress to him in any of your earlier conversations?'

'No, we had not.'

'And what items of clothing were found near Evelyn Bates's body?'

'A dress and a pair of high-heeled black shoes.'

'What colour was the dress?'

'Green.'

A murmur all around court, from upstairs in the gallery, and in the well, behind us.

'So would it be fair for me to suggest that there is no way the accused could have known the colour of the victim's dress unless he'd met her that night?'

'That would be a fair suggestion, yes,' DCI Reid said.

'Thank you, Detective Chief Inspector. No further questions at this time.'

DCI Reid stood down.

A short recess.

The courtroom emptied. We stayed put.

'If I didn't know better, I'd swear he was guilty,' Christine said.

Twenty minutes later DCI Reid was back on the stand for Christine's cross-examination.

'DCI Reid, you've been a police officer for fourteen years – correct?'

'Yes.'

'How many arrests have you made in that time?'

'Uh ...?'

'I don't need an exact number. Is it over a hundred?'

'Yes,' she said.

'Can you explain to the court what the correct arrest procedure is, when you first visit a suspect in connection with a crime?'

'Yes,' DCI Reid said. 'An officer must initially identify themselves as police and give their name and rank. Then they inform the individual of the reason for their visit. If they decide to arrest the suspect and take them into custody, the officer has to inform the suspect that he or she is under arrest for suspicion of committing whatever offence prompted the visit.'

'Did you do all of that when you visited Vernon James at his offices?'

'Eventually.'

'*Eventually?*'

'We introduced ourselves to him when we walked into his office, but he immediately started talking to us.'

'He was making these "unsolicited outbursts" about a party in his hotel suite and the damage that was done?'

'Yes.'

'And you let him finish?'

'Yes.'

'Why?'

DCI Reid didn't answer.

'According to the rules of procedure you've just outlined, you're supposed to inform the suspect of the reason for your visit. After all, it's not a social call, is it?'

'He didn't give us a chance.'

'He didn't give you a *chance*? You're *the police*. *You* give the chances, not a suspect.'

'The way Mr James was talking – babbling, really – I thought he might admit to murdering Evelyn Bates,' DCI Reid said. Her earlier poise was gone.

'So you let him "babble" away on the off chance he'd incriminate himself?'

'Yes,' she said.

'But he didn't, did he?'

'Not exactly.'

'Not *exactly*? Did he tell you he'd killed Evelyn Bates?'

'No.'

'Then Mr James didn't incriminate himself at all, did he?'

'No.'

Christine stared across at DCI Reid. DCI Reid lowered her gaze.

'Approximately how long into your visit to Mr James's office was it before you informed him that a body had been found in his hotel suite?'

'I'm not sure,' she said.

'It wasn't immediately, was it? It wasn't the first thing you said to him, right after introducing yourselves?'

'No,' she said. 'It was some time later.'

'How much later?'

'I'm not sure,' she repeated.

'I will suggest an estimated time to you,' Christine said. 'DS Fordham marked the time you entered Vernon James's office as 10.23 a.m. He marked the time you informed Mr James that he was under arrest as 10.57 a.m. Which means you spent over thirty minutes – half an hour – talking to him in his office. Is that right so far?'

'Yes.'

'I'd say, judging from the testimony you gave my learned friend, it was a good twenty minutes before you informed Mr James he was a murder suspect.'

'I don't know if it was that long,' DCI Reid said.

'But it was still a considerable amount of time. In the course of this time, did you ask him about the injuries to his face?'

'Yes,' she said.

'And what did he tell you?'

'He said that he'd tried to break up a fight between guests and got caught in the middle of it.'

Christine turned a page in her pad.

'Did you caution Mr James at any point in this first meeting?'

394

'Yes,' she said. 'After we'd informed him that he was under arrest for suspicion of murder.'

'So at 10.57? Over thirty minutes after you'd first walked in to his office?'

'That's what it says in the notes.'

'In other words, for a full half-hour Mr James had no idea he was a murder suspect?'

DCI Reid didn't answer. She looked at Carnavale, then at Christine, then at me for a second.

'Detective Chief Inspector Reid, could you please answer my question?'

'I don't know what Mr James was thinking.'

Christine looked down at her pad.

'You told my learned friend that when you first spoke to Mr James in his office you didn't think he was drunk. What is the drink-driving limit?'

'Eighty milligrams of alcohol per 100 millilitres of blood.'

'In plain English?'

'Roughly four units. So two pints of standard beer, two normal glasses of wine, a double shot of spirits.'

Christine scribbled this down.

'Moving on, after that first interview at the police station, what's the procedure with a suspect?'

'After they're first interviewed?'

'Yes.'

'The suspect is fingerprinted, photographed and blood, hair and DNA samples are taken in the form of—'

'How much blood?'

'A hundred millilitres, or so – maybe more.'

'And why is blood taken?'

'For DNA analysis, to match against any blood found at the crime scene, and it's also sent for toxicological analysis.'

'Toxicology being a test for the presence of narcotics and alcohol in the body, yes?'

'That's right.'

Christine made a big show of thumbing through a sheaf of papers on the lectern.

'I have the toxicology report on Mr James's blood sample. It states that he was more than twice over the limit. So eight-plus units.

'Mr James told us – and this is confirmed by eyewitnesses – that he'd been drinking vodka on the rocks the night before the murder. Double shots. The receptionist at the Blenheim-Strand told this court that

Mr James appeared to be drunk when he checked out of the hotel at 6.30 a.m.

'Now, it's medically confirmed that alcohol is eliminated from the body at the rate of roughly one unit per hour. So, assuming Mr James didn't drink alcohol between leaving the hotel and the time his blood was taken at Charing Cross at 15.39 p.m. the same day, we can say that he eliminated nine units of alcohol.

'This means he left the hotel with seventeen units in his system. You started talking to him about four hours later, so four less units, therefore thirteen. Thirteen units of alcohol is approximately three times over the limit. Legally that makes him drunk as a skunk.'

DCI Reid didn't respond.

There was silence in the courtroom. The jury had followed everything.

'And alcohol wasn't the only intoxicant found in Mr James's bloodstream was it, DCI Reid?'

'No,' she said.

'What else did the toxicology report reveal?'

'Rohypnol.'

'Rohypnol is commonly known as the date-rape drug, is it not?'

'Yes.'

'Have you investigated rapes where Rohypnol was used on a victim?'

'Unfortunately, yes.'

'What are the general effects of Rohypnol on an individual?'

'It's a sedative. It causes drowsiness and physical incapacitation. Mixed with alcohol, it's known to cause blackouts, amnesia, disorientation,' DCI Reid said.

'So you not only interviewed a drunk, Detective Chief Inspector, but someone under the influence of a powerful drug?' Christine said.

'We had no way of knowing that at the time,' DCI Reid retorted.

People laughed. Christine didn't.

'Vernon James was drugged and drunk when you interviewed him at his office. And he was still somewhat under the influence of both when you first interviewed him at the police station.

'Furthermore, DCI Reid, I will suggest that both you and DS Fordham knew that Mr James was in no fit state to be interviewed and you didn't care. You took down anything and everything he said, called it testimony and jammed it through as evidence. Didn't you?'

'That's not correct,' DCI Reid said.

'I'm suggesting it is. You saw an open and shut case and an opportunity to make a quick arrest.'

'That's not correct.'

'You failed to note – for the record – that the suspect was drunk when giving evidence.'

'He appeared sober.'

'Appearance is not fact, DCI Reid,' Christine said.

'Testimony given by someone under the influence of alcohol is admissible in court,' DCI Reid said.

'Yes, it is, Detective Chief Inspector. As long as it's made perfectly clear to the jury in advance. Which is not the case here,' she said. '*In vino veritas* goes the saying. Latin for "in wine there is truth". But we all know that's complete rubbish. No one takes the words of a drunk remotely seriously. My husband was a drinker. After he'd had a few, he'd tell me he loved me. Unfortunately he stopped drinking in 2000. Our marriage hasn't been the same.'

Half the jury laughed. The rest smiled. They'd been transfixed, following the exchanges between Christine and DCI Reid, their eyes moving from barrister to witness as each spoke.

'One further question,' Christine said, closing her pad. 'Do you believe Vernon James killed Evelyn Bates?'

The question took DCI Reid by surprise.

For a few seconds she looked completely stunned.

And that was enough for the jury – especially the foreman, who frowned in confusion.

'Based on the evidence at hand at the time, I believed the accused to be guilty,' she said, eventually.

Believe*d* . . .

Past tense.

The jury heard it loud and clear. They *all* made a note.

I saw Carnavale clench his pen hand into a fist.

'No further questions,' Christine said.

I got up to help her to her chair but she waved me off and stayed standing.

She waited until DCI Reid had left the courtroom and then addressed the judge.

'My Lord, would it be possible for us to see DS Fordham's original notebook from March 17th? My learned friend has only provided us with a typescript.'

'Mr Carnavale?' the judge said.

Carnavale stood up.

'The notebook has been logged into evidence, My Lord. It's Exhibit 14.'

A few minutes later the court clerk passed the notebook to Christine. The pertinent pages had been marked with Day-Glo page tags.

Still standing at the lectern, Christine rifled through the notebook. 'My Lord, is DS Fordham in the building?'

'Mr Carnavale?'

'Yes, he is.'

'With the court's and my learned friend's permission, I would like to call him to the stand.'

'On what grounds, Mrs Devereaux?'

'To explain his note-taking process to the jury,' she said.

'Mr Carnavale?'

'DS Fordham will appear as a witness later this week. Is his appearance now strictly necessary?' Carnavale said.

'This relates to the credibility of DCI Reid's testimony, My Lord. Part of the evidence she gave the court relied extensively on the contents of DS Fordham's notebook. I would merely like to be satisfied that the notes he made on that initial visit to Mr James's offices were taken according to police procedure.'

'Very well,' the judge said. 'Call DS Fordham.'

Fordham came into the courtroom. Cheap grey suit over a light-blue shirt and tie.

'Detective Sergeant Fordham, did you accompany DCI Reid to Vernon James's offices on March 17th?' Christine asked.

'I did, yes.'

'And you took notes of the conversation you had?'

'Yes, I did.'

'In your notebook?'

'Yes,' he said.

'You wrote down both DCI Reid's questions and Mr James's responses, yes?'

'That's correct.'

'Is it not standard procedure to have a suspect read through the statements you've taken down in your notebook and initial or sign after every answer, to make sure they acknowledge that you've taken down their words accurately?'

'Yes, it is,' he said.

'And you also initial every answer?'

'That's right.'

'So, after every answer there should be two sets of initials, yes?'

'Yes,' he said.

She leafed through the notebook.

'Why do I only see one set of initials here? "M.F." Yours, I presume?'

'The accused – Mr James – didn't sign my book.'

That caused a murmur in court.

'Why not?'

'I . . . I failed to get him to do this.'

'Why?'

'I neglected to do this.'

'Did you show Mr James your notebook at all?'

'No,' he said.

Another murmur, louder. I thought that was going to prompt another Blumenfeld glare, but it didn't.

'Was Mr James aware that you were taking down everything he was saying when you were talking to him in his office?'

'I'm not sure.'

'Was Mr James drunk at the time, in your opinion?'

'He smelled of alcohol, but he seemed *compos mentis* to me.'

'Did you know he was under the influence of Rohypnol when you first interviewed him?'

'Not then, no. I read about it in the toxicology report later.'

'As DCI Reid told the court a few moments ago, Rohypnol can cause amnesia when mixed with alcohol. So wouldn't it be fair to say that Mr James was telling you the truth when he claimed he couldn't remember what he'd said to you earlier?'

'He didn't say anything about Rohypnol,' Fordham said.

'Probably because he didn't know he'd taken it, DS Fordham. Probably because one of the many drinks he'd had the night before had been spiked.'

Carnavale stood up.

'My Lord, my learned friend is leading the witness. She's asking him to comment on something of which he wasn't aware – and couldn't have been aware of.'

'I wasn't leading the witness, Mr Carnavale,' Christine said. 'I neither asked him a question, nor solicited his opinion. I was merely making a point.'

'Do you have a question for the witness, Mrs Devereaux?' the judge asked.

'No further questions, My Lord.'

Christine sat down.

Carnavale tried to salvage the situation. Had Fordham – to the best of his knowledge – taken down every word the accused had said accurately? Yes, he had.

But the damage was done. Procedure hadn't been followed. And Christine had told the jury VJ's drink had been spiked.

After Fordham left the courtroom the judge ruled the statements VJ had given in his office inadmissible, and told the jury to disregard them.

He also admonished Carnavale for entering the notebook into evidence, and for wasting half a day of both the court's time and the jury's.

'What the fuck just happened?' VJ asked, with a smile.

'In order of importance?' Christine said. 'DCI Reid effectively let the jury know she doubts your guilt. They *definitely* picked up on the way she hesitated before she answered. Secondly, the prosecution can't now legally say you lied to the police, because they bungled that first interview. And the jury knows you were drugged. In short, we had a good day.

'Now, don't get your hopes up. This is still the prosecution's trial to lose. Procedural mishaps are common, and juries tend to overlook them unless they're major cock-ups. But I've planted that all-important seed of doubt in the jury's mind.'

VJ rubbed his temples and then his eyes.

'How did you know I hadn't initialled the notebook?'

'When Janet first called me about taking your case, she sent over copies of the statement she'd taken from you at Charing Cross, as well as her notes. She wrote that she'd advised you not to sign anything without her being present,' Christine said. 'This is a good start.'

78

Dinner for one: a prawn stir fry I managed to mess up with too much oil and too high heat. It was a soggy brown mess, the prawns shrunk to the size of fingernail clippings and all the nutrients of the vegetables floating about the kitchen in a pall of oily smoke.

I turned on the TV to BBC News 24.

Breaking news on the Strand shooting.

Anchor:
'. . . has taken a new turn, after it was revealed that the gunman shot by police on Adam Street was an Israeli citizen, and a former member of Sayeret Matkal – Israel's equivalent of the SAS.'

Jonas's face popped up on the screen. Some kind of black-and-white ID photo. Square head, dimpled chin, small porcine eyes and a hint of a smile. He was younger and had hair – albeit clipped short – but it was the same man who'd tried to kill me.

Anchor:

'The gunman has been named as Daniel Bronstein. The Israeli Embassy released a statement this morning disassociating its armed forces from Bronstein. He was discharged from the Israeli Army four years ago.'

Cut to: Shaky, low-res mobile phone footage from Saturday. The car had stopped in the road after running over the traffic light and people were attacking it.

Cut to: A reporter standing outside Charing Cross Station, talking live to camera.

Anchor:

'Jim O'Born is outside the police station where one of the people in the vehicle is currently being interviewed. Jim.'

Reporter:

'The suspect – a woman said to be in her early thirties – is still being questioned by police following her arrest on Sunday morning. Police have until tomorrow morning to charge her, or apply for an extension from magistrates.

'A third man – believed to be the driver of the Megane – is in hospital under armed guard. He is still in a critical condition.

'Police now believe the man seen fleeing the scene may have been the victim of an attempted kidnapping, after several eyewitnesses confirmed they saw Bronstein and a woman bundling him into the Megane.

'Police are appealing to the man to contact them immediately. They have issued a new photograph of him, taken from CCTV.'

I braced myself.

And then I didn't understand what I was looking at.

There was a picture up on screen, but it wasn't me.

It *did* sort of match the general description – tall, dark-haired, white – and our clothes were the same, minus the pink bandanna that had slipped off his face.

I recognised the face.

It was the person who'd been running just behind me, to my right. The wild-eyed sprinter.

I checked the other news channels to make sure the BBC hadn't made a mistake. They hadn't.

First thought: Thank God! What a relief ... One less thing to worry about.

Second thought: Wait a minute ... How had the police got it so wrong? *Or had they?* There were half a million CCTV cameras in London. That's roughly one for every fourteen people. It's estimated you're filmed an average seventy times a day. I'd been in the *middle* of central London, a hive of cameras; electric eyes on you everywhere, all the time.

Overriding thought: The police hadn't made a mistake at all.

What about Rudy Saks? What had happened to him? What if he was the driver, the one in the coma? What would that do to the trial?

I turned on the computer to check my emails.

A message from Albert Torena, sent this morning; the information I'd asked him to get me.

Two attachments – a list of hotel security personnel who'd worked the nightshift on March 16th, and keycard data for Room 474, where Evelyn Bates and Penny Halliwell had stayed.

The keycard info.

474 – Door Lock

Day   Time

16.3.11:   15.46pm (gk1100696)
16.3.11:   18.11pm (gk1100696)
17.3.11:   02.19am (pk15t)
17.3.11:   11.12am (gk1100696)

gk – Guest Key
pk – Passkey

17.3.11: 02.19am (pk15t)

Bingo.

Evelyn had *never* gone back to her room after she left for the hen party.

Yet Penny Halliwell had found a note from her on her pillow, when she'd finally returned to the room the next morning.

@ Private party @ Suite 18. Evey x

Who'd left it there?

Not Evelyn, but the person who had used a passkey to open the door at 2.19 a.m. on March 17th. And it was the same passkey they'd used to get into VJ's room.

Next, the list.

That confirmed what I'd suspected:

402

Jonas Dichter – aka the late Daniel Bronstein, the Strand shooter – had worked that night, on hotel security.

I was now sure he was also the 'big bald bugger' who'd helped raid David Stratten's house. Just as I was sure he was the man Fabia had seen Evelyn Bates talking to in the corridor.

What was he doing there?

He'd been following VJ.

Which meant he'd been in the nightclub first.

Which meant . . .

I fed the Casbah club CCTV disc into the computer drive and hit play.

I watched

. . . Evelyn Bates come in; Evelyn with her back to the dancefloor, talking on the phone; VJ approaching her, their brief exchange; the conga line bursting in and Evelyn flying forward . . . Evelyn leaving the club, hurrying out, bent over . . . Then VJ leaving the club a few moments later . . .

I let it play on after I'd always stopped it.

Ten seconds passed.

Twenty.

Then . . .

Bingo.

Jonas Dichter – shaven-headed, broad shoulders stuffed in a suit, and an earpiece wire clearly visible – walked hurriedly past the bar and out the door.

What was that Swayne had said to me on the phone after he dropped off this DVD?

Evelyn Bates is on it. So's the Strangler.

I'd thought he meant VJ.

He hadn't.

He'd meant *Jonas*.

He'd *known* who'd really killed Evelyn Bates. And he'd *told* me.

And I'd missed it.

Completely.

79

Day 3

Forensics.

In his opening statement, Carnavale had billed this as one of the showpieces of his case – absolute, undeniable proof of VJ's guilt:

'Science – unlike people – does not lie,' he'd said, with a melodramatic flourish. 'Science is honest. Science is certain. We may sometimes doubt science, but science never doubts us. And science will prove – beyond *all* doubt – that Vernon James killed Evelyn Bates.'

A whiteboard had been set up near the witness stand. It was a line diagram of Suite 18, sectioned into three parts – 'Area A (Crime Location)', 'Area B (Bedroom)' and 'Area C (Lounge/Couch)'.

Dr Derek Beales was called to the stand. He'd headed up the team that analysed the evidence. Bald and round of cranium, long and thin of body, Beales had the mirthless expression of someone who'd never heard a joke in his life.

Carnavale began by asking his witness to explain how evidence was gathered at a murder scene. This was a populist ploy. The jury was about to be deluged in all manner of data – chemical, biological, physical and mathematical. They couldn't be thrown in at the deep end. They had to be spoonfed, starting with the easiest bits. And what's easier than picking something up from the floor?

Beales cleared his throat and started speaking.

'A SOCO team—'

'What does "SOCO" stand for?' Carnavale asked.

'Scene of Crime Officers,' Beales said. 'They're responsible for gathering all physical evidence. They usually arrive on site within an hour of the police and medical services. The teams vary in size from four to six officers. While SOCO personnel are trained in all aspects of evidence harvesting, some are better at certain aspects of it than others. For example, not everyone can take a good crime-scene photograph, and fingerprint lifting requires a certain deftness of touch as well as patience. The best duster I knew once sourced a print from a victim's eyeball.'

That last detail didn't impress the jury. Several of them looked queasy. Carnavale missed it. Beales didn't notice.

'The body is photographed first – full shots with background, then close-ups of the face – and injuries. Bags are then placed over the body's hands and feet to preserve evidence under nails or on the skin. The bags are sealed with rubber bands. The body is then photographed again.

'Once that's done, an outline is drawn around the body and markers are placed in all pertinent parts of the crime scene – where significant evidence is visible. The area is photographed again.

'The body is removed and the SOCO team search the scene for trace evidence – hair and fibre, tissue, footprints, paint chips, soil/dirt, bodily fluids including blood, and, of course, fingerprints.

'Once harvested, the evidence is placed in bags and envelopes, logged on to a computer and placed in containers. Everything is sent to the lab for analysis, which is where I come in.'

Now . . .

This all *should* have been fairly interesting to the jury – especially the crime writer – but they were bored rigid; eyes glazed over or wandering every which way, mouths quivering as they fought yawns, hands constantly fidgeting.

Beales didn't speak in sentences but multiple paragraphs, delivered in the bored, monotonous drone of a professor giving the same lecture for the thousandth time.

Carnavale moved on to the evidence itself.

Hair. Beales explained that he'd analysed a total of seventeen hairs – eight from Area A, the floor near the three steps leading to the bedroom, where the murder happened, two from the bedroom, three from the couch and the remainder from VJ's suit. The hair was DNA matched against a sample taken from Evelyn Bates during the autopsy. It was hers.

Carnavale asked him how sure he was of the match. Beales talked percentages, probabilities and likelihood ratios.

'Is that a yes or no?' Carnavale asked him at the end of that long, jargon-laden answer.

The courtroom laughed. The jury smiled. Christine yawned. The judge rolled his eyes.

'That's a yes,' Beales said.

We broke for coffee.

In the canteen Christine swallowed some pills and looked longingly at my cup of steaming black coffee.

'Couldn't Carnavale find a more interesting witness?' I said.

'Witnesses are like family,' she said. 'You're stuck with what you get.'

Fibres took us up to lunch. These mostly came from the floor, but several were found on the couch and in the bedroom, and one was discovered in the rubbish bag taken from VJ's office, where he'd bundled his dirty suit and left it for his PA to dispose of.

Again Beales took the slow scenic route around the answers.

I could see Carnavale wanting to hurry him, but the scientist's sentences were so long and technical he didn't know where to interrupt. His witness ran and overran in his dreary flatlined voice . . . univariate projections based on the first principal component . . . .. multivariate kernel density estimates . . . until he finally came to the conclusion that the fibres matched Evelyn's green dress. Same colour, same composition.

I yawned. The jury foreman saw me and stifled a laugh. Carnavale's junior looked at her watch. The public grew restless. Bodies shifted on their uncomfortable seats, legs were stretched, feet shuffled, shoulders rolled.

As for the jury – they were all the way gone, zoned out, no longer listening but willing themselves to stay awake. Carnavale had lost them.

Fluid and tissue evidence took much of the afternoon and used up everyone's patience – including Carnavale's.

He wrapped it up by asking Beales for his brief conclusions as to what had happened in the room – based on the evidence.

'Evelyn Bates was murdered on the floor of the living room – designated as Area A – hence the abundance of hair and fibre there, as well as the presence of urine, saliva and a trace of faecal matter. The pattern of the urine stains and the preponderance of hair indicate that the victim was lying on her back while being strangled. Her killer then carried her into the bedroom post-mortem, where she was stripped naked and laid on the bed.'

Now it was our turn.

The judge looked at the clock. We had half an hour left.

'Mrs Devereaux, how long is your cross-examination likely to take?'

I helped Christine to her feet.

'Not long, My Lord,' she said.

A few of the jury scowled.

Christine looked to the witness stand.

'Dr Beales, I'm sure you're very busy and would rather not have to return tomorrow. Could you please therefore limit your answers to "Yes" and "No",' she said, raising laughter from the public and smiles and smirks in the jury. There was even a smattering of applause. The judge banged his gavel, but he was smiling too.

'Very well,' Beales said, acting oblivious to the mockery.

'How much of the victim's hair was found in the bedroom?'

'Two strands.'

'Only two?'

'That's right. On the pillow.'

'And how many on the couch?'

'Eight strands.'

'And on the carpet of Area A?'

'Seventeen.'

'Which led you to conclude that Evelyn Bates was strangled on the floor, as opposed to the couch or the bedroom?'

'Correct.'

406

'Did you recover any relevant fingerprints from the bedroom – either the accused's or the victim's?'

'No.'

'None whatsoever?'

'No.'

'Did you recover any of the accused's hair or fibres from the bedroom?'

'No.'

'None whatsoever?'

'No.'

'So would it be fair to say that the accused never entered the bedroom?'

'Not necessarily,' he said. 'If the accused wore gloves to commit the crime, he wouldn't have left any prints on the door.'

'But not all gloves obscure fingerprints, do they?' she said. 'Cloth gloves will leave prints, leather ones leave an impression, as do surgical gloves.'

'Thick latex gloves won't.'

'We'll return to that shortly,' she said.

The jury were back. They were listening.

'Can you tell the court which of Mr James's clothes were tested for DNA.'

'His shirt, trousers, shoes, socks, boxer shorts and his jacket.'

'Were traces of the victim's bodily fluids found on any of these?'

'There was a slight amount of saliva on the collar of his shirt, mixed in with the victim's lipstick,' Beales said.

'Anything else?'

'No.'

'You found no other traces of the victim's bodily fluids on Mr James's clothes?'

'No.'

'Strangulation's a messy death, wouldn't you agree?'

'It can be.'

'How many such murders have you had to analyse over the course of your career, Dr Beales?'

'I don't keep tallies,' he said. 'But it's quite a few.'

'Did any of those previous victims void their bowels and bladders, as happened here?'

'In most cases, yes.'

'And in those cases, when you examined those suspects' clothing, did you find traces of their victims' bodily fluids?'

'Where the clothes were recovered, yes. Very often.'

'Yet, there were no traces on Mr James's clothes.'

'No.'

She paused. The four main jurors were writing furiously. She waited until they'd finished.

'It's been determined that Evelyn was lying on her back when she was murdered, so facing her killer,' Christine said. 'This means the killer was very close to her, on his knees, straddling her. The pattern of bruising at the back of her neck tells us his hands were all the way around her throat, and he'd interlaced his fingertips around her nape. For him to have done this, Evelyn Bates's head would have to be off the ground, and her killer would have been leaning very close to her, using his full body weight to apply pressure on her throat. All the while, Evelyn was fighting hard – fighting for air, fighting for her life. So, Dr Beales, why was no trace of the victim's saliva found on the front of Mr James's shirt?'

'I don't know,' he said.

'Could it be it's because Mr James didn't kill Evelyn Bates?'

Beales looked at Carnavale before answering.

'I don't wish to speculate on the reasons,' he said.

Christine paused there.

She'd scored a definite point in the reasonable doubt area.

'Were there any fingerprints found on the victim's neck?' she asked.

'No.'

'But you looked for them?'

'Of course.'

'So, not a *single* fingerprint was found on the neck and throat. Any explanation for that?'

'The killer most likely wore gloves. It's the only explanation.'

'Were any gloves found at the crime scene?'

'No.'

'Were any gloves found in the search of the accused's property and workplace?'

'No.'

'How would you explain that?' she asked.

'It's unlikely the killer would have kept them. Perhaps he threw them away.'

80

Day 4

Rudy Saks was due to give evidence first thing.

*

We filed into court.

As always, Judge Blumenfeld asked the barristers if they had any pending issues before he called the jury and let the public in.

Carnavale got to his feet.

'My Lord, it appears that Rudy Saks has left the country.'

So he *wasn't* the driver in the Megane.

The judge had two faces; one for the jury, another for us. When addressing the former, he was charm personified, speaking to them with humility and respect, as if they were his equals – which, of course, in here they almost were. With us he was the incoming storm, thunder massing in his pendulous jowls.

That's what Carnavale was getting from him now.

'*When* did he leave the country?'

'Saturday, My Lord.'

'It's Thursday today, Mr Carnavale. Why am I only hearing about this now?'

'The police were initially unaware he'd left. They'd made numerous attempts to contact Mr Saks about his court appearance. When he didn't respond, they went to his address yesterday and were told that he'd had a family emergency in Portugal. His mother is apparently terminally ill.'

'How was he allowed to *leave*?'

'We're looking into that, My Lord.'

The judge beckoned his clerk over and whispered something. She picked up the phone and made another of her silent calls.

'I've issued a summons for his immediate return.'

If witnesses fail to appear in court a judge can force them to attend and give evidence. If they don't come of their own free will, the police drag them to the stand. Not that there was any way that was going to happen with Saks. The summons was as good as nominal. Saks probably wasn't even in Portugal any more. He was in the wind.

According to Janet, Saturday's events wouldn't affect the trial, because none of my three kidnappers were directly linked to Evelyn's murder – at least not yet. Their only connection was the house one of them had shared with Saks, and that wasn't proof of anything.

Still, Saks's no-show was great for us. A major pillar in the prosecution's case had been kicked away.

Christine didn't react, but Redpath gave me a discreet thumbs-up.

'Are your other witnesses already in the building, Mr Carnavale?'

'They are, My Lord.

'Let's proceed then, shall we?'

•

The nightclub CCTV footage was cued up on the courtroom flatscreen.

Carnavale called two waitresses who worked at the club. Eastern European, pretty, pert, twenties, hair scraped back. Swayne and I hadn't interviewed either of them.

Waitress 1: Dead nervous, voice like stilettos stamping on sheet metal. She saw VJ and Evelyn talking for 'a while'.

Why did she notice them in particular?

'Because of her dress. Green is an unusual colour to wear at night.'

Christine cross-examined. How long did Waitress 1 see them together?

'Only for a second.'

'But you said you saw them talking "for a while".'

'They looked like two people in the middle of a conversation.'

'I think what *actually* happened is you only looked at them for a second, before you went about your business? Would that be a fair comment?' Christine says.

'Yes. I think that's how it was.'

'So, you only assumed they'd been talking for a while?'

'Yes,' the waitress said. Then she looked at Carnavale, blushing scarlet. 'I'm sorry.'

'We all make mistakes,' Christine said.

Carnavale let that one go, called Waitress 2.

She was a lot more confident. She saw VJ and Evelyn 'dancing together, really close, like a couple'.

Christine asked her if she remembered the conga line bursting through the door. She did.

Christine played the video, narrating for the jury. The dancers came in-between the bar and where Evelyn was standing, so the waitress couldn't have seen her.

She saw what happened *after* Evelyn had been knocked over by the conga line and fell on top of VJ. Then they both got up, and he might have helped her to her feet, or been checking that she was all right.

Waitress 2 insisted she saw them 'slow dancing'.

Christine played the rest of the tape. Evelyn left the club, one hand clutching at her torn dress strap. Christine pointed to the timer and said that less than four minutes elapsed between Evelyn getting knocked over and her leaving the club. So they either weren't 'dancing' like the waitress thought, or it was the fastest slow dance in history. That got a laugh from the public and a smile from half the jury. They were warming to her, I noticed.

The waitress said she was sure of what she saw.

Christine knew the rest of the video showed Jonas Dichter following

410

VJ out of the club, but she couldn't raise it in court, because it proved nothing.

'No further questions.'

At lunch, Redpath told Christine he thought it was going well – better than well, even.

'Trials are won one day at a time. Every trial has a tipping point, a moment when you know which way it's going to go. We're not there yet,' she said.

Then I sensed I was being stared at. I followed the sensation to a small old man in a thick, battered grey tweed jacket, unshaven and sweaty-faced, the remains of his hair clinging unkempt to his temples. He was sitting alone, an open Tupperware container in front of him, unwrapping a tin foil package. He was looking right at me.

DCI Reid was sitting next to him. She was staring at me too.

Gary Murphy was the last witness of the day. Redder and rounder than when I'd last met him, he gave me a nod as he passed. I didn't reciprocate.

Carnavale started with a couple of scene-setting questions, and then cut to the chase.

'Please tell the court what happened on the night of March 16th?'

'It'd been a very quiet night, only two or three customers. Around half-eleven or thereabouts he came in—'

'Who?'

'The fella in the dock.'

'Vernon James?'

'Yeah.'

'Was he with anyone?'

'Yeah, a woman. Tall, blonde, green dress.'

The court clerk passed Murphy a photo.

'Was that her?' Carnavale asked, and then turned to the jury. 'For the record: the witness has just been handed a police photograph of Evelyn Bates post-mortem.'

'I never really saw her face,' Murphy said.

Carnavale's mouth was poised to launch his next question – lips quarter-parted and puckered into a tense moue. Then his brain registered the words that had passed through his ears. He blinked a couple of times, looked down at the lectern, his brow corrugating.

'That's not what you said in your police statement.'

'That's *exactly* what I said.'

'Not according to this,' Carnavale said, holding up his statement. 'DS Fordham showed you that photograph of the victim and asked you, "Is

411

this the woman you saw him with?" – to which you replied, "Yes".'

'That's not what I *said*, though. I said, "Yes. Maybe. But I didn't get a look at her face." The copper must've stopped at "Yes."'

'Mr Murphy, you *signed* the statement, acknowledging it to be true,' Carnavale said. He was keeping his cool, but the edge of his neck and the backs of his ears were starting to flare up.

'I read it quickly, skimmed it really,' Murphy said.

'Why?'

'I was busy. He interviewed me at work. There were customers to serve. Anyway, I trusted the bloke. He's a copper, right?'

Mild laughter from the public.

'Are you therefore now telling me – telling this court – that you *didn't* see Evelyn Bates – the woman in the picture – with the man before you, in the dock?'

'I'm not saying I did, I'm not saying I didn't,' Murphy said. 'It might've been her, but I didn't get a look at her face.'

'And you served them at 11.30 that night?'

'I served the fella. The woman went and sat in the corner.'

'And you saw them leave together?'

'Yeah.'

'What time was this?'

'Around midnight.'

Carnavale sat down, took a deep breath, and exhaled it back as a long pissed-off sigh. His junior said something to him, which earned her a sharp look.

Christine rose. She asked the court clerk to hand the witness Exhibit 17 – the Facebook photo of Evelyn Bates in her green dress, taken on her iPhone before she went out to the hen party. A copy of the photo was also handed to the jury. She waited until the foreman had it before she started speaking.

'Was this the woman you saw with Vernon James?'

'No.'

'You're absolutely sure of that?' Christine said.

'Absolutely sure,' Murphy said. 'The woman I saw the fella with was tall. She had long straight blonde hair, past her shoulders. And then there was her dress ... It was down to her ankles with this split up the thigh. You saw most of her leg, most of the thigh. And the back was exposed too. And ... erm ... the dress was ... it was pretty darn tight. Like paint.'

'Paint?'

'Like she'd painted it on, if you know what I mean,' Murphy said, embarrassed.

The public guffawed. The judge smirked. The Asian juror covered her mouth to giggle.

Christine asked for copies of the forensics photos of Evelyn's dress to be given to both the witness and the jury.

'Was it this dress?'

'No. Nothing like it. The only thing in common was the colour, but even *that* was different. The blonde I saw, her dress was *dark* green. This one here's wrong.'

'How?'

'It's got a back for a start. And it's too short. The one I saw was more like a gown or something.'

'When you say the woman you saw with Mr James was tall, how tall would you estimate her to be?'

'About his height,' Murphy said, nodding in VJ's direction.

'Vernon James is six foot two. So was she roughly that tall?'

'Yeah, I'd say, give or take.'

'What about her build?'

'Fit.'

'As in athletic?'

'And that.'

More laughter. Even the judge chortled.

'So she was curvaceous?'

'Yeah . . . well fit.'

'One further question – did you notice anything in particular about Mr James. About his appearance?'

'Yeah, he was in a bit of a state. Dishevelled. His suit was dirty – damp, like he'd had something thrown on him. And he had scratches on his face too.'

'Where?'

'On his cheek,' he said. 'Oh, and he seemed a bit pissed – I mean, drunk. He was slurring his words.'

'Thank you.'

She sat down.

Most of the jury made notes.

Carnavale got up for the cross.

'Mr Murphy, would you care to tell the court about your conviction for perjury?'

Murphy gawped in shock.

The public muttered.

Christine was taken aback. Redpath too.

As were judge, jury, court clerk and even the stenographer.

I was confused. Was Carnavale *attacking* his own witness?

413

'In 2007 you were convicted for lying under oath during an insurance fraud trial, were you not? You served six months in prison,' Carnavale said.

'I ... I ... I ... errr ...'

Christine stood up. The judge waved her to sit down.

'Mr Carnavale, *what* are you doing?' the judge asked.

'My Lord, the witness contradicted his statement, and I'm trying to determine the reason why.'

'He is *your* witness.'

'But, My Lord, this concerns his credibility.'

'Of *your* witness?' The judge was incredulous.

'Yes.'

'Mr Carnavale. This is *your* case. Therefore it's *your* responsibility to determine the credibility of *your* witnesses *before* you bring them to court – not *while* they're in court. Secondly, as you *knowingly* put a convicted perjurer on the stand, I don't think you're in any kind of position – moral, legal or otherwise – to cross-examine him about his past. Now, unless you have any questions relating directly to the matter *at hand*, then please ask the witness. If not, I will discharge him.'

Carnavale stood there, glowering at the barman for a good few seconds. The jury watched the stand-off with glee. The foreman had his mouth open. He'd be dining out on this one for a good long while.

'No further questions.'

'You may step down,' the judge said to Murphy.

The barman walked away, shaken.

There was a buzz of voices from the press and public gallery.

I shot VJ a quick look. He was impassive, but the big guard behind him was fighting back a gale of laughter.

'Mr Carnavale, see me in chambers. Court is dismissed until tomorrow morning at ten.'

The judge banged his gavel and it sounded like an explosion.

81

Day 5 (a.m.)

VJ couldn't hide his happiness at the way things were going, at that glimpse of freedom coming out from under the horizon like a blessed sunrise after a long night. He entered the cramped meeting room in a top of the morning good mood.

His jolliness fell away in big chunks when he heard our news:

'Ahmad Sihl may be testifying against you today,' Christine said.

'*What?*'

'The prosecution wants to call him as a witness.'

We'd only found out an hour ago, when Carnavale had told us.

'Why?' VJ said, staying on his feet.

'The prosecution contends that Ahmad Sihl paid off women on your behalf – women you allegedly battered. They'll use it to bolster their argument that you believe your wealth puts you above and beyond everybody, that you'll always be able to buy your way out of potential trouble.'

'Well that's obviously not the fucking case, is it?'

'Focus, Vernon, focus,' Christine said. 'This is happening whether you like it or not. I'm going to need any ammunition you can give me. Stuff I can throw at Ahmad, to undermine his credibility.'

We lost the legal argument. The judge ruled that Ahmad Sihl could give evidence. He'd be heard this afternoon.

After the public had taken their seats, Carnavale called his first witness.

'Dr Louis Martindale.'

'Who's that?' I whispered to Redpath.

'Vernon's doctor.'

'His *doctor?*'

'They entered his medical records into evidence.'

'*When?*'

'June.'

When I'd been grounded and kept out of the loop.

Martindale was a tanned slip of a man in his forties. He'd come to court in a double-breasted pinstripe suit with a crisp, bright white handkerchief capping the breast pocket. The heaviest, bulkiest thing about him was his hair, which was so thick and helmet-like I wondered if it wasn't really a wig.

'How long have you been practising, Dr Martindale?' Carnavale asked.

'Just shy of twenty years.'

'Is your practice public or private?'

'A bit of both.'

'How long has Vernon James been your patient?'

'Fifteen years. We met when he was in the City.' The doctor's voice was deep and family-tree posh, his manner respectful yet relaxed, perfectly at ease in his surroundings.

'And is he a private patient of yours?'

'Yes.'

415

'How often do you see him?'

'A minimum of twice a year. Mr James has a full body check-up every six months.'

'Is he in good health?'

'Generally, yes, although he occasionally suffers from anxiety attacks.'

'Can you please describe – in general terms –what you mean by "anxiety attacks"?'

'Sudden onsets of tension, worry, irritability. Symptoms also include an accelerated heart rate, heightened blood pressure and headaches.'

'What triggers these attacks?'

'From what I understood from him, it was work-related. It's a fairly common condition in the world of finance.'

'Did you prescribe any medication to Mr James?'

'Yes.'

'What?'

'Flunitrazepam.'

'Does it have a more common name?'

'Rohypnol.'

Collective whispers fizzed and hissed around the public gallery like jets of steam waking a nest of snakes.

'Would you usually prescribe Rohypnol to someone suffering anxiety attacks?'

'No. I'd choose a milder sedative.'

'Why did you prescribe Rohypnol to Mr James?'

'He requested it. He told me he'd had a similar episode in America a few months before, and that he'd been given Rohypnol by a doctor there. He said it solved the problem.'

'When was this?'

'In 2007.'

'Was it the only time you prescribed Rohypnol to Mr James?'

'No. There were two other occasions. In 2009, and in February of this year.'

Carnavale asked for Exhibit 21 to be shown to the witness.

The court clerk passed the doctor a small white cardboard box in a clear sealed evidence bag.

'Let the record show that the witness has been handed a box of Rohypnol tablets recovered from the accused's office during a police search of the premises on March 17th. The item was found in the bottom drawer of his desk. There were originally twenty-four tablets in the box. Three were missing,' Carnavale said. 'Dr Martindale, is that the Rohypnol you prescribed to the accused in February?'

Martindale turned the bag over and looked at it.

416

'Yes. It has the address of my surgery on the back.'

The clerk passed the bag to the jury. The crime writer had a *good* look at it.

'Did you have any reason to believe your patient was lying when he said he had anxiety issues?'

'No,' he said.

'So when he said he specifically needed Rohypnol, because he'd been prescribed it before, you believed him?'

'I had no reason to disbelieve him.'

'Did you subject him to a check-up of any kind, before prescribing the drug?'

'No.'

'Why not?'

'He showed me the Rohypnol he'd been given in America. It was a legitimately prescribed item.'

'Thank you.'

Carnavale sat down.

I helped Christine to her feet.

'You said anxiety attacks are not uncommon among people working in the financial sector. By that I take it you've treated others working in that field?'

'I have, and I continue to do so.'

'What other common ailments have you treated them for?'

'Depression, insomnia, stress disorders.'

'Have you ever prescribed Rohypnol to these patients?'

'On a couple of occasions, yes.'

'Why did you prescribe them Rohypnol specifically?'

'I'd tried milder sedatives which hadn't worked. Rohypnol is stronger and acts faster.'

'So, in that context, Mr James's request wasn't odd – or uncommon?'

'No,' he said.

'Rohypnol isn't illegal, is it?' she said.

'As long as it's on prescription, and used for its intended medical purpose.'

'But it's also classified as a Class C drug.'

'Yes.'

'Is there only one variety of Rohypnol available?'

'There are three. The commercially available variety is 1mg in strength and is a green tablet, which gives off a blue dye and is harder to dissolve in liquid. This was introduced by the manufacturer as a safeguard to prevent the drug being used to spike drinks,' he said. 'There are also the laboratory variants, which come in either liquid form or as white tablets which dissolve very quickly and leave no physical trace. They're also twice the strength.'

'And which variety did you prescribe Mr James?'

'The commercial kind, of course. I wouldn't have access to the lab variants.'

'So, the green tablet?'

'Yes.'

'And was he given the green tablets in America?'

'Yes.'

Christine let a few moments pass before she asked her next question. 'Dr Martindale, does Rohypnol cause blackouts?'

'Memory loss is a common side-effect, yes. Especially when the drug is mixed with alcohol.'

'Do these memories return at all?'

'Generally, yes. Depending on the individual, of course. It's common for rape victims to wake up with little to no initial recollection as to what happened. Then, when the drug wears off, their recall gets better and better.'

'How long does it take for the drug to wear off?'

'Rohypnol is at its most potent in its first four to six hours. Then its effects start diminishing.'

'No further questions.' Christine sat down.

Dr Martindale left the witness box.

Carnavale was only calling one escort as a witness, as opposed to the three originally listed. He was making way for Ahmad Sihl, obviously confident in his testimony.

When Rachel Hudson walked into the courtroom, I immediately thought of how Fabia might've looked with blonde hair. She was the same type. Tall, long-haired, attractive but forbidding with it. She'd make your head turn and poke your eyes out for looking.

She was wearing a loose grey flannel suit that only slightly hinted at her curves. Her hair was scraped back tightly from her high forehead, exposing her full face, with its unlined brow and thin dark eyebrows. Before she took the oath, she stared right at VJ. I couldn't quite fathom her look. Fear, loathing or gloating?

'Ms Hudson, when did you first meet the accused?' Carnavale asked.

'In 2007,' she said.

'How did you meet?'

'I was working for an escort service called Essence.' Her voice was soft and demure.

'Can you please explain for the record what being an escort entails?'

'An escort service is a glorified dating agency,' she said. 'They set people up on dates.'

'When you say "people", you mean men?'

'Usually, but not exclusively.'

'Women also used the agency?'

'Couples, occasionally. Husbands and wives, boyfriends and girl-friends.'

The middle-aged female juror winced. The foreman smiled. He was going to be dining out on *this* as well.

'The way it works is that the agency introduces the client to the escort. The escort meets the client for a pre-agreed fee. If they get along and the escort chooses to, she'll sleep with a client. Almost like a standard date.'

'How did the accused find out about you?'

'Via the agency's website.'

'Did you use your real name?'

'No.'

'Why not?'

'Everything about escorting's fake. And you never know who you're going to meet.'

The jury was riveted. The witness was good. Classy, respectable, obviously educated – not what they were expecting. She was the last person in the world you'd think was an escort. And listening to her now, she could be talking about any profession in the world *except* the oldest one going.

'Please tell the court about your first meeting with Mr James.'

'It happened in the bar of the Franklin Hotel in Docklands. We talked for a couple of hours.'

'How did the meeting go?'

'Very well. He was charming, funny. I was attracted to him. Genuinely.'

'Did you have sex with him that night?'

'Yes.'

'Did he pay you?'

'No,' she said. 'I'm an escort, not a prostitute.'

'He *didn't* pay you?'

'No.'

'You slept with him for *nothing*?'

'An escort is paid for her time, not her body.'

'I don't follow.'

'If we have sex with a client, it's at our own discretion.'

419

'So you're saying you're *not* a prostitute?'

'A prostitute guarantees sex, an escort does not. I slept with Mr James because I wanted to.'

Carnavale looked at his notes.

'You weren't *expected* to have sex with the client?'

'If I charged for it, I'd charge a lot more than £500 an hour,' she said.

Some laughter. Disapproving frowns from both female jurors. Smirks from the younger men.

'Did you receive money directly from the man in the dock?'

'Yes,' she said. 'He gave me cash gifts.'

'After you had sex?'

'Yes. Sometimes before.'

'How much?'

'The first couple of times it was £1500. And then it went up – no pun intended.'

That earned her a few laughs from the press.

'How many times did you meet the accused?'

'Eight times.'

'When?'

'Between 2007 and 2008.'

'Did you sleep with him on every occasion?'

'Yes,' she said.

'How would you describe your sexual relations with the accused?'

'He was into rough sex.'

'By "rough", you mean violent?'

'Yes. He slapped and choked me.'

'He slapped and *choked* you? You mean he *strangled* you,' Carnavale said.

'Yes.'

There was absolute silence in the courtroom, as if the whole place had caught and held its breath as one. Not even the wood creaked.

I scanned the jury. The foreman glanced at VJ, the Asian woman bit her bottom lip, the writer looked from the witness stand to Carnavale, and then at us – at me. We locked eyes for a second before he flicked his eyes to the judge.

'Did he do this to you every time?' Carnavale asked.

'Yes. The first few times he didn't slap me that hard. They were more like heavy taps to the face. They stung a little, but that was it. Nothing serious,' she said, batting her hand quickly back and forth, swiping the air. 'But then it got worse. We'd agreed a safety word, something I'd say or shout if he was going too far. But he ignored it. Or said he hadn't

420

heard it. He went further and further, hitting me harder and harder, until he started giving me bruises and black eyes, and split my lip.'

'But you kept on seeing him?'

'He'd compensate me when he went too far. He'd give me £500 more. "To pay for the damages," he'd say.'

'You said he also choked you?'

'Yes.'

'From that very first date?'

'Yes.'

'How did he choke you?'

'With his belt. He'd put it around my neck and pull it tight, when he was taking me from behind. Again, we'd agreed a safety sign, which he ignored. The last time I saw him, he almost killed me.'

'In choking you?'

'Yes. I kept signalling for him to stop. I thought I was going to die. I blacked out.'

'Then what happened?'

'I came to, on the floor, gasping for air, dizzy and in a lot of pain.'

'What did he do?'

'He asked if I was OK. I told him to get out and never contact me again,' she said. 'Then I took pictures of all my injuries with my mobile and went to hospital. He'd slapped me around that time too, even worse than before.'

'Did you contact the police?'

'No. The hospital did. The police came to see me, the next day.'

'What did you tell them?'

'I told them what had happened.'

'Did you give them the accused's name?'

'Yes.'

'How did you know his name? Did he tell you?'

'No. He used to change it every time we met. It was a joke we had – at least at the beginning.'

'How did you find out who he was?'

'I knew he worked in finance.'

'How?'

'Escorting's a very small world. I knew other women who'd been with him, who he'd done the same things to,' she said. 'And once, while he was asleep, I went through his wallet. Not to steal, you understand, but to find out who he was.'

Carnavale took a pitstop there, had a quick consultation with his junior.

'Mr James was never arrested in connection with the assault,' Carnavale said. 'Why was that?'

'I withdrew the charges.'

'Why?'

'I hadn't told the police I was an escort.'

'Why not?'

'Because I didn't think they'd take me seriously,' she said. 'I also weighed up what might happen on the off-chance there was a trial. I'd be in the public eye and my reputation would be ruined. Everyone would know what I did for a living. And it would follow me around. That's when I thought of pursuing the matter out of court.'

'In other words, you decided to get a pay-off from Mr James?'

'An escort's career is short. You don't find too many over thirty. I'm now thirty-three,' she said.

'Is that a "yes", Ms Hudson?'

'Yes.'

'How did you contact Mr James?'

'By email. I sent him the pictures I'd taken of myself after his assault.'

Carnavale asked the court clerk for Exhibit 26 – Rachel Hudson's photos.

'Let the record show that these photographs came not from the witness, but were recovered from the accused's laptop.'

She confirmed that they were of her, and that she'd taken them.

The photos were passed to the jury.

They saw Rachel Hudson's heavily bruised face, one eye swollen and closed to a slit; the bruises all over her arms and legs and back, the black rectangular patches and bloody scratches on her neck, no doubt made by the belt.

The jurors were all horrified. One young man went pale. The Asian woman gasped. The writer couldn't look.

'Did he reply to your email?'

'No. But I got a phone call from someone a few hours later – a man with a London accent. He said he was calling on behalf of the person I'd emailed. He offered me £10,000 in cash. I negotiated. We settled on £100,000. It was going to be paid in staggered amounts over a two-year period. If I agreed, I'd get half upfront, the rest over the next two years.'

Carnavale paused there, let the jurors write that one down. And they *all* did. We no longer had three decision-makers to worry about, but twelve.

'How did you receive the money?'

'In cash, always. And in person. I arranged to meet the man who'd called me at a Burger King on Oxford Street. I took a friend of mine along – mostly for protection, and to have a witness, just in case. She sat in a corner and got a photo of the man on her mobile. He gave me two copies of a non-disclosure agreement to sign. I read it through and signed. He took one copy and left the first instalment of £50,000 in an envelope on the table. He said he'd be in touch next year.'

Carnavale looked at the court clerk.

'Can the witness be shown Exhibit 27, please?'

The clerk handed her a single photograph of David Stratten, dressed in a beige raincoat. He was sat at a small table in front of Rachel, with his hand on a padded envelope.

'Is that the man?'

'Yes.'

'Can the record show that the man with the witness has been identified as David Stratten, a freelance private investigator. Mr Stratten died in April.'

The jury was passed the photo.

'Did Mr James ever contact you again?'

'No.'

'Are you still an escort?'

'No, I left the business after that.'

'Thank you.'

Carnavale sat down without another word.

I helped Christine to her feet.

'Ms Hudson, you stated that Mr James choked you with his belt?'

'Yes.'

'Did he ever use his hands to choke you?'

'No.'

'Never?'

'No. He only used his hands to slap me.'

'You said you talked about Mr James with others in your profession. How many people did you talk to?'

'Three or four.'

'Which was it, three or four?'

'Three.'

'All escorts?'

'Yes.'

'Did you discuss what he did to them?'

'Yes.'

'Did he choke them too?'

'Yes.'

'With his hands or his belt?'

'His belt.'

'Not his hands?'

'No.'

Christine paused, turned a page in her pad, turned it back again.

'About these three women, how would you describe them, physically?' she asked.

'They're all blonde. Long hair. And tall.'

'Approximately your height?'

'Yes.'

'Would you say Mr James has a type?'

'Obviously.'

Christine beckoned to me and whispered for me to hand her a couple of pages from my file – any old pages would do.

'Did these three tall blondes tell you they'd also been paid off by Mr James, so they wouldn't press charges?'

Rachel Hudson didn't reply. She looked at Carnavale. Blinked.

'Ms Hudson, you're under oath,' Christine said, very calmly.

'Can you repeat the question?'

'Did the three escorts you spoke to about Mr James tell you he'd paid them off so they wouldn't go to the police.'

'Yes,' she said.

'Did they tell you the sums of money they received?'

Rachel took a deep breath. Looked at Carnavale again. Unfortunately I couldn't see his face.

'Ms Hudson,' Christine said, a little more sternly. 'Would you like me to repeat—'

'No,' she said, a little louder than before.

'"No", what, *Mizz* Hudson? "No", you don't need me to repeat the question, or "No", they didn't tell you about the settlements, the hush money they'd received from him?'

'Yes,' she said. 'They told me they'd got pay-offs.'

'Did they tell you how much?'

'Yes.'

Christine lifted up the sheets of paper I'd given her – a list of unused evidence. Rachel Hudson stared at the paper.

Carnavale's hands were clenched – no, clasped – on the desk in front of him.

'Ms Hudson, do you remember how much, roughly, each of the women got from James?'

Rachel Hudson blushed now.

'One got £15,000, one got £20,000, and one £30,000.'

'Did any of these women tell you they'd pressed charges?'

'No.'

'Do you know if they did?'

'I don't think they did.'

'Why did one woman get £15,000 and another £30,000?'

Rachel looked at the floor, sighed heavily.

'Ms Hudson, may I once again remind you—'

'That I'm under oath? I know,' she snapped. 'And, yes. One escort got paid less than the other, because she didn't look as bad.'

'By "bad", you mean—'

'Beaten up. And the woman who got the least money told me if she'd known he was that rich, she'd have let him beat her up worse and threatened to press charges so she could get more.'

A couple of jurors gasped.

'And that's exactly what you did, wasn't it, *Mizz* Hudson? You encouraged Mr James to go further, didn't you? You didn't yell out the safety words at all, did you? You didn't signal for him to stop. You encouraged him to hit you harder and harder, so you could get more money out of him. What's a little extra pain if you're getting an extra £500? Then you played your ace. You let him almost kill you by choking you, so you could take your injuries to the police – not for justice, but to satisfy your own personal greed. Isn't that the case, *Mizz* Hudson?'

The witness blinked, looked at Carnavale, then at the jury, then at the public.

'I wanted to get out of the business,' she said, finally.

'So you admit to effectively setting Mr James up in a sting?'

'He deserved it,' she said. 'He's a violent man, a sadist. He gets off on hurting women. I took that bastard for everything I could.'

There was a commotion in the public gallery, and from the press, and even among the jurors.

The judge banged his gavel for silence.

Carnavale rose as I helped Christine down to her seat.

'Miss Hudson, thank you for your candour,' he said. 'I have a few more questions. Are you OK to carry on?'

'Yes,' she said.

'Were any of your other clients rough?'

'Some were.'

'Were they as rough as Vernon James?'

'No. They respected the boundaries.'

'Did you ever – for want of a better word – blackmail any of your other clients?'

'No.'

'Would you have blackmailed the accused if he hadn't hurt you?'

'No,' she said.

425

'Do you regret not pressing charges against Vernon James?' he asked.
'Yes, I do.'
'And why is that?'
'Because Evelyn Bates would still be alive today,' she said.
There were sighs in the jury, more commotion in the gallery.
'Thank you, Miss Hudson,' Carnavale said. He turned to his junior and she smiled at him.

82

Day 5 (p.m.)

Ahmad Sihl came into the courtroom. He avoided looking at the dock as he took the stand.

'Mr Sihl, how long have you known the accused?' Carnavale asked.
'Twenty years.'
'In what capacity?'
'I've been his business lawyer from the time he made his first deal, to the present day,' Sihl said. Was it me or was his Scottish brogue that much more pronounced today?
'Would you say you're friends?'
'Aye.'
'Is that a yes?'
'Aye.'
Some laughter in the gallery. A couple of smiles from the jury.
Carnavale checked his papers, made a few scribbles. I got his shtick now: break his cross-examination up into small info blocks, with a pause between each so the jury could swallow and absorb what they'd just heard.
'Do the following businesses mean anything to you – the Camelia Group, Orchid and Essence?'
'They're escort agencies.'
'All three were shut down last year for prostitution. The owners are currently serving custodial sentences. When the police went through their books, they found copies of invoices, including sent to Sihl-Bose. What is the name of your law firm, Mr Sihl?'
'Sihl-Bose.'
Murmur from the public.
'Would you care to tell the court why three escort agencies invoiced your firm to the tune of £80,000?'
'We used their services.'
'Who's "we"?'

'The firm.'

'Your firm?'

'Aye.'

Carnavale craned forward, making me think of a crow spotting distant prey.

'You mean to tell me your whole firm of twenty-nine lawyers *used* escorts?'

That line was delivered with a hint of nasal sneer, to some laughter. This was the infamous 'kazoo' Christine had warned us about, the tone Carnavale adopted to mock a witness.

'*We* didn't *use* them in the sense you mean – as in sexually,' Sihl said, unflappable. 'I meant the firm – the organisation, not the people who work there. Twice a year we throw parties for clients – actual and prospective – one in the summer, one at Christmas. Because our clientele is heavily – though not exclusively – male, we hire attractive women to mingle among the guests. A lot of our clients like the sight of a pretty girl.'

'Did your clients know they were prostitutes?'

'They were escorts, no prostitutes.'

'*Aaaaah,* yes. Semantics strike again,' Carnavale kazooed.

Mild to medium laughter – but not from the jury. They were fascinated. They could sense a reveal coming.

'Did your clients know they were escorts, then?'

'They're not stupid,' Sihl said.

'Wouldn't you say that's at best a chauvinistic way of doing business – and at worst a kind of pimping?'

'It's called getting a client laid.'

More mild laughter. Sihl was holding his own.

'So you agree the women were there to have sex with your clients?'

'If they wanted to.'

'Did your clients pay these women for sex?'

'I don't know. I never asked.'

'Or did your firm pay the escorts extra – a retainer, if you will – to have sex on demand?'

'We did no such thing. We employed the women for the night, for the duration of the parties.'

'Who chose them?'

'We all did, at the firm.'

'Do you employ women at your firm?'

'I do.'

'Were they involved in choosing the escorts?'

'They were.'

427

'And they didn't think there was anything backward or even misog-
ynistic about using women as ornaments?'

'No one complained,' Sihl said.

'Would you have taken those complaints seriously?'

'Of course.'

'So you wouldn't have hired the escorts if one of your employees had
complained?'

'I would have excused them from attending the party.'

That earned Sihl a grumble from the public gallery. He didn't react.
Carnavale was making him look like a sleazy sexist pig.

'Did you know the accused cheated on his wife?'

'We never discussed his marriage.'

'You've known the accused twenty years, and you've *never* discussed
his private life?'

'It's none of my business.'

'Did it come as a surprise to you when he was arrested for murder?'

'No . . .' Sihl said. 'It came as a complete shock.'

Eh?

I thought that was the moment Sihl was going to turn on VJ.

Carnavale made another pitstop; ticked things off in his pad, turned
a page, took his time looking it over.

'Do you know someone called David Stratten?'

'I knew him, yes. He died recently.'

'What was your relationship with him?'

'David was a private investigator my firm used from time to
time.'

'So he worked for you?'

'He did, but not exclusively. He was freelance.'

'What kind of work did he do for you?'

'Background checks into potential clients, business partners, that sort
of thing.'

'Did he do any work for you between 2008 and 2010?'

'Aye.'

'What kind of work?'

'Background checks.'

'After Mr Stratten's death, the police were handed his appointments
diaries going back to 2007. In the 2008 and 2009 diaries they found four
names – women's names – as well as their mobile numbers, and alongside those, in brackets, sums of money – £15,000, £20,000, £30,000,
£50,000. There was also a tick near each. These women were all escorts
who'd been employed by the three agencies your firm did business
with – including Rachel Hudson, who gave evidence today.'

Sihl looked at Carnavale nonplussed.

'You were the first person the accused called after his arrest, weren't you?' Carnavale asked.

'Yes. I'm his lawyer.'

'You're his *business* lawyer.'

'At the time he didn't have a criminal lawyer, because he didn't need one,' Sihl said. 'He contacted me to get him appropriate representation, which I did.'

Pitstop time.

I checked the jury. Inscrutable. They were waiting for someone to crack or fold. No sign of that from either of them. I wondered if Christine would even need to get Ugly on Sihl, drop the A-bomb of filth VJ had handed her on him in a sweary three-minute monologue down in the cells this morning. Sihl had been staunch so far.

'After the police arrested the accused for Evelyn Bates's murder, they searched his offices and his home. Among the items removed were several laptops. One of these laptops was used by the accused exclusively for his dealings with escorts. Computer forensics examined the machine and found the accused had had numerous encounters with escorts, including all four listed in Mr Stratten's diaries. Don't you think that's more than just a coincidence, Mr Sihl?'

'I don't understand the question,' Sihl said.

'I suggest that you employed David Stratten as more than just an investigator. He was your bag man. He paid off escorts like Rachel Hudson so they wouldn't report your biggest client to the police.'

Sihl was as cool as frost on an iceberg.

'I may be a business lawyer, Mr Carnavale, but I took the same oath you did. And I would never break, let alone demean that oath. You can suggest, insinuate, even *intimate* all you want, but you have absolutely no proof whatsoever to back it up. What you're suggesting is little more than a sordid conspiracy theory at best,' Sihl said.

That stung Carnavale. But Sihl hadn't finished.

'You're fond of that little word, aren't you? "Suggest". It's the fig leaf you're hiding your totally inadequate case behind, isn't it? You can't flat out accuse me of perverting the course of justice in a court of law, because you have absolutely no proof or evidence I did. That wouldn't just be inadmissible and get struck from the record, it would also be slander.'

Carnavale sighed impatiently.

'One final question, Mr Sihl. Did you ever share escorts with Mr James?'

'*Share* them? As in what? Go Dutch?'

Loud laughter.

'I meant use the services of the same one, based on Mr James's recommendations.'

'No.'

'Have you ever used an escort service?'

'Personally or professionally?'

'Personally.'

'No.'

'Have you ever met a woman called Rachel Hudson?'

'No.'

'Her working name was Tina Hart.'

'I've never met her.'

Carnavale sat down.

Christine was up next.

'What are you doing here, Mr Sihl?'

'I was legally compelled to come,' he said.

'By the prosecution?'

'That's correct.'

'But you wouldn't be here otherwise, giving evidence against Mr James?'

'No, of course not. Besides, as you've heard, there's no evidence to give against him on my part.'

A few moments later Sihl stepped down.

Carnavale only had one more witness to call – Nikki Frater, VJ's PA.

But he told the judge he'd decided not to call her after all, as her evidence was merely to confirm that the police had followed correct procedure when searching VJ's office.

'Rubbish,' Christine whispered to me. 'He doesn't think she'll make any difference.'

Carnavale rested his case.

The judge dismissed us for the weekend.

83

The weekend.

Rain. Constant solid downpour. Rain so hard and fast it was almost white outside, the buildings shrouded in a mobile mist that made the estate look even more miserable than usual.

I sat on my hands and watched the TV news as I'd been doing all week. Things had gone dark about the Strand shootings. Really dark. As in pitch black and no matches or a cheap lighter. There was no mention of the Israelis in custody, nor the man the police were looking for instead of me. Nothing whatsoever. It was as if the whole thing had never happened.

I washed my five shirts and ironed flawless creases in my two suit trousers.

I spit-polished my shoes and got them gleaming like every cop bright.

I ate ready-meal macaroni cheese and stared at the digital photoframe on the mantelpiece. My kids got older and a little taller. Amy didn't stop laughing. Ray got more knowing and wary. Karen gained a little weight, lost much of the glow she'd had at the start of our relationship, and her smiles grew more wan. Or maybe I just didn't know how to take a good picture of her.

What I *didn't* do was dwell on Scott Nagle and Sid Kopf and why they'd set VJ up. I didn't want to go there, didn't want to think about it. I'd almost died the way others had: Evelyn Bates, Fabia Masson, David Stratten and Andy Swayne.

The thought of that was just too much to cope with right now.

And I couldn't shake the feeling that I was at least partly responsible for two of those deaths.

I wanted to see my kids again. I wanted to watch them become adults and be there to guide them through their young lives, so that when they'd have kids of their own they'd have something positive to pass on to them.

Mostly, I wanted to leave this all behind, bury it somewhere and forget where I'd put it.

And here was the thing that was bothering me the most. VJ may have been innocent of Evelyn Bates's murder, but he was a danger to women all the same.

I couldn't get Rachel Hudson's testimony out of my mind, no matter how conniving she'd been. I kept on juxtaposing her with Fabia.

Why was VJ hurting women the same way he'd seen his father hurt his mother?

Karen called on Sunday.

'How's things going with the trial?' she asked.

'See the news?'

'Yeah. And I've been following it online too. It's not looking too good for him, is it?'

'So they'd have you believe,' I said.

According to most of the papers and the TV stations, it looked like we were losing the trial. They'd only reported on the sensational stuff –

that VJ was into S&M, and beating up prostitutes (the distinction didn't bother them).

I wasn't supposed to talk about the trial, but I told Karen about it from my perspective.

All things considered, Sihl had been the biggest surprise. He'd thrown all of us, except for Janet. Talking to her afterwards, reading between the lines, I strongly suspected she'd secretly prepped him for the cross-examination, told him exactly what Carnavale was going to ask and how to reply. If true, it was a gross violation of ethics.

We were winning this.

Sid Kopf's plan had backfired.

Christine had been brilliant so far. She hadn't destroyed the case against VJ, but she'd seriously damaged it.

'When's it over?'

'Thursday, Friday at the latest. Then the jury's out and we wait on the verdict.'

'Is it safe for us to come home now?'

'Give it till Friday,' I said.

'See you on Saturday, then?'

'I can't wait,' I said.

84

Day 6

The jury spent the morning at the Blenheim-Strand, touring Suite 18.

Redpath went as an observer.

Christine and I waited in the Bailey canteen.

She looked about as well as I'd ever seen her, practically healthy. Her eyes were sparkling, the whites actually white instead of a shade of cheap rosé. The puffiness had gone from her face, and her breathing didn't sound ventilator-assisted. I was guessing the trial going a lot better than expected had something to do with it. Or perhaps being back in court, in her element, was keeping her illness at bay.

She popped one of her pills and chased it with distilled water.

'Nineteen eighty-four,' she said. 'That was the year I tried my first case here.'

'What was it?'

'A rape. Those were the only cases I used to get back then.'

'How come?'

'The law was a very different institution. It was a man's world – a gentle*man*'s club. All boys together. Women had to fight three times as hard and be five times as good as their male counterparts. And even then it wasn't enough.'

'The old glass ceiling?'

'More like concrete lined with titanium. You can break *glass*.' She smiled. 'The chambers I was working for at the time gave me cases that weren't just unwinnable but always involved defending men who hurt women. It wasn't even a test. Those you can pass. They wanted to get me to quit. I knew this, of course. So I looked at those cases as challenges – not just within themselves, but to the system itself. Chauvinistic, backward, elitist. It was a paradox of the most twisted kind: there I was trying to beat a male-dominated institution by representing men who'd committed atrocities to women.'

'Did you win the trials?'

'More often than not, yes.'

'Knowing they were guilty?'

'They're almost always guilty, Terry,' she said. 'But that was never the point. And it still isn't. It was, is, and always will be about the law. Do you know what a legal defence really is? It's highlighting the mistakes the police and prosecution have made on their way to trial. The shortcuts, the illegal moves, the witnesses they didn't fully vet, the confessions they coerced.'

There was something I had to ask her, something that had been bugging me ever since the trial started.

'Why am I not impressed with Carnavale?' I asked.

'I thought about that very thing this morning,' she said. 'The Franco I know has barely turned up here. Do you know he's booked up all the way to March? That's seven trials to prepare for. That could be the reason. I also think he took this too lightly. He saw the case as cut and dried. An easy win. There's the body in the room, no sign of forced entry, a suspect who flees, a suspect who seems to confess to the crime, eyewitnesses who place the suspect with the victim at the right time, DNA ...'

She gave me a complicit look.

'And he probably thought I was past it too.'

'How wrong he was,' I said.

And I didn't just mean Carnavale.

The defence started in the afternoon.

Christine asked for VJ's bill and the keycard data to be introduced into evidence. She also recalled Albert Torena.

Carnavale had no objection.

*

433

Our first witness was Dr Pam Wong, the pathologist who'd compiled the toxicology reports on both VJ and Evelyn Bates.

This was an unusual move, using a witness from the prosecution's side. Defence teams habitually fight fire with fire, bring in their own expert witness to argue the evidence.

Pam Wong was in her thirties, with black hair, cut in a bob.

'Dr Wong, are you familiar with the chemical properties of Rohypnol?'

'I am,' she said, in a loud, clear voice.

'In very basic layman's terms, can you please tell the court how you identified the presence of Rohypnol in both Mr James – the man before you in the dock – and in the victim, Evelyn Bates.'

'May I start with the victim?'

'Please.'

'There are three tests for Rohypnol. If a person has taken it, there will be traces of the drug in the blood, hair and also, for up to seventy-two hours post-ingestion, it'll be found in urine.

'As the victim was less than twelve hours dead, whatever substances she'd taken had not metabolised. We tested her blood and found Rohypnol present.'

'Did you test her urine?'

'Yes. Her bladder was empty, post-mortem, but we managed to test urine found on the carpet from Area A, where it's believed the strangulation took place. This also tested positive for Rohypnol.'

'Can you specify roughly what the dose might have been?'

'From our samples there was a high enough quantity of Rohypnol in both her urine and blood. I'd assume it was quite a high dose.'

'Am I right in saying that Rohypnol tablets come in two strengths, 1 and 2 milligrams?'

'Correct,' Dr Wong said. 'But the only tablets legally available in the UK are the 1-milligram variety. I should say that Rohypnol is also available in clear liquid form, sold as ampoules. But those are only available for licensed scientific purposes, not public consumption.'

Christine paused.

The jury were following all this without a problem.

'You also tested Mr James's blood and urine?'

'Yes.'

'And you found Rohypnol there too?'

'Yes, in both samples.'

'So, in your opinion, Mr James was still under the influence of the drug during his arrest and up to the time he gave the samples?'

'Yes,' she said. 'The levels found in his blood and urine were consistent with those of someone who'd taken the drug within the last twelve hours.'

Another pause. Christine asked for Dr Wong to be given the box of Rohypnol tablets found in his study.

'Dr Wong. You'll see that one tray of tablets has been removed from the box for ease of inspection. What colour are the tablets?'

'Green.'

'Why are the tablets green?'

'They contain a blue food dye, which is automatically released if the pills are mixed with drink.'

'In your experience of testing urine samples for Rohypnol, is the dye usually present?'

'Yes, depending on the time of consumption. The drug is at its most potent in the first six hours, and then gradually the effects taper off as the body eliminates it. In those early stages, the urine is stained blue.'

'Was that the colour of Mr James's urine?'

'No. It was a normal colour.'

'Was there any blue food dye in his urine?'

'No.'

'But you tested for it?'

'Yes, as soon as we found the presence of Rohypnol.'

'Was any blue food dye found in Evelyn Bates's urine?'

'No.'

'Would it therefore be fair to conclude that the Rohypnol consumed by both Mr James and Evelyn Bates did not come from that box?'

'Yes. The dye would have shown up.'

'Would it be therefore equally fair to say that both the victim and the accused consumed a non-prescribed, illegal variety of Rohypnol?'

'Yes.'

'Thank you, Dr Wong.'

Carnavale had no questions.

The witness was excused.

Next, DCI Reid was called.

'When you took statements from witnesses at the Blenheim-Strand, who were the primary interviewers?'

'Myself and DS Fordham.'

'When did you conduct your first witness interview?'

'March 17th.'

'The day of Mr James's arrest?'

'Yes.'

'Who did you interview first?'

435

'The hotel receptionist.'

Christine jotted a few things down. DCI Reid was composed, looking straight at her interrogator. She knew the drill, that the questions were going to get progressively trickier from now on.

'Moving on to your interview technique, generally. Do you have pre-prepared questions when you interview, or do you play it by ear?'

'A mix of both. Set text and improv. We're determined to get as much pertinent information as possible out of a witness – information that'll help us build a picture of what happened. I think of a crime as a jigsaw puzzle. Half the pieces are right in front of you – the victim, the physical evidence. The rest of the pieces are in the hands of other people – the witnesses, the suspect. It's our job to get as many pieces as possible, so we can finish the puzzle as best we can.'

'Why didn't you ask the receptionist if Mr James was drunk when he checked out of the hotel?'

'It didn't occur to me to ask that question,' DCI Reid said.

'Why not?'

'Because he wasn't as drunk as you'd like to think he was. He was lucid enough to lie.'

No comeback from Christine. She wasn't going to get drawn into a firefight.

'Who interviewed Gary Murphy, the barman?'

'That was DS Fordham.'

'Were you present?'

'Yes.'

'Do you recall the interview?'

'Yes.'

'Did Mr Murphy positively identify Evelyn Bates as the woman he saw Mr James with?'

'Positively enough,' Reid said. 'He was shown a picture of the victim and said, "Yes, it could've been her."'

'He didn't say it *was* her, though, did he? He said it *might've* been her. *He* wasn't positive. But you accepted that anyway?'

'At the time of the interview he seemed more certain than uncertain. This was a day after the murder, so we assumed his memory was fairly fresh,' she said.

'You asked him to identify the woman he saw from a post-mortem photograph of Evelyn Bates, didn't you?'

'Yes.'

'When our investigator showed the barman a picture of Evelyn Bates – alive – wearing the same dress she had on at the hotel he said it wasn't her at all.'

'We could only use the material we had to hand at the time.'

'We found the picture of Evelyn alive on her Facebook page,' Christine said.

'When you have a suspect in custody, you only have a limited amount of time to get the evidence to charge them with. You're going to use what you have.'

A few jurors nodded along in agreement.

'In his testimony to this court, Gary Murphy described the woman he saw with Mr James as six feet tall, with long straight blonde hair and wearing a green dress that only had a passing similarity to the one Evelyn wore. That similarity was their colour, but the shades were different – as were the styles. He told us he informed DS Fordham of this, yet his statement makes no mention of it at all.'

'That's because he never told us that. He described the woman he saw as blonde and wearing a green dress. That was it.'

'Are you suggesting the witness lied to the court?'

'No,' DCI Reid said. 'I think his memory's on the blink.'

'Did you ask him to describe the dress to you?'

'Not beyond the colour.'

'Why not?'

'We were investigating a murder not a dress style.'

Laughter.

Christine scribbled and underlined something in her pad, and then turned a page.

'Were you in court on Friday, DCI Reid?'

'Yes.'

'Do you recall Rachel Hudson's testimony?'

'I won't forget that in a hurry.'

Laughter from the press.

'*Mizz* Hudson told us Mr James has a type of woman he likes. Tall, long blonde hair. That describes the woman Mr James insists he took up to his room, does it not – the one called "Fabia"?'

'In broad strokes it does, yes,' DCI Reid said.

I saw what Christine was doing. The question wasn't aimed at DCI Reid. In fact it wasn't a question at all. She was making a statement camouflaged as a question. The point being that VJ wouldn't have fancied Evelyn Bates.

'Who interviewed Rudy Saks?'

'DS Fordham was the primary.'

'Were you present?'

'Yes.'

'There are two glaring inconsistencies with Saks's evidence—'

Carnavale was up at the lectern.

'My Lord, I must object here. Mr Saks's evidence has not yet been heard.'

The judge nodded. 'Mrs Devereaux, please refrain from that line of questioning.'

'My Lord, with all due respect, I'm trying to establish whether certain points of procedure were followed in the gathering of evidence.'

'I'll allow it, as long as you do not make any reference to Mr Saks's statement.'

'Of course, My Lord. I apologise to the court,' Christine said with due humility. 'DCI Reid. One of the items entered into evidence was a bottle of Cristal champagne in an ice bucket, and two glasses. These were found on the coffee table in the lounge in Suite 18. To your knowledge, were any of these items tested for fingerprints?'

'Yes. All of them.'

'Were any fingerprints found?'

'No.'

'None whatsoever?'

'The bottle and bucket were both wet when delivered, so fingerprints wouldn't necessarily have formed on the surfaces.'

'But the glasses were dry.'

'I believe so.'

'Yet they didn't have any fingerprints on them either.'

DCI Reid said nothing.

'Didn't you find that odd?'

'No. Maybe the waiter who brought them up was wearing gloves.'

'Did you ask him?'

'I don't recall.'

'Did you fingerprint him?'

'Yes, we did.'

'Why?'

'He'd been in the suite. It was so we could eliminate him if his prints turned up. We did that with everyone who entered the room after Mr James had left, including all police and medical personnel.'

Christine paused.

'DCI Reid, was Evelyn Bates strangled by hand?'

'Yes.'

'There were no fingerprints found on her neck either.'

'Maybe her killer wore gloves,' DCI Reid said.

'Just like Mr Saks,' Christine replied.

85

Day 7 (a.m.)

Albert Torena took the stand.

Christine started by getting him to explain why only the nightclub CCTV footage was available. He talked about the overloaded circuits, the hotel management's 'working hours-only' contract with the camera maintenance firm, and the generic security keypad code on the fuse-boxes themselves. He also mentioned that the hotel's fuse room was locked electronically, like the rooms themselves. Entry was keycard-only.

'Could anyone with a passkey access the fuse room?' Christine asked him.

'Yes.'

Christine then asked for two sheets of keycard evidence to be distributed to the witness and jury: lock data for Suite 18 and Room 474, where Evelyn and Penny Halliwell had stayed.

Torena explained how the lock system worked. The guests were given pre-programmed keycards, which let them into their rooms for the duration of their stay. The cards expired as soon as the guests checked out, or from midday on their last day. They were then deactivated. The cards also served other purposes. They could be used to buy things in the hotel, including food and drink.

VIP guests staying in the tower had exclusive use of two express lifts to take them to their rooms. The lift doors could only be operated with their room keycards.

Certain members of staff – maids and security – were given passkeys. These allowed them access to all rooms. Security had their passkeys on them at all times, in case of emergencies. Maids were only issued the cards on their shifts and had to hand them back at the end.

Every time a card was used to open a door in the hotel, data was logged into a central server. The data was archived for a year, before being wiped.

Christine asked Torena to identify the prefixes for the two different types of card that appeared on the lists.

GK – Guest Key.

PK – Passkey.

'Looking at the data for Suite 18, I note that Mr James – using the card starting "GK" – entered his room only twice during his stay. Once at 5.38 p.m., shortly after he checked in, and then at 11.57 the same night, which is when he returned to his room after going to the nightclub. Would I be right in assuming that he only used his key to open his door twice?'

'That seems to be true, yes,' Torena said.

'Mr James attended the award ceremony function from roughly 8 p.m. onwards, where he was seen by many people. Yet these records show that someone, using a passkey, entered his room at 8.52 p.m., while he was out. Who was that?'

'It could have been the maid, for the turndown service.'

'For the benefit of the jury, what is a turndown service?'

'It's when the sheets of the bed are folded down so that the guest can get in. It usually happens in the evening.'

'So that's it, just the sheets are turned back?'

'No, the pillows are plumped up and mints are left on top of each.'

'What kind of mints?'

'Mints,' he shrugged.

'Are they in wrappers?'

'Yes, blue plastic wrappers.'

She asked me for the pictures of Evelyn on the bed.

She went through them on the lectern, then looked at the court clerk. 'Can the witness be handed Exhibits 9b and . . . 10e, please. And can copies of both be passed to the jury.'

9b was a shot of the row of pillows to the right of Evelyn's head.

10e showed the bed after Evelyn's body had been removed.

'Looking at photograph labelled 9b. Is that a mint on the pillow?'

'No, it's a chocolate. They're placed on the pillow the first day the guest arrives.'

'But not as part of the turndown service?'

'No.'

'Never?'

'Not to my knowledge. This could have been a mistake, though.'

Christine cleared her throat.

'Now please look at photograph 10e. Has that bed been turned down?'

'No.'

The sheet was covering the bed, the edge covered by the bank of pillows.

'So would it be fair for me to suggest that the bed was never turned down that night?'

'Yes.'

'Then who used a passkey to open the door to Suite 18 at 8.52 p.m. – while Mr James was out?'

'I don't know,' he said.

'But someone definitely opened the door then?'

'According to this print-out, yes.'

'Did the police question you about this data?'

'No.'

Christine killed a few seconds at the lectern, crossing off her list of questions.

'Moving on to the second data sheet, for Room 474. Evelyn Bates was a guest in that room, wasn't she? She shared the room with Penny Halliwell, who organised the hen party she was attending on March 16th.'

'Yes, I believe so.'

'According to the data, Evelyn or Penny last opened the door at 6.11 p.m. on March 16th. They went out. That was the last time a guest key-card was used to open the door until 11.12 a.m. the following morning.

'We have a statement from Penny Halliwell, saying she returned to the room at around 11 a.m. on March 17th,' Christine said. 'However, that wasn't the only time the door was opened. When does the turndown service stop, Mr Torena?'

'Usually around 9 p.m.'

'Not later?'

'No.'

'So there wouldn't be a turndown service at 2 a.m.?'

'No.'

'Then why is there a record of a passkey being used to enter Evelyn Bates's room at 2.19 a.m.?'

'I don't know.'

'You're head of security, Mr Torena. The keycard's full code is "PK15t". That's the same card that was used to enter Mr James's room at 8.52 p.m., was it not?'

'It's a generic code,' he said. 'All the passkeys are called PK15t.'

'So you don't actually know which individual members of staff are accessing the rooms?'

'No.'

'It's hardly secure, is it?'

'I don't make the rules,' he said.

'Our clerk here obtained the information from you, didn't he?'

'Yes, he did.'

'Did you not notice that someone had entered the victim's room at around two in the morning?'

'I just copied and pasted the data and emailed it to Terry, as he requested.'

'So you didn't look at it?'

'I'm not a cop any more,' he said. 'I just work in a hotel.'

'Thank you, Mr Torena.'

DCI Reid was recalled and handed the keycard information.

'Do you recognise the data for Suite 18?' Christine asked.

'Yes.'

'So you should, DCI Reid. It's your evidence.'

DCI Reid didn't flinch.

'Did you notice that someone had used a passkey to enter Suite 18 while Mr James was out?'

'Yes.'

'Did you find out who it was?'

'We thought it was a maid.'

'Did you *confirm* it was a maid?'

'No. It's a fancy hotel, we assumed it was a turndown service.'

'We've just spoken to the head of security, who informed us that the bed wasn't turned down at all.'

The policewoman didn't reply.

'DCI Reid?'

'What's your question?'

'Did you notice the bed hadn't been turned down?'

'No.'

'Do you know what a turned-down bed looks like?'

'Yes,' she said, with a hint of indignation.

'Did you ask who had entered the room at 8.52 p.m., using a passkey?'

'We assumed it was a maid.'

'For the turndown service that never happened? I will suggest that you made the wrong assumption, DCI Reid. I will in fact suggest that you completely overlooked a small, but potentially vital discrepancy. In fact, I'll go further. Your investigation was downright sloppy.'

DCI Reid didn't answer.

Christine had chalked up another major point in the police-not-doing-their-jobs-properly tally.

'Can the witness please be shown Exhibit 5. And can copies of Exhibit 5 also be circulated among the jury,' she said to the clerk.

That was Evelyn's note, written on hotel stationery.

@ Private party @ Suite 18. Evey x

'DCI Reid, what is Exhibit 5?'

'It's a message written by Evelyn Bates to the person she was sharing her hotel room with, Penny Halliwell. Ms Halliwell found it on Evelyn's pillow when she returned to the room the next morning.'

'What steps did you take to confirm that this note was actually written by Evelyn Bates?'

'The letter was shown to members of her family and we had a handwriting expert compare it to a sample. They're an exact match. We also tested the paper for fingerprints. Her prints are on there.'

'Were there any other prints?'

'Yes.'

'How many?'

'Two different sets.'

'Did you make any attempt to find out who they belong to?'

'It's from a hotel room notepad. It could have been a guest or a maid.'

'*Another* assumption, DCI Reid. I'm seeing a pattern here, aren't you?'

DCI Reid stayed calm. 'Anyone could have handled that pad. It's a popular room.'

'Did you think to track down previous guests?'

'No.'

'Why not?'

'We didn't think it was relevant.'

'Did you even think about doing that at all?'

DCI Reid sighed. 'Probably not.'

Christine put lines through a couple of questions.

'Penny Halliwell said she only saw the note when she returned to the room on March 17th.'

'Yes.'

'Please look at Sheet 2 of the keycard information, for Room 474. Take your time over it, please, DCI Reid.'

DCI Reid studied it for a few seconds and looked up.

'Have you ever seen that data before?' Christine asked her.

'No.'

'So you never accessed keycard data for the victim's room – just the suspect's?'

Silence.

'Is that a yes or a no, DCI Reid?'

'No, I did not access the data for Room 474.'

'Surely, in *any* investigation – but especially a *murder* investigation – you want to track the victim's last movements every bit as much as the suspect's?'

'Yes.'

'Yet you didn't even attempt to find out whether Evelyn had gone back to her room that night.'

'We'd found the note.'

'And you didn't want to know when she'd left it? Isn't establishing a timeline of events *elementary* police work?'

DCI Reid swallowed and tightened her jaw. 'We'd found the note. We deemed that sufficient proof that the victim had been back in her room. We also deemed it sufficient proof that she'd gone up to Suite 18 – especially since she was found dead there.'

'You didn't do your job properly did you, dear?' Christine said.

DCI Reid finally lost her cool. She flushed, and gave Christine a ferocious look, but said nothing.

'Because from the data, I cannot understand how Evelyn Bates could possibly have left this note in her room. She didn't have her keycard with her when she went out. That was found on the bedside table.

'Someone else put the note there, someone employed at the hotel, someone with a passkey. I'm going to suggest that her killer placed the note there. Her *real* killer. Not Mr James.'

DCI Reid looked at Christine a moment, and then at Carnavale.

'Evelyn could quite easily have given the note to a receptionist, or another member of staff with a passkey to put in her room,' DCI Reid said.

'Unlikely,' Christine snapped. 'DCI Reid, over the course of this trial, it's become obvious that you and certain members of your team cut corners in this investigation.'

DCI Reid didn't reply.

When Christine sat down, I wasn't sure who the jury had sided with.

Janet joined us in the canteen for lunch.

'I've just got off the phone with Melissa James. She doesn't want to give evidence,' she said.

I'd completely forgotten about that. I'd been focusing on the bigger event – VJ's turn on the stand, which was happening this afternoon.

'Why not?' Christine asked.

'She said she doesn't want to commit perjury.'

86

Day 7 (p.m.)

VJ left the dock and crossed over to the witness stand.

The jury saw him at ground level – their level – no longer the elevated entity behind a bulletproof shield. His walk was unhurried and stiff-backed, his head held high. The jurors followed him with their eyes.

Janet had joined us on the benches. She was sat behind me, next to Carnavale's clerk.

'What were you doing at the Blenheim-Strand on March 16th?' Christine asked VJ after he'd settled in.

'I was there to attend an award ceremony . . .'

And they went through his version of what happened, from the moment he walked into the hotel to the instant the police told him he was under arrest for murder.

He was immediately impressive and stayed that way. He abided by the SQUID rules. He looked Christine in the eye the whole time. He got the tone absolutely right. They'd worked on it in Belmarsh. She'd got him to speak in a slightly bemused manner, as if he'd just woken up and didn't recognise his surroundings. It made him sound powerless and vulnerable, even in his shortest answers.

But he'd added an ingredient of his own – his accent. The Stevenage Estuary was flowing through his vowels again, easy to hear when his speech took too sharp a corner. He was someone who'd had most of his rough edges rubbed smooth by the pumice stone of polite company, yet retained the grain of his background too – aka his soul. He hadn't changed, his circumstances had.

I watched the jury throughout. No reaction, but they were hanging on to his every word.

And I watched Carnavale too. He was also paying strict attention and continuously making notes. As was his junior, who passed him messages on Post-its from time to time.

'One final question,' Christine said. 'Did you kill Evelyn Bates?'

No,' VJ said. 'I did not.'

'Mr James. Did you kill your father?'

That was Carnavale's opening.

There were a few baffled gasps and grunts from the public.

Christine was on her feet.

'My Lord, we object to the question on the grounds that it is not only completely irrelevant to this trial, but it's also a gratuitous attempt by the prosecution to prejudice the jury against the defendant.'

Judge Blumenfeld nodded and looked to Carnavale for a retort.

'This isn't the first time the accused has been suspected of murder, My Lord.'

'I think "suspected" is too strong a word,' Christine countered. 'Mr James was neither arrested nor charged in connection with the tragic murder of his father. He was merely questioned, along with his mother

445

and his sister. As my learned friend well knows, it is standard police procedure to question immediate family during murder investigations.'

Carnavale was quick on the comeback.

'My Lord, the police interviewed the defendant's mother and sister once before eliminating them from their inquiries. However the defendant was interviewed under caution on five separate occasions. He was quite obviously the main suspect.'

The judge sighed heavily.

'Mr Carnavale, the defendant is not on trial for the murder of his father.' He turned to the jury. 'Please disregard the question.'

Christine sat down.

'You didn't like him much, did you?' Carnavale said to VJ.

Christine was back on her feet. The judge cut in before she could speak.

'Mr Carnavale, *what* is the relevance of the defendant's relationship with his father?'

'Credibility, My Lord. On March 16th the accused gave a speech expressing his love and admiration for his father. Yet on the day his father was murdered, the accused was seen having a violent argument with him. The police later discovered that the accused and his father had had a volatile relationship.'

The judge nodded and turned to VJ.

'Please answer the question.'

Christine sat down, pissed off.

'Our relationship was troubled,' VJ said.

'That's not what I asked you,' Carnavale said. 'I asked if you *liked* your father.'

'Then no, I didn't like him. I didn't like him at all,' VJ said. 'My father was a very angry, bitter man who resented everything about his life, including his family. He considered us a burden rather than a blessing. It's hard to like someone like that.'

'In other words your award speech was a complete lie?'

'No, it wasn't. As I got older and when I became a father myself, I understood the man who made me. He'd suffered when we moved to England, financially and professionally. He went from being a somebody in a small country to a nobody in a big one. He took it out on those nearest to him. Yet, despite that, he always put food on our table and kept the roof over our heads. I'd like to think that if he were alive today we'd be friends.'

The SQUID rules had gone out the window, but the Asian juror was moved.

'You had an alibi for the night your father was murdered, didn't you?'

'Yes. I was with friends.'

Oh no . . .

Here it comes . . .

The judge banged his gavel hard.

'Mr Carnavale,' he said, wearily. 'You may not have exhausted this particular line of questioning, but you've exhausted my patience. The defendant is *not* on trial for killing his father. Irrespective of what the police at the time thought or suspected, they had no proof to back it up. So you may not ask the defendant any more questions about this. Is that clear?'

Then Carnavale turned and looked straight at me.

My heart started pounding, my mouth went suddenly dry. The prosecutor's eyes were burning into me. I didn't want to look at him, but couldn't look away.

'Do you have any questions to ask the defendant relating to the case at hand – the murder of Evelyn Bates?' the judge asked.

'I do, My Lord.'

'Then please ask him *those*. Thank you.'

What had just happened?

Christine tossed me a handkerchief.

'You're sweating,' she whispered.

I touched my brow with cold fingertips, which came away wet.

Carnavale's junior passed him some sheets of paper. He took his time looking them over on the lectern.

'What was the name of the award you were accepting?' he asked.

'The Ethical Person of the Year.'

'Ironic, don't you think?'

VJ didn't answer.

Carnavale craned forward.

'You're not "ethical" at all, are you? Not this year, not last year, not *any* year.' That was a pre-prepared line if ever there was one. He'd delivered it with an adenoidal sneer, a full blast of the dreaded kazoo. 'After all, you *have* cheated on your wife, haven't you?'

'It wasn't the Ethical *Husband* of the Year award,' VJ said. 'If it had been, I'd have turned it down.'

Laughter. Smirks from the jury. Carnavale had walked right into that one. He blushed at the nape.

'How many homes do you own, Mr James?'

'Five.'

'How many in London?'

'One.'

'Where?'

'Chelsea.'

'That's less than ten miles from the hotel. Why didn't you spend the night at home?'

'There was a party after the ceremony. I thought it was best to stick around.'

'You could easily have caught a cab.'

'I wish I had.'

'I suggest you stayed at the hotel because you planned to pick a woman up.'

'That wasn't my ulterior motive. The award ceremony was at the hotel. I was expected to attend the afterparty, and I did.'

'Did you bring Rohypnol with you to the hotel?'

'No.'

'I suggest you did.'

'I did not.'

'There was Rohypnol in Evelyn Bates's blood.'

'There was also Rohypnol in mine. Didn't that strike you as odd, Mr Carnavale?' VJ shot back.

'Not at all, Mr James,' Carnavale said. 'You're a highly intelligent man with a first from Cambridge – top marks from one of the top universities in the world.

'I suggest *you* took Rohypnol after you murdered Evelyn. You knew you'd be arrested. But you also knew there'd be a blood test and the drug would show up. You were already thinking ahead, to what your defence would be. Namely that you were drugged by persons unknown, out to get you, out to "set you up".'

'That's utterly ridiculous!' VJ snapped.

All twelve jurors were startled.

'After you got back to your office, you threw your clothes away, didn't you?'

'I put them in a bin bag to be disposed of.'

'You were getting rid of evidence, weren't you?'

'No.'

'Didn't you put a note on the bin liner instructing your PA to get rid of the clothes?'

'Yes.'

'So you were getting rid of them, weren't you?'

'Yes, but not the way you're implying.'

Carnavale paused and straightened up.

'What did you do with the gloves?'

'I didn't have any gloves.'

'I suggest you threw them away after you left the hotel.'

'I didn't have any gloves. And Evelyn Bates was never in my room.'

'Oh, but she *was* in your room, Mr James. She was found dead there on March 17th, remember?'

VJ was stumped.

For the first time he looked at us – in mounting panic.

'You don't like women much, do you?' Carnavale said.

'That's not true,' VJ said.

'You don't consider them your equal.'

'That's not true either.'

'You claimed that a woman called Fabia assaulted you in your suite. Why didn't you report this?'

'I was passed out on the couch. I didn't come to until the next morning.'

'Why didn't you report it then?'

'I had to get to work.'

Carnavale pulled an exaggerated frown.

'You mean to tell me, you were the victim of a serious assault – we've all seen the pictures of your bruised torso – and you were *too busy* to report it? There was also extensive – and very expensive – damage to the suite. Didn't it occur to you that you'd be held accountable for that by not reporting what happened?'

'I wasn't thinking straight that morning. Unbeknown to me, I'd been drugged a few hours earlier. I had a deal to do that afternoon. A piece of land I was going to bid on. That was all that was on my mind.'

Carnavale shook his head.

'Mr James, would you have reported the assault if it had been a man?'

VJ hesitated.

'Mr James?'

'I might have, yes. But I was passed out.'

'But you didn't report it because it was a woman?'

'No.'

'Is that "No", you didn't report it *because* it was a woman?'

'The fact that it was a woman had nothing to do with why I didn't report it,' VJ said.

'But you've just told the court you *might* have reported it if it had been a man. Were you embarrassed to have been beaten up by a woman?'

'I suppose it was a little embarrassing, yes.'

Oh dear . . .

'Was that why you didn't report it?'

'Maybe . . . That could've been a . . . a subconscious reason.'

Bad answer.

449

'You really *don't* consider women equal to men at all, do you? They're just objects to you. Objects you can use and abuse at will.'

'That's not true.'

'Yes it is, Mr James,' Carnavale said, contemptuously.

The prosecutor looked at his papers.

'When the police emptied the pockets of the jacket you were trying to dispose of, they found Evelyn Bates's broken iPhone. What were you doing with it?'

'She dropped it in the nightclub. I picked it up,' said VJ.

'Why?'

'I was going to hand it in at reception.'

Carnavale cleared his throat.

'I don't think that's what happened at all. I think she tried to call for help from your suite. I think you grabbed the phone and smashed it.'

'That's not what happened,' VJ said.

'You killed Evelyn Bates, didn't you?'

'No.'

'I suggest you did,' Carnavale said. 'You took Evelyn up to your suite. You drugged her with Rohypnol. As you waited for it to kick in, you ordered champagne from room service. The Rohypnol didn't work on her as fast as you'd expected. You tried it on with her.

'Evelyn didn't want anything to do with you and tried to leave. You lost your temper. You were indignant and angry because you're used to having your way with women. Not because you're charming. Not because you've got some kind of foolproof technique. No, Mr James. The kind of women you have your way with are the kind you have to pay for that privilege. The kind that charge for their company – who take your money and put up with your bad jokes and cheesy patter. You've been doing it for so long, your perspective's become warped. You believe *all* women are escorts. A few thousand pounds and they're yours for the night. Evelyn wasn't like that, though. Evelyn wasn't an escort. But you no longer know the difference.

'You're also a violent man, Mr James. Especially towards women. You like to hit and choke them for some sick, twisted thrill.

'Evelyn tried to fight you off. She fought hard, but not hard enough. You strangled her on the floor and then you carried her body into the bedroom, where you stripped her and left her on the mattress, with her legs apart. You not only took her life, but you even took her dignity in death. No further questions.'

87

Day 8

The last day of the trial. Wednesday.

The two sides were to sum up their respective arguments; then the judge would give the jury his directions, before sending them out to deliberate the verdict.

It was almost over.

VJ thought he'd done badly yesterday. I agreed. Carnavale had been impressive, *very* impressive. Even though I knew VJ was innocent, I almost believed he could be guilty. Luckily, I wasn't asked for my opinion.

Christine reassured VJ he'd done brilliantly, especially when she'd cross-examined him. She claimed the jury had seen through Carnavale, how he'd not so much asked questions as framed his preferred version of events *as questions*. Janet and Redpath had said nothing.

The court was packed now, as it had been from the start. But today it felt like there were even more people here. The public gallery was stacked with faces. I spotted Melissa, in a corner. Sid Kopf was right next to her, looking straight at me. I wondered if VJ's mum had come, or maybe his sister.

Christine leaned over to me.

'Janet told me your theory – about Sid,' she whispered. 'We'll talk about that afterwards.'

'Do you think it's possible?'

'Janet does,' she said.

Turning to the jury, Franco Carnavale delivered his pitch for a guilty verdict. Gone were his snide tone, his leaning over the lectern, his pauses, the kazoo. He was now a salesman on a mission.

He started by reminding the jurors who Evelyn Bates was; her age when she died, the loving family and friends who'd never see her again and the life cruelly and callously ended. He was empathetic, his delivery powered by restrained moral outrage.

He recapped the forensics and the emotion went out of his tone. He spoke plainly and matter-of-factly.

The bulk of his summary was devoted to his theory that the accused led a double life. To the public he was the award-winning *ethical* multimillionaire businessman and devoted husband and family man. In private he was a sexual sadist who got his kicks hurting women, hitting and choking them.

'In the past, when he was choking women,' Carnavale said, 'Vernon James was at the threshold of murder. It was only a matter of time before he took that final fatal step. On the morning of March 17th he did, when he took Evelyn Bates's life.'

Then, to conclude, he said this:

'Vernon James is a danger to women. To set him free would be to put more young women's lives at risk – women like Evelyn. If she died for something, then let it be to rid the world of people like her killer, the man in the dock.'

And with that Carnavale thanked the jury and sat down.

He looked *mighty* pleased with himself.

After a short recess it was Christine's turn.

Like the prosecutor, she also faced the jury. Unlike him, she had no notes in front of her.

'When I first spoke to you, ladies and gentlemen, I told you I didn't like Vernon James. Well . . .

'I *still* don't like him. Why? Because he's a depraved man beholden to his appetite for violent, sadistic sex. An appetite so rampant, so destructive, so all-consuming it's brought him here, before you, accused of a serious, heinous crime. So, in that respect, Vernon James *is* guilty – guilty of weakness, stupidity, and a complete and utter lack of self-control. But those, ladies and gentlemen of the jury, are personal failings, not crimes.

'I'll be honest with you. When I heard about the case on the news, my first reaction was *He did it. He's guilty.*

'Evelyn's body was found in his hotel room. He checked out of the hotel without reporting it. He *must* be guilty. She's dead. He ran. Fair cop. Case closed. Right?

'*Wrong.* Let's reconsider the case in the light of everything we've heard over the past two weeks.

'When the police first interviewed the defendant, Vernon James, mere hours after finding Evelyn's body, he was not only drunk, he was also – unbeknown to both them *and* himself – still under the influence of Rohypnol.

'As we've heard, from both a medical professional *and* the detective in charge of this investigation, Rohypnol mixed with alcohol causes disorientation and blackouts.

'The police interviewed a man who could only remember very confused fragments of what had happened the night before. They accused him of lying, of changing his story. They said he'd made up the woman he said he was with – a tall, attractive, long-haired blonde in a green dress. And they made much of the fact that when they showed him a picture of Evelyn Bates and asked him if that was the woman he was with, he said, "I'm not sure."

'Ladies and gentleman of the jury, Mr James wasn't lying when he said those words. *He really wasn't sure.* He wasn't sure of where he was, where he'd been, who he'd been with. He probably wasn't entirely sure that what was happening to him then was even real.

'A single dose of Rohypnol has a cycle of between eight and twelve hours. It's at its most effective in the first six hours. After that it starts to weaken, and the person who's taken it slowly regains clarity of mind. Their memory comes back.

'And so it proved with Mr James. The first official police interview took place at Charing Cross at 1 p.m. That was when he was initially shown the picture of Evelyn.

'The second police interview took place three hours later. He was shown the photo of Evelyn again and said, "No. That wasn't her." And he also told the police his version of events. He told them he'd gone up to his room with a tall blonde in a dark-green dress. He remembered her name – Fabia. He tried to seduce her in his suite and she viciously assaulted him.

'Yes, he'd changed his story to a completely different version of events. Of course it was different, because it was based on the memories that were coming back to him as the drug was wearing off.

'And Mr James has stuck to that version ever since. It hasn't changed at all. It's the same version he told me, and it's the same version he told the court. And it is also, in my opinion, *exactly* what happened.

'You'll remember that the defendant's doctor gave evidence on behalf of the prosecution. He said that he'd prescribed Rohypnol to Mr James for an anxiety disorder.

'The prosecution contends that the defendant deliberately drugged himself after he'd murdered Evelyn, to give himself an alibi of sorts – to make out that he'd been set up for the murder.

'That is absurd. It assumes that Mr James somehow managed to stay in full possession of all his mental faculties while under the twin influences of alcohol and Rohypnol – a combination well known to cause temporary amnesia.

'Secondly, where did the Rohypnol found in both the victim *and* the suspect come from? Not from the *legally prescribed* packet found in Mr James's office. That would have left traces of blue dye in both the victim's and the suspect's urine.

'No. The Rohypnol used on both the victim and the defendant on March 16th or 17th, was of the illegal variety. The kind that leaves no traces, and is completely undetectable when mixed with drink. There is no evidence that Mr James ever possessed that type of Rohypnol.

'Now let's consider the actual evidence against Mr James. As you saw, from the CCTV footage, he *did* meet Evelyn Bates; very briefly, in the hotel nightclub. They spoke for approximately ten seconds, before Evelyn was knocked over by a passing crowd of dancers. She was on the phone at the time. The phone went flying, as did Evelyn. She landed on Mr James. The two of them fell over. As she tried to get up, the strap of her dress broke, her hair got entangled and she accidentally scratched his cheek. A witness saw them rolling around on the floor together.

'This explains the very few hairs found on Mr James's person. It also explains the reason he had scratches on his cheek, and why his blood and skin were found under Evelyn's fingernails. As for the phone in his pocket – he picked it up off the nightclub floor because he was going to hand it in to reception.

'After he left the club, Mr James was seen at a bar on the eleventh floor of the hotel, at around 11.30 p.m. The barman – Gary Murphy – said he noticed the scratches on the accused's face. So they were definitely made *before* he went up to his room.

'Secondly, the defendant was not alone. Mr Murphy told the court that Mr James was with a tall woman – at least six feet in height. She had long blonde hair, and was wearing a dark-green dress. Mr Murphy was very specific in describing the dress. It was skin tight, split to the thigh, and the back was exposed. That was *not* the dress Evelyn Bates wore. Hers was a much brighter shade of green, and a completely different style.

'Mr Murphy insists he told the police this, yet they chose to ignore the details. They were selective in the way they took down his statement. For them it was enough that the defendant was seen with a blonde in a green dress.

'When this came out in open court, the prosecution brought up Mr Murphy's previous criminal record for perjury, effectively suggesting he was lying again.

'Yet, why would he lie? He had no reason to. He doesn't know Mr James. He has nothing to gain, except a clear conscience that he told the truth – the whole truth, and not an edited version.

'The barman described the very same person Mr James has always insisted he went up to his room with. Fabia. Not Evelyn. *Fabia.*

'I'm sure you'll remember Rachel Hudson, the escort who gave evidence. She was tall and blonde. So too, according to her, were three other escorts Mr James had been with. *He has a type,* she said. Tall, attractive, blonde, with long straight hair.

'Granted, Evelyn Bates was blonde. Her hair was medium length and curly. She was five feet four inches in height. She was not tall. And she was not Mr James's "type".

'You will also – I am sure – never forget what *Mizz* Hudson had to say about the defendant's sexual practices. He liked slapping and choking her during sex. He choked her with his *belt* while he was taking her from behind.

'Evelyn Bates was strangled by *hand*. And she was *facing* her killer. There is absolutely no medical evidence of sexual activity. And neither was there any bruising to her face – only to her neck, made by the killer's *hands*, not his belt.

'And what of those hands? No fingerprints were found on the victim's throat or neck. The pathologist stated that this is because her killer wore gloves. Yet no gloves were found at the crime scene. And no gloves were found in Mr James's office, where he went directly from the hotel. No gloves were found in the rubbish bag Mr James put his dirty clothes in, although Evelyn's phone was found there.

'The police and the prosecution contend that he must have disposed of the gloves en route. Yet, if that's the case, surely he would have had the wherewithal to get rid of Evelyn's phone too?

'The fact that the killer used gloves disproves the prosecution's case for premeditated murder in a fundamental way. Because it would mean that Mr James would have had to have come to the hotel with the *intention* of strangling someone – anyone – to death. That's not why he went to the hotel at all. He went there to receive an award.

'Ladies and gentlemen of the jury, it is my opinion that the bulk of the prosecution's case is little more than grasping conjecture masquerading as fact.

'Now I usually have infinite respect for the police, both as an institution and as individuals. But on this occasion, with this case, I find my sympathies challenged. Why? Because they didn't do their jobs properly.

'In investigating a murder, the police must focus on the victim as much as the suspect. They must reconstruct to the best of their ability the victim's last movements. On this occasion, they didn't.

'We know that Evelyn Bates left the hen party she was attending early to go back to the hotel. We know that she went to the nightclub. We also know that she met – or rather, encountered – Mr James there. We know she left the club at around 11.15 p.m.

'Some time after that Evelyn Bates wrote a note informing her roommate that she had gone up to a private party in Suite 18. That she actually wrote the note is not in dispute. How the note got into her room is. What is certain is that it was put there at 2.20 a.m. But not by her.

'You will recall that I cross-examined DCI Reid over keycard entry data for Suite 18, where Mr James stayed, and Room 474, where Evelyn Bates stayed. DCI Reid told the court that she was seeing the data for 474 for the first time. She – the head of this investigation – had not thought to check it.

'Had she done so at the very start, she would have found that someone using a hotel staff passkey had entered Room 474 at 2.20 a.m. on March 17th – well within the agreed timespan of Evelyn's murder.

'The police didn't know this had happened until I pointed it out to them, here in court.

'This wasn't the only occasion they failed to act on discrepancies in the keycard data. On March 16th, shortly before 9 p.m., while Mr James was downstairs in the ballroom attending the award ceremony, someone used a hotel passkey to enter his suite.

'The police had this information, yet made no effort whatsoever to find out who that person was and what they were doing in a room that several hours later became a crime scene.

'Why were they so sloppy, so negligent? The only explanation I can give is that they assumed they had their man. To convict someone of murder, you need much more than assumption. You need *absolute* certainty.

'You will shortly be asked to deliberate your verdict. You will be told that you have to be satisfied that the prosecution has proved its case beyond reasonable doubt.

'The prosecution concluded its summary by telling you to find Vernon James guilty, because his murder of Evelyn was part of an escalating pattern of violence towards women.

'I will conclude by reminding you that our legal system punishes people for things they have done, not for things they may yet do. Vernon James did not kill Evelyn Bates. I firmly and *wholeheartedly* believe that. And I have every good faith that when you re-examine the evidence in your deliberations, you will come to the same conclusion. Thank you.'

I helped Christine sit down. For once, she actually needed my help. She was exhausted, sweating and shaking. She'd given it her all.

I wanted to pat her on the back, but it had to wait.

Judge Blumenfeld gave his directions, the final summary.

We knew he wasn't going to tell the jury whether to convict or acquit, but he could strongly hint at what he thought their verdict should be – in so many words. And the general rule of thumb, when predicting a verdict, is:

As goes the judge, so the jury.

We listened carefully..

Judge Blumenfeld highlighted the pros and cons of both arguments, giving each equal time and weight. Then he said this to the jury:

'The prosecution had access to all the evidence it needed to make a convincing case, but you should ask yourselves whether you were presented with enough of it to be convinced of the defendant's guilt. The fact that Evelyn Bates was murdered in the defendant's hotel room may be enough to convict him in the court of public opinion, but it is *not* enough to convict him in a court of law.'

In other words . . .

He didn't think the case was as strong as it should have been.

Christine allowed herself the slightest of smiles.

Carnavale couldn't hide his dejection.

'All rise!'

88

We got out of court at 12.30 and were going to go straight down the cells to see VJ.

But DCI Reid marched straight up to me, ignoring Christine and Redpath.

'Can I have a word, please?'

'Remember we took your fingerprints in Southend nick? They were all over this,' DCI Reid said, tapping on an evidence bag on the table between us.

We were in a windowless cubbyhole on the second floor. Nothing but a table, and a couple of plastic chairs.

She opened the bag and unfolded the contents. The first thing I noticed were yellowy brown oval smudges on the surface, where the paper had been iodine-fumed by forensics.

It was the building plan I'd found in Swayne's locker in Frant station.

'It was in the Renault Megane you were in two weeks last Saturday,' she said.

'Took your time getting to me,' I said.

'We *bided* our time. We didn't want to disrupt the trial in any way,' she said.

'I'm sure you didn't,' I said, sarcastically. She ignored that.

'Now, about what happened that day. As I'm sure you know we have two people in custody—'

'And another in the morgue.'

She paused long enough to skewer me with a glare.

'There have been some significant developments,' she continued. 'But before I go there, I need you to promise me that whatever's said here, stays here. Is that understood?'

'Yes.'

'We have a man and a woman in custody. We believe the man was the driver. He's being treated for third-degree burns and a wound to the back of his neck,' she said. 'In the next twenty-four hours, we're going to charge the woman with the murder of Fabia Masson in Southend. It was her on the station CCTV. She'll also be charged with your attempted kidnapping. You're our main witness. I'm going to need a statement from you.'

Before I had time to react, DCI Reid had placed a digital tape recorder in front of me.

'Ready?'

And off I went, spilling in an unchecked freeform blurt:

Meeting Swayne on Wellington Arch . . . the woman we'd seen standing by the Australian War Memorial . . . Sid Kopf rigging the defence team to lose the trial (she didn't so much as blink at that) . . . exchanging coats . . . going to Swayne's flat, being followed . . . ditching my tail at Tunbridge Wells . . . the drawing in the railway locker . . . getting bundled in the car by the woman and Jonas Dichter . . . the syringe, the gun, the petrol bomb . . . being rescued by rioters . . . running away.

DCI Reid pressed stop.

'Who were my kidnappers?' I asked.

'Ex-Israeli Special Forces, now working for the private sector as killers for hire. Well trained, highly skilled, very dangerous. We're finding out more and more about them as we go along,' she said. 'They were based in a house in Ealing. Two of them had – very briefly and until fairly recently – been working at the Blenheim-Strand. One in security, one in housekeeping. They got the jobs through Beverley Wingrove at the Silver Service Agency.'

I stayed calm.

'When did you find all this out?' I asked.

'Over the course of the past week,' she said.

I thought back to what Swayne had told me on Battersea Embankment:

The Wingroves – the White Ghosts – *Mossad* . . .

He'd been trying to tell me where to look.

'When we searched their place in Ealing, we found fake passports, stacks of money, and a gun. We also found vials of the same poison used on Fabia.'

A chill travelled from the edge of my neck to my toes at lightning speed. I shuddered.

'This changes everything, right?' I said.

'What does it change?'

'You know Vernon didn't kill Evelyn Bates.'

'No, we don't,' she said. 'All the evidence says he did.'

'Come on!'

'For an apprentice lawyer who's just sat through a trial, you're pretty stupid, Terry. You should know how things work in court by now. It's not how things are, it's how they look. And, above all, it's about what you can prove.'

I could've got angry, but there was no point. This was ultimately all about the law; about what did and didn't stand up in court.

'Did you ask the Israelis who they were working for?'

'I don't think you have anything more to worry about now, Terry.'

'And what was I worried about?'

'You don't have to fear for your safety – or that of your family. They can come home now.'

My family?

How did she know they were away?

Had the police been watching me?

I wanted to ask her, I really did . . . But I didn't want to know.

Let it go, walk away. And be grateful you can. She's telling you this is over.

She folded Swayne's drawing up and handed it to me.

'You can go back to work now.'

89

Something had happened in the Great Hall. A small crowd was gathered in the middle. Admin staff, security, uniformed cops all mingling with the legals, as if there'd been a drill or an alarm had gone off.

I spotted Janet and Redpath off to one side. Redpath was on his phone.

'Christine's collapsed,' Janet said.

'*What?*'

'We were standing here talking and she keeled over. She was unconscious when the medics got here. I thought she'd fainted. But it could be a stroke.'

'Jesus.'

'She's on her way to hospital. We've informed her family. They're on their way there.'

Christine had seemed well all through the trial – her health even improving with each passing day, especially when things had gone our way. But when she finished her summing-up she looked ashen.

'What's going to happen now?' I asked.

'He takes over,' she said, hiking her thumb in Redpath's direction.

Great, I thought. Our mute barrister.

'I doubt the jury'll come back today,' Janet said. 'They won't start deliberating until two. We might know tomorrow morning.'

'How's the rule go again?' I asked. 'Quick – you're nicked/Slow – you can go.'

The faster the jury comes back, the likelier a guilty verdict.

Janet shook her head.

'It's a myth,' she said. 'But I've got another rule for you: "Expectation is the mother of disappointment and the father of resentment." You'd best remember that if you decide to continue in the legal profession.'

I started heading off.

'Where are you going?' Janet called after me.

'Lunch,' I said.

90

For my sins I found myself going back to Croydon. That was where the headquarters of the Land Registry department was situated.

The receptionist made me wait as she phoned to see if anyone was around to help me. I was in luck. I paid £15, gave my details and got given a visitor's pass and a name to ask for on the first floor.

My designated official was a pale blond man in his fifties with translucent eyelashes. I showed him Swayne's drawing and explained that I had neither an address nor a postcode, just the reference number in the legend.

He looked at it for all of five seconds.

'The postcode's right here,' he said, pointing to the first part of the legend in the box. 'See? E15 1LW. The other numbers – 1960 – probably correspond to the year the drawing was made, and the others – 0507 . . . I dunno. Company code maybe?'

'E15? That's east London, isn't it?'

'Yes. Stratford,' he said.

As with the last time I'd come here, there was a van parked outside the Stratford Friends House, but it wasn't serving soup to the homeless now. It was a removal van.

I recognised Fiona, pushing a box inside. When she'd finished she massaged her upper arms.

460

'It's Terry, isn't it – Terry from Kopf-Randall-Purdom?' she said, offering me her hand and then withdrawing it almost as quickly and wiping it on the side of her jeans.

We stood there awkwardly for a moment, clueless in the vacuum of aborted decorum.

She'd been much friendlier before, when I was a stranger.

'I see you're moving out?' I said.

'Last bits and bobs. We've got a centre in Walthamstow,' she said. 'The diggers are coming in tomorrow. They're knocking it down Tuesday. Hard to believe it'll be gone this time next week.'

She turned to look at the decaying building, its layers of grime mixing with the early afternoon shadows to make it resemble something that had been dredged up from a peat bog, dragged here and left behind.

'So the sale went through, then?' I said.

'Oh, it went through all right,' she said, sarcastically.

'What happened?'

'Don't you know?'

Yes, I did, but not the way she was implying – as in: I'd known all along, from when we'd first met. I only found out when the man in Land Registry told me the postcode.

But I wanted to hear it from her. Her take.

'No,' I said, feigning ignorance and confusion.

A man came out of the building with two boxes stacked one on top of the other. She waited until he'd gone back into the warehouse.

'Remember how we wanted to sell the building to a reputable buyer? Someone who'd carry on some of our tradition here, helping out the less fortunate? Hal Peterson, the Canadian, seemed ideal. *Too* ideal, as it turned out.'

'How so?'

'He ...'

She couldn't bring herself to say it, so I did.

'He was dodgy?'

'Not exactly ... I mean, yes. It was our fault for being too ... too trusting. But how were we to know? Everything seemed on the level. Peterson submitted his bid. One of our board had been to school with him and vouched for his integrity. He came in and met everyone. He told us what he'd do with the land. He told us exactly what we wanted to hear,' she said. She sighed and shook her head. 'We should've seen it. It was right there, in front of us. All we had to do was *look*. Look past him, *into* him.'

She wiped sweat off her brow with the back of her hand.

'Hal Peterson was a Trojan Horse,' she said.

'A front?'

461

She nodded slowly and sadly.

'For someone you would never have sold to?' I said.

Another heavy nod.

'It was Scott Nagle, wasn't it?' I asked.

I thought back to when I'd gone to the newspaper archive and looked up Nagle. He'd been exposed using a frontman and a shell company to try to buy Battersea Power Station, because the owners wouldn't have sold to him directly on account of his reputation. But how much had he got away with; how many principled, unsuspecting sellers had he duped before?

'I thought you said you didn't know, Terry?'

'How come *you* didn't?'

'It never occurred to us to double-check. All we had to do was go on the Companies House website and look up Hal Peterson Associates. If we had, we'd have seen that it was a shell company not even a year old, and that one of those "Associates" was Scott Nagle. He was listed as a director. And we *definitely* wouldn't have sold to him,' she said. 'I *cared* about this place, this area. It turned my life around.'

'So how did you find out?' I asked.

'Because of you.'

'*Me?*'

'The last time you came, you gave me your card,' she said. 'After the deal went through, I was asked to photocopy all the paperwork – the contracts and lawyers' letters. I recognised the name of your firm on some of the letters – Kopf-Randall-Purdom.'

'*They* did the deal for Peterson?' I asked. 'Do you remember the name of the lawyer?'

'Yes, Kopf. Sid Kopf.'

It shouldn't have come as a surprise, but it did. I'd have thought Kopf would stay in the background, not get directly involved.

'You *really* didn't know, did you?' she said, scrutinising my face.

'It's a big firm with separate divisions. And I'm little people,' I said. 'Scott Nagle's father – Thomas Nagle – built this place, didn't he?'

'He left it to us in his will.'

His *will?* I'd seen it in Kopf's office. There'd been no mention of Quakers.

'Thomas was a good man, by all accounts,' she continued. 'He grew up in Stratford, you know? His family were poor. Quakers looked after them. He never forgot that.'

'I didn't know that,' I said.

'You wouldn't believe it from the way his son turned out, would you?' she said. 'Scott Nagle's been trying to buy this land for decades. *Decades.*

462

I suppose if you hang around long enough you get everything you want.'

'Or learn how to take it,' I said.

'You know what else I found out?' she said. 'Vernon *was* going to put a bid in after all. One of the directors told me he'd booked a meeting with them.'

'Do you remember when it was supposed to be?'

'March 17th.'

The day he was arrested.

A short while later we said our goodbyes. I shook her hand and wished her the best. She told me to ask VJ to come visit them in their new place when he was free – in both senses of the word. I said I would. I'd never told him I'd come here, never told him they'd been praying for him.

It was warm going on hot as I set off back across the baked ground, with the rattle and thudding reports of construction work from the nearby Olympic Village strafing the air.

I stopped and turned back to look at the building.

The first thing I noticed was that I couldn't make out the massive mural of Quaker Oats man at all, not even the faintest outline. The afternoon sun was falling on the building selectively, brightening up the left side but leaving the right deep in deep shadow.

There was something suddenly very familiar about the warehouse, something that hadn't registered the last time I was here. That was because I'd seen it in the morning, when the sun was at its highest.

Then it came to me.

I'd seen this place before I ever visited it.

On Kopf's office wall. It was the most prominent of the dozen framed photographs he'd hung behind his desk – the heart of the display, larger than the others, pride of place. Everyone who sat facing him would notice it. He'd photographed the warehouse from roughly where I was standing now, and at almost the same time of day.

What was that Swayne had told me?

KRP is the house Scott Nagle built.

A few things started connecting.

Kopf had had VJ framed and arrested to get him out of the way, so Scott Nagle could buy this building and the land it stood on.

It's very likely VJ would have won the bid, had he been around to place it. He was the ideal buyer. He'd built up a good relationship with the centre over the years – *and* he'd just been crowned Ethical Person of the Year. He couldn't lose.

463

He'd also researched his rival bidder. Ahmad Sihl had put David Stratten on the case. Stratten was due to give Sihl his report on March 17th. Except he never made the meeting. He got raided by the Israelis, posing as tax inspectors. They took away his computers and hard drives containing all the information he'd gathered. He'd found out Peterson was a Scott Nagle proxy. VJ would have mentioned that in his pitch for sure.

Swayne knew this *all along*.

He told me oblique clues:

The Israeli hitmen, the Wingroves, Michael Zengeni, the building.

I had all the pieces, but how did they fit together?

Scott Nagle had been trying to buy back the land for *decades* . . .

He wanted it badly.

But why?

VJ owned the rest of the land.

What was worth killing four people over?

91

Thursday

Pepe Regan's trial had started the day before. There was a picture of him on the front page of the *Daily Chronicle*, walking next to Adolf. They made an odd couple. Regan, every inch the gormless multi-millionaire thug with lucky feet, his conservative suit and tie emphasising rather than masking his failings, making him look like he was playing a banker in a rap video. Adolf, on the other hand – despite barely reaching his shoulder – was the picture of ascetic professionalism; black suit, white blouse and that all-important documents trolley. She looked good, I had to give her that.

The jury spent all day deliberating, and I spent all day in the canteen, drinking cups of so-so black coffee and observing the comings and goings. Cops briefing reporters. Reporters filing stories. Defendants and their legal teams keeping to themselves. Freelance clerks eating packed lunches. Court administrators on their tea breaks.

At the end of the day, the judge sent the jury home.

No verdict yet.

Christine was in Barts Hospital. She'd had a stroke. She'd been put in a medically induced coma to reduce the swelling in her brain.

I went to see her.

I met Carnavale coming down the corridor. He recognised me and slowed down to talk.

'How is she?' I asked.

He shook his head and walked away.

Friday

More of exactly the same, right down to the faces.

No verdict yet.

The judge sent the jury home for the weekend.

Saturday

My family returned in the early afternoon.

I was elated – but mostly relieved.

Karen was relaxed and chatty, full of things she couldn't wait to tell me.

Both the kids seemed to have grown a little taller.

We came together in the middle of the living room and gave each other a big impromptu hug. I swore I'd never be apart from them again, never let anything get between us, and – most of all – never *ever* put them in harm's way.

Later I took Ray to Battersea Park. It's the most beautiful public garden in London. It even looks good in bad weather.

The sun was starting to lose its brightness, but the air was balmy and scented with cut grass and flowers and a hint of drying Thames mud. I bought us ice-cream cones and we sat on the only free bench, close to the pagoda and looking out across the river.

'I found your flashdrive,' I said.

'Are you angry?'

'No, just worried.'

'Why?' he asked.

'You mustn't lie to us, Ray.'

'I didn't lie, Dad. You never *asked* if I had a secret flashdrive.'

I wanted to laugh at his innocent logic, and the serious frown on his face. I smiled instead.

'There's more to lying than just saying things,' I said. 'Why were you looking at videos about Vernon James?'

'I'm interested in what you do,' he said. 'And you and Mum were always talking about it at night.'

I'd thought we'd been so quiet then – and that the kids were asleep.

465

'Did I really do something wrong?' he asked.

'No. You just didn't do it the right way.'

I realised we were facing roughly where Melissa lived on Cheyne Walk. I couldn't see the house because of the thick trees. I wondered if she was home, and what she was thinking. Was she hopeful about how the trial would turn out? Was she still going to get a divorce?

'Does Mum know you go to the spare room at night?' Ray asked, licking melted ice cream off his finger.

'No.'

'That makes you a liar too, then,' he said.

'Yeah, I suppose you're right,' I said. 'But it doesn't mean you can be one.'

'Then you're a hypocrite.'

I did a double take. The boy was *eight*. I don't think I could even pronounce that word when I was his age, let alone know what it meant.

'I heard it in religious studies last term,' he said, reading my surprise. 'Our teacher told us what it meant.'

'You should really think of being a lawyer, Ray.'

'I already am,' he said, crunching his cone. 'Why don't you hang your old college picture up?'

'Nowhere to put it,' I said.

'There's plenty of space.'

'Don't want to mess up the walls.'

'We'll have it,' he said.

I didn't reply.

One day soon I'd have to tell my children the cautionary tale of how I'd screwed up my life before I'd been old enough to realise what I was doing . . .

Although . . .

No. How could I really say I'd screwed up my life? Not when I was sitting next to a little miracle, and going home to two more. My life had actually turned out all right. It was just the getting here that had been hell.

'I'll say this to you now, Ray. We both know I'm not your father, but I am your dad. And you'll always be my son. All right? I want you to think of me as someone you can always come to with anything, someone you can count on. I may not always have the right answers, and I may not always be able to help you, but I'll always try my hardest for you anyway. OK?'

He gave me his best cauliflower frown, and then he smiled and nodded.

'Just no more sneakiness, all right?'

'As long as you promise the same,' he said.

'Deal.' We shook hands like *hombres*.

In the kitchen, after dinner, I told Karen almost everything that had happened since they'd been away, including the trial.

True to form, I omitted a few things: the attempted kidnapping, Melissa (*obviously*), my drinking (*especially* that) and my theory about Kopf – even if that theory was almost as good as fact. She really didn't need to know just yet. I would tell her, though, when enough time had passed and I'd put the right amount of distance behind it – or if justice was done, and the truth came out anyway. Whichever came first.

Her only response was:

'Thank God this is almost over. Let's talk some more tomorrow.'

I couldn't sleep at all that night, so I went to the living room and turned on the TV. The screen was orange, yellow, red and black. It wasn't Tripoli, Baghdad, Beirut or Gaza. It was north London; Tottenham. Buildings and cars had been set on fire, shops had been looted, and the police were being pelted with bricks and bottles. It all had something to do with a police shooting in the area two days before. A peaceful protest had turned into a full-scale riot.

92

Monday

3.15 p.m.

I was in the canteen eavesdropping on two detectives talking about the rioting going on in east London. It had started mid-morning. Hackney was a warzone. Crowds were attacking the police, looting shops, setting fire to cars and buses. It was barricades, bricks and bottles.

Trouble was spreading to other parts of the city too. Lots of it, kicking off simultaneously. They were saying it was all being plotted and coordinated via Blackberry messenger and Twitter. The riots as flash-mobs. The police were overstretched and losing control. They were talking about getting the army in.

I rang Karen.

'There's going to be trouble in Clapham Junction,' she said.

'How d'you know?'

'It's usually noisy around here, what with all the kids being on holiday.

But it's quieter than Christmas today. That's 'cause they're all out in the town. I'm keeping Ray and Amy indoors. You be careful getting home.'

'I will.'

Just then Janet came into the canteen.

'We're wanted in court,' she said. 'The verdict's in.'

The Verdict – Monday, August 8th, 2011

The courtroom wasn't full. The press bench was half empty. They were out covering the riots. The public gallery was threadbare, more wooden space than people. Melissa had come. She was in her corner seat. We locked eyes. She broke the stare first.

Kopf was sitting next to her, looking at me too.

VJ was brought in and led to the dock.

We turned to face him. Me, Janet and Redpath. He flashed us the briefest of smiles. He was nervous. A strange sight. All through the trial he'd been a study in trance-like calm.

Judge Blumenfeld addressed the jury.

'Have you reached a verdict upon which at least ten of you agree?'

The foreman stood up. He'd had a haircut and was wearing a freshly pressed suit – which meant they'd pretty much made their decision on Friday, but run out of court time.

'We have, My Lord,' he said in a high-pitched voice, which may or may not have been the weight of the moment pressing on his nerves.

I knew exactly how he felt.

I was nervous too.

I took a quiet and very deep breath. My heart was pounding away like heavy feet on a treadmill.

The court clerk stood up.

'Will the defendant please rise.'

VJ stood. And so did we – Redpath and I, Janet on the row behind.

I wished Christine was here.

The judge looked at the foreman.

'How do you find the defendant, guilty or not guilty, on the charge of murder?'

His eyes on the judge, his hands clasped in front of him, the foreman said:

'Guilty.'

93

Downstairs, in the cells, VJ was in shock. He sat very still at the table, palms on the surface, looking through Janet, who was talking to him.

The judge had deferred sentencing until next month. She explained that he'd probably get the standard tariff for a first-time murder – life with a fifteen-year minimum term. He'd be eligible for release when he was fifty-three.

She'd start working on his appeal immediately, she promised.

VJ didn't reply.

I was still numb as I crossed the Great Hall and made for the stairs.

'Were you surprised?' a man's voice said behind me. I thought it was a reporter.

But it was Redpath.

'Shocked, more like,' I said.

'I wasn't,' he said. 'Jurors are simple people who understand simple things. The prosecution had the body in the bed, eyewitnesses, DNA, a prime suspect who left the scene, lied to the police – *and* who also liked strangling women for kicks. Ergo he did it. What did we have? Accusations of dodgy police work. That was it.'

And there I was, thinking Redpath had been useless, when really he'd been underused.

I'd really thought we'd win. Christine hadn't sunk the prosecution's case, but she'd definitely flooded the basement. Or had that just been the way I'd seen things?

'Why didn't you say anything?'

'Christine hates me. She didn't want me on the case. When she wasn't talking down to me, she was talking over me – and that's when she was talking to me at all.'

'What would you have done differently, then?' I asked.

'Persuaded the defendant to plead guilty to manslaughter. He'd be looking at half the time now,' Redpath said.

'But he *didn't* do it.'

'We couldn't prove that,' he said. 'And when you can't prove something, you cut a deal.'

Liam Redpath was a bright and cynical young man, forged by bitterness and disappointment. I knew this, because I recognised in him the same things I saw in the mirror every day.

I didn't reply. I was suddenly tired. Utterly drained.

It was over.

VJ was going to jail.

Nagle had got his building.

Sid Kopf had won.

'Fancy a quick drink?' Redpath asked.

'I've got to get back to the office,' I said. To get fired, I thought.

'Some other time, then?'

'Sure,' I said.

DCI Reid was reading a statement to the assembled press when I came out of the Old Bailey; TV cameras, microphones, tape recorders all crowded around her like big blunted spikes.

I didn't hang around to listen. I'd catch the highlights on TV.

I went up the road to get the Tube. It was a beautiful day again. The wrong kind of weather. I wouldn't have minded rain now. Lots of it. Lashings of it. And thunder. And lightning.

I wanted to feel something raw and sharp – anger, outrage, turmoil – but I was numb. I had too many questions in my head about why and how the jury could have reached that verdict.

'*Guilty!*'

That had come from an old man, standing on the pavement, right in front of me. Where had he popped up from? Who was he? Some nutty beggar?

'Finally! *Guilty!* They got that fucker! They got him!'

Now I recognised him . . .

The thick grey tweed jacket, the lank grey-white hair, the flushed greasy face, and *that* stare . . . I'd seen him in the Bailey canteen, looking at me as he was now with his piercing little eyes. *A cop look.*

And then I realised who he was.

'*Quinlan?*' I said.

'That's *Detective* Quinlan to you, Terry Flynt.'

'What are you doing here?'

'What d'you think?' he snapped. 'I come to see James get his deserts. What did I tell you back then? Told you he'd do it again, didn't I? Told you he'd kill someone else, just like he did his dad.'

'I haven't got time for this,' I said and tried to walk around him, but he got in my face, bobbing up and down like a buoy in a stormy sea. He stank of old sweat and dirty clothes.

'And you're *still* defendin' him, inn't ya? Still lyin' for him! You're a snivellin' little bitch, you know that, Flynt? A snivellin' little bitch. I reached out to you, 'cause I thought you was different to the rest of your dirty little family. You weren't. You're all the same.'

Two people were standing watching us from the opposite pavement.

470

Two men. One of them was very tall, and had a huge grin on his face. The other was pointing a camera at us and snapping away.

I tried to walk round Quinlan, but he was quick on his feet and kept on blocking me.

The tall man came over, still smiling.

It was Kev Dorset. Mr Adolf.

Oh ... *shit.*

'Hi Terry,' he said. 'I'm doing a big piece on Vernon James for Sunday's *Chronicle.* Centre-page spread. It's all about the unsolved murder of his dad and how he was the main suspect. Do you care to comment on the alibi you gave him back then?'

So my face, my name and my past were about to be splashed all over the country's biggest-selling Sunday newspaper.

'Detective Quinlan's told me all about it.'

Quinlan cackled.

I barged past him and started walking away.

Kev followed me on his big long legs. The photographer shadowed us on the opposite pavement.

'Come on, Terry. Give us a quote. Better still, give me your side of the story. I know you lied for him,' he said behind me, that big dumb voice of his booming so loud I swore Lady Justice herself could hear him.

I stopped and turned.

He was only a couple of feet away from me, still grinning, tape recorder in his outthrust hand.

'Sure, I'll give you a quote, Kev. It's this: Go fuck yourself.'

94

I'd planned my exit. No face-to-face goodbyes, no announcements.

I'd written a resignation letter to Janet, which I was going to leave in her in-tray as soon as I'd finished typing up and filing my court notes.

Then I'd walk out.

And never come back.

> *Dear Janet,*
>
> *I am writing to inform you that I wish to resign my position as legal clerk with immediate effect.*
> *While I have enjoyed my time at the firm and have learned a lot, I do not feel that the law is the right career for me.*

Thank you for giving me the opportunity all the
same.
With best wishes for the future,

Terry Flynt

That was it. Bland and formal. No details. No fuss. And absolutely nothing whatsoever about jumping before I was pushed (or *got* pushed ... in every sense of the word). A real damp squib of a thing. But what else could I do?

There was a massive bunch of flowers on Adolf's desk. A mushroom cloud of blue and white blossom, garlanded with pine sprigs and dried leaves, wrapped in shiny blue paper and tied up in white bows.

Thanks for everything.
Love, Pepe

My soon to be ex-colleagues were standing in the middle of the office, toasting Adolf with plastic cups. They'd opened a bottle of champagne. Pepe Regan's case had collapsed a few hours earlier and he'd been discharged. A key witness hadn't turned up. He was probably hanging out with Rudy Saks.

But I guessed that wasn't all they were celebrating.

Adolf must have heard she'd got the paralegal's job and the degree – and all about my reunion with Quinlan, and looming tabloid infamy.

All things being equal, I wasn't as upset about that as I would otherwise have been. I was still reeling from the verdict. Still mostly numb.

The jubilation dipped a little when the Gang of Three saw me walk in, then sprang back with force. The voices rose. Iain giggled.

My phone rang as I turned on my computer.

'Terry?' It was Edwina.

'Yes.'

'Sid wants to see you .'

Kopf was sitting at his desk, watching the riots on his flatscreen. Hackney, Enfield, Brixton, Croydon ... It had spread, and it was still spreading. Shops, buildings, buses and cars wrecked and torched. The police were either nowhere to be seen, or cowering behind plastic shields in thin lines, getting driven back by hails of projectiles.

'It's 1981 all over again,' Kopf said, motioning me to a chair opposite his desk. 'A recession, a Royal Wedding and a riot.'

472

I didn't say anything, just glared at him. He'd tried to have me killed. I owed him that much.

'Thirty years ago, I empathised. They had a cause or two. Something worth fighting for,' he continued. 'But now? Look at them! Nothing but vandals and thieves. Stealing things they don't even need. Stealing just to steal. Mark my words, this generation here will make exactly nothing of itself. It won't leave a mark on history. It won't create, it won't invent, it won't leave anything behind. It'll pass through time like it never existed.'

He turned off the TV, leaned back in his chair and studied me. He had a small, inscrutable smile on his face.

My eyes strayed to the photo of the Quaker warehouse above him, on the wall. It looked more striking in black-and-white; more decrepit and desolate, forbidding even.

And then I slowly brought my gaze back to his. He understood.

And he smiled at me a little more, flashing a hint of pearly white veneer. Suddenly I realised we weren't alone.

Janet was sitting in the chair next to mine.

I'd been so focused on Kopf, I hadn't noticed her.

So it was the three of us, exactly like the first time I was summoned here.

Janet spoke first.

'Everyone loses in this game, Terry. It doesn't matter how brilliant your argument, how straight your facts, how credible your witnesses, the surest things often go to hell. The thing to remember is, it's never about winning or losing. It's about *how* you lose.'

'An innocent man is in jail. I'd say we lost pretty fucking badly, wouldn't you?'

Janet was about to counter, but Kopf beat her to it.

'I know this isn't how you saw things ending, Terry. But what do you want me to say? That you'll get over it? You *won't*. That it'll pass? It *won't*. That things'll get better? They *won't*. What you've been through these past few months, what you've experienced, what you've seen and learned, it'll stay with you. It'll probably haunt you. But it will also define you and therefore guide you in the future. So accept this defeat. Embrace it. Learn from it. Just don't go expecting a happy ending next time, because the law – like life – is not a movie. Good guys lose. The innocent get convicted, the guilty walk free. Everyone dies, and everyone cries. Happens all the time. You've just got to accept that. And move on. That's very important. *Always* move on. And keep moving.'

OK, I thought. This is the bit where you tell me I'm fired.

Hurry up and get it over with. I've got to get home before the intifada hits Clapham Junction.

But Janet still had things to say.

'There'll be some big changes here over the next few months. The criminal division is going to expand. I'm going to be running it as before, but some new people will be coming in, and there'll also be some moves.'

She was looking right at me, smiling broadly.

Kopf was smiling too.

'The hours'll be gruelling,' Janet continued. 'You'll be expected to balance full-time study with paralegal work ...'

Eh?

'And, as you'll see in your contract, you'll be expected to qualify with at least an upper second – preferably a first. Anything lower and you'll have to repay your tuition fees.'

What the HELL was this?

Had I just ... been *offered ... the ...*

PARALEGAL JOB?

Kopf stood up and held out his hand.

'Welcome to the firm, Terry.'

Surprises obviously come in fives. First the verdict, then Redpath, then Quinlan, then Kev, and now *this—*

'You're offering me *a job?*'

'No,' Janet said. 'You've already got a job here. We're promoting you to paralegal, and the firm's putting you through university so you can qualify to be a solicitor. You also get a payrise.'

'But ...'

'Do you accept?' Kopf asked me.

'I ... I'm ... I'm going to need to think about it,' I said.

'What's there to think about?' he said. 'It's a gift horse. You either throw a saddle on it or look it in the mouth.'

I was still sitting down.

So I stood up. Janet too.

'Take tomorrow off,' she said. 'Let us know on Wednesday.'

'All right.'

'I'm sure you'll make the right decision,' Kopf said, nodding at his still extended hand.

I shook it. And as I did, I felt something small and sharp and metallic pressing into my palm.

When I pulled my hand away, I saw what he'd just given me.

Or, rather, *given me back.*

And I was confused as to why he'd had it in the first place.

Then I remembered.

It was one of my lucky four-leaf clover cufflinks – the ones my kids had given me. I thought I lost it at Melissa's house that time, but it must've come off when I went through Kopf's filing cabinet.

That was why he put the Israelis on to me.

Because he thought I'd found something out.

And why had he just given it back to me?

For the same reason I'd been offered the job.

He didn't know what I had on him and Nagle, what Swayne had told me, what I might be sitting on.

So he was buying me off, offering me a future – a career, for my silence.

Him, I understood. I knew exactly where he was coming from.

But what about Janet? She knew what I did.

Whose side was she on?

'Mind yourself getting home,' Kopf said as I left. 'It's dangerous out there.'

95

I didn't know what I was going to do.

If I accepted the job I was a criminal. If I turned it down I was a fool. And I had to be one or the other. No in-betweens, no grey areas, no sitting on the fence.

Did I want to sleep at night, or did I want my kids to eat in the morning?

That was the question.

What would you do?

The back exit of Clapham Junction station had been closed, and two worried-looking security guards were blocking the barriers. I had to go out the front way.

I stepped out into mayhem. People were running down St John's Hill, heading for the intersection where all the big stores were. Groups had formed around shop entrances, trying to lever up the metal shutters. Windows were being battered with bars and bats, or kicked and body-slammed. So far nothing had been broken into, but it was only a matter of time.

No police around at all.

Someone ran past me in a Spider Man mask. I thought it was one of the fancy dress clubbers from the Clapham Grand, except they wore the whole cape and tights clobber. This passer-by only had the mask on. Was he a vigilante? How funny would that be?

I turned left on to Falcon Road. And stopped dead in my tracks.

Both pavements were choked and teeming with people, coming at me fast in regimented bobbing flows of hoodies and baseball caps, faces covered in bandannas and balaclavas, like a pair of parallel mass marathons for the underclass. It was way too dangerous to go forward.

I doubled back and ducked into the Falcon pub. Moments later the staff bolted the doors and pushed big chairs against them. Then they dimmed the lights and killed the music.

The place was rammed. Regulars and refugees, all flat-out terrified. Everyone moved away from the windows and huddled in the centre.

For the next two hours we had front-row seats to the mass looting and all-round destruction that followed, as our once-safe familiar high street was overrun and trashed by the rampaging mob.

They got past the metal shutters in the big Debenhams department store, bending and peeling and wrenching back a corner, making enough of a gap to crawl through. Bodies disappeared so fast inside, it was as if they were being sucked in by some centrifugal force.

They smashed their way into the two sports shops. They tenderised front windows with constant hammering, beating and kicking, until the panes gave up their resistant properties and came away whole from their frames, flopping softly to the ground like disembodied sails. People poured in with a triumphant roar. We watched them tearing down armfuls of clothes and then trying to fight their way out of the influx with their loot. Some slipped and fell on the glass and scattered their spoils, which were suddenly snatched up by fast hands.

Those who hadn't come with facial disguises raided a party shop. That was when the superheroes and supervillains started joining in the riot. Batman had a flatscreen TV under his arm. Wonder Woman was cradling a coffee machine. Beetlejuice was making off with a brand-new microwave. Frankenstein's monster had a Dyson over his shoulder.

The women were the most proactive, the most sensible and organised. They'd headed straight for the luggage section in Debenhams and grabbed the biggest suitcases they could find and stuffed them to splitting. Then they walked out of the shop, wheeling or dragging their loot through the crowds, as if they'd just got back from a long holiday.

By now, in the pub, fear had given way to morbid jokes. The ashtrays had come out and smokers were chugging away on cigarettes, and the Falcon was like all pubs used to be ten years ago. People had their phones out, filming, clicking, or reassuring family and friends, babbling away excitedly. Some were giving running commentaries.

A single police car appeared on the corner of Falcon Road. Then it reversed sharply and shot up a sidestreet, followed by a storm of bottles and an almighty cheer.

The mood in the pub swiftly changed when the party shop went up in flames. First the ground floor, then the first floor, the second and finally the third. There were mutterings that the building could blow up because there were helium canisters inside. Everyone moved even further back from the windows, cramming into the lounge, cowering.

A round metal table came flying out of nowhere and slammed into one of the windows, cracking the glass straight across in a diagonal streak. A load of people jumped and quite a few screamed and shouted. We braced ourselves for an all-out assault. The barstaff brandished knives and rolling pins from the kitchen. Bottles and chairs were grabbed. Someone shouted, 'What if they fuckin' petrol bomb us?' Nobody answered.

Karen kept on calling, and I kept on reassuring her that I was OK, that it would be over soon, not to worry, I'd be home in one piece. It didn't even occur to me to drink.

Sometime after midnight the police arrived in big numbers, kitted out in riot gear, armed with truncheons and German Shepherds. They cleared the streets by driving armoured vans up and down at high speed. Then they moved in on the defiant stragglers.

The crowds vanished.

And then it was all over.

Clapham Junction, swathed in thick grey smoke from the burning shop, was ringing with the sound of pointless shop alarms. The streets were glittering with so much smashed glass they looked like frozen rivers after a deep frost.

'Thank God!' Karen screamed when I finally got home.

We hugged and kissed and hugged some more.

The kids were fast asleep.

The TV was on, the volume low.

I watched the replay.

London burning.

London erupting.

London turning in on itself and spitting out the pieces.

Clapham Junction hadn't come off too badly, compared to other places. Parts of Croydon looked like they'd been drenched in lava. There'd been home invasions and arson attacks in Ealing. Hackney had been a warzone. Peckham another. A picture of a woman jumping from the window of her burning building was shown on every station.

Outside, on the estate, there was an eerie quiet, a desolation wrapped in emptiness, as if a plague had passed over the area. It was a warm, dry summer's night, a rarity this year. The kid posses would have been congregating on the benches now with their bullshitting and their tinny hip-hop, but they weren't there tonight. They had better places to be.

The silence was intermittently broken by screaming sirens, and, for nearly an hour we heard the thrum of a police helicopter circling the vicinity, its searchlight beam splicing through the darkness.

'I knew something like this was coming,' Karen said. 'You could just feel it, you know? These kids around here ain't got nothing better to do with themselves.'

We watched TV. The carnage and fires and street battles were on a loop. There were first-hand accounts. Fingers were already being pointed, most of them at the police for their slow response.

At around two, Karen said she was off to bed.

On her way out, she stopped in the doorway.

'D'you get the verdict today?' she asked me.

No surprise it hadn't made the news.

'Yeah,' I said, yawning. 'Guilty.'

She wasn't shocked or baffled or puzzled, or even curious.

'That's that, then,' she said and closed the door behind her.

I stayed up until the early morning, staring at the TV, standing guard.

I didn't think anything more would happen, but you never knew around here.

Downstairs I heard the Serbs talking loudly among themselves. They were doing the same as me. Not a peep from Arun next door. I bet he'd been out in the Junction.

At around dawn, with the night starting to fade and birdsong coming through the window, I closed my eyes and fell asleep, thinking that was two riots I'd been mixed up in this year.

When I woke it was broad daylight.

The kids had had breakfast. I could hear Amy and Karen in the kitchen.

The TV was still on.

I rubbed my eyes and yawned.

The morning after . . .

Images of:

Clapham Junction – the centre completely shut down, the streets cordoned off with police tape.

A burned-out car – WELLCOM 2 HACKNEY – spray-painted in green capitals on the charred hood.

West Croydon – House of Reeves, a 150-year-old furniture store, had been burned to the ground by an arsonist.

Stratford ...

A huge pile of charred, still smoking rubble filled the screen. Firemen were hosing it down.

I turned up the volume.

'It's still far too early to determine exactly what happened here,' a male reporter was saying. 'It's thought a group of rioters attempted to raid the nearby Olympic Village, but they were driven back by armed police. They targeted this building instead. Until recently it was a shelter for the homeless run by a local Quaker group. The land had been sold to a property developer. Ironically, the building was due to be demolished today.

'Rioters are believed to have commandeered a digger that was already on site, and driven it into the building. Firefighters think the building was set on fire by the rioters and subsequently collapsed. Police sources tell me there were no casualties.'

The camera pulled back. There was nothing left standing of the warehouse. It had collapsed into a rectangular crater, a blackened mound of smashed masonry, brick and tile. A fire engine, two police cars and a couple of press vans were parked on the wasteland.

And then, in the background, a familiar figure appeared, still dressed in the grey suit she'd worn in court yesterday.

It was DCI Reid.

THE NEWS

(2011–2012)

Evening Standard, September 5th, 2011

Vernon James Sentenced to Life

Millionaire banker Vernon James was given a life sentence for the murder of Evelyn Bates at the Old Bailey this morning. He will serve a minimum of twenty-five years before becoming eligible for release.

In pronouncing sentence, Judge Adam Blumenfeld branded James 'a depraved, predatory individual'.

James was arrested on March 17th for the murder of Bates, whose body was found in a suite at the Blenheim-Strand hotel, where James had been staying, after being named the Hoffmann Trust's *Ethical Person of the Year*.

James, who had pleaded not guilty, showed no emotion as the sentence was read out.

Guardian, September 6th, 2011

Respected Barrister Dies

The legal profession has been paying tribute today to Christine Devereaux, QC, who died in hospital yesterday morning. Ms Devereaux had been in a coma since collapsing outside court in August.

Over a successful career spanning more than twenty years, Ms Devereaux built up a reputation for her tough no-nonsense style in court, and her merciless cross-examinations were the stuff of legend in legal circles.

Ms Devereaux defended Vernon James in his recent murder trial. James was found guilty and sentenced to life imprisonment yesterday.

Franco Carnavale, QC, said, 'When I was first called to the bar, Christine Devereaux was my mentor and I her pupil. She taught me everything I know.'

Ms Devereaux is survived by her husband and four children.

The Law Times, September 8th, 2011

End of an Era – Kopf Retires

Sid Kopf, senior partner and co-founder of Kopf-Randall-Purdom, announced that he is to stand down as CEO at the end of the month. He will be succeeded in the role by Janet Randall.

Kopf, who founded the firm with his colleague Stephen Purdom, in 1962, was famously dubbed 'The Blond Assassin' by colleagues, for his fearsome reputation as both a litigator and a corporate lawyer.

Janet Randall has announced that the firm will be expanding its criminal division, and extending its brief to take on Legal Aid cases as well as continuing to represent private clients.

Daily Chronicle, September 9th, 2011

Stratford Riot Warehouse – Human Remains Found

Police confirm that bones discovered in the foundations of a collapsed warehouse in Stratford, east London, last week are human. A spokesman described the remains as being 'over fifty years old'.

The warehouse collapsed when rioters involved in last month's disturbances bulldozed their way in with a digger. The building, which was structurally unsound, had been earmarked for demolition.

The warehouse, previously used as a homeless shelter by the Stratford Society of Friends, a Quaker charity, was close to the Olympic Village.

Detective Chief Inspector Carol Reid, who is heading up the investigation, has appealed to the public for information. 'At the moment we're keeping an open mind as to how the body got there,' she said. 'We're definitely not ruling out foul play.'

Daily Chronicle, September 19th, 2011

The Stratford Skeleton – It WAS Murder!

DCI Carol Reid of the London Met Police announced a murder investigation last night, after the human remains known as 'The Stratford Skeleton' were identified as those of Michael Zengeni, half-brother of controversial property tycoon Scott Nagle.

Zengeni was originally believed to have been kidnapped and murdered in Rhodesia (now Zimbabwe) in 1961.

At an inquest held in London in 1962, Rhodesian police captain Oliver Wingrove told the coroner he had identified a badly decomposed body as Zengeni's, through dental records and a passport found at the scene.

It is now almost certain Zengeni arrived in the UK from Rhodesia on November 28th, 1961, and that he was murdered the same day. Tests on the remains confirmed the cause of death as a single gunshot to the head.

The body was subsequently buried in the recently dug foundations of a warehouse which later housed the Stratford Quaker hostel. Construction started on the building on November 29th, 1961.

Police believe Mr Zengeni was lured to his place of death by someone familiar to him. They have named that person as Andrew Swayne, a private investigator who worked for the law firm, Kopf-Randall-Purdom. Swayne died of an alcoholic seizure in July this year.

Zengeni was the illegitimate, mixed-race son of property developer Thomas Nagle, and half-brother to Scott Nagle, the controversial property tycoon.

Sun, March 8th, 2012

Pepe Gets Two Years

Disgraced Chelsea midfielder Pepe Regan was yesterday jailed for two years after being found guilty of intimidating a witness in his assault trial last year. The 2011 trial collapsed when the witness, who had been granted anonymity, changed his testimony.

During proceedings the court heard how Regan found out the identity of the witness when he was given a transcript of a phone conversation recorded by a private detective employed by the *Daily Chronicle*.

Regan's two co-defendants, ex-*Chronicle* journalist Kevin Dorset and his girlfriend, Arabella Hogan, were each handed one-year suspended sentences and 150 hours' community service.

Dorset admitted giving the transcript to Hogan, who was working for the footballer's defence team during the initial trial.

Regan, who is expected to serve a year inside, has started his sentence at Wandsworth Prison.

BBC Online News, May 22nd, 2012

Shock Confession Sparks Brawl at the Old Bailey

There were astonishing scenes in Court 1 of the Old Bailey this morning at the trial of three Israeli nationals, when a brawl broke out in the dock between the defendants. They had to be restrained by security.

The defendants – Deborah Levin, Sam Dreyfus and Rudy Cohen – are accused of the murder of a Swiss prostitute in Southend police station in April 2011, as well as the attempted kidnapping that led to the shootings on the Strand in London last August, where two people, and the gunman – Daniel Bronstein, the fourth member of the team – were killed.

The accused are former members of an elite unit in the Israeli Defence Force, famed for its black ops missions, including assassination. Since leaving the army, they are believed to have worked as contract killers.

The fight erupted at the very start of proceedings, when Cohen unexpectedly announced, through his barrister, Ann Sanlon, QC, that he wished to change his plea to guilty, and would give evidence for the prosecution.

When the judge asked Cohen to confirm this, he said:

'Yes. And, by the way, you might as well know that we all killed Evelyn Bates. May God have mercy on our souls.'

He was then physically attacked by his co-defendants. The trial was suspended until tomorrow.

Guardian, June 6th, 2012

Scott Nagle Arrested

Police yesterday arrested property tycoon Scott Nagle at his home in Kent on suspicion of conspiracy to commit murder.

The arrest follows an ongoing investigation into the 1961 murder of Nagle's half-brother, Michael Zengeni, whose remains were found last August in the foundations of a warehouse in Stratford built by Nagle's father's construction company.

DCI Carol Reid of the Metropolitan police issued a brief statement confirming that an eighty-three-year-old man was in police custody.

Evening Standard, August 8th, 2012

Vernon James to be Freed

Vernon James is likely to be freed from prison by the end of the week. His murder conviction is expected to be overturned by the Court of Appeal at a hearing on Friday.

This follows revelations of a set-up made by Rudy Cohen, one of four ex-Israeli soldiers involved in the shootings in central London last year.

The millionaire hedge fund owner was sentenced to life in September 2011, for the murder of Evelyn Bates in his hotel room.

The appeal will be heard at the Royal Courts of Justice.

Epilogue

The Whole Point
of No Return

'We all set for tomorrow?' VJ asked me.

It was just us in the Belmarsh visiting room.

'Good to go,' I said.

Tomorrow morning his appeal would be heard. A mere formality, and then he'd be free.

You'd have thought they'd have released him the instant the Israelis were convicted, but the decision had to be ratified by the courts, and the process took time. Free slots had to be found, other cases juggled and moved. If anything, I was surprised at how quickly this had happened.

'What are my chances?' he asked, smiling.

'Best not get your hopes up. This game is played one move at a time,' I quipped.

'Spoken like a true lawyer,' he said.

We laughed. We could do that now.

Yeah, you guessed right . . .

I was still at KRP.

Everyone has their price. Mine was the lives of my children, an easier life for my wife and, yeah, a second chance at a future.

So, I'd taken the job.

I was working as a paralegal and studying for a law degree at UCL.

I was done being a fool.

It was different at the firm now that Kopf was gone. Janet had moved into his office, and expanded the criminal division.

I was Janet's right-hand man. I had her ear, and she was mentoring me. I didn't know what to make of her. And I still don't know how she got Kopf to quit and hand her the keys to his kingdom. Was it blackmail, or something they'd planned?

On the one hand, justice had been done. Evelyn Bates's killer was dead, Fabia Masson's were in jail, and an innocent man would soon walk free.

Yet the real culprits, the ones who'd instigated this, were also free – for now.

I'd given evidence in court about my attempted kidnapping by the Israelis; and also – finally – recounted what Fabia had told me in Southend nick before they killed her.

But I wasn't the star witness. Rudy Cohen – aka Rudy Saks – was.

He spent two days on the witness stand, reeling off the whole story of VJ's fit-up, from his team's recruitment to the moment of his arrest at Gare du Nord in Paris.

It was chilling. How they selected Fabia Masson as the 'ideal victim' based on their intel on the type of woman VJ liked. How Evelyn Bates was brought up to the suite when they were forced to improvise after Fabia fled. Why her? 'She was convenient. A woman on her own, no friends.' Daniel Bronstein (aka Jonas Dichter) had strangled her on the suite floor. They hadn't even noticed the colour of her dress.

Normally they should all have split the country once the job was done, but Fabia was a loose end they had to tie up first. Why had they bothered? 'We wouldn't get paid in full, and our reputations would be damaged. Just like in any other job,' Cohen had said.

He admitted the group raided David Stratten's house posing as taxmen, but denied killing him. He also denied killing Andy Swayne, but admitted they'd 'wasted' two days 'following him'.

The two surviving members of Cohen's team got life, with a minimum of thirty years. Cohen got life with a minimum of fifteen – for his cooperation.

That wasn't the whole story.

The police had raided the Silver Service Agency and arrested Beverley Wingrove, but they'd let her go because there wasn't enough evidence to charge her. She said she didn't know the Israelis' true identities. As for Oliver Wingrove, her husband had never talked about the work he did back then, she said. There was no proof either way.

Scott Nagle had been released on bail and was under house arrest, pending the ongoing investigation into Michael Zengeni's murder. KRP wasn't representing him. Janet cited a 'conflict of interest'. Nagle may have allowed himself a wry laugh, if he found humour in irony.

The critical piece of evidence linking him and Zengeni, and thus providing the motive for his murder – their father's second will, dividing his estate and businesses between them – had disappeared from Sid Kopf's filing cabinet. Kopf had covered both their tracks.

As for Kopf himself, he'd voluntarily gone to the police for questioning, and been released without charge three hours later. Janet accompanied him. Not that he needed her.

VJ, now knowing Scott Nagle had bought the warehouse, suspected it was him who'd had him framed, but he hadn't made the connection with KRP. Not yet, anyway.

Andy Swayne:

Everyone now thinks he killed Michael Zengeni.

Everyone except me.

I don't think he had it in him. I don't even think he knew what was going on. He thought he was delivering a letter. Just as he thought he was picking Michael up from Heathrow and taking him to a building site in Stratford to meet his dad.

He witnessed the murder, though. Of that I was sure.

He'd been traumatised and guilt-ridden for the rest of his life, which is why he turned to drink.

Why hadn't he simply confessed, told me everything?

He couldn't. He was as implicated as Kopf and Nagle were. And he was scared of Kopf. Kopf had a hold on him.

So he needed me – a KRP employee, a clerk just going about his job – to blow the whistle. He was pushing me towards the truth all along, and I didn't realise it.

'What happens tomorrow, then?' VJ asked.

'I expect the verdict will be ruled unsafe, your sentence will be quashed and you'll be set free.'

'But I won't be acquitted?'

'You need a retrial for that, which won't happen because the CPS won't seek one. Trials cost taxpayers' money. Why acquit an innocent person when they can send a guilty one to jail?'

'So my name won't be cleared?'

'Technically, no,' I said.

'I'll always be the guy who killed Evelyn Bates?'

'To people who don't know any better, yeah. But at least you'll be free.'

'It's not fair,' he said, with a sigh of disgust.

Finally, the right moment had come – the moment I'd been waiting for, ever since I first found myself in the same room as him again: the opportunity to bring up the past – our past.

'It's like what happened to me with your diary,' I said.

'What?'

'Your diary, remember? The one you accused me of stealing?'

He gave me a puzzled look; a look that stayed on his face for so long I wondered if he hadn't completely forgotten what he'd done.

'Oh . . .' he said after close to a minute of silence. '*That*.'

'Did you ever find it?' I asked.

He shook his head.

'Did you ever find out who took it?'

Another shake of the head.

'But you know I never stole it, right?'

'I can't believe we're even talking about this.'

'It was a pretty big deal to me,' I said.

He sat back in his chair and crossed his arms over his chest. He'd bulked up quite considerably over the past year, said he took out his frustrations on free weights.

'That was twenty years ago, Terry.'

Yes, it was. And it was petty and trivial; and – in the current circumstances – totally insignificant. But not to me. This was my one and only chance to put the matter to rest, to ask him the question that had been bugging me for . . . yeah, '*twenty years*'. Tomorrow he'd be free.

'Didn't you figure out what happened?' he asked.

'No,' I said.

'I thought you would've done by now. I thought you *had*. I thought you'd understood.'

'"Understood"?'

I really didn't know what he was on about. And, suddenly I wasn't sure I wanted to know. But if I left it here, I'd never stop thinking about it. No closure, no peace. No peace, no progress.

'You might as well tell me,' I said.

'Do you remember what you were like at Cambridge? What you turned into?'

'What do you mean?'

'You were pissed the whole time. An embarrassment.'

'To who?'

'Me, of course – and people I knew.'

'Your fancy new friends, you mean?'

'There you go again,' he sighed. 'You haven't changed a bit, have you? Still balancing a chip on each shoulder. Still with that small-town mentality of yours – suspicious of anything and everything beyond the end of your nose. The world's flat and you're too scared to go too far in case you drop off the end.'

His contempt cut deeper than it should have. He'd looked down on me then. He was still looking down on me.

'At least I wasn't a social climber,' I said.

'You don't get it, do you? People like us – state school kids, no connections, no rich parents – if we're not climbing, we're sinking. And I
didn't get into Cambridge to sink. That wasn't me. But, most of all, that
never used to be *you*.'

'What are you saying?'

'What do you *think* I'm saying?' he said.

I knew.

I didn't want to believe he would have gone that far, been that ruthless. I thought I knew him, knew his limits.

'You never had a diary, did you?' I said.

'No.'

'You made it up – the theft?'

'Yeah.'

'Why?'

'Why d'you think?'

'Tell me.'

'What's it matter? It's trivial. Kids' stuff,' he said.

'It matters to me.'

'All right, then,' he said. 'I wanted you out of my way and out of my
life. You were holding me back. I'd be talking to people, making those
all-important contacts you do in places like Cambridge. And what
would happen? You'd turn up. Pissed out of your skull, lairy, aggressive,
insulting everyone. And it'd reflect badly on me. You're known by the
company you keep. And I was known by *you*. My pisshead twat mate
from *Stevenage*. I couldn't have that.

'But I couldn't just cut you off. That wouldn't have looked good. It
would've looked weak. So I needed a good excuse to get rid of you, a
convenient incident.'

That hit me like a wrecking ball to plywood. I'd never guessed I was
holding him back.

'You lied to the college,' I said. 'You told them I'd stolen from you.'

'I didn't want it to go *that* far, believe me,' he said. 'But I didn't have
a choice.'

'Yes, you did.'

'What? Take it back? Have you been listening to a word I said? I
wanted you out of my life.'

'You got me kicked out of Cambridge.'

Anger flashed across his face and his eyes narrowed to shiny black
slits.

'No, I didn't, Terry. You know why you got sent down? It wasn't for
stealing my non-existent diary. They wouldn't have cared about that.
You got kicked out because you failed your exams. It wasn't because of

497

me or anything I did. It was because of you and everything you *didn't* do.

'And that was work. You never did any the whole time you were there. I kept on telling you. I kept on warning you. You didn't listen. You didn't want to know. You were too busy going down the pub. All those essays you never wrote, or when you did, you dashed them off an hour before they were due. You just couldn't be arsed. Life was a drink and you got drunk.'

I didn't answer. I *had* no answer.

I was angry and I was disgusted. Disgusted with him – even if he was fundamentally right in everything he'd said.

Yes, I *had* thrown my life away then. I'd messed up an opportunity people like me barely even catch a glimpse of. And for that, I deserved what had happened.

But that didn't make it all right. Not one bit.

And I hadn't even mentioned Melissa.

Over the past few months, working on his appeal, talking to him regularly, I'd managed to separate the person he was now, from the one he'd been. It had been easy. The man across the table from me had been sent to prison for a crime he hadn't committed. He wasn't a person, he was a cause. I even started to like him . . .

Not any more.

I sensed those old wounds that had finally started healing starting to open again.

I sensed that dormant anger turning over, opening an eyelid.

I suddenly wanted to bring up Rodney's murder and the alibi . . . Kev Dorset's story never did run in the *Chronicle*. The riots and their aftermath had ensured VJ's conviction wasn't even news.

But right then I heard Karen's voice, loud and clear, ringing around my head like church bells tolling across a flat, frozen meadow:

'You can't cheat karma.'

Over and over, like a mantra.

You can't cheat karma.

She was right.

VJ *hadn't* cheated karma.

All my life I'd wanted him to pay for what he'd done to me.

In a roundabout way, he had.

My life had been damaged by a lie he told. And his life had been ruined by a frame-up – a different kind of lie, but a lie all the same.

You can't cheat karma. No one can. It's not instant, but it always gets you in the end.

I could have pointed that out to him, but what would have been the point?

He'd be a free man tomorrow, sure. But what would that freedom look like? He'd lost his business. Melissa was divorcing him. And everyone knew what kind of person he was. He'd get back on his feet, without a doubt, but he wouldn't stand quite as tall, nor be looked at the same way. And yes, there'd always be someone who thought he was a killer.

'If you'd known about the diary, would you still have helped me out the way you did?' he asked.

Good question

Very good question.

Would it have made a difference?

I thought about that.

The person I was on March 17th, 2011, wouldn't have raised a finger to help him.

The person I was now would have helped him regardless.

'I'm not a lawyer yet,' I said. 'But I started becoming one the minute I got given your case. The law is founded on the abiding principle that everyone is entitled to a fair trial, irrespective of who they are and what they've done – to others, or to yourself.'

He chuckled.

'You hate me, don't you?'

'No.' I shook my head. And I meant it too. For the very first time. I didn't hate him at all. Not any more. We were even. Life had redressed the balance. I saw that now.

'I had a friend, a long time ago,' I said. 'He was a good friend. My best friend. We were really close, like brothers. Then we grew up and went our separate ways. I never saw him again. I don't know where he is or what happened to him. Chances are, if we passed each other in the street a month, a year from now, I wouldn't even recognise him. But you know what? That's OK. Because this way I'll always remember him for what he was, not what he became.'

With that, I stood up and went over to the cell door and banged on it for the guard. Seconds later the door was opened and the sounds of the prison came flooding in, the machine of confinement running off its trapped souls.

I didn't even turn round to look at him. I was never going to turn round again, never ever look back. From now on I was moving forward.

'I'll see you in court, Vernon.'

About the author

Nick Stone was born in Cambridge in 1966, the son of a Scottish father and a Haitian mother. His first novel, *Mr Clarinet,* won the CWA Ian Fleming Steel Dagger, the International Thriller Writers Award for Best First Novel and the Macavity Award for Best First Novel, and was nominated for The Barry Award for Best British Novel.